T0354551

"One historical mystery series that never gets boring or dull."
—*Midwest Book Review*

WHAT WOULD SCOTLAND YARD DO
WITHOUT DEAR MRS. JEFFRIES?

Even Inspector Witherspoon himself doesn't know—because his secret weapon is as ladylike as she is clever. She's Mrs. Jeffries—the charming detective who stars in this unique Victorian mystery series. Enjoy them all . . .

The Inspector and Mrs. Jeffries
A doctor is found dead in his own office—and Mrs. Jeffries must scour the premises to find the prescription for murder . . .

Mrs. Jeffries Dusts for Clues
One case is solved and another is opened when the Inspector finds a missing brooch—pinned to a dead woman's gown. But Mrs. Jeffries never cleans a room without dusting under the bed—and never gives up on a case before every loose end is tightly tied . . .

The Ghost and Mrs. Jeffries
Death is unpredictable . . . but the murder of Mrs. Hodges was foreseen at a spooky séance. The practical-minded housekeeper may not be able to see the future—but she can look into the past and put things in order to solve this haunting crime . . .

Mrs. Jeffries Takes Stock
A businessman has been murdered—and it could be because he cheated his stockholders. The housekeeper's interest is piqued . . . and when it comes to catching killers, the smart money's on Mrs. Jeffries . . .

continued . . .

Mrs. Jeffries on the Ball

A festive Jubilee celebration turns into a fatal affair—and Mrs. Jeffries must find the guilty party . . .

Mrs. Jeffries on the Trail

Why was Annie Shields out selling flowers so late on a foggy night? And more importantly, who killed her while she was doing it? It's up to Mrs. Jeffries to sniff out the clues . . .

Mrs. Jeffries Plays the Cook

Mrs. Jeffries finds herself doing double duty: cooking for the inspector's household and trying to cook a killer's goose . . .

Mrs. Jeffries and the Missing Alibi

When Inspector Witherspoon becomes the main suspect in a murder, Scotland Yard refuses to let him investigate. But no one said anything about Mrs. Jeffries . . .

Mrs. Jeffries Stands Corrected

When a local publican is murdered, and Inspector Witherspoon botches the investigation, trouble starts to brew for Mrs. Jeffries . . .

Mrs. Jeffries Takes the Stage

After a theatre critic is murdered, Mrs. Jeffries uncovers the victim's secret past: a real-life drama more compelling than any stage play . . .

Mrs. Jeffries Questions the Answer

Hannah Cameron was not well-liked. But were her friends or family the sort to stab her in the back? Mrs. Jeffries must really tiptoe around this time—or it could be a matter of life and death . . .

Mrs. Jeffries Reveals Her Art

Mrs. Jeffries has to work double-time to find a missing model *and* a killer. And she'll have to get her whole staff involved—before someone else becomes the next subject . . .

Mrs. Jeffries Takes the Cake

The evidence was all there: a dead body, two dessert plates, and a gun. As if Mr. Ashbury had been sharing cake with his own killer. Now Mrs. Jeffries will have to do some snooping around—to dish up clues . . .

Mrs. Jeffries Rocks the Boat

Mirabelle had traveled by boat all the way from Australia to visit her sister—only to wind up murdered. Now Mrs. Jeffries must solve the case—and it's sink or swim . . .

Mrs. Jeffries Weeds the Plot

Three attempts have been made on Annabeth Gentry's life. Is it due to her recent inheritance, or was it because her bloodhound dug up the body of a murdered thief? Mrs. Jeffries will have to sniff out some clues before the plot thickens . . .

Mrs. Jeffries Pinches the Post

Harrison Nye may have had some dubious business dealings, but no one expected him to be murdered. Now Mrs. Jeffries and her staff must root through the sins of his past to discover which one caught up with him . . .

Mrs. Jeffries Pleads Her Case

Harlan Westover's death was deemed a suicide by the magistrate. But Inspector Witherspoon is willing to risk his career to prove otherwise. Mrs. Jeffries must ensure the good inspector remains afloat . . .

Mrs. Jeffries Sweeps the Chimney

A dead vicar has been found, propped against a church wall. And Inspector Witherspoon's only prayer is to seek the divinations of Mrs. Jeffries . . .

Mrs. Jeffries Stalks the Hunter

Puppy love turns to obsession, which leads to murder. Who better to get to the heart of the matter than Inspector Witherspoon's indomitable companion, Mrs. Jeffries . . .

continued . . .

Mrs. Jeffries Speaks Her Mind

Someone is trying to kill the eccentric Olive Kettering, but no one believes her—until she's proven right. Without witnesses and plenty of suspects, Mrs. Jeffries will see justice served . . .

Mrs. Jeffries Forges Ahead

The marriageable daughters of the upper crust are outraged when the rich and handsome Lewis Banfield marries an artist's model. But when someone poisons the new bride's champagne, Mrs. Jeffries must discover if envy led to murder . . .

Mrs. Jeffries and the Mistletoe Mix-Up

When art collector Daniel McCourt is found murdered under the mistletoe, it's up to Mrs. Jeffries to find out who gave him the kiss of death . . .

Mrs. Jeffries Defends Her Own

When the general office manager of Sutcliffe Manufacturing is murdered, Mrs. Jeffries must figure out who hated him enough to put a bullet between his eyes . . .

Mrs. Jeffries and the Merry Gentlemen

Days before Christmas, a successful stockbroker is murdered and suspicion falls on three influential investors known as the Merry Gentlemen. Now Mrs. Jeffries won't rest until justice is served for the holidays . . .

Visit Emily Brightwell's website at emilybrightwell.com

Also available from Prime Crime:
The first four Mrs. Jeffries Omnibus Mysteries
Mrs. Jeffries Learns the Trade, Mrs. Jeffries Takes a Second Look, Mrs. Jeffries Takes Tea at Three, and *Mrs. Jeffries Sallies Forth*

Berkley Prime Crime titles by Emily Brightwell

THE INSPECTOR AND MRS. JEFFRIES
MRS. JEFFRIES DUSTS FOR CLUES
THE GHOST AND MRS. JEFFRIES
MRS. JEFFRIES TAKES STOCK
MRS. JEFFRIES ON THE BALL
MRS. JEFFRIES ON THE TRAIL
MRS. JEFFRIES PLAYS THE COOK
MRS. JEFFRIES AND THE MISSING ALIBI
MRS. JEFFRIES STANDS CORRECTED
MRS. JEFFRIES TAKES THE STAGE
MRS. JEFFRIES QUESTIONS THE ANSWER
MRS. JEFFRIES REVEALS HER ART
MRS. JEFFRIES TAKES THE CAKE
MRS. JEFFRIES ROCKS THE BOAT
MRS. JEFFRIES WEEDS THE PLOT
MRS. JEFFRIES PINCHES THE POST
MRS. JEFFRIES PLEADS HER CASE
MRS. JEFFRIES SWEEPS THE CHIMNEY
MRS. JEFFRIES STALKS THE HUNTER
MRS. JEFFRIES AND THE SILENT KNIGHT
MRS. JEFFRIES APPEALS THE VERDICT
MRS. JEFFRIES AND THE BEST LAID PLANS
MRS. JEFFRIES AND THE FEAST OF ST. STEPHEN
MRS. JEFFRIES HOLDS THE TRUMP
MRS. JEFFRIES IN THE NICK OF TIME
MRS. JEFFRIES AND THE YULETIDE WEDDINGS
MRS. JEFFRIES SPEAKS HER MIND
MRS. JEFFRIES FORGES AHEAD
MRS. JEFFRIES AND THE MISTLETOE MIX-UP
MRS. JEFFRIES DEFENDS HER OWN
MRS. JEFFRIES TURNS THE TIDE
MRS. JEFFRIES AND THE MERRY GENTLEMEN
MRS. JEFFRIES AND THE ONE WHO GOT AWAY

Anthologies

MRS. JEFFRIES LEARNS THE TRADE
MRS. JEFFRIES TAKES A SECOND LOOK
MRS. JEFFRIES TAKES TEA AT THREE
MRS. JEFFRIES SALLIES FORTH
MRS. JEFFRIES PLEADS THE FIFTH
MRS. JEFFRIES SERVES AT SIX

MRS. JEFFRIES
PLEADS THE FIFTH

EMILY BRIGHTWELL

BERKLEY PRIME CRIME, NEW YORK

THE BERKLEY PUBLISHING GROUP
Published by the Penguin Group
Penguin Group (USA) LLC
375 Hudson Street, New York, New York 10014

USA • Canada • UK • Ireland • Australia • New Zealand • India • South Africa • China

penguin.com

A Penguin Random House Company

MRS. JEFFRIES PLEADS THE FIFTH

Berkley Prime Crime Books are published by The Berkley Publishing Group.
BERKLEY® PRIME CRIME and the PRIME CRIME logo are a registered
trademark of Penguin Group (USA) LLC.

Berkley Prime Crime trade paperback ISBN: 978-0-425-26976-3

Library of Congress Control Number: 2014942219

PUBLISHING HISTORY
Berkley Prime Crime trade paperback edition / April 2014

Cover illustration by Jeff Walker.

CONTENTS

CONTENTS

MRS. JEFFRIES TAKES THE CAKE

CHAPTER 1

Maisie Donovan pulled the heavy trunk up the last two stairs and heaved a sigh of relief that she'd got the ruddy box this far. She gave the thing a vicious kick and then plopped down on the top of the flat lid to catch her breath. Only one more flight to go, she told herself. Too bad that wretched boy had taken it into his head to run off; by rights this should have been his job, lugging the mistress's trunk up to her room. But the household had awoken this morning to find Boyd gone and she'd got stuck with the job. Sighing, Maisie rose to her feet. She'd better push on. They'd be here any minute now and she didn't want to get caught sitting on the landing.

In the fading evening light, the landing was so dark as to be almost black. Perhaps that's what caught Maisie's eye—the streak of light seeping out of Mr. Ashbury's door. Blast. She swore softly and fluently to herself. Now, why was he home? "What's that old tattletale doin' here?" she muttered. She wondered if he'd heard her kicking the truck.

Maisie didn't think she'd get the sack, not after Boyd's runnin' off like that. But she wasn't sure. Mr. Frommer could be a right old tartar. Breaking the silliest rule could find you out on the street, she thought, remembering what had happened to Emma only a few days before the household had gone to Ascot. Poor girl had been sacked over a ruddy flowerpot. Blast. It'd be just like that old Ashbury to pretend he wasn't here and then tell the master he'd heard her kickin' their precious trunk. Well, she wasn't having it. She wasn't going to spend the next few hours or even days wondering if the ax was going to fall. She glared at the doorway and then, when she heard nothing, boldly decided to take matters into her own hands. Maybe Mr. Ashbury hadn't come in yet.

"Mr. Ashbury?" she said softly as she pushed the door open. "Are you in here, sir?"

There was no answer.

She stepped inside and gazed sharply around the spacious sitting room. Empty. But he'd been here.

The heavy curtains were wide open, letting in the last rays of the fading sun. A fully loaded tea trolley stood next to his favorite balloon-backed chair. Bloomin' odd, she thought stepping farther into the room. She could see that the door to the connecting bedroom stood open and the top of the spread was rumpled. "Mr. Ashbury, sir. Are ya here?"

No one replied.

The hair on the back of Maisie's neck stood up. Something was wrong. Very wrong. Tentatively she took a step closer to the tea trolley. "Mr. Ashbury?"

Silence.

"Oh, this is stupid," she muttered, more to give herself courage than for anything else. The back of Mr. Ashbury's chair faced the door. Maisie walked over to it and peeked around the edge. She gasped in surprise. The old man himself was sitting there, staring straight at her.

"Oh, I'm sorry sir," she began as she backed away. "I didn't realize you was in here."

He said nothing; he merely gazed at her out of his pale, washed-out hazel eyes.

"I thought there might be something amiss, sir," she explained, "when I saw the door open a crack, sir. I mean, we didn't think you were due home till tonight, sir."

He continued to stare at her.

Maisie stopped. She realized he hadn't so much as blinked. She walked back across the room and knelt right in front of him.

He didn't move a muscle.

She waved her hand in front of his eyes.

He didn't blink.

Relieved, she sighed. At least he wouldn't be running to Mr. Frommer telling tales now. "Old blighter's kicked off," she murmured. Death was no stranger to Maisie. She'd buried both her parents and three brothers by the time she was fourteen. Matter-of-factly she reached over to close Mr. Ashbury's eyes. Not because she liked him, but out of respect for the dead in general. As she touched him he toppled to one side.

It was only then that Maisie saw the blood on the back of the chair and the gaping hole in the side of the man's skull.

"Looks like the poor bloke didn't know what hit him," Constable Barnes said to Inspector Witherspoon. "Shot directly in the side of the head." He clucked his tongue sympathetically. The constable was a tall, craggy-faced man with iron-gray hair beneath his policeman's helmet.

Inspector Gerald Witherspoon suppressed a shudder. If he could have managed it, he'd have avoided examining the body altogether. But as it was a necessary part of the investigation, he steeled himself to do his duty. "It doesn't appear as if the man put up a struggle," he replied. He swallowed heavily as he gently moved the victim's head to one side. Witherspoon was no expert on gunshot wounds, but even he could see that the weapon had been fired at close range. Very close range.

"No," Barnes agreed, "he didn't struggle. Just sat here like a lamb to the slaughter and let the killer do his worst."

"Perhaps he didn't see it coming," Witherspoon suggested.

Barnes nodded in agreement. "Could be the killer come up on his blind side, sir. With these kind of chairs"—he tapped the heavy side padding—"you can't see a ruddy thing unless you stick your head out."

"Yes, I expect the killer was counting on that." Gerald Witherspoon was a tall, robust man with thinning dark brown hair and a neatly trimmed mustache. He had a long angular face with a sharp, rather pointed nose and, behind his spectacles, clear, blue-gray eyes. "Most people don't generally sit calmly and wait for someone to put a bullet in their head. Not if they see it first, that is. Do you think it might possibly have been suicide?"

Barnes shook his head. "I shouldn't think so, sir. For starters, if he'd done himself in, the gun should be somewhere right here." He pointed to the area around the body. "And we've looked, sir. It's not."

"I see what you mean. Suicides don't generally hide the gun after they've used it." Witherspoon pursed his lips and stepped back to survey the scene. The walls were decorated with nice but unimaginative paintings of hunting scenes and wildlife. There was a decent but well-worn camel-colored Turkey carpet on the floor and terra-cotta-colored muslin summer curtains hung at the windows overlooking the back garden. To one side of the chair where the victim reclined was a settee upholstered in thick, navy-blue cloth. A fully loaded tea trolley stood at the far end of the settee. A dark-colored cake with a large sliver missing was next to a pink-and-white-rose teapot. Two dessert plates, both used, two forks and two cups and saucers testified to the presence of two people.

Barnes grimaced. "Seems wrong, doesn't it, sir? Sitting down and havin' tea with someone you're plannin' on killin'."

"Breaking bread with a murderer," Witherspoon replied, shaking his head sadly, "seems somehow so very, very, awful. More awful, really, than just getting murdered in the course of one's day."

Barnes's gaze dropped to the two dessert plates, one scrapped clean and the other spotted with several tiny rocklike mounds. "One of them didn't like walnuts." He sighed and straightened his spine. "Well, sir, do you want to begin taking statements now?"

"We might as well get cracking. The police surgeon's on his way and we've had a good look at the victim. Do we know the poor fellow's name?"

"It's Ashbury, sir." Barnes flipped open his notebook. "According to the maid, Miss Maisie Donovan; she's the one who found the body. The victim is one Roland Arthur Ashbury."

"He owns the house?"

Barnes shook his head. "He lives here, sir, with his daughter and son-in-law, Andrew Frommer. They are at their country house in Ascot; they're due back later this evening."

"Frommer," Witherspoon repeated with a frown. "Now, why does that name sound so familiar?"

"He's an MP, sir." Barnes sighed again. "So that means this case'll probably get sticky. I expect we'll have the home secretary and half of Westminster puttin' their oars in on this one."

"Oh dear," Witherspoon groaned. "I'm afraid you're right, Barnes. Unless, of course, we get very lucky and this turns out to be a simple case."

"Simple, sir?" Barnes snorted in disbelief. "I don't see that happening. They never are, sir. I expect that's why the chief sent you out on this one. He's got a nose, he does, our chief inspector. A call comes in and he can tell by the smell if it's goin' to be a clean one or a right old tangle to sort out. But you're right good at it, sir. If I do say so myself."

Witherspoon's narrow chest swelled with pride. "Thank you, Barnes, but I don't solve cases alone. You're just as important as I am." He sighed, thinking of the tremendous responsibility he would have to shoulder. "All right then, complex or not, let's get this sorted out." He darted a glance at the door to the hall. The maid who'd discovered the body and the other servants had been asked to remain in the kitchen. "We'll search the room thoroughly and then get on with taking statements. I suppose I ought to send a message home, telling them not to wait up for me."

"I've already taken care of that," Barnes said as he hurried toward the bedroom door. "As soon as we got the call, I sent a street arab off to both your home and my missus. No sense in worryin' people when we don't get home on time, is there?"

The street arab, one Jeremy Slaven, age eight, stared at the coin the pretty blonde maid had just dropped into his dirty palm. A whole shilling. He couldn't believe it. Fearing she'd made a mistake and might snatch it back, he quickly closed his fingers on it and stepped out of reach.

"Thanks for bringing us the message," Betsy, housemaid to Inspector Gerald Witherspoon, said as she smiled brightly at the filthy, spindly-legged lad on the backdoor stoop. She was aware of exactly what was going on in his head. Having been poor herself, she knew precisely how suspicious one could be of unexpected generosity. The boy looked as though he'd not had a decent meal in days. "Don't worry," she said reassuringly, "I'm not going to take it back. You've earned it. If you've a mind to, you can come in. There's a bit of pudding left from supper. You're welcome to it."

For a moment Jeremy studied her, and then shrugged as though the matter was of no importance. "All right, seein' as you've asked."

Betsy turned and started down the back hall, the boy following right at her heels. As they came into the kitchen Jeremy had second thoughts. A whole ruddy bunch of people was sitting at the table. Everyone stopped talking and stared at him.

"The lad's just come in to finish up that bit of pudding," Betsy said brightly, ushering him toward the table where the others sat. "As he's come all the way from Charing Cross with a message from the inspector, I thought he might be a bit peckish."

"Is the inspector going to be in for dinner?" Mrs. Goodge, the cook, asked. She studied the street lad over the top of her spectacles. He was filthy enough to make her squirm. But she held her tongue. Something was happening, she was sure of that.

"No, he's been called out to a possible murder." Betsy said the words carefully, not wanting to indicate any excitement whatsoever in the presence of a stranger. Even one who was only a youngster. The household's investigations on behalf of Inspector Witherspoon were a secret.

"I see," Mrs. Goodge replied, with equal care. Her round face broke into a welcoming smile at the lad. What did a bit of dirt being tracked into her kitchen matter? There was plenty of carbolic in the washroom. "Do sit down, then," she said briskly, getting up and heading toward the larder, "and I'll get the pudding."

Jeremy stopped a few feet from the table as everyone in the kitchen broke into broad, welcoming smiles. These were an odd lot, that was for sure. But he was hungry, so he'd take his chances. He'd not had a bite all day and only half a slice of stale bread the day before.

"'Ere." Wiggins, the inspector's young footman, pointed to an empty chair next to him. "This is a nice seat. Come on, now, don't be shy."

Jeremy hesitated for a moment and then plopped down in the seat. "Ta," he muttered.

Wiggins smiled brightly, his round apple cheeks flushed with excitement. He was barely out of his teens and not as good at hiding his feelings as the others.

"I understand you brought a message to the house?" Mrs. Jeffries, the inspector's housekeeper, asked.

Jeremy looked at her and decided she was all right. He couldn't say why he thought that way; it was something you just knew. He'd gotten good at sussin' out people. She reminded him of someone he used to know, but he couldn't say who. He only knew he'd decided she could be trusted. Her eyes were a bright brown, kindly-like. She had red-brown hair streaked with gray at the sides and a ready smile that made him glad to be sitting at this table.

"Here you are, boy." Mrs. Goodge popped a plate heaped with food under his nose. "You might as well help us get shut of this food, seein' as how you've come so far."

His eyes widened in disbelief. He'd been expectin' a bit of puddin', but this was a feast fit for a king. He stared at the slab of chicken pie, the mashed potatoes and the peas, and his mouth watered.

The cook handed him a fork and knife. "They'll be treacle pudding for afters," she said lightly. Brushing a bit of flour off the apron covering her ample girth, she sat down next to the housekeeper.

Jeremy wasn't one to look a gift horse in the mouth. He snatched up the fork and tucked right in.

"As the young man's been taken care of"—Mrs. Jeffries flashed a quick smile at Betsy—"why don't you tell us the rest of the inspector's message."

"Oh it's not much," Betsy replied airily. "Just that the inspector's been called out on a case and won't be home until late."

"I wonder what kind of a case?" Wiggins mused. "I mean did he know fer sure it were a murder, or were it an accident of some kind?"

"It were a murder," Jeremy volunteered. "The copper that sent me told me so. Seems some old fellow got himself shot in the 'ead."

Mrs. Goodge clucked her tongue. "Shocking. Absolutely shocking. You didn't by any chance happen to hear the name of the poor man, did you?"

"Nah." The lad shook his head. "But I heard the old bas—copper tellin' another copper the address. It were on Argyle Street. Number twenty-one. That's over near the Midland Railway Terminus."

Using various indirect means, they questioned the lad closely. But it was soon evident he'd told them everything he knew.

"Blimey," he finally said, scraping the bowl and spooning the last of the pudding into his mouth. "I'd best get movin'. I've got to tell that old copper's missus he's not comin' home till late too."

Betsy walked him to the back door. Reaching into the pocket of her lavender broadcloth skirt, she pulled out another shilling. "Here," she said, handing it to the boy, "hang on to this. You might need it for a rainy day."

"'Ow come you're bein' so nice to me?" Jeremy was no longer suspicious; now he was just plain curious. These were a strange lot of people, they were. He'd never in his life had so many grown-ups listening to every word he said.

Betsy shrugged. She wasn't sure she could explain it properly, even to herself. But she'd been young and poor herself once. "No reason not to be, is there? Besides, I've been skint myself a time or two," she said, yanking open the back door. "You look like you could use a bit of coin in your pocket. Go on, now. Get off with you. Constable Barnes's missus is probably getting worried."

With a jaunty wave he hurried across the small terrace toward the side of the house. "Thanks for everything," he called over his shoulder as he disappeared around the corner.

When Betsy got back to the dining room, the others were already discussing what needed to be done.

"I think I ought to get over to Argyle Street and suss out what's up," Wiggins volunteered.

Mrs. Jeffries thought about it for a moment. The staff had been helping their dear inspector with his cases for several years now, but, as always, it was imperative they be discreet. Inspector Witherspoon wasn't aware that he was getting any help in his investigations.

"I think you ought to wait for Smythe," Betsy said before the housekeeper could reply to Wiggins's query. "He should be back any minute now."

Smythe was the household's coachman. He'd gone the station to collect their neighbor Lady Cannonberry.

"But it might take ages for him to get back 'ere," Wiggins protested. "And you know what Mrs. Jeffries always says; the trail goes cold if you don't get right on it."

"It doesn't go that cold," Betsy told him. "Besides, you know we're not supposed to go off snooping about on our own. It's not fair, is it? Especially at the beginning, everybody should have a chance."

Mrs. Jeffries listened carefully, hoping to be able to nip any incipient rivalry in the bud. Over the course of their investigations, they'd all become just a tad competitive with one another. Everyone, it seemed, wanted to be the one who discovered the clue that solved the case. To that end, they'd informally agreed to a set of rules. Everyone was to have a chance to hear all the pertinent information about the case as it was gathered. Yet the housekeeper could understand the footman's eagerness to get started. They had an address. They had a body. It did chafe a bit to have to wait. Then she realized there might be a way to accommmodate both points of view.

"You're both right," she said briskly. "On the one hand, it's only fair to wait for Smythe to get here before we leap into action, so to speak."

"Are we goin' to wait for Luty and Hatchet as well?" Wiggins asked.

"I'm getting to that," the housekeeper replied. "Actually, what I was going to suggest is that you escort Betsy down to the high street and put her in a hansom. She can go get Luty and Hatchet. You can nip over to the murdered man's house and try and pick up a bit more information, and by the time everyone gets back here, Smythe ought to have returned."

"The killer left us a present, sir," Barnes muttered. He was on his knees in front of the tea trolley, his nose to the carpet. "Looks like there's a gun here." The constable carefully reached behind the wheel and slowly pulled the weapon out. Getting a grip on the handle, he straightened up and held it out to Witherspoon. "A revolver, sir. An Enfield."

Grimacing, Witherspoon took it and held it to his nose. He wasn't certain what, exactly, it was supposed to smell like. As far as he could tell, the only scent was a slightly smoky metallic one. But he'd seen other policemen put a gun barrel to their nose and then pronounce on whether it had or hadn't been fired. The inspector supposed that if it hadn't been fired, there wouldn't be a scent at all. "It's been fired," he concluded. "Here, have a whiff and see if you don't think I'm right."

Barnes took the gun and gave it a good long sniff. "Right, sir," he agreed, "it has been fired. I'd say this is our murder weapon. Odd that the killer left it here and didn't take it with him."

Witherspoon almost sagged in relief. "Well, then, that would rule out suicide."

"Right, again, sir. That trolley is a good ten feet from the victim." Barnes pointed at the expanse of carpet between the chair and trolley. "Ashbury wouldn't have shot himself in the head and then heaved it under that far."

"Agreed. And it certainly wasn't an accident." The inspector shook his head. "But why leave the weapon at all?"

"Maybe the killer panicked sir," the constable suggested. He'd been a policeman a lot longer than the inspector, and in his day, he'd seen some pretty stupid criminals.

Just then another constable appeared in the doorway. "The police surgeon's just here, sir," he said to Witherspoon, "and the mistress of the house, a Mrs. Frommer, has arrived. She's getting upset. What do you want me to do?"

"Send the police surgeon in here, but make sure Mrs. Frommer is kept downstairs. I don't think she ought to see her father this way. It would be most shocking, most shocking, indeed. We'll be down in a few moments to have a word with her." Witherspoon handed the gun to Barnes. "Would you take charge of this?" The constable was far more experienced with firearms than himself, and frankly he didn't want to risk shooting off his big toe by carrying the gun himself.

"Yes, sir." Barnes took the gun, opened the thing up and peered into the cylinder. "There's only five bullets here, sir. That means that one's been fired." He popped the bullets out of the gun and put them into his pocket. "We'll place it in evidence when we get back to the station."

"Er, ah, yes, Constable, that's a good idea," Witherspoon muttered.

He wished he'd thought to open the gun himself, but the truth was, he was a bit frightened of them.

The two men went down the stairs to the ground floor. As they neared the front door Barnes veered off and gave the weapon to the constable who was stationed there. Witherspoon went on into the drawing room.

The lady of the house was a plump, middle-aged woman with light auburn hair peeking out of an ornate bonnet and pale blue eyes. Dressed in a dark green traveling dress, she leapt up from the settee when the inspector stepped through the door.

"Who are you?" she demanded. Her voice was thin, reedy and edged with hysteria. "Why are all these police here? What's happened? Where's my father? Where are the servants?"

"I'm Inspector Gerald Witherspoon, madam," he replied sympathetically. "I take it you're Mrs. Frommer."

She clasped her hands in front of her. When she spoke, her voice shook. "Yes, I'm MaryAnne Frommer. Mrs. Andrew Frommer. What's happened? Where's my maid?"

The inspector could tell by her demeanor that the woman was well aware that something awful had happened. One doesn't come home to find one's house full of police without realizing that something terrible has occurred. But even with that, he wanted to break the bad news to her in as kindly a way as possible. "Your maid and the rest of the servants are in the kitchen, madam," he said gently. "I'm afraid I've bad news. Very bad news. Was your father expected here today?"

"Yes." She paled even further. "We've all been out at our country house. Father came home on an earlier train today. He should be here. Where is he? For God's sake, has there been an accident?"

"I'm afraid he's dead, ma'am." The inspector hated this part of his job. Watching someone learn of the death of a loved one was heartbreaking.

MaryAnne Frommer stared at him for a long moment. Her mouth parted slightly and she cocked her head to one side, as though she hadn't heard correctly. "Dead?" she finally whispered. "But that can't be. He was fine at luncheon . . . he ate two apple tarts for dessert. How can he be dead? How did it happen? Was it his heart? A stroke?"

"He was shot, madam." Witherspoon dearly wished the lady's husband would get here. He wasn't sure what to do if she had hysterics.

"Shot?" She shook her head in disbelief. "No, I don't believe it. Father?

But who . . . how . . . ? I don't understand. But he didn't keep firearms in his room. All the hunting rifles are kept at the country house. How could he have been shot?"

"He wasn't shot with a rifle, ma'am. He was shot with a revolver," the inspector replied. "And it doesn't appear as if it was an accident of any kind. It appears to have been done quite deliberately." Witherspoon generally didn't like to use the word *murder* until he absolutely had to.

Her eyes widened to size of scones. "Are you saying he was murdered?"

"I'm afraid so, ma'am," Witherspoon replied. Drat. He noticed that Barnes hadn't come in to take notes.

She swayed on her feet and, before the inspector could reach her, sat down heavily on the settee. "I don't believe this," she whispered as her eyes filled with tears. "Father dead. Shot."

"What's all this, then?" A booming voice sliced into the quiet drawing room.

Witherspoon looked up just as a short, rather stout, dark-haired man in thick spectacles strode into the room. "Now, see here," he began, as soon as he spotted the inspector. "I demand to know what's going on? That blockhead of a constable wouldn't say anything. I demand to know why my house is swarming with policemen."

Wiggins mingled with the small crowd that had gathered on the pavement in front of number twenty-one. The huge, pale gray-brick house was at the end of the fashionable street and set back behind tall, spear-pointed black fencing. A police constable stood guard at the front gate. Two more stood like sentinels on the wide doorstoop of the house. Wiggins thought the one on the left looked familiar. So he quickly darted behind two tall women, both servants from the look of their clothes. No reason to stick his face out where he might be spotted.

Staying to the center of the crowd, well behind the women, he kept a sharp eye out, hoping that none of the police constables coming and going would notice him. Too many of them knew who he was and that he worked for Inspector Witherspoon.

"What's 'appened?" Wiggins asked the youngest of the women.

"The old bloke wot lives here 'as got done in," she replied excitedly. "Shot he was, while he was havin' his tea."

"Now, Vera. You don't know that fer sure," the other, older woman cautioned.

"Do too," the one called Vera replied. "Heard it from our Agnes, who got it directly from that young police constable that's sweet on her. She spotted him comin' back from raisin' the alarm and he told her that old man Ashbury 'ad been shot in the 'ead. So don't tell me I don't know what's what." She folded her arms over her chest and glared at her companion.

"Your Agnes was wrong about that robbery over at that Yank's house, wasn't she?" the other woman shot back. "And she'd supposedly got that from the constable too. If you ask me, he don't know what's what."

"He does too," Vera countered hotly. "Anyone could have made a mistake on that other one. The door and the window was wide open."

"But nothing was taken, was it?" her companion said triumphantly. "So there weren't no robbery."

"Does this Mr. Ashbury live on 'is own?" Wiggins asked quickly, before the two women could get into a full-blown argument.

"'Course he don't live on his own," Vera snapped. "Lives with his daughter and her husband. Mr. and Mrs. Frommer. He's an MP. He just went inside a few minutes ago. Stopped and had a right old dustup with that constable on the door." She giggled. "Mind you, I expect by the time the night's over, the police'll be wishin' it were Andrew Frommer that'd been shot. He's a nasty one, he is."

"Nasty fellow, is 'e?" Wiggins knew he couldn't stay much longer, but he wanted to learn as much as he could before going back to the others.

"Won't give ya the time of day," Vera said flatly, "and treats the help like they was dirt." She jerked her head toward the house. "Most of the staff there is untrained. They can't keep proper servants. They've even got a footman that's a half-wit."

"Really?" Wiggins edged away. He wanted information about the murder. About what had gone on this evening, not about what kind of employer Frommer was. That could come later. He worked the crowd, keeping up a discreet but steady stream of questions. By the time he left, he'd found out enough to get the household started.

"Lady Cannonberry's train was late," Smythe the coachman explained. "And by the time I got 'em loaded up and on the way, it was later than I'd thought." He was a tall, muscular, dark-haired man with brutally heavy features. Were it not for the kindness in his brown eyes and the good-natured set of his mouth, he could easily be mistaken for a ruffian. But nothing was further from the truth. The coachman was as kindhearted as he was strong.

"Them?" Mrs. Goodge queried. "I thought it was just Lady Cannonberry you were bringing home."

"She's brung a houseguest with 'er." Smythe took a quick sip of tea and glanced at the clock. "Some sort of distant cousin of her late 'usband. Fellow's name is Pilchard. Morris Pilchard. Bit of a toff. I could tell it niggled 'im that she were so friendly to me."

"How foolish of him," Mrs. Jeffries murmured. "We are all Lady Cannonberry's friends." Ruth Cannonberry was the wife of a late peer of the realm. She was also the conscience-driven daughter of a clergyman, a bit of a political radical and halfway in love with their dear Inspector Witherspoon.

"She didn't pay any mind to 'im," Smythe replied. "She were just 'er usual nice self." He shot a fast glance at the clock. "Blimey, it's gettin' late. What's takin' 'em so long?" He hated for Betsy to be out in the evening on her own. "By rights, Betsy's had plenty of time to get Luty and Hatchet back here."

"There are dozens of valid reasons why they might have been detained. Luty may have had guests or they might have been in the midst of something," Mrs. Jeffries replied. "She's not been gone all that long. Just a little over an hour. Besides, we can't start until Wiggins gets back. So far the only thing we know is that someone's been murdered. We don't even have the victim's name."

"But we've got their address," Mrs. Goodge said brightly. "And believe me, in that neighborhood I know I can find out who the victim is pretty quick. You know my sources; they cover this whole city."

The cook wasn't simply bragging. From her own cozy kitchen here at Upper Edmonton Gardens, she had a veritable army of people to call upon. Deliverymen, milkmen, butcher's boys, chimney sweeps, costermongers, rag-and-bones men and fruit vendors to name but a few. She did her bit in the investigations in her own way, but she never left her kitchen. She could also call upon a circle of acquaintances that included cooks from some of the wealthiest houses in all of England. She could find out any scrap of gossip, any breath of a scandal about anyone in the city.

Mrs. Jeffries gave an understanding smile. She too was eager to begin, but as she had told Wiggins earlier, it wouldn't be fair not to wait for the others.

Their patience was soon rewarded. Smythe heard the carriage first. "That's them," he said, rising to his feet and heading for the back door. "Now let's just hope that Wiggins gets himself back here quick."

A few moments later Betsy and two others hurried into the kitchen. Leading the charge was an elderly, white-haired woman with sharp dark eyes. Her frame was small and her body frail looking, yet she marched into the kitchen like a general leading her troops. Wealthy, American and some would say eccentric, Luty Belle Crookshank loved investigating murders more than anything.

Directly behind her was her butler and archrival in the game of gathering clues. Hatchet too had white hair, but he was a vigorous fellow in late middle age. Proper and proud, he was devoted to his plainspeaking and blunt mistress. "I trust we haven't kept you waiting too long," he said by way of a hello.

"We got here as quick as we could," Luty said as she took the chair next to Mrs. Jeffries. "But wouldn't you know it, Myrtle and some of her friends had dropped by and we couldn't get rid of 'em without bein' rude."

"I believe that suggesting they take their 'fat little fannies' elsewhere could constitute being rude, madam," Hatchet corrected her.

"Fiddle." Luty waved her hand dismissively, unmindful of the way the diamond and sapphire rings she wore caught the light. "They knew I was just funnin' with 'em. Besides, they'd been there long enough. If I'd had to listen to Myrtle much longer, I might have run screamin' from the room." She flashed an impish grin at the others around the table. "What kind of a killin' we got here?"

"A man has been shot," Mrs. Jeffries replied. "That's really all we know. We're fairly certain Inspector Witherspoon has the case. Wiggins is at the scene of the crime now, trying unobtrusively to find out more information. He ought to be back any moment."

"Do we have a name?" Hatchet inquired.

"No, only an address," Mrs. Goodge replied. She sighed and reached for the teapot. "Though if that boy doesn't get back soon, I've a mind to box his ears. This waitin's awful."

"It shouldn't be much longer," Smythe said easily. He'd cocked his head to one side. "I fancy there's a 'ansom pullin' up outside."

Within minutes a breathless Wiggins rushed into the kitchen. "Sorry it took so long," he said, "but there was ever so much gossip goin' on I couldn't tear myself away. You'll not believe what all I've learned." He yanked out a chair and plopped down. Fred, the household mongrel, bounced up and down next to the chair, deliriously happy to see his friend. Wiggins absently patted his head.

"Take a moment to compose yourself," Mrs. Jeffries instructed as she poured him a cup of tea, "and then tell us everything you heard."

"What's the victim's name?" Betsy asked eagerly. It niggled her that Wiggins had got to go to the scene of the crime and she'd been sent to fetch people. But that was a woman's lot in life, gettin' stuck with the borin' bits.

"His name was Roland Ashbury," Wiggins replied. "He lived with his daughter and son-in-law. You'll never guess who his son-in-law is, either." He paused dramatically. "Andrew Frommer. Member of Parliament."

CHAPTER 2

"Have you gone deaf, man?" Frommer snapped. "I said why are policemen swarming all over my house? There's an ungodly crowd outside. I demand to know what is going on?"

Witherspoon glanced at Mrs. Frommer. He'd kept quiet, thinking that bad news might be less shocking coming from a member of the family. But apparently his was a minority opinion.

MaryAnne Frommer didn't say a word to her husband. She ignored him and huddled in one corner of the settee. She seemed to have visibly shrunk in size.

The inspector silently chided himself for being so insensitive. Why, the poor woman was probably so overwrought, she wasn't capable of saying anything. How could he have been so impolite? Mrs. Frommer was in shock. It would be his duty to relay the terrible news. He took a quick step toward the angry man striding impatiently through the doorway.

"I'm sorry, sir," he said quickly. "I'm Inspector Gerald Witherspoon. I'm afraid I've very bad news for you."

Frommer stopped abruptly. He tilted his head in a gesture which had the unfortunate result of fattening his face by adding another chin. "Bad news? What sort of bad news? Has there been a robbery?"

"I'm afraid it's worse than that, sir," the inspector said. "Your father-in-law is dead. He's been shot."

"Shot? Roland? But that's ridiculous. He was a bit of a windbag and a fool, but I can't see why anyone would want to shoot him." Frommer didn't so much as glance at his wife as he spoke. "When did it happen?"

"We're not sure," Barnes interjected softly. "We think it was sometime late this afternoon."

"I can't believe this." Frommer began to pace the room, the thud of his footsteps masked by the thick carpet of the drawing room. "It couldn't happen at a worse time. The party doesn't need this sort of thing. I'll have to make some sort of statement. Good Lord, this isn't going to look good at all. A murder in an MP's home." Without so much as a glance at any of the others in the room, he whirled on his heel and stalked back toward the hallway.

"Excuse me, sir," the inspector called just as Frommer reached the door, "but I do need to ask you some questions." Witherspoon was appalled by the callous way the man treated his wife. Good gracious, the poor woman had only just learned her father had been murdered, and here her husband couldn't be bothered to offer one word of comfort.

"Questions? Me?" Frommer looked outraged. "Whatever for? I haven't seen Roland since breakfast this morning."

"That's not true," Mrs. Frommer said. "I saw you talking to him in the garden before he left." She straightened from her slumped position and stared at her husband speculatively. "It looked to me as if you were having quite an argument about something."

Clearly stunned, Frommer gaped at his wife. "Don't be absurd," he said. "I merely stopped to tell the old fellow to be careful and to say good-bye."

"You two were arguing," she countered, pointing a finger at him. "Papa was all puffed up like a bullfrog and your face was as red as a cherry. So don't tell me you weren't having words." She smiled maliciously at her spouse. "And you've never told my father to be careful in your entire life."

Witherspoon felt some of his sympathy for Mrs. Frommer evaporate. What on earth was wrong with these people? He stifled a sigh. Unfortunately, as a policeman, he'd seen all too often that many families not only weren't happy, but positively loathed one another. He was beginning to think that might be the case here.

He looked at Mrs. Frommer. "What time did your father leave the country house?" he asked.

"It must have been around two o'clock," she replied. "He took the two-fifteen train. I believe he was planning on going by his office."

"His office?" Barnes asked. "And where would that be?"

"On Russell Street near the East India Docks," she replied. "He wanted to have a word with—"

"Look, Inspector," Andrew Frommer interrupted, "if you need to ask me questions, please do so now. You can question *her*"—he jerked his head toward his wife—"later. Considering that old Ashbury's managed to get himself murdered in my house, I've a number of things to take care of, so please get on with it."

MaryAnne Frommer stared at her husband with undisguised loathing. Then she giggled, apparently delighted that her husband was so annoyed.

Frommer's jaw dropped. His mouth opened and closed rapidly, as though he were trying to say something but couldn't quite find the right words. Mrs. Frommer, seeing her husband silenced—perhaps for the first time in their marriage, Witherspoon caught himself thinking—giggled again and said, "Dear, dear, Andrew, don't you think you ought to wait before you answer any questions? Unless, of course, you have a perfect alibi for where you've been this afternoon."

"Why . . . you . . . how dare you . . ." Frommer sputtered as he finally found his voice.

"Oh, now that dear old Papa is dead," she hissed, "you'll find I dare quite a bit."

Whatever was going on, the inspector thought, enough is enough. "All right, Mr. Frommer," he said firmly. "If you'll please sit down, we'll take your statement." He turned his attention to Mrs. Frommer. "Madam, you have my deepest sympathies. If you don't mind, we'd like to take your husband's statement now."

She gazed at him curiously. "Does that mean you want me to leave?"

"Just for a little while," Witherspoon said.

She nodded regally and then, completely ignoring her husband, rose to her feet and left the room. The inspector wondered what had happened to change her so completely and so quickly. When Mr. Frommer had first entered the room, she'd cringed like a kicked pup. But within minutes she was baiting the man and virtually accusing him of being a liar.

Frommer sat down on the settee his wife had just vacated. He tapped his fingers restlessly against his knee. "Well, get on with it, man. I don't have all evening."

The inspector glanced at Barnes, making sure the constable's notebook was out and ready before beginning. This was one statement he wanted taken down word for word. Having not been invited to sit, he stood next to the ornate marble fireplace. "When was the last time you saw your father-in-law?"

"As my wife said, it was in the garden after lunch." He shrugged his shoulders casually. "I'd quite forgotten seeing Roland then."

"Your wife was quite sure you were having an argument with her father," Barnes said.

"She was mistaken," Frommer returned disdainfully. "To be perfectly truthful, my wife tends to imagine things. I saw Roland leaving and stopped to say good-bye and to wish him a safe journey."

"What were you doing in the garden, sir?" Witherspoon asked. It sounded a bit like a silly question, but the inspector was amazed at the number of times seemingly stupid questions had led to the arrest of a murderer.

"I was getting some fresh air," Frommer replied. "We'd had a rather heavy lunch and I had a lot of work to do. I'd gone to the garden to get some air, hoping to refresh myself so I could take care of a number of important matters."

"Your servants have said that the entire household was coming back this evening. Is that correct?"

"That's right."

"Did everyone in your household come back to the city separately?"

"I don't understand the question?" Frommer wrinkled his nose in distaste. "What do you mean?"

"Exactly what I said, sir," Witherspoon explained. "Apparently the victim, Mr. Ashbury, came up early, as did the other servants. It was your 'tweeny, Maisie Donovan, who discovered the body," the inspector continued. "Then your wife came home and you arrived a good fifteen minutes after she did. I was merely curious as to what your traveling arrangements had been."

"I don't see how my household's movements can have any bearing on Roland's death, but if you must know, the servants came back with our cases by coach."

"How many servants do you have?"

Frommer thought about it for a moment. "Well, let's see, there's the butler and the cook, of course. Then there's a housemaid and an upstairs maid and a 'tweeny . . . oh yes, and we've a scullery maid and a footman as well." He was counting on his fingers as he spoke. "That makes seven servants, Inspector. Though I fail to see how the number of people I have in my employ has anything to do with Roland's death."

"You'd be surprised, sir," Witherspoon muttered. In his experience, the more staff there was the more opportunity there might be for a good policeman to find out a great deal about a household. So many people, he had observed, tended to think their servants were like pieces of furniture. Deaf, dumb and existing only to serve. He strongly suspected that Andrew Frommer was this kind of person. No doubt Mr. Frommer would be absolutely stunned to know that amongst his own staff there were people of keen intelligence and perception. "What time did your staff leave Ascot for London?"

"Right after lunch."

"At the same time that Mr. Ashbury left for the train station?" Barnes asked.

Witherspoon nodded approvingly. That might indeed be useful information to have.

"Yes, the servants were packing up the coach when Roland and I were chatting in the front garden." Frommer stroked his chin.

"When did you and your wife return to London?" Witherspoon asked. "Apparently, from what Mrs. Frommer said to you, you weren't together."

"She was correct about that," he admitted. "We did come back to town separately. Mrs. Frommer went to visit the vicarage and I came on ahead on the four o'clock. MaryAnne was supposed to take the five o'clock."

"You've been in the city since late this afternoon?" The inspector mentally calculated how long it took to get from Ascot to London. "Since about four forty-five." He pulled out his pocketwatch and noted the time. "It's well after seven, sir. Where have you been?"

"That's none of your business"—Frommer blustered—"but you can't possibly think I had anything to do with Ashbury's death. I'd no reason to dislike Roland."

"I've no doubt that's true, sir. In which case you can have no objection to telling me where you've been since four forty-five. It doesn't take two hours to get here from the station."

"Actually"—Frommer cleared his throat—"I did a bit of shopping. That's why I came on early; I wanted to stop off on Bond Street and see my tailor. Trouble was, fellow wasn't in, so it was a wasted trip."

"What's the name of your tailor, sir?" Barnes asked.

Frommer's eyebrows shot up. "Are you implying you don't believe me?"

"It's merely routine, sir," Witherspoon put in hastily. "We have to confirm everyone's whereabouts."

"That's absurd." Frommer's eyes snapped angrily and a crimson flush spread up his neck. "I'm a respected member of the community, Inspector. A member of Parliament. I'll not be questioned like some common criminal. Now, if you don't mind, sir, I'll say good day." With that, he turned on his heel and strode from the room.

Barnes looked at the inspector. "What do you make of that, sir?"

"Difficult to say, Constable." Witherspoon sighed. "He might be one of those people who feel they're so important they're above the rules that govern ordinary people."

"Or he might be scared."

"Yes, that's definitely a possibility as well." Witherspoon shrugged. "It doesn't really matter, though, does it? We'll have to confirm his alibi."

"How can we do that, sir? He never told us the name of his tailor."

"I daresay his wife will," the inspector replied. "I don't think she likes him all that much."

A wide smile flashed across Barnes's craggy face, making him appear years younger. "Right, sir, I should have thought of that. Do you think he'll cause us a bit of bother, bein' an MP and all? He could go running to the home secretary."

"I expect he will," Witherspoon replied. "But it won't make any difference in our investigation. We must find out the truth; it's our duty."

Barnes nodded somberly. Sometimes he wasn't sure whether his superior was a saint or a fool. Politicians could cause no end of bother. But either way, the constable was firmly in the inspector's corner. "Shall I go and get Mrs. Frommer?"

"Yes, please. I'll be very interested in hearing what she has to say."

"An MP, cor blimey." Smythe shook his head. "That's a bit of 'ard luck for our inspector."

"Why?" Wiggins asked.

"'Cause politicians got friends in high places," Luty said darkly, "and the right kind of friends can make life awfully miserable for an honest policeman tryin' to find a killer."

"Let's not jump to any conclusions as yet," Mrs. Jeffries put in quickly, though she too was a bit worried about this latest turn of events. "Wiggins still has to tell us the rest of what he found out this evening."

"It were dead easy, Mrs. Jeffries," Wiggins continued eagerly. "A whole crowd had gathered in front of the 'ouse. There were police everywhere."

"You made sure that none of them saw you?" Hatchet asked. They were all aware that one slip and the whole game could come down around their ears. The inspector was a dear man, quite naive and innocent, but he wasn't a fool. Seeing a member of the household staff at the scene of all his crimes would not be a wise thing.

"'Course I did, I kept a right sharp eye out; there was two women as tall as pine trees standin' in front of me. One of 'em was fairly wide too. I kept well behind 'em." He waved a hand in dismissal. "I know what's what."

"Of course you do," Mrs. Jeffries said, "but Hatchet has a valid point. It's imperative we keep firmly in the background on the inspector's cases." The last few cases had thrust one or more of them firmly in the forefront of an investigation, and this time the housekeeper wanted to nip that sort of thing in the bud.

"We understand, Mrs. J." Smythe answered for all of them. "Believe me, everyone knows we've shaved it fairly close in the last year. Now go on, lad"—he encouraged the footman—"tell us the rest."

"Well, like I said, the victim's name was Ashbury," Wiggins continued. "'E's an older gent, probably up in his late seventies. He's lived in the Frommer 'ouse for a good number of years, moved in after his wife passed on." He leaned forward eagerly. "And you'll never guess what else I 'eard. Seems 'e's a bit of a snob and there's some dark 'ints that 'e's done 'is daughter wrong."

"Are you sure of this information?" Mrs. Goodge asked. Sometimes, she thought, the lad could get ahead of himself and say things he only thought were true instead of knowing for sure. As she'd been guilty of that herself a time or two, she was especially sensitive to it in others.

"'Course I'm sure," Wiggins said defensively. "I'ad a nice natter with two 'ousemaids from the place right next to the Frommer 'ouse, and after I'd gotten everythin' I could out of them, I found a talkative footman. He actually works for the Frommers."

"No one's doubting your truthfulness, Wiggins," Mrs. Jeffries soothed, "it's simply that in the heat of the moment people will say anything. After all, you were in a crowd just outside the victim's house. I remember my late husband once telling me there was a near riot in York when a suspected child killer was rumored to be hiding out in the attic of a boarding-house."

Mrs. Jeffries's late husband had been a constable in Yorkshire for over twenty years. She often thought it was through him that she first got her love of snooping.

"The truth was," she continued, "it was only a man who merely had had a drink with the felon who was actually in the house. But by the time the story made the rounds of the crowd, they became so enraged it took several dozen policemen to hold them back."

Wiggins nodded in understanding. "Don't worry, Mrs. Jeffries, I was right careful about 'ow I put things. I'm pretty sure what I 'eard is true."

"How had he done his daughter wrong?" Betsy asked curiously.

"Neither of the maids 'ad any details," he replied. "They just said they'd 'eard some gossip from the Frommer servants that Mr. Ashbury had a right old dustup with 'is daughter a while back, and even though they live in the same 'ouse, she's barely spoken to 'im since."

"How long ago was the alleged altercation?" Hatchet asked.

"I'm not sure of the actual date—they couldn't remember—but it were after the new year, they knew that much," Wiggins answered.

"That was months ago," Betsy said. "That's a long time to go without speaking to someone."

"Did you ask the footman about it?" Mrs. Goodge asked. "You know, just to suss out if what the maid told you was the truth and not just some talk she made up to make herself look important?"

"I were goin' to"—Wiggins shook his head—"but all of a sudden the lad took off like the 'ounds of hell were on 'is 'eels."

"Ya followed him, didn't ya?" Luty asked eagerly.

"Almost," Wiggins admitted, "but then I decided not to. I knew every-one was waitin' fer me, so I came on 'ome."

There was a collective groan around the table. Wiggins looked crest-fallen.

"That's enough," Mrs. Jeffries chided them. "Wiggins did just as he ought. The first thing we must do is to get started on the this case, not go haring off after someone who may or may not know anything pertinent about it." She too was a bit disappointed, but she wouldn't let it show. She'd not have the lad starting off on this hunt thinking himself a failure. "Now, I suggest we decide what we're all going to be doing."

"I'll nip out tomorrow morning and have a go at the shopkeepers in the area," Betsy said. She was quite good at that; she'd done it enough times that she knew exactly how to poke and prod until she found someone who had information.

"You'd best be back by eleven o'clock," Mrs. Goodge told her bluntly. "If you'll recall, Lady Cannonberry is comin' round for morning tea."

There was another collective groan. This time Mrs. Jeffries didn't try to silence them. Ruth Cannonberry was their neighbor and a delightful friend, but all of them hated postponing their snooping for a social occasion.

"Can't we put 'er off?" Smythe asked. "I'm itchin' to get out. I want to 'ave a go at the cabbies and the pubs in the area."

"I'm afraid we can't get out of it." Mrs. Jeffries sighed. "Ruth's been gone for over two weeks; she'll be very hurt if everyone isn't there."

"Well, at least Madam and I can make a good start," Hatchet stated conversationally.

"'Fraid not," Luty said. She looked a bit shamefaced. "We were invited too, and I accepted. Ruth's expectin' us."

"Really, madam." Hatchet's eyes narrowed. "I do wish you'd let me know when you've accepted a social invitation."

"Cor blimey," Wiggins whined. "We'll be ages gettin' started if we 'ave to 'ave tea."

"You're not goin' to tell 'er what's goin' on?" Smythe asked anxiously. His concern was quite valid. Lady Cannonberry had been involved in several of their other cases. She considered herself an excellent detective. As a matter of fact, she frequently hinted that she'd love nothing more than to be asked to join all the cases.

"Of course I'm not going to mention it," Mrs. Jeffries replied. "In any case, as she has a houseguest, I don't think she'd want to become involved."

Luty snorted. "Fiddlesticks. She'd dump her guest in two seconds flat if you'd let her into the case. She loves to snoop more'n I do."

Hatchet raised his eyebrows. "I hardly think that's possible, madam."

"I suggest that we all meet here at ten o'clock," Mrs. Jeffries said firmly. "That will give us plenty of time to have our meeting before we have tea with Ruth. It will also give the early birds who want to get out and about a few hours to do so before the meeting. Is that agreeable to everyone?"

"Sounds fine to me." Wiggins nodded. "It'll give me time to get over to the Frommer 'ouse and see if I can find that footman. Maybe I can get 'im to talk."

"If you haven't any luck with the footman," Mrs. Jeffries suggested, "try making contact with another servant from the house. Try and find out as much as you can about the events leading up to the murder."

"I'll get onto my sources down at the bank," Luty said. Her connections into the heart of the British financial community were legion. When she said "down at the bank" she was referring to the Bank of England. "If this Frommer is an MP, there ought to be plenty I can dig up on 'im."

"But if you'll recall, madam . . ." Hatchet sniffed. "Mr. Frommer isn't the victim. His father-in-law was."

"I know that," Luty shot back. "I'll find out what I can about the victim and the rest of the household too."

"Very well," he replied, unperturbed. "I, of course, will be using my own rather extensive network of resources for information."

Luty glared at him. She and Hatchet were fiercely competitive when it came to hunting clues.

"What are you going to do?" Mrs. Goodge asked Mrs. Jeffries. Everyone already knew that the cook was going to bake up a storm so she'd be able to feed the army of people she'd have trooping through her kitchen.

Mrs. Jeffries thought for a moment. "I'm not really sure. I think I'll hear what the inspector has to say before I decide what I need to do."

"Do you think Dr. Bosworth will be doing the postmortem?" the cook asked. "He comes in handy every now and again."

"He most certainly does," Hatchet agreed.

Dr. Bosworth was a young physician who'd helped them on several of their cases. As he'd practiced the healing arts for several years in San Francisco, he knew an awful lot about gunshot wounds. Americans, Mrs. Jeffries thought wistfully, had so many more murders than the English. Accordingly Dr. Bosworth had developed some very interesting theories. She found them most fascinating. "Dr. Bosworth is the police surgeon for the Westminster area. I don't know if the victim's home is in his district," Mrs. Jeffries replied. "But it would certainly be convenient if it were."

MaryAnne Frommer smiled wearily as she sat back down on the settee she'd vacated only half an hour earlier. "You wanted to question me, Inspector?" she said.

"Only if you feel up to it," Witherspoon replied. Her earlier bravado was gone; now she merely looked like a very weary, very tired middle-aged woman doing her best to cope with bad news.

"You've a lot of questions, Inspector," she said, shrugging her shoulders, "and I'd like to answer them now and get it over with. I still can't believe he's gone."

Witherspoon couldn't make head or tails of the woman. She certainly didn't seem cold or callous, yet he had the sense that she was more shocked than grieved by her father's demise. Interesting and also very sad. "I'm sure it's most difficult for you," he began, "and I appreciate your cooperation. I'm sure you're as eager as I am to get to the bottom of this."

"I'd like to know who did it," she replied softly, her attention focused on the window across the room. "And why."

Witherspoon cleared his throat and glanced at Barnes. The constable had his trusty notebook open and his pencil at the ready. "Mrs. Frommer, who's your husband's tailor?"

She started in surprise. "Pardon? Did I hear you correctly? Did you ask who was my husband's tailor?"

"That's correct." He hesitated for a moment. "Your husband claims he's been on Bond Street shopping since four forty-five this afternoon. He says he went by his tailor's. Unfortunately he neglected to give us the man's name."

She smiled broadly. "He goes to Barkham's."

"Thank you." Witherspoon suddenly went blank. Now that he'd asked the one question on his mind, he found he simply couldn't think of another one. Oh dear, this wouldn't do. It wouldn't do at all. "Er . . . Mrs. Frommer . . . er . . . uh, can you tell me what you think your husband and your father might have been arguing about when you saw them in the garden today?" Yes, he thought, that was a good one.

"I've no idea," she answered. "Neither of them took me into their confidence."

"But you're certain they were arguing?" he prompted. What if she were merely guessing or, even worse, simply making things up so her husband would look guilty? From what he'd seen of both the Frommers, there was no love lost between them.

"As certain as I can be without having actually heard what they were saying." She shrugged. "But as I told you earlier, they looked like they were quarreling fiercely."

"How long has your father lived here?" Barnes asked.

"Since my mother died sixteen years ago." She clasped her hands together in her lap.

"Yes, I understand, your poor father probably couldn't stand to be alone after losing your mother," Witherspoon murmured sympathetically. He'd often found that a small dose of understanding went quite a long way and got one a great deal of information.

"Oh no, that wasn't it at all," she explained. "He came here because after Mama died, he'd nowhere else to live."

Witherspoon frowned. "You mean he'd no home of his own?"

"That's right. You see, he'd lived in my mother's house all of their married life. Mama was a Sheridan," she said proudly, dropping the name of one of England's oldest and wealthiest families. "I was already married and living here, so when she passed away, he had to leave. The house naturally went to one of my mother's cousins. He was most put out about it too. He'd always thought Mama had left the house to him, but she couldn't, could she? I mean, it belonged to her family, not to her. I don't think Mama was always truthful with Papa, but then again, why should she be? He certainly wasn't truthful with her."

"I see." Witherspoon nodded encouragingly. "So your father couldn't afford a home of his own—"

"Oh he could afford it," she interrupted. "He just didn't want to live on his own. Not when he could live in an MP's home."

"I see," the inspector said. "Do you know if your father had any enemies?" That was always a good, straightforward question. Generally, though, it always got the same response. The victim was universally loved and hadn't an enemy in the world.

"Oh, lots of them, I should imagine," she replied airily.

"Oh, and who would these enemies be?" the inspector said quickly. Goodness, he hadn't expected that reply.

"I expect most of the neighbors disliked him," she replied. "He was quite a nosy sort, my father. And he loved the sound of his own voice. He monopolized conversations and had opinions about everything. It didn't matter to him whether his opinions were informed or intelligent, either. He wasn't at all shy about sharing them. The neighbors used to run when they saw him coming down the street."

"That must have been difficult for him," Witherspoon suggested.

"Not at all," she answered. "He never noticed. Honestly I've no idea how the man lived so long without realizing that he was so disliked. He could clear a room faster than a bad smell. People would make their excuses the moment he walked in."

"Other than the neighbors, who else disliked him?" Witherspoon asked.

"None of the servants were fond of him," she said. "He was such a tattle-tale. One small infraction and he'd go running to Andrew." She held up her hand and ticked off her fingers as she spoke. "Let's see, the neighbors and the servants. Then there are his business colleagues. He wasn't terribly popular with any of them. Not that he does much work these days; he simply sticks his head in his office every once in a while to annoy poor Henry."

"Henry?" Witherspoon queried.

"Henry Alladyce. The son of my father's late business partner," she replied. "Oh yes, of course, I almost forgot. I loathed the man." She looked up at Witherspoon and Barnes and smiled brightly. "I thought I might as well tell you myself rather than have you learn it from the servants. I didn't like my father. I've barely spoken to him for months."

Witherspoon was so scandalized he could barely speak. He knew he oughtn't to be so shocked; as a policemen, he'd seen enough horror to convince him that human beings were capable of anything. Yet still, he was stunned by the cheerful way she spoke of hating her own father, her own flesh and blood. "I see," he finally said.

Barnes asked, "Why did your father come into town early?"

"He wanted to stop by his office and check on things." She smiled. "At least that's what he told us. But it was obviously just a ruse to get away early."

The inspector regarded her quizzically. "Why do you say that? From the manner in which you describe your father and your relationship with him, why would he need a ruse to get away?"

"Oh, he wouldn't care about offending me." She laughed. "Not one whit. But he walks on eggs not to offend Andrew. Andrew's important, you see. He'd walk over burning coals rather than offend my husband. So he needed a ruse, you see. That's why he came up with that sad tale of going to his office."

The inspector's head started to ache and he found himself wishing he wasn't getting all this information quite so quickly. He could barely take it all in. "I'm not sure I understand." He shook his head, almost to try and clear it. "What makes you think there was a ruse . . . I mean—"

"What the inspector means," Barnes interrupted, "is why did your father want to come home early in the first place? Why not just wait and come with either you or Mr. Frommer."

"I should think that's obvious," she declared. "He was meeting someone. Someone he didn't want the rest of us to know about."

"You think he planned to meet someone here?" Witherspoon said. "Why? What makes you think so?"

"Because he was having tea with whoever killed him," she replied proudly. "I overheard one of the constables talking when I was waiting for you to question me. Plus I saw the tea trolley being taken out of the room. So it must have been planned, mustn't it?"

Witherspoon hazarded a guess. "He could have met someone when he was at his office and invited them back for tea?" He'd have a quiet word with the constables later. It was easy to slip and talk about the circumstances of the murder, he could understand that, but he would warn them to be a bit more careful when there was a possible suspect in the area.

Mrs. Frommer shook her head. "He wouldn't have done that. He was neither generous nor kind and he never ever did anything impulsively. Every aspect of his life was planned out to the last detail. Believe me. I know the man. He came back early to meet someone. Furthermore, the house had been empty for two weeks."

"Yes, we know that," the inspector said.

"But you don't understand the significance of it," she insisted. She pointed in the direction of her father's quarters. "The man was shot while having tea. But the house had been empty, which means there wasn't a scrap of food to be had. Yet someone had bought milk for tea and stopped at a bakery to buy a cake. That someone could be only one person. My father. So you see, he planned to be here this afternoon, and whoever he planned to meet killed him."

Witherspoon forced himself to speak with the servants. His head pounded and he'd heard more information than he could possibly understand in a very short time, but he felt it imperative he question the servants himself.

He smiled at Maisie Donovan. She was a tall, buxom young lady with dark blonde hair and a wide, intelligent-looking face. "Now, Miss Donovan.

Could you tell me again how it was that you went into Mr. Ashbury's quarters and discovered his body?"

Maisie nodded vigorously. "I might not have noticed if I'd not stopped on the landing to rest. That trunk of Mrs. Frommer's weighs ever so much. If that bloomin' Boyd hadn't run off, I'da not been stuck draggin' the ruddy thing up to the attic, but it's a good thing it were me and not him, if you know what I mean. A bit slow is our Boyd. He'd have not noticed the light comin' out of Mr. Ashbury's door." She paused to take a breath.

"I'm afraid I don't quite understand." Witherspoon frowned. "Are you saying a member of your staff has gone missing?" This was rather important news.

"Oh yes. We woke up this morning and Boyd had scarpered," she said cheerily. "His clothes were gone too, so we knew he'd gone, you see. Mind you, everyone was quite shocked seein' as how attached to Mrs. Frommer Boyd was. Loved her, he did. But maybe he got tired of bearin' the brunt of Mr. Frommer's temper all the time. He used to always say he was fixin' to go off to Australia someday. Claimed he had a cousin in Adelaide."

Witherspoon thought about this statement. "So the lad was gone before anyone, including Mr. Ashbury, left the Ascot house? Is that correct?"

She nodded. "That's right. And Boyd wouldn't 'ave killed anyone, 'specially not Mr. Ashbury. He's simple, you see. That's why it were a good thing it were me on the landin' and not him. Boyd wouldn't have gone into Mr. Ashbury's quarters under any circumstances. Dead scared of Mr. Ashbury he was. Used to run and hide every time the old man came through the kitchen."

Witherspoon didn't see how a footman who'd gone off hours before the murder could have anything to do with its commission, but one never knew. "But you did go into Mr. Ashbury's quarters, correct?"

"That's right."

"Did you hear anyone else in there?" Barnes asked.

She shook her head. "No, I didn't hear anything."

"Did you see anything odd or unusual?" Witherspoon asked. "You know, when you first arrived back at the house. Was there any sign that someone had been in here? Any doors left open? Any windows?"

"Nothing like that," she replied firmly. "The back door was locked tighter than the vault at the Bank of England."

"How about the front door?" Barnes asked. "Was it locked?"

"I think so." Maisie seemed less sure now. "I mean, I didn't go to the front of the house and look. That would be the butler's job. Not mine. But I'll tell you one thing; whoever left, didn't go out by the back door. Not unless they had a key."

CHAPTER 3

"You didn't need to wait up for me, Mrs. Jeffries." Witherspoon handed her his hat. "But I'm very grateful that you did."

"I was curious about your new case, sir," she replied, hanging the bowler on the coat tree and then starting down the hall. "Do come and have a sit-down, Inspector. I've made a fresh pot of tea."

He followed her into the drawing room and sat down in his favorite chair while she poured tea for the both of them. He closed his eyes for a moment, trying to clear some of the muddle out of his mind. But everything about this evening was a jumble. The dead body, the gun being left on the scene, the apparent hatred between the Frommers, Maisie Donovan's interview and the missing footman. It was no good. He couldn't make heads or tails of anything. The only thing which would do any good at all was having a nice long chat with his housekeeper.

"Here you are, sir," she said, handing him his cup. She sat down on the chair opposite him and waited patiently for him to begin. Mrs. Jeffries had no doubt he'd tell her everything. He always did.

"It's very good of you to have tea waiting for me," he began after he'd taken a nice long sip. "I'm going to become spoiled and expect it."

"You deserve it, sir," she said truthfully. He was the best of employers. He'd inherited this house and his fortune from a rather eccentric aunt, and having not been born to wealth, he'd never learned to treat servants badly. Unlike most men of his position, he actually treated the staff like human beings and not objects put on this earth for his pleasure and amusement. Even if he hadn't been a police inspector and hadn't given Mrs. Jeffries a chance to do what she most loved doing, solving mysteries, she thought she still might wait up for him when he came in late. "Now, sir, do tell me all about this case of yours."

"It's going to be one of those dreadful ones, Mrs. Jeffries." He sighed. "I just know it. Why, already I've learned so much that I can't quite keep everything straight in my mind. Does that ever happen to you?"

"Of course," she answered promptly. "It happens to everyone, but I'm sure it must be especially difficult for you, sir. After all, your mind is quite different from the rest of us. Your mind, sir, is always on the hunt, so to speak."

He gazed at her blankly, as though he couldn't quite decide whether she was complimenting him or insulting him. "Yes," he said slowly, "I suppose it is . . . I mean, I suppose I am a bit different. Well, I must be, mustn't I?"

"But of course, sir," she said briskly. She realized he needed a bit of a confidence boost here. The dear man sometimes took it into his head that he wasn't up to the task at hand. "I'm sure that even as we speak there's a corner of your mind that's sorting through everything you've learned today. Why, you're sure to be cataloging and analyzing all of it, sir. Now, what happened, sir?"

Her words made him smile. She was, of course, correct. Even though he couldn't sort things out yet, he was certain his "inner voice" was doing its job properly. Eventually he'd clear the muddle up. He always did. "A fellow named Roland Ashbury was shot this afternoon," he replied. "While he was having tea, of all things."

"How awful, sir." She didn't have to force the note of disgust in her voice. Mrs. Jeffries thought murder was the worst of all crimes. "When did it happen?"

"As near as we can tell, it must have been around half-past three," he continued.

"Do you have a witness that heard the shot?" she asked hopefully. To be able to pinpoint the time precisely would give them an excellent starting point.

"Unfortunately, no. That's actually quite a puzzle too. No one seems to have heard the shot at all. It must have been quite loud too."

"Then how do you know what time it happened?"

"One of the neighbors saw him going into his house at about ten minutes to three. Maisie Donovan, the maid, discovered the body at around four o'clock. If you factor in the time it must have taken him to make tea and exchange some pleasantries with his guest, we venture to assume the

shooting probably took place around three forty-five," he said proudly.
He and Barnes had worked out that particular timetable. He was quite
pleased with it.

"Why do you think he entertained his guest?" she asked curiously.
"Maybe the killer murdered him as soon as he arrived at the house."

"He couldn't have." Witherspoon smiled with pride. "He ate the cake.
Both of them did. We found their empty plates right next to the empty
teacups. One of them hates walnuts and the other cleaned his plate of every
last crumb."

"I see," she murmured. "And from that you've deduced that he not
only knew his killer, he trusted him enough to have tea with him?"

"Right," Witherspoon said enthusiastically. "It's obvious they spent
some time talking and enjoying their tea before the killer pulled out the
gun and shot him in the head. Besides, from the position of the body, it
doesn't look as if the victim knew what hit him. His posture wasn't in the
least defensive." The inspector continued on, telling her every detail that
he could remember from the crime scene. Talking to her helped him; now
that he'd shared the horror of the hole in that poor man's skull, he sincerely
hoped he'd be spared nightmares.

"He was shot in the head, sir?" she asked. She already knew some of
these particulars, but she couldn't let on that she did. Mrs. Jeffries didn't
want the inspector to become suspicious at her lack of curiosity.

"Oh yes." He took a sip from his cup. "At very close range too."

"And no one heard the shot?" she pressed again. That was an important
fact; she wanted to make sure it was absolutely correct.

"Not so far," Witherspoon replied. "But we've still got lads doing
house-to-house interviews. Something may turn up tomorrow. The whole
situation is very odd. Except for the killer, Ashbury was apparently alone
in the house. Quite deliberately so, it seems. The rest of the household was in
the country and they didn't come home till later this afternoon. According
to the evidence and statements made by the victim's family, Ashbury connived to get to the house early so that he could meet the person who probably killed him."

"So you're assuming he knew his killer and had actually invited him
to tea, is that it, sir?" Mrs. Jeffries was beginning to get a tad confused
herself.

"That's the assumption we're working on." He sighed again and continued specifying the other details of the investigation. Carefully he gave

her a moment-by-moment account. As he spoke he felt as though a huge weight were being lifted off his shoulders. By the time he'd finished his narrative, he felt positively cheerful.

"So you can see why I thought this might be a difficult one to solve," he said. "After all, this is going to be one of those cases where the victim wasn't well liked by anyone but doesn't seem to have done anything bad enough to actually make someone want to shoot him. Yet someone did shoot the poor chap, and it's my job to find out who. Most puzzling."

"But you're very good at solving puzzles, sir," she reminded him. "I must say, his daughter's behavior seemed rather odd."

"Very odd, indeed," he replied, then took another sip from his cup. "As was her husband's behavior. About the only behavior that wasn't odd was the servants'. They were all just frightened, of course. Except for the one that found the body; she didn't seem to be scared. Mind you, I'm going to have another chat with the staff. It was so late by the time I got to them that everyone was tired."

"Are you going to look for the missing footman?" Mrs. Jeffries sipped her tea.

Witherspoon considered this. "I'm not sure. The lad left hours before the killing happened. I don't see what it could have to do with the murder, but then again, I'm not sure I quite believe it was a coincidence. But yes, I'll try to find the boy. He may know something."

Mrs. Jeffries nodded and went on to her next question. "Are you sure the gun you found under the tea trolley was the same one used to kill the victim?" She'd learned never to take anything for granted.

"We won't know more until after the postmortem's been done," he replied. "The revolver had been recently fired."

"Did anyone in the household recognize the gun?"

Witherspoon stared at her blankly. "Pardon?"

"Oh, how silly of me." She waved her hand dismissively. "Please, forget I asked that question. Of course you won't show the gun to the servants until after you find out whether or not it's likely to be the murder weapon."

The inspector gazed at her for a moment and then broke into a wide smile. "You're never silly, Mrs. Jeffries. But you are right in that I wouldn't show it about until after I have the results of the postmortem. Of course, even a good autospy can't tell us precisely if it is the murder weapon, but if the bullet is retrieved, it can narrow it down quite a bit. And, at that point, I'll try and find out if anyone recognizes it."

They talked for a good half hour more. Mrs. Jeffries listened carefully and occasionally asked a pertinent question or two. By the time a yawning Inspector Witherspoon took his leave and headed for the stairway, she was sure she'd learned all the details of the case. She knew the names of the two suspects, the number of servants in the household and the time everyone claimed they arrived at the Frommer house. She knew how many cups were on the trolley, that walnut cake had been served and the name of Andrew Frommer's tailor. What she didn't know yet was how many more people would turn up who had the motive, means and opportunity to murder one Roland Arthur Ashbury.

"The police'll have a hard time findin' out what's what," Nat Hopkins said as he plunged his hand into the soapy water and grabbed the washrag. "Not with Frommer bein' a bloomin' politician. Thinks he's above the law, he does."

"Why do ya say that?" Wiggins asked. He glanced up the street, hoping that the inspector or, even worse, Betsy didn't see him chatting up this shopkeeper. Of the two, he'd rather face his employer. At least the inspector wouldn't tear him off a strip for poaching on his territory. When it came to shopkeepers, Betsy thought they were hers by right. "I mean, wouldn't a member of Parliament want to find out who murdered his father-in-law?"

Nat slapped the washrag against the window and energetically stroked it from side to side. "Frommer'll make like he does, but take my word fer it, he's not losin' any sleep over the old man's death."

"I guess 'e musta not liked 'im much," Wiggins said casually. "'Course, seems to me it were pretty decent of 'im to let the bloke live with 'im, seein' as 'ow 'e didn't like him."

Nat slopped the rag across the bottom of the window and then dropped it back in the bucket. "Don't be daft, boy. Frommer only let the old man stay on because he had to. That one"—he jerked his dark head in the direction of the Frommer house—"doesn't do anything out of the kindness of his heart. If he'd tried to toss him out, Ashbury would have blabbed to everyone who stood still for thirty seconds about Frommer's mistress. That'd not done his career any good."

"Cor blimey," Wiggins exclaimed, "you know a lot."

"Sure I do," Nat said conversationally. He reached into the bucket of rinse water and grabbed a clean rag. Wringing the water out, he started mopping the suds off the top of the pane. "My niece Emma used to work for the Frommers. She was the upstairs maid. Treated her like dirt, they did. A couple of weeks ago the old bastard sacked her because she broke a flowerpot. Can you believe it? Sackin' someone over a trifle like that. Well, I can tell you, we've no reason to keep quiet about Mr. Holier-Than-Thou Frommer. Not now. We kept our peace even though Emma used to come home tellin' these bloomin' awful tales about the rows the mister and missus'd have, but now we're tellin' the whole neighborhood, we are. They wouldn't even give the girl a bloody reference."

"Cor blimey," Wiggins said sympathetically. "That's a bit of 'ard luck. It's tough to get a position without a reference."

Nat shrugged. "Yeah, but what can you do? Poor girl'll just have to do the best she can. She's a right pretty girl; it's just as well she's not livin' in that house. I'd not trust a man like Frommer to keep his hands to himself." He sighed. "Still, it's one extra mouth to feed. The shop's doin' all right, but well, you know how it is. I only wish one of them coppers would come along and ask our Emma a few questions. She could set 'em straight."

That could be arranged, Wiggins thought. "Did she ever see Mr. Frommer's mistress?" He could feel himself blush as he asked the question, but he wanted to have as much information as possible before this morning's meeting.

"That she did." Nat grinned broadly and dropped the rag into the water. A few drops shot up and splattered over the apron spread across his wide belly. "Twice."

Wiggins nodded encouragingly. He'd come out this morning to try to find that footman who'd scarpered off the previous night. Failing that, he'd hoped to make contact with a servant from the Frommer house. But no one had so much as stuck their head out the door this morning, and rather than go back to Upper Edmonton Gardens empty-handed, he'd come along to see if any of the tradespeople could give him any clues about the footman's whereabouts. He'd only had to mention the murder to the dark-haired grocer and Nat Hopkins gave him an earful. "Cor blimey, then she actually saw him with his fancy woman." He shook his head in pretended amazement. "That wasn't too smart of the fellow, lettin' himself be seen that way."

"Frommer's not too smart." Nat picked the bucket up and started for the edge of the pavement. "He's arrogant and stupid. Probably didn't even realize that Emma was in the house when he had his woman there." He dumped the dirty water into the street and looked up at Wiggins speculatively. "You're a curious one, aren't you?"

Like a bolt from the blue, Wiggins was suddenly inspired. There was a way to kill two birds with one stone. "'Course I'm curious," he admitted. "Murder always makes a body ask questions like. Especially if they work for Inspector Gerald Witherspoon. He's in charge of this killin' and I'll bet my next quarter's salary 'e'd be right interested in anythin' your Emma 'ad to say."

"Here we are, Constable." The inspector stopped in front of a door upon which a faded sign reading ASHBURY AND ALLADYCE, SHIPPING AGENTS was attached. They stood in front of a tall, rather scruffy-looking office building on a small, narrow street just off the East India Docks. On one side of the building was a long, fully occupied warehouse; its front doors stood wide open, and despite the narrowness of the street, vans, carts and freight wagons were lining up to pick up and deliver goods. On the other side was a smaller but equally busy goods depot. In the bright morning sunshine, the blue-black Thames glittered through the spaces between the buildings.

Witherspoon knocked once, opened the door and they stepped inside. They found themselves in a small, rather dim room. The inspector blinked, trying to adjust his eyes to the gloom. What light there was crept in through the rather dirty transom over the front door.

"May I help you gentlemen?"

Witherspoon jumped and turned to see a tall, cranelike man stepping out of a door on the other side of the room. "Er, we'd like to speak to Mr. Roland Ashbury's clerk," he said, squinting so that he could see the fellow better. "I say, it's awfully dark in here."

"I haven't drawn the curtain yet," the man replied. He sounded rather petulant. His hair was dark blond and curly, his face bony and his mouth a thin line slashed across a jutting chin. "I've only just unlocked the door and come inside." He swept a heavy curtain down the entire wall, revealing a set of windows and letting the sun inside the gloomy room. At once the place was brighter, but not much else.

The furniture, such as it was, consisted of two huge desks overflowing with papers and cluttered with boxes, bags and baskets along the top. The floor was gray linoleum. A straight-backed chair sat before each desk. Along the wall was a row of cabinets, their tops cluttered as well with all manner of things. Above the cabinets was a chalkboard covered with rows of names and dates.

"Are those references to ships?" Witherspoon asked curiously as he pointed to the chalkboard.

"Yes, and their estimated departure dates. We are a shipping company." He waved them toward him. "I suppose I'm the person you need to see, but I'm not Roland Ashbury's clerk."

"I'm sorry," Witherspoon said sincerely. "No offense was intended. I'm Inspector Witherspoon and this is Constable Barnes. We were told that Mr. Ashbury had a clerk and that it was this clerk he stopped to see yesterday—" He broke off as he realized he wasn't making a great deal of sense.

"What's your name, sir?" Barnes asked quickly.

"Henry Alladyce." He sat down on one of the chairs. He was dressed neatly in a crisp white shirt, black tie and yellow waistcoat. His outer coat, the same pearl-gray color as his trousers, was hung neatly on the coat tree by the door. "I'm the only one here. As I said, I'm not a clerk; I own half of this company."

Witherspoon hesitated for a moment. He did so hate telling people bad news, but there was nothing he could do to soften the blow. "I'm afraid I've some bad news Mr. Alladyce—" he began.

"Yes, yes, I know," Alladyce interrupted impatiently. "Old Roland's got himself murdered. It was in this morning's papers. Well, it's too bad, I suppose, but let's be frank, Inspector. Roland was quite old and not particularly well liked. I shouldn't think he'll be missed."

"Apparently not," the inspector murmured. "Er, Mr. Alladyce, when was the last time you saw Mr. Ashbury?"

Alladyce leaned back in the chair, steepled his fingers together and stared up at the ceiling. "Let me see, I suppose it must have been over a fortnight ago. Yes, that's right. It was the day before Roland went off to the Ascot house with his daughter and her husband."

"You didn't see Mr. Ashbury yesterday?" Barnes asked. "He didn't call here in the afternoon?"

"No," Alladyce replied. "As I said, I haven't seen him since before he left for Ascot."

"Were you here all afternoon?" Witherspoon asked.

Henry spread his hands. "Where else would I be? I'm the only one here and I've a business to run."

"You don't have a clerk, sir?" Barnes asked.

"Roland claimed we didn't need one." Henry pursed his lips. "But of course we did, and do."

"Did you see anyone yesterday afternoon, sir?" Barnes pressed. "Anyone who can verify you were here all day?"

Henry's expression didn't change. "No, I didn't. I spent the afternoon going over the accounts. I didn't leave until almost seven last night. I saw no one and no one saw me."

"You're sure Mr. Ashbury didn't come here?" Witherspoon asked.

"Quite sure," Alladyce replied. "If he were coming here, he'd have sent a message or a telegram. He did neither."

The inspector nodded. "Did Mr. Ashbury have any enemies?"

"No more than any other businessman." Alladyce shrugged casually. "You mustn't judge the firm by the appearance of our office." He waved his hand around the room. "This is quite a successful venture, sir. It's a bit untidy just at the moment, but that's only because Roland was ridiculously cheap and absolutely refused to spend a penny on proper furniture and fittings."

"So you're saying that Mr. Ashbury had made enemies in the course of running his business?" Barnes clarified.

"Not exactly." Alladyce sighed. "What I meant was that it was entirely possible that Roland had made enemies. When he and my father were building this business, Roland wasn't above undercutting someone else's rates."

"I see," Witherspoon replied. This interview wasn't getting them much information. But at least they'd confirmed that Ashbury hadn't called here before going to the Frommer home. "Well, thank you, Mr. Alladyce. You've been most helpful. Do get in touch with us if you can think of anyone who might have had a reason to want to harm Mr. Ashbury."

"Oh." Alladyce brightened immediately. "Then you'd best sit down, Inspector. I can think of lots of people who would have loved to harm Roland."

"I do hope you don't mind my bringing Morris with me." Ruth Cannonberry whispered the words to Mrs. Jeffries as they walked across the small terrace behind Upper Edmonton Gardens. They headed toward the oak table which sat invitingly underneath the shade of a large tree. Her houseguest, who'd been introduced to them as Morris Pilchard, was at the far end of the gardens. He stood beneath a yew tree, staring fixedly at the trunk.

"Of course we don't mind," Mrs. Jeffries assured her. The others were already at the table, which was set for a splendid morning tea. "Your guests are always welcome."

"Thank you." Ruth smiled brightly and her pale, middle-aged face was transformed. "I really didn't know what else to do with him. He's not terribly interested in seeing the sights of London." She sighed and turned her head, seeking her houseguest. "He must be watching ants," she muttered when she spotted him.

"Is he a naturalist, then?" Mrs. Jeffries tried to move Lady Cannonberry along a bit faster. The others were champing at the bit to get started, and if the truth were known, she was rather in a hurry herself.

"Oh no." Ruth shrugged. "He simply likes watching bugs. Oh, this looks lovely," she exclaimed as they finally reached the table. "Mrs. Goodge"—she beamed at the cook—"you've outdone yourself. It looks wonderful."

The table was loaded with food. There was a large brown pot of tea, a plain seedcake, scones, cream, jam, a Victoria sponge and a bowl of quince sprinkled with sugar.

"Thank you," the cook replied briskly. Naturally the reason she'd baked so much was to feed her sources when they came trooping into her kitchen. But it didn't do any harm for Lady Cannonberry to think the display had all been laid out for her. "We wanted to welcome you home right and proper."

Mrs. Jeffries took her seat. "Wiggins, please go and fetch Mr. Pilchard while I pour the tea."

Wiggins was off like a shot. For a few moments they made small talk and filled their plates. The footman returned with the errant houseguest, who blushed when he realized none of the others had touched their food and were waiting for him.

"I'm so sorry," he apologized quickly as he took the seat next to Lady Cannonberry. "Sometimes I do get carried away. Nature is so very fascinating."

Morris Pilchard looked to be in his fifties. Tall and thin, he had a long, melancholy face with deep-set hazel eyes and a rather protruding nose. His complexion was pale, his hair a nondescript beige blond streaked with gray.

"Please don't apologize, Mr. Pilchard," Mrs. Jeffries said briskly. "We all quite understand. The garden is a fascinating place." She was determined to get this tea moving right along so they could finish their meeting and get back on the hunt. Unfortunately they'd been in the middle of Wiggins's report when Lady Cannonberry and her houseguest had turned up.

"Has the inspector any interesting new cases?" Ruth asked brightly.

They all looked at the housekeeper, waiting to follow her lead before opening their mouths and risk giving the game away. Everyone liked Ruth Cannonberry and no one wanted to lie. She was too good a friend for that.

Mrs. Jeffries smiled, delicately reached for a scone and laid it on her plate. She was desperately trying to think of how to answer. "Actually, he's been rather busy lately."

"Oh goody." Ruth leaned forward eagerly. "Has he a good murder?"

"Lady Cannonberry!" Pilchard stared at his hostess in utter shock. "Surely you're jesting. You can't possibly have meant what you just said."

"Of course I did," she declared. "I don't condone the taking of life, Morris. But let's do be honest here: murder is fascinating."

Morris pursed his lips and shook his head. "I think it's quite distasteful."

"Here's your tea, Mr. Pilchard." Her eyes twinkling behind her spectacles, Mrs. Goodge handed him his cup. "Would you care for a scone or a slice of cake, sir?"

Momentarily distracted, he turned away from his hostess to study the offerings. "A small slice of sponge, please." He whipped his head back around, apparently ready to take up the argument again, but Ruth was a step ahead of him.

"It's only distasteful if you think it's right that killers can take life with impunity," she charged.

"It's very . . . common. Yes, that's right, murder is common and almost always done by the lower classes." As soon as he said the words, a bright blush crept up his cheeks as he realized whom he was having tea with. "Oh dear, I don't mean to imply that any of you would ever do such a thing—"

"Hello, hello." The inspector's cheerful voice interrupted the terribly embarrassed Mr. Pilchard. "I was just on my way to the Magistrates' Court and thought I'd pop in and welcome our dear neighbor home." He smiled happily at Ruth Cannonberry as he approached the table. "I do hope I'm not interrupting, but when Mrs. Jeffries mentioned this morning that you were coming around for morning tea, I just had to stop in and see you."

"Gerald, I'm delighted to see you as well," Ruth said quickly. Her eyes suddenly sparkled with pleasure, a flush crept up her cheeks and her mouth curved in a wide smile. "I'm so happy you came. It seems as if it's been far more than a fortnight since we've seen one another."

"Uh . . . uh." Morris Pilchard cleared his throat loudly. The indelicate sound grated loudly in the quiet garden. Ruth dragged her gaze away from Witherspoon's and made the introductions.

Mrs. Jeffries looked at the others. Luty, Smythe and Hatchet seemed to be amused. Betsy and Mrs. Goodge looked impatient, and Wiggins was too busy stuffing his face with seedcake to notice anything.

"Wiggins," she ordered gently, "could you go and fetch the inspector a chair?" The lad nodded and leapt to his feet.

Mrs. Jeffries hoped the inspector wouldn't say anything about the murder. If Ruth found out they were "on the hunt," she'd want to help, and as she had a houseguest in residence, that wouldn't be a wise course of action. "Would you care for tea, Inspector?" she asked.

"Thank you, that would be lovely. I've not got long. Constable Barnes is meeting me here in a few minutes." His smile was strained as he spoke and his eyes seemed to dart between Morris Pilchard and Ruth. "Oh, thank you, Wiggins," he said as the lad returned and shoved a chair under him.

He took the tea his housekeeper handed him and then reached for a plate. Witherspoon put a scone and a slice of seedcake on it and then slapped on a huge dollop of heavy, clotted cream. "Are you staying long, Mr. Pilchard?" he asked. He forked a quarter of the cake into his mouth.

"I'm not really sure," Pilchard replied. He glanced at his hostess and smiled. "It all depends."

"On what?" the inspector asked. He reached for a knife and slathered the cream across the top of the scone.

Morris shrugged. "Oh, this and that."

"This and that, you say?" Witherspoon nodded encouragingly. His smile was quite strained by now. When Mr. Pilchard remained silent and merely kept smiling at Lady Cannonberry, the inspector stuffed the remainder of the cake into his mouth and then took a huge bite of the scone.

Luty's eyebrows shot up and she gave Mrs. Jeffries and Mrs. Goodge a knowing grin. Seeing the glance that passed between the two women, Hatchet poked his employer in the ribs.

Betsy, a surprised expression on her pretty face, glanced at Smythe, who shrugged ever so faintly. Wiggins finally looked up from his plate, with a puzzled expression. "'Ow come it's gone all quiet?" he asked.

Mrs. Jeffries decided she'd best do something. The situation was getting more and more awkward by the minute. "We're all enjoying the nice sunshine," she explained brightly. "Would anyone care for a slice of sponge?"

"I would," Witherspoon said, handing his plate to Mrs. Jeffries. He glanced at Lady Cannonberry. "Er, I'm rather tied up at the moment, but I would so like to take you for ride in the country soon. We want to take advantage of the weather while we can."

"I should love that, Gerald," she began enthusiastically.

"That would indeed be nice," Morris interrupted. "Do let us know when you're free." He smiled and rose to his feet. "Now, if you'll excuse us, Lady Cannonberry and I are off to the Natural History Museum." He reached over and helped her to her feet.

"Thank you for the tea," Ruth said, her expression uneasy. "It was lovely." She gave the inspector one long, meaningful look and then allowed Morris to lead her off toward her own home at the far end of the communal gardens.

Witherspoon didn't take his eyes off them. But even with his attention firmly diverted, his fingers managed to grab the plate full of sponge cake that the housekeeper handed him. He forked the cake in his mouth without blinking, his attention completely focused on the retreating man and woman. Finally he sighed. "I'm so glad she's come home," he said.

"We are too," Mrs. Jeffries said stoutly. "And we're so glad you found the time to join us for tea this morning. Now, sir, do tell, what have you been up to today? You know how fascinated all of us are by your investigations."

Witherspoon nodded absently. His gaze was still fixed on the huge four-story brick home at the far end of the garden. *Her* home. "Yes, thank you," he muttered. "I'd love another scone."

Mrs. Jeffries smiled softly. She felt rather sorry for her dear inspector. The poor man was so obviously wrestling with the demons of jealousy he wasn't even listening. "Right, sir. Another scone."

Mrs. Goodge looked outraged, but she managed to reach for his plate without smacking his fingers. She'd never seen anyone stuff himself so full of food. What was wrong with the man? If he kept eating at this rate, she'd not have enough provisions to feed her sources this afternoon.

"Me too." Wiggins started to take a scone but stayed his hand when the cook glared at him. "Uh, maybe I'll not."

"Inspector." Luty raised her voice quite a bit to get his attention.

Blinking, he came out of his daze and turned to look at the American woman. "I'm sorry, were you speaking to me?"

"Yes, sir, I was," Luty said. "I was jes' wonderin' if you wouldn't mind tellin' me a bit about this here murder you've got. You know how Hatchet and I like hearin' about all your investigations."

"Oh well, of course." He smiled proudly. "Uh, let me see, I suppose Mrs. Jeffries has told you some of the details." He picked the scone up in his fingers and took a bite.

"She sure did." Luty leaned toward him and dropped her voice. "What I want to know is what were ya up to this morning? Did ya catch the killer yet?"

"Not quite," the inspector replied. "Actually, I've only just got started. But we're making progress. We confirmed this morning that the victim didn't go to his office yesterday afternoon. We spoke to his partner. Fellow named Henry Alladyce. Alladyce claimed that Roland Ashbury had no intention of going to his office. If he had, he'd have sent Alladyce either a message or a telegram. He sent neither."

Smythe opened his mouth to speak, thought better of it and leaned back in his chair. Betsy noticed. But then she noticed most everything about the coachman. She cocked her head and looked at him speculatively.

"Do you think he planned on going back to the Frommer house all along, sir?" Mrs. Jeffries asked. "And that his telling the family he had to go to his office was only a ruse to leave Ascot earlier than the others?"

Again Smythe seemed to lean forward, his expression clearly indicating that he wanted to say something, and again he thought better of it.

"I don't know," Witherspoon replied. Absently he plopped another dollop of cream on the small sliver of seedcake left on his plate. "Yet his daughter is convinced he lied about needing to go to his office. She's sure it was a ruse to get away without offending Andrew Frommer. But if what Mrs. Frommer thinks is true, that means he'd planned to meet his killer there all along. . . ." His voice trailed off as he tried to think of the best way to say what he was thinking. But he couldn't seem to find the right words. "I mean, it seems to me that—"

"Of course, sir," Mrs. Jeffries said quickly. She knew exactly what he was trying to articulate. "What you're saying is that he planned to meet his killer and he kept that plan a secret. As a matter of fact, he connived to get the privacy he needed for the meeting. Therefore, the meeting must have either been with someone he didn't want his family to know about or it must have been about something he didn't want made public. Is that what you're trying to tell us, sir?"

Witherspoon brightened immediately. "Yes, that's it precisely. Well, you can see what that would imply, can't you?"

"I can't," Wiggins said honestly.

"It would imply that the victim might have something to conceal," Hatchet said softly. "Secret meetings usually mean both parties have a vested interested in hiding something."

"Do you think Ashbury was being blackmailed?" Luty asked.

Witherspoon licked the last of the cream off his fork. "I'm definitely leaning in that direction," he answered. "But, of course, if he were being blackmailed, why would the killer murder him?"

"Maybe *he* was the blackmailer?" Betsy guessed.

"That's possible too," the inspector replied. "But we've no evidence either way. Oh dear, I'm getting way ahead of myself. The only thing we know for certain is that he's dead. We don't know for certain that he didn't go to his office. I mean, we only have Henry Alladyce's word, and from what I understand, he benefits from Ashbury's death."

"You think this Alladyce feller is lyin', then?" Luty asked eagerly.

Witherspoon shook his head. "Not really. I mean, I suppose it's possible. But it didn't strike me as likely. He was actually quite candid with us. He gave me a long list of people who didn't like the victim. Of course, if he's the killer, that could have been a ruse as well. What better way to throw the police off the scent than by giving them false information."

"He gave you a list of people, sir?" Mrs. Jeffries clarified.

"Oh yes." Witherspoon eyed the bowl of sugared quince. "According to Alladyce, there were quite a number of people who disliked the victim rather intensely."

At hearing this, everyone at the table went to full attention. Even Wiggins. They all gave the inspector their complete concentration.

"Really, sir?" Mrs. Jeffries encouraged. "A whole list? That might make your task much more complicated. But then again, perhaps it will make it easier." She desperately wanted to get the names out of him, and the only way to do that was to keep him talking.

"Yes, that's just what I was thinking," he agreed. He licked his lips, picked a crumb off his plate and popped it into his mouth.

"Are the people on this list going to be easy to . . . uh—" She broke off deliberately, hoping he'd jump right in.

"Investigate." He smiled. "Why, yes, indeed they are. As a matter of fact—"

"Hello, Inspector," Barnes called from the side of the house. "If you don't mind, sir"—he pointed toward the street—"I've got a hansom waiting."

"Oh dear." Witherspoon leapt to his feet. "I must go. Thank you ever so much for the lovely tea. Don't wait dinner on me," he called over his shoulder. "I expect I'll be quite late."

CHAPTER 4

"Bloomin' Ada," Smythe muttered as the inspector and Barnes scampered out of sight. "'Ow'd we let him get away without spillin' the beans?"

"A list of the victim's enemies would have been most useful," Hatchet agreed.

"Useful, hmmph," Mrs. Goodge snapped. "Necessary, if you ask me. We need a few more suspects. I can't question anyone unless'n I have names. Not that they'd do me any good now." She gestured furiously at the table. "Just look at this, it's practically all gone. What am I goin' to feed my sources? The man sits here and stuffs himself fatter than a Christmas goose then has the nerve to scarper off without being any help at all."

"I don't think he meant to eat so much," Mrs. Jeffries murmured. She too was a tad annoyed at their dear employer. Not so much that he'd made a pig of himself—after all, it was his food—but at the way he'd dashed off without giving them the information they so desperately needed. "I think seeing Lady Cannonberry with her houseguest must have made him a bit anxious."

"He was as jealous as an old tom," Betsy declared. "But it's his own fault; he should have paid more attention to Ruth."

"He gives her lots of attention," Smythe countered. "She's the one that's always going off to the country."

"She's got relatives to visit," Betsy said, defending her friend. "Her own and her late husband's. She got stuck with that lot too, you know. What do you want her to do, ignore them?"

"She could stay home for a change and give a fellow time to court 'er properly." The coachman frowned darkly, an expression that was known to clear a path in the roughest of pubs, but Betsy wasn't in the least intimidated.

"She's given him plenty of chances," she shot back. "But like most men, he's not got the sense to see what's right under his nose. He just assumes she'll be sittin' there waiting for him when he decides he's got time for her."

Smythe's jaw dropped in outrage, but before he could form the words to protest, Mrs. Jeffries interrupted.

"Smythe, quickly, follow them."

"Huh?" Confused, he still got to his feet. "Follow the inspector?"

"Yes, now. Hurry; if you run you might be able to catch their hansom up at the corner. There's always a dreadful traffic jam there."

"What do you want me to do?" he called over his shoulder as he raced toward the side of the house.

"See where they go," she called back to him. "And then get back here this afternoon."

Without another word, the coachman disappeared around the corner.

Mrs. Jeffries turned and smiled at the others. "Let's hope he can catch the inspector's hansom." She'd sent Smythe on the errand to halt the squabble that was developing between him and Betsy. The maid hadn't really been complaining about Witherspoon's shortcomings in the court- ship department; she was sending Smythe a message. Had she not sent the coachman off, the argument might have become very heated and very personal. A fact that both the parties involved would soon regret once they'd calmed down.

"You want poor Smythe to hotfoot it after the inspector's 'ansom all day?" Wiggins asked incredulously.

"Of course not," she replied. "I'm quite sure Smythe will have enough intelligence to hire a hansom of his own."

Hatchet frowned slightly. "Excuse me, Mrs. Jeffries. But I don't quite see the point of sending Smythe off."

Of course you don't, Mrs. Jeffries thought, you're a male. She could tell from the smug expressions on Luty and Mrs. Goodge's faces that they knew precisely what she'd been doing. But naturally she kept her thoughts to herself. "The point is we want to know who was on that list of names the inspector got from Henry Alladyce. The inspector may not be home until very late tonight. If Smythe follows him for a few hours today, we might find out the names of some of the suspects."

"Meaning that the inspector will go and interview them." Hatchet nodded knowingly.

"That's correct. I'm sure all of you realize that we don't have much to go on so far. Even a couple more names might be worthwhile."

"But I don't understand," Betsy said. "Aren't we going to concentrate on finding out as much as we can about the victim. That's how we usually do it."

Betsy had a valid point. That was generally how they'd conducted their previous investigations, and usually the method had been most successful. "Of course we are," the housekeeper replied quickly. "But even with doing that, we frequently have several other suspects to concentrate on as well." That much was actually true. "So far, we've only got the Frommers. If neither of them is the murderer, we'll be at a loss to help the inspector solve this case."

"Oh. I guess then I'd best wait until this afternoon's meeting to tell everyone what I found out early this morning." Betsy sank back against her chair, her expression glum.

Their plan to meet before Lady Cannonberry and her guest arrived had gone awry. No one, save Mrs. Jeffries and Mrs. Goodge, had been available at the o'clock. Everyone else had been late.

"Well, it wouldn't be fair to Smythe to have a meeting now," the housekeeper offered.

"Fiddlesticks," Luty cried. "I'm bustin' to tell what I found out. I was out at the crack of dawn this mornin'."

"I don't see why you're so proud of yourself, madam." Hatchet sniffed disapprovingly. "You ought to be ashamed. Waking up a member of the House of Lords at six A.M. is unforgivable."

Luty grinned. "You're just jealous 'cause I got to him first."

"Hmmph." Hatchet pursed his lips.

"Can it wait, Luty?" Mrs. Jeffries asked. "I really don't like the idea of Smythe missing out, especially as I'm quite sure he had something to tell us all too. He acted quite eager when the inspector was here."

Luty made a face. Eager as she was to share her information, she wanted to be fair too. "Oh, all right, then. I'll wait till this afternoon. But if someone else comes up with the same thing I found out, I'm goin' to be madder than a wet hen."

"What time are we meeting this afternoon, then?" Mrs. Goodge asked bluntly. "I need to know, as I've got a lot to do. I'm going to have to restock my supplies." She glared at the inspector's empty plate. "Never seen the man eat so much at one sitting."

"Why don't we meet at five o'clock?" Mrs. Jeffries suggested. "Hopefully Smythe will have returned by then."

"And what do we do in the meantime?" Wiggins asked. He didn't fancy talking to any more shopkeepers. One time Betsy might forgive; she was a good-hearted girl, after all. But twice, no; she'd box his ears if he poached on her patch again.

"We do precisely as Betsy has suggested." Mrs. Jeffries smiled kindly at the maid. "We concentrate on learning as much as we can about the victim. Wiggins, I think you ought to visit the Frommer house and see if you can make contact with a servant. Perhaps locate the footman who left before you could speak to him yesterday." She looked at the maid.

"I know," Betsy said. "I'll go back and have a thorough go at the shopkeepers and"—she gave Wiggins an impish grin—"anyone else I see hanging about."

"There's still plenty for me to do," Luty announced gleefully. "I'll drop in on a new friend of mine that's got a few connections. She knows what's what in this town."

"Who?" Hatchet demanded suspiciously. "Is it someone I know?"

"Now just never you mind." Luty brushed him off with a wave of her hand. "You just drop me off on Park Lane and send the carriage back at four."

"Hmmph." Hatchet stood up as well. "In that case, madam, I shall endeavor to follow up on my own leads. I take it we're free to find out whatever we can about the entire Frommer household?"

"Of course," Mrs. Jeffries replied.

The cook began stacking plates onto a tray she whipped out from under the table. "I'd best get crackin'. Mrs. Collins from next door has a laundry boy comin' in about ten minutes, and later this afternoon Lady Afton's dressmaker will be in the neighborhood. She always stops in for a cuppa." She frowned at the empty scone plate. "Let's just hope they like Victoria sponge; that's about all I've got left."

Panting heavily, Smythe skidded around the corner just in time to see the inspector's hansom—at least he hoped it was the inspector's—halt at the Uxbridge Road. Thanking his lucky stars for the heavy traffic, he spotted a four-wheeler dropping off a fare just up the road. Keeping his gaze glued to the cab he was almost sure contained the inspector, he ran toward the wheeler and leapt on board. "Follow that hansom," he ordered the surprised driver. "And don't let 'im see ya."

"Now 'ow am I goin' to do that?" the driver asked. "Anyone with eyes in 'is 'ead can turn about and see a bloody great thing like this"—he smacked the seat—"on his tail."

"All right, then, just keep back and try not to get spotted," Smythe snapped, and pulled a fistful of cash out of his pocket. "I've got a guinea here on top of the fare if you can do it."

"You're on, mate," the driver said cheerfully.

As it turned out, the four-wheeler had no trouble keeping up with the hansom. Smythe breathed a little easier as they followed the cab up the Uxbridge Road and approached the neighborhood where the murder took place. That increased the likelihood that he was following the right hansom. Any lingering doubts vanished when the hansom turned onto the Grays Inn Road and few minutes later onto Argyle Street.

Smythe kept his eyes glued to the cab as it pulled up in front of the Frommer house. "Go past them and pull up a bit farther up the road," he ordered the driver.

The four-wheeler moved another fifty yards and then pulled into the pavement. "This far enough?" the driver asked.

Smythe hesitated. It was close enough for him to get a good look at what was going on, but was it far enough away to keep the inspector from getting suspicious? "This'll do," he called softly.

He stuck his head out and watched as Witherspoon and Barnes stood on the pavement talking softly. Finally they turned and started toward the row of houses, but it wasn't the Frommer home at which they stopped; it was the one next door. Taken aback, Smythe watched the inspector and Barnes walk up to the front door and bang the knocker.

"Cor blimey," he muttered. "That's odd." Mrs. Jeffries had already told them that the police had taken statements from the neighbors, none of whom had heard or seen a thing. If that were true, what was the inspector up to?

"Wait 'ere," he instructed the driver.

"Not to worry, mate," he said, "I'm not goin' nowhere. Not without my guinea."

Keeping a sharp eye on the doorway through which the inspector and Barnes had disappeared, Smythe got out. He'd have to be quick about this;

he didn't want the inspector coming out and haring off on him. Smythe stood on the pavement and examined the surrounding area, looking for anyone who could give him the information he needed. "Ah." He grinned as he saw a housemaid scrubbing the front steps of a grand house just up near the corner. She'd do. She'd do just fine.

"I'm sorry, Inspector. I don't really know what I can do to help you. I've already made a statement." Charles Burroughs smiled disarmingly. He was a tall, handsome, dark-complected man who appeared to be in his late thirties. His mouth was wide and generous under a sharp blade of a nose, and his eyes were a dark, almost sapphire blue. As the sun spread out across his high cheekbones, it revealed deep lines on his face. "Yesterday two police constables interviewed me and my entire household. We told them everything we knew, but I'm afraid it wasn't very much."

"Yes, sir, we're aware of that," Witherspoon replied. "But we'd like to ask a few more questions if you don't mind."

"Fine, then." Burroughs stepped back from the door and held it open. "Do come in."

As soon as the two policemen stepped inside, Burroughs closed the door behind them and started down the hall. "I'm afraid I can't offer you tea," he said. "It's the staff's day out. I'm here alone."

"That's quite all right, sir," Witherspoon replied as they walked through a set of wide oak double doors into the drawing room. "We're not thirsty." He took a quick look around, carefully noting that the place was exquisitely and expensively furnished. The drapes were heavy red damask, the carpet a richly patterned Wilton and the settee and chairs upholstered in bold, bright reds and blues. A huge, hand-carved rosewood cabinet dominated one end of the room. Through its glass doors, china figurines, gold plates and silver knickknacks could be seen. Tables covered with delicate cream-covered lace were at both ends of the settee, and opposite the door, a fireplace with a carved marble mantel held a triple set of ornately gilded mirrors.

Burroughs gestured at the settee. "Please be seated, gentlemen." The inspector and Barnes settled themselves as Burroughs took a seat on the chair next to them. He clasped his hands together and smiled, waiting patiently.

"Mr. Burroughs, how long have you lived here?" Witherspoon asked.

Burroughs raised his eyebrows slightly. "Three months, Inspector."

"And where did you live before you moved to London?"

Burroughs crossed his legs. "I don't see what my movements have to do with Mr. Ashbury's death," he said.

"I realize it sounds quite an unusual question," the inspector replied, "but we do have a valid reason for asking."

"May I know that reason?"

The inspector hated situations like this. On the one hand, he was such an essentially honest man that it was difficult to look another human being in the eyes and tell a lie. On the other hand, if he let Burroughs know the real reason he was asking, it might harm the investigation.

"We've had a report that you're in the habit of quarreling with your neighbors, sir," Barnes said quickly. "And that these quarrels led to violence at your last place of residence."

Burroughs stared at them for a moment and then burst into laughter. "I don't know who you've been talking to," he finally said, "but I assure you, gentlemen, I do not quarrel with my neighbors. I'm actually considered quite an amiable fellow. However, if you want to confirm my story, you'll have to send someone to Denver, Colorado. That's where I last resided. My next-door neighbors were a lovely family called Robb. I left all of them hale and hearty, and most kindly disposed to me, when I came here."

Witherspoon shot his constable a grateful look. Barnes had managed to get the needed information out of the witness without revealing everything that Henry Alladyce had told them. The inspector made a mental note to send a cable to the authorities in Denver.

"You're an American, sir?" he asked. "Born and bred." Burroughs replied.

"Then you never met Roland Ashbury before you came to live next door to him?" The inspector wanted to be crystal clear on that point.

"Absolutely not, sir." Burroughs shrugged. "Unless, of course, he happened to come to Denver. In which case, I don't recall ever meeting the man."

"Had you ever met Mrs. MaryAnne Frommer?" Barnes asked.

"No, not until I came here." He uncrossed his legs and leaned toward them. "But I will tell you, if anyone had a reason to end up with a bullet in his brain, it's that brute of a husband of Mrs. Frommer's. He's the most diabolical man I've ever met. He treats her terribly."

"In what way?" Witherspoon didn't want to be sidetracked, but at the same time he wanted to gather as much information as possible. "How did he treat her badly? Did he beat her?"

"He did." Burroughs hesitated. "Well, I never actually saw the man raise his hand to her; if I had, I'd have stopped him. Where I come from we don't take the beating of helpless females lightly."

"Then how do you know he beat his wife?" Witherspoon pressed. Gracious, he was getting a lot of information at one time. He only hoped that Mrs. Jeffries was right and that his "inner mind" was cataloging it all correctly. He wasn't sure he could even remember much of it.

"I've seen the bruises," Burroughs stated flatly. "Her upper arms were black-and-blue. When I asked her about them, she insisted she'd bumped into the side of a tallboy. I didn't believe her."

"So you're friendly enough with the Frommers to ask such a personal question?" Barnes asked.

Burroughs hesitated for a split second before answering. "That's a difficult question. I'm not quite sure how to reply. I'm not really all that friendly with anyone in the Frommer household. As a matter of fact, after seeing what kind of people they really are, I've taken some pains to avoid them."

"Then how did you come to see the bruises?" the constable pressed. "Did she show them to you?" Barnes had seen enough domestic violence to know that most women who'd been beaten were so ashamed they went to great pains to hide the marks of their ill-treatment.

"No," he admitted. "It's a rather awkward situation and I wouldn't like you to get the wrong impression. I saw the bruises out in the garden. As you know, our gardens are joined at the back; they're separated by a stone wall. I was out watching some starlings in the oak tree when I happened to see Mrs. Frommer in her nightdress; she was confronting her father, having some sort of argument with him. They were on the other side of their garden, which is quite wide, so I couldn't hear what they were saying. . . . Also, I believe both of them were deliberately keeping their voices down. Mr. Ashbury started to walk away; she grabbed his arm and pulled the old man back, then she yanked the sleeve of her nightdress up to the shoulder and shoved her arm right under his nose." He pursed his lips in disgust. "Ashbury pushed her aside and walked away. I couldn't believe it. Even from where I stood, I could tell she was terribly distraught, terribly upset."

"How did you see the bruises if they were so far away you couldn't hear what they were saying?" Witherspoon asked.

"There's a stone bench on their side of the wall," he explained. "Mrs. Frommer rather stumbled over to the bench and sat down; then she covered her face with her hands and wept. I saw the bruises because her sleeve was still rolled up. I guess I must have walked toward her, wanting to offer comfort or something. I don't know; I simply found myself standing behind her, shocked as I realized what she'd been showing to her father. Without thinking, I asked her about them." He shook his head sadly. "She was quite startled and jumped up. As she ran off back toward her house she called out that she'd banged up her arm by running into a tallboy. It was nonsense, of course. Frommer had beat her."

"But you don't know that for a fact, sir," Witherspoon reminded him.

"Oh, but I do," Burroughs declared. "Later that day, Fiona, my parlor maid told me she'd heard gossip from the servants at the Frommer house. There'd been a terrible row that morning, Andrew Frommer had gotten furious at his wife for something or other, and like most cowards, he'd used his fists on his wife. Apparently her own father had done nothing to help her, but had barricaded himself in his quarters and pretended that nothing was amiss."

"Did your parlor maid happen to mention what the row was about?" Witherspoon decided if he was going to listen to gossip, he might as hear all of it.

Burroughs wrinkled his brow in thought. "Let's see . . . ah, yes, now I remember. Mrs. Frommer didn't want to go to the house in Ascot. She wanted to stay in town."

"You do understand we'll have to confirm this information with your servants?" Witherspoon said.

"Of course. They'll be back later this afternoon."

The inspector wasn't at all sure what it would mean even if the servants confirmed the rumor that Frommer beat his wife. That might be useful knowledge if it had been Andrew Frommer who was the victim. But he wasn't. "Mr. Burroughs, are you absolutely certain you've no prior acquaintance with the victim?"

Burroughs shrugged. "As far as I know, I never even saw the man until I moved in next door to him."

"Do you own a gun?" Barnes asked.

"Yes, I own a revolver. An Enfield." He laughed. "I'm afraid it's a carryover from my living in the American West. Everyone has guns."

Witherspoon nodded. "May we see it, sir?"

"It's locked in my desk"—he stood up—"in my study. If you'll come with me, I'll show it to you."

The policemen followed him down a long hall to a wood-paneled room. Bookcases lined two of the walls, a huge rolltop desk sat in the corner and several huge, overstuffed chair were planted in front of the fireplace. Burroughs pulled a small brass key out one of the many cubbyholes on the top of the desk. He unlocked the bottom drawer and removed a small, flat blue case.

Carefully he put the case on the desk and flipped open the lid.

Then he gasped. The case was empty.

"Prompt as always." The tall, gaunt-faced man smiled pleasantly at Hatchet and stepped back, pulling the door wide open. With a dramatic flourish, he waved Hatchet inside. "Do come in and make yourself comfortable."

"Thank you." Hatchet stepped inside, took off his top hat and gloves and sat down in a Queen Anne chair that had certainly seen better days. But then, virtually everything in Newton Goff's life had seen better days. Hatchet ought to know: he'd once worked for the man. But he'd worked for him before Goff became a thief. "How have you been keeping yourself?" he asked.

"I've managed to avoid being arrested"—Goff grinned—"if that's what you're asking. I'd offer you something to drink, but I'm afraid all I've got is whiskey and I know you don't indulge." He walked over to a small cabinet sitting under the window. Opening the door, he reached inside and took out a bottle. "You don't mind if I indulge? I always find it's so much more civilized to conduct business over a nice drink."

Hatchet nodded. He didn't care how much Goff drank as long as the man was still able to ferret out information. "By all means, drink up."

Goff set the bottle on the top of the cabinet and reached inside, pulling out a glass.

"Do you still have reasonable sources of information available to you?" Hatchet asked, watching as Goff poured the whiskey into a shot glass that didn't look altogether clean.

"Of course. That's how I've managed to stay alive all these years. What is it you want to know?"

"I'm not certain," Hatchet admitted. "A man by the name of Roland Ashbury was shot the other day. He ran a shipping agency. It's down near the East India Docks. He lived with his son-in-law, Andrew Frommer."

"The politician?" Goff raised an eyebrow.

Hatchet nodded. "That's right. I want you to find out what you can about either of them."

Goff looked doubtful.

"Is there a problem?" Hatchet pressed. "I thought you said you had numerous resources."

"I do." Goff tossed the drink back. "But getting information on a politician might be expensive. They cover their tracks pretty well—if, I mean, there's anything to be covered. Do you think he did the shooting?"

"I don't know." Hatchet was grasping at straws. He'd no idea what was going on and he had the distinct impression that none of his cohorts did either. He wasn't even sure that coming here had been a wise move. But there was nothing else he could think of to do. They needed more information. "But I want you to find out what you can about him. See if there's any skeletons in his closet. Don't worry about what it costs; I can afford it."

"All right," Goff agreed. "Check back with me tomorrow. I might have something for you then." He tossed back the rest of the drink and studied Hatchet for a long moment. "Why do you care?" he asked.

"Pardon?" Hatchet had gotten to his feet. Goff's question took him by surprise.

"Why do you care who killed this fellow?" Goff pressed. "Did you know him?"

"No, but I care all the same. There is such a thing as justice."

Goff gazed at him and then shook his head, his expression puzzled. "Do you really expect me to believe that? That you're sticking your nose in this murder simply because you're interested in justice? That you're getting nothing out of it for yourself?"

"Yes," Hatchet replied. "I do." He clamped his mouth shut, refusing to say another word on the subject. Goff could think what he would. He wasn't here to convince the man of anything.

"I'm not sure I believe you, Hatchet." Goff shrugged and turned toward the dirty window. "All I know is you sure have changed. Used to be you didn't give two figs about anything except yourself."

"As you said, Goff," Hatchet replied softly, "I've changed."

"He's plum disappeared, 'e 'as." The small, ruddy-faced gardener slapped the stack of straw mats down on the ground next to the black currant bushes.

Wiggins quickly looked around, wanting to make sure that there weren't any policemen still hovering in the garden of the Frommer house, which was right next door. He'd made the acquaintance of the gardener by offering to help him carry these flat straw mats from a wagon out front of the house into the garden. It was a proper kitchen garden too, he noted, similar to the ones Mrs. Goodge was always going on about. Rows of black currant bushes trailed along the back wall. Gooseberry and red currant bushes flanked the side wall and rows of vegetables were planted in straight lines running up toward the house. Several fruit trees were planted in the grassy space between the currant bushes and the vegetables.

"Thanks fer the hand, lad," the gardener said. "I'd like to pay ya, but I've no coin with me."

"That's all right, I don't mind 'elpin' out. Matter of fact, like I told ya, I was 'opin' to see my friend from next door. But when I went round to the back, they told me 'e'd gone."

"That's right; that's what our scullery maid heard. The lad hasn't been seen since the day of the murder." The gardener bent down and picked up a long pole which was lying beside the stack of mats. He stood up and plunged the pole directly into the center of the bush. "He were out in the country, and then, on the day of the murder, he completely disappeared. But Minnie—that's our scullery maid—said she can't believe Boyd had anything to do with the killin'. He'd no reason to want to harm the old man."

"But Boyd was supposed to see me today." Wiggins was making it up as he went along. "I've brought him a message from home."

The gardener laughed and picked up a mat. Taking a ball of thin rope from his pocket, he quickly looped it around and between the straws on the top of the mat and then drew it tight, forming a sort of skirt. "Message from home? For Boyd? You're jokin', lad. Boyd ain't got no 'ome. Afore he got taken in by Mrs. Frommer, 'e was at St. George's Workhouse in Hanover Square."

"I mean I brought him a message from my home, from my auntie Jeffries. She was invitin' 'im to come for Sunday tea." Wiggins watched, fascinated, as the gardener looped the twine through a hole in the top of the pole and then, standing on his tiptoes, hoisted the mat skirt over the top, anchoring the thing to the top of the pole. The entire top part of the bush was now covered with the mat.

"Oh." The gardener picked up a third mat and placed it carefully around the base of the bush, taking care to make sure the mat was loose enough not to crush the tender shoots on the tips of the branches. "I see. Well, you're goin' to have to disappoint yer auntie. Boyd's gone, and I don't think he's comin' back."

"Why'd he leave like that? I wonder."

The gardener shrugged. "Probably saw something that made him uneasy." He fitted a fourth mat onto the bush, effectively covering it completely. Then he stepped back and surveyed his handiwork. "He were right fond of Mrs. Frommer, he was."

Wiggins didn't wish to push his luck, but he had to find out more. He'd learned that you could get a lot more information if you were a bit sly about how you asked your questions. "What's that for?" he asked, pointing at the matted bush. "It looks like a wigwam. You know, one of them houses that indians live in America. I saw a drawing of one in the *Illustrated* last month."

The gardener laughed. "It's a covering to keep the currant bushes from ripening all at once. Mind you, these bushes should have been covered a month ago. Bein' as we're in July, it might already be too late. If you can keep the sun off it, it'll delay the fruit ripening. That's the idea." He grabbed another pole and started for the next black currant bush. "I've not tried it before, but my wife's the cook and she's mighty tired of having to put up jams and jellies by the bushelful because all these currants ripen at once. So I'm tryin' this to see if we can push some of the bushes back."

"You're right clever." Wiggins was sincere about the compliment, but he's also found that people tended to keep talking to you if you said nice things to them.

"Thanks, lad. I'm sorry about yer friend."

He sighed dramatically. "I am too. Boyd's a nice lad. My auntie was lookin' forward to seein' 'im again. She's goin' to be right disappointed."

"You might try havin' a look over on Hanover Square," the gardener suggested as he plunged the pole into the next bush. "Boyd still went over that way occasionally. I think he was friends with one or two of them poor blighters at the workhouse."

"Thanks," Wiggins said. "I'll do that. I would like to find 'im. 'E's a good friend. At least now I know where to start lookin'. Good thing I run into you." He jerked his head toward the Frommer house. "They'd no idea where 'e'd gone."

The gardener frowned, his eyes growing speculative as he glanced at the house next door. "They'll have plenty of ideas soon enough," he said darkly. "As soon as everyone realizes what Boyd takin' off like that means, they'll be fallin' all over themselves with ideas about where to look for the lad."

"What do ya mean?" But Wiggins knew what the man meant.

"There's been murder done there, son," the man said darkly. "And when murder's been done, they like nothing better than to blame it on the likes of us. Take me word fer it, they'll be runnin' to the coppers soon enough with all kinds of tales about the poor lad. Everyone would rather it be some poor servant than one of their own kind."

"Well . . ." Wiggins hesitated, he didn't want to overplay his hand here, but he did want to hear as much as possible. "It *is* odd, Boyd leavin' like that. I mean, it's not like 'im. Makes you wonder."

The gardener gave him a sharp look. "I thought you said you was his friend."

"I am," Wiggins protested. "But it's odd."

"It's not a bit odd." He yanked a mat off the stack. "He's devoted to Mrs. Frommer, he is. I reckon he took off for one reason and one reason only. Because she told him to."

"I'm thinkin' maybe a guinea's not enough," the cabbie said to Smythe. They were trotting along St. Martin's Lane. Bored with sitting in the four-wheeler, Smythe had come up and taken a spot next to the driver. "I mean, you've tied my rig up all day."

"Bollocks," Smythe retorted. "Who do you think you're kiddin', mate? You'd not make a guinea for one day's work, so don't go tryin' to up the price 'ere." It wasn't the money he objected to, it was the idea of being taken advantage of that set his teeth on edge. He glared at the driver.

The intimidating expression obviously worked, for the poor fellow almost fell off the seat as he tried to pull away from his frowning passenger. "All right, all right," he said quickly. "You can't blame a bloke fer tryin'. It's tough to make ends meet these days. I'm out on this rig for twelve, sometimes even fourteen hours a day. I've got a wife and three kids to feed. I didn't mean no harm."

Smythe sighed and stifled the shaft of guilt that crawled out of his gut. He didn't like being taken advantage of, but he couldn't really blame the man for trying. He knew what it was like to be poor. He'd been poor most of his life. "No offense taken. Just a minute, now; they've stopped. Drive on past and pull on ahead of them."

Smythe turned his body away from the hansom as they trotted past. As soon as the four-wheeler pulled in at the curb, he whipped his head around and saw the inspector and Barnes get out. They had just started up the stairs of a lovely, small white house when the door flew open and one of the most beautiful women Smythe had ever seen stepped out.

Elegantly dressed in a teak-colored afternoon gown, matching hat and gloves, she had exquisite features and a slender figure. She spoke to the two men, and a moment later they disappeared inside the house.

Smythe jumped down off the seat. "Stay here," he ordered the driver in a soft voice. Taking care to avoid being seen, he nipped across the road to a tobacconist's on the corner. He didn't waste time trying to be subtle. What was the use of being rich as sin if he couldn't use his money to serve the cause of justice? Reaching into his pocket, he pulled out a couple of florins and slapped them on the counter. The old woman folding newspapers didn't even look up; she merely put her wrinkled hand on the coins. "What can I get you, sir?"

"Information," he said. She looked up then, her expression curious. He pointed to the house. "Who lives there?"

"There? That house." The old crone laughed. "Why, it's that fancy woman that lives there, sir. Her name is Hartshorn, Eloise Hartshorn."

CHAPTER 5

"Please sit down, gentlemen," Eloise Hartshorn said as she led them into a small, very feminine-looking sitting room and gestured at an ivory-colored settee. The walls were done in pale pink, the curtains were cream-colored lace and a fawn-colored carpet covered the floor.

Barnes and Witherspoon both sat. The inspector tried not to stare, but it was really very difficult. Miss Hartshorn was quite a lovely woman. Small, slender and titian-haired, she had delicate features and lovely blue eyes.

Removing her gloves, she gracefully sat down on the love seat opposite the settee. Tossing the gloves to one side, she folded her hands in her lap and smiled patiently. "How can I help you, sir?"

"Er, uh, we'd like to ask you a few questions about Roland Ashbury," Witherspoon said.

Her smile disappeared and her expression became serious. "I'm surprised it took you this long to get around to me. I haven't been hiding, you know."

"Hiding?" Witherspoon repeated in confusion. "Goodness, Miss Hartshorn, we know that. We simply didn't realize you'd anything to do with Mr. Ashbury until after we'd spoken to Henry Alladyce."

"So you learned about me from Henry, did you?" She shrugged, the gracefulness of her movement making the gesture look eloquent. "I knew we wouldn't be able to keep it quiet much longer. Not that it mattered." She laughed. "Roland was such an idiot. He actually was stupid enough to think I'd care if he went running to Andrew."

"Running to Andrew?" Witherspoon said. "You mean Andrew

Frommer?" Alladyce had only said that Miss Hartshorn disliked the victim; he hadn't told them why.

"Who else would I mean, Inspector." She sighed and leaned back against the overstuffed pillow of the settee. "Roland was a despicable man. I loathed him. He tried to blackmail me. But I wasn't having any of it. I told him to go right ahead and tell Andrew everything. I was finished with Andrew anyway. God knows what I ever saw in the man in the first place." She gestured helplessly. "Perhaps he turned my head because he was a member of parliament. In any case, it doesn't matter. Once I discovered what a brute he was, I wasn't interested anymore." She laughed again. "It really took the wind out of Roland's sails when I told him that too, silly fool. I didn't care if he did tell Andrew about Charles and me."

Barnes looked at the inspector. So far, they were getting far more than they'd hoped. "Are you saying you were once . . . er . . . involved with Mr. Frommer and that Mr. Ashbury tried to blackmail you because he'd discovered you were now involved with Mr. Burroughs?"

Witherspoon nodded gratefully at the constable. Fellow knew just the right way to put things.

"That's exactly what happened," she said. "There's no reason for me to lie about it. Far too many people know about me. Most of Andrew's servants knew and MaryAnne suspected we were seeing each other. Not that she cared, mind you. And after having gotten to know Andrew better, I can understand why."

"How long were you involved with Mr. Frommer?" Witherspoon asked.

"About six months," she replied. "Roland Ashbury found out that Andrew and I were seeing each other. I think he followed Andrew here one afternoon. The day before he went to their country house in Ascot, Roland showed up on my doorstep. He demanded money to keep quiet. I laughed in his face. He said if I didn't give him money—quite a bit of money—he'd tell Andrew I was now seeing Charles Burroughs. I told him to go right ahead, that it would save me a great deal of trouble and a very unpleasant scene."

"I see." Witherspoon was flabbergasted. "Did he go to Mr. Frommer?"

"I'm sure he did," she said nonchalantly. "But I don't think that's why Andrew killed him. Andrew would murder for money or power, but he certainly wouldn't kill over losing me."

"You're accusing Mr. Frommer of murdering his father-in-law?" Barnes exclaimed. "What reason could he have for wanting Mr. Ashbury dead?"

That was precisely what the inspector wanted to know.

Eloise Hartshorn hesitated for the briefest of moments.

"I'm not sure," she began. "All I know is that Roland Ashbury didn't seem unduly surprised when I told him I wasn't paying him a penny. He simply sneered at me and said if I wouldn't pay, there was someone else who would. I can only guess that he meant Andrew."

"But I thought he was in awe of his son-in-law?" Witherspoon said. "Our information has made it very clear that Mr. Ashbury wanted nothing more than to stay in Mr. Frommer's good graces. Are you sure he wasn't referring to Mr. Burroughs?"

"Don't be absurd. Charles was no more likely to pay that pompous fool than I was," she snapped. "Why should he?"

"Perhaps to protect both his and your reputation," Witherspoon suggested. He was only guessing, of course. But sometimes even the wildest conjecture might turn out to hit the mark.

"You are joking, Inspector, aren't you?" She looked very amused. "Women like me don't have reputations. I should have thought someone in your profession would have realized that. Besides, Andrew Frommer wanted Roland dead. Furthermore, he was there the afternoon the man was shot. I know; I saw him coming out of the house."

"You *saw* him?" Barnes prompted. "Where were you?"

She smiled triumphantly. "Right next door. You can see the back of the Frommer house from Charles's bedroom window. At four o'clock, Andrew Frommer came running out the back door like the devil himself was on his heels."

Everyone was on time for the afternoon meeting. Mrs. Jeffries, who'd gone on an errand of her own and then spent the remainder of the day going over what little information they'd acquired, was eager to hear from the others. "Who would like to start?" she asked.

Wiggins bobbed his head. "Let me. I've 'eard plenty and I'm afraid I'll forget it if I don't get it out." When no one objected, he plunged straight in. "I've got two things to tell. The first one I 'eard this mornin'. I 'ad a chat with a shopkeeper." He tossed Betsy an apologetic glance, even though he'd apologized special-like before their botched-up morning meeting. "And 'e give me an earful." He gave them all the details he'd learned from his encounter with Nat Hopkins. His voice rose in excitement as he told them of Andrew Frommer's "fancy woman" and the fact that young Emma had actually seen her.

"Did you get her name?" Betsy interrupted eagerly.

Wiggins's face fell. "No, I was goin' to, but ya see, I think I might 'ave made a muck-up of the whole situation."

"Muck-up?" Mrs. Jeffries repeated. "In what way, Wiggins?"

He swallowed nervously. "I told Nat Hopkins who I worked for; I told 'im I worked for the inspector. Well, I 'ad to say somethin', I'd been asking the feller questions and 'e was gettin' a mite suspicious, so when he was moanin' that the coppers weren't goin' to come around and question 'is niece, I thought 'ere's my chance to learn even more. So I told 'im who I worked for, thinkin' 'e'd keep on talkin'." Wiggins sagged in his chair. "But it didn't work out, ya see. Right after I said that, is wife come along and shouted for 'im to come 'elp 'er. I was thinkin' I'd find a way to tell the inspector 'e ought to go along and interview this Emma. I was goin' to do that at tea this mornin' when the inspector showed up so unexpectedly, but there weren't a good way to bring it up, not with Lady Cannonberry bringin' that Mr. Pilchard with 'er and the inspector actin' so funny."

No one said a word. It was a given that while in the midst of the investigation none of them were supposed to mention they worked for Inspector Witherspoon. Better to be discreet than take the chance of their inspector finding out members of his own household were questioning witnesses. But as they'd all found reason in the past to violate this rule, no one wanted to criticize Wiggins.

Mrs. Jeffries's expression was thoughtful. "Don't worry, Wiggins, we'll find a way to get the information to him. What's this girl's full name?"

"All I 'eard was 'Emma,'" he replied, "but she lives with Nat Hopkins and 'e owns the shop down on Badgett Street around the corner from the Frommer house."

"Too bad you didn't get the name of Frommer's fancy woman," Mrs. Goodge mused. "That would have been right useful. At least it gives a reason why Andrew Frommer might want to murder his father-in-law. Maybe he got tired of putting up with the old bloke and did him in to make sure he couldn't tell anyone anything."

"I'm sorry." Wiggins shook his head, his expression glum. "I didn't 'ave time to get 'er name."

"Not to worry, lad," Smythe said cheerfully. "I think I know who she is. Eloise Hartshorn. She's one of the people the inspector interviewed today. She's a right beautiful woman, that's for certain. I can see why Frommer . . ." He trailed off as he caught sight of the fierce glare Betsy was directing at him.

"You said there were two things you needed to tell us, Wiggins," Mrs. Jeffries said briskly. "What was the other one?"

Wiggins took a deep breath. He wanted to get this part right. "I learned a bit more about that missin' footman from the Frommer household," he said. He told them what he'd learned from the gardener. He took great pains to make sure he got every detail right and made doubly sure he repeated the gardener's assertion that the lad had disappeared to protect MaryAnne Frommer. "Anyway," he finished, "I was thinkin' I'd 'ave a nip over to St. George's and see if anyone there knows anythin' about this lad. It's important we find 'im."

"Do you really think this boy knows anything?" Hatchet asked.

"'Course 'e does," Wiggins declared. "'E scarpered, didn't 'e?"

"But 'e scarpered the morning before the murder took place. So 'ow could 'e know anythin'?" Smythe asked thoughtfully. "Unless, of course, 'e 'eard somethin' or saw somethin' earlier that scared 'im."

"You should pursue locating the lad," Mrs. Jeffries said. "But do please be careful."

When Wiggins nodded, she looked at the others. "Who would like to go next? Betsy?"

"I didn't learn anything." Betsy wrinkled her nose at the footman. "None of the shopkeepers I spoke to had anything interesting to say. Mr. Frommer pays his bills promptly and most of the household shopping is done by the housekeeper, not Mrs. Frommer. No one knew anything about Mr. Ashbury."

"Don't be discouraged, Betsy," Mrs. Jeffries said stoutly. "You'll do better tomorrow."

"I might as well go next," Smythe said. "I've not got much, but I did follow the inspector to a couple a places. The first one was right next door to the Frommer 'ouse. Bachelor lives there and 'is name is Burroughs, Charles Burroughs. I couldn't find out anythin' else about 'im, though. There wasn't time before the inspector come out. Then 'e went to talk to this Eloise Hartshorn."

"The pretty one?" Betsy asked archly. She smiled sweetly at the coachman.

"Right." He grinned. "She were pretty. The inspector was in there a fair amount of time. When he come out he went back to the station. As it were gettin' late, I decided to nip on back 'ere." Smythe didn't tell them that he'd also nipped into his bank and taken out a wad of cash. He had an appointment tonight and he was going to need it.

"Mrs. Goodge, have you anything to report?" Mrs. Jeffries's own news wasn't so important that she was in any rush to impart it.

"Not really. I only had a couple of people stop in today." She shook her head in disgust. "Good thing, too, as I'd not much to feed them. But I've got the word out, and tomorrow, there'll be an army of people trooping through here. Now that I've got them names from Smythe"—she shot the coachman a grateful smile—"that'll give me a lot to work with." Her broad face suddenly creased in a thoughtful frown. "But there's something I'd like to know. Where'd that cake that Ashbury served for tea come from?"

"The kitchen?" Wiggins suggested.

"Of course it come from a kitchen," Mrs. Goodge said impatiently. "But what kitchen? The Frommer household had been on holiday for two weeks. You don't leave a cake sittin' in the larder for weeks on end."

"But you bake our Christmas cake in August," Wiggins argued.

"This wasn't a bloomin' Christmas cake," the cook snapped.

"It was walnut," the housekeeper murmured.

"Thank you," Mrs. Goodge said promptly.

"And you're right to wonder where it came from," the housekeeper continued. She looked at the maid. "As a matter of fact, that's something you ought to do straightaway. Tomorrow. Check with all the bakers in the area. Find out who bought that cake."

"Are you thinkin' it might 'ave been the killer?" Smythe asked. "Surely no one is that stupid."

"You'd be surprised how stupid some criminals are," Mrs. Jeffries replied. "But you're probably right. I doubt the killer walked into a local baker's shop and bought it. But someone must have. I do think that we ought to know who."

"Maybe Ashbury brought it from the country," Luty suggested. "From what I hear, he's about as cheap as they come."

"Is that all you found out, madam?" Hatchet grinned broadly. "That the victim was a cheapskate?"

Luty frowned at her butler. "It's early days yet in this investigation. Don't ya worry yourself about me, Hatchet. I'll find out plenty."

"In other words, madam"—the butler smiled gleefully—"that is all you found out."

"But I thought you was eager to tell us something earlier today?" Mrs. Goodge said. "Something you heard from your friend in the House of Lords."

"I was," Luty replied. "But seein' as how Wiggins and Smythe has already mentioned Eloise Hartshorn, they've kinda stole my thunder. That's really all he had to tell me. He was just repeatin' some gossip. The only other thing he mentioned was the scandal involvin' Ashbury's son, Jonathan, but that was years ago."

"He disinherted the boy, didn't he?" Mrs. Goodge nodded. "That's what my sources said. The lad married a servant girl, a Russian immigrant, and they left the country."

Luty nodded. "The boy and his family died when the wagon they was in got washed away. Just goes to show what kind of man Ashbury was. He wouldn't even help his own flesh and blood."

"You saw Dr. Bosworth today?" Betsy asked Mrs. Jeffries. She rather liked the good doctor, and better yet, she knew it niggled Smythe that she would bring the man's name up. She shot the coachman a quick glance out of the corner of her eyes. He looked annoyed.

"Yes, I went around to the hospital right after tea." She pursed her lips thoughtfully. "He'd not done the postmortem, but he'd managed to have a look at Dr. Potter's report. It's as we thought. Ashbury was killed by a bullet, probably from a revolver."

Smythe pushed his way through the crowded, noisy pub, one hand over his pants pocket to protect against pickpockets as he scanned the small room. He spotted a familiar figure leaning up against the bar.

"Hello, Blimpey." Smythe wedged himself in next to the short, rotund fellow. "Glad to see yer on time."

"Am I ever late when there's money involved?" Blimpey asked with a wide grin. He wore a brown-and-white-checked coat that had seen better days, a dark, porkpie hat covered with so much grime its original color was anyone's guess and a wilted gray shirt that had once been white. A bright red scarf was tossed jauntily around his squat neck. Blimpey nodded at his empty glass. "Wouldn't say no to another."

Smythe caught the publican's eye. "Another one 'ere," he called, pointing to Blimpey, "and I'll 'ave a pint of yer best bitter."

"Ta," Blimpey said amiably. "Well, me lad, how ya been keepin'?"

"I'm doin' all right," Smythe replied, pulling out a handful of coins and slapping them on the counter as the barman put their drinks in front of them. "Same as always."

"How's that sweet girl of yours?" Blimpey said chattily. "My, but she's a lovely one. When the two of you tyin' the knot? I could tell by the way ya hovered over her so carefully that she's right special to ya."

"You saw me and Betsy? Where?"

"At the Crystal Palace." Blimpey smiled slyly. "A few months ago. It was at the Photographic Exhibition. Grand, wasn't it?"

Surprised, Smythe retorted, "You was at the exhibition?"

"Don't sound so shocked," Blimpey countered. "You're not the only one who can get out and about. I like lookin' at interestin' things too."

"More like ya was pickin' pockets." Smythe reached for his beer. He wasn't sure how he felt about someone like Blimpey knowing too much about his courtship of Betsy. It made him feel vulnerable. He didn't mind Mrs. Jeffries and the others knowing he was crazy about the girl; that was different, that was family.

Blimpey's face fell; he actually looked hurt. "I'll have you know, I don't do that anymore," he said with dignity. "I don't have to. My current occupation is far too lucrative. Now, why don't you tell me what it is you're wantin' from me tonight?"

Blimpey's current occupation was the reason that Smythe had arranged to meet him. After years of petty thieving and picking pockets, the man had realized his phenomenal memory could be put to much better use than dodging coppers.

So now he bought and sold information. His clients ranged from people like Smythe to politicians and, on occasion, even Scotland Yard itself.

"No offense was meant," Smythe said apologetically. Not that he was overly concerned with hurting Blimpey Groggnis's tender feelings; he just didn't want him so annoyed he didn't do a good, quick job. Smythe felt a bit funny about his current mission. Somehow, it didn't seem fair. Especially as it was becoming a bit of a habit. He'd hired the man on several of the inspector's cases now. But in his own defense, he thought quickly, he did plenty of investigating himself. It just seemed silly to run all over London trying to find out things when for a few bob he could pay Blimpey and be sure of getting it fast and quick. And it wasn't like he couldn't afford it, either.

He had plenty of money. More than he knew what to do with, and that was causing him no end of bother as well. It was one of the reasons he couldn't "tie the knot" with Betsy.

"None taken." Blimpey's good humor was restored as quickly as it had disappeared. "Now, who am I onto this time?"

"Did you hear about that murder at the MP's house?"

"All of London's 'eard of that one." Blimpey chugged his drink. "Andrew Frommer. It was his wife's father who was killed, wasn't it?"

"Right," Smythe agreed. "And I want to know everything there is to know about both of them. The husband and the wife."

"You think she might have done her old man in?" Blimpey asked conversationally. Nothing surprised him.

"It's possible." Smythe shrugged. "I've got a few more names fer you as well. Find out what ya can about Charles Burroughs; 'e lives right next door to the Frommers."

Blimpey didn't bother to write anything down. "Who else?"

"Eloise Hartshorn. She lives at number four Tacner Place in Chelsea. I think she might be Frommer's mistress. Then there's a bloke named Henry Alladyce. 'E was the victim's partner. They ran a shipping agency over on Russell Street. That's right off the East India Docks."

"I know where it is." Blimpey finished off his pint. "Is that it, then?"

Smythe nodded. "Yeah, for right now. How long do ya think it'll take to find out anythin'?"

"Meet me here at noon tomorrow," Blimpey replied. "I ought to have something by then."

The inspector arrived home for dinner only an hour past his usual time. "I do hope dinner is ready," he commented as he handed his hat to Mrs. Jeffries. "I'm quite famished. By the way, do you happen to know how long Lady Cannonberry's houseguest is staying?"

"Dinner is on the table, sir." Mrs. Jeffries led him down the hall and into the dining room. "Mrs. Goodge has made a lovely meal for you, sir." She gestured at the table. "She thought you might enjoy a cold supper, sir, as it's so hot today." Actually, the cook had been too busy using her ovens to bake for her sources to bother making much of a meal for the inspector. Betsy and Mrs. Jeffries had been the ones to put together his dinner from what fixings they'd found in the dry larder.

"Excellent." He pulled out his chair, whipped his serviette off the plate and reached for the platter of sliced ham. He speared a double portion and dumped it onto the china. "This does look good."

"I've no idea how long Mr. Pilchard is staying with Lady Cannonberry," she continued. She reached for a bowl of fresh mixed greens and handed it to him. "How was your day, sir? Are you making any progress on the case?"

"Well"—he made a face as he popped two hard-boiled eggs next to the greens—"I think so. I interviewed two other people who might have had a reason to kill the victim. But honestly it's all such a muddle, I can't make heads nor tails of it."

"Really, sir? And who were they? If, of course, you don't mind my asking."

"One of them is a neighbor. Charles Burroughs. Nice enough chap." Witherspoon shook salt onto his eggs. "Very cooperative. He told us something most interesting." As he ate he told her about the interview, taking care to get all the details correct. Talking the case out with Mrs. Jeffries was always so helpful. "So you see," he said, "I had quite a good impression of the fellow, thought he was being honest and everything until I spoke to Eloise Hartshorn. That's when it all got terribly, terribly confusing. As a matter of fact, I think Miss Hartshorn might be lying. Could you pass me those greens?"

She complied with his request, nothing that not only was he demolishing the last of the greens, but he'd also eaten all the ham. "Why do you think she might be lying, sir?"

"Because"—he scraped some more greens onto his plate—"I think she's in love with Charles Burroughs and she's trying to protect him. She claimed she saw Andrew Frommer leaving his own house by the back door at a quarter to four on the afternoon of the murder. She said she witnessed this from the window of Charles Burroughs's bedroom." He broke off as a bright, red blush swept his cheeks, and then forced himself to go on. "But that's not true. We interviewed Mr. Burroughs's servants on the way home this evening, and all of them testify that Miss Hartshorn wasn't in the Burroughs house the afternoon of the murder. So she couldn't have been in his bedroom and couldn't have seen what she claimed she saw." He shook his head and popped another bite into his mouth. As he demolished his dinner he told Mrs. Jeffries about his interview with Eloise Hartshorn.

As always, she listened carefully, storing every little bit of information in her mind. Finally, when it appeared he'd told her everything, she said, "But I don't understand why Henry Alladyce wanted you to interview Charles Burroughs in the first place. I can see why he'd give you Eloise Hartshorn's name. But why Burroughs?"

"Oh." Witherspoon looked surprised. "Didn't I tell you?"

"No, sir, you didn't. From what you've told me, Burroughs's only connection to the family is that he lives next door. The fact that he knows Andrew Frommer beats his wife couldn't be the reason that Alladyce sent you to him in the first place. Not unless Burroughs told Alladyce what he'd seen."

The inspector swallowed a huge bite of egg. "He hadn't. Alladyce thought I ought to see him because he knew that Burroughs had a gun."

Incredulous, she stared at him. "That's it? He was suspicious of the neighbor because of a gun? But, sir, half of London owns weapons of some sort."

"True." Witherspoon scanned the empty serving bowls. "But most of them aren't revolvers. Burroughs has a revolver. The same kind of weapon used in the murder."

"How did Alladyce know what kind of gun had been used?"

"From the newspaper." He frowned. "Stupid of us, really, letting that information get out to the public."

Mrs. Jeffries knew it was common practice for the police to keep some details out of the press. "How did Alladyce know that Burroughs had the gun? Are they well acquainted?"

"Not really. Alladyce only met him once, in front of the Frommer house. He knew about the gun because he happened to see Burroughs cleaning it a few weeks back. He'd taken the weapon in the garden to clean and Alladyce saw it over the fence. He said Burroughs wasn't trying to hide what he was doing, he was simply sitting at the lawn table in his shirtsleeves cleaning his gun. Burroughs confirmed this. He admitted he'd been doing just that. Even knew when it must have happened. It was the day before the Frommer household went to Ascot."

"I still don't think that's enough of a reason to consider the man a suspect," she said, shaking her head.

"Normally I'd agree with you." Witherspoon licked his lips. "But in this case, considering what I learned from Eloise Hartshorn, I'm glad I went to see Charles Burroughs. You see, the revolver he owns is missing. It's completely disappeared."

They only had time for a brief meeting the next morning. Mrs. Jeffries brought them all up-to-date on what she'd heard from the inspector. She also assured Wiggins that she'd managed to plant the idea in the inspector's mind that he ought to interview any servants who'd recently left the Frommer household. Therefore, he could stop worrying about Emma not being able to tell her tale. By the time everyone had left to do all their own snooping, she'd still not decided what she ought to do. She sat at the table, gazing blankly ahead, trying to sift all the bits and pieces of information into some sort of coherent pattern. But nothing, absolutely nothing came to mind.

Mrs. Goodge ushered in a young man wearing a footman's livery. "Oh," she said, when she spotted the housekeeper sitting at the table, "you're still here? I thought you'd gone off with the others."

The words weren't rude or even unfriendly, but Mrs. Jeffries had the distinct impression the cook wanted to pump her source in private. She finally decided what she ought to do. "I was just leaving," she said, smiling at the skinny lad as she rose to her feet and hurried over to the coat tree. Reaching for her hat, she said, "I ought to be back by tea."

She left by the back door, hurried up to Addison Road and from there onto the Uxbridge Road. She found a hansom in front of Holland Park Gardens. "Take me to Chelsea," she ordered, getting inside.

"None of the alibis are right, sir," Barnes said as he and the inspector waited on Ladbrook Road for a passing hansom cab. The police station, where they'd just come from, was directly behind them. "I don't know why people bother lyin' to us. Do they think we don't check up on them?"

"I'm afraid that's precisely what most of them think." Witherspoon raised his arm as a cab clip-clopped toward them. "Argyle Street," the inspector instructed the driver when the hansom pulled over. As soon as he and the constable were safely inside, he allowed a sigh to escape him. Not only was this case becoming a bit of a muddle—don't they all, he thought—but he was rather distressed about Lady Cannonberry. He'd popped over early this morning hoping to have a word with her before breakfast, only to discover that she and Mr. Pilchard were already out and about. They'd taken the early train to Brighton. Drat. He'd so wanted to ask her to dine with him later in the week.

"Well, sir?" Barnes asked.

Witherspoon came out of his daze to find the constable staring at him expectantly. "I'm sorry," he said, "I'm afraid I didn't quite hear you."

Barnes nodded sympathetically. He'd arrived at Upper Edmonton Gardens this morning just in time to see the inspector leaving Ruth Cannonberry's front porch. The glum expression on Witherspoon's face and a discreet question or two had elicited enough information for the constable to guess at the cause of the inspector's preoccupation. Ah, first love, he thought, it didn't matter whether one was fifteen or fifty. It hit with the force of a gale, spun the unlucky man to and fro a few times and then knocked him on his backside. Poor fella. "I asked who we wanted to question first?"

The inspector forced himself to keep his mind on the case. "Why don't we see who's available?" he finally said. "It could well be that Mr. Frommer is at his office."

But Mr. Frommer wasn't at his office; he was at home. When the butler led the two policemen into the study, Frommer looked up from his desk with a puzzled, abstracted expression. It took him a moment before he recognized his visitors. "Back again? Have you caught the killer yet?"

"No, sir, we haven't," Witherspoon replied.

"Why not?" Frommer put down his pen and leaned back in the chair. "What's taking so long? It's most awkward for me, being part of a household where an unsolved murder has been committed. My constituents don't like it. The party doesn't like it. I don't like it. Now, why can't you fellows catch the lunatic that did this thing?"

Witherspoon hadn't much cared for Mr. Frommer the first time he met him. Since hearing Burroughs's contention that the man was a wife beater, he cared even less for him. He'd no doubt Burroughs had been telling the truth, though as to why he felt that way he couldn't say. But the inspector had long ago learned to listen to his inner voice, and right now that voice was telling him this man was a blackguard and a cad. However, that didn't mean he was a killer. "I expect it would be easier to catch the murderer," he said carefully, "if we didn't have to waste so much time sorting out the lies people tell us."

Frommer's self-satisfied expression vanished. His eyes grew wary. "I don't know what you mean."

"Don't you, sir?" Witherspoon walked closer to the desk. "You told us you came to London on the four o'clock train, sir. But that's not true. We've a witness who placed you on the two forty-five."

Frommer shot to his feet. "Your witness is lying. You were already here when I arrived, and that was well into the evening. It had gone half-past six."

"Our witness isn't lying, sir," Barnes said firmly. "He's a policeman. He stood right next to you on the platform at Ascot and then watched you get into a first-class compartment. When the train arrived at London, he saw you get off."

"He's mistaken," Frommer sputtered. "It wasn't me."

"It's no mistake, sir," Witherspoon said. "He knew quite well who you were. You're the MP for his district. Now, sir, why don't you tell us where you were on the afternoon of the murder?"

Speechless, Frommer gaped at the two men and then flopped back into his chair. "All right," he muttered, "I'll tell you. But it's to go no further than this room. You must give me your word on that."

"I'm afraid I can't do that," Witherspoon said gently. "I may have to give evidence in court and I can't promise to keep any information secret."

"Now, see here," Frommer snapped. "It's a matter vital to the national interest—"

"No, sir, I'm afraid it isn't." Witherspoon sighed inwardly. Honestly, people sometimes thought the police were such fools. "The chief inspector has already been in contact with the home secretary and Whitehall. You were doing nothing official or even unofficial in your capacity as a member of Parliament that afternoon. As a matter of fact, according to your chief whip, you missed an important meeting of your own party that day. Now, could you please tell us where you were?"

"Yes, Andrew, do tell us."

The inspector and Barnes swiveled around to see MaryAnne Frommer standing in the open doorway. Though she was covered from head to toe in mourning black, the bonnet on her head and the black parasol she carried signaled the fact that she was getting ready to go out. She didn't take her eyes off her husband. "Well, where were you?" she goaded. "You weren't at Ascot. You weren't at your office and you certainly weren't helping any of your constituents."

"I don't have to answer to you," he finally sputtered.

"True, you don't." She smiled sweetly, a smile that took fifteen years off her middle-aged face. "But I do believe the inspector is waiting for a reply."

"Your wife is correct, sir," Witherspoon interjected hastily. He wasn't sure what he was trying to do; he only knew he didn't wish to give Mr. Frommer further reason to get angry with his wife. "We do need an answer." He looked at Barnes. "Could you please escort Mrs. Frommer into the drawing room and take her statement?"

"That won't be necessary," Mrs. Frommer said. "I know why you're here and I'm quite prepared to tell you the truth."

The inspector was very, very confused. "Er, if you'd like to go with the constable . . . I'm sure he'll be pleased to take your statement."

"There's no reason to go anywhere," she said flatly. "You're here to find out why I lied about the day my father was killed, aren't you?"

Frommer shot to his feet again. "What are you talking about, MaryAnne?"

"Don't look so shocked, Andrew." She pushed past the policemen and flopped down on the chair opposite her husband's desk. "I was on the two forty-five train that day. With you."

"Now, lad, why don't you drink up?" Mrs. Goodge handed the footman a third cup of tea. "Would you like more sponge?"

"Umm. yes." Matthew Piker nodded vigorously as he stuffed the last bite of scone into his mouth. He completely ignored the crumbs that fell from his lips and dotted the chest of his dark blue footman's uniform. "This is good. Mrs. Hampton's a good mistress, but she's a bit stingy with food. I'm always hungry."

"So many of them are like that." Mrs. Goodge clucked her tongue sympathetically and silently sent up a prayer of thanks that her aunt Elberta had finally come in useful. She'd accidentally dropped the box containing Elberta's rambling letters when she'd been rummaging about in her bureau drawer for one of her "special" recipes. When she'd picked the letter up, it had opened onto a page that mentioned Elberta's late husband's two nephews worked for Eugenia Hampton, a dreadful shrew of a woman to be sure. But she lived just up the road from the Frommer house. Mrs. Goodge hadn't wasted a moment. She'd sent off a note to young Matthew Pike inviting him to come around for tea on his afternoon off. He'd arrived wary, but curious. It wasn't often the likes of him got invited to tea in a fine kitchen. "We're very lucky," she went on. "The inspector's quite the generous man."

"Must be funny, workin' for a copper?" Matthew gasped quietly as he saw the slab of sponge cake the cook loaded onto his plate.

"It's not so bad," she said, handing him the cake. "We get to hear all about his cases. They're interesting."

"Well, we had us a murder," he boasted. "Bet you've 'eard of it; it were in all the newspapers. Old man up the road got himself shot while he was havin' tea."

"Oh yes." She nodded. "I know all about that one. His name was Roland Ashbury."

"Is your inspector on that one, then?" Matthew asked, somewhat disappointed because he'd been looking forward to having all the details coaxed out of him with more cake and tea.

"He is indeed," Mrs. Goodge replied. "And he likes to discuss his cases, he does. For instance, I'll bet you didn't know that the man was murdered with a revolver."

"The whole neighborhood knows that," Matthew shot back, "and just about everyone knows whose gun it were too."

"Charles Burroughs's."

His mouth dropped in surprise. "Blimey, I guess you do know all about the case." He pursed his lips and stared at his plate. Then he brightened. "But I'll bet you didn't know something else. Something that no one except me knows."

CHAPTER 6

Mrs. Jeffries eyed the small but elegant house warily, wondering if she was about to do something very foolish. She hesitated by the letter box, in her hand an old envelope she'd found in her skirt pocket. Using the envelope as a prop, she pretended to double-check the address, all the while keeping her gaze on the white-painted door of the house across the street. What if the woman refused to answer her questions? Refused to cooperate at all? What if she told the inspector? Mrs. Jeffries pursed her lips as she weighed the odds. To go in or not to go in, that was the question. She smiled at a maid who was vigorously sweeping the door stoop of the house behind her. The maid simply stared back, no doubt beginning to wonder why someone was lingering so long in front of a letter box.

Mrs. Jeffries was just about to start across the road when the front door opened and a tall handsome man emerged. A woman, small, elegantly dressed and quite beautiful, came out right behind him. He gave the woman his arm and the two of them descended the stairs and began walking up the street.

Mrs. Jeffries didn't hesitate. She turned and walked in the same direction the couple had taken, but she stayed on her side of the road. Traffic was brisk. Hansoms, four-wheelers, drays and loaded wagons kept up a moving screen between her and the two on the other side. When she reached the corner, she saw them turn onto Guildford Street. She hurried after them, taking care to keep them in sight yet staying far enough behind not to be noticed.

They went past the Statue of Coram, the Foundling Hospital and from there onto Lansdown Place and into Brunswick Square. Mrs. Jeffries was breathing heavily by the time the couple in front of her circled the square and headed into the burial grounds. From the way they kept their heads close together in conversation without so much as a glance behind them, she was fairly sure they'd no idea they were being followed.

The man suddenly led the woman off the path and into the cemetery itself. Mrs. Jeffries was close enough now to see the expression on his face. He was worried, very worried.

They finally stopped in front of a large marble statue of a winged angel surrounded by a grouping of cherubs. Mrs. Jeffries halted as well. She desperately wanted to know what her prey were discussing, but she needed to stay out of sight. She surveyed the scene carefully and, after the briefest of hesitations, decided the headstone might be large enough to conceal her. Moving cautiously, she darted off the path and crept up on other side.

"But why must I leave?" she heard the woman ask. "I've already spoken to the police. They know about us."

"You shouldn't have told them anything," the man insisted. "They're not fools. Now they know you had a motive. The old bastard tried to blackmail you."

She gave a cynical laugh. "He tried, but he didn't succeed. I told him to go ahead and tell. I was going to break it off anyway. But it's not me I'm worried about, Charles, it's you. Why did you admit to having a gun?"

"Because I had to," he said harshly. "Too many people have seen it."

Mrs. Jeffries could hear the shuffle of feet as the man's agitation increased. She huddled closer to the headstone.

"It doesn't matter, darling. The police will realize the gun must have been stolen," the woman cried. "You didn't have any reason to kill him."

There was a long silence, so long that Mrs. Jeffries was beginning to think they might have discovered her presence and were in the process of tiptoeing away. But finally the man spoke. "That's where you're wrong, my dear. I had the best reason of all to want him dead."

"But you didn't even know him till you came here?" The woman sounded as though she couldn't believe what he was saying. "You couldn't have hated him enough to murder him. You just couldn't."

"You don't really believe that, dearest," he said softly. "If you did, you wouldn't have made up that lie about seeing Andrew Frommer."

"It wasn't a lie," she hissed. "I did see him."

"Darling, I'm touched by your devotion, but you weren't even at my house that afternoon. The police will find that out soon enough. My servants won't lie." There was the thump of feet and the rustle of clothing as they began to move. "Come on," Mrs. Jeffries heard him say, "let's walk."

Mrs. Jeffries waited a few seconds, giving them time to move farther away. The moment she judged they were far enough down the path not to hear her, she hurried out from her hiding place.

Her face fell in disappointment. Coming directly toward her was a huge black coffin, in front of which walked a sad-faced cleric. Somehow a funeral procession had gotten between her and her quarry. She stepped to one side so they could pass. By the time she could politely make her way past the mourners, her prey were gone.

The inspector and Barnes followed Mrs. Frommer into the drawing room. Witherspoon waited until she'd sat down on the sofa before quietly closing the door. He didn't think Mr. Frommer would dare interrupt them, especially as he'd left a fresh-faced police constable on duty outside the study. But he was taking no chances. The man had been furious at his wife. Witherspoon, despite not knowing what to make of MaryAnne Frommer, didn't wish to conduct the interview in her husband's presence. He was afraid her answers might enrage Frommer to the point that he'd do violence to his wife the minute the house was empty of police. The inspector wasn't having any of that.

MaryAnne Frommer cocked her head to one side and gazed at him quizzically. "You're wondering why I lied earlier, aren't you?"

"Yes, madam, I am." He crossed the room and, without being invited, sat down on the other end of the sofa. "You originally told us you'd come back to London on a late train because you'd gone to the vicarage."

"I knew you'd find out the truth." She laughed. "I suppose expecting a vicar to lie for one is expecting a bit much, don't you agree? Of course, when I arrived home and found out that Papa was dead, lying no longer mattered."

Witherspoon didn't think he could be any more confused. "Could you explain yourself, please."

"I told everyone I was going to the vicarage so I wouldn't have to come home on the same train as Andrew." She broke off with a short, harsh laugh. "I thought he'd be going on the four o'clock train. Imagine my surprise when I came hurtling onto the platform and saw him. I jumped back so fast I almost tripped."

"I take it your husband didn't see you?" Witherspoon asked.

"Andrew isn't particularly observant." She shrugged. "Once the train pulled in, I waited till he got into a first-class carriage and then got on myself. When we arrived at Waterloo, I kept well back, making sure that he didn't see me. When I saw him leave the station, I hurried out and hailed a hansom. Then I went to Mortimer Street, to the offices of Henley and Farr."

"Who is that, ma'am?" Witherspoon asked.

"They're a firm of solicitors." She smiled wanly.

The inspector nodded encouragingly. "What time was your appointment?"

"I didn't have one. I went to them because they were the only solicitors in town who I thought might represent me. They aren't frightened of Andrew, you see."

Witherspoon didn't see, but before he could formulate a question that didn't sound too terribly odd, she continued.

"What I needed from them was rather delicate. The sort of thing most solicitors wouldn't want to handle in any case." She sighed. "Especially when the husband in question is an MP. Andrew isn't averse to using his position to make someone's life miserable. He's done it before. Frequently. That's why I had to go to Henley and Farr. They've gone up against Andrew several times and won."

"What did you want them to do for you, ma'am?" Barnes asked softly.

"I wanted to find out if I could obtain a divorce." She smiled sadly. "You see, I had grounds now. Andrew's got a mistress. I have witnesses. Several of them."

"I see." Witherspoon knew that obtaining a divorce was very difficult. From what he'd learned of Frommer's character, he didn't much blame Mrs. Frommer for wanting to leave this marriage, but something was bothering him. Something she'd said. He frowned, trying to remember precisely what it was.

The constable, after waiting a moment of two for the inspector to speak, finally asked, "Who did you see at Henley and Farr?"

She made a disgusted face. "No one. The whole trip was absolutely wasted. The office was closed; there weren't even any clerks there. There was a notice on the door saying that they were closed until Monday next. Can you believe it? The whole office gone on holiday at the same time."

Barnes glanced at Witherspoon. The inspector's face still wore an expression of fierce concentration. The constable carried on. "What did you do then?" he asked.

"What did I do?" she repeated, with a cynical laugh. "What could I do? Nothing. I was very disappointed, of course. Who wouldn't be? I didn't want to face going home, so I went for a long walk."

Again the constable glanced at his superior. He didn't want Witherspoon thinking he was getting above himself by asking so many questions. But the inspector still looked preoccupied, so the constable pressed on. "Did you see anyone you know?"

She shook her head. "Not that I recall."

Barnes scribbled her answers in his notebook, more to give the inspector time to finish his thinking than anything else. The constable had quite a good memory. But he'd learned that putting something in writing didn't hurt. Especially when one had to give evidence in court. He glanced up. Witherspoon was now stroking his chin, his expression still preoccupied. There was nothing for it but for him to keep on. "Where were you between three-thirty and four o'clock?" he asked.

She looked puzzled by the question. "I just told you." Her expression cleared as she realized the implications of what was being asked. "Gracious, that must have been when Father was killed."

"Yes, ma'am." Barnes wondered if the inspector was ever going to ask another question. "As far as we can tell, that would be the time of death."

"And I've no alibi now." Again she laughed. "I assure you, Constable. Much as I disliked my father, I certainly didn't kill him. I was nowhere near the house at that time."

Witherspoon started slightly, as though her answer had pulled him back into the conversation. As a matter of fact, her statement had reminded him of what was bothering him. "You admit you didn't like your father."

"I admit that," she replied. "I told you that before. I didn't like my father at all. He was never a real father to me. He always put his own interests first, but much as I disliked him, I didn't murder him."

Witherspoon nodded slowly. He wanted to ask this next question very carefully. "Could you tell me why you said that once you'd found out your father was dead, lying wouldn't matter." He was rather annoyed at himself for taking so long to recall that particularly interesting comment she'd made. Especially as she'd made it only a few moments ago. He admonished himself for being so distracted. He really must keep his mind on the interview at hand. But gracious, it was so very easy to get muddled.

She started down at her hands and a long, heartfelt sigh escaped her. "I meant that if I'd known Papa was dead, I wouldn't even have bothered going to the solicitors. I'd have left. I've some money of my own. With my father dead, Andrew couldn't have forced me to come back. That's what he did, you know. One other time when I left him, he made me come back by threatening me."

"How did he threaten you?" Witherspoon asked quickly. "If you've money of your own, how could he have made you come back?"

She looked away for a moment, and when she turned back to the inspector, her expression was grim. "He told me he'd toss Father out into the streets if I didn't come home. At the time I was sure he meant it. But after I found out what my father did, after the way he'd behaved recently, I wouldn't have cared about what Andrew could do to him. I wouldn't have let anything stop me. I was quite prepared for the worst."

Witherspoon thought back to his conversation with Henry Alladyce. He'd gotten the impression that Roland Ashbury was cheap, but certainly not destitute. "Your father, then, couldn't afford his own home?"

"That's not the point, Inspector." MaryAnne Frommer smiled bitterly. "My father has plenty of money. But he claimed he couldn't live on his own because he had a weak heart. It was rubbish, of course. He was as healthy as a horse. He only made the assertion because he wanted to stay on here."

"What did your father do to you?" Witherspoon asked. "You said a few moments ago that once you found out what he'd done . . ."

"He told Andrew where I was living," she cried angrily. "I'd written to him to give him the address of the rooming house where I was staying. I hadn't wanted him to worry. But instead of taking my part, instead of helping me get away from that monster I was married to, my own father led him right to me. I never forgave him for that. Never."

Witherspoon looked at the constable, making sure that Barnes was getting all of this down. Whether Mrs. Frommer realized it or not, she'd just given them a motive for murder. "So you hated your father," he prodded gently.

"Of course I did. My father couldn't have cared less about me," she countered flatly.

"You realize you've just given us a motive, don't you?" Witherspoon warned. He wasn't quite at the point of cautioning her officially, but she was definitely climbing to the top of the suspect list.

MaryAnne Frommer didn't look in the least alarmed. "Why would I kill him? I'd devised the perfect revenge against the man. I was going to leave. Andrew would have tossed him into the street. That would have hurt my father ten times more than getting a bullet in his skull. He wouldn't have been able to stand the humiliation of being a nobody."

"Living here meant that much to him?" Barnes queried.

"It meant everything to him," she said passionately. "He stayed because despite Andrew treating him like a half-witted servant, he loved basking in Andrew's limelight. He loved living in a big house with an important man, an MP. Don't you understand, as long as he was a member of this household, people treated him with respect. He got invited to the best gentlemen's clubs, he was asked out to dine, his opinion was solicited. If he was tossed out on his ear, all that would end. My father was terrified that if he lived on his own, he'd just be another stingy businessman with no entrée into the circles of his betters."

"Stingy businessman," Witherspoon repeated. "But your father's business partner says the business is doing well." He really didn't know what to make of all this; it was most odd. Most odd indeed. Tonight, when he got home, he'd have to have a good long think about the whole situation.

MaryAnne Frommer's brows came together. "Business partner? You mean Henry?"

"He said he was your father's partner," Witherspoon replied. "Isn't that correct?"

She looked doubtful. "Well, I suppose he *would* say that. But actually Papa and Josiah Alladyce had quite a different arrangement worked out. Papa set it up when my brother Jonathan went to live in the United States."

"I'm sorry," the inspector said, "but I don't quite understand." He didn't know if this matter would turn out to be pertinent to the case, but he'd learned that the most seemingly unconnected events could end up being important.

"It's an old story, Inspector"—she sighed again—"and one that does none of us any credit. For when it happened, I was just as unreasonable as Father. Pride, I suppose. Anyway, it doesn't matter now. My brother and his wife and son have been dead for over fifteen years. They died in California. They were killed when the wagon they were sleeping in was washed away in a flood. But the point is, when my father disinherited Jonathan and had no son to leave his half of the business to, he forced

Josiah Alladyce—that's Henry's father—to draw up an agreement about the disposal of the company's assets when they either died or retired. The agreement is very specific in its terms. Whoever died first would leave his half of the business to the other one until both partners were dead or retired. Then the business would be sold and the assets split between my father's heirs and the Alladyce heirs. That's why I'm surprised that Henry calls himself a partner. He's not. Well, I suppose he is now that Father's dead. But he wasn't before."

Barnes asked, "How much is the business worth?"

"I'm not certain," she replied. "Quite a lot, I think. I know Father hadn't spent a penny of the profits that he didn't have to after Josiah Alladyce died. I do believe that annoyed Henry. Mind you, Henry does pull his living out of the firm."

Again Barnes glanced at Witherspoon. The inspector nodded slightly in acknowledgment. It was obvious now that they had one more suspect on their hands.

There was an air of suppressed excitement around the table as they all took their places for their afternoon meeting. For once, Mrs. Jeffries thought, everyone is on time. She could tell by their expressions that most of them had found out something useful. She couldn't wait to tell them what she'd learned.

"Can I go first?" Luty asked eagerly as she scanned the faces of the others, daring someone to deny her request. "I'm gonna bust if I don't git it out."

"Go ahead, Luty," Mrs. Jeffries replied. Her own information, important as it was, could wait.

"Well, as you all know, I've got plenty of ways of findin' out things." She shot her butler a glare as a faint snort of derision issued from his direction. "And I found out something real interestin' about Andrew Frommer. He's broke. He spent a bundle campaignin' in the last election. So much so that he's up to his nose in debt and that fancy house of his is mortgaged to the hilt. That means he's got a motive for murderin' his father-in-law."

"I don't see how his financial condition could be that affected by Roland Ashbury's death," Hatchet said thoughtfully. "Even if Mrs. Frommer inherits from her father, it would be her money, not his."

"So?" Luty demanded.

"So"—Hatchet gave her a sly smile—"we know that Mrs. Frommer loathes her husband. If she inherits from her father, I don't think she'll be sharing it with her spouse. Furthermore, how much could the victim actually have to leave to anyone? He didn't even own his own home and his business certainly doesn't appear to be all that prosperous. I know. I went along and had a look at the place."

"He's got plenty to leave," Mrs. Goodge said darkly. "He hasn't spent a penny of the profits off that business since his partner died five years ago. MaryAnne Frommer's the heir, you see. That business may not look like much, but I found out that Ashbury and his partner bought the building some years back, and the warehouse next to it. The whole lot's worth a fortune now."

"Seems to me that just about everyone 'ad a reason for wantin' Mr. Ashbury dead," Wiggins said. "Even 'is own kin."

"Especially his own kin," Mrs. Goodge declared stoutly. "Ashbury was a horrible man. He disinherited his own son because the boy married a servant, and forced Mrs. Frommer to stay with that brute of a husband of hers. But now that he's dead, she can leave him. She'd left him before, you see. But her own father told Frommer where she was stayin' and he went and drug her home."

"Whaddaya mean, 'he drug her home'?" Luty asked, her eyes narrowed dangerously.

"Just what I said," Mrs. Goodge replied. "Frommer went to the flat where his wife was living and made her come home with him. He's a wife beater."

"And she went with him?" Luty exclaimed, her expression incredulous.

"What else could she do?" Mrs. Goodge said. "He was her husband. I'm sure her landlord didn't want that kind of trouble, especially as Frommer was an MP."

"MP or not," Luty snapped, "they'd be havin' snowball fights in hell before I'd let some wife-beatin', no-good cowardly varmmit come draggin' me home."

"My sentiments precisely," Mrs. Jeffries agreed. Gracious, the information was coming along so fast she could barely absorb it all. They must be a tad more orderly or she, along with the rest of them, would get confused. "But let's let Luty finish talking and then we'll move along to Mrs. Goodge. Both of you seem to have found out an awful lot."

"I'm done," Luty announced. "All I learned was that Frommer was broke and iffen Mrs. Frommer ain't gonna share with him, I guess that leaves him out as a suspect."

"Not necessarily," Mrs. Jeffries murmured. She made a mental note to ask Lady Cannonberry about the Married Woman's Property Act. One of the delightful things about being friends with a radical is that they were usually well up on all the most recent legislation. "We'd better check on what Mrs. Frommer's position would be. Legally she might not have been able to stop her husband from using her money or selling her property. Especially if it was left to her in trust and that trust is administered by her husband."

"But even Ashbury wouldn't have done that," Betsy cried. "It wouldn't be right. Surely he knew Frommer was a brute."

"He'd do it all right," Mrs. Goodge interjected. "Any man that would let his own son and his wife lose their home and almost starve to death wouldn't care tuppence for his daughter's happiness."

"Ashbury let his son's family starve?" Smythe asked.

"Almost." The cook shook her head in disgust. "He disinherited the boy when he married. The girl was a servant, a Russian immigrant. They, along with the wife's family, moved to the United States and bought a small farm somewhere out west. There was a drought or something horrid like that; you know how things like that are always happening in America. The family lost the farm. Jonathan Ashbury wrote his father for help, begging him to lend him some money. Ashbury never even answered. A few months later, when the family had been forced out of their home, the wagon they were sleeping in was washed away in a flood. All of them were killed except for the daughter-in-law's brother."

"Cor blimey," Wiggins muttered. "Ashbury really was a monster."

"That's right," Mrs. Goodge agreed. "So it's no wonder his own daughter stopped speakin' to him. I only hope the stupid old fool didn't tie up the girl's inheritance and give Frommer control of it."

"We don't know what Frommer can or can't do," Mrs. Jeffries said. "I think it may well depend on how Ashbury wrote his will. Apparently he spent more time trying to please his son-in-law than he did worrying about his daughter's well-being."

"And as Frommer's an MP," Smythe muttered, "there's no tellin' what he could do even if the money was left free and clear to his wife." He caught Betsy's eyes and gave her a wary smile. He didn't want her thinking he approved of any man hitting a woman. He'd noticed that when women heard about another female being knocked about, they tended to tar all men with the same brush.

"Does this mean that Mr. Frommer is still a suspect?" Wiggins asked.

"Of course," Mrs. Jeffries replied.

"But 'e's got an alibi," the footman pointed out, "and so does Mrs. Frommer."

"What difference does that make?" Luty exclaimed. "We've had half a dozen cases where the one with the best alibi ended up bein' the killer."

"I don't think it's Mr. Frommer," Wiggins stated, shaking his head. "I think it's her, Mrs. Frommer. She really hated her father, especially after he come and drug 'er 'ome."

"How do you know that?" Mrs. Goodge demanded.

"Because I talked to Bobby Vickers," he said casually. "'E's a good friend of that footman that's taken off from the Frommer household. He told me that Boyd—that's the lad's name—'ad said that 'e was worried that Mrs. Frommer was goin' to do somethin' awful. She were desperate to get away from 'er 'usband."

"Oh bother, Wiggins." Mrs. Goodge crossed her arms over her chest. "That's silly. If Mrs. Frommer was goin' to commit murder because her situation was so awful, why would she murder her father? Seems to me she'd have killed her husband."

"You have a point, Mrs. Goodge," Hatchet agreed. "My sources of information all agreed that Mrs. Frommer despised her husband and would have done anything to get away from him."

"Why'd she marry him in the first place?" Betsy murmured.

"She married him because her father made her," Hatchet replied. Goff had come through with a bit of information. Not much, but at least he could contribute something. "Andrew Frommer is from an old and well-respected family. But like many such families, they've no money. The estate was lost years ago and there was only a small yearly income for Andrew. Not enough to support his political ambitions and certainly not enough to finance a campaign. Then he met Roland Ashbury at a party political dinner. Ashbury was in trade, of course, but he'd money and a daughter. Frommer, to his credit, at first resisted Ashbury's attempts to buy a husband for his daughter. But he eventually gave way and asked MaryAnne to marry him." He toyed with the handle of his teacup. "But the marriage went sour from the start and Andrew Frommer made no secret of the fact that he considered it his father-in-law's fault. He blamed him for getting him stuck in a loveless marriage."

"He wants an heir too," Mrs. Goodge added. "I've got that on good authority. He dreams of startin' a political dynasty. 'Course, he can't do that without a son." She smiled, thinking of the way the poor lad had blushed earlier today when he'd told her about overhearing Frommer bragging to one of his associates that as his wife was barren, he'd have to "take matters into his own hands" to procure a son. It had taken her ten minutes to pump that bit of information out of Matthew Piker. "But Frommer's been talkin' about the neighborhood that he's got that problem well in hand," she finished.

Mrs. Jeffries knew she had to take control of this situation. There was far too much information being bandied about. So much so that she wasn't sure she'd even remember it all.

"Please, everyone, can we do this one at a time? I'm getting very confused." She looked at Luty. "Now let me see if I understand you. You found out that Frommer finances are in a mess."

Luty nodded vigorously. "That's right."

"And I found out that he's a wife beater and that Mrs. Frommer had run off from him and that he and her father had drug her home," Mrs. Goodge announced proudly. She'd also found out another bit or two, but she was saving this for their next meeting. Sometimes she'd found her sources could be most unreliable and she could have dozens of people through the kitchen without learning a ruddy thing. Well, it wasn't so much that she'd found out anything as it was that she'd thought of something and she considered it might be important.

"I see." Mrs. Jeffries nodded encouragingly and then looked at Hatchet. He repeated what he'd learned and she turned her attention to Smythe and Betsy, both of whom had been somewhat quiet. "Betsy?"

The maid smiled and shrugged. "No luck yet, Mrs. Jeffries, but I'll keep at it. I'm going back out before supper to have a word or two with one of the housemaids who works for Charles Burroughs. I'm meeting her at the Lyons Tea Shop on Oxford Street." She glanced at the clock and then got to her feet. "I'd best be off. I told her I'd be there at five o'clock."

Smythe hated for Betsy to be out late in the afternoon; he was always worried that she'd get caught up in her investigation and end up on the streets after dark. "Now, why would you want to talk to Burroughs's 'ousemaid?"

"She might know something." Betsy shrugged. "After all, it might have been Burroughs's gun that killed Ashbury." She was desperate to find out something and at this point she was willing to talk to anyone.

"But 'e'd no reason to murder the old man," Smythe persisted.

"We don't know that," Betsy said. "We don't know that at all."

"Betsy's right," Mrs. Jeffries interjected. "Burroughs did have a good reason to murder Ashbury. Unfortunately I don't know what that reason is."

Andrew Frommer seemed to have aged ten years in the past half hour. He sat slumped behind his desk, his expression morose, all arrogance gone. "What did she tell you?" he asked.

"Quite a bit," Witherspoon replied. Without being invited, he took a seat on a cane-backed chair opposite Frommer's opulent desk. He nodded for the constable to take the empty one next to him. "Your wife states that both of you came back on the early train. That, along with the PC who saw you on the earlier train, is more than enough evidence to warrant further questioning."

"Where was she when the old man was killed?" he asked.

The inspector certainly wasn't going to answer that question. Eventually there wouldn't be any police constable on the premises, and who knew what kind of vengeance Frommer would take on his wife if the man knew she'd gone to a solicitor. "More to the point, sir, where were you?"

He jerked his head up. "I went for a walk," he mumbled. "I had a lot on my mind."

"Did anyone see you, sir?" Barnes asked.

"Lots of people saw me," he replied.

"Anyone who actually knew you?" the constable persisted. "Anyone who could confirm your whereabouts between the hours of three and four o'clock?"

Frommer shook his head. "No. Not that I recall."

"Where did you walk, sir?"

He swallowed heavily. "Look, Inspector, if I tell you the truth, can you promise to keep it confidential?" He held up his hand as he saw the inspector start to protest. "I swear, this has nothing to do with Roland's murder. But it isn't the sort of information I want made known. It could ruin my career."

Witherspoon mentally debated his options. He didn't like Andrew

Frommer; the man was a brute and a bully, but that didn't necessarily mean he was Ashbury's murderer. Also, there was the small matter of Eloise Hartshorn's statement that she'd seen him leaving here on the afternoon of the murder. Not that Witherspoon was accepting her statement at face value. Not yet. "I'll try to keep what you tell me confidential if, indeed, it has no bearing on this case."

Frommer heaved a sigh of relief. "Good, good. It doesn't, believe me. Well, let's see, where to begin?" He gave a weak laugh and put his elbows on the desk. "I did come back to London on the early train. There was someone I wanted to see. I got to the station and I took a hansom to Tancer Place; that's over near the Foundling Hospital in Chelsea."

"Who were you going to see, sir?" The inspector already knew the answer to that question, but he wanted to see how genuinely honest Frommer would be.

"A woman by the name of Eloise Hartshorn," he replied, his expression was now speculative. "But I expect you already knew that."

Witherspoon nodded but kept quiet.

"Eloise wasn't home. I was disappointed, but as I hadn't told her I was coming, I couldn't really get angry."

"What time was it that you were at Miss Hartshorn's?" the inspector asked.

"I believe it was close to three-fifteen or so. After that I went for a walk. I had a lot of thinking to do."

Witherspoon said nothing for a moment. "What were you thinking about, sir?"

"I don't think that's any of your concern," Frommer snapped.

"I'm afraid it is, sir. You see, I think you were thinking about the awful row you'd had with your father-in-law before you both left Ascot."

Frommer's face darkened with anger. "Are you back to that? I've told you, Roland and I didn't *have* an argument. My wife imagines things. She's a dreadfully stupid woman . . . just because she couldn't abide her father she thinks that everyone hated him. I'd no reason to quarrel with Roland. No reason at all."

"But you did, sir," Witherspoon said calmly. He hoped the information he'd received from Ascot was reliable. "You were furious with him because he wouldn't loan you any more money."

"Who told you that ridiculous story?" Frommer leapt to his feet. "It's a lie. A damned lie."

"Are you denying that you asked your father-in-law for a loan?" Barnes queried.

Frommer hesitated and the inspector pressed his advantage. "We know all about your financial situation, sir. We know that you're completely without funds. Roland Ashbury has made the last two payments on your bank loan, hasn't he, sir?"

"All right, I'm a bit short at the moment, I'll admit that. Roland was glad to help me. He was always glad to help," Frommer insisted.

"Not this time, though," Witherspoon said. "This time he told you he wouldn't do it and you were angry. Very angry. I believe you actually threatened him, didn't you? Told him if he knew what was good for him he'd pay up."

Frommer paled. "I didn't mean I'd kill him," he said, his voice a hoarse whisper. "I only meant that I'd ask him to leave this house. It's still my house, you know."

"But it wouldn't be for much longer, would it, sir? Not if you stopped paying your bank loan." Witherspoon watched Frommer carefully.

"You can't possibly believe I killed him," Frommer insisted. "Why, I was at Chelsea at three-fifteen. Eloise's maid will testify to that."

"But you could easily have made it here by three thirty-five," Barnes pointed out. "And as the body wasn't discovered until almost four, you'd have had ample time to murder the man."

CHAPTER 7

"What do you think, sir?" Barnes asked as they walked toward the hansom station at the corner.

"I'm not sure," Witherspoon replied. "Frommer could have murdered him, but we've no real evidence. That's the mucky bit about this case, Constable. There are so many who could have killed him, so many who apparently wanted him dead, but we've no proof that any of them actually did it. Mrs. Frommer could just as easily have done it, as could Henry Alladyce or the servants . . . or—I don't know; we'll just have to keep digging. Any word on that missing footman yet?"

"No, sir, nothing. We've sent the lads around the workhouse, but no one there admits to seein' the boy. Mind you, that lot isn't all that happy to be cooperating with us in any case, so who knows if he's been there or not. Do you think he's important?" Barnes ran his hand over his forehead, wiping off a line of perspiration trickling out from under his helmet onto his cheek. The day was waning, but the summer air was heavy and humid.

"I'm not sure. According to Miss Donovan and the other servants, the boy hasn't been seen since the morning of the murder. Which would mean he'd disappeared hours before the murder and probably has nothing to do with it. But I don't like it, Barnes. I don't like it at all. But there's not much about this case that I do like. It certainly is turning into a muddle, isn't it?"

They'd come to the curving junction of Manchester Street and Grays Inn Road. This late in the afternoon, traffic was heavy. On the pavement, a boardman advertising this evening's performance of a pantomine spotted

Constable Barnes in his policeman's uniform and made a mad dash in the other direction. As did a young shoe-black. A mush-faker pushing a ginger-beer cart yelled a catcall at the retreating boy and boardman and then grinned broadly as the policeman came steadily on, seemingly oblivious to the consternation their appearance on the street had caused.

A row of hansoms formed a line across the road, some of them disgorging passengers in front of the Throat and Ear Hospital. Barnes didn't know what to think; he was as confused as his inspector. " It *is* a muddle, sir. But about the missing footman, well, coincidences do happen," he ventured. "Should I get us a cab, sir?"

"Let's walk." Witherspoon pointed to his left. "There's a grocer's up a ways."

"You're going to do the shopping?"

"Oh no, no." The inspector laughed. "There's a witness we need to interview. It may come to nothing, but I want to stop in and have a word with the grocer's niece. She used to work for the Frommers."

Witherspoon started briskly up the street. He was glad he'd remembered this bit of information; why, goodness, poor Wiggins had mentioned the girl almost two days ago. "She might be able to help us. Oh, I say, look, there's a fruit vendor. Yoo-hoo, boy." He waved his hands at a boy pushing a large coster's cart just up ahead. "Hang on, lad," he called. He quickened his steps and Barnes had to run to catch up with him.

The coster stopped and waited for the policemen to catch up to him. He bobbed his head respectfully as Witherspoon and Barnes trotted up. "What can I get ya, guv?" he asked. "The fruit's good and ripe."

"My, my, these do look good." The inspector licked his lips as he eyed a basket of ripe peaches. "How much?"

"Fourpence each, sir," the lad replied. "But I'll let you 'ave two at that price seein' as 'ow it's gettin' late and they'll not keep overnight."

"I'll take them." Witherspoon reached in his pocket and pulled out some coins. Dropping them into the boy's hand, he deftly scooped up two of the ripest-looking fruits and tossed one to Barnes.

"Thank you, sir." The constable watched as the inspector stuffed the peach in his mouth and took an enormous bite. This was twice now that Witherspoon had stopped to buy something to eat. Earlier, on their way to the Frommer house, he'd bought a lemon halfpenny ice from an Italian iceman. Barnes had been horrified; everyone knew those ices weren't fit to eat. But before the constable had been able to protest, Witherspoon had gulped the thing down. What on earth was wrong with the man?

"Aren't you going to eat yours?" the inspector asked. "They're awfully good."

"I'm sure they are, sir, but I'm not really hungry now. If you don't mind, I'll save mine till after supper."

"As you like, Constable. Ah, here we are. Hopkins Grocers." He stopped beneath the green-stripped awning and polished off the rest of the peach. He pulled out a pristine white hankerchief and delicately wiped his fingers, taking care not to get the fabric near the dripping pit he held between his left thumb and forefinger. "Hmm . . . what can I do with this?" he asked, frowning as he glanced at the tables of assorted goods out on the pavement. "There doesn't seem to be a dustbin out here."

"Can I help you gentlemen?" The grocer stepped out of the front door.

"Have you a dustbin?" Witherspoon held the pit out.

The grocer, to his credit, made only the slightest of faces. "Give it to me, sir. There's one inside. Is that all you needed?"

"Actually we've come to speak to a Miss Emma." Witherspoon smiled at the grocer. "I believe she used to work for Andrew Frommer."

"That she did, sir." He broke into a huge, satisfied grin. "That she did. You're the police, then, come about that murder at the Frommer house?"

"I'm Inspector Gerald Witherspoon and this is Constable Barnes."

"Come inside, gentlemen, and I'll get the lass. I'm Nat Hopkins, the proprietor." He bustled back through the door with the two policemen right behind him. They stopped in front of the counter and waited. Hopkins walked to the back of the store, opened a door and stuck his head inside. "Emma," he shouted. "Come down here, lass. There's some coppers want to have a word with you."

"All right," a muffled female voice replied.

Nat hurried back to them, his expression bright with anticipation. "Nice of that lad of yours to pass on my message," he said, bobbing his head at the inspector. "Smart lad. Come in to buy some boiled sweets and we got to talking. When he found out that our Emma used to work for that rotter, he was right excited. Said you wasn't like other coppers, said you'd take the trouble to listen to the girl. She's heard plenty, she has."

"You wanted to see me, sir?"

Witherspoon and Barnes whirled about to see a young girl of about sixteen standing behind them. Small and slender, she was a beauty. Her hair, so dark a brown it was almost black, was pulled back off her face and lay in a thick braid down her back. Her features were perfect, her eyes a dark luminous green. Witherspoon knew that if Wiggins had seen the girl, he'd have fallen in love on the spot. "Yes, miss, we understand you used to work for the Frommer family. Is that correct?"

"Yes, sir," she replied calmly. "But Mr. Frommer sacked me a few weeks back. He wouldn't even give me a reference, sir, so I've been unable to find another position."

The door opened and two customers, both women, stepped inside. They'd been chatting to each other, but their conversation died when they caught sight of Barnes in his uniform.

"Would you like to step back to the parlor?" Hopkins offered quickly. "Emma'll show you the way."

They followed the girl and a few moments later were standing in a small, neat room comfortably but not opulently furnished.

"Would you like to sit down?" Emma offered, gesturing at the sturdy horsehair settee.

"Now, Miss Emma," Witherspoon said as soon as the three of them were settled. "Can you think of anyone who might have had a reason to dislike Mr. Ashbury?" He started with that question because he'd realized the girl wouldn't know anything about the murder itself and he thought he might as well take the bull by the horns.

"Oh, sir, I expect there's lots of people that didn't like Mr. Ashbury; he weren't a very likable person, if you take my meanin' sir." She smiled timidly. "I don't like speakin' ill of the dead, sir. But he wasn't a good man."

Witherspoon nodded encouragingly. As he couldn't think of the kinds of questions he ought to be asking, he'd decided that perhaps just keeping the girl talking might be the best way to proceed. "Would you elaborate on that a bit, please?"

Emma's perfect brows drew together in a confused frown. "Pardon?"

"He means would you tell us exactly in what way Mr. Ashbury wasn't very nice?" Barnes interjected.

"Oh." She gave him a bright smile. "That'll be easy. He was awful particular, he was. Worse even than Mr. Frommer. He was the one got me sacked." She broke off and looked at them, her expression earnest. "It's true, it is. I swear. I'm a good girl and I worked right hard. It weren't fair of them to sack me because of an accident. It could have happened to anyone."

"I'm sure you're a very hard worker." Witherspoon offered her an encouraging smile. "Why don't you tell us what happened."

"Well, it was a few days before the family was set to be goin' to the house at Ascot," she began. "The whole staff was to go. My aunt and uncle weren't happy about me goin' off. The reason they liked me workin' for the Frommers was because it was close to home, but there was naught they could do about it. Anyway, I'd gone up in the attic to fetch Mr. Ashbury's boxes so he could pack. As I said, he's a right particular sort, and as there was three of them up there, I weren't sure which one he wanted, so I had Boyd haul down all three of them."

"You took them to Mr. Ashbury's quarters?" Witherspoon added, hoping to hurry her narrative along a bit.

"Oh no," she replied. "We took them out to the garden to be aired. Well, I'd forgotten that Mr. Burroughs was comin' round for tea that afternoon, so I left the boxes out next to the table so they could get the afternoon sun."

"Open or closed?" Barnes asked.

"Closed." She frowned. "They was locked, so I couldn't open them. I remember I was goin' to ask Mr. Ashbury for the keys so I could give them a proper airing. Anyway, then I went about my business. I was upstairs polishing the railings when Boyd come runnin' up sayin' that I'd best help him get them cases moved, as Mr. Ashbury and the others were outside and that Mr. Burroughs had arrived for tea." She made a face. "I flew down the stairs, I did. But it was too late. They was already outside. Mr. Ashbury started to give me the back of his tongue for leavin' them out where everyone could see them, but that nice Mr. Burroughs made a jest of the whole thing. I still think that Mr. Ashbury would have sacked me right then, he were so angry. He hated looking like he was lower class, sir. Hated it worse than anything, and those cases of his were a right tatty-looking bunch. But he was too cheap and mean to buy new ones, even though Mrs. Frommer had been after him about it the week before."

Barnes asked, "Why didn't he sack you then?"

"Mr. Alladyce arrived to give Mr. Ashbury some papers."

"Henry Alladyce?" the constable clarified.

"Yes, sir. I was ever so pleased to see Mr. Alladyce. He took Mr. Ashbury's mind right off me." Emma grinned. "He started giving poor Mr. Alladyce a tongue-lashing for leaving the office in the middle of the day."

"So Mr. Ashbury was distracted? That's why you didn't get the sack?"

Witherspoon was finding her story just a bit difficult to follow. Plus, he wondered why Charles Burroughs was having tea at the Frommer house. He'd made it perfectly clear he didn't think much of his neighbors.

She nodded eagerly. "That's right. Anyway, Mr. Alladyce took no notice of Mr. Ashbury. He was too busy staring at Mr. Burroughs. He was downright rude. He kept on and on, asking Mr. Burroughs if they'd ever met. Mr. Burroughs laughed and said not unless Mr. Alladyce had been to Colorado, but Mr. Alladyce wouldn't leave it alone. He kept sayin' he never forgot a face and he was sure he'd met Mr. Burroughs before. Well, by that time Boyd and I had finished moving the cases, so I thought I'd best ask Mr. Ashbury for the keys so they could be aired out before we brung 'em upstairs. Mr. Ashbury didn't like bein' interrupted, but he didn't want to make any more of a fuss. I think Mr. Burroughs had shamed him, sir; I think he'd made some kind of comments about how it were only lower-class people that were mean to servants in front of guests. But Mr. Ashbury were still angry with me, I know that."

"How do you know?" Barnes asked. His weathered face was creased in a frown, as though he too were having trouble seeing the point of her story. But like the inspector, he'd learned to be patient. Especially with the very young.

"Because he was givin' me that funny smile of his, the one he used when he was feelin' like he'd pulled one over on you."

"I'm sorry." Witherspoon's eyes narrowed behind his spectacles. "I don't quite understand."

"It's the truth, sir," she said earnestly. "He did have a mean smile. Ask anyone. Every time he'd gotten one of us in trouble or told some big tale or just done something horrid to someone, he had this nasty, smary smile that just made you wish you could smack him in the face. Beggin' your pardon for bein' so bold, sir. But that's how it made all of us feel, sir."

"All right." Witherspoon decided to accept her statement at face value. "Go on, what happened then?"

"Well, I asked him for the keys, sir," she repeated. "He kept them in his pocket, on a small brass ring. He pulled off the three little keys and said that only two of the cases was to be aired. The other one was nothing but old letters and daguerreotypes and stuff like that. It was to be taken back upstairs. The first case I unlocked was the one with the papers, so I sat it next to the back door so Boyd could haul it back up to the attic. Then I opened the other two and took them to the other end of the terrace so they could get the best of the sunshine. I could hear Mr. Ashbury goin' on and on on the other side of the garden. Anyway, I got up and turned around, thinking I'd slip back in through the door off the terrace so I wouldn't have to face Mr. Ashbury again. Well, blow me, if I didn't run smack into a big terra-cotta pot. Someone had moved the ruddy thing till it were almost directly behind me and I'd slammed straight into it. It toppled over against the stone tiles and smashed into dozens of pieces." She sighed. "I knew I was in for it then. Breakin' their things would get you sacked right fast, and this was an expensive pot. Everyone come runnin' to see what had happened. I tried to explain that someone had moved the pot, but it were no good; Mr. Ashbury kept on and on until Mr. Frommer sacked me. I left that very day. It didn't even help when Boyd went to Mr. Frommer and told him that I were tellin' the truth: someone had moved that pot, someone who wanted to get me sacked. I thought it had to be Mr. Ashbury. He never liked me. It was the kind of mean thing he'd do."

Witherspoon didn't know what to say. The story was quite sad and unfair; the girl shouldn't have lost her position merely because of an accident, regardless of the circumstances. "I'm sorry, my dear," he said. "You were treated very badly."

"They treated everyone like dirt, they did."

"Even Mrs. Frommer?" Barnes asked.

Emma smiled cynically. "She was all right, but no one took any notice of her. Not her husband and certainly not her father."

Barnes smiled kindly at the girl. "Do you really think it was Ashbury who moved the pot?"

Witherspoon couldn't tell if he was humoring her or not. But to Emma, the question was deadly serious.

"That's just it," she said. "The only person who I think would be mean enough to do it was Mr. Ashbury. But when I asked Lottie the kitchen maid if she saw him come around to where I was, she claimed that Mr. Ashbury hadn't moved from his chair, so it couldn't have been him. Lottie's got no reason to lie to me, and as she was the one whose job it was to keep an eye on the tea party to see if they needed anything else, then she'd know. Besides, I could hear him talking while I was opening the cases. He couldn't have nipped around and moved that pot and then nipped back."

"So no one left the table while you were opening the cases?" Witherspoon asked. He too was now curious as to how the pot got moved.

"No one, sir." She shrugged. "It's a right mystery. That pot was in its proper place by the back door when I went around to the terrace, that's for certain. I'd have noticed if it wasn't."

"Wouldn't you have heard it being moved?" the inspector asked curiously. "Terra-cotta pots are quite heavy."

"This one wasn't, sir," she answered. "It were one of them thin ones. Come from Italy it did. They'd only bought it a few days earlier. Besides, it was empty, so it wouldn't have weighed much. And I wouldn't have heard it in any case, not with Mr. Ashbury brayin' loud enough to wake the dead on the other side of the terrace wall."

"I see." Witherspoon frowned thoughtfully. Deep inside his mind, something slid into place and then just as quickly slipped away. Before he could grasp the elusive thought, it was gone. His frown intensified. He chewed on his lip as he tried to will the idea back, but it was no use.

"Sir?" Barnes voice was concerned. "Are you all right?"

"Yes, yes, I'm fine. Right as rain, as it were." He forced himself to smile. Apparently, his inner voice didn't wish to speak to him anymore today. But he'd learned one thing. Everything the girl had told him was important. Most important. Either that, or her statement had triggered him into thinking about something else, something connected. Too bad he couldn't recall what it was. Oh well, he'd think of it sooner or later. As Mrs. Jeffries always said, he had to learn to trust his instincts. "Are you absolutely certain that no one left the table? They were all still there taking tea, both the Frommers, Ashbury, Mr. Alladyce and Mr. Burroughs?"

"Mr. Alladyce had gone, sir. He'd left while Mr. Ashbury was giving me the keys." She laughed harshly. "Just like the old tartar not to invite the poor man to stay to tea. He was like that, he was. Unless you were big and important, he couldn't be bothered with you. Not like that nice Mr. Burroughs. He was nice to everyone. Even poor Boyd."

"Boyd?" Witherspoon queried. "What was wrong with Boyd?"

"He's not right, now, is he?"

The inspector had no idea what she was talking about. "What's not right about the lad? I know he's gone missing, but I didn't know there was anything wrong with him."

She frowned angrily. "He's gone missing? When?"

"The morning of the murder," Barnes replied. "But what's wrong with him?"

"He's a bit slow," she replied, with a shake of her head. "You know, he's not too smart. Not so stupid that he couldn't work, but not very bright either. I can't believe he'd run off. He's devoted to Mrs. Frommer. He'd do anything for her."

"Well . . ." Witherspoon sighed. This case was even more complicated than he'd thought. "He's gone now."

Emma studied the two policemen. "You don't believe that poor Boyd had anything to do with it, do ya?"

"We've no evidence that he did," Barnes replied. "But as he's disappeared, he is a suspect. Especially as we know that Mr. Ashbury wasn't very kind to him." The constable had tacked that part on; in truth, they didn't know anything at all about the way Ashbury had treated the footman. But given what they'd learned of the victim, Barnes was fairly certain the man hadn't been good to the lad.

"Boyd wouldn't hurt anyone," she insisted. "He's not smart, but he's the sweetest lad you'd ever meet. And he wouldn't know how to shoot a gun. He's scared of them, he is."

"Most people are frightened of weapons," Witherspoon said kindly. "But we've found that being afraid doesn't stop people from using them."

The inspector tried to keep his spirits up as he turned the corner onto Upper Edmonton Gardens. He was terribly confused about this case, but he refused to be down-hearted about it. As Mrs. Jeffries always said, he'd figure it out in the end.

Just then a four-wheeler pulled up, and the inspector, thinking it might be an urgent message from the station or the Yard, stopped. He smiled as Lady Cannonberry emerged. His smile faltered as Morris Pilchard got out right behind her.

She spotted him immediately. "Oh Gerald, this is lovely. I had so hoped to see you."

"I was just on my way home." He swept his bowler off and bobbed his head. "I'm happy to see you too."

"Good evening, Witherspoon." Morris Pilchard elbowed his way between them. "How is your case going? Caught the killer yet? Of course, one doesn't expect you to work miracles, does one? Actually I'm amazed that you chappies manage to catch anyone at all. No offense meant, but the police don't seem to be very good at it. They never caught that Ripper fellow, did they?"

"Well, no—" Witherspoon began.

"Don't be ridiculous, Morris," Ruth interrupted. "The police do a fine job and I'll have you know that Gerald is a brilliant detective. Do you have any idea how many murderers he's caught?"

"Now, now, dearest." Pilchard patted her arm. "Don't upset yourself. I wasn't casting aspersions on your neighbor's good character. I'm sure he does the best he can."

Dearest? Witherspoon's heart sank as the meaning of Pilchard's familiarity toward Ruth sank in. Her defense of him was nice, but she was the sort of person who would defend anyone who was being berated unfairly. "Thank you, Ruth. But you're much too kind. I don't catch murderers all on my own. It's a team effort. I could do nothing without the rest if the force."

"You're much too modest, Gerald. You're the best detective they have at the Yard," she said earnestly. "I know you're probably terribly busy, but can you dine with us tonight?"

"Dinner?" The inspector's spirits soared. "At your house? Gracious, I should love to."

"Good, then it's settled." She smiled and patted his arm.

"Are you sure it won't put your cook to any trouble?" Witherspoon asked.

"Not at all, Cook always prepares far more than we eat," she assured him. She smiled at her houseguest. "Gerald can tell you about some of his more interesting cases," she told the sour-faced man. "You'll be fascinated."

Pilchard's mouth curved in disapproval. "I hardly think murder is a proper topic for dinner conversation."

"I think it's a better topic than dung beetles," she said sweetly, "and that's what you talked about last night."

"I must go home and tell the staff," Witherspoon said eagerly. "Then I'll pop right over, shall I?"

"That'd be lovely, Gerald." She took Pilchard's arm and, ignoring his frown, led him toward her front gate. "We'll expect you in fifteen minutes. That will give us time for a glass of sherry before dinner."

"I shall be there," he called happily. Turning, he dashed up the road toward his own front door. Taking the steps two at a time, he fairly flew inside, almost crashing into Mrs. Jeffries. "Oh gracious," he exclaimed. "I *am* sorry. But I'm in a frightful hurry."

"Oh dear, sir," Mrs. Jeffries said sympathetically. "Has something happened on the case? Are you going to make an arrest?" She certainly hoped that wasn't true. She couldn't make heads or tails of what was going on with this murder, and unless the inspector had had a confession or an eyewitness turn up, she didn't see how he could have solved the crime.

"No, no, no, Mrs. Jeffries," he said happily. "I'm going to Lady Cannonberry's. She's invited me for an impromptu supper. Do tell Mrs. Goodge that I'm ever so sorry," he called over his shoulder as he vaulted up the staircase to his room. "I hope she didn't go to a lot of trouble with tonight's dinner."

"She didn't, sir," Mrs. Jeffries replied. "It was only a cold supper. It'll keep." This also meant that she wouldn't have a chance to find out what the inspector had learned until late tonight when he came home. She hoped he wouldn't be so tired that he'd go right to bed. She didn't want to wait until breakfast tomorrow.

Upstairs, the inspector washed his hands, combed his hair and changed into a fresh shirt. He'd just called down the backstairs that he was leaving when there was a knock on the front door. Mrs. Jeffries, coming in from the drawing room, reached it first.

As it was after dark, the inspector frowned as he saw her turn the doorknob. "I say, Mrs. Jeffries, do let me get it." He hurried up the hall, but his words were too late. She'd already pulled the door wide open.

Witherspoon's frown intensified. A police constable, a rather familiar-looking one, stood on the door stoop. "Beggin' your pardon, sir," the lad said, talking over the housekeeper's shoulder directly to the inspector, "but I've been sent to fetch you to the hospital."

"Hospital? I'm sorry, Constable . . ."

"Martin, sir. Theodore Martin. We met a few months back on that murder at old man Grant's house."

"Oh, yes, yes, I thought you looked familiar. What's happened? Why do I have to go to the hospital?"

"There's been a shooting, sir," Martin explained. "Constable Barnes was just goin' off duty when the word come in and he thought you'd want to know right away. It's a Mrs. Frommer, sir. She's been shot."

As soon as the front door closed behind the inspector, the household sprang into action. Betsy was dispatched to Lady Cannonberry's to express the inspector's regrets about dinner, Smythe was sent off to Howard's, the livery where the inspector's carriage and horses were stabled and Wiggins was put in a hansom to deliver the news to Luty and Hatchet. Mrs. Goodge and Mrs. Jeffries settled in the kitchen to discuss this new turn of events. Their main concern was how they could learn all the details of this latest development without having to wait for the inspector to return home and tell them.

In less than an hour all of them, except Smythe, were back and gathered about the kitchen table.

"This is sure puttin' the fox amongst the chickens," Luty declared. "Just when I was fixin' to figure this one out too. Do we know who did the shootin'?"

"Not yet," Mrs. Jeffries replied. "Smythe has taken the horse and carriage to the hospital. He's using the pretext that the inspector may need it this evening. Naturally he'll find out what he can."

"Which hospital is it?" Hachet asked.

"The one on Grays Inn Road," she answered. "The Royal Free."

"Smythe might not be able to get away," Betsy said. "He'll probably be stuck there as long as the inspector is."

Mrs. Jeffries nodded. "I know, dear. But knowing Smythe, even if he's stuck, he'll find out what he can."

"Why do they git to go?" Luty asked, glaring at her butler. "I can go just as easily."

"It wouldn't be right, madam," Hatchet said quickly. "A lady such as yourself doesn't go about the streets at this time of the evening."

"Oh, pull the other one, Hatchet," she snorted in disgust. "I've been out more times at night than you've had hot dinners. Why don't you just admit it, you like hoggin' all the fun."

"Really, madam, I hardly think that's fair."

"Fiddlesticks," Luty snapped. "I'd be in the carriage, and besides, I'd have Dickson with me."

"Dickson, madam, wouldn't say boo to a goose in barnyard," Hatchet shot back. "He is an excellent driver, but he certainly couldn't defend you against any street ruffians."

"I don't need defendin'," Luty countered. She was getting tired of always being the one waiting for news. "I'm pretty danged good at takin' care of myself. You just don't want me to go because you're afraid I'll git the jump on you."

Since this was absolutely true, Hatchet would have died before admitting it. But as he'd not found out much of anything, even after paying Goff to snoop about, he was getting quite desperate for clues. "Don't be ridiculous, madam. Our investigations are a cooperative effort."

"Indeed they are," Mrs. Jeffries said quickly. "And as there is quite a bit I haven't had a chance to share, we women will have a brief meeting of our own while the two of you"—she smiled at Wiggins and Hatchet—"go over to the hospital and find out what Smythe has learned. You ought to be back in a couple of hours or so. We can compare notes then."

MaryAnne Frommer lay upon the narrow bed at the end of the ward. Her eyes were closed and she was deathly pale. A coarse but clean white sheet was drawn up under her chin. A gray-haired doctor stood opposite her. "I don't mind admitting I don't know all that much about gunshot wounds," he said. "But we'll do the very best we can."

"Is she going to live?" Witherspoon asked.

"I don't know. She's lost a lot of blood." The doctor shook his head. "The surgeon got the bullet out. It's a clean wound; it entered her side and doesn't appear to have damaged any of her internal organs. If she dies, it'll be because of blood loss or infection."

"Can I speak with her?" Witherspoon asked. "It's important. We have to know who did this to her, especially if there's a chance she's"—he hesitated, torn between his duty as a policeman and his compassion as a human being—"not going to recover. It's imperative we try and find out if she knows who did this to her."

"You can try"—the doctor looked doubtful—"but I don't think she'll be able to tell you very much. I doubt she'll respond at all."

"Who brought her in?" Barnes asked.

"A young man," the doctor replied. "He brought her in a hansom. He and the driver carried her inside to the casualty ward. As soon as we realized she'd a bullet in her, we sent her directly into surgery."

Witherspoon looked around the ward. Except for two nursing sisters and another doctor, all of them tending to patients, no one else was about. "Where did this young man go?"

"I can't help you there. I didn't see him. I'm Dr. Hall," he said. "I've got to finish my rounds. Have one of the sisters come find me if you need me. We'll keep a close eye on her." He nodded toward Mrs. Frommer. "You can depend on that."

"Thank you, Doctor," the inspector replied. "We won't be long. We've only a few questions to ask."

"If she does respond, try not to upset her. She's in pretty bad shape." Dr. Hall smiled briefly and moved on to the patient in the bed across the aisle.

Witherspoon looked at Barnes. "What do you think? Should I try to ask her what happened?"

Barnes hesitated, his expression uncertain. He'd been a copper for a long time. Sometimes, no amount of experience prepared you to make the best decision. "I don't think we've any choice, Inspector," he whispered. "She might die. At least if we can find out who did this to her, they'll not get clean away with it."

Witherspoon took a deep breath and leaned over the bed, placing his lips as close to her ear as he dared. "Mrs. Frommer," he whispered.

She moaned softly.

"Mrs. Frommer"—he tried again—"can you hear me?" His instincts were to go away and let her rest, but he couldn't do that. The constable was right: if she died, he wanted to make sure he arrested her murderer.

She moaned again, but this time it sounded a bit like a "yes."

"Do you know who did this to you?" Witherspoon pressed. "Did you see who shot you?"

"Tashaa . . ." she muttered. "Tash . . . bro . . ."

"Can you understand her, sir?" Barnes asked anxiously.

The inspector shook his head and cocked his ear only inches from her lips. "I'm sorry," he said, "but you'll have to try again. Do you know who shot you?"

"I'm afraid she's probably not going to make any sense at all," Dr. Hall interrupted. He'd come back when he heard Mrs. Frommer moan. "We gave her quite a bit of laudanum after the surgery."

Witherspoon straightened up. "Are you saying that even if she says something, it might not be true?"

"I ought to have mentioned it before, but frankly I didn't think you'd get any reaction at all from the poor woman. I wouldn't put too much stock in anything she tells you," he said. "Her system is full of opium. She probably doesn't even hear you. I'd suggest you wait until tomorrow to question her."

"We can't," Witherspoon said simply. "By your own admission, she might not live through the night."

She spoke suddenly.

This time they heard her quite clearly. She said one word.

"Andrew."

CHAPTER 8

Hatchet and Wiggins, with Smythe in tow, were back within the hour. "The inspector is spendin' the night at the 'ospital," Smythe explained as he dropped into the chair next to Betsy, "so he sent me along home. I ran into these two 'ere and we 'otfooted it back as soon as we could."

"Unfortunately, we left so quickly we hadn't a chance to ask very many questions," Hatchet said disapprovingly. "Smythe, for some reason of his own, seemed to feel it was imperative we get back right away."

"Yeah, 'e 'ustled us out of there right fast," Wiggins agreed as he shot the coachman a quick frown. "I didn't 'ave time for much of anythin' except a quick word or two."

"If you'll just give me a chance to tell you," Smythe charged, "you'll see it were right important we got back here as quick as we could. We may be going out again."

Wiggins's frown vanished. "Goin' out?" he said eagerly. "Where?"

"Oh, that sounds most interesting," Hatchet added. "Where are we going? Back to the hospital? Over to the Frommer house?"

"That's not fair," Mrs. Goodge protested. "We've been stuck here for an hour waitin' to find out what's what, and you're thinkin' of dashin' off again?"

"How come you git to go out?" Luty demanded.

"Please, everyone." Mrs. Jeffries held up a hand to silence them. This was becoming ridiculous. Now they couldn't even start a meeting without things getting completely out of hand. Men, she thought in exasperation, sometimes they were all little boys. The merest hint of adventure could get them completely offtrack. "Let's hear what Smythe has to say before we start deciding who does or doesn't need to go out tonight." She turned to the coachman. "Tell us what happened?"

"MaryAnne Frommer was shot." Smythe reached for the teapot and poured the hot brew into his mug. "She's still alive, but the doctor don't know if she'll make it through the night. 'Er 'usband's nowhere to be found, neither. I overhead one of the police constables tellin' Constable Barnes that they couldn't find the fellow. The Frommer servants said 'e weren't 'ome and they didn't know when 'e was expected."

"Poor lady was shot right in 'er own back garden," Wiggins said in disgust. "She'da died if it 'adn't been for Boyd turnin' up like 'e did. 'E's the one that sounded the alarm."

"How did you find that out?" Hatchet demanded.

"I 'ad a quick word with the lad after 'e finished talkin' to Smythe," Wiggins admitted. "You were busy listening to them constables natterin' on down at the end of the ward."

"The missing footman's turned up?" Mrs. Goodge said. "When?"

"This evening," Hatchet interjected smoothly. He gave Wiggins a quick grin. "Eavesdropping is sometimes most rewarding. According to the statement the butler gave to the police, they knew the footman was back when he started pounding on the kitchen door and screaming for help. The butler raced outside and found Mrs. Frommer lying on the ground unconscious. The footman had gone to fetch a hansom. It was Boyd and the hansom driver who got the woman to the hospital."

"Why didn't he fetch a policeman?" Mrs. Jeffries asked. "There should have been constables nearby. The Frommer house had a murder in it only a few days ago."

"Apparently the only constables left in the area were doing rounds on foot," Hatchet explained. "Frommer had enough influence with the Home Office to get rid of the policeman who'd been watching the house."

"Seems to me she owes 'er life to Boyd," Wiggins declared. "If 'e'd not come to meet 'er, Mrs. Frommer woulda laid there bleedin' to death."

"Didn't anyone hear the gunshot?" Luty demanded. "They ain't exactly quiet, you know."

All three men answered at once.

"Someone may have," Hatchet said. "The constable I overheard said they'd been instructed to do a house-to-house for witnesses who may have seen or heard something."

"Boyd said 'e been about the neighborhood for a good few minutes waitin' for Mrs. Frommer to come out, and 'e never 'eard nothin'," Smythe offered.

"No one 'eard the shot when Ashbury were killed either," Wiggins added firmly. "Maybe the killer's got a special way—"

"*Please*," Mrs. Jeffries shouted. She was almost out of patience. "We really must hear from you one at a time." Her expression was stern as she looked at the three men. "I don't know about any of you, but the more I learn about this case, the more confused I get. So far, we've a lost footman who now turns up at a very suspicious time, an attempt on Mrs. Frommer's life and a missing husband. None of it makes any sense. Now, the only way I'm going to be able to make heads or tails out of anything is if all of us share our information in a calm, logical fashion. Is that absolutely clear?"

"You tell them, Mrs. Jeffries," Betsy exclaimed. "I'm so confused I don't know what I should even be asking when I'm out and about."

"Me too," Mrs. Goodge muttered. "I've had half a dozen sources through this kitchen today and I'm so addled, I couldn't think of a ruddy thing that made any sense."

Mrs. Jeffries softened her expression as she gazed at the now shame-faced men. "I realize you weren't deliberately trying to confuse us. I'm sure you're all doing your best, but it would be so much easier for the rest of us if you would speak one at a time."

Everyone was silent for a moment, then Smythe grinned. "Looks like you've finally found a way to shut the three of us up." He laughed. "Sorry, everyone. It'll not 'appen again. And I know what you mean about this case. It's right confusin'. So much as 'appened tonight, I'm not sure 'ow to begin."

"Why don't you just tell us what happened this evening?" the house-keeper suggested. "Start from when *you* arrived at the hospital."

Smythe nodded in agreement and took a quick sip of tea. "By the time I got there, the inspector had already gone into the ward. I was right surprised, though, because I'd expected to see Mr. Frommer or someone from the household awaitin'. But there weren't no one but a scared-lookin' lad. It turned out that was the missin' Boyd."

"Was he wearing his uniform?" Mrs. Jeffries asked. She didn't know why, but for some reason, that seemed a pertinent question.

"No, but as 'e were the only one sittin' on the bench outside the ward, I figured 'e might 'ave something to do with Mrs. Frommer. I asked 'im who 'e was, and the lad were so surprised to be spoken to, he answered me without thinkin'. The boy were right torn up about Mrs. Frommer, that was for certain," Smythe said sympathetically. "Anyway, as soon as I 'eard 'is name, I asked 'im where 'e'd been. 'E were a bit skittish at first, but after we'd chatted a few moments, I got 'im to talkin'."

He'd had gotten the lad to speak by being honest. He'd told Boyd whom he worked for and assured him that Inspector Witherspoon wouldn't rest until he'd found MaryAnne Frommer's assailant. "'E told me 'e'd been in 'idin' since the day of the murder."

"Hiding?" Luty said. "Why? Did he shoot Ashbury?"

"No, but he were in the house when the killer did."

"He was a witness?" Mrs. Jeffries asked. "He saw who did it?"

Smythe shook his head. "No, 'e only heard it. 'E was up in the attic when the killin' was done."

"The attic," Betsy said. "What was he doing there?"

"He'd gone up to get somethin' for Mrs. Frommer. That's why 'e'd slipped off early that mornin' from the 'ouse at Ascot. Boyd 'adn't run off," Smythe explained. "Mrs. Frommer 'ad sent 'im on an errand."

"What kind of errand?" Mrs. Goodge asked. She felt calmer now that Mrs. Jeffries had laid down the law.

"Money," Smythe replied. "Seems that Mrs. Frommer 'ad some money 'idden up there. She sent Boyd into town fer it and told 'im to meet 'er in front of 'er solicitors' office. She were so desperate to get away from Frommer, she were willin' to pay out all she could get 'er 'ands on to the solictors so they'd take 'er case. But Boyd never showed up. 'E claims that while 'e was up in the attic, 'e 'eard Ashbury come into 'is rooms below. Scared the boy to death; 'e'd been told the 'ouse was empty. He laid low for a few minutes and then 'e 'eard someone else come in, but 'e couldn't tell who it was."

"Not even if it were a man or a woman?" Luty asked incredulously.

"Not even that," Smythe replied, his expression somber. "The walls in them old 'ouses is thick. Boyd says for a good 'alf ' our 'e couldn't 'ear anything, so 'e made up 'is mind to get the cash and slip down the stairs and out the back way. Then all of a sudden, a muffled poppin' sound."

"The gunshot," Mrs. Goodge muttered. "Probably done through that pillow that's gone missin'. Sorry." She waved her hand. "I'm doing it again, aren't I? Jumping in without waiting for my turn. Go on, Smythe, finish up."

"Well, as I said, Boyd 'eard this poppin' sound and 'e really got scared. 'E started down the stairs, but 'e stopped when 'e 'eard footsteps runnin' out of Ashbury's rooms. Poor lad flattened 'imself against the wall, but 'e needn't 'ave worried. The killer were in such a 'urry to get away, 'e wouldn't 'ave stopped to look behind him up to the attic."

"What did Boyd do then?" Mrs. Jeffries asked.

"'E was real confused, 'e didn't know what to do," Smythe explained. "At that point 'e didn't know that Ashbury was dead. All 'e'd 'eard was a funny noise; 'e didn't know it was a gun. He knew 'e had to get out of there, so 'e started down as quiet as 'e could. 'E'd got to the other side of Ashbury's door when he accidentally dropped the carpetbag containing Mrs. Frommer's money."

"Cor blimey, she must 'ave 'ad a lot of it" Wiggins exclaimed, "if it took a carpetbag to carry it!"

"It wasn't all filled with money." Smythe motioned impatiently with his hand. "There was some old papers and letters in there too. Mrs. Frommer had told Boyd to get them from one of her bureau drawers. Anyway, 'e dropped the ruddy thing on the floor and it make a bloomin' racket. Boyd said 'e were sure that Mr. Ashbury'd come barrelin' out and box 'is ears. But 'e didn't."

"Why didn't he leave then?" Mrs. Goodge asked curiously. "That's what I'da done. That's what most people would have done."

"He were too scared," Smythe replied. "Boyd's not too bright, but 'e's not dumb as a lamppost, neither. 'E knew something were wrong. Bad wrong. So 'e stuck 'is 'ead in the room and didn't see anything. But 'e 'ad a feelin', as it were, so even though 'e was so scared 'is knees were shakin', he went inside. He told me peekin' over the back of the old man's chair was the 'ardest thing 'e ever did. But 'e did it and 'e saw Ashbury sittin' there all wide-eyed and starin', so 'e gently moved the bloke's 'ead. That's when 'e saw Ashbury'd been shot."

"Why didn't he raise the alarm right then?" Mrs. Jeffries asked.

"'E was scared the police'd think 'e did it. 'E'd moved the body, 'e'd got blood on his 'ands and 'e'd got the blood on 'is clothes too. 'E took off and went into 'idin'."

"What about Mrs. Frommer?" Luty demanded. "If he's so devoted to her, why didn't he meet her in front of the solicitors' office and tell her what had happened. I know Ashbury weren't much of a father to the woman, but Nell's bells, Boyd knew the man was dead."

"The lad weren't thinkin' clearly," Smythe said defensively. "Besides, 'e'd been stuck up in the attic so long, 'e'd already missed his meetin' with her. Remember, there was blood all over 'im. All 'e could think to do was run and hide. That's what'e did. 'E took off and hid out down on the docks by the river."

Mrs. Jeffries tapped her finger against the rim of her empty teacup. "What made him go to the Frommer house today?" she asked curiously.

Smythe smiled sadly. "Boyd couldn't stand bein' separated from 'er, from Mrs. Frommer. 'E'd decided to tell her the truth about what 'appened, about what 'e'd ' eard."

"Did he bring the money with him?" Betsy asked.

Smythe grinned broadly. "No, but 'e told me where 'e'd put it. Gave me real good directions too. It's over near the Greenland Dock. That's why I wanted to get right back 'ere tonight. I thought you might want the three of us"—he indicated the other two men with a nod in their direction—"to go out and see if we can find this 'ere carpetbag."

Mrs. Jeffries eyed the coachman speculatively. Smythe was doing his best to appear calm and collected, as were the other two, but it was quite clear from the sudden sparkle in his eyes that he wanted nothing more than to go. On the other hand, the woman were getting a bit tired of sitting and waiting for the menfolk.

"That's a very rough area this time of night," she said thoughtfully. She had no choice except to let the three of them go and collect the bag. But, really, there was no point in making it easy for them.

"But I think it might be important, Mrs. Jeffries," Smythe argued. "Not the money so much as the papers. I mean, Mrs. Frommer was goin' to take 'em to her solicitors. She told Boyd they was as important as the money."

Mrs. Jeffries pretended that she had to think about it. If she gave in too quickly, Betsy and Luty might have a fit. "Do you think you could find Boyd's hideout in the dark?"

"'Course I could." Smythe looked slightly offended.

"I wasn't doubting your abilities," the housekeeper said quickly. Really, men were so easily affronted. "All I meant is that it's quite dark and the docks are rather notorious for having poor lighting."

"I'll take a lamp," he offered. "I don't know why, Mrs. J, but I got a feelin' this is important. The carriage is right out back. We could get over there and back in a couple of 'ours."

"I'll be most happy to accompany you," Hatchet offered.

"Now just hold yer horses here," Luty put in. "I kin go just as well as you. As a matter of fact, I've got my Peacemaker right outside in our carriage. . . ."

"Really, madam," Hatchet rebuked. "You promised me you'd leave that wretched thing at home."

"I did no such thing," she shot back. "I promised I wouldn't carry it in my muff. I didn't say a thing about not hidin' it under the seat in the carriage."

"Luty," Mrs. Jeffries said quietly. This was precisely what she'd feared would happen. She considered it only luck that Betsy wasn't demanding to go as well. "I really would like you to stay here."

"Why?"

"If the inspector should unexpectedly return while Smythe is gone, at least with Hatchet gone as well we'd have a reasonable answer as to why you were here so late at night. We could always say that Hatchet had taken your carriage to go rescue Smythe because he'd thrown a wheel." It was a very weak excuse, but it was the very best Mrs. Jeffries could come up with at the moment. She didn't want their elderly friend out on the docks at this time of night. Even with a Colt .45 for protection.

"Oh cowpatties, Hepzibah, you never want me to have any fun." Luty tossed her butler a quick glare and then turned back to the housekeeper. "But seein' as how you put it like that, I guess I'll have to stay. But I'm tellin' ya, I'm gittin' tired of the men havin' all the fun."

"Not to worry, Luty," Mrs. Goodge said. "Our turn's coming. I can feel it in my bones."

"You really ought to go on home, Constable," Witherspoon whispered to Barnes. They'd gone out to the hallway and sat down on a bench. The ward sister had promised to call them if there was any change in Mrs. Frommer's condition. "There's no point in both of us missing a night's sleep."

Watching for changes in the wounded woman's condition wasn't the only reason the inspector was staying. Whoever had shot Mrs. Frommer hadn't killed her. He was afraid the murderer might try again. To that end, he'd stationed police constables on the front door and the door leading to this ward. They were to report anyone acting suspiciously.

At the end of the hallway, the double doors suddenly flew open and a woman swathed in a bold, emerald-green evening cloak charged through.

"My goodness," Witherspoon murmured. "It's Miss Hartshorn. What on earth could she be doing here?"

Eloise Hartshorn, an anxious expression on her lovely face, hurried up to the inspector. "Is it true?" she asked without preamble. "Has MaryAnne Frommer been shot?"

"Yes, I'm afraid she has," the inspector replied. He was very confused now. But he was also rather curious as to how the woman had learned the name so quickly. "How did you find out about it?"

"One of the Frommer servants came to my house. They were looking for Andrew," she replied. "He wasn't there, of course."

"I see," Witherspoon said. He was very puzzled. Why would Andrew Frommer's former mistress be so concerned about the man's wife that she rushed to the hospital upon hearing the wife had been shot? He wasn't quite sure how to phrase the question, though. "Er, uh, why have you come here, Miss Hartshorn? Do you know anything about this?"

Eloise ignored his question. "Is she dead?"

He hesitated, not certain of how much information he ought to provide. "No, but she's lost a lot of blood," he finally admitted. "The doctor doesn't know if she'll live. Have you any idea where Mr. Frommer might be? We'd like to inform him of his wife's condition." He watched her face carefully, hoping that he could see something in her expression that might help with this baffling case.

"Oh, I shouldn't worry about telling Andrew." She sneered. "I'll wager he already knows all about it. As a matter of fact, Inspector, that's why I came. I think Andrew Frommer murdered Roland Ashbury and then shot his wife." She clutched Witherspoon's arm. "You've got to help me. I think he's going to come after me next. Andrew's desperate for money."

Smythe was as good as his word. It was almost two hours to the minute when he, Hatchet and Wiggins returned to the warm, cozy kitchen of Upper Edmonton Gardens.

He grinned as he put the worn carpetbag in the center of the table. "Would you like to do the 'onors, Mrs. J?"

"I think the three of you have earned that right," the housekeeper replied. She ignored the disgruntled expressions on the faces of the female contingent around the table. They, of course, had had the advantage of discussing all the details of the case in the warmth of the cozy kitchen.

Mrs. Goodge had proposed an interesting theory. "Go on," she ordered with a smile, "open it."

"I'll do it." Hatchet reached for the top of the bag and unclasped the heavy, brass prongs in the center. Opening it wide, he eased back, nodding at Smythe and Wiggins to have the first look inside. The others crowded closer as well, their gazes on the open bag.

"Cor blimey," Wiggins cried. "Looks like she 'ad a bundle stashed in that attic."

Smythe whistled and then reached inside. He pulled out a stack of pound notes tied with blue ribbon. The stack was a good two inches thick.

"Wonder 'ow much that is," Wiggins whispered in awe.

"What else is in the bag?" Mrs. Jeffries said. She was quite sure that the money had nothing to do with Ashbury's murder. They already knew that the footman had been dispatched on his errand hours before the killing. Which, of course, should imply that the money had been in the attic for a good while. Now she wanted to make sure that whatever else was in the carpetbag was equally innocent.

Smythe reached inside again. The sound of rustling paper filled the quiet room as he pulled out a small stack of letters tied with string. "Just this," he said, handing them to the housekeeper.

"Are they letters?" Mrs. Goodge demanded to know. She wanted to get on with this bit so she could think further about her theory.

"Just a moment." Mrs. Jeffries slipped off the string, which was quite loose, and laid the stack on the table. She picked up the first envelope and gazed at the address. "It's a letter to Roland Ashbury," she murmured.

"Roland Ashbury," Betsy repeated. "Why would Mrs. Frommer want her father's old letters?"

"I don't know. Let's have a look." She slipped the top one out of the envelope, taking care not to damage the fragile page. "It's dated October tenth, 1875."

"Read it," Betsy said. "I'll bet it's important. I'll bet it's something to do with the murder."

"'My dearest father,'" Mrs. Jeffries began to read:

I am writing to you because I am in desperate need. I had hoped that time would soften you somewhat and make you want to heal the breach between us. But as you did not respond to my earlier missive wherein I informed you of the birth of your first grandchild, I can only

conclude that you are still angry at me for disobeying you and mar-
rying Natasha. I'm sorry that such is the case. But she has made me a
good wife and I love her dearly.

I will get right to the point. We are in dire need of money. There has
been a series of calamities recently. I will not bother you with the
details; suffice to say, if you do not send me my share of my dear late
mother's estate, I will be ruined. The bank will foreclose on our farm
and we will lose everything.

Surely you must see the rightness of my request. If you do not wish
to communicate with me, kindly have your bank send the particulars
of the transfer of funds directly to the First Bank of Boulder.

Your loving son,
Jonathan Ashbury

Mrs. Jeffries, not understanding how this could have any bearing on the case, yet feeling instinctively that it did, frowned as she put the letter to one side. "This is very peculiar."

"It couldn't have anything to do with the murder," Hatchet murmured. "That letter is fifteen years old."

"Maybe it does," Betsy countered. She bobbed her head at the other letters. "What's in those?"

Mrs. Jeffries picked up the next one and scanned it quickly. "It's another one from Jonathan. He appears to be getting more desperate. Listen to this: 'The bank has already started foreclosure proceedings. They've already taken my plow to be sold at auction. We are desperate. Natasha's brother lost his job at the mine, so the last of our income has disappeared. If you ever had any vestige of feeling for your own flesh and blood, you'll send the money without delay.'"

She shook her head in disgust and picked up the next envelope off the stack. After she'd studied it for a few moments, she said, "More of the same. Jonathan's family is virtually starving." She grabbed the next one, read it quickly and sighed. "Poor Jonathan just gets more and more desperate in each letter."

"How many are there?" Luty asked.

"This is the last one." Mrs. Jeffries picked up the buff-colored envelope. As she extracted the letter something dark fell out and landed onto the table. "It's a photograph," she exclaimed, laying the letter to one side and picking it up.

She studied it for a moment and then smiled sadly. "I think it's a picture of Jonathan and his family." She held it up and they all leaned closer.

The picture showed a tall, dark-haired man dressed in a morning suit standing next to a woman with a baby in her arms. Next to the woman stood a young man who couldn't have been more than twenty.

"It's sad, isn't it?" Betsy murmured. "Seeing them like that, all done up in their nice clothes, and knowing what's going to happen to them."

"What does the letter say?" Mrs. Goodge asked eagerly, trying to push things along a bit.

Mrs. Jeffries opened it up. "There isn't a salutation," she said, "it simply begins, 'I hope you are happy now. We are ruined. The bank has taken the farm and anything else they could get their hands on. Natasha's brother is so sick with the fever that he'll probably be dead by the time you get this. I want you to know you have my undying hatred. How anyone could let their own flesh and blood be turned out is beyond me. You are a mean and miserable man and a thief. You stole my inheritance. One of these days you'll stand before the Almighty and have to accept judgment for what you've done.'"

"Cor blimey, Ashbury was a mean-'earted bloke, wasn't 'e?" Smythe pursed his lips in disgust. "'Ow could'e do it?'Ow could'e let his own family suffer like that?"

Betsy sighed. "They must have died right after." She picked up the picture, her gaze on the baby held in Natasha Ashbury's arms. "How awful, turned out and hungry and then washed away in a flood."

"Yes it *is* awful," Mrs. Jeffries agreed. She, like the others, was saddened by the fate of that poor family. But she couldn't see what connection it could possibly have with Ashbury's murder. "I wonder if the photograph came with the letter."

"Probably," Luty stated. "I imagine Jonathan wanted to rub old Ashbury's nose in it—by sending that there photograph, he'd make him see who he was hurting. Then when the family died, I expect the old feller really felt bad."

"I wonder why it was mixed in the stuff that Mrs. Frommer wanted?" Betsy asked. She continued to hold the picture. "What could she want with these letters and this picture?"

"I don't know," Mrs. Jeffries replied, and reached for the picture. As her gaze scanned the somber faces in the photograph, something nudged her in the back of her mind and then just as quickly disappeared. "Like you, I can't think of one reason why she'd want to show them to a solicitor. Perhaps she only wanted to put them in a safe place."

"What shall we do now?" Hatchet asked, nodding at the open carpet-bag on the table. "How are we going to get this to the inspector? We can hardly admit we went haring off down to the docks and pinched evidence that by rights should have gone directly to the police."

"Don't worry about that," Mrs. Goodge said resolutely. "We'll think of something. We always do. Now, I've got this idea—"

"And it's quite an interesting idea," Mrs. Jeffries interrupted. She rose to her feet. "But we're all so tired tonight, none of us can think straight. Smythe, I'd like you to take charge of the bag. We'll meet again tomorrow morning at nine. Is that all right with everyone?"

"But what about my idea?" the cook protested. She was sure she was right. "It's a foolproof way to catch the killer. I need an answer if it's to work. Getting the ingredients this time of the year won't be easy. I'll have to send over to Covent Garden directly tomorrow morning so I can do the bakin'."

"That'll be fine," the housekeeper replied. "Now, I suggest we all get some rest. We're going to have long day tomorrow."

Mrs. Jeffries didn't bother to light the lamp as she stepped into her small sitting room. From outside in the hall, she could hear the creak of the floorboards as Smythe and Wiggins marched up the stairs to the own quarters. She made her way across the darkened room to the chair by the window. Sitting down, she stared out into the night.

A long, heavy sigh escaped her. This case was perplexing. Perhaps one of the most confusing ones they'd ever had. She wasn't one to admit defeat, but for once, her usual optimism was at a very low ebb. She leaned her head back against the chair and took long deep breaths, trying to force her body to relax. She'd discovered her mind worked better when she was calm. Soon she felt a lightness of spirit as her breathing became slow, rhythmic and even. She let her mind drift aimlessly, deliberately keeping herself from worrying about what had gone wrong on this case.

Thoughts and ideas floated in and out of their own accord. To begin with, the victim was a monster. Virtually anyone who was close to him might have a motive to murder him. Any of them could have done it too, she thought. None of the alibis were worth much.

She took another long deep breath as the details of the case seemed to sort themselves into a semblance of order of their own accord. The victim had been murdered by someone he knew very well. Someone he planned to meet that afternoon. It could be any of the suspects. Andrew Frommer could have followed him into town and murdered him. With his father-in-law dead, he might have access to his wife's estate.

Henry Alladyce could have done it as well. He certainly benefited from Ashbury's death. As could Eloise Hartshorn. They had only her word for it that she was going to end her relationship with Frommer. She might have decided that she didn't want Ashbury telling Frommer about her affair with Charles Burroughs . . . Mrs. Jeffries caught her breath as the face from the photograph flashed into her mind. She thought back to the day she'd followed Eloise Hartshorn and Charles Burroughs into the burial grounds. She remembered his face. His handsome, worried features. She remembered his words.

Suddenly she sat bolt upright in her chair. Now she knew why something had bothered her about that photograph. Charles Burroughs was Natasha Ashbury's brother.

Of course he had a reason to murder Roland Ashbury.

He wanted revenge.

CHAPTER 9

Mrs. Jeffries's immediate problem was the inspector. How could she communicate what she'd learned to him? The carpetbag was useful evidence, of course. But how to get it to him without admitting their part in the investigation?

She got up and began pacing her sitting room. She knew the room well enough that even in the dark, she easily managed to avoid crashing into furniture.

For several hours she paced and thought, considering all the angles of the problem. Finally, long after midnight, she hit upon a solution, and thus allowed herself a few hours rest before getting up and setting her plan in motion.

In the interests of fairness, she ought to tell the others what she was up to, but there really wasn't time, she thought as she climbed the stairs to the attic box room.

Knocking softly, she roused Wiggins from a sound sleep. "What is it, Mrs. Jeffries?" he asked, sticking his head out. "Is somethin' wrong?"

"No, Wiggins," she whispered softly. "But I do need you to help me. Do you remember how to find Boyd's hiding place?"

"'Course I do," he said, yawning.

"And you can find it again?" she clarified.

"'Course I can." He rubbed the sleep out of his eyes. "Why?"

"Because I've thought of a way of our getting the carpetbag to the inspector without his knowing of our involvement," she answered. "However, I do need you to take the bag and get over to that hiding place."

"You want me to find Boyd?"

"For this plan to work, we need him."

"But what if 'e's not there," Wiggins hissed softly. "What if 'e's scarpered off again?"

"I've thought of that," she replied. From inside the room, she heard Smythe snoring. "And I don't think he'll have gone off anywhere. He's no place else to go. I think he'll go right back to his hiding place. He was safe there."

"If you say so, Mrs. Jeffries," Wiggins said halfheartedly. "I'll give it a look."

"Excellent, Wiggins," she replied quietly. "I knew I could count on you. I wouldn't be sending you out at this time of the morning, except that I think it's important."

"Do you know who did it, then?" he asked excitedly.

Mrs. Jeffries allowed herself a small, smug smile. "I think so," she replied. "And if all goes well, the rest of you will understand everything by tonight."

"I'll nip out, then," he said. "Just give us a minute to get ready. Where's the bag?"

"It's in my quarters," she said. "Come along as soon as you're dressed and get it. I'll give you the money for a hansom as well."

She hummed as she went down the stairs a little while later. As she neared the kitchen she stopped in the doorway, surprised to find Mrs. Goodge already up and about. The cook generally didn't stir herself until seven-thirty.

Mrs. Goodge glanced up and saw her standing there. "Good morning," she said cheerfully. "Lovely day, isn't it? I do hope it's not goin' to be too hot. I want these to bake properly." She was standing in front of the worktable by the sink, kneading a mound of white dough on a marble slab.

"Good morning," the housekeeper replied. Her heart sank as she saw what the cook was preparing. Mrs. Goodge apparently hadn't given up on her idea. Well, Mrs. Jeffries thought magnanimously, there was no reason why the cook's theory couldn't be correct as well. The two ideas weren't mutually exclusive. "Goodness, you are up and busy early today. Are you baking something delicious for your sources, then?" she asked hopefully.

"Oh no, this isn't for them," Mrs. Goodge said. "It's for the inspector. I know I'm right. All he's got to do is take these round when he interviews the suspects. Once I explain to him what to look for, we'll have our killer by the end of the day."

"Now, Mrs. Goodge, your idea was only a theory," Mrs. Jeffries warned.

"Most ideas are only theories until they're proved right." The cook picked up her rolling pin and gave the dough one very light roll across. The cream-colored substance was spotted with dark brown dots. "These'll be ready in twenty minutes or so. We should know by then what the inspector'll be up to today. If I need to, I'll take these along to him wherever he is."

Mrs. Jeffries didn't have the heart to continue this conversation. There was no point in telling the cook that even though her theory might be right, the killer would be caught because his motive was now exposed and not because of his eating habits. "I don't expect you'll have to take them anywhere," she replied. "I think he's here."

Through the small window at the other end of the kitchen, she saw the wheels of a carriage pulling up in front of the house. Mrs. Jeffries hurried over and had a good look. "He's just now getting out of a hansom."

"I'm ready for him." Mrs. Goodge pointed at the table, where the teapot, creamer, sugar bowl and several cups and saucers were stacked on a brown wooden tray. "Just give us a minute and I'll get the kettle onto the boil so he can have some tea."

A few minutes later Mrs. Jeffries found the inspector in the drawing room. His face was drawn and tired, his eyes red-rimmed from lack of sleep and his hair stood straight up as though he'd just run his hands through it.

"Good morning, Mrs. Jeffries." He greeted her with a wan smile. "I trust all is well with the household."

"We're fine, sir," she replied. "You're the one we're concerned about. Smythe told us what happened. You must be exhausted. Mrs. Goodge has made up a nice tray for you, sir. There's some toast and tea. We weren't sure if you wanted a full breakfast."

"That's most kind of her," he replied. "Most kind, indeed. Actually I'm not very hungry. Constable Barnes and I ate a quick meal in the wee hours of the morning. The nursing sisters at the hospital took pity on us and got us some breakfast from the hospital kitchen. The food wasn't very good, but one doesn't like to complain. I should love a cup of tea, though."

Mrs. Jeffries put the tray down on the table next to his chair and poured him a cup of the steaming brew. "Is Mrs. Frommer still alive?" she asked, handing him his cup.

"Yes." He smiled happily. "Her breathing improved enormously this morning. The doctor thinks she might be past the worst. She was well enough to be moved into a private room. It'll be easy to keep a watch on her if she's not on the ward. There's simply too many people coming and going on the wards. Until this killer is caught, I won't risk her. He's tried once. I expect when he realizes he's failed, he might try again. That's why I left a police constable outside her room when I decided to come home and freshen up."

"Aren't you going to have a rest, sir?" she asked in alarm. "You've been up all night."

"I'll be fine," he assured her, taking a huge gulp from his cup. "I've too much to do today to sleep."

"Really, sir?" She set a plate of toast on the table next to him. "The investigation is going well, then?" She needed to keep him here until Wiggins returned.

He made a slight face. "I wouldn't exactly say that; it's still all a bit of a muddle. But after last night we've a number of new leads to follow up. For starters, we'll have to open an investigation into who tried to kill MaryAnne Frommer."

"You think it's the same person who shot her father, don't you?" Mrs. Jeffries asked. Her own theory would fall apart if it wasn't. But she was fairly confident that wasn't going to happen.

"Oh yes, the two are definitely connected." He gulped more tea. "And with that in mind, the first thing on my agenda today is to locate Andrew Frommer."

"Didn't he come to the hospital at all last night?"

"He hadn't been there by the time I left this morning, nor has he returned home. I don't mind telling you, Mrs. Jeffries, this looks quite bad for the man. I didn't take Eloise Hartshorn's accusations all that seriously last night."

"Eloise Hartshorn," Mrs. Jeffries interrupted. "Was she there?"

"Oh yes." Witherspoon nodded vigorously. "She's convinced that it was Andrew Frommer who shot his wife. She's equally convinced she's going to be next. Though her reasons for thinking so don't really make all that much sense."

"What are those reasons?"

"Miss Hartshorn seems to feel Frommer has gone insane. As I said, it's all a bit of a muddle. No one heard the shot or has any information about the attempted murder of Mrs. Frommer."

"What about the servants?" Mrs. Jeffries asked. "Weren't they able to help?"

He frowned slightly. "Not really. All any of them could tell us was that she'd gone up to the attic late in the afternoon, come back downstairs, washed her hands and then had tea. That was the last anyone saw of the poor woman until they found out she was lying in the back garden with a bullet in her side." He sighed. "It's most annoying. We can't locate Mr. Frommer, the footman who helped get the poor woman to the hospital has disappeared—"

"No 'e 'asn't sir," Wiggins said. "'E's right 'ere."

Witherspoon turned sharply. Wiggins and a young lad of fifteen or so, stood in the open doorway of the drawing room. The boy was holding a worn carpetbag in his hand. His hair was dark blond and cut close to his scalp. His face was thin, his complexion a pasty pale color and his expression anxious. He wore a dirty white shirt, a brown short-waisted jacket with the two top buttons missing and a pair of badly wrinkled and stained russet trousers. Under the inspector's scrutiny, he shifted his slight weight from one foot to the other and then eased behind Wiggins.

"It's all right," Wiggins assured the boy, patting his arm. "No one 'ere'll 'urt you. The inspector's a nice man, 'e is. Like I told ya, you just tell 'im the truth and everythin' will be all right."

Witherspoon smiled gently. He wasn't precisely sure what was going on, but he realized this poor lad was scared out of his wits. "Wiggins is right," he said softly. "No one here will hurt you. Please, do come closer and sit down."

The boy hesitated and looked at Wiggins, who nodded encouragingly. "Go on. You can 'ave some tea."

Mrs. Jeffries had already poured the boy a cup. She held it out as he slowly made his way across the drawing room and, still staring at the inspector out of wide, frightened eyes, sat down on the end of the settee. He dropped the carpetbag by his feet. She handed him the tea and then moved quietly to the other end and sat down herself. Wiggins, who'd followed the lad, propped himself against the side of the settee next to the housekeeper.

"Did you bring that bag for me to have a look at?" Witherspoon asked the boy.

"Yeah." He gulped some tea. "It's Mrs. Frommer's. She wanted it."

"She told you to bring it to her?" he asked.

"Yeah."

"When?" Witherspoon prompted.

"I don't know." The lad sniffed and rubbed his nose. "Before it were done."

"Before what were done?" the inspector pressed.

"The murder. Mr. Ashbury's murder. She sent me before."

"I see."

"Was it on the day you were all to come back from Ascot?"

Boyd bit his lip in confusion. "I don't know. I don't remember so good."

"Why don't you tell me what you do remember?" Witherspoon suggested.

"I hid," the lad replied. "I was scared."

"I see." He nodded, trying to encourage the boy to keep on talking. But Boyd shut up and stared down at the carpet.

"You got the bag from the Frommer house on the day of the murder, right?" the inspector said.

"I guess." Boyd didn't sound so certain. "I think, I'm confused."

Mrs. Jeffries realized that at this rate of questioning, they'd be here all day. "Excuse me, Inspector. I don't mean to interrupt, but, well, sir—" She broke off and jerked her head toward the hall.

"Is something wrong, Mrs. Jeffries?" he asked. "You seem to have devloped a twitch . . . oh . . . yes." He leapt to his feet as he realized she was trying to tell him something.

"If you'll excuse us, boys," Mrs. Jeffries said, "we'll be right back."

As soon as they were in the hall, she said, "I'm not trying to tell you your business, sir, but I've had some experience in dealing with people like Boyd." When he continued to stare at her blankly, she went on: "I mean, sir, he's scared of you, and probably of me as well. I think if we let Wiggins get him talking, you'll find out that you can get all of your questions answered far more quickly."

The inspector thought about it for a moment. "You know, I think you're right," he agreed. "Wiggins," he called, sticking his head into the drawing room, "Could you come here, please?"

The plan worked like a charm. Within half an hour Boyd had told his tale and departed with Wiggins downstairs for a hearty breakfast.

Meanwhile Witherspoon, with a very helpful Mrs. Jeffries making comments as they went along, was giving the contents of the carpetbag a very thorough going-over.

"How on earth did she manage to get all this money?" he asked as he put the stack of notes to one side.

"She'd money of her own," Mrs. Jeffries said, and then clamped her mouth shut as she realized that she'd not got that bit of information from the inspector. "I mean, perhaps she'd money of her own," she continued as the inspector shot her a puzzled look, "or perhaps she'd managed to save it out of the household accounts over the years. Some women are quite clever money managers."

"I expect it's the former," Witherspoon replied as he pulled out the stack of letters. "From what the constable and I learned, she did inherit some money from her mother. Which, of course, explains Miss Hartshorn's hysterics last night. Though why she thought she'd be next is beyond me."

"So that's why Miss Hartshorn felt that Frommer had attempted to kill her?" Mrs. Jeffries queried. She wanted to cover her mistake as thoroughly as possible, seeing as how she might have to do some very fancy juggling to lead the inspector down the path she wanted him to go. "I'm afraid I don't understand."

"That was one of the reasons." Witherspoon peered at the faded ink on the front of the top letter. "She claimed that Frommer is desperate for money. According to her rather convoluted reasoning, Frommer murdered his father-in-law so Mrs. Frommer would inherit Ashbury's half of the business. Then he tried to murder Mrs. Frommer so he'd inherit her money. Supposedly he was going to kill Miss Hartshorn because she was the only one capable of putting all the pieces together and ruining Frommer's plan."

"You don't believe her, do you?" Mrs. Jeffries task would be much more difficult if the inspector thought that Andrew Frommer was the killer. Much more difficult indeed.

Witherspoon sighed and put the letters down on the tea tray. "I don't know what to believe." He picked the first one up and tapped it absently against the side of the tray. "At first I dismissed her ravings as hysteria, but as I said, it doesn't look good that we can't locate Frommer. Where could he be? We've checked his office, his club, even with his party's chief whip, but no one's seen hide nor hair of the fellow. But be that as it may, I don't believe he's our killer."

"You don't?" Mrs. Jeffries held her breath.

"No, to begin with, if Mrs. Frommer had died, her husband would lose all rights to Roland Ashbury's half of the shipping agency," he explained. "The constable and I had a word with Ashbury's solicitors yesterday." He stopped tapping the envelope and slipped the letter out. "Remember when I told you he'd changed the will when he disinherited his son?"

"Yes, sir, I remember," she said patiently.

"Apparently in an effort to ensure that Jonathan Ashbury had no claim on the estate whatsoever, Ashbury and Josiah Alladyce did their wills up so that only one chosen heir would inherit. For Ashbury, that heir was MaryAnne Frommer." He settled back in the chair and flipped open the letter. "So the last thing Frommer would want is his wife dead. If she dies, the estate all goes to Josiah Alladyce's heir."

"You mean it's a bit like a tontine," she remarked. "Whoever is left gets it all? Isn't that illegal?"

"It does sound a bit like that," he murmured. "But apparently it's not illegal if it's worded correctly in the will."

"Did Frommer know about Ashbury's will?" she asked.

"Oh yes, Ashbury made it quite clear to Frommer sometime back," Witherspoon replied as he turned his attention to the paper in his hand.

Mrs. Jeffries sagged in relief. She knew Andrew Frommer wasn't the killer. He was a monstrous human being, but he wasn't a murderer.

Witherspoon's brows drew together as he read the first letter. Absently he handed it to Mrs. Jeffries to read and then picked up the next one.

His expression changed to disgust as he read the others. By the time he finished the last one, his mouth flattened into a grim, hard line. "It's unbelievable, isn't it, Mrs. Jeffries? How could the man have treated his family so abominably."

She pretended to read the letter before she looked up and met his gaze. "Yes, sir, it is awful." She scanned the area quickly, looking for the photograph. With dismay, she realized it hadn't fallen out of the envelope as it had last night. "Is there anything else in the envelope?"

The inspector picked it up and peered inside. "No, why did you ask? Do you think the letter sounds as if it were missing a page."

Blast, she thought. Now what? "Oh no, sir, I simply wanted to make sure." She forced herself to laugh. "I'll be honest, sir. I know what a thorough policeman you are. I was just trying to impress you with my own, rather feeble attempt at efficiency."

"Dear Mrs. Jeffries," he scoffed. "You've no need to impress me at all. Why, you know how much I've come to rely upon you to be my sounding board, as it were. But, as you say"—he reached for the bag, just as she'd hoped he would—"I am thorough. Let's see if there's anything else in here." He pulled it closer and held it wide open. "Goodness, there is something else."

Mrs. Jeffries sent up a silent prayer of thanks. They were heading back in the right direction. This was becoming increasingly difficult and now she had a new fear. What if Constable Barnes arrived before she could use the photograph to get the inspector moving toward the real killer. "What is it, sir?" she asked.

"It looks like a photograph," he murmured. He held it up and stared at it, a look of curiosity on his face. "Oh how sad. I think it's Jonathan Ashbury and his family."

"May I see, sir?" she asked. She kept her ears cocked toward the front of the house. Were those footsteps coming up the front stairs?

"Of course." He handed it to her and then put the carpetbag on the floor. "Have a good look. I think it's quite a good photograph. Amazing what they can do these days."

She didn't answer for a minute. She was trying to determine what was the fastest course of action here. From down the hall, she heard the pounding of the door knocker.

"You know, sir," she said loudly, hoping to distract him, "there's something very familiar about this face."

"That's probably Constable Barnes at the front door." He started to get up. "And yes, there is a resemblance. I think Jonathan Ashbury looks very much like his sister."

"Do sit down and finish your tea, sir," she ordered. "Betsy'll get the door. I expect the constable could do with a cup of tea as well." Panic set in as she realized that she wasn't supposed to have ever seen any of the principals in this case. Blast.

He eased back into his chair as footsteps echoed in the front hall. "He's probably in a hurry, Mrs. Jeffries. As I said, we've much to do today."

"What I meant, sir"—Mrs. Jeffries tried again—"was that I wouldn't know about the resemblance of Jonathan Ashbury to his sister; I've never seen her." She took a deep breath and hoped she could manage to pull this off without arousing his suspicion. "But I have seen one other principal in the case."

Witherspoon raised his eyebrows. "Really? Who?"

She heard Betsy's voice and then Constable Barnes. This was no time for to be subtle. "Charles Burroughs," she announced bluntly. "I accidentally saw him, sir."

"Really?" Witherspoon repeated.

Betsy's and Barnes's footsteps came toward the drawing room. Mrs. Jeffries only had few more seconds to make her point. "Really, sir. It was quite accidental, I assure you. I'll tell you the circumstances later, but what is important"—she held up the photograph and pointed to the young man standing next to Natasha Ashbury—"is this. Don't you see it, sir?"

Witherspoon squinted at the picture. "I'm afraid I don't see what you're getting . . . good gracious, you're right."

"Good morning, sir," Barnes said easily as he slipped in behind the maid.

"Barnes, do come have a look at this." Witherspoon pointed at the photograph.

The constable, to his credit, didn't bat an eye; he simply crossed the room and did as he was instructed. "All right, sir," he finally said. "It's a nice enough picture, but I don't . . . yes, sir, I see what you mean. This young fellow"—he placed his finger on the figure next to Natasha—"is very familiar. Now, where have I seen that face?"

"It's Burroughs, man. Charles Burroughs." Wither-spoon leapt to his feet. "And that means we'd best get over there right away. We've found our killer, Barnes, and it isn't Andrew Frommer." He charged out into the hall with the constable on his heels. A moment later the front door slammed.

A satisfied smile on her face, Mrs. Jeffries relaxed back against the settee. It had been touch and go for a moment or two there. Thank goodness the inspector had put two and two together and realized that the motive on this murder wasn't money but revenge. As to all the other bits and pieces, well, she was sure that once Burroughs was in custody and had told his tale, they'd sort out the puzzling things that didn't add up as yet.

"I take it from the expression on your face that you know what that was all about," Betsy said.

Mrs. Jeffries started. She'd quite forgotten the girl was in the room. "Oh, I'm sorry, Betsy. I was thinking." She got up. "But yes, I do know what it was about. If you'll come downstairs, I'll tell you at the same time as I tell the others. Is Boyd still here?"

"Wiggins took him upstairs so he could have a rest," she replied. "The boy hasn't slept well since Ashbury's murder."

The two women made their way downstairs. Mrs. Goodge, who was taking a tray of scones out of the oven, turned as they came into the kitchen. "What's happened?" she asked.

"We really should wait till the others are all here before I say anything," Mrs. Jeffries said. "I do so want to be fair."

Mrs. Goodge slammed the tray of scones down hard on the worktable. "Wiggins'll be back as soon as he gets Boyd settled, and Smythe has gone to fetch Luty and Hatchet."

Mrs. Jeffries realized the cook was most put out. "Mrs. Goodge," she asked, "is something wrong?"

"Wrong? What could be wrong?" She put her hands on her hips and glared at the other two women. "Wiggins seems to feel you've solved the case all on your own."

"Now, Mrs. Goodge," Mrs. Jeffries said gently, "that's not true. I'll admit I had to act quickly today. But only because it was the only way I could think of to get the carpetbag back here and into the inspector's possession without him realizing what we'd done."

"Then you haven't solved it?" the cook asked hopefully.

"I wouldn't precisely say that," Mrs. Jeffries hedged. She wanted to let the cook down easily and tried to think of a way to go about it.

"Then you have solved it," she charged.

"Well, more or less." The housekeeper winced as Mrs. Goodge's expression turned thunderous. For the first time she realized the others might consider that she'd been just a tad hoggish on this case. But what could she have done differently?

"You could have at least given me a chance to test me theory," the cook cried. "Was that too much to ask? I've gone to a lot of trouble here. I've been up since before dawn, sendin' street lads to Covent Gardens and over to other places sussin' out information, and for what? So you can come along and solve the case without so much as a by-your-leave. Well, I tell you, I'm annoyed. Right annoyed. I know I was right and all it woulda took was a few minutes with each of the suspects."

"You're not bein' fair," Betsy said. "Mrs. Jeffries had to act fast. We had to get that carpetbag to the inspector and she figured out a way to do it."

"It couldn't have waited a day or two?" Mrs. Goodge asked archly.

It could have, Mrs. Jeffries thought. Charles Burroughs wasn't going anywhere and the police were watching over Mrs. Frommer, so he couldn't make an attempt on her life again. "Yes, Mrs. Goodge," she admitted, "it could have waited a day or two. I'm terribly sorry. I should have let you test your theory. Or at least told the others about it."

"Test what theory?" Smythe asked easily as he came in from the back hall. Luty and Hatchet were right on his heels.

"My theory," Mrs. Goodge declared. "But it's too late now; Mrs. Jeffries has already solved the ruddy case." With that, she dusted off her hands and went to the sink to fill the kettle.

No one said anything for a moment. Luty and Hatchet quietly slipped into their chairs. Smythe, with an inquiring look at Betsy, sat down, and Mrs. Jeffries, her conscience troubling her greatly, took her place at the head of the table.

"I'll just go get Wiggins," Betsy said softly.

"Please do," Mrs. Jeffries said, "and when you both come down, we'll have our meeting."

"Will you arrest him, sir?" the constable asked as they got out of the cab. The inspector had briefed him on the drive over.

"I'm not sure," the Inspector admitted. "But I will ask him a number of questions."

"Do you think he really is Natasha Ashbury's brother?" Barnes persisted. He gave a quick, worried glance at the front door of the Burroughs house. "Seems to me it could just be a coincidence; the way he looks, I mean. Lots of people resemble each other. Let's face it, sir, your whole case would fall apart if it turns out he's nothing to do with the Ashburys."

"What about both of them being from Colorado?" Witherspoon argued. "Burroughs has already told us he was from Boulder. Jonathan Ashbury's letters prove that they were in Colorado as well. I don't think that's a coincidence." He sincerely hoped it wasn't. "It's at least worth asking a few questions over."

Barnes banged the door knocker. "I suppose so, sir. But for my money, I'd like to get my hands on Andrew Frommer. We still haven't found the man, and in all my years as a policeman, I've seen that it's generally the guilty that disappears."

The door opened and Eloise Hartshorn stuck her head out. "Hello, Inspector, Constable. Have you located Andrew yet?"

"No, ma'am," Witherspoon replied. "Not yet. But we're still looking. May we come inside, please. We need to ask Mr. Burroughs a few questions."

"He's not here," she said quickly.

"When is he expected back?" Witherspoon asked. He wasn't sure that Miss Hartshorn was being entirely truthful.

She slipped out of the front door and closed it behind her. "He didn't say," she said. "I'll have him get in touch with you when he comes back, all right?"

The door suddenly flew open behind her, revealing a grim-faced butler and an even grimmer-faced Charles Burroughs. "Oh, for God's sake, Eloise, don't be so ridiculous. Did you think the butler wouldn't come and fetch me when you ordered him away from the front door?"

"I didn't want you disturbed," she countered, lifting her chin defiantly. "You need your rest. You were up most of the night."

"Please stop trying to protect me, Eloise." He sighed in exasperation. "Inspector, Constable." He nodded at the two policemen and opened the door wide. "I've been expecting you. Do come in."

Mrs. Jeffries told her story quickly and efficiently. "So you see, as soon as I realized that the boy in the photograph was Charles Burroughs, I realized that he had to be the killer. He came back for vengeance."

"But why try and kill Mrs. Frommer?" Luty asked. "She didn't have anything to do with what Ashbury did to his son."

"But she had money of her own," Mrs. Jeffries countered, "and it doesn't appear she had been willing to help her brother either."

She turned to Mrs. Goodge. "I'm really sorry if you felt I acted untoward here, but honestly I didn't realize that your theory was so very important to you. I'm quite sure you're right."

"Do you think so?" the cook asked. She appeared to be somewhat mollified by Mrs. Jeffries's apology.

"Absolutely."

Mrs. Goodge smiled happily. "Then that's all right."

They discussed the case for a while, asking questions and speculating on what the real answers would be when the inspector came home and gave them all the details. No one had any doubts that Mrs. Jeffries was right about Charles Burroughs being the killer.

No one that is, except Mrs. Goodge.

To her credit, she waited till the others had left the kitchen. Then she got up, packed the freshly baked scones into a wicker basket, covered it with a clean cloth and took off her apron. She put on her hat, took one last look around the kitchen to make sure everything was in order, picked up the basket of scones and then slipped out the back door.

CHAPTER 10

Burroughs took them into his drawing room and bade them to sit down and be comfortable. He smiled tenderly at Eloise, his irritation of a few moments ago clearly forgotten. "My dear, I think it would be best if you left us alone."

"I'm staying," she said flatly. She crossed the room and stood next to him. "I'm not leaving your side."

He stared at her for a few seconds and then took her hand and kissed it. "All right, my love. But let's sit down." The two of them went to the love seat across from the settee and sank down on the cushions. Burroughs turned his attention to the policemen. "Gentlemen, I believe you wanted to ask me some questions. But before you do, I've a question I need answered. How is Mrs. Frommer? Eloise told me she'd been shot."

"She's alive," the inspector replied.

"Will she live?"

"Perhaps," he said cautiously. He wasn't sure how much information he wanted to give just at this moment. "You know that she was probably shot in her own back garden?"

"Yes, my servants told me you'd questioned them, but none of them heard the shot."

"That's correct. I understand you weren't home yesterday evening."

"I was at Eloise's house," he replied. "Her servants will verify that."

Witherspoon was in a quandary. He was sure that whoever had shot Mrs. Frommer was also the same person who'd murdered her father. But how could Burroughs be the killer if he wasn't here last night? Eloise Hartshorn's servants might be well paid, but they weren't paid enough to perjure themselves in a murder inquiry, and both the maid and the cook had sworn that Charles Burroughs was at the Hartshorn house all afternoon and evening. Oh well, there was nothing for it but to press on. Eventually the truth would out; it always did.

"Yes, sir." Witherspoon cleared his throat and stifled a yawn. "We know." Perhaps he ought to have had a nap, because all of a sudden he was feeling a bit muddled. "Is Charles Burroughs your real name?"

"Charles Burroughs is my legal name."

Witherspoon was taken aback. "You realize we will check everything you say with the authorities in America," he warned.

"I would expect nothing less," Burroughs replied easily.

"Is Charles Burroughs the name you were born with," Barnes asked.

Burroughs grinned. "Very good, Constable, you're obviously aware of the fact that many people change their name when they go to America. Quite rightly too. For many of us it is a new life. Too bad it didn't turn out that way for my sister and her family. But as to your query . . ." He looked at the inspector as he spoke. "I was born Mikhail Ilyich Buriyakin. That's a bit of mouthful for most Americans, so I had it legally changed to Charles Burroughs."

"What was your sister's name?" Witherspoon asked.

"Natasha Buriyakin Ashbury," he said. "Her husband was Jonathan Ashbury. They, along with my ten-month-old nephew, were killed when the wagon they were sleeping in was washed away in a flash flood. They'd lost their home, you see, and Roland Ashbury, Jonathan's own father, hadn't lifted one damned finger to help them."

Witherspoon was suddenly overwhelmed with sadness. There was something most likable about Burroughs, most likable indeed. Now he was going to have to arrest the fellow. Maybe. "Why weren't you killed?"

"I wasn't in the wagon," Burroughs said. "I'd recently been very ill; I'd almost died. One of our neighbors had taken me in to nurse. They'd offered to let Jonathan and Natasha sleep in their barn that night too, but Jonathan was too proud. He'd pulled the wagon onto a dried-up riverbed. Jonathan wasn't from the west, he didn't know about storms in the mountain and floods roaring down so fast that you couldn't do anything to save yourself. That's what happened to them. They were swept away. It took us two days to find the bodies."

"You blamed Roland Ashbury," Witherspoon stated.

"Who else?" Burroughs shrugged. "It wasn't as if Jonathan asked for what wasn't his. Jonathan's mother had left him money; quite a bit of it. All Jonathan wanted was what was his by right. But the old bastard never sent it. He never even answered Jonathan's letters. The day we buried them, I swore I'd get even with him. I swore I'd make him pay."

"So you came to London for the express purpose of exacting vengeance against Roland Ashbury?" The inspector needed to be very clear about the man's actions, since he would, eventually, have to give evidence in court. This murder, apparently, wasn't a heat-of-the-moment sort of crime. That would make a difference to the court.

"It took me fifteen years of hard work," Burroughs admitted, "but I did it. I ended up with a fortune from silver mining. Right before Christmas, I sold up and came here."

"When exactly did you arrive in London?" Barnes asked.

"February fourteenth. I used a private inquiry agent to locate Ashbury," he said. "Luckily, the house next door to my prey was for sale. I bought it and moved in."

"Why didn't you kill Roland right away?" Witherspoon asked.

Burroughs looked at Eloise Hartshorn before he replied. "I found out, Inspector," he said firmly, "that much as I loathed Ashbury, I couldn't kill him in cold blood."

"Are you saying you didn't murder him?" Witherspoon pressed. "Are you saying you didn't shoot him?"

"I did not," Burroughs said flatly. "How could I? I'd spent years dreaming of the day I would put a bullet into that man's skull, but after seeing the suffering of his daughter, after living next door to him, I couldn't find it within myself to actually do it. I kept putting it off and putting it off, and then I met Eloise and everything changed. Vengeance didn't seem important to me anymore."

"Remember, sir," the inspector warned, "it was your gun that was found at the scene of the murder. You've admitted you had a motive and you could easily have manufactured the opportunity, yet you expect us to believe that you suddenly had a change of heart because you felt sorry for Ashbury's daughter and you fell in love."

"It's true," Eloise cried. "Everything did change when we met each other. Besides, that gun was stolen."

"Now, Eloise, we don't know that," Burroughs cautioned. "We only think it might have been taken."

"When was this, sir?" Barnes asked.

"A few weeks back. We came home from the theater and found a window wide open but nothing missing."

"That's what we thought at the time," Eloise added, "but Charles never checked to see if the gun was still here."

Witherspoon eyed them speculatively. The tale had the ring of truth to it. "Did you fetch the police?"

"We sent for the constable up on the corner," Burroughs replied. "But by the time he came round, we realized nothing appeared to be missing and told him to go. But you can check with him."

"Rest assured we will, sir," Witherspoon said.

"I tell you, Charles didn't do it," Eloise insisted. "He couldn't. He's too decent a man to kill someone, even an odious pig like Roland Ashbury."

"Ashbury tried to blackmail you, didn't he?" Barnes reminded her. "So you had reason to hate him as well."

"Now, see here." Burroughs got to his feet. "Eloise had nothing to do with Ashbury's death or with the attack on Mrs. Frommer. Why would she? She told me herself about her past. Ashbury couldn't blackmail her."

"And it didn't bother you, sir," Barnes said easily. "It didn't bother you that the woman you loved was the mistress of the son-in-law of a man you hated. Seems to me, sir, that it adds a bit more fuel to the fire."

The inspector wondered what his constable was up to, but he wasn't going to interfere. The man did have a point.

"Of course I hated it, Constable," Burroughs snapped. "But I never hated enough to kill in cold blood."

"We were going back to America," Eloise cried shrilly. "I'd already gone and booked the tickets. I'd made arrangements to get both our household things shipped to San Francisco. Show them, darling, show them the tickets. We bought them days before the murder."

"I should like to see them, if you please," the inspector said.

Burroughs nodded, crossed the room and rang the bellpull. A moment later the butler appeared. "You rang, sir."

"Yes, could you please go to my study and bring me the envelope you'll find in the top left-hand drawer."

"Yes, sir." The butler withdrew to do his master's bidding.

While they waited the inspector tried to think of something else to ask. He'd been so very certain of Burroughs's guilt before he spoke to the man; now he wasn't quite so sure. "Er, which shipping company did you arrange to have your things shipped with?" he finally asked.

Eloise laughed harshly. "The only one I could think of was Ashbury and Alladyce. Ironic, isn't it? I hated Roland Ashbury, yet without even thinking about it, I gave him my business. I suppose I didn't realize he was still a part of it. I thought Roland had retired and was completely out of it."

"Will Mr. Alladyce verify that you came to see him and made arrangements through his company?" Witherspoon asked.

"I don't see why he shouldn't," she replied.

"How long before the murder did you go and see Mr. Alladyce?"

She thought for a moment. "Let me see, now. It must have been two, possibly two and a half weeks before Roland's murder. I told him what ship we were leaving on and left a deposit for the packing and shipping charges."

The butler returned and handed a large, buff-colored envelope to Charles Burroughs. "Thank you," he said, dismissing the servant. He opened it, pulled out the contents and nodded in satisfaction.

"Have a look at these, Inspector; the invoice is right on top. You'll see the purchase date is three days before Roland Ashbury's murder, but the sailing date of the ship is two weeks from now. If I'd killed Ashbury, I'd have left town immediately. I certainly wouldn't have hung around packing up two houses."

The inspector took the proffered documents and studied them carefully. There were two first-class tickets for a mid-month sailing of American Lines flagship vessel the *Elizabeth Kristina* to New York. The invoice for the purchase of those tickets was indeed dated three days before Ashbury's murder.

The inspector wasn't sure what to do. The tickets didn't really prove anything, but their very existence argued against arresting Charles Burroughs. Furthermore, Witherspoon thought, the man had made some powerful points in his own defense. If he had committed the murder, why hang about waiting to be caught? Surely he must have expected that there was a risk the police would find out his true identity. Once that had happened, it would be only a matter of time before his motive became apparent. Then, of course, there was the attempt on Mrs. Frommer's life. Burroughs couldn't have done that. He had an alibi. But he could have paid to have had it done. Witherspoon had seen that happen a time or two. Paid assassins were, unfortunately, all too common.

"Excuse me, sir." The butler had quietly come back into the drawing room. "But there's a rather . . . unusual woman who insists on seeing the inspector."

"Do send her in," Burroughs said. He smiled at Eloise and patted her arm. "Don't worry, darling, everything will be all right."

"This way, ma'am." The butler ushered in a plump, gray-haired woman carrying a wicker basket over her arm.

"Gracious," Witherspoon yelped. "Mrs. Goodge, what are you doing here?"

"I didn't mean to disturb you, sir." She shot the butler a malevolent glare. "I asked him to fetch you out to the hall, not march me inside."

"Yes, yes," the inspector murmured, somewhat surprised at the appearance of his cook. "I'm sure you . . . ah . . . ah—what are you doing here?" he finally repeated. "Is everything all right at home."

"Everything's fine." She nodded politely to Barnes and the others. "It was you that we was worried about. Mrs. Jeffries mentioned how you'd been up all night at the hospital with Mrs. Frommer. Well, sir, seein' as how you didn't even take the time for a proper breakfast—"

"I ate at the hospital," he interjected quickly; he had a horrible feeling he knew what was coming next. Barnes was already trying to hide a smile and even the two suspects looked amused.

"That's not decent food," she charged. "But anyway, my point is, sir, you'll be needin' your strength. I've made up a batch of my special scones, sir. They'll keep you going all day. As I said, I didn't wish to disturb you, but I felt it necessary to bring them round." She opened the wrapping cloth, walked over to the inspector and shoved the basket under his nose. "Here, sir. Have one."

Witherspoon had no choice but to take a scone. Before he realized it, she'd darted to Barnes, forced a scone on him and then dashed across the room to the love seat. "Here, sir." She offered the basket to Charles Burroughs. "They're excellent scones, sir. They've got walnuts in them. Do have one."

Burroughs, looking as though he were having a hard time keeping a straight face, took a scone and bit into it with gusto. "You're right, these are good. Do try one, Eloise."

Eloise Hartshorn gaped at the cook. "I'm not really very hungry," she began. Burroughs reached in the basket, snatched a scone and handed it to her. "Eat it," he ordered. "You've not had a thing in your stomach since you heard about Mrs. Frommer."

Eloise shrugged and took a bite. "They *are* nice," she agreed, a few moments later. "Very nice indeed. These are quite different than your usual scone. They're excellent, Charles; do please remind me to get this recipe from the inspector's cook before we leave for America."

"Of course, dear," Charles replied. "I must say, Inspector. You're quite lucky to have such a devoted cook. I do hope she doesn't mind sharing her recipes."

"We're all devoted to our inspector," Mrs. Goodge said cheerfully. She watched the two of them as they demolished her scones. "And I don't mind sharin' my recipes at all. At least not with the two of you."

"Thank you, Mrs. Goodge." The inspector gulped down the rest of his scone and got to his feet. The pastry was jolly good. How very clever of Mrs. Goodge to think to add walnuts to the recipe. They added quite a crunchy flavor.

"Mr. Burroughs," Barnes said, "I trust you and Miss Hartshorn won't be leaving London until your ship sails." He too had wolfed down his scone. He'd not eaten anything since that pathetic meal at the hospital.

"No," Charles replied as he stuffed the last bite in his mouth, "we'll be right here."

The policemen, followed by Mrs. Goodge, made their way outside. The cook gave the butler a smug smile as she went past.

As soon as they were outside, she seized the initiative. "Inspector," she said, "please forgive me, but I had to bring you these." She poked at the basket hanging off her arm. "I remembered what you said the day after the murder. You are brilliant, sir. Absolutely brilliant."

When Mrs. Goodge walked back into her kitchen, the place was in an uproar. Smythe was just getting ready to go for the carriage, Mrs. Jeffries was pacing the floor, Betsy was ringing her hands and Wiggins had just suggested they drag the river.

Smythe spotted her first. "Where 'ave you been?" he demanded. "I was getting ready to go to 'oward for the carriage. Then I were goin' to find the inspector and tell 'im you was missin'."

"We've been worried sick," Betsy added.

"Cor blimey, Mrs. Goodge, you shouldn't give us a scare like that. Me and Fred was just fixin' to go out and search the riverbank for your 'at."

"Mrs. Goodge?" Mrs. Jeffries queried gently. "I do believe I apologized for my earlier actions. Surely you're not so angry at me that you would scare everyone so badly."

"I'm not at all angry at you," Mrs. Goodge declared as she took off her hat. "I'm sorry I give everyone a fright. I know I don't usually git out of my kitchen, but sometimes a body's got to do what a body thinks is right."

"Where've ya been, then?" Wiggins asked. Relieved that she wasn't floating facedown in the Thames, he'd bounced back to his usual cheerful demeanor.

Mrs. Goodge bustled across to her stove, grabbed the kettle and put it on the boil. When they heard what she'd done, they were all going to need a cup of tea. "Well, I've done something I thought was necessary." She was determined to stall for time until she could think of just the right way to put it.

"Yes, but what was it that was necessary?" Betsy prodded. Unlike Wiggins, she was still a mite upset. It had frightened her badly when she'd seen that the cook was gone without so much as a by-your-leave. That wasn't like Mrs. Goodge. She was of the old school. Before this incident, Betsy would have bet her next quarter's wages that the cook would never leave the house without permission from the housekeeper.

"Just give us a moment to get the teapot ready." Mrs. Goodge started for the china hutch.

"I've already done that," Mrs. Jeffries said quietly. "As a matter of fact, I've done up a tray. Smythe, will you fetch it from the dry larder, please. You must be tired after your outing, Mrs. Goodge," the housekeeper continued smoothly. "Do sit down and rest your feet. Betsy and I will get the tea."

Mrs. Goodge sat down. A few moments later the tea was ready and the rest of them had joined her at the table. Everyone gazed at her expectantly. She cleared her throat, a bit nervous at being the center of attention. "Well, now, when you hear what I've done, I don't want any of you kickin' up a fuss, not till you hear me out."

"I think we can all manage that," Mrs. Jeffries said.

"All right, then." She took a deep breath. "I wanted to make sure you were right about the killer bein' Charles Burroughs, so I went over there with my scones. Burroughs isn't the killer and neither is Eloise Hartshorn. Both of them ate every bite of them scones, walnuts and all. So despite us findin' out who Burroughs really is, someone else killed Roland Ashbury," she finished.

No one said a word. They were too surprised. Finally Mrs. Jeffries said, "But, Mrs. Goodge, maybe it was Ashbury who picked the walnuts out of his cake. Had you considered that? In which case your theory that the killer didn't like walnuts would be categorically incorrect."

"I don't understand," Wiggins interjected. "What's the killer got to do with walnuts?"

"He picked them out of the cake," Mrs. Goodge replied. "The inspector said that one of the dessert plates found at the scene of the murder had walnuts on it. That's been nigglin' at me ever since we started this investigation. I'm a cook. I know a lot about food and how people pick and choose what they'll eat. And I know our killer didn't like walnuts. He probably doesn't even realize what he did can point the finger of guilt at him, but I know it and I know that Ashbury liked walnuts," she declared gleefully. "He had to; he's the one that bought the cake. No one in their right mind buys a cake with nuts in it if they don't like them."

Everyone glanced at one another, wondering if anyone at the table would have the nerve to argue with the cook. No one did. The truth was, her idea made a sort of sense.

"What did the inspector say when you showed up?" Betsy finally asked. In her lap she crossed her fingers, hoping and praying that the cook hadn't mucked things up completely.

"He were a bit surprised," Mrs. Goodge admitted. "But I've worked with Mrs. Jeffries long enough to understand what I need to do in a situation like that. I handled it right well, even if I do say so myself. He's got that basket of scones with him. He ought to be feeding one to Andrew Frommer anytime now."

Andrew Frommer belched loudly and scratched at the stubble on his face. His clothes were dirty and wrinkled, his hair uncombed, and he was missing one of his shoes. He sat on the settee in his drawing room, oblivious to the fact that he had two policemen staring at him suspiciously.

"Where have you been, Mr. Frommer?" Witherspoon asked. Though it really was a rather foolish question: one could tell from the smell emanating off the fellow that he'd been drinking.

"I don't think that's any of your business," he replied. "I don't have to answer your questions. I'm not under arrest."

"Not yet, sir," Barnes muttered.

"Mr. Frommer," Witherspoon began sternly, "your wife is in very serious condition. She's been shot. She's in the hospital."

"And I'm in a pretty miserable state myself," Frommer replied morosely. "What am I going to do? The bank's going to foreclose and I know that cow I'm married to won't lift a finger to help me."

Witherspoon thought he was beyond shock. "We need to know where you were last evening at seven o'clock."

"Seven o'clock?" Frommer repeated. "I don't remember. Damnation, man, how am I supposed to know where I was at any particular time yesterday? My whole life is in ruins. The party's withdrawing their support, I'm losing my home, I've no money and that tart I was sleeping with is running off to America with that lout who used to be my neighbor."

Barnes stuck the basket of scones in his face. "You look like you might be a bit hungry, sir," he said. "Eat one."

Frommer, so lost in his own misery that the incongruity of a policeman offering his a pastry completely slipped past him, absently reached into the basket and helped himself. "Thanks," he mumbled as he took a bite.

The inspector watched him carefully. He wasn't precisely sure how Mrs. Goodge had jumped to the conclusion that he expected her to make pastries with walnuts in them, but for some odd reason, she had. Though he did rather think it beyond the call of duty for her to come across town to bring them to him while he was interviewing suspects. But then again, his staff was quite exceptional. Even the constable thought so.

"Mr. Frommer," Witherspoon began again, "perhaps you don't understand that your wife is gravely, gravely ill."

Frommer dismissed him with a wave of his hand. "Quit harping on that, man. She'll be all right. She's too much like that old father of hers to go quietly out of this life. She'll do all right now that Roland's gone. She and Henry are both going to dance on the old bastard's grave. I tell you, she'll not die."

He chomped away on the scone. Witherspoon wondered if it was a fair test. He was almost sure the man was still a bit drunk. If he did dislike walnuts, perhaps all the drink had made him forget that fact.

"But don't you think you ought to go and see her?" The inspector tried one last time. He simply couldn't believe that the man was so callous about his wife's condition.

"Why should I?" Frommer gave an ugly bark of a laugh. "She doesn't need my company. Hospital or not, Henry will go see her today. He told me this morning that he was looking forward to it."

"You saw Mr. Alladyce this morning?" Witherspoon pressed.

Frommer stuffed the last bite into his mouth. "Yeah, he told me about MaryAnne."

"He told you your wife had been shot?" Witherspoon wanted to make absolutely sure he'd heard that correctly.

"That's what I said, man." Frommer sniffed pathetically. "I tried to get him to loan me some money now that he's got so much of it. But he cried poor, just like he always does and sent me on my way."

"What do we do now?" Betsy asked. Like everyone else at the table, she was confused. "If Charles Burroughs isn't the killer, then we're back where we started."

"Not quite," Mrs. Jeffries replied. "We do have Mrs. Goodge's idea, of course. It's actually quite an excellent one. I should have listened to you earlier," she told the cook. "If I had, we might have the killer under lock and key now." She suddenly frowned. "But if one or more of the suspects doesn't eat the scones, then what will we do? Just because they refuse to eat in the presence of the police won't necessarily mean that they don't like walnuts."

"Not to worry." The cook beamed proudly. "I thought of that already. That's why I sent out one of my sources early this morning." She glanced at the carriage clock on the hutch. "As a matter of fact, Jeremy ought to be back anytime now. He's a clever lad, he'll do well, I know it."

"Jeremy Slaven, the boy who first brung us news of the murder?" Wiggins asked. "'E's one of your sources?"

"Now he is," she said. She cocked her ear toward the hall as she heard the clink of the back door and then footsteps coming their way. "Maybe that's him now."

But it wasn't. It was Luty and Hatchet.

The staff quickly brought them up-to-date with all that had happened. When they were almost at the very end of their narrative, Jeremy Slaven finally came racing into the kitchen. He skidded to a halt as he caught sight of the entire group at the table.

"It's all right, boy," Mrs. Goodge said reassuringly. "They know everything. Now, you just get on over here and have some tea while you tell us what's what."

"Are there any of them nutty scones left?" Jeremy demanded as he popped down in the chair next to Wiggins. "I could do with more of them; they was right good."

"Nary a one, boy," Mrs. Goodge replied. "But if you've found out what I wanted you to, I'll bake you a batch tomorrow all your own. You'll not have to share 'em with anyone."

"Except Sally," he replied promptly. "That's my little sister. I'll share with 'er. Can't I 'ave a slice of bread? I'm hungry."

"Certainly." Mrs. Jeffries shoved the plate of bread and the butter crock toward him. He grabbed a slice and slathered it with butter as the housekeeper poured him a mug of tea. "Ta," he said, when she pushed it next to his plate.

"Well, go on, then," Mrs. Goodge encouraged. "What did you find out?"

"Mr. Frommer's 'ome now." Jeremy took a huge bite out of his bread. "Accordin' to the 'tweeny that works fer 'im, he were on a powerful drunk and come in smellin' like a pub. But she said he likes walnuts well enough. The girl said Mrs. Frommer likes 'em too. That Mr. Burroughs—none of his servants would talk to me, so I didn't find out anything. But Miss Hartshorn ain't got nothin' against 'em. I couldn't find out anything about Mr. Alladyce either. His 'ouse was locked up tight and his neighbor said he was leavin' London as soon as he got back from visitin' Mrs. Frommer in the 'ospital."

"That doesn't tell us much more than what we already know," Smythe muttered. "Too bad this isn't like some of our other cases. All you 'ad to do then was keep yer eye on who ended up with the money."

Mrs. Jeffries's head jerked up. "What did you say?"

Taken aback, Smythe stared at her. "When?"

"Just now. What did you say? Repeat it, please," she ordered.

"I said it's too bad this isn't like some of our other cases. All we 'ad to do then was see who ended up with the money," he repeated. "Well, you've said it many a time yourself, Mrs. Jeffries. The one who ends up with the goods at the end of the day is usually the one that did it."

Mrs. Jeffries couldn't speak for a moment. She stared blankly at the far wall. Then she shook her head. "I've been a fool. A stupid, arrogant fool."

"Now, Hepzibah," Luty began, "don't be so hard on yerself. We've all made mistakes. So you thought the killer was Burroughs. Based on what we knew at the time, it was a right good assumption."

Mrs. Jeffries looked at the faces staring at her from around the table.

"Do you still trust me?" she asked them. "Even after the dreadful mistake I made about this case. Are you still willing to do what I ask."

"'Course we are," Wiggins volunteered. "You're right smart."

"I trust you," Betsy declared. "Why? What's happening?"

"Hatchet and I always trusted ya," Luty said, speaking for the two of them. "What's wrong? Why you lookin' like a fox that just figured out the farmer's got a gun?"

"Mrs. Goodge?" The housekeeper looked at the cook.

"You know I trust you too," she said. "You've not been wrong very often."

Smythe was already getting to his feet. "What do I have to do, Mrs. J? Just tell me what ya need and I'm on my way."

CHAPTER 11

Mrs. Jeffries glanced at Jeremy. The lad was working on his second piece of bread. Mrs. Goodge, seeing the direction of the housekeeper's gaze, acted quickly.

"Jeremy, boy," she said, reaching across and patting him on the arm. "You've done a fine job. But we've a number of things to take care of now, so you'd best be off." She got up as she spoke and made her way to the pine china hutch. "Let me wrap up this loaf of bread for ya. That way, you can take some to your sister." She yanked open the top drawer and pulled out a big sheet of brown paper and a bit of string.

Jeremy slanted a quick, suspicious look around the table. He knew he was being shown the door, but there was nothing he could do about it. He was curious as to what was going on, but not so curious that he'd risk losing the bread by being overly bold. He watched as the cook deftly wrapped the bread and neatly tied the package with the string.

"Ta," he said as she handed him the wrapped loaf. "Do you want me to come by tomorrow?"

"You might as well," she replied. "We might have somethin' for you to do."

With one last look around the table, he nodded and scampered out to the back door.

They all called out their good-byes as the lad left. As soon as he was gone, Mrs. Jeffries turned to the coachman. "You've got to get to the hospital. I think Mrs. Frommer is in terrible danger."

Smythe started for the hall. "Wait," she called. "Take Hatchet with you." She turned to him. "That is, if you're willing to go."

"You need have no fear on that account." Hatchet nodded at Luty as he got up and joined the coachman.

"What do ya want us to do when we get there?" Smythe asked. "There'll be a police constable on duty. What do we tell 'im?"

"Whatever you have to, to get into Mrs. Frommer's room," Mrs. Jeffries ordered. "But hurry. We'll find the inspector and get him there as soon as possible. Don't worry; I'm sure that between the two of you, you'll think of something to get you inside. But it's imperative you stay with Mrs. Frommer until the inspector arrives."

As soon as the men had left, she turned her attention on Wiggins. "Go upstairs to my sitting room," she instructed, "and get me the cigar box from the the bottom drawer of my desk."

Wiggins was off like a shot. Sensing the rising excitement in the air, Fred bounced after him.

"Do you know where the inspector was going after he left Mr. Burroughs's?" she asked Mrs. Goodge.

"Well . . ." The cook thought hard. "Just as I was walkin' away I thought I heard Constable Barnes sayin' somethin' about the Frommer house, but I couldn't hear exactly what. Why? What are we goin' to do?"

"We've got to find the inspector," Mrs. Jeffries said, "and we've got to get him to the hospital."

"Knowing you, I expect you've got a plan," Luty said gleefully. "Goody. I'm itchin' to git out and about."

Wiggins dashed into the room. "'Ere you are," he said, sliding the box on the table. "What now?"

Mrs. Jeffries flipped open the lid, reached inside and pulled out her supplies one by one. A bottle of black ink, cheap writing paper and a pen. "I'm going to write several notes," she said. "One for each of us. We don't know where the inspector might be, so we've all got to go out, so to speak, and find the fellow."

"Even me?" Mrs. Goodge asked.

Mrs. Jeffries stared at her for a moment. "I thought that after this morning you might like getting out and about as the rest of us do. Don't you want to go?"

"To be perfectly honest, Mrs. Jeffries"—the cook sighed—"this mornin' was a bit of an emergency, at least to my way of thinkin'. If it's all the same to you, I'd like to stay here and keep my eye on things. Wouldn't want to start any bad habits now, would we? Out and about is good for them that likes it, but for some of us, stayin' close to our kitchens is what's important."

Mrs. Jeffries smiled. "I think that's a fine idea. As a matter of fact, we do need someone here. Just in case the inspector comes back. But you'll need a note all the same."

"What are these notes goin' to say?" Luty asked.

"They'll all say the same thing." She took the cap off the ink bottle. "And naturally, I'll disguise my handwriting."

For several minutes she worked in silence, concentrating on making her handiwork as authentic as possible. Bad spelling, poor grammer and barely legible handwriting. When she finished the first one, she held it up, studying it critically.

Inspectaur Withiespon

Hurry to hospitel. Danger. Lady killed.
Hurry up or you'll be late and she'll dy.

"I think this will do nicely," she said. "Now, to make one for each of us." She pulled another sheet of cheap paper out of the box. "Each of us will have one. Betsy, you'll take yours to the station, in case he or the constable comes there."

"I'm to tell him what," Betsy asked, "that a lad showed up at the house with this note?"

"Precisely. But please, all of you, use your own judgment and take care who you show either yourselves or the note to."

"In other words, ask if the inspector's about before we bring out the paper, right?" Luty said.

"Right. It doesn't matter so much if the inspector hears that five different people from his household were looking for him. We can always say we enlisted all of you to help locate him when the note arrived." She finished writing and slipped the note across to Betsy. Then she started the next one. "But it is imperative that he doesn't hear that each of us had a note with us. I think you all get my meaning. You show the note only to Inspector Witherspoon, no one else."

"You want us to keep our mouths shut and use our 'eads, right?" Wiggins said bluntly.

"Excellent, Wiggins, I knew you'd understand precisely. We'll all meet back here later this afternoon and see how we've done."

"Hurry, man, hurry," Hatchet yelled at the coachman through the window. "A life may be at stake."

Deacon Dickson, Luty's coachman, took the butler at his word and urged the horses onward. The coach careened around the corner, cutting it close and narrowly missing a letter box.

"He's goin' pretty ruddy fast," Smythe muttered darkly. In truth, the only person he trusted to drive this fast was himself. "I'd like to get there in one piece."

"Never fear," Hatchet said calmly. "Our coachman is an expert. He's fairly useless at anything else, but at driving a coach, no one can beat him."

Smythe, looking worried, stuck his head out the window as the coach rushed past slower traffic, veering dangerously around coopers vans and hansoms. Up ahead, he could see the entrance to the Royal Free Hospital.

"We're almost there," he called, more to calm himself than to give any information to Hatchet, who was looking out the other window. Throughout the ride, he'd been trying to think of a way to get them into Mrs. Frommer's room.

A lot of the police constables knew him by sight; he'd been with the inspector often enough. But what if there was one on that didn't know him? If the inspector had left instructions that the lady wasn't to be disturbed, then how could he and Hatchet get inside? How could the killer get inside? he wondered. But he already knew the answer to that. Desperate people could be bloody resourceful and this man had murdered once. He was ruddy desperate by now.

The coach pulled up in front of the hospital and Hatchet and Smythe leapt out before it even came to a full stop. Ignoring the startled glances of pedestrians, patients and nursing sisters, they ran for the huge double front door. Smythe reached it first. He yanked it open and they charged inside. They skidded to a halt in front of the reception desk.

The sister behind the desk studied them with a disapproving expression on her face. "Please do not run in hospital."

Hatchet stepped forward. He doffed his hat and bowed politely to the woman. "I'm terribly sorry, ma'am, we certainly didn't mean to disturb the peace of your fine establishment. But we're in rather a hurry. Would you be so kind as to direct me to the room of Mrs. Andrew Frommer? It's most urgent we get there quickly. We've a message for the police constable from his superior, Inspector Witherspoon."

The sister eyed him suspiciously, apparently, still annoyed at their heathen manners. Finally she said, "Mrs. Frommer is down the hall. It's on the left at the first corridor. She's in room number twenty-nine. But please don't run. The constable's gone to get something to eat and won't be back for a half hour or so. Another policeman came along a few moments ago to relieve him."

Smythe stepped forward. "Was this copper wearin' a uniform?"

"He was in plain clothes," she replied.

Smythe spun on his heel and charged down the hall, Hatchet hot on his heels.

"I told you not to run," the sister shouted after them, but they ignored her and kept going. Smythe swung around the corner and leapt to his left to avoid crashing into a man on crutches.

"Watch where you're goin', mate," the man snarled, and then broke off as he flattened himself against the wall to avoid the other gent that come crashing around the corner.

They hurtled down the hall. Smythe scanned the numbers on the top of the rooms as he went. Dodging gurneys, patients, doctors and instrument carts, he ran as fast as he could, oblivious to the yelps and protests coming from behind him.

Twenty-three . . . twenty-six . . . twenty-eight . . . His heart was in his throat as he finally reached number twenty-nine. Grabbing the doorknob, he yanked it open and flew into room.

Directly across from him, a cranelike man stood over MaryAnne Frommer's bed. He was holding a pillow over her face.

The man looked up, an expression of surprise on his face. Smythe leapt at him, but the man dropped the pillow and scurried to the end of the bed, only to run flat into Hatchet, who grabbed him by the arm.

"Here now, you blackguard," the butler yelled as he jerked him around to the other side of the bed. Incensed because he too had caught a glimpse of what the fiend had been doing. "You'll hang for this."

"Watch out." Smythe called out a warning, but it was too late. The bastard used his free arm to pull a derringer out of his coat pocket. "He's got a gun."

"And it's aimed right at your heart," Henry Alladyce snarled. He shoved the gun against Hatchet's chest. "Now let me go."

Hatchet released the man's arm.

"I don't know who you are," Alladyce snapped, "but get the hell out of my way."

With a fast, worried glance at the woman on the bed, Hatchet raised his hands and stepped away. Alladyce, a mad expression on his face, kept the gun leveled in the direction of the two men, backed toward the door . . .

. . . and collided straight into Constable Barnes. Who whacked him lightly on the back of his head with his policeman's baton.

Alladyce moaned, dropped the gun and fell to his knees.

Hatchet dived for the weapon as it hit the ground. Everyone breathed a sigh of relief when it didn't go off.

Smythe leaned toward Mrs. Frommer as the inspector rushed toward the bed. "Goodness, what's happened? Did he try and kill her?"

"He was smotherin' 'er with a pillow when we walked in," Smythe said. "Then he pulled a gun on us and threatened to shoot Hatchet."

The doctor, followed by a nursing sister, hurried into the room as Constable Barnes hauled Henry Alladyce to his feet.

As the doctor tended to his patient Witherspoon walked over to Alladyce. "Henry Alladyce, you're under arrest for the murder of Roland Ashbury and the attempted murder of MaryAnne Frommer."

Several hours later all of the staff plus Luty and Hatchet gathered back at Upper Edmonton Gardens. They'd discovered that none of them had had to use their notes. The inspector, in one of those strange quirks of fate, had gone back to the hospital of his own volition.

"Odd, weren't it," Betsy said as she poured herself tea, "him going back there on his own?"

"He said he had a feeling," Mrs. Jeffries said calmly, "that he ought to. I, for one, am most grateful he arrived when he did. If Constable Barnes hadn't been able to stop Alladyce—" She broke off and shuddered. "Well, we might have had several dead bodies in that hospital room."

"I don't believe he'd have actually shot me, Mrs. Jeffries," Hatchet said thoughtfully. "I think at that point he just wanted to escape. He was quite surprised to see us. But of course, as soon as we came into the room, his plan was ruined."

"I think 'e knew it were all over," Smythe added. "'E'd failed to murder Mrs. Frommer. Weak as she was, 'e'd not been able to kill 'er."

"How did he think he'd get away with killin' her right there in hospital?" Mrs. Goodge wondered. "He must have known the nursing sister would tell everyone he'd masqueraded as a policeman, and the police constable he'd sent off to get something to eat would certainly remember him."

"I expect Alladyce's plan was quite simple," Mrs. Jeffries guessed. "I imagine he was going to say he simply wanted to see an old friend and that the only way he could get into the room was by pretending to be a policeman."

"But she'd be dead," Betsy insisted. "Surely he must have known the police would suspect him."

"They can suspect all they want," Mrs. Jeffries replied. "But they couldn't prove he'd killed her. Not if he claimed she was already dead when he entered the room."

"Is she goin' to be all right, then?" Wiggins asked.

"For the tenth time, Wiggins," Betsy said impatiently, "she'll be fine. Smythe said he overheard the doctor telling the inspector she'd be right as rain soon."

Luty looked at Hatchet and sighed heavily. "You silly old fool, you ought to know better than to let a man like that get the drop on ya. I've told ya a dozen different times ya ought to carry a Peacemaker. It was right in the carriage too. Why didn't you take it in with ya?"

Hatchet, who could see the worry in her face despite her words, merely reached over and patted her hand. "Next time I will, madam," he promised.

"Are you going to tell us how you figured out it was Alladyce?" Betsy asked.

"It wasn't all that difficult," Mrs. Jeffries said. "We can thank Mrs. Goodge and her theory for that."

"You mean I was right?" the cook asked.

"Absolutely. One of the things I did when I was out was have a chat with Emma Hopkins. You remember her; she's the maid who was sacked. She confirmed that Alladyce hated walnuts. As a matter of fact, she told me that every time Roland Ashbury invited Alladyce for tea, he bought a cake with walnuts."

"Deliberately?" Betsy asked.

Mrs. Jeffries nodded. "I'm afraid so. He knew the man hated the nuts, but he bought it anyway, just to be mean."

Mrs. Goodge shook her head. "It's no wonder Ashbury was murdered.

He was a nasty sort. But anyway, all that aside, go on, tell us how you sussed it out."

"Well, as I said," the housekeeper continued, "because your theory eliminated so many suspects, there was really not much left to choose from when Smythe happened to mention money. That's when it all clicked into place. The one person who was going to come out of all this with any advantage was Henry Alladyce. He stood to inherit a financially sound business and several very valuable buildings."

"Do you think you'd have figured it out if it hadn't been for the walnuts?" Mrs. Goodge pressed.

"Eventually," the housekeeper replied. "Even without the nuts, there were plenty of clues. First of all, the story that Emma Hopkins told the inspector should have raised a warning flag. If you'll remember, she was sacked for breaking a flowerpot. But she claimed someone had moved the pot so she'd deliberately run into it. She was exactly right too: the person who'd moved it was Henry Alladyce. He did it to raise a commotion to buy him time."

"Time for what?" Luty asked.

"Time to look in that suitcase of old letters that Emma had put by the door. She said she'd put it there for Boyd to take back upstairs. Alladyce took the letters that we found in Mrs. Frommer's carpetbag. Those letters weren't addressed to Mrs. Frommer; they were to her father. Someone had given her those letters and I'll wager that someone was Henry Alladyce. He wanted her to suffer, he wanted her to be racked by guilt, but most of all, he wanted her to be so angry at her own father that when Alladyce murdered him, she wouldn't cooperate all that much with the police. What he hadn't counted on was her desire to leave Andrew Frommer. She was going to take the letters to her solicitor. I think we'll find that she'd planned on using them to stop her father from interfering this time. Even Roland Ashbury wouldn't have wanted people to know how abominably he'd treated his own son."

"Mrs. Jeffries." Betsy's pretty face puckered in confusion. "I still don't understand."

"It's actually very simple once you see the sequence of events," Mrs. Jeffries said. "The first thing that happened was Henry Alladyce recognizing Charles Burroughs when he saw him in the garden one afternoon cleaning his gun. You'll recall that Burroughs claimed the gun was stolen. Well, I think it was—by Henry Alladyce. He recognized Burroughs as

Natasha Ashbury's brother and the plan sprang into his mind. He'd murder Ashbury and Mrs. Frommer so that he could inherit the business. Charles Burroughs coming to London and taking the house next door to Andrew Frommer gave him the perfect opportunity to carry out his plan."

"But Emma told the police that Alladyce went on and on about having seen Mr. Burroughs somewhere before," Wiggins said. "If he were settin' 'im up to take the blame for this crime, why'd 'e do that?"

"To make certain that no one else recognized him," she replied. "It was an integral part of his plan that it be the police and not the Frommer household who discovered Burroughs's real identity. Look what happened when the police did find out who he was; they immediately went to arrest him. It was only Alladyce's bad luck that it was our inspector on the case. Anyone else would have clapped Burroughs into jail and brought him to trial."

"So you're sayin' that Alladyce plotted the whole thing from the time he recognized Burroughs?" Luty clarified.

"I think he plotted it long before Burroughs arrived on the scene," she said. "But Burroughs's arrival provided an opportunity he wasn't going to miss. There's still a number of details to work out and questions that need to be answered, but I think that once the inspector gets home, we'll know everything."

"We shouldn't have to wait long," Wiggins murmured, his gaze on Fred, whose tail had begun to wag. "I think he's comin' now."

Fred, as always, was right. A few moments later Inspector Witherspoon trudged into the kitchen. "Oh, everyone's here."

"But of course, sir. You know how all of us eagerly await the latest development on your cases," Mrs. Jeffries said easily. She had her lies all ready. "Luty and Hatchet couldn't bear to leave without hearing what happened."

"Alladyce confessed," Witherspoon said as he sank into a chair. He nodded his thanks as Mrs. Goodge pushed a plate of tea cakes under his nose. "He murdered Roland Ashbury and tried to murder MaryAnne Frommer."

"How did he get Ashbury to come back to London earlier than the rest of the family?" Mrs. Jeffries asked. "You told us that none of the servants recalled Ashbury getting a telegram. Was it arranged before Ashbury went to Ascot?"

"He sent a messenger," Witherspoon replied. "A street lad. The boy waited till Ashbury came out in the garden and gave him the message that Alladyce needed to meet him in London on urgent business. Roland told the lad to tell Alladyce to be at his home at three-fifteen for tea. Alladyce came and killed him." He shook his head wearily.

"Then he tried to murder poor Mrs. Frommer?" Wiggins murmured.

"He tried, but luckily he failed. With her dead, he got the entire business." The inspector yawned widely. "He knew that Burroughs wasn't home that evening and so he waited in his garden. Remember, Alladyce had been around the Ashbury family all of his life; he knew their habits. He knew that Mrs. Frommer escaped outside every evening after dinner to get away from her husband. Alladyce hid behind the stone wall in the Burroughs garden, and when he saw Mrs. Frommer, he shot her. He used a pillow to muffle the noise. That's why no one heard the shots from either crime. Pillows. Resourceful of him, wasn't it?"

The question was rhetorical and no one replied.

"You've had a very tiring few days, sir." Mrs. Jeffries clucked her tongue sympathetically.

"Yes, indeed I have." He gave himself a small shake. "But I do want to tell all of you how very much I appreciate your efforts on my behalf."

Everyone froze. Wiggins, who'd been reaching for a bun, stopped with his hand in midair. Smythe, who'd been sneaking a quick peek at Betsy, went rigid. Hatchet and Luty went perfectly still. Mrs. Goodge swallowed nervously. Mrs. Jeffries's heart skipped a full beat.

"I don't quite understand, sir," the housekeeper finally managed to say.

"Oh, now, I don't want you pretending you don't know what I'm talking about," he said airily. "All of you do. Let's not be coy. Sometimes your devotion is a bit misplaced, but it's always, always appreciated."

"That's good to hear, sir," Mrs. Jeffries replied. He didn't appear to be angry, of that much she was certain.

"I do believe I'm the envy of the entire Yard," Witherspoon continued. "Everyone was most impressed with Mrs. Goodge and her scones."

"I'm so very glad, sir," the cook mumbled.

"They weren't just impressed with the fact that you were devoted enough to bring me food because I'd been up all night," he said eagerly. "They were amazed at my cleverness about those walnuts. Thank you, Mrs. Goodge. Naturally I told everyone that it was your cleverness in interpreting my meaning that helped in this case."

As the cook wasn't in the least sure what he was referring to, she merely smiled and nodded at her employer.

"Smythe, you and Hatchet both deserve a great deal of thanks," he continued. "Had it not been for the two of you, that poor woman would be dead. Now tell me again, why had the two of you come to the hospital?"

Smythe was ready for this one. Mrs. Jeffries had briefed him as soon as he and Hatchet had returned home.

"We was lookin' for you, sir," he said, his expression earnest. "We got this 'ere note." He pulled one of the five that had been written out of his pocket and handed it to the inspector. "Hatchet and Luty 'ad dropped by when the boy brung it, and as I didn't want to waste time, Hatchet took me to the hospital, 'opin' we'd find you. Instead, well"—he shrugged modestly—"you know what we found. Alladyce tryin' to murder poor Mrs. Frommer."

Witherspoon squinted at the spidery handwriting. "I wonder who sent this?" he muttered. He folded it and tucked it in his breast pocket. "Oh well, as we've a confession, I don't suppose it matters. But I must say, we do seem to get a jolly lot of notes sent here."

"It's probably from one of Alladyce's servants or someone else who suspected what he was going to do, sir," Mrs. Jeffries said cautiously. "You must admit your reputation has grown so that it's only natural that people would think to, well, tip you off."

"Tip me off?" Witherspoon repeated.

"Yes, sir," she replied eagerly. "That's probably why you're always getting those sort of notes on your cases. People who normally wouldn't trust the police feel very comfortable dealing with you."

Witherspoon's brows rose. "Do you think that could be it?"

"Oh, absolutely, sir," she said fervently.

The others around the table nodded in agreement.

"You've a fine reputation," she added for good measure. "You're considered one of the fairest policemen in London. You ought to be proud that people send you notes, sir. I'm sure you get information from the sort of people who normally wouldn't give the police the time of day."

"You know, Mrs. Jeffries"—he straightened up as he spoke—"I do believe you're right. Goodness, I'm such a very lucky man. A devoted staff and people out there"—he waved his hand to indicate the rest of the world—"who trust me above all others. It's a burden, but one that I accept with the utmost humility."

"Yes, sir," she murmured, trying to hide her amusement. "I'm sure you do."

They talked about the case a bit longer until the inspector, yawning with fatigue, took his leave and went to bed. Luty and Hatchet quickly followed suit.

Witherspoon was up and out in the garden early the next morning. The sun shone brightly, birds warbled from the tops of the leafy trees and the air had the crisp, clean scent of a new day. The inspector took a deep breath of air and turned to look a the house at the far end of the communal garden. *Her* house.

He told himself he wanted to enjoy a few moments of sunshine before he went to the station. There would be a mountain of paperwork to get through and a long and involved interrogation. He sighed. The truth was, he'd come out here to see if he could catch a glimpse of Lady Cannonberry. He missed her dreadfully.

His stomach rumbled with hunger. Maybe he'd ask Mrs. Goodge to make more of those walnut scones; they were certainly tasty. His fingers drifted to the waistband of his trousers. Perhaps he ought to ask the housekeeper to take these to the tailor's. They were getting a bit snug around his middle.

"Good morning, Gerald." Ruth's soft voice had him spinning around on his heel. "I saw you from my bedroom window and couldn't resist the chance to see you."

"Ruth," he exclaimed with pleasure. "I'm so glad you did. It seems ages since I've seen you."

"It's only been a few days," she replied, stepping close and taking his hand, "but it does seem a long time. How is your case going?"

"It's over," he stuttered, staring down at the hand she held so gently in hers. "How is your houseguest?"

"Morris is going to be leaving today," she replied, stroking his fingers tenderly. "He doesn't know it, but he's going to be taking the train back to Chester. Frankly I'm sick to death of him. Gerald, would you be so kind as to have dinner with me tonight?"

"I should love to, Ruth," he said fervently. "Is it a dinner party, or will it be just the two of us?"

"Just the two of us," she whispered. "I've got to go now. I'll see you this evening at seven."

Witherspoon watched her disappear through her back door. He turned and hurried into his own house.

"Good morning, sir," Mrs. Goodge called as he flew past her, heading for the backstairs. "Breakfast will be ready in a few minutes. There's bacon and eggs, porridge, toast and kippers. Will that be enough, sir?"

"Oh, don't bother with breakfast, Mrs. Goodge," he hollered over his shoulder. "I'm going to skip it today. I believe I've gained a bit of weight."

MRS. JEFFRIES ROCKS THE BOAT

CHAPTER 1

Malcolm Tavistock unlocked the heavy, spiked gate and pushed it open. "Come along, Hector," he said, yanking gently on the bulldog's lead. Hector, with one last sniff at an errant dandelion that had poked up between the stone squares of the footpath, followed his master.

"Humph," Tavistock glared at the dandelion as he and the dog stepped into the gated garden in the middle of Sheridar Square. He made a mental note to have a word with the gardener. The place certainly looked scruffy. He pulled the gate shut behind him and made sure he heard the lock engage before carefully pocketing the key.

Sheridan Square was for residents only. It wasn't a public garden and Malcolm, for his part, would do his best to insure it never became one. It rather annoyed him that some of his other neighbors on the square weren't as diligent as he was about insuring the security of the garden. Tugging at the dog's lead, Tavistock strolled up the footpath toward the center of the large square, his eagle eye on the lookout for more signs of neglect on the part of the gardener. The animal trudged along next to his master, keeping his nose close to the ground and sniffing happily at the bits of grass and clumps of leaves.

Suddenly, Hector came to a dead stop and his thick white head shot up. He sniffed the air and then lunged up the path, yanking his master along behind him.

"Hold on, old fellow," Malcolm ordered as he pulled back on the lead. He wasn't through ascertaining exactly how much of a tongue-lashing to give that wretched gardener. "Humph," he sniffed as he surveyed the area. The place was abysmal. The bushes along the perimeter had grown high and unwieldy. The footpath was scattered with stems and leaves and bits of dried grass, the flower beds were filled with weeds, and the lilac bushes were completely overgrown. "Well, really," Malcolm muttered. "Am I the only one that cares how this garden looks? The garden committee shall certainly hear about this."

Hector lunged again, almost yanking Malcolm off his feet.

"Oh, all right." Malcolm finally decided to let the poor dog have his walkies. He looked around, saw that he was the only one in the garden, and then dropped the lead. "Go on, boy. I'll catch up in a moment." Hector took off like a shot. Malcolm reached down and picked up a dirty bit of paper that was littering the path. "Honestly," he muttered as he crumpled the paper into a tight ball, "some people have no consideration for others."

From the center of the square, Hector howled.

Malcom was so startled, he jumped. He stuffed the paper in his pocket and ran towards his dog. His heart pounded against his chest. For all his grumbling, he loved that silly dog, and Hector might look like a terror, but he was easily upset.

Flying up the path, Malcolm skidded to a halt. Hector was perfectly all right. He was standing next to a bench upon which a woman lay stretched out sound asleep.

"Well, really," he exclaimed. "What has become of this neighborhood! Hector, come away from that disreputable person immediately." This wasn't the first time such a thing had happened. Because the garden was shielded by the high foliage from the eyes of passing policemen, vagrants occasionally climbed the fence. But this was the first time Malcolm had ever seen a woman do it. "What is the world coming to?" Malcolm muttered. He marched toward the bench. "I blame those silly suffragettes," he told Hector. "Puts stupid ideas in women's heads." He bent over the sleeping woman, frowning as he realized her clothes were new and expensive. Not the sort of clothes a vagrant would wear. He was suddenly a bit cautious. "Uh, miss." He poked her gently in the arm. "Is everything all right?"

The woman lay silent.

Hector whined softly.

Frightened now, Malcolm looked around him at his surroundings and wished he were visible from the street. The hair on the back of his neck stood up, and he shivered. But he couldn't just leave the woman lying here. "Miss," he said loudly, "are you all right?"

Hector whined again and stuck his nose under the wooden slats. But his head wouldn't go in very far as the lead had got tangled around the base of the gas lamp next to the bench. Malcolm bent down and untangled the lead; as he stood up, he saw what was under the bench. Stunned, he blinked and then forced himself to look again. But the view didn't change. In the pale morning light it was easy to see exactly what it was. Blood. Lots of it. Grabbing the dog's lead, he pulled him hard toward the gate. "Come on, Hector, we've got to find a policeman. That poor woman's dead. There's blood everywhere."

Hepzibah Jeffries, housekeeper to Inspector Gerald Witherspoon of Scotland Yard, stepped into the kitchen and surveyed her kingdom with amusement. Wiggins, the apple-cheeked young footman, sat at the kitchen table. Beside him sat a scruffy young street arab named Jeremy Blevins. In front of them was an open book, a pencil and a large sheet of paper. At the far end of the long table, Betsy, the blond-haired maid, sat polishing silver. Mrs. Goodge, the gray-haired, portly cook stood at the kitchen sink scrubbing vegetables for the evening stew.

The only one missing was Smythe, the coachman. But as it was almost morning teatime, Mrs. Jeffries expected him in any minute.

"Shall I make the tea?" Mrs. Jeffries asked the cook as she came on into the kitchen.

"No need." Mrs. Goodge jerked her chin to her left, toward a linen-covered tray that rested on the counter. "It's all done. But if you could just put the kettle on to boil, I'd be obliged. My hands are wet."

"Certainly." The housekeeper did as she was asked.

"Come on now, Jeremy," Wiggins said to the lad, "Concentrate. You know what that letter is. You learned it yesterday."

"I am concentratin'," the boy shot back. "But it's bloomin' hard to remember every little thing." His thin face scrunched as he stared at the book. "Uh, it's a 'C,' right?"

"It's a 'G,'" Wiggins corrected. "Can't you remember?"

"Leave off, Wiggins," Betsy interjected. "Jeremy's doing well. He's learned ever so much in just a few days."

"Ta, miss." Jeremy beamed at Betsy. "I reckon I've done well too . . . mind you, I don't know why I'm botherin' with book learnin'. It's not like the likes of me'll ever get a chance to use it much."

"You don't want to be ignorant all yer life, do ya?" Wiggins cuffed the lad gently on the arm and closed the book. "Besides, you never know what the future holds. At least if you know your letters and can read a bit, you'll be able to sign your own name."

"Fat lot of good that'll do me," Jeremy grumbled. He'd only told this lot he wanted to learn to read as a means of getting into the house and having a bite of food every now and again. He'd not expected they'd take him at his word and whip out this silly book every time he came around because his belly was touching his backbone. Still, Jeremy mused, they were a decent lot. Treated him well, even if they did expect him to learn his bleedin' letters. He glanced at the covered tray and wondered what sort of goodies were under the linen. He'd already been fed, but it never hurt to get some extra. When you lived like he did, you never knew when you might next eat. "Are ya havin' a fancy tea, then?"

"No," Betsy replied. She tossed her polishing cloth to one side and stood up. "Just our usual. Why? Are you still hungry?" Having been raised in one of the poorest slums of London, she was well aware of what the lad was up to. She'd lived on the streets for a time herself and knew what it was like to try and survive. "Help yourself to some more buns if you're still feeling peckish. There's plenty in the larder." She lifted the heavy tray of silver and started for the pantry.

Surprised, Jeremy gaped at her and then quickly scrambled to his feet. He didn't bother to look at the others; he simply followed Betsy down the hallway. He'd known as soon as he asked the question that he should have kept his mouth shut. When people were doling out charity, they didn't like you to be greedy. He couldn't believe she wasn't cuffing him on the ears or giving him a lecture.

"The buns are in the dry larder," Betsy called over her shoulder. She indicated a closed door she'd just passed and grinned as she heard it creak open behind her.

"Thanks, miss," Jeremy called as he darted inside the larder. "I'll 'elp meself if ya don't mind."

At the far end of the hall, the back door opened and a tall, dark-haired fellow with heavy features stepped inside. He took one look at the maid and frowned ominously . . . it was a scowl that could send strong men running for cover, but it had no effect whatsoever on Betsy. "You oughtn't to be liftin' that 'eavy tray." He came forward and took it out of her hands.

"Don't be silly, Smythe," she replied. "It's not at all heavy. It's only a bit of silver."

Smythe, the coachman, had been courting Betsy for some time now. Though they seemed quite mismatched, they were, in fact, very devoted to one another. He glanced up the hall to make sure the coast was clear and then leaned forward and snatched a quick kiss.

Jeremy chose that moment to pop out of the pantry. "I only took . . ." His voice trailed off as the two adults sprang apart.

Betsy whirled about, her face crimson at having been caught, even by a street lad. "Did you get some buns, then?"

Jeremy, who was almost as embarrassed as the maid, held up two of them. He'd been tempted to take more but decided against it. "I took these for me sister," he explained honestly. "She's only four. I'd best be off then," he mumbled as he pushed past the couple and headed for the back door. "Tell Wiggins I'll be back in a couple of days," he said as he scurried out and slammed the door behind him.

"I do think we embarrassed the boy." Smythe's voice was amused.

"You shouldn't have kissed me," Betsy hissed. "He'll tell Wiggins, you know."

Smythe only grinned. The entire household knew that he and Betsy were sweethearts. Knew and approved. But unfortunately, their courtship kept getting interrupted by the inspector's murder cases. "Help me take this to the pantry," he said softly.

"You don't need any help," Betsy protested. She looked quickly back toward the kitchen. "The others will wonder what we're up to."

"The others will understand we're doin' a bit of courtin'," he insisted. He started for a closed doorway opposite the wet larder.

"All right." Betsy followed him. "What have you been doing this morning?"

He opened the pantry door and stepped inside. "After I dropped the inspector off, I took Bow and Arrow for a good run," he replied. "They needed the exercise. Where do ya want this?"

"Put it over there." Betsy pointed to an empty shelf on the opposite wall. The tiny butler's pantry was too small for furniture. It consisted mainly of shelves of various sizes running up and down the length of the walls. Smythe carefully eased the tray into its place and then turned and pulled her close in a bear hug. Betsy giggled.

In the kitchen, Wiggins glanced toward the hallway. "I thought I 'eard Smythe come in." He started to get up. "And where's that lad got to?"

"Sit down, Wiggins," Mrs. Jeffries ordered. "Smythe has come in, and

I think he's probably helping Betsy put the silver away. I expect that Jeremy has helped himself to some buns and left." Unlike the footman, she knew precisely what was going on down the hallway.

"But I need to 'ave a word with Smythe." Wiggins started to get up again. "'E promised to—"

"Sit down, boy," Mrs. Goodge said sharply. "You've no need to go botherin' Smythe now. He'll be in for his tea in a few minutes. You can talk to him then."

"But Betsy's talkin' to 'im now . . ." Wiggins's voice trailed off as he realized what the two women already knew. His broad face creased in a sheepish grin. "Oh, I see what ya mean. They're doin' a bit of courtin'."

"That's none of our business." Mrs. Goodge placed the tray of food in the center of the table. She pushed a plate of sticky buns as far away from Wiggins as possible and shoved a plate of sliced brown bread and butter in front of the boy. He ate far too many sweets. Then she put the creamer and sugar bowl next to the stack of mugs already on the table. Lastly, she put the heavy, brown teapot in front of the housekeeper and then shoved the empty tray onto the counter behind her.

Mrs. Jeffries smiled her thanks and began pouring out the tea. She'd done a lot of thinking about Betsy and Smythe. They were, of course, perfect for one another. She certainly hoped that Smythe would ask the girl to marry him. She wasn't foolish enough to think a change of that significance wouldn't have an effect on the household. It would. A profound effect.

To begin with, she wondered if the two of them would want to stay on in the household if they married. Normally, a maid and a coachman who wed would simply move into their own room and stay on. But these weren't normal circumstances. Smythe would want to give his bride her own home. A home she suspected he could well afford. The housekeeper was fairly certain that one of the main reasons he'd not yet proposed was because he couldn't think of a way to tell the lass the truth about himself. But that wasn't what was worrying the housekeeper. Smythe could deal with that in his own good time. What concerned her was what would happen to their investigations if Smythe and Betsy married and moved out.

She sighed inwardly. There was nothing constant but change in life, she thought. When she'd come here a few years back, she'd never thought she and the others would get so involved in investigating murders. But they had. They'd done a rather good job of it as well, she thought proudly. Not that their dear inspector suspected they were the reason behind his success as Scotland Yard's most brilliant detective. Oh dear, no, that would never do.

Mrs. Jeffries put the heavy pot down. They'd come together and formed a formidable team. The household, along with their friends Luty Belle Crookshank and her butler Hatchet had investigated one heinous crime after another. Those investigations had brought a group of lonely people closer to one another. In their own way, they'd become a family. Now they had to make some adjustments. Murder, as interesting as it was, couldn't compete with true love. Especially, she told herself, when they didn't even have one to investigate. Not that she was thinking that someone ought to die just so she and the rest of the staff could indulge themselves. Goodness, no, that would never do. Murder was a terrible, terrible crime. It was impossible to think otherwise.

Still, if someone did die, she thought wistfully, it would break the monotony of the household routine and give all of them a much-needed bit of excitement. She shook herself when she realized where her thoughts were taking her. Then she looked up and found the cook gazing at her with an amused expression on her face. There were moments, Mrs. Jeffries thought, when she was sure Mrs. Goodge could read her mind.

"Mr. Tavistock, if you'll just tell us how you came to find the body, please," Inspector Gerald Witherspoon said gently to the portly, well-dressed gentleman.

"Yes, I will, just give me a moment, please." He swallowed and glanced down at the fat bulldog that sat at his feet, seeming to take strength in the animal's presence. He lifted his head and ran a hand nervously through his wispy gray hair. His blue eyes were as big as saucers, and his elderly face was pale with shock.

Inspector Witherspoon, a middle-aged man with thinning dark hair, a fine-boned, pale face and a mustache, smiled kindly at the witness he was trying to interview. The poor fellow was so rattled, the hands holding the dog's lead trembled. Witherspoon didn't fault the man for being upset. Finding a corpse generally had that effect on people. To be perfectly frank, it still rattled him quite a bit.

"I've already told those constables." Tavistock pointed a shaky finger at two uniformed police guarding the bench on which the body still lay. "I don't think I ought to have to tell it again. It's most upsetting."

"I'm sure it is, sir," the inspector replied. He glanced at the policeman standing next to Tavistock. Constable Barnes, an older, craggy-faced, gray-haired veteran who worked with Witherspoon exclusively, stared impassively out at the scene.

"Constable," Witherspoon said, "have one of the lads take Mr. Tavistock home. We'll have a look at the body and then pop over and take his statement when we're finished."

Tavistock slumped in relief. "Thank you, Inspector. I live just across the Square." He pointed to a large, pale gray home on the far side. "I don't mind admitting I could do with a cup of tea."

Barnes signaled to a uniformed lad, and a few moments later the witness, with his dog in tow, was escorted home. Witherspoon stiffened his spine and started up the footpath toward the body. He'd put off actually having to see it till the last possible moment. But he knew his duty. Distasteful as it was, he'd look at the victim.

He simply hoped it wasn't going to be too awful.

"She's right here, sir," the PC standing guard called out as soon as he spotted the inspector. "We did just like Constable Barnes instructed, we didn't touch anything."

"Good lad." Witherspoon swallowed heavily. He stopped next to the bench and looked down at the victim.

"She's not all that young," Barnes murmured. He'd come back to stand at the inspector's elbow. "And her clothes don't appear to be tampered with."

"True," Witherspoon replied. The victim was a middleaged woman with dark brown hair peeking out of her sensible cloth bonnet. The hat skewed to the side revealed a few strands of gray at her temples. She wore a deep blue traveling dress with expensive gold buttons. Her feet, shod in black high button shoes, dangled off the end of the bench. "She's tall," Witherspoon muttered. "That bench is over five and a half feet long." For a moment, he forgot his squeamishness. Except for the blood pooling underneath the bench she could almost be asleep. Her skin hadn't taken on that hideous milk blue color he'd seen in other corpses. He rather suspected that meant she'd not been dead long.

"She's not got any rings on sir." Barnes pointed to her hands, both of which were splayed out to one side of the body. "So unless the killer stole them, I think we can assume she's not married."

"But the killer may very well have stolen her jewelry," the inspector said. "As you can see, she's not got a purse or a reticule with her. Not unless it's underneath the body."

Taking a deep breath, he squatted down next to her. Barnes did the same. "Let's turn her over," Witherspoon instructed. Gently, the two men turned her on her side. The inspector winced. "She's been stabbed. I rather thought that might be the case."

"Poor woman." Barnes shook his head in disgust. "And from the looks of that wound, it weren't a clean, quick kill either."

Witherspoon forced himself to examine the wounds more closely. The constable was right, the woman's dress was in ribbons, and it was obvious, even to his untrained eye, that she'd been stabbed several times before she died.

"How many times do you reckon?" Barnes asked.

"It's impossible to tell. The police surgeon ought to be able to give us an answer after he's done the post mortem."

"She might have screamed some," Barnes said grimly. "As it looks like the first thrust didn't kill her, maybe someone heard something."

"Let's hope so," Witherspoon mumbled. "But I don't have much hope for that. There's a constable less than a quarter mile from here. Why didn't someone go get him if they heard a woman screaming?"

Barnes shrugged. "You know how folks are, sir. Lots of them don't want to get involved."

Together, they gently lowered the body back down. Witherspoon stared at the poor woman and offered a silent prayer for her. There was nothing more they could learn from her. She'd gone to her final rest in the most heinous, awful manner possible. Now it was up to him to see that her killer was brought to justice.

Witherspoon cared passionately about justice.

"There's nothing on her to identify her, sir." Barnes stated. He stood up. "Nothing in her pockets and no purse or muff."

"Hmmm." The inspector frowned heavily. "We must find out who she is. Let's give the garden a good search. There may be a clue here. You know what I always say, Barnes, even the most clever of murderers leaves something behind."

Barnes blinked in surprise. He'd never heard the inspector say anything of the sort. "Right, sir."

"We'd best send a lad back to the station to see if there are reports of any missing persons matching the victim's description."

"Right, sir."

"And I suppose I ought to send a message home"—Witherspoon stroked his chin thoughtfully—"and let them know I'm probably going to be late." Drat. Tonight he'd planned on sitting in the communal gardens with Lady Cannonberry, his neighbor. But duty, unfortunately, must come before pleasure. "You'd better let your good wife know as well, Constable. Can't have people worrying about us when we're late for supper."

"I'll take care of it, sir." Barnes replied with a grateful smile. He was touched by Witherspoon's thoughtfulness. His good wife would worry if he was late.

They spent the next half an hour searching the area, but even with the help of five additional policemen, they found nothing in the square that gave them any indication of who their victim might be.

When the body had been readied for transport to the morgue, Witherspoon and Barnes followed it out to the street. They left two constables inside to guard the area and also to keep an eye out for who came and went in this garden.

The attendants loaded her into the van and trundled off. Witherspoon turned to his constable. "Right, we've a murder to solve, then. Let's get cracking. Send some lads around on a house to house to see if anyone heard or saw anything." His gaze swept the area. "I daresay, this is quite a nice area."

"Very posh, sir," Barnes replied. "And the garden is private, sir. That ought to make it easier." He pointed to the gate. "You need a key to get inside. But there wasn't a key on the victim, so that means she either knew her killer and came in with him or her, or the gate was already unlocked when she got here."

"I suppose she could have scaled the fence," Witherspoon muttered. He looked at the high, six-foot spiked railings and then shook his head. "No, that's not likely. Not a woman of that age."

Barnes smiled. "I agree, sir. I can't see her leaping the ruddy thing."

"I suppose she could have had a key and the killer took it with him after he'd stabbed her," Witherspoon said thoughtfully.

"The only people with keys are residents of the square," Barnes said. "Malcolm Tavistock said he'd never laid eyes on the woman before and he ought to know. He's lived here for years."

"Who?"

"Tavistock," Barnes replied. "The man who found her."

"Ah yes." Witherspoon nodded sympathetically. "Poor fellow. Finding a body isn't a very nice way to start one's day."

"Neither is getting stabbed."

"Right," Witherspoon sighed. Sometimes he felt a bit inadequate for the task at hand. But then again, he'd try his very best. "Let's get on with it. Where does Mr. Tavistock live?"

"This way, sir."

The Tavistock house was directly across from the entrance to the garden. Like its neighbors, the dwelling was a pale gray, three-story townhouse with a freshly painted white front door. The inspector banged the shiny gold knocker, and almost instantly Malcolm Tavistock stuck his head out. "I suppose you want to come in?" he said grudgingly.

Witherspoon didn't take offense at the man's words. "That would be helpful, sir," he replied. He was inclined to give the poor fellow the benefit of the doubt. The shock of stumbling across a body could make someone behave in the most appallingly rude way.

Tavistock gestured for them to step inside. "Hurry up, then. Let's get this over and done with. I've an appointment in a few moments." He turned on his heel and stalked toward a set of open double doors off the foyer.

"I do beg you pardon, sir. But we'll need a complete statement," Witherspoon said as he and the constable followed Tavistock. They came into a large drawing room. The decor was nicely done, but hardly opulent or unusual. The walls were painted a dark green and the windows covered with heavy gold damask curtains. A huge fireplace, over which hung the requisite portrait of an ancestor, dominated the far end of the room. Fringe-covered tables, bookcases and overstuffed furniture completed the picture.

Tavistock flopped down on a mulberry-colored leather chair and gestured at the opposite settee. "Do sit down, then. I'd offer you tea, but I've no staff at the moment."

"You're here alone, sir?" Witherspoon asked. The house was large and well maintained. He'd be surprised if one person could take care of it alone.

"My servants aren't due back until tomorrow," Tavistock explained. "They weren't expecting me home until the end of the week. I've been abroad."

"On business, sir?" the constable asked. He'd taken out his notebook and flipped it open.

The inspector nodded approvingly at the constable's initiative. He encouraged Barnes to participate in questioning witnesses.

"Hardly. Frankly, I can't see that my reasons for being out of the country are anyone's business but my own. Now, can we please get on with this? As I said, I've an appointment in a few moments."

The inspector sighed inwardly. He did wish that people were a tad more respectful of the police. It wasn't as if they came around disrupting people's lives because they'd nothing better to do. "We'll try to be as quick as possible. Can you tell us precisely how you came to find the body?"

"I didn't find it," Tavistock said. "Hector did. He dashed off down the footpath and a few moments later, he was kicking up a terrible fuss. Not like him, he's generally such a good dog, quite well behaved."

Hector, licking his chops, ambled into the drawing room at just that moment. He took one look at the two policemen, snorted in a loud, bulldog fashion and then trotted over and planted his rather large behind firmly next to his master's feet.

Witherspoon couldn't help smiling. He liked dogs. Mind you, he didn't think this one looked quite as intelligent as his own dog, Fred. But as Tavistock's expression had brightened noticeably at the animal's appearance, the inspector wisely kept his opinion to himself.

"What time was this, sir?" Barnes asked.

Tavistock thought for a moment. "Let me see, usually I take Hector out for his walkies at seven every morning, but as we're a bit off our schedule, overslept as it were, I think it was closer to seven fifteen when we finally managed to get outside."

Hector's head snapped up at the word "walkies." He whined softly. Tavistock reached down and absently patted him on the head. "Now, now, old fellow, we'll go walkies later."

"You went straight out your front door and directly into the garden, is that it?" Witherspoon asked. He'd learned it was most valuable to get time sequences sorted out correctly. He'd had some rather substantial success in the past solving crimes with the help of timetables.

Tavistock's thin eyebrows rose in surprise. "Where else would I go? I was taking Hector for his morning walk. Of course I went straight from the house to the garden. Why would I pay a substantial amount of money each year for the upkeep of a private garden if I didn't use it?"

"We're only trying to establish all the facts, sir," Barnes said smoothly.

"You left here at seven fifteen and went straight across? You didn't stop to talk with anyone?"

Tavistock nodded. "There was no one to speak to, Constable. Seven fifteen is quite early."

"Is the garden always locked?" Witherspoon asked.

"Always. We're most particular about that. Any resident that leaves it unlocked is subject to a fine."

"I see." The inspector nodded. "And how many people have keys?"

Tavistock frowned thoughtfully. "Well, there's seven houses on the square. Each household is issued a key of course . . . no, no, I tell a lie. Mrs. Baldridge down at number one doesn't have one."

"Why not?" The inspector asked.

"She did have one, but you see, she doesn't anymore. There was a terrible row over the hollyhocks." He waved his hand dismissively. "The woman simply couldn't get it through her head that the wretched flowers wouldn't grow properly in that soil. So the garden committee decided to plant something else. She was most upset. She chucked her key at us and told us to go to the devil."

The inspector tried not to smile. "But there are seven keys in existence, correct."

"No, there's eight. The gardener has one, of course." Tavistock crossed his legs and leaned back.

"Could you give us the names of the other residents?" Barnes asked.

Tavistock glanced pointedly at a clock on the top of a cabinet a few feet away from where he sat. He sighed. "I'm going to be dreadfully late, Inspector. Can't we do this another time? Say this afternoon perhaps?"

"We're sorry to inconvenience you, sir," Witherspoon explained. "But the sooner we begin our investigation, the sooner we can get this sorted out."

"All right." Tavistock shrugged. "Let's, see, there's Mrs. Baldridge at number one. She's just across the square, but as I said, she had no key."

"Who does have her key, sir?" Barnes asked.

Tavistock frowned thoughtfully. "I'm not sure. Mr. Heckston, I imagine. He's the head of the committee . . . yes, he's bound to have it. Mrs. Baldridge was aiming at his head when she chucked the key. Quite a good aim for a woman her age. Smacked him right in the nose."

Barnes ducked his head to hide a smile. "And who else, sir?"

"Mrs. Lucas at number two has a key." He held up his fingers and ticked them off one by one as he spoke. "The Heckstons at number three, Colonel Bartell at number four, the Prospers at number six . . ."

"Who's at number five?" Witherspoon asked.

"No one," Tavistock said. "The owner died last year and the place has been empty ever since. I believe the rest of the family are in India or Canada. Let's see now, where was I, oh yes. The Prospers, number six and lastly, there's me, of course. I live here at number seven."

"There's only seven houses on the square." Barnes could have sworn there were more than that.

"Oh yes." Tavistock beamed proudly. "The houses are all quite large, sir. Not like some other places I could mention. There's only the seven of us."

"What's the gardener's name and where can I locate him?" Witherspoon asked. He was confident that Barnes had written down all the necessary particulars about the square's residents, and he wanted to make sure he took care of this bit of information before it completely slipped his mind.

"Jonathan Siler," Tavistock said. "I don't know where he lives. You can get that information from Mr. Heckston. But I'm sure that Jonathan hasn't anything to do with this poor woman's death. He's been taking care of the garden for years and he's a decent fellow, certainly wouldn't go about stabbing his betters. Not, of course, that we don't have to keep after him to keep the place up to our standards. You know how that class of person is. They'll do a fine job as long as you keep a close eye on them."

Witherspoon said nothing. He could easily have argued the point. He'd seen more than one case of murder where someone's "betters" got a bullet in the brain or a knife in their back. "I'm sure your gardener is most trustworthy. But you do understand, we have to talk with him."

"He's due here this morning," Tavistock said. "As a matter of fact, he ought to be turning up any moment now."

"When did you arrive back from your trip abroad?" Witherspoon asked.

"Yesterday evening. I stopped and had a bite to eat in a restaurant near Victoria, fetched Hector and came on home."

"And how long have you been gone, sir?" Barnes asked.

"Two weeks. I'd planned to stay longer." Tavistock smiled sheepishly, "but I found myself missing home." Again he leaned down and patted his dog. "You know how it is, sir. One goes off expecting to have a marvelous time and one finds that one misses the comforts of home. I know everyone says Italy has such superb weather, but frankly, this time of year it's simply too hot. I'd fully planned on staying a month. I sent the staff a telegram telling them I was coming home early."

"I see," Witherspoon said slowly. He didn't think there was much more this witness could tell him. Nodding at Barnes, he rose to his feet. "You've been most helpful, sir. Pity you weren't in the garden last night . . ."

"Who says I wasn't?" Tavistock exclaimed. "Of course I went into the garden. I had to take Hector walkies before we retired. Mind you, it was quite late when we went in, around midnight I should say."

"Why were you there so late?" Barnes asked.

Tavistock shot him a disgruntled look. "You obviously don't have a dog, Constable. Especially a dog that's quite excited to see you."

"Oh." The constable nodded in understanding. "Took him out to do his business, I see."

"Precisely, sir. We went all the way into the garden too."

"And there was nobody there," Witherspoon said.

"Precisely," Tavistock replied. "If there had been, Hector would have found them. He's quite good at finding things."

CHAPTER 2

Betsy broke into a welcoming smile as she opened the front door. "Constable Griffiths, how nice to see you. What brings you here? Inspector Witherspoon was up and out hours ago." She could tell by the pleased expression on his face that he hadn't come bearing bad news about their inspector.

"I've brought a message for the household, miss." He smiled bashfully. "Inspector Witherspoon's been called out on a murder case. He won't be home till quite late."

"A murder. Really?" Betsy threw the door open wide. "Come in, then."

"I'd love to, Miss Betsy," he explained, "but I've got to get over to Constable Barnes's house and tell his missus he won't be home in time for supper."

Betsy wasn't about to let the details of a murder slip through her fingers so easily. "Oh, but you must have a cup of tea," she implored him with a pouting smile. She hated using such tactics to get her own way, but she simply couldn't risk his going without telling them the details. "You simply must. It's so warm out today, I'm sure you're tired from coming all the way over here. Come down to the kitchen with me."

Constable Griffiths hesitated. He was quite sweet on Miss Betsy. She was ever such a pretty girl. But he didn't wish to be derelict in his duty. "I really shouldn't, miss."

"Nonsense, if you're worried about getting the message to Mrs. Barnes, don't be." She reached out, snagged his arm and tugged him into the house. Surprised by her aggressiveness, he found himself inside before he could stop her.

"It's still quite early, you'll have plenty of time to get to the Barnes house." Betsy slammed the door shut on her victim and gave him another dazzling smile. "Inspector Witherspoon would be most upset if he knew we'd let you leave without giving you refreshment." Still holding his arm, she tugged him towards her, whirled about and ran smack into Smythe.

He glared at the dainty hand on the constable's sleeve.

Betsy glared right back at him. "Constable Griffiths's come to give us a message," she blurted before Smythe could run the poor lad off. "There's been a murder, and the inspector won't be home till late. We're just on our way to the kitchen to have tea."

With the men in tow, Betsy led the way downstairs.

When the three of them trooped into the kitchen, Mrs. Jeffries and Mrs. Goodge, who were sitting at the table, making up menus for the week, looked up in surprise.

"There's been a murder," Betsy blurted, "and Constable Griffiths's come all this way just to let us know the inspector'll be home late. I insisted he have a cup of tea before he goes on to the Barnes house."

"But of course he'll have tea." Mrs. Goodge snatched up the menus and stuffed them in her apron. "And something to eat as well."

Within moments, Wiggins had appeared and the entire household gathered around the table to have tea with the constable. They looked expectantly at the housekeeper. No one wanted to be the first to speak. They'd leave that up to Mrs. Jeffries. The wrong question, the wrong attitude could have terrible consequences. Constable Griffiths wasn't stupid. If they didn't handle this just right, he could easily guess it was the household helping to investigate the inspector's cases that gave the man such success. None of them was prepared to do anything that would injure their employer. He'd been far too good to all of them.

With a barely perceptible nod of her head, Mrs. Jeffries acknowledged that she understood. Then she smiled at the constable, leaned back and fired her first salvo. "I must say, Constable, I do so admire you policemen. I don't think I could start my day by doing something as dreadful as investigating a murder. I think it's terribly, terribly brave of you." Flattery always worked.

"Oh, there's nothing to it, really. It's all part of the job," Griffiths replied modestly. "Mind you, a murder like this one doesn't come along every day."

"Who got killed?" Wiggins asked eagerly. Now that Mrs. Jeffries had taken the lead, the rest of them instinctively understood how to play their own parts. Wiggins, because he was young, could get away with asking blunt, straightforward questions.

"Now that's a right interestin' question," Griffiths replied. "We don't know. The woman didn't have anything on her to make an identification."

"It's a woman, then," Mrs. Goodge commented brusquely.

"Oh, how sad," Betsy cried. Like the footman, she too stepped into her part with ease. "Some poor woman gets murdered and they don't even know who she is. How awful . . . I'll bet she's some poor street woman down on her luck."

"This woman weren't poor," Griffiths said. "She were well dressed, well fed and laying on a bench in a private garden in a posh part of town."

"What private garden?" Smythe asked. "Someplace near here?"

"Sheridan Square."

"That's too close for my liking." Mrs. Goodge shook her head in disgust. "We'll all be murdered in our beds, we will. What's the world coming to when a decent woman can't even walk the streets of London without being murdered for her money?"

"We don't think she were murdered for her money," Griffiths said quickly. Then he blushed. "I mean, the inspector doesn't. I overheard him talking to Constable Barnes. The garden where she were found is private. You had to have a key to get in and out. She didn't have one on her and she weren't no young woman, so we don't think she nipped over the fence. Besides, it's six foot tall and it'd be hard for even a man, let alone a middle-aged woman to get past them spikes running along the top."

"What's that got to do with 'er bein' killed fer 'er money?" Wiggins asked. He wasn't playing a part now; he really wanted to know.

"It means whoever killed her probably had the key and let her into the garden with it," the constable explained. "The inspector and the others reckon she must have known her killer."

Mrs. Jeffries nodded in encouragement. "I see. Well, I expect you gentlemen will have it all cleared up in no time."

Stealthily, they questioned the constable until they'd wrung every little detail about the murder out of him, and then Betsy escorted him to the door.

As soon as the two of them had disappeared up the front steps, Smythe leapt to his feet. "I think I know how we can identify the victim."

"How?" Mrs. Jeffries asked.

"She didn't fly into that garden and if she weren't layin' there last night when that Tavistock fellow took his dog out, that means she musta gone there early this mornin'. There's a hansom stand not more than a quarter of a mile from Sheridan Square. I'll nip over there and see what I can find out."

"You think she went there by hansom cab?" Mrs. Goodge asked.

"She 'ad to get there someway," Smythe reasoned, "and a respectable well-dressed woman walkin' the streets in the dead of night or early of a mornin' woulda been noticed by the constable on patrol. But accordin' to what Griffiths said, no one saw hide nor hair of her."

"You're right, Smythe." Mrs. Jeffries nodded. "There's a good chance the victim did use a cab. Go on and see what you can find out. We'll meet back here this evening."

Smythe nodded and took off towards the back door.

"Where's he goin'?" Betsy asked as she came back to the kitchen.

"To see if the victim got to Sheridan Square by a hansom cab," Mrs. Goodge said. "And I don't think it's fair. Smythe gets to do something, and the rest of us have to sit here twiddling our thumbs because the silly woman managed to get herself murdered without anyone knowing who she was."

"We've plenty to do," Mrs. Jeffries said calmly. "For starters, you've got to get that provision list ready and off to the grocer's so you can prepare to feed your sources. The larders are empty."

"I suppose so," Mrs. Goodge agreed grudgingly. But she was still annoyed that Smythe had got the jump on them. There was just the teeniest bit of natural competition between the males and the females in the household.

"The larders really are empty," Mrs. Jeffries said again. "If we manage to identify that woman quickly, you're going to be in a bit of a pickle if you haven't anything on hand to feed people."

The cook decided to give in gracefully. "You're right. I'd best be ready. Let me see, where did I put that list? Ah yes, here it is, in my pocket with the menus."

Mrs. Goodge did her investigating in her own way. She baked enough to feed an army and then opened her kitchen to dozens of London's working people. Costermongers, servants, delivery boys, rag-and-bones men, flower girls, and shoeblacks; one and all traversed through Mrs. Goodge's kitchen. While they were there, she pumped them for every morsel of gossip about the suspects in a particular case. But she didn't stop there. She also had her own network of servants from other households feeding her information. She'd cooked for a number of England's finest families, and she still had connections all over the country. She was quite ruthless about using them as well.

Betsy frowned. "It's all well and good that Mrs. Goodge has something to do, but what about Wiggins and me? Are we just supposed to sit about twiddling our thumbs?"

"Of course not," Mrs. Jeffries replied. She quite understood Betsy's complaint. "There's plenty we must do. I'd like you to nip over to Luty and Hatchet's and tell them what's happened. They'll need to be here this afternoon for our meeting."

Luty Belle Crookshank and her butler, Hatchet, were friends of the household. They frequently helped on the inspector's cases. Luty Belle, in particular, threw a fit if she was left out.

Mollified, Betsy nodded. "Right. Do you want me to get on over to Sheridan Square afterward and see what I can suss out?"

"Absolutely," Mrs. Jeffries agreed, "but do be careful. You mustn't let the inspector or anyone who might recognize you catch even so much as a glimpse of you."

"I'll be careful," Betsy promised.

"What am I goin' to do, then?" Wiggins asked eagerly.

"You're going to get over to Sheridan Square as well," she replied. "But unlike Betsy, you're to make yourself known as a member of the inspector's household."

"What?" Wiggins jaw dropped. "Are you 'aving me on, Mrs. Jeffries?"

"No," Mrs. Jeffries said bluntly. A plan was rapidly forming in her mind. "I'm not having you on, so to speak. But I do have an idea. We need to know the identity of our victim as soon as possible. I'm going to have Mrs. Goodge make up a parcel of food for you to take to our inspector. But you're not to give it to him. You're to hang on to it and use it as your excuse to poke about and see what's going on."

By the puzzled frown on the lad's face, she could see he didn't quite get what she was trying to tell him. "What I mean is that you're to make sure you don't make contact with our inspector until the last possible moment . . . but having the food with you will give you an excuse to be hanging about listening and, if you're very clever, asking a few questions.

If anyone asks what you're doing there, you can say you're bringing the inspector something to eat."

"Now I get it," he bobbed his head eagerly. "I'm to hang about and learn what I can and use the food parcel as my reason for bein' there."

"Correct."

"Give me a minute and I'll have the food ready," Mrs. Goodge said as she bustled toward the pantry. "There's some buns and cheese I can put in as well as a few plums."

"What are you going to be doing?" Betsy asked as she slipped her hat off the coat tree. "Will you be out asking questions as well?"

"No, I'll be right here," Mrs. Jeffries replied firmly. "Holding down the fort as it were."

"Should we start here, sir?" Barnes pointed to the door of the house next to the Tavistock residence. Number six was much like its neighbor. As a matter of fact, it, along with virtually every other house in the square was almost identical. All of them had freshly painted white doors, and all of them were of the same uniform light gray color. The only difference between the Tavistock home and the one the constable pointed at was the color of the curtains. The ones in the windows of number six were a dark midnight blue.

Witherspoon nodded. "I suppose this is as good a place as any." He started up the pavement toward the short set of stairs leading to the front door. "This is going to be quite tedious, Constable. We're going to have to talk to every household on the square."

"Yes, sir," Barnes replied glumly. "I know."

The door to number six was opened before they even knocked by a cheery-faced maid. "Good morning, gentlemen," she said chattily. "You're the police, aren't you?"

"Good day, miss. You're quite correct, we are the police," Witherspoon replied. "We'd like to speak with the head of your household if we could."

"That'd be Mr. Prosper," the maid replied, "and he ain't here. He's in Edinburgh on business. Will Mrs. Prosper do?"

"That will be fine."

The maid nodded and ushered them inside. "Just go on into the drawing room, sir," she instructed, pointing to an open doorway down the hall, "and I'll get the mistress."

"Thank you," the inspector replied. He blinked in surprise as he entered the drawing room.

"Blimey, sir," Barnes muttered with a quick look over his shoulder to make sure he wasn't overheard, "there's enough in here to open a shop."

Settees, overstuffed chairs, ottomans, bookcases and cabinets crowded the huge room. Along the walls, portraits, hunting and pastoral scenes and boldly garish wall sconces competed for attention. Along the tops of the cabinets and bookcases there were knickknacks of porcelain and silver. Chinese vases, fringed shawls and elegantly draped midnight-blue curtains gave the room an air of oriental mystery. Witherspoon shook his head. "You're quite right, Constable. I do believe one could easily stock a shop, and it appears that the stock would be quite expensive too. None of this looks cheap."

The constable pointed to a pair of ceramic shepherds sitting atop a small cherry wood table in the corner. "The missus saw just one of them in a shop window a few weeks back, wanted a pretty penny for it too."

"I understand you want to see me?" A cool female voice said from behind them.

Witherspoon, blushing to the roots of his thinning hair, whirled about. "I'm dreadfully sorry, madam," he said to the tall, elegantly dressed woman standing in the doorway. "I didn't hear you come in. We were just admiring your porcelain. It's quite lovely."

"Thank you." She nodded regally. She was a woman who was in her early thirties. Her hair was a light brown, her eyes blue and her face thin and fine boned. Slender and tall, she wore a morning dress of brilliant blue with white lace flounces along the neck and wrists. "I'm Annabelle Prosper. The maid said you wished to speak with me."

"Yes ma'am," Witherspoon introduced himself and the constable. "We do hate to disturb you," he continued, "but we're in the position that we must get statements from all the households in the square."

"Please sit down." She nodded toward the nearest settee while she took a seat on the one opposite. "What is this about?"

"I'm afraid something rather unfortunate has happened in your garden," the inspector said. "There's been a murder."

She started in surprise. "A murder. In our garden? But that's absurd. It's locked."

"Absurd as it may be," the inspector assured her, "it still happened.

The victim was a middle-aged woman. She had nothing on her person to identify her. Is anyone from your household missing?"

"No." Mrs. Prosper shook her head. "Everyone's here."

"Are you quite certain about that, ma'am?" Barnes asked. "This is a big house. Have you seen all your staff?"

Annabelle Prosper raised one delicately arched eyebrow. "I'm quite sure, Constable. In my husband's absence, I preside over morning prayers. I assure you, the entire staff was present."

"We weren't doubting your word, ma'am," Witherspoon interjected hastily.

"Annabelle, I've heard there are some policemen here . . . Oh, goodness, it's true, then." A short, dark-haired rather plump woman of middle years hurried into the drawing room.

"Really, Marlena, must you be so precipitous?" Annabelle shot the woman a disapproving frown.

The woman ignored her and advanced toward the two men. "Hello, I'm Marlena McCabe, Mrs. Prosper's sister-in-law."

Witherspoon and Barnes both got to their feet. He looked pointedly at Mrs. Prosper, who rather grudgingly introduced the two policemen. "We were just having a word with Mrs. Prosper," he explained after the pleasantries had been exchanged.

"About the murder in the garden?" Marlena said eagerly.

"How did you know about that, ma'am?" Barnes asked.

She laughed. "Really, Constable, did you think you'd be able to keep it a secret? There's police all over the square. I heard it from Maggie, our tweeny, and she got it from Colonel Bartell's scullery maid. Is it true that a woman's been stabbed and her head cut off?"

"Marlena!" Annabelle Prosper snapped. "Must you be so . . . so . . ."

"No one got their head cut off, ma'am," Witherspoon said quickly. "But we did find the body of a woman. That's why we're here. We're trying to determine who she might be."

"How exciting," Marlena flopped down next to her sister-in-law. "Maybe I can be of some help."

"You don't know anything," Mrs. Prosper chided. "Honestly, Marlena, you ought to be ashamed of yourself. You mustn't interfere with an official police inquiry simply because you find it exciting."

"I do too know something," she replied, glaring at her sister-in-law.

She looked at the policemen. "Was the woman quite tall, wearing a plain hat and a blue traveling dress?"

Witherspoon and Barnes straightened to attention. "She was," the inspector said. "Do you know her? Can you tell us who she is?"

"Well, no, not exactly," she replied. "But I can tell you when she arrived at the square. I saw her getting out of a hansom about five this morning."

"You saw her?" Barnes prompted.

"From the front hall," Marlena explained. "I'd come downstairs to get a glass of water. No one was up at that hour, of course, and it was very quiet. I heard a carriage come into the square—they make a terrible racket, you see. It's the horses' hooves on those cobblestones on the north side."

"You're digressing, Marlena," Mrs. Prosper said. Now, she too looked interested. "Do go on."

"Well." Marlena nodded importantly. "As I said, I heard a carriage come in. Of course, I thought it might be Eldon back from Scotland . . ."

"Eldon's not due until this evening," Mrs. Prosper interrupted.

"Yes, I know that. But he does hate being away from home, and I thought he might have come back early, you see." She paused for breath. "As I was saying, I heard the carriage and, thinking it might be Eldon, I went to that window." She pointed toward the end of the room facing the square, "and had a look. But it wasn't Eldon, it was this woman. She got out of a hansom right in front of Mr. Tavistock's house. Of course, that's right next door."

"Did you see her go into the garden?" Witherspoon asked.

She shook her head. "No, I went back upstairs."

"Did you hear anything after that? Anything at all that struck you as odd." Witherspoon didn't wish to put words in the woman's mouth, but perhaps she'd heard a scream or a scuffle.

"I'm afraid not." She shrugged apologetically. "My room is on the second floor at the back of the house. I heard nothing."

"And you're sure about the time," Barnes pressed. "It was five o'clock in the morning."

"Quite sure," Marlena McCabe said firmly. "The clock in the hall had just struck the hour when I heard the hansom come into the square. I'm sorry I can't be more helpful."

"You've been most helpful, indeed, ma'am," Witherspoon said gratefully. "At least now we know the victim was still alive at five this morning." He got to his feet.

Barnes, flicking his notebook shut, got up as well. "Do you remember if the garden gate was closed?" he asked as he tucked the book in his pocket.

Mrs. McCabe's brows drew together in thought. "I don't think, I know. Frankly, I wasn't looking at the garden. I was looking at the hansom. My attention was turned toward the Tavistock house. I've no idea if the gate was open or closed."

"I quite understand, ma'am." Witherspoon wished that people were more observant. But he could hardly say so. Especially as this woman was the first helpful witness they'd come across. "As I said, you've been most helpful."

"Thank you," she replied. But she wasn't looking at the policemen; she was smirking at Mrs. Prosper. "Well, what do you think, Annabelle, have I been helpful or not?"

Annabelle smiled thinly. Clearly, she didn't like being shown up in front of strangers. "As the inspector said, dear, you've been most helpful. Most helpful indeed."

"Look, it's not as if I'm askin' ya to fly to the moon and back," Smythe said in disgust. "All I want is a bit of information."

The cabbie yawned and rubbed his face. He leaned against the side of the small building that housed the hansom stand. Inside his mates were drinking tea and having a bit of a rest. "You may as well ask me to fly to the moon. It's not as if you're wantin' to know if someone picked up a fare at Sheridan Square. You're wantin' to know who took a fare there. It coulda been from anywhere in the city, mate. It'da been a mite sight easier if it were the other way around. It woulda have to have been one of the local blokes if it were a pickup, but as it were a drop, it coulda come from anywhere."

Smythe knew it was pointless getting irritated. The cabbie was right. As the victim had been dropped off and not picked up at the square, she could have come from anywhere around London. The two-mile rule only covered picking up passengers, not dropping them off. He sighed and shoved away from the lamppost he'd been leaning against. This had been a blooming wasted trip. He'd had sod all luck. No one knew anything. "All right, then, thanks for yer 'elp."

"Weren't much 'elp, mate." The cabbie shrugged sympathetically. "Not much I can tell ya. None of us around here took that fare."

"What fare?" A tall, rawboned cabbie with red hair poking out of a battered bowler strolled up to the men.

"A fare to Sheridan Square."

"Harry did," the cabbie said slowly as he raked Smythe's plain working clothes with a practised eye. "Why? What's it to you?"

"I'm lookin' fer someone," Smythe replied. "A woman."

"Your woman?" the other cabbie asked.

"Never you mind whose woman she is," he said. "Let's just say that whoever can help me find out which of you drovers took a fare to Sheridan Square this morning will be in fer a pretty penny." He'd decided that greasing their palms with silver would work far better than trying to come up with some silly story explaining why he wanted to track the woman down.

"How much?" the red-haired man asked.

Smythe wasn't stupid enough to whip out his roll of bills in front of all and sundry. Nor was he going to part with cash until he had some information. "First you tell me which one is 'arry and then we'll talk about how much."

The cabbie eyed him suspiciously. "How do I know you'll pay?"

"You don't," Smythe sighed impatiently. He didn't want to stand here all day. "Look, you take me to this 'arry feller and I'll make it worth yer while. Does that sound fair?"

The man thought about it for all of two seconds. "Fair enough." He turned on his heel and started off down the road, away from the cab stand. "Come on, then. Get a move on. Harry's not goin' to be there long."

Smythe nodded his thanks to the other cabbie and hurried after the tall redhead.

Wiggins tucked his small parcel neatly under his arm as he stood on the cobblestone road and gazed onto Sheridan Square. Opposite him was the garden where the poor lady had met her untimely death . . . to Wiggins any death not taken in a nice soft bed at the age of ninety was untimely. Wiggins bobbled to one side. He could see see the helmet of a constable on the far side of the garden. Probably a police constable guarding the entrance, he thought. He tucked the parcel of food under his arm, straightened his spine and strolled toward the action. After all, if anyone stopped him, he had a reason for being there.

He rounded the corner of the garden and saw that the gate was open. The constable on guard was a lad not much older than himself. Wiggins stood on tiptoe, trying to see through the thick bushes into the interior of the square. But all he could see were passing police helmets or the flash of a dark uniform as the lads searched the grounds.

He moved his gaze from the garden to the square itself. The houses were huge, well kept and reeking of money. Wiggins chuckled lightly. Most of the residents were too well-bred to show any interest in the police presence right under their noses, but they'd sent their servants out to pick up what gossip they could. In front of number six a tweeny energetically swept the doorstoop. Across from Wiggins, windows were being washed at another house and at a third, a footman was outside polishing the brass carriage lamps. None of them were paying more than passing attention to their tasks; they were all watching the garden.

Wiggins took a deep breath and started in the direction of the tweeny. A lad had to start somewhere and she was as good as any.

The girl didn't even hear him approaching. She was staring hard at the garden. Wiggins, thinking she might have a better view from this end of the square, stopped a few feet away from her and took a gander himself. He could see nothing but bushes and hedges. He glanced back at the girl. Her attention was still fixed on the square, the broom in her hands moving rhythmically back and forth as she brushed the same spot over and over. He headed towards her, taking care to walk heavily so that his footsteps sounded along the pavement. The girl started and whirled about.

"Sorry, miss," he said quickly. "I didn't mean to frighten you."

"You didn't scare me," she said defensively, "you startled me, that's all."

She was really very pretty, he thought. Beneath her conical maid's cap, her hair was a deep brown color. Her eyes were hazel and her skin was perfect. "I didn't mean to," he said. "You was staring at that garden so hard you musta not 'eard me coming till I was right behind you. What's happened?" He jerked his head at the square.

"Someone's got murdered," she replied. She turned her back on him and went back to sweeping.

Wiggins didn't think this was a particularly good sign. But the fact that he'd have to talk to her back didn't stop him. "Murdered? Really? How?"

"I don't know," she muttered.

He knew that was a lie. By now, he knew that every servant in the square knew how the victim had died. "Well, I can see talkin' about it upsets you, miss," he said sympathetically. "So I'll not trouble you with any more questions. But could you tell me if you've seen a policeman . . ."

"I've seen half a dozen coppers," she snapped over her shoulder. "They're all over the garden and the square."

"But I'm lookin' for a particular one, miss," he continued calmly. "An inspector. He's my guv, he is. I've got a packet of food our cook sent over for 'im."

The girl turned and stared at him. "You work for one of them policemen?"

"I work for the man in charge," Wiggins bragged. "Inspector Witherspoon. If you've 'ad a murder 'ere, 'e'll find the killer. 'E's ever so good at it, 'e is. Do you know where 'e is?"

She stared at him for a moment. "I don't know where he's gone," she finally said. "He were here earlier talkin' to the mistress, but then he left."

"Left? You mean 'e's gone back to the station?"

"How should I know?" Once again she turned her back on him and began to sweep. "It's not for the likes of me to stick my nose into anything that don't concern me."

"But murder concerns everyone," Wiggins protested. Then he clamped his mouth shut. His instincts were screaming at him to keep quiet for a moment. Something was going on here, something wasn't right. He'd had dozens of conversations with servants that had been close to crimes or a crime scene, and not one of them had ever acted like this girl. She wasn't excited or curious, and that just plain wasn't right. He knew what a domestic's life was like. Anything out of the ordinary, anything that took you away from the drudgery of your work, even for a few moments, was cause for excitement.

But the girl wasn't excited.

She was angry. Wiggins chewed his lower lip as he thought about what to do next. He noticed her hands were clamped around the broom handle so tightly that her knuckles were white. Her shoulders were hunched defensively, and her expression was closed and grim.

"Uh, miss," he said tentatively, "I'm really sorry I startled you."

"It's all right," she muttered. "Now get on with you. I've work to do."

"I didn't mean to interrupt you," he continued, racking his brain for some way of prolonging the conversation. "I really didn't. You won't get in trouble will ya? I mean, you'll not get the sack just because I stopped and spoke to ya?"

"Not if you go away now," she said. "But if you hang about chatting, they'll toss me out on my ear. Now get off with you."

"Cor blimey, you must work for a strict household."

The girl laughed. "You could say that. Go on, go find your inspector."

Wiggins hesitated. He sensed he'd missed his opportunity to get any more information out of the girl, but he was loath to give up so easily. He opened his mouth to ask another silly question when the front door flew open and an older woman stuck her head out. "Fiona, get in here. You're not to spend all day sweeping that pavement."

"Yes, ma'am," she replied, "I'm just coming." She picked up her broom and disappeared around the side of the house.

Wiggins watched her leave and promised himself he'd come back later. He glanced at the house number and made a mental note that it was number six. It wouldn't do to forget where the girl lived. That Fiona knew something. He'd bet his next meal on it.

Timothy Heckston sat behind his huge rosewood desk and tapped his fingers impatiently on the desk pad. He was of late middle age but still had a head of thick blond hair, a sharp-pointed chin, thin lips and prominent cheekbones. "I'm sorry to be so unhelpful, gentlemen," he said with a shrug. "But there's little else I can tell you."

"Are you absolutely certain there are only seven keys to the garden, sir?" Inspector Witherspoon asked.

"Eight, Inspector," Heckston corrected. "Eight keys. Each house on the square is issued one, and the gardener has one as well."

"Yes, of course, Mr. Tavistock told us that." Witherspoon nodded.

"Are you still in possession of Mrs. Baldridge's key, sir?" Barnes asked. "I believe she, uh, gave it back to you."

Heckston broke into a grin. "Heard about that, did you? She didn't give it to me, sir. She threw it at my head."

Barnes smiled. "We understand Mrs. Baldridge is a great lover of hollyhocks."

"Silly woman couldn't understand that the wretched things wouldn't grow in the garden." He stood up, walked across the room to a small cupboard next to the door. Taking a small key out of his pocket, he unlocked the cupboard and opened it. "You'd have thought we were deliberately trying to upset her. I was as gentle as possible . . ." he stopped and a frown crossed his face. "That's odd. It's not here."

Witherspoon glanced at Barnes and then said, "What's not there, sir?"

"The key." Heckston turned and stared at them, his expression puzzled. "Mrs. Baldridge's key isn't there. It's gone."

"Are you sure, sir?" Barnes asked. He and the inspector had both risen to their feet. They crossed the room and stood behind Heckston's shoulder. The cupboard was lined with three rows of hooks. The top two rows had keys of various sizes hanging from them with small, white labels affixed beneath them. The bottom row, the row labeled "Garden Keys" was completely empty.

Heckston pointed to the last hook on that row. "Mrs. Baldridge's key was right here."

"Could it have been misplaced, sir?" Barnes asked.

Heckston shook his head. "No one opens this cupboard but me, sir. I always keep it locked."

"What about other members of your household?" Witherspoon prodded.

"Other than myself, there's only my wife who has a key. She'd have no reason to bother with garden keys."

"When was the last time you saw the key, sir?" the inspector asked quickly. He'd found that if one kept up a steady stream of questions, one sometimes found that the person one was questioning didn't have time to make up any lies.

"The last time." Heckston frowned. "Let's see. I suppose it must have been last week. Yes, yes, that's right. I opened up the cupboard to get the key to the wine cellar."

"Was it possible the key fell out or was accidentally taken?" Barnes pressed.

"No, as you can see, the hooks are rounded so that keys can't be knocked off accidentally."

"Was anyone else in the room with you?" Witherspoon asked. "I mean, did anyone else know where the key was kept?"

Heckston hesitated. "Well, I suppose so. I opened the cupboard in front of the whole garden committee. We were having a meeting, you see. We always meet in the study. It keeps things more businesslike, moves the whole process along a bit faster, if you know what I mean. Long meetings are so tireseome."

"So you're saying, sir," Barnes said quietly, "that everyone on the square knew where the spare key was kept?"

Heckston nodded glumly. "I'm afraid so."

"Which means that anyone could have taken the key. No offense meant, Mr. Heckston, but that lock doesn't look to be very sturdy." Witherspoon said. Drat. This wasn't going to be an easy one to solve.

CHAPTER 3

The household gathered back at Upper Edmonton Gardens at four that afternoon. Everyone was there, even Luty Belle Crookshank and her butler Hatchet. Luty Belle was an elderly, wealthy, rather eccentric American. White haired and dark eyed, she had a penchant for brightly colored clothes and an acerbic tongue that masked a heart as big as her native country. Hatchet, her butler, was tall, dignified and constantly trying to force his mistress to watch her manners.

"Really, madam." Hatchet sniffed as they took their places at the table. "You might have managed to be a bit kinder to Countess Rutherford. I don't believe she much appreciated being told she had to leave because you had something important to do."

"Then she ought to have taken the hint," Luty shot back quickly. "I'd spent ten minutes droppin' little niceties to git the woman outa my drawin' room. But she didn't budge. I don't like being mean to people, but Nell's bells, that woman could talk a grizzly into a cave. I didn't think I'd ever git rid of her."

Mrs. Jeffries smiled at the two of them. She knew perfectly well that Hatchet was speaking more out of habit than anything else. She was sure that if Luty hadn't gotten rid of Countess Rutherford, he would have. He wouldn't let anyone, titled or not, stand in the way of a murder investigation. Both of them enjoyed snooping far more than entertaining. After Luty had inadvertently gotten involved in one of the household's first cases, she'd come to them for help to find a missing girl. After that, it would have been difficult to keep either her or Hatchet out of their investigations.

"I'm sorry you had to get rid of your guest," the housekeeper said apologetically, "but I thought you'd want to be here. Even though at this point we don't know all that much."

"You thought right," Luty said. "What have we got? Betsy's message this mornin' weren't real detailed."

"Sorry about that," Betsy smiled. "I know I should have stayed and told you everything, but I was in a hurry to get out and about."

"Don't concern yourself, Miss Betsy," Hatchet said. "Your message was fine. Unlike Madam, I realized immediately that you'd not learned more than the bare facts of the case."

"Speakin' of which," Luty said, "maybe you could rest yer tongue a minute so Hepzibah can share those details with us." She was the only one to ever call the housekeeper by her Christian name.

Mrs. Jeffries quickly said, "We still don't know who the victim was." She told them about the woman being found in the locked garden and about how the victim had been stabbed.

"A locked garden?" Puzzled, Luty shook her head. "Why go to so much trouble? Nell's bells, there's half a dozen places to stab someone in the middle of the night."

"I agree," Mrs. Jeffries replied. "I've spent a good part of today thinking the same thing. The circumstances of the murder are very, very strange."

"Not if the killer planned on meetin' the victim in that garden," Wiggins said. "I've seen the place. It's a right good place for murder. The bushes and such is so high you can do what you like and not be seen from the street."

"But she was killed in the middle of the night," Betsy said. "You don't need bushes for that. All you need is darkness. I agree with Luty and Mrs. Jeffries. Luring someone into a garden in the dead of night is a strange way to commit murder. Why go to all that bother? Why not just meet them on a deserted public street and wait till their back is turned?"

"It's hardly convenient," Mrs. Jeffries said. "Especially as we know that the killer had to have had a key."

"Or the victim had one," Hatchet said thoughtfully. "And the killer took it with him when he left."

Mrs. Jeffries knew that too much speculation at this point might be dangerous. On more than one of their past investigations, they'd done their snooping with a whole set of preconceived notions that had turned out to be just plain wrong. She didn't want that to happen here. "Well, let's keep an open mind, shall we? I do hope that one of you has learned something useful today? Otherwise we'll have to wait until the inspector comes home, and that might not be till quite late."

"I think I might know a few things," Wiggins volunteered eagerly. "'Angin' about was a right good idea, I overheard 'alf a dozen coppers talkin'."

"Excellent, Wiggins." Mrs. Jeffries beamed proudly at the lad. "Do tell us everything."

Wiggins took a fast sip of his tea. "For starters, I overheard the one of the coppers sayin' that the inspector 'ad found a witness who'd seen the victim arrivin' in the square."

"That's a good start," Luty encouraged. "What time did she git there?"

"It weren't the middle of the night. It were five in the mornin'," he continued, "and she come by hansom."

"Who's the witness?" Smythe asked softly.

"A lady who lives at number six, her name's McCabe. Mrs. McCabe." Wiggins frowned. "Why do ya want to know? Don't you believe me?"

"Of course I do, ya silly git," Smythe said. "As a matter of fact, I found the driver that brung the woman there. I just thought it might be important to know who else was up and about at five in the mornin', that's all." He turned his attention to the housekeeper. "To tell ya the truth, Mrs. J, we're in a bit of a pickle. Ya see, I didn't just find the hansom driver. I think I found out who the victim was. I can't for the life of me think of a way to let the inspector know."

"You know who she is?" Luty exclaimed. "Hell's fire and apple butter, that'll put us way ahead of the police."

"Excellent work, Smythe," Hatchet said proudly. "We really are good, aren't we?"

"Goodness, you're ever so clever, Smythe." Betsy smiled at him and patted his arm. "I wish I'd been able to find out who she was."

"Good work," Mrs. Goodge said. "Knowing who our victim is will save us a lot of time and trouble."

"Gracious, Smythe," Mrs. Jeffries said, "you've managed quite a feat. Who was she?"

"That's just it." Smythe shook his head. "She weren't nobody. I mean, she were somebody, but she couldn't be somebody anyone would want to kill. Not unlessin' they was a lunatic like that ripper feller. Ya see, the woman couldn't have had any enemies in England. She'd just arrived here the day before from Australia. Why would anyone want to kill a perfect stranger?"

"We're not doing all that well, are we, sir?" Barnes asked glumly as they made their way to the last house on the square. "Mrs. Lucas at number two was sound asleep, and so were her servants. What do you think of Colonel Bartell, sir? Do you think he was telling the truth?"

"About being awake but hearing nothing." Witherspoon smiled sadly. "Oh, yes, I'm quite sure he was telling the truth. I don't think his hearing is all that good. If you'll recall, he kept his head cocked toward us the whole time we were there. As for him being awake, I imagine that's true too. Many elderly people have difficulty sleeping through the night. It's too bad there aren't more people like that helpful Mrs. McCabe at number six. She, at least, saw something useful."

"Most people aren't up at five, sir," Barnes said with a frown. "I'll tell you the truth, sir, I'm not looking forward to this one." He jerked his chin toward the house they were rapidly approaching. "Mrs. Baldridge sounds like she's got a bit of a temper."

Witherspoon hadn't been looking forward to it either; that's why he'd left it to last. "Let's hope she'll be more cooperative with the police than she was with the garden committee." He sighed as they reached the Baldridge house. He couldn't put this off any longer, he thought, as he started up the short flight of steps.

The front door flew open, and a round-faced, smiling girl with a maid's cap on stuck her head out. "You must be the police," she said cheerfully. She pulled the door open wide and gestured for them to come inside. "Do come in, sirs. The mistress has already ordered tea. We've been waiting for you. She wondered what was taking you so long."

Bemused, Witherspoon glanced at Barnes. The constable looked as puzzled as the inspector. They followed the maid down a long hallway, their footsteps echoing loudly on the polished oak floor. From what the inspector had heard of Mrs. Baldridge, he certainly wouldn't have thought she'd be in any hurry to speak with the police. So few people were.

The girl led them through a set of double oak doors and into a large, elegant drawing room. There were cream-colored damask curtains at the windows, a lovely Persian carpet and several comfortable-looking settees and love seats arranged imaginatively about the room. On the settee far-thest from the door sat a well-dressed woman. A silver tea service was spread out on a low table in front of her. She stared at the two men curi-ously as they approached. Middle-aged and with fading brown hair pulled up in a topknot, she had dark, rather intelligent-looking brown eyes, a full mouth and a long, straight nose.

The inspector was rather surprised. Though well past her first youth, she was rather an attractive, pleasant-looking person. Not the kind of woman one would imagine hurling a set of keys at someone. He really didn't know what to make of this. "Good day, madam. I'm Inspector Gerald Witherspoon and this is Constable Barnes."

"I know who you are, Inspector," she replied. A hint of a smile crossed her face. "I've been waiting for you. Please sit down and make yourselves comfortable. As you can see, I've taken the liberty of ordering tea. I do hope you and your constable will have it with me."

"Thank you, ma'am," Witherspoon said gratefully. His mouth watered. He tried not to stare at the food, but he'd not had much to eat since break-fast. Temptingly spread out on the table before him were trays of sand-wiches, scones, Madeira cake and sliced buttered bread. "That's very kind of you."

"Do help yourselves to something to eat," she said matter-of-factly as she poured the tea. "I'm sure you're both hungry. You've been out on the square for hours. I don't quite see how you do it. All that investigating on an empty stomach."

"Actually, my footman brought us a spot of lunch," the inspector said as he helped himself to a slice of thick brown bread. But as he'd shared most of it with Barnes and two uniformed lads, they'd not had enough to fill them up.

"Most of which you shared with me and the other lads," Barnes put in.

"Then I'm sure you're both quite hungry. Please, do help yourselves," she ordered briskly. She handed each man his tea and then picked up her own pink and white porcelain cup. "I expect you want to ask me a few questions, don't you?"

Witherspoon finished loading a scone on his plate before answering. "Did you hear or see anything early this morning? By that, I mean, did you hear or see anything out of the ordinary? Anything that struck you as odd."

"Of course I did, Inspector." She smiled. "That's why I wanted to speak with you."

"How very fortunate for us," he replied. Perhaps this time he'd be very lucky on a case, and there would actually be a useful witness to the murder. He slapped a piece of buttered bread next to the scone. "What did you see, ma'am?"

"I didn't see anything."

"I beg your pardon?" He put his plate down and gave her his full attention.

She raised an eyebrow. "I didn't see anything, sir. I heard something."

"What would that be ma'am?" Barnes asked. He too put his plate down and whipped out his little brown notebook.

"Before I give you the details," she said thoughtfully, "there's something you need to understand. Since my husband passed away, I've had a great deal of trouble sleeping. Consequently, I find myself wide awake at the most ridiculous hours."

"Was that the case last night?" the inspector asked.

"Very much so," she sighed. "I awoke at half past four this morning. I know exactly what time it was because I got up and looked at the clock. Well, of course one can't wake their servants up at such an awful hour, so I put on my robe and decided to go downstairs for a cup of tea. I was just coming down the front stairs when I heard someone outside in the street."

"Heard someone?" Witherspoon frowned. "Precisely how? Did you hear a hansom?"

"I heard footsteps," she said. "It's extraordinary how quiet it is at that hour of the morning."

"Yes, ma'am," Witherspoon agreed slowly. "Er . . . uh, it is very quiet at that time of the morning."

"You don't understand," she said impatiently. "I didn't make that comment as an idle observation, Inspector. I made it because it is quite pertinent to your case."

"Pertinent," Witherspoon echoed. "Yes, yes, I'm sure it is." He was rather puzzled. "But are you positive it was half past four when you heard these footsteps?"

"The very latest it could have been was four thirty-five," she said firmly. "It doesn't take long to don a robe and come down one flight of stairs."

"I'm sure it doesn't," he replied quickly. "I'm not disputing your word, ma'am. I'm merely making certain I understand you completely."

"You're not asking the right questions, sir," she admonished. "Aren't you at all curious as to why I think those footsteps are pertinent?"

"I was just getting ready to ask that," he said.

"Good, because if you must know, I'm quite sure the footsteps must have been those of the killer." She leaned forward eagerly. "You see, the reason I made the remark about the quiet is because whoever was walking by the front door took care to be as quiet as possible. But they couldn't mask their footsteps completely, and I heard them."

Witherspoon thought he understood what she was saying. "You mean you think they were taking care not to make any noise."

"Whoever it was out there was creeping about on his tiptoes," she said.

"How can you be sure of that, ma'am?" Barnes asked curiously.

"Because I don't sleep much," she said bluntly. "And I've heard all manner of people go by outside at night. Whoever was out there early this morning was deliberately trying to be quiet. And not because they were being considerate of their neighbors, either, but because they had murder in their hearts. Believe me, I know what I'm talking about. There's plenty of people around here who don't give a toss for whether or not they're disturbing their neighbors."

The inspector wasn't quite sure how to take this sort of evidence. He didn't wish to offend the lady, but he couldn't quite see how she could be so sure about the sound of footsteps. Still, his "inner voice," the one that Mrs. Jeffries always assured him would keep him on track, was telling him not to discount this lightly.

His consternation must have shown on his face because Mrs. Baldridge suddenly sighed. "Inspector, I can imagine what you've heard about me. But I assure you, I'm neither an hysteric nor a shrew."

"Really, ma'am," Witherspoon blustered. "Such a thought never crossed my mind."

"Let us be frank, Inspector." She waved her hand dismissively. "I'm sure you've heard all about the garden key incident. But I only tossed it at Mr. Heckston because he was making such a fool of himself."

"Not because of the hollyhocks?" Barnes asked.

"Certainly not." She grinned broadly. "I don't care what kind of flowers they plant in that stupid garden. I was only fed up because Mrs. Prosper snidely remarked they were 'common' when I suggested them. Well, really.

Who on earth did she think she was fooling? The woman was nothing more than a lady's maid before she married Eldon Prosper, and of course that love-struck fool Heckston agreed with her."

"Her name was Mirabelle Daws," Smythe said softly, "and this was her first visit to England. She come in on the *Island Star*, and that only come into port late yesterday afternoon."

"Which port?" Hatchet asked quickly.

"Southampton," Smythe replied. "Miss Daws took the last train up last night. It was supposed to arrive at the station at midnight, but there was some trouble on the line and it didn't get in till half past three. That was where the cabbie picked her up. He didn't want to take her all the way over to Sheridan Square, but she offered to pay him double, being as it was in the middle of the night."

"Gracious, you've learned far more than we'd hoped," Mrs. Jeffries said.

Smythe grinned. "The cabbie were a bit of a talker but more importantly, so was Miss Daws. Seems she told him what she thought of British trains, British ships and British weather before she even got into the hansom. Didn't like us much, that was fer certain. But that's 'ow come he came to know the name of the ship and all. She was goin' on a mile a minute about the ship being late, the train bein' late and the air smellin' to 'igh 'eaven." He suddenly sobered. "I know we've learned a lot. Now I want to know 'ow we're goin' to get this information to the inspector. It's not like you can drop a few 'ints and 'ave 'im suss out what you're goin' on about."

"I know," Mrs. Jeffries murmured thoughtfully. "We do seem to have a problem. But we'll think of something; we always do. In the meantime, there's no time to lose." She hesitated for a brief moment. "I know it's late, but do you think you can take the carriage and get to Southampton tonight? I think it's imperative that we find out who else might have been on that ship with Mirabelle Daws."

"That's not goin' to be easy," Luty put in. "The ship come in yesterday. Most people don't hang around that long. They git on about their business and go home."

"But the crew's still there," Hatchet said gleefully. "Surely there's a porter or a steward who'll be able to help us." He rose to his feet. "If it's all right with madam, I'd like to accompany Smythe. The two of us can cover far more territory together than apart."

Luty snorted derisively. "Since when have you ever asked my permission to do anything? But I'd like to go with ya . . ." her voice trailed off as everyone at the table protested at the same time. She glared at all of them. "You all think I'm too old to be gallavantin' out at night having adventures, do ya?"

"No, Luty, of course not," Mrs. Jeffries said soothingly. But, of course, that's precisely what they thought. "We simply think you'd better stay here and help the rest of us come up with a plausible way to get the information we received to the inspector. You've a much better imagination than I have. All I can come up with is the same silly old idea I always have, an anonymous note."

Luty eyed the housekeeper suspicously for a few moments. "You sure you ain't just sayin' that cause you think I'm too old?"

"We're all gettin' old," Mrs. Goodge interrupted. "But that's not why we want you to stay. Like Mrs. Jeffries says, we've got some hard thinkin' to do, and your mind is sharp as one of my best kitchen knives. Now sit down, drink your tea and let's get these men out of here so we women can have a good think on how to get us out of this mess. And don't think it's not a right old mess, because it is. We're honor bound to give the inspector the woman's name, but I, for one, don't want him gettin' any more suspicious about us than he already is."

"Does that mean I ought to go too?" Wiggins asked eagerly. "I'm one of the men. With the three of us, we could cover even more territory."

"I reckon I ought to stay then." Luty leaned back in her chair. "I do have an idea or two about how we can let the inspector know who the woman was. Like Mrs. Goodge says, we don't want him gettin' any ideas about us. No offense meant, Hepzibah, but you're right, that anonymous note trick is wearin' thin."

They'd used it several times before in their investigations, so Mrs. Jeffries could hardly take offense.

Smythe rose to his feet. "Which carriage should we take? Ours or Luty's?"

"Take mine," Luty said quickly. "I can always get a hansom home. That'll save you havin' to go over to Howards and gettin' your own livery out."

"Can I go too?" Wiggins asked again as he got up. "I really think I ought to; I am one of the men." Fred, seeing his beloved Wiggins move, uncurled himself from his comfortable spot on the rug and trotted over to the footman.

"How are they going to find out anything?" Betsy asked. "By the time they get down there, it'll be late at night."

"Don't worry about that, Miss Betsy," Hatchet said cheerfully. "It'll not take all that long to reach our destination. There's a train at six for Southampton and once we're there, I've an idea finding out which pub the ship's crew hangs about is going to be easy."

"But I thought we was goin' to take the carriage," Wiggins said.

Hatchet shook his head. "We'll take the carriage to the station. The train's much faster than even the madam's fine team of horses."

"What if the ship has already sailed?" Luty asked. "What then?"

"She won't have sailed," Smythe said confidently. "I've taken ships between here and Australia. They always need at least two days portside to take on provisions and make repairs. It's a hard trip."

Betsy's eyes narrowed. "Exactly how many times have you done it, then?" He'd only mentioned one trip to Australia.

"Three, maybe four times," he answered honestly, thinking she was doubting his knowledge of the ships' port time. It was only when he saw her jaw drop that he realized what he'd just let slip. "I've told you about my trips to Australia," he said. He had a horrible feeling in the pit of his stomach.

"You most certainly have not," she shot back, "and considerin' how much we talk, I'm surprised all your world traveling hasn't come up in the conversation."

Smythe could have kicked himself for being so stupid. He'd not mentioned the last couple of trips to Australia because he'd not wanted to tell her the reason he'd made them. Mainly, to check on his rather substantial holdings in that country.

"They really ought to get going right away," Mrs. Jeffries interjected. She could tell by the expression on Betsy's face that a real storm was in the making. But the lass would just have to hold her peace until she and the coachman could be alone together. Besides, Mrs. Jeffries rather suspected she knew the reason Smythe hadn't mentioned his other trips to Australia.

"Do I get to go?" Wiggins asked for the third time. "And Fred too?"

"You can come, but not the dog," Smythe said as he edged toward the back door. "The inspector will want to know where he is when he comes home. You know he likes to take him for a walk before he goes to bed." He was watching Betsy as he made his way across the room. Cor blimey, the lass was boiling. Maybe when he had a moment or two, he'd tell her the truth. But just as quickly, he decided maybe he wouldn't. He loved Betsy too much to risk losing her over the lie he was living.

"You will be careful going home, madam," Hatchet said as he trotted after Smythe. Wiggins was right on his heels.

"You worry about yerself, Hatchet," she snapped. "I may be old, but I can still take care of myself."

"I don't doubt it for a moment, madam."

"Stay, Fred," Wiggins told the dog. "Smythe's right, the inspector will want to take you walkies when he gets home."

"I'm not sure what time we'll be back," Smythe said. "But don't wait up for us." With that, they disappeared down the hall.

"We won't," Betsy yelled. She turned to the housekeeper. "Who does he think he is? Even if they take the ruddy train, they'll not be back until tomorrow. What are we going to tell the inspector?"

"We'll tell him that Smythe took the horses for a good, long run and that he took Wiggins with him." Mrs. Jeffries was fairly sure Inspector Witherspoon wouldn't notice his footman and coachman were gone. Not when he was in the middle of murder investigation. "Now, I think we'd better put our heads together and decide how we can tell him who the victim was."

"I know what we should do," Luty stated. She picked up her teacup and took a dainty sip. "And I must say, I think it's right imaginative."

"Are you goin' to tell us, then?" Mrs. Goodge demanded. She was a bit put out that the victim was such a nobody, and a foreign nobody at that. She'd be hard put to contribute much to this investigation.

"Course I'm goin' to tell ya. We're in this together, ain't we?" She took another sip of tea. "I know exactly how we'll tell the inspector."

"How?" Betsy demanded. She was in a bit of testy mood herself.

"We'll send him a telegram."

"A telegram?" Mrs. Jeffries said with a puzzled frown. "I'm afraid I don't see how that would be all that different than sending him an anonymous note."

"Sure it would," Luty stated flatly. "Cause this won't be anonymous. We'll sign it. We just won't use our own names."

"I must say, the house is very quiet this evening," Witherspoon said as he picked up the glass of sherry his housekeeper had so thoughtfully had poured and waiting for him when he arrived home.

"That it is, sir. There's only you, me and Mrs. Goodge here. We weren't sure what your schedule might be, sir," she said. She gave an embarrassed shrug. "I'm afraid that Smythe and Wiggins had planned on taking the horses out for a long run and, well, they weren't sure whether or not you'd need them, so they went ahead with their plans. I do hope you don't mind, sir. I don't expect them back until late tonight."

"They didn't take Fred, did they?" Witherspoon asked quickly. He did look forward to his nightly walk with the dog. Especially as he and Lady Cannonberry generally used that time to have a few moments alone together.

"Of course not, sir." Mrs. Jeffries smiled. "Fred would be very put out if he missed his evening walkies, sir. You know how devoted the animal is to you."

"Oh, Fred likes everyone." He frowned suddenly. "Uh, where is Betsy? She didn't go with them, did she? I know that she and Smythe seem to have some sort of an understanding, but I don't think we ought to . . . uh . . . you know . . . uh . . ."

"Betsy has accompanied Luty Belle home in a hansom cab. She'll be back shortly, sir."

Witherspoon blushed. "Er, I didn't mean to imply anything untoward about Betsy and Smythe. It's just that I feel responsible for the girl . . . not that Smythe would ever do anything dishonorable . . . oh dear, I'm not very good at this sort of thing, am I?"

Mrs. Jeffries knew precisely what he meant. "On the contrary, sir. You're excellent at it, sir."

"You're most kind, Mrs. Jeffries," he sighed. "I must admit, I do wish that Smythe would get on with it. I think we could all sleep a good deal better if he'd just make his intentions clear to us all. I'm sure he wants to marry Betsy."

"I'm sure he will marry her," she replied. "Eventually. But I don't think that either of them is in any hurry." She really didn't want to discuss

Smythe and Betsy's courtship. She wanted to talk about the murder. "How did your investigation go today, sir? Was it dreadful?"

"Oh, not as awful as it could have been." He made a face and took another quick sip of sherry. "The poor woman had been stabbed in the back. But it wasn't as messy as some I've seen."

"Do you have any idea of why she was killed?"

"None at all."

"Were there any witnesses, sir?"

"Not really," he sighed again. "Though we do have two people who heard some unusual activity last night. I say, Mrs. Jeffries, it's the oddest thing. I don't quite know what to make of it."

"Oh, do tell me, sir," she pleaded with a smile. "You know how interested I am in your cases."

He smiled happily. It was always such a relief to talk his cases out. It always gave him a new perspective on the crime. "Let's see, where should I begin?"

"Why don't you tell me what you thought was so odd, sir?" she suggested. "I'm terribly curious."

"Good idea." He reached for his glass again. "You know the victim was found in Sheridan Square. That's quite a nice area. Rather expensive and large houses. There's only seven residences around the square, and what was odd was that we had someone from a house at each end of the square hear something early this morning."

"What did they hear, sir?"

"Mrs. Baldridge—she lives at number one, that's at one end of the square—claims she heard someone creeping by her windows early in the morning. Yet we've evidence from Mrs. McCabe, who lives at the other end of the square, that she heard a hansom come into the square a good half hour after Mrs. Baldridge swears she heard footsteps. It's most mystifying."

Mrs. Jeffries didn't find it in the least mystifying. "How so, sir?"

"I'm not sure," he muttered, "it just is. I mean, was it the killer creeping about at half past four, and or was it the victim?"

"I should think it was the killer," Mrs. Jeffries said firmly. "Why would the victim try to be quiet? By the way, have you any idea who the poor woman might be?"

"No," he sighed again. "We haven't a clue. I tell you, it's all very, very, confusing."

"It's always confusing in the beginning, sir," she said stoutly. "But you know how very, very good you are at solving murders, sir. You'll catch the killer in the end. You always do."

"It's reassuring that you have such faith in my abilities," he said sofly. "But sometimes I doubt myself."

"Nonsense, sir. You should never doubt yourself."

"Thank you, Mrs. Jeffries." He smiled. "I must admit, it does help to talk about it. You know, the people on that square were a tad uncooperative. You'd think they'd do everything they could to help us solve this case, especially as it was right on their own doorstep, so to speak."

"Indeed, you would, sir," she agreed.

He continued talking about the murder. Mrs. Jeffries occasionally clucked her tongue or asked a question. By the time he'd finished his sherry, he'd told her every little detail about the crime.

"You must have had quite a day, sir," she commented, when it was apparent he'd told her everything he knew. "I expect you'd like your dinner now."

"Oh yes, I am a bit hungry." He got up and started for the dining room. "What's Mrs. Goodge laid on for us this evening?"

"Lancashire hot pot, sir." She followed him out into the hall, "and there's lemon tarts for dessert, sir."

They were almost at the dining room when there was a loud knock on the front door. Mrs. Jeffries turned and started in that direction.

"No, Mrs. Jeffries." Witherspoon gently pulled her back. "This time of night I don't want you or Betsy answering the door."

"It's not that late, sir," she protested.

"Nevertheless, I'd feel better if you let me get it." With that, he marched down the hall and threw open the front door.

"Telegram for Inspector Witherspoon, sir," a young lad in a messenger's uniform said.

"I'm Inspector Witherspoon." He reached for the pale brown envelope the boy held out. "Thank you," he said as he took the telegram in one hand and reached in his trouser pocket with the other. Withdrawing a coin, he handed it to the lad. "For your trouble."

"Thank you, sir," the boy said as he pocketed the money.

Witherspoon closed the door and stared at the envelope as though he'd never seen one before.

"Aren't you going to open it, sir?" Mrs. Jeffries asked.

"Oh, yes, I suppose I ought to." The inspector grinned sheepishly and tore it open. Taking out the slender, thin yellow paper, he read it quickly. His eyebrows rose, and Mrs. Jeffries noticed he read the page again. "Good gracious," he exclaimed. "This is most extraordinary. Most extraordinary, indeed."

"What is it, sir?"

"Let me read it to you. 'Dear Inspector,'" he read, " 'The woman who was stabbed in Sheridan Square is one Miss Mirabelle Daws. She arrived from Australia yesterday evening on a ship called the *Island Star.*'"

"Goodness, sir, that is extraordinary." Mrs. Jeffries wondered if it were Betsy's or Luty's idea to provide the name of the vessel. She wasn't sure they ought to have given so much away, but it wasn't her plan. "Who is it from?"

"That's extraordinary as well." He shook his head. "I've no idea."

"You mean it's unsigned?"

"It's signed; it's just I've never heard of this person." He shook his head and glanced back at the message. "It's signed, 'Your humble servant, Rollo Puffy.'"

"And you've no idea who he is?" she asked. Really, where did Luty come up with these strange names?

"I've no idea. No idea at all."

"You're certain, sir?" She pressed. She wanted to make sure there wasn't a real Rollo Puffy out and about somewhere in London. Occasionally, Luty's sense of humor overcame her good sense.

"Absolutely, Mrs. Jeffries," he insisted. "I don't think I'd ever forget meeting someone with a name like that."

CHAPTER 4

The next morning, Betsy was still furious. She ignored the admiring glances of the young lad sweeping the sidewalk in front of the fishmonger and charged toward her destination, a grocer on the far corner. She wasn't on Sheridan Square, but the nearest shopping street to it. She was determined to have something useful to tell the others this afternoon.

When Smythe—she kicked a small pebble out of her way—finally took it into his head to come home today, she wanted to make damned sure she had something better to report than he did.

She dodged around a fruit-loaded hand cart blocking the pavement in front of a greengrocer and kept on walking. She might as well see what the shopkeepers had to say. At least now she had a name.

It wasn't simply rivalry that had prompted her to leave the house so early this morning in search of clues. Yesterday she'd been deeply, deeply hurt. She'd been so sure she and Smythe were coming to an understanding, had truly gotten to know each other. She'd told him things about herself she'd never shared with anyone, and he, the ruddy sod, hadn't bothered to tell her a blooming thing. Though that wasn't quite true, she was in no mood to be fair.

Luckily, by the time she arrived at the grocer's she'd walked some of her anger off. Pulling open the door, she stepped inside. As it was just past opening, she was the only customer in the place.

"Can I help you, miss?" a thin-faced young man said from behind the counter.

"Yes, thank you." Betsy gave him her most dazzling smile. "I'd like a tin of Bird's Custard Powder, Epps Cocoa and some Adam's Furniture Polish, if you have it."

"We've all those things, Miss." He blushed deeply. "I'll get them for you."

In a few moments, the items she'd ordered were on the counter in front of her. "I say, isn't it awful about that poor woman they found murdered over on Sheridan Square?"

"It's dreadful, miss. Right dreadful." He tallied up the bill on a sheet of brown paper. "We don't often get things like that in this neighborhood. Well, you can see by the houses and such it's a very nice area."

"I hear she was stabbed clean throught the heart," Betsy continued. "Poor Miss Daws, she simply didn't stand a chance, did she? Not with someone out to murder her."

He looked up from his figures. "Daws?" he repeated.

"Yes," Betsy said quickly. "I heard it was a lady named Mirabelle Daws . . ."

"I'm afraid you must be mistaken." He shook his head. "Awful isn't it, how people simply don't get things right?"

"What do you mean?" she demanded.

"Well." He dropped his pencil onto the countertop. "There was a Miss Annabelle Daws in this neighborhood . . ."

"Is she dead too?"

"No, no, she's not dead, she's married. She's now Mrs. Eldon Prosper. She's also alive and well, so I don't think she could be the woman who was murdered."

Betsy stared at him so hard that he blushed again.

"I'm sorry, I didn't mean to sound so . . ."

"Don't apolgize." She gave him that dazzling smile again. She'd struck gold. "It's I who should be apologizing to you. I must say, you must be ever so clever to know so much about the people in your neighborhood."

"I'm not really very clever," he replied, "it's really my mum. She owns this place. She'd talk the hair off a dog, she would. She doesn't mind asking the most impertinent questions. A lot of housemaids and tweenies come in here, Mum talks them half to death before they can get what they're after an' make an escape. Mind you, she doesn't mean any harm, she simply likes to know about people. That's how come I know the name *Daws*. Mum knows everything about everyone around here."

Betsy dearly wished it was the mother standing in front of her and not the son. "Your mum sounds a right nice person," she said stoutly. "There's nothing wrong with wanting to know a bit about people, is there? It's natural, isn't it? Uh, is your mum going to be here anytime soon?"

"Nah, she's gone to Cheshire to visit my gran." He shrugged. "She'll not be back till next week."

"That's too bad," she said. She clucked sympathetically. "It must be lonely for you, all on your own."

"Well, it is a bit," he admitted. "You get used to having a bit of company."

"Maybe I ought to hang about awhile and talk to you," she offered. "After all, it's not like you've got much business this morning, is it?"

"I've never heard of Rollo Puffy either," Barnes admitted. He handed the inspector back the telegram. "But at least we've got the victim's name now. That's a good place to start."

"If it's the right name," the inspector replied.

"Well, sir, it's the only one we've got," the constable pointed out. "So we might as well ask about if anyone's heard of the woman."

"Of course, Constable. Yet I can't help wondering if it might have been the killer who sent the message. I mean, who else could have known who the woman was? Why send a telegram? Why not, if one were innocent, simply come along to police and identify her?"

"I don't know, sir," Barnes said. He stopped in front of Malcolm Tavistock's house. "It's a puzzle. What did the telegraph office say? Could they remember who'd sent it?"

"Vaguely. I went along to there myself early this morning. The night clerk was just going off duty. But he remembered who sent the message. It was a street arab. A young lad came in with the money and the message already written out."

"Would the clerk be able to identify the boy?" Even as he asked the question, the constable knew the answer. Street arabs were thick as fleas on dogs in London.

Witherspoon shook his head. "No, boys come in all the time to send messages. The clerk doesn't even bother to look at them. He merely takes the money and sends the telegram. But perhaps now that we've a name, we'll be able to connect the woman with someone on the square."

"Let's hope so, sir," Barnes muttered. "Otherwise, we might have a devil of a time trying to locate all the passengers who came in with the woman on the *Island Star.*" He knocked on Tavistock's front door and announced his business to the maid. A few minutes later, he and the inspector were sitting in Tavistock's drawing room for the second time.

Malcolm, with Hector trotting at his heels, made his appearance a few moments later. "Good day, Inspector," he said politely, but he looked less than pleased to see them. "I do hope you've made some progress on the case. We'd like to be able to use our garden again. Was the gardener able to help you any with your inquiries? I must say, I never really liked the fellow, doesn't want to look you in the eye when he speaks, if you know what I mean."

Witherspoon pursed his lips in annoyance. Only yesterday Tavistock had virtually assured them that the gardener wasn't capable of murder. Now that he'd had a night to think it over, it had suddenly become far more likely that the murder was done by someone poor like Jonathan Siler rather than one of their own. He wasn't surprised that Tavistock was trying to cast suspicion on the man. He'd seen that trick done many times in his investigations. "Your gardener was most cooperative. Mr. Siler was at home when the crime was committed. He knew nothing about it."

"That's what he would say, isn't it?" Tavistock insisted.

"We've no reason not to believe him," Witherspoon continued. "Just as we've no reason not to believe you and the other residents of Sheridan Square. None of you, it seems, have any idea who the victim might have been. But he was able to confirm that there were only eight keys. His was safely in his possession."

Tavistock looked taken aback. "Well, really, what are you implying?"

"Nothing, sir." The inspector didn't have a lot of time to waste. He was going to have to talk to everyone in the square and possibly the entire neighborhood. Again. "We do have some more questions for you, sir. Have you ever heard of a woman named Mirabelle Daws?"

"Mirabelle Daws," Tavistock repeated. "Are you sure you don't mean Annabelle Daws? Daws was Mrs. Prosper's maiden name . . ." his voice trailed off and his jaw gaped. "Oh God, how awful. Of course, of course, Mrs. Prosper has a sister named Mirabelle. She lives in Australia."

"Are you sure, sir?" Barnes asked.

"Absolutely," Tavistock bobbed his head furiously. "I saw a letter from the woman a few months ago. I mean, I didn't read it, of course, I merely handed it back to Mrs. Prosper. She'd dropped it in the garden."

"How did you know who it was from?" Witherspoon asked. "If you didn't look at it?"

"The signature on the bottom was quite visible when I handed it to Mrs. Prosper. When I realized the name was so similar to her Christian name, I commented upon the matter, and she said the letter was from her sister in Sydney."

"Exactly when was this?" Witherspoon asked. He wondered if the sister might have mentioned a forthcoming trip to England.

Tavistock's brows drew together as he concentrated. "Let me see, I think it must have been no more than two months ago. It was in March."

"You're certain, sir?"

"Of course I am. There were several of us in the garden that day. Mrs. Prosper, Mr. Heckston and myself. We chatted about how mild the weather was for March. The letter had slipped out of Mrs. Prosper's pocket. I found it under the bench, the one in the center . . ." His voice trailed off when he realized what he was saying.

"The one where the victim was found stabbed?" Barnes finished.

Tavistock shook his head sadly. "Poor woman. Not much of a welcome to England, is it?"

Barnes and Witherspoon exchanged a glance. "Did you know that Mrs. Prosper's sister was coming for a visit?"

"No, no, I didn't."

"What do you think, sir?" Barnes asked as they started toward the Prosper house.

"I don't know what to think," he admitted. "Surely Miss Daws would have let her sister know that she was coming . . ."

"Inspector Witherspoon," a voice called from behind them.

They turned to see Mr. Heckston hurrying toward them. He doffed his hat politely. "I thought you ought to know that I've found that key that had gone missing."

"Really, where was it, sir?" Witherspoon said. In truth, he'd actually forgotten about the missing key.

"It was on the floor, Inspector." Heckston shrugged in embarrassment. "The maid must have knocked it off when she was dusting, and it got wedged in between the carpet and floorboards. She found it today when she was sweeping. I am sorry I didn't look more carefully when you were there."

"No harm done, sir. At least we know where all the keys are now," the inspector replied. He was actually quite pleased. Knowing that all the keys were accounted for narrowed the range of suspects. But then again, he thought, as they now knew the victim had a relationship with one of the residents here, it was already narrowed quite a bit.

"Well, I'll be off, sir." He nodded at the two men. "I've a lot to do today."

"Before you leave, sir," Witherspoon said, "may I ask you a question?"

"Certainly." Heckston said politely.

"Are you acquainted with Mrs. Prosper, sir? I mean, are you more than neighbors?" The moment the words left his mouth, he realized he'd been very indelicate. Judging by Heckston's ominous frown, he'd found it indelicate as well. "I am sorry," Witherspoon amended. "I didn't mean that quite the way it sounded. I do need to know if you're acquainted enough with Mrs. Prosper to verify that she has a sister. It's quite important that we know."

Heckston's expression changed from anger to surprise to shock as he realized the implication of the question. "Good Lord, I do hope this doesn't mean what I think it does." He swallowed. "I'm well acquainted with Mr. and Mrs. Prosper. As is my wife. Mrs. Prosper does have a sister. An older sister named Mirabelle."

"Does that sister live in Australia?" Barnes asked. He always liked to double-check his facts.

Heckston nodded.

Witherspoon's expression was somber. "Then I'm afraid we may have some very bad news for Mrs. Prosper. Is Mr. Prosper home?"

"Yes, I think so." Heckston closed his eyes briefly, then looked sympathetically at the Prosper house. "Poor Mrs. Prosper. This will come as a dreadful shock. Absolutely dreadful. She was very fond of her sister." He began to back away. "Perhaps I ought to let you get on with it, sir. If you need to speak with me again, I'll be home later this afternoon."

As soon as the man had cleared off, the inspector looked at Barnes. "I suppose we'd better go and talk with Mrs. Prosper."

"Are you going to ask her to look at the body?" Barnes asked as they started walking.

"I'm afraid I don't have a choice," the inspector replied. "That may be the only way we can possibly have the woman identified."

"Did Betsy say where she was goin'?" Smythe asked anxiously.

Mrs. Jeffries shook her head. "Not really, only that she had a few things she needed to do this morning. She told us to go ahead and have our meeting."

Smythe started to ask another question, then realized it would be useless. He'd just have to wait till the lass came home to make his peace with her. But cor blimey, he'd not thought it was that big a sin he'd committed. So he'd never told her about all his trips to Australia. He'd told her about one of them. But he knew why she was hurt. She'd told him everything about her own past. A past that had been pretty grim in parts too, and here he was, keeping secrets.

"Can we go ahead and talk, then?" Wiggins wanted to know. "We learned ever so much."

"I'll just bet ya did," Luty muttered. She gave Hatchet a good glare and picked up her teacup.

"Being childish is most unbecoming, madam," Hatchet chided.

"Being pompous isn't very becomin', either," Luty shot back.

"Were you able to figure out 'ow to let the inspector know the poor murdered lady's name?" Wiggins asked quickly.

"Luty came up with an excellent idea," Mrs. Jeffries replied. "We sent him a telegram . . ."

"A telegram?" Hatchet said increadulously.

"From Rollo Puffy," Luty snickered at the gasp of indignation that escaped her butler. "You remember him, don't ya?"

Hatchet's eyes narrowed. "Of course I remember him, madam."

"Who's Rollo Puffy?" Wiggins asked, "and why is 'e sendin' the inspector a telegram?"

"He's not," Mrs. Goodge said impatiently. "We are. We just used his name. Now can we get on with it?"

"That's a good idea," Mrs. Jeffries interjected quickly. It was obvious from the smug expression on Luty's face that she'd deliberately picked this particular name to annoy her butler. Later, perhaps, the women would get the entire story, but for right now, they'd best get a move on. "Do tell us what you've learned."

"It were right easy," Wiggins said. "We got to Southampton, lickety-split and then we found a pub where some of the ship's crew 'ung about. The *Island Star* was still there. She's not due to sail for another two days." He paused and took a quick sip of tea. "Anyways, at first we didn't have much luck. Mainly we only found workers from below decks. Then Hatchet 'ere," he nodded toward the butler, "'e cornered a couple of stewards who knew all about Miss Daws. Seems the lady weren't exactly shy. She talked to anyone who'd stand still and listen to 'er."

"All ya talked to was a couple of stewards?" Luty asked.

"That was quite sufficient, madam," Hatchet sniffed. "Not only were they able to tell us quite a bit about the deceased, but they also supplied us with several names of other passengers who'd talked at length with the deceased."

"What, precisely, did you learn?" Mrs. Jeffries asked. Honestly, between Smythe's long-faced silence over Betsy, Luty and Hatchet's sniping at each other, and Wiggins gushing enthusiasm, they weren't getting anywhere.

"For starters," Smythe said glumly, "We found out how the victim is connected to Sheridan Square. Mirabelle Daws is the sister to Mrs. Eldon Prosper."

"Very good work, gentleman," Mrs. Jeffries said. Now they were starting to get somewhere. "At least now we know where to focus our investigation. Odd that she didn't tell the inspector her sister was expected and hadn't arrived."

"It gets even stranger," he said. "Mirabelle Daws told everyone aboard the ship that the family's fortunes had changed and they'd never have to serve anyone again."

"Serve anyone?" Mrs. Goodge said. "How do you mean?"

"It seems the family was in service," Hatchet explained. "Mirabelle Daws ran a boardinghouse out in the outback, and her sister Annabelle was a lady's maid. At least, Annabelle had been one before she'd married Eldon Prosper. Apparently, though, their brother, Andrew Daws, had struck it rich in mining. Mirabelle supposedly wore a rope of opals around her neck that she never took off."

"How very curious," Mrs. Jeffries murmured. "There wasn't any jewelry found on her when she was killed. Perhaps this will turn out to be a simple robbery after all."

"If it were just a simple robbery," Mrs. Goodge pointed out, "why go to all the trouble of lockin' the woman in that garden? Like we discussed before, that took some doing." She shook her head vehemently. "It weren't no robbery. It were murder and whoever done it couldn't resist pinching the opals. How much would they be worth?"

"A lot," Smythe said bluntly. "It weren't just opals on this necklace. There were diamonds, too, and accordin' to what the stewards said, the two center ones were bigger than currants. I'd say Mirabelle Daws was wearing a fortune around her neck and the silly woman let herself be lured out in the middle of the night to meet her killer."

"Lured?" Mrs. Goodge repeated. "How do you know that? She might have been forced out."

"I hardly think so ma'am," Hatchet said. "From what we learned of Miss Daws, the only way she could have been forced to do anything would have been at gunpoint. She left the vessel of her own free will."

"What time was this?" Mrs. Goodge asked.

"An hour after the vessel docked," Hatchet replied. "That would have been around six in the evening the night that she was murdered."

"So she got from Southampton to Sheridan Square in the space of what, ten hours?" Mrs. Jeffries drummed her fingers lightly against the tabletop. "How? And where is her luggage?"

"We don't know," Smythe admitted. "Not yet anyway. And I didn't think to ask that cabbie I talked to if she had any when he picked her up."

"We'll find out," Luty said confidently. "We always do. Now what were those names you fellers got hold of? Come on, give. The rest of us want somethin' to do here."

Hatchet nodded. "Miss Daws was supposedly quite friendly with a woman named Judith Brinkman. She lives in a small village named Boreham outside of Chelmsford. She ought to be easy enough to find."

"The other one she were well acquainted with was a young man named Oscar Denton," Wiggins offered. "He'll be easy to find as well; he lives over the family business. An estate agency over on Cormand Lane near Bond Street."

"Gracious, you have done very well indeed," Mrs. Jeffries said. In truth, she wasn't quite sure what to do next. They'd gone from having no clues to having almost more than they could cope with.

"That's not all," Smythe said. "We got the names of a couple of other people who were hangin' about the woman as well. Lady Henrietta Morland and her butler were all over her, accordin' to the stewards. We ought to look them up too."

"You're back, Inspector." Mrs. Prosper didn't look pleased at the sight of the two policemen sitting in her drawing room.

Witherspoon and Barnes both rose to their feet. Neither man looked forward to what they had to do next. "Yes, I'm afraid we are. Uh, Mrs. Prosper, is your husband at home?"

"He's in his study. I've already called him," she said calmly. "Was there some reason you needed to speak with him? He wasn't even here the night that poor woman was killed."

"We know, ma'am," the inspector replied. He broke off as the door opened and a tall, slender gentleman of late middle age came into the room.

"Good day, sirs, I'm Eldon Prosper." His face was long and bony, his eyes a pale gray and his hair, what there was left of it, heavily sprinkled with gray.

The inspector introduced himself and his constable. "We wanted you to be here, sir, because we may have some very unfortunate news for your wife."

"Unfortunate?" Prosper said. "I don't understand?"

"Do you have a sister, Mrs. Prosper?" Constable Barnes asked. She looked puzzled. "A sister. Yes, I do, but she lives in Australia."

"You weren't expecting her for a visit?" Witherspoon prodded. He wanted to make sure he got this part perfectly clear. It could have a great deal of bearing on the case.

"Not in the immediate future," Mrs. Prosper replied. "Why? What on earth are you getting at?"

"I'm afraid we've reason to believe that the woman . . . uh . . . we think perhaps that the victim found in Sheridan Square might have been Miss Mirabelle Daws."

Stunned, Annabelle Prosper gaped at them for a few moments. "That's impossible. My sister is in Australia. What would she be doing in Sheridan Square? I'd have known if she was here."

"Nevertheless," the inspector insisted. "We must ask you to accompany us . . ."

"For God's sake, man," Eldon Prosper exclaimed. "Even if that dead woman is Mirabelle, you've no reason to arrest my wife."

"We're not arresting her, sir, we're asking her to accompany us to the hospital morgue," Witherspoon explained. "We do need a positive identification."

Mrs. Prosper had gone completely pale. "This is absurd. I tell you my sister is in Australia."

"But we'd best go with them, dearest," Prosper said gently. He patted his wife's arm. "We must make sure."

She looked at the hand on her arm and then slowly raised her eyes to meet her husband's gaze. "Of course, Eldon," she murmured. "I suppose I'd better go with them. But my sister is in Australia. This is all a mistake."

"If you think it'll be too difficult, ma'am," Witherspoon said, "we have contacted the shipping company. They're sending over the ship's purser. He could identify the victim if you think you'll be unable to face it."

"The ship's purser?" she muttered. "What ship?"

Witherspoon felt terribly sorry for the poor woman. She looked absolutely dazed. "From the *Island Star*, ma'am. We think that's the vessel your sister took from Australia to England. Luckily, the ship hasn't sailed yet."

"I see," she murmured. She took a long, deep breath and stared off blindly through the front window.

"Shall I call for your maid or Marlena?" Eldon Prosper asked his wife anxiously. "Would you like one of them to accompany us?"

She straightened her spine and took another slow, deep breath and then stepped away from him. "That won't be necessary. I'm quite all right. Wait here and I'll be right back. I'll just get my things."

As soon as she'd left, Prosper turned and glared at the two policemen. "This is unspeakably cruel. I'll not have my wife upset."

"We're not doing it deliberately, sir," Witherspoon pointed out. "And we did give your wife an alternative to actually viewing the body. The ship's purser can identify Mirabelle Daws."

"Even if this woman is Mirabelle Daws," Prosper shot back. "It could well be nothing more than a coincidence of names, sir."

Witherspoon hadn't thought of that. "Yes, I suppose it could," he mumbled. "But two women, both of them from Australia and both of them having the name Daws?"

"Mirabelle is quite an unusual name, though. Isn't it?" Barnes said softly.

Prosper clamped his mouth shut and said nothing else until Mrs. Prosper, now wearing a blue hat with a midnight blue veil, gloves and carrying a dark green parasol, returned to the drawing room. "Shall we go, gentlemen? I'd really like to get this over with."

"Mrs. Prosper did quite a bit better than her husband," Barnes said as he and Witherspoon came out of the mortuary at St. Thomas's hospital. "For a few minutes there it looked like he might bring up his breakfast."

"I don't blame the poor fellow," the inspector said. He stopped and took in several large gulps of air. "It really was quite awful. I don't see how you and the medical people are able to stand these sort of places."

"Well, sir, I don't have much of a sense of smell." Barnes grinned. His inspector really was quite a squeamish sort, not that it kept him from doing his duty, it didn't. That made the constable admire Witherspoon even more. It was hard facing things that literally made you sick to your stomach. But the inspector did it without complaint. "Makes it easier when you don't smell the place. I think that's how some of the doctors do it, too. Old Doctor Potter once admitted to me he couldn't smell much. Not that he was much of a doctor. I'm glad you had Mrs. Prosper come in to identify the body, sir. I'd have felt uneasy relying only upon the purser's identification. Not that I think the fellow is lying, but only to make sure we'd actually got Mrs. Prosper's sister and not just someone using her name."

Witherspoon nodded his agreement. "Yes, er, quite. Do you think she's telling the truth?"

"About it bein' her sister," Barnes asked. "Why, yes, sir, I do. At first I thought she was a real cold woman, but the way she hung back and couldn't hardly make herself set foot in the viewing room got me to thinking that maybe I was wrong. It was hard for the lady, sir."

"It was hard for the purser, and he wasn't even related to Miss Daws," Witherspoon pointed out. "He was quite green about the gills himself."

They'd seen the purser leaving with a police constable as they were approaching the mortuary room. After escorting the man to the street and putting him in a hansom, the constable had come back and confirmed the purser's identification of the victim.

Barnes chuckled. "You'd think a seaman would have a stronger stomach, wouldn't you, sir? But it just goes to show that there's no tellin' how dead bodies are goin' to affect people. By the way, while you were talking to Mrs. Prosper, Constable Edmunds slipped back and told me that if we needed the purser to give identification evidence in court, he'd be available.

He won't be sailing on the ship. The fellow's retiring to his family home in Chiswick."

"That's good to know, but I don't think we'll need him. Mrs. Prosper's evidence ought to be sufficient." Witherspoon sighed and stopped in the middle of the busy pavement. "I do wish I knew what to make of it all. Why on earth would a woman take it into her head to come halfway around the world and not even tell her family she was on her way? It simply doesn't make any sense."

Betsy dashed into the kitchen. She skidded to a halt when she saw that it was empty. "Drat," she mumbled. "And I've got ever so much to tell."

"Have ya now?" Smythe stepped out from the front hall and into view. He'd been waiting for her. "Well, I'm glad you've had such a good day, lass."

"Where is everybody?" she demanded with a frown.

"Out and about," he said easily. "Why don't we sit down? I'd like to 'ave a word with you."

"Mrs. Goodge isn't out and about," Betsy said. She moved towards the kitchen table, pulled out a chair and took a seat. She was still a bit miffed at the coachman, but she might as well sit down and rest her feet.

"She's out in the garden shelling peas," he said, taking the chair across from her. "She's got one of 'er sources lendin' a 'and."

"Where's Mrs. Jeffries and the others?"

"She's out doin' some snoopin' of her own," he replied. "Wiggins is up changin' his shirt and Luty and Hatchet are probably on their way 'ere as we speak. Everyone's meetin' 'ere in a few minutes."

"Good," she said flatly. "I've a lot to report. Maybe I ought to put the kettle on." She started to get up.

"Give it a minute," he ordered. "We need to talk. I've got somethin' important to tell you."

Starting at him, she sank back into her seat. "All right. Go ahead."

Smythe wasn't quite sure how to begin. But he knew he had to tell her the truth. If it changed her feelings for him, well, that was a risk he'd take. He cleared his throat. "Uh, I know you're a bit annoyed with me . . ."

"More than just a bit," she shot back. "Just so you'll know, Smythe, I'm furious. I've told you everything about myself, and you haven't returned the favor. I thought you'd only been to Australia the one time. But you've been a lot more than that."

"Not that many times," he said defensively, "but I'll admit to bein' a bit vague. But I had a reason, Betsy."

"What reason? It's not that I give a toss how many times you've gone. What hurt me was the fact that you'd not bothered to tell me at all, and I've told you everything." She broke off and looked away as her throat closed a bit.

Smythe's heart broke as he watched her struggle with her emotions. But he knew her well enough to know that if he reached out a hand to her, she might just tear off his arm. He'd hurt her badly and that was the last thing he'd ever wanted to do. "Betsy, I'm sorry, lass. You're right, you've trusted me with so much of your own life. I think it's time I trusted you with mine."

She dragged a deep breath into her lungs and turned to stare at him. "What do you mean by that?"

He decided to plunge straight in. "I've been to Australia five times. The first time I went there to make my fortune. The last four times I went was to check on my investments. I've also been to America a time or two for the same reason."

Betsy didn't say a word. She simply started at him. Finally, she said, "Smythe, are you sure you're feeling all right?"

It took a moment before he understood. She didn't believe him. "Cor blimey, Betsy, of course I'm all right. Do ya think I'm makin' this up?"

"No, no," she said quickly, "of course not. But perhaps you're exaggerating just a bit."

He was dumbfounded. Of all the reactions he'd expected her to have, this one had never occurred to him. "I'm not ruddy well exaggeratin'," he snapped. "No one goes on a long, borin' trip all the way to Australia for the bloomin' fun of it."

"No, but they do go for other reasons." She reached across the table and patted his arm. "Exactly when did these trips take place? I've known you for four years, and the longest I've ever seen you gone was a couple of days."

"I went in the three years before the inspector inherited this house from Euphemia," he yelled. Euphemia Witherspoon had been the inspector's aunt. She'd also been a special friend of the coachman's. She'd left this house and a fortune to her nephew. She'd also extracted a promise from Smythe.

"That's right." Betsy nodded. "You worked for Euphemia Witherspoon, didn't you? You and Wiggins."

"Originally, yes, I did," he was almost shouting now. "But I wasn't workin' for her when she died, and it's all because of a promise I made to her that I'm in this mess now."

"Promise, what promise?" Wiggins bounced into the kitchen. Fred was right on his heels.

"We'll continue this talk later," Smythe hissed. "I'd be obliged if you'd keep what I've told you to yourself."

"I'll not say a word." Betsy, who was quite enjoying herself now, giggled.

"Am I interruptin'?" the footman asked innocently. He pulled out a chair and flopped down.

"It's nothing important," the maid shot the coachman a cheeky grin. "Smythe was just telling me some interesting tales. Right imaginative ones they were, too."

CHAPTER 5

It was obvious to both the cook and the housekeeper that while Betsy's frame of mind was much improved since the morning, Smythe's had taken a turn for the worse. Mrs. Jeffries sighed silently and glanced at Mrs. Goodge, who shrugged. She took her place at the head of the table. There was nothing she could do to insure that the course of young love ran smooth. These two would have to work their troubles out for themselves.

"I'm glad we're all here on time," Mrs. Jeffries said briskly. "I've a feeling we've a lot to tell one another."

"I had the most interesting chat with a grocer's clerk this morning," Betsy said enthusiastically, "and I've found out how the murdered woman is connected with Sheridan Square."

"I know how the woman was connected," Mrs. Goodge said bluntly.

"So do I," said Luty.

"Me too, I'm afraid," Hatchet added.

"All of you know?" Betsy asked in exasperation.

"I'm afraid so, Betsy," Mrs. Jeffries said apologetically. "Once we had the name . . ."

"Yes, yes, I know." The maid waved her hand dismissively. "Once we had the name, finding out the connection was easy. But I bet you didn't know that that Annabelle Daws Prosper used to be a lady's maid."

Mrs. Jeffries winced guiltily.

Betsy gasped. "How did you find that out?"

"I had rather a long chat with a Miss Varsleigh. She's the housekeeper for Colonel Bartell, one of the other residents of Sheridan Square. I saw her leaving the Bartell residence and followed her. When she went into the

Lyons Tea Shop on Oxford Street, it seemed far too good an opportunity to miss. As a matter of fact, Betsy, we ought to bring you up to speed on what Hatchet, Smythe and Wiggins learned in Southampton. You missed this morning's meeting." Quickly and efficiently she told the maid what they'd learned.

"Oh?" Betsy frowned thoughtfully. "I see."

"What all did this Miss Varsleigh tell you?" Hatchet asked the housekeeper.

"Quite a bit, actually," Mrs. Jeffries mused. "I don't know how much of it is pertinent to our case, but she gave me an enormous earful regarding the Prosper family. But I really think we ought to let Betsy say her piece first, she was out awfully early this morning."

"Thank you," Betsy said. "As I was saying, I found out that Mrs. Prosper used to be a lady's maid when she lived in Australia."

"We know that," Wiggins said. "What we don't know is 'ow she end up bein' the mistress of that big 'ouse?"

"If you'll let me finish, you'll find out," she said tartly. "Mrs. Prosper worked for a family called Moulton before she married Mr. Prosper. No one knows how it happened, but Annabelle Daws, as she was then, started corresponding with Eldon Prosper. He'd made a fortune in copper and pipe fittings. He's got a factory up in Lancashire somewhere. But despite all his money and success, he was a lonely sort and wanted to get married . . ."

"Couldn't 'e find someone 'ere to marry 'im?" Wiggins asked.

"Apparently not," she snapped.

"But if 'e 'ad all this money and all," the lad protested. "Why'd 'e 'ave to bring someone all the way from Australia?"

"There could be any of a dozen reasons for his actions," Mrs. Jeffries said firmly. "Now do let Betsy finish."

"Thank you." Betsy nodded at the housekeeper. "As I was saying, after a year or so of regular correspondence, Eldon Prosper proposed to Annabelle Daws."

"Did he care that she was a maid?" Luty asked curiously. "Not that there's anything wrong with bein' a maid," she said quickly, "but you English put a lot of store in things like that. I guess I'm wondering why with all his money he wanted a woman that had to work fer her living?"

"That's a good question," Mrs. Jeffries said thoughtfully. She looked at Betsy. "Do you have an answer?"

"Actually." She smiled proudly, pleased that she'd had the foresight to find out the right information. "I do. Prosper wasn't born wealthy, and he's got plenty, but he's not so rich that he looks down his nose at them that's had to work. Besides, he was absolutely captivated by Annabelle's letters. He's supposedly a very sensitive man. He fell in love with her because they both shared a love of poetry and nature. She might have been a maid, but she is educated and can read and write. Apparently the Daws family fortunes tend to go up and down, and both the girls managed to get some education when times were good."

"That's what I heard too," Mrs. Goodge put in. "From my sources, that is. Prosper was besotted with her from the letters. But even when he proposed, it took a few months before she agreed to leave her family and come here to marry him."

"Really?" Betsy said. "I didn't know that part."

"I only know about it because my sources knew more about the family that Annabelle Daws worked for than they did about her," the cook replied.

"Would you like to explain that?" Luty demanded.

Mrs. Goodge reached for the teapot and poured herself a second cup. "Like the rest of you have found out, once we had the victim's name, the connection to Sheridan Square was easy. But the only thing my sources knew about Annabelle Prosper was that she'd once worked for Henry and Abigail Moulton. Mrs. Moulton was one of Lord Tanner's nieces, you know. Henry and Abigail had gone to Australia to work for his family business, and it hadn't turned out well at all. There was right old scandal at the time, that's how my sources knew the maid's name, ya see."

"No, I'm afraid I don't," Mrs. Jeffries said quickly. Sometimes the cook had a tendency to assume that all of them were as familiar with the British upper class and their comings and goings as she was.

"Henry Moulton was accused of embezzling money from the business. His family would have hushed it up, of course." Mrs. Goodge was thoroughly enjoying herself. She took a long, slow sip of her tea. "But the other principals insisted he be prosecuted. Rather than face that, he put a bullet to his head. His wife was forced to close up their house and come back to England. Some say it was that that caused Annabelle Daws to accept Prosper's proposal. With Henry Moulton dead and her mistress coming here, she had lost her position."

"She got married because she lost her job?" Wiggins sounded absolutely scandalized.

"Not just because of that," Betsy put in. She was a tad miffed that the cook had stolen her thunder. "She wasn't all that young, you know. Besides, what else could she do? Her own family didn't have much, and she probably didn't want to be a burden to them."

"She didn't end up a burden, that's for certain." Mrs. Goodge chuckled. "Eldon Prosper sent her a ticket for a first-class suite on the *Island Star* and a bundle of cash as well."

"How come the gossipmongers know so much about the Moultons' lady's maid?" Hatchet asked. "That's a bit odd, don't you think?"

Mrs. Goodge's eyes twinkled. "It's not in the least odd when you hear what else I found out. It seems that there weren't even enough money for Mrs. Moulton to buy herself the cheapest passage back to England. Annabelle bought her a ticket. The two women came back together on the same ship. Only before the vessel even got to England, Abigail Moulton had become so embarrassed at havin' to come home and live as a poor relation with one of her cousins up in Northumberland, she got off the ship when it docked in Cherbourg."

"What happened to her then?" Wiggins asked.

Mrs. Goodge shrugged. "No one really knows. Though her family did receive a postcard from her a few months after she got off the vessel. It was from Italy and said she'd found work as a governess."

"I guess she thought that was better than comin' back and bein' a poor relation." Wiggins sighed deeply. "Maybe she's found 'appiness in 'er new life. Let's 'ope so." Stories like this tended to affect Wiggins deeply. He had quite a romantic nature.

"This is interestin' and all," Luty said, "but we really need to know more about Mirabelle Daws than we do her sister. Mirabelle's the one who's dead."

"Yes, you're quite right," Mrs. Jeffries said. "We have to discover why someone would want Mirabelle Daws dead. More importantly, we need to know why she didn't tell anyone she was coming to England."

"How do you know she didn't tell anyone?" Mrs. Goodge asked.

"Because if she had, her sister would have reported her missing when she didn't arrive at the Prosper house."

"And she didn't do that, did she?" Smythe said thoughtfully. "Maybe instead of just talkin' to one or two people that was on the ship with Mirabelle, we ought to talk to more of 'em. Seems to me if she didn't write and tell 'er sister she were comin', she musta 'ad a reason. Maybe she told someone on the ship what that reason might be."

"But we are goin' to be talkin' to the people who were on board with 'er," Wiggins reminded him. "We just ain't tracked 'em down yet."

"You don't' understand." Smythe shook his head. "I'm thinkin' we ought to round up as many of 'em as possible to talk to. We only got a couple o'names when we was in Southampton. Like Luty said, it's Mirabelle that's dead, not 'er sister. We need to find as many as we can that was on that ship with 'er. Someone's bound to know something, or they might 'ave seen something, when the vessel docked. It's a long voyage and there's something about all that water surroundin' you that draws people together. Makes 'em tell things they'd normally keep to themselves."

"You'd know all about that, wouldn't you?" Betsy gave him a smile that didn't quite reach her eyes. "Considering how much you've traveled."

Smythe opened his mouth to protest, but before he could say anything, Mrs. Jeffries intervened. "I think that's a very good idea, Smythe. The only problem is, how do we go about finding the names of the others that were on board with her?"

"I can take care of that," Luty volunteered.

Everyone stared at her. Clearly enjoying her moment of glory, she grinned broadly. "The *Island Star* is owned by the Hamilton-Dyston Steamship Line. Jon Dyston was a close friend of my late husband's. All I got to do is ask, and he'll git me a copy of the passenger manifest."

"And pray tell, madam," Hatchet asked archly, "precisely what will you tell Lord Dyston when he asks you why you want it?"

If possible, her smile widened. "Don't you worry yerself about that, Hatchet, I'll think of somethin'. As soon as we're finished here, we can drop by Dyston's townhouse on the way home. I'll have that manifest first thing tomorrow morning."

"That would be very helpful, Luty," Mrs. Jeffries said.

Annoyed that his employer had one-upped him so neatly, Hatchet contented himself with a faint sneer and turned to Mrs. Jeffries. "Does this mean we're not to focus on any of the other residents of the square?" he asked.

"Not at all," Mrs. Jeffries replied. "Contacting the other passengers is a good idea. But as we've learned in the past, we mustn't investigate with preconceived notions. And we must keep in mind that because the victim was connected with one of the residents of the square, it doesn't mean someone else didn't kill her. For all we know, someone from the ship could well be the murderer."

"If it was someone she met on the *Island Star,* why kill her at Sheridan Square?" Betsy asked. "Why not just shove her overboard late at night when there was no one about? Why wait until she got all the way to London?"

Mrs. Jeffries shook her head. "I don't know, Betsy. I'm simply saying that we mustn't ignore any possibilities. There may even be someone from Sheridan Square who had a reason to want her dead."

"That'd be a bit of a stretch, wouldn't it?" Mrs. Goodge pushed her glasses up her nose. "Not that I've any objections to keeping my sources on the hunt, so to speak. But I can't see that anyone else on Sheridan Square could possibly have a reason for wanting Mirabelle Daws dead. Take that Mrs. Isadora Lucas, the widow lady that lives at number two. Why would she want to kill a foreigner she'd never set eyes on?"

"How do we know she'd never set eyes on her before?" Betsy asked as she tossed a quick glance at Smythe. "Seems to me that half of London's been to Australia dozens of times."

"We don't know anything as yet," Mrs. Jeffries soothed. Goodness, were they all deliberately being obtuse. "And though I tend to agree with Mrs. Goodge; we must still keep an open mind." She looked at the cook and asked. "What did you find out about this Mrs. Lucas?" She knew good and well that name hadn't been dropped into the discussion by accident.

"Isadora Lucas hasn't left her house in over ten years," she replied. "One of my sources told me she went in and shut herself up after she was jilted by her fiancé."

"But you said she was a *Mrs.* Lucas," Wiggins pointed out.

"She's been a Mrs. for years. She was widowed young," Mrs. Goodge said.

Mrs. Jeffries made a mental note to ask the inspector about this. The only thing he'd said about the Lucas woman was that she hadn't seen or heard anything. "Well, perhaps things will be a bit clearer the more we investigate. Is there anything else anyone wants to add?" She paused and looked pointedly at the men.

"I'm afraid I didn't have much luck with Miss Brinkman today," Hatchet explained.

"And that Oscar Denton weren't 'ome either," Wiggins put in. "I wasted hours today 'angin' about waitin' fer 'im to come 'ome."

"In that case," Mrs. Jeffries said, "let's decide what we're going to do next."

"I'd like to nip back round to the square and find out what I can about the rest of the 'ousehold," Wiggins volunteered. "Then I'll 'ave another go at this Denton feller. But I don't think there's much of a 'urry about it. The estate agency were locked up nice and tight."

"All right," the housekeeper agreed. "Don't give up on Denton, though. He is one of the few clues we have about Mirabelle."

"Does Mrs. Prosper have a maid?" Betsy asked.

"I don't know," Mrs. Jeffries replied. "Does anyone else?"

None of them did.

"I think I'll try to find out," the maid continued, "and if she does, I'll have a go at her. It should be interesting to see how Annabelle treats her own maid, if she has one."

"I'll have a go at the local pubs," Smythe rose to his feet. "There ought to be some infomation I can suss out tonight."

"I thought you and Hatchet was a'goin' to talk to the people Mirabelle met on the ship?" Luty asked. "Just because this Brinkman woman wasn't home don't mean you should give up. If you're not wantin' to do it, I'll have a . . ."

"Absolutely not, madam," Hatchet put in quickly. "I've already made inquiries concerning Miss Brinkman, and I'll thank you to let me continue at my own pace."

"Meanin' that she didn't want to talk to you," Luty said gleefully.

As that was precisely what it meant, Hatchet blustered even more than usual. "Certainly not, it's simply that it wasn't convenient today . . ."

"Bet she slammed the the door in yer face?" Luty asked. "Not to worry, she'll not be slammin' the door on a poor old soul like me."

Since that was just what had happened, Hatchet sighed in exasperation and then gave in gracefully. "Actually, madam, it might be a good idea for you to have a try. While you're doing that, I'll have some of my sources come up with whatever information is available on Lady Henrietta Morland. I didn't have time to make any inquiries concerning her today."

Luty nodded. "Suits me."

"I think I might keep on investigating the others on the square," Mrs. Jeffries said. "At least until Luty gets a copy of that passenger manifest."

Inspector Witherspoon sighed gratefully and sank down onto his seat at the dining table. He oughtn't to be so hungry. Generally viewing a dead body put him off his food for days, but for some odd reason, this evening he was famished.

He picked up his serviette and flicked it onto his lap. "Are you sure I can't persuade you to join me?" he asked his housekeeper as he sliced off a bite of roast beef and popped it into his mouth.

"No, thank you, sir." She smiled serenely. "I ate earlier with the others. We were getting a bit concerned when you were so late this evening."

"Murder investigations are never simple," Witherspoon said. "One never knows what's going to crop up next. Take today, for instance. Once we got that telegram, things began to happen quite quickly. Very quickly, indeed." He told her about his visit to the Prosper residence and then the trip to the mortuary to identify the body.

"How very dreadful, sir." She clucked her tongue sympathetically.

"It certainly wasn't very pleasant," he replied, "but Mrs. Prosper managed it quite well. Mind you, the poor ship's purser turned a bit green about the gills . . ."

"Ship's purser?" she queried. "You mean the purser from the *Island Star?*"

"Yes, we had a bit of luck there." The inspector smiled briefly. "The fellow's retired. This voyage in from Australia was his last. He was most cooperative and didn't mind coming in to have a look at the body. We warned him it wouldn't be very pleasant."

"But if you had Mrs. Prosper to make an identification," she asked, "why did you want the purser?"

"Just to double-check." He nodded vigorously and stuffed a huge bite of roasted potato in his mouth. "We wanted some verification as to whether or not it was Miss Daws. He confirmed her identity. Poor fellow, even with the warning that it wouldn't be pleasant, it was quite upsetting for him. I was quite glad I'd had the foresight to ask the purser for his help. It was a bit worrying whether or not Mrs. Prosper was going to be able to go in."

"I take it she was squeamish, sir?"

Witherspoon frowned. "Not at first. She was fine until we got just outside the viewing room. Then all of a sudden, she stopped, began sobbing and threw herself in her husband's arms. She made an awful lot of noise, startled the constable escorting the purser out. But to her credit, she got hold of herself and insisted on going in and having a look. Barnes thinks it was the smell that finally got to her. The air does get rather horrid in those places."

"I see." Mrs. Jeffries nodded absently. She was racking her brain, trying desperately to think of a way to let the inspector know some of what she and the others had learned today. "Was Mrs. Prosper expecting her sister?"

"No." The inspector speared another piece of beef. "She says Mirabelle never said a word about coming for a visit."

"How sad that she came all this way to end up murdered." She sighed. "Was the purser able to supply you with any names of the other passengers? I mean, was he useful at all?"

"Quite." He smiled. "Miss Daws wasn't shy. Apparently, she told everyone on board with her that she was coming to England to 'talk some sense into her sister and make her come home.'"

Mrs. Jeffries couldn't believe her ears. Inspector Witherspoon had apparently got the jump on them about this particular bit of information. "She wanted her sister to come back to Australia?"

"Oh, yes." He nodded cheerfully. "It seems their brother, one Mr. Andrew Daws, had struck it rich in the outback mining. Now that the family had money, Mirabelle seemed to be of the opinion that she could persuade her sister to leave her spouse and come back to Sydney. Apparently, the Daws family doesn't take the bonds of matrimony very seriously." He sobered. "That reminds me, I might have to consult with Inspector Nivens on this case."

"Inspector Nivens?" Mrs. Jeffries exclaimed. "But why, sir? How on earth could he possibly help you?"

Inspector Nivens was one of the few people that the housekeeper actively disliked and, more importantly, distrusted. He'd tried on several occasions to imply to the powers that be at Scotland Yard that Gerald Witherspoon had help solving the heinous murder cases that were assigned him. The fact that this was perfectly true made no difference to Mrs. Jeffries or the rest of the household. They didn't like Inspector Nivens one bit, and they certainly didn't trust him near their dear Inspector Witherspoon.

"I need to ask him to be on the lookout for a necklace of opals and diamonds," Witherspoon replied. "Mirabelle Daws was wearing it the night she left the vessel. According to the purser, she wore it all the time. But it wasn't on her body when she was found."

"You think the killer took it?"

"Yes, I don't think he could resist."

"Then you're leaning toward the idea that it was robbery after all?" she prodded.

"Oh, no." He waved his hand. "Someone lured her to that garden, and that person killed her. I think whoever did it simply couldn't pass up a valuable treasure."

Mrs. Jeffries cocked her head to one side. "You realize, sir, that the obvious suspect is Annabelle Daws Prosper. Who else could have possibly had a reason for wanting to kill the woman?"

The inspector finished off a last bite of potato before he answered. "I've thought about that all day," he finally said. "And I've come to the conclusion that I simply don't know enough to form any theories whatsoever. Mrs. Prosper seemed to be genuinely shocked that the dead woman was her sister. She certainly wasn't expecting her to come to England and had no reason to want to murder the woman even if she had been expecting her. Mrs. Prosper allowed me to read some of her correspondence from Mirabelle. It was quite obvious the sisters were very fond of each other."

"Did Mrs. Prosper know that her brother had struck it rich?" she asked.

"Indeed she did." The inspector pushed his empty plate to one side. "But it wasn't just her brother who'd struck it rich; it was Mirabelle as well. She owned half the mine. Yet I don't see money as motive for murder in this case. Mrs. Prosper simply doesn't need it. Her husband is very, very wealthy. Much wealthier than he lets on. He made it quite clear that his wife wanted for nothing. From the way he behaved today, I rather had the impression he was very devoted to her as well."

"It's a puzzle, isn't it, sir?" She rather thought that perhaps she wouldn't try so hard to share what they'd learned with him. He seemed to be doing quite well on his own. "But I'm sure you'll solve it."

"I certainly hope so, Mrs. Jeffries." He looked around the table. "Uh, is there dessert this evening?"

If ya keep on starin' at people like that," Wiggins said to Smythe, "we'll not find anyone who wants to talk to us."

Smythe shot the footman a fast glare, realized the lad was right and tried to force a more amenable expression onto his face. He and Wiggins had come out tonight supposedly to find someone at this ruddy pub that could tell them a bit more about the murder. But the truth was, he didn't much care if they found out anything at all. His mood had darkened as the evening progressed. The more he thought about it, the madder he got. He still couldn't believe it. He'd bared his ruddy soul to the lass, and she'd acted like she thought he was telling tales. He elbowed his way through the crowd to the bar. "Two bitters," he told the told the publican.

"This is right nice," Wiggins said enthusiastically as he gazed around at the noisy public bar. There were several small, round tables with people crowded round them in front of the open stone fireplace. Long slate benches with chairs facing them lined the other two walls and along the bar, the patrons were two deep. It had only been Smythe's size that had gotten them near the bar.

Wiggins hadn't been to many pubs. Truth was, he'd just about fallen over in shock when Mrs. Jeffries had suggested he accompany the coachman.

"Grab us a seat at that bench over there." Smythe pointed to a spot to the left of the fireplace. Three men were getting up and leaving. Wiggins made a run for it. He slid his bottom on the bench against the wall and slapped his foot on the chair opposite, saving it for Smythe. An elderly man sitting in the spot next to him looked up from his tankard and stared hard at the lad but said nothing.

A moment later, Smythe ambled across and handed Wiggins a glass of beer. He lowered his big frame into the chair the boy had saved him. "See any likely prospects?" he asked absently.

Wiggins was taken aback. He was also flattered that the coachman would ask his opinion. "Prospects? You mean people to talk about the murder?"

"That's why we came," Smythe replied. He wasn't at all in the mood for chasing after clues. He was too busy brooding over Betsy. Just like the lass to take it into her head to be stubborn. He didn't know what was worse, his worrying about how she'd take the truth or her not believing him when he tried to tell her.

"You a copper?" the old man who'd glared at Wiggins asked.

Smythe cringed; he hadn't realized how loud he'd been talking. Blast, if there had been a decent prospect around, his surly expression probably scared them off.

"Course I'm not a peeler," he sneered. "We was just curious, that's all. My friend and I." He jerked his head at Wiggins. "We got us a bet goin'. I say it's that ripper feller up to 'is old tricks, and 'e says it's someone else what done it."

"It's not the bleedin' ripper." The old man drained his beer. "She weren't sliced up."

"Maybe the ripper's changed the way he does things," Smythe pressed. "Besides, 'ow do you know what the feller did to her?"

The man smiled faintly. "I know 'cause I was there. I work just across the street, and I saw 'em bring her out."

"If ya saw 'em bringing 'er out, 'ow do you know she weren't sliced? She'da been covered with a sheet," Smythe goaded. "They always cover 'em with somethin'."

"Everyone knows that," the fellow sneered. "But I know what I knows 'cause I went into the garden the next day. Soon as the coppers cleared off, Jon took me in and showed me where she'd been killed." He lifted his tankard and drank. "There weren't enough blood on the ground fer it to have been the ripper," he said, wiping his mouth. "Siler showed me the spot, and there weren't enough blood."

"Who's Siler and 'ow does 'e 'ave anything to do with it?" Smythe asked belligerently. He couldn't back off now; otherwise the fellow might dry up completely. He'd learned that some kinds of people told you more if they were just that bit annoyed. He also deliberately played up his accent. A working man like this one was far more likely to trust one of his own rather than someone from a different class. Besides, Smythe was beginning to enjoy himself. Acting the part cheered him up a little. At least it took his mind off a certain fair-haired lovely that could drive a decent man to drink.

"He's the ruddy gardener over on Sheridan Square and a good mate o' mine," the man shot back. His thick, calloused hands wrapped around the base of the tankard, and his watery gray eyes looked mournfully into its empty depths. "He could tell them coppers a few things about what's what, but they never asked him much. Just kept goin' on about how many ruddy keys there was to the garden. As if that made any difference. Jon says people are always slippin' in there at night an' unlockin' the gate."

Smythe stiffened. He'd struck gold. Pure gold. He hesitated a split second wondering what tactic to use now. He didn't want to risk shuttin' the fellow up by sayin' the wrong thing now.

But it was Wiggins who hit upon just the right note.

"It's shameful the way them coppers won't listen to what a workin' man 'as to say," Wiggins agreed sympathetically.

"More their 'ard luck." The fellow shook his head emphatically. "They're the ones that ain't goin' to solve this 'ere murder. Not with the sort of silly questions that inspector was askin'. Mind you, Jon did say this bloke was polite like, better than most peelers. Treated him with respect."

"Ooh, I'd love to talk to yer friend. I bet 'e knows what's what," Wiggins said eagerly.

"Maybe you'll get yer chance," a quiet voice said from behind the coachman.

Smythe turned and saw a tall, gaunt-faced fellow with dark hair and a ruddy complexion standing staring down at them. He was dressed in a dark coat and heavy, black trousers that were creased and stained. He wore brown, workingman's boots.

"You Mr. Siler?" the coachman asked.

"Who wants to know?"

Smythe eased out of the chair and rose to his feet. He extended his hand. "My name's Smythe. Yer friend there." He jerked his chin at the man they'd been talking with. "He's told us all about that awful murder over on Sheridan Square. I'd be pleased to buy ya a drink if you'll let me."

Siler hesitated a split second and then shook the extended hand. "I'll not turn down a free drink."

"It's a cheap enough price to pay fer satisfyin' me curiosity." Smythe grinned broadly, playing the part of a curiosity seeker as well as he could. "It's not often ya get to meet someone that's been there and seen where it 'appened."

Wiggins got up as well. "I'm Wiggins," he introduced himself. "And we've 'eard all about ya."

"Beer or whiskey?" Smythe asked as he started for the bar.

Siler looked surprised at the offer. Whiskey was ruddy expensive. "Whiskey," he called before the fellow changed his mind.

"You can get me one too," the man next to Wiggins yelled.

"'E will," the footman assured him. "What's yer name?"

"Bill Trent." The fellow slid over to make room for Jon Siler.

Smythe came back with the drinks and handed them round. Wiggins looked down at his now-empty glass and said, "Don't I get another one?"

"Maybe later, lad." The coachman took his seat. "We don't want you goin' 'ome all wobbly kneed, do we? Now, Mr. Siler, yer friend 'ere,"

"'Is name's Bill Trent," Wiggins interrupted.

"'E says you know a lot more than yer lettin' on to the coppers? That right?"

Siler stared at him suspiciously. "Why you so interested?"

"Just curious. Like I told ya, it ain't often ya can talk to someone who's been to the scene, so to speak." Smythe shrugged and tossed back a swig of the whiskey he'd ordered for himself.

"Can't blame a man for bein' interested." Siler took another sip from his glass and then wiped his hand across his mouth. "It ain't that I know more than I'm sayin'. It's that the coppers ain't askin' the right questions. They was only interested in who had keys to the ruddy garden."

"That's kinda important, isn't it?" Wiggins asked.

"Not really," Siler replied. He grinned broadly. "That garden was very convenient for a lot of people livin' on that square, if you get my drift."

"You mean there was them that was usin' the place to 'ave a bit o'privacy?" Smythe guessed.

"More than one was doin' it." Siler chuckled. "Well, it stands to reason, don't it? If you're a married feller and you want to have a safe place to meet your sweetie, all ya got to do is wait till old Tavistock walks his dog and then nip out and unlock the gate. Late at night, the wifey's sound asleep, the garden's empty, and you've got the place to yourself."

"Cor blimey," Smythe said. "That's a right good little idea. But if these people was meetin' at night, 'ow did you find out? No offense meant, but I thought most gardenin' took place during the day?" He wanted to verify that Siler was telling the truth and not just making up tales. Then he'd try and figure out exactly who the man was talking about.

"'Ere, you sayin' he's makin' it up?" Trent asked bellingerently.

"Don't get shirty now, Bill," Siler said easily. "It's a reasonable question. I know about what was goin' on 'cause I saw it with my own eyes. A time or two they left the front gate unlocked when they was finished. Well, I knew that if Tavistock saw that, it'd be my job. I also noticed it almost always happened on Sunday night. So after I found the gate open for a third time when I come in on Monday morning, I decided to suss out what was goin' on. The following Sunday I waited till after I saw Tavistock take his stupid dog walkies, then I used my key and let myself in. I hid in the bushes behind the bench. Didn't have to wait long, either. About half past one, that Mr. Heckston came waltzing in as big as you please. Whistling, he was, like he didn't have a care in the world. He plopped down on the bench, and within ten minutes his ladyfriend had shown up."

"Who was she?" Wiggins asked.

Siler smiled broadly. "It was that toffee-nosed cow that lives at number six. Mrs. Prosper."

CHAPTER 6

"She's a right old tartar, she is," the girl declared. "You'd think that havin' been a maid herself she'd be a bit nicer, but no, not her. Acts like the bloomin' Queen of Sheba, she does." The homely young woman lifted her glass and tossed back the gin in a single gulp. It was her third drink in fifteen minutes. "Wouldn't even have my day out if it weren't for Mr. Prosper," she declared. "She tried to make me stay in today, tried to tell me that she needed me because of all that bother with her sister gettin' stabbed. But that was just an excuse to keep me at her beck and call."

Betsy nodded sympathetically. The pub was noisy and crowded and reeked with the stench of tobacco, gin and unwashed bodies. She resisted the urge to cover her nose. She didn't want to give offense. It'd been hard enough to follow the girl into this dirty place without doing something that might cause her to stop talking altogether. Added to that, Betsy's conscience bothered her. She'd bought Alice Sparkle, Annabelle Prosper's maid, three drinks now and, somehow, that didn't feel right. Betsy had flirted with men before to get them to shed their secrets, but this was the first time she'd followed a pathetic young woman into a horrid, smelly little pub and plied her with alcohol. But she couldn't stop now, not when the woman was finally starting to talk. Betsy hadn't been comfortable going into a pub without an escort. But this place was filled with serious drinkers, and no one had even noticed the two women coming in on their own. God knows she'd done it before coming to live at the inspector's house, but that had been a whole lifetime ago.

She sighed silently, knowing that if she'd not been lucky enough to collapse on the inspector's doorstep, she might be in just the same shape as the girl sitting opposite her.

Alice was able to hide her need now. Her clothes were clean and pressed, and she could talk without slurring her words. But in a few short years, the brown eyes would be bloodshot, and she'd be dropping things because her hands were shaking. She wouldn't be working as a lady's maid either.

Overwhelmed with pity, Betsy smiled at Alice and wished there was something she could do to ease her misery. But there was nothing. Maybe Alice might have had a chance at a better life if she'd not turned to drink.

"Why do you think Mrs. Prosper's like that?" Betsy asked. "I mean, it's horrible that it's her sister that was stabbed, but why is she tryin' to take it out on you?"

"Because she's a cow." Alice shrugged and pushed a strand of frizzy brown hair off her sunken cheek. "She's mean and nasty. She's got everyone else fooled, but she can't fool me." She looked down at her empty glass and made a face.

"Let me buy you another," Betsy said quickly. She raised her hand, caught the barman's attention and jerked her chin at Alice. He nodded, poured another gin and handed it to the barmaid to bring to their table.

"Ta," Alice said as the woman set the glass in front of her. "This is right nice of ya."

"Oh, it's fine," Betsy replied. "I had a good night." She forced the ugly words out knowing that if Alice thought she was a prostitute, it'd loosen her tongue even more. She wanted to get this over with as quickly as possible. Betsy didn't think she could stomach buying the woman another drink. It was too much like drowning a kitten. So she'd pretend she was something she wasn't. She'd noticed that people tended to speak freely around those at the bottom of the ladder and watch their tongues around those closer to the top. She forced herself to laugh gaily. "If you know what I mean. Do go on with what you were sayin'"

Alice's brows came together in a frown. "What was I sayin'?"

"That Mrs. Prosper could fool everyone else, but not you," she reminded her. "What'd ya mean by that?"

Alice sighed. "Oh, she's got everyone thinkin' she's heartbroken about her sister. But it's all a ruddy lie."

"Really?"

"God, yes." Alice continued eagerly. "She used to pull faces everytime she got one of her sister's letters. She'd read 'em and then rip 'em in half and toss 'em in the trash. You can't tell me she cared one whit for the woman. Why, she almost had a fit when she got that letter six weeks ago tellin' her that Mirabelle was comin' for a visit."

"She had a letter?" Betsy prodded. She had to be careful here. It wouldn't do to slip and put the maid on guard that she knew more about this murder than she'd let on.

"Oh, she didn't tell anyone about it." Alice took a gulp from her glass and wiped her mouth with the back of her hand. "She didn't want Mr. Prosper knowin' that family was comin' to visit. Right ashamed of 'em, she was. I could tell by the look on 'er face when she was readin' the letter. She went all pale and shaky like. Honestly, you'd think she'd been born to the gentry the way she acts. It's not as if Mr. Prosper didn't know what kind of a family she'd come from."

"Did she tell you her family was comin' then?" Betsy asked carefully. "Is that how you know?"

"She never told me anything." Alice sneered. "But I can read, ya know."

"I didn't mean to say you couldn't," Betsy apologized. "I was just wonderin', that's all. To tell the truth, sometimes when one of me customers falls asleep, I have a quick look through the pockets. Surprising what all ya can learn that way. Well, a girl's got to take care of herself in this old world, don't she?"

"That's the God's truth." Alice grinned. "I started readin' them letters after I saw Mrs. McCabe fishin' them out of the trash and havin' a snoop."

"Who's that?" Betsy asked innocently. She wasn't sure she quite understood everything that was going on here, but then again, she wasn't used to questioning people at eleven in the morning in a workingman's pub.

"That's Mr. Prosper's sister," Alice explained. "She used to keep house for Mr. Prosper before he married Mrs. Prosper."

"Is she jealous of Mrs. Prosper then?" Betsy guessed. "For comin' and takin' her place."

"No, she was happier than a cow in clover," Alice said. "She wants to go off and do a bit of travelin' with her friend Miss Beems. She couldn't do that while she was takin' care of Mr. Prosper."

"Why not? You just said she were a widow."

"She's a widow, but she's a poor one." Alice laughed. "And Mr. Prosper might be a nice man, but he does keep his mitts on the purse strings. He give Mrs. McCabe a generous allowance as long as she stayed and took care of him."

"But didn't he have servants?"

"That's not the same, is it?" she said. "He wanted a bit of company, said he couldn't live on his own. Mrs. McCabe was delighted that he got married. Took the burden off her some. Mind you, I don't think she likes her sister-in-law all that much. But she sure is glad she's there, or she'd be stuck for the rest of her life with her brother."

Betsy looked puzzled. "If she was so glad the woman had married her brother, why was she readin' her mail? I mean, that sounds like she was tryin' to git somethin' on her, doesn't it?"

"More like she was making sure she didn't run off with someone else." Alice smiled cynically. "It's not like Mrs. Prosper actually loves her husband, ya know. And I know fer a fact that she's got a lover. If I can figure it out, I expect Mrs. McCabe could too." She snickered. "She probably is thankin' her lucky stars that someone murdered that Miss Daws. Otherwise, Mrs. Prosper probably would have gone back to Australia with her sister."

"You mean she'd run off and leave her husband?" Betsy's head was beginning to spin. She didn't know if it was because of the cigar smoke or the few sips of gin she'd had.

"At the drop of a hankie." Alice nodded wisely. "Mrs. McCabe weren't worried while Mrs. Prosper was havin' her fun with that Mr. Heckston. At least as long as she was playin' about with him, Mrs. McCabe knew she wouldn't be leavin'. But they had a blazin' old row a few weeks ago, and she's not gone out to see him since. Then when that letter arrived tellin' Mrs. Prosper that her sister was on her way and that the family in Australia had struck it rich," she laughed, "that put the fear of God in Mrs. McCabe. I overheard her talkin' to her friend not two days before the murder."

Wide-eyed, Betsy dropped her voice to a whisper. "And what was she sayin' then?"

"She was tellin' Miss Beems that their plans to go off to Araby might be up in smoke. She said that Mrs. Prosper was no better than she ought to be and that now that Mr. Heckston had told Mrs. Prosper he'd not sneak out and see her anymore, she was scared that Mrs. Prosper would go back home with her sister."

"You mean she'd divorce Mr. Prosper?"

"Who knows? I don't think she cares all that much whether she's legally wed or not. She thinks she's above everything and everyone. You know, like she's royalty or something. Like the normal rules don't apply to her. Besides, if the family in Australia has more money than Mr. Prosper, she'd be gone like a shot. She'd do anything for money, she would. Anything at all."

Inspector Nigel Nivens deliberately ignored them. He kept his head lowered and his gaze focused on the paper on the top of his desk. Constable Barnes knew good and well that Nivens knew they were standing right in front of his desk, but the bloomin' sod refused to look up.

After a few moments, Inspector Witherspoon cleared his throat. "Er, Inspector Nivens, I do so hate to interrupt . . ."

"Then why are you?" Nivens asked rudely. He still didn't look up.

"Probably because he has something rather important to discuss with you." The voice came from behind them and belonged to Chief Inspector Jonathan Barrows.

Nivens's head jerked up, and he leapt to his feet. He was a man of medium height with dark, blond hair that he wore slicked straight back from his face. His nose was prominent, his cheeks ruddy and his eyes pale blue and mean-looking. "I'm sorry, sir. Witherspoon," he ignored Barnes in his apology. "Do forgive me. I didn't mean to be rude. It's just I've been so busy. Most of these cases are so difficult, and there's a lot of pressure on."

Chief Inspector Barrows nodded curtly. Inspector Nivens was a disgusting toady, but the fellow had some rather powerful political connections. The police were supposed to be above politics and all that, but the chief inspector dealt with the realities of life rather than the ideals one spouted for the press. He'd let Niven's obnoxious behaviour toward a fellow officer pass. This time. "No more difficult than this murder Witherspoon's got. Which brings us to why he needs your attention. You're to give him any help and cooperation he needs."

"Certainly, sir," Nivens agreed eagerly.

"Right, then, I'll leave you to it." Barrows nodded brusquely and went back to his office.

Nivens turned his attention back to Witherspoon and Barnes. "What did you want to see me about?" he asked grudgingly.

Barnes glared at the man. There were empty chairs on either side of Nivens's desk, but the constable was sure that now that the chief was back in his office, they'd not be invited to sit down.

The large room was relatively quiet, but a few detectives were working quietly at their desks, and a couple of uniformed lads puttered about.

"We'd like some information about some jewelry," Witherspoon replied. "We've just found out that a rather valuable opal necklace might have been stolen during that murder on Sheridan Square."

"Opals aren't particularly valuable," Nivens said. "But I'll have my lads keep their eyes open."

"It's got diamonds on it," Barnes added. He smiled maliciously. "Lots of 'em. We need to know if it turns up in any of the usual places." The constable didn't have to be specific. Nivens, despite being a rude little sod, was enough of a copper to know that the "usual places" meant anywhere a fence might try to pass stolen merchandise.

"Diamonds?" Nivens was suddenly interested. "How many of them?"

"They're only small ones," Witherspoon said, "but there are quite a number of them. They lie between the opals."

"How long is the necklace?"

"The purser said it hung halfway down the victim's chest," Barnes replied. "So it's a good long rope of a piece. It's got to be worth a pretty penny."

"So it would seem," Nivens agreed. "All right. We'll do some snooping for you. But I've not heard of anything fitting that description being flogged on the street."

"We'd appreciate any information you happen to come across," Witherspoon replied.

"I'll have my sources look into it," Nivens said importantly. He pulled a watch out of the pocket of his jacket.

Barnes fought to keep a sneer off his face. Nivens's sources were generally petty crooks who sold their own out for pennies.

"Anything else?" Nivens looked pointedly at his watch.

"That's all we need. But, of course, we'd be most obliged if you passed on any information you might hear about the murder. Thank you, Inspector." Witherspoon nodded politely and turned toward the stairs. Barnes, with one last glare, followed him.

Neither of them spoke until they were out of the building and on the street. "Where to now, sir?" the constable asked.

"The train station," Witherspoon said. "I want to have a word with that woman the purser mentioned. You remember, the one who was so friendly with Miss Daws."

"Judith Brinkman?" the constable queried.

"That's right." Witherspoon nodded and stepped off the curb. Raising his hand, he hailed a passing hansom. "Perhaps she'll be able to tell us a bit more about Miss Daws."

Mrs. Jeffries took a deep breath and slammed the knocker on the front door against the wood. She wasn't sure what she hoped to accomplish. She wasn't certain she could even get Mrs. Lucas to talk with her, but she felt she ought to try. People who didn't leave their houses frequently saw more than one would expect. Their windows were quite literally their only connections with the outside world.

The door creaked open, and a gaunt, middle-aged woman wearing a maid's uniform stuck her head out. "Yes? Can I help you?"

"I'd like to see Mrs. Lucas," Mrs. Jeffries said boldly. She gave the maid a confident smile.

"Mrs. Lucas doesn't see people."

"Oh dear, that is too bad." Mrs. Jeffries sighed. "I've come a great distance, you see. All the way from Yorkshire." That wasn't precisely a lie; she had come from Yorkshire. The fact that it had been five years ago, when her dear, late husband had passed away was of no consequence whatsoever.

"Are you sure it's important?" The woman asked uncertainly. "Madam doesn't like to be disturbed."

"It's very important." Mrs. Jeffries nodded eagerly. "I need her help in locating someone."

The woman's thin lips cracked in a ghost of a smile. "She couldn't help you there, ma'am. The mistress never leaves the house."

"Who is it, Mary?" a woman's voice called from the depths of the house.

"It's a lady from Yorkshire," the maid turned and shouted down the hall. "She says she wants you to help her find someone."

"Ask her in," the voice commanded. "Bring her into the drawing room."

"That's a bit of a surprise." Mary smiled widely, stepped back and held the door open. "Come in, ma'am."

Mrs. Jeffries stepped inside and followed the maid down the hall and into a large, airy reception room. Sitting on the settee and staring at her curiously was a stout woman with fading blond hair, blue eyes and exceptionally white skin. "Mrs. Lucas, I presume," she asked by way of introduction.

"Correct. Who might you be?"

"My name is Hepzibah Jeffries," she replied. "And I've come to see you about a matter of some importance."

"A matter of some importance," Mrs. Lucas repeated slowly.

"Shall I bring tea, madam?" the maid asked.

"That would be nice, Mary," she agreed. "Oh goodness, where are my manners? Please, do sit down." She gestured to the chair next to the settee.

Mrs. Jeffries quickly took a seat. She'd won half the battle; she was inside the house. "I do thank you for agreeing to see me. As I said, it's a matter of some urgency."

Isadora Lucas inclined her head graciously. "I've no idea why you think I'd be able to help you. As I'm sure my maid told you, I rarely leave my home."

Mrs. Jeffries took another deep breath and decided to trust her instincts. There was something about this woman that convinced her she wouldn't be easily fooled. She decided to toss her well-thought-out plan out the window and simply tell the truth. "Do hear me out, ma'am. I work for Inspector Gerald Witherspoon."

"The policeman who is investigating that awful murder we had in the garden?" she asked. "I liked him. He seems a very gentle sort of man. Not at all like what one thinks a policeman might be."

"He is a true gentleman," Mrs. Jeffries said firmly. "What I'd like to know from you is some more information about the inhabitants of the square. Specifically, about anyone who might be connected in any way with the Prosper household."

Mrs. Lucas gaped at her for a moment. "Do they have women police now?" she asked.

"No, no, I'm not with the police . . ."

"But you said you worked for Inspector Witherspoon," she protested.

"Yes, I know, I'm his housekeeper," Mrs. Jeffries admitted. "I know this sounds odd, but you see, myself and the rest of our staff are very devoted to our inspector. We like to help him on his cases. Not that he knows we're helping, mind you. But nevertheless, we've found we can learn things that he can't. People will talk to us, you see."

"People like me." Mrs. Lucas stared at her for a long moment, and then a slow smile spread across her face. "Your inspector is very fortunate in his staff. Of course, I am as well. I've got my devoted Mary and her sister Hilda to take care of me."

"And we takes good care of you, ma'am," Mary said as she came back into the room pushing a delicate wicker tea trolly. The kettle must have already been on the boil and the tray made up because she'd been gone only a few minutes. She eased the trolly into an impossibly small space between the settee and a red, silk-fringed footrest.

"Indeed you do." Isadora Lucas smiled gratefully at the maid and reached for the teapot. "Thank you, Mary. I'll ring if I need anything else."

As soon as she'd poured their tea, she studied Mrs. Jeffries openly. Whatever she saw on the housekeeper's face must have reassured her because finally, she said, "All right, I'll try and help. But I'm not really certain I understand exactly what it is you need from me. When you say you want to know anything connected to the Prosper house, does that mean you want to know which married man on the square is having an improper relationship with Mrs. Prosper? Or does it mean you'd like to know that Mr. Prosper is well aware of his wife's behaviour but deliberately shuts his eyes to it?"

Mrs. Jeffries stifled a feeling of elation. It would, of course, be wrong to gloat. But her instincts had been right! This woman knew a great deal about what went on in Sheridan Square. "Actually, I think I'd quite like it if you could tell me everything."

"Then I hope you've plenty of time." She laughed in delight. "Because there's plenty to tell. After dark, our garden has more foot traffic than Oxford Street."

The inspector decided that Miss Judith Brinkman was a sensible, no-nonsense sort of woman. Much like his housekeeper. Dressed in a serviceable lavender day dress and plain black shoes, she sat ramrod straight in the middle of her drawing room and listened to them without interruption. She asked no questions and made no comments. She merely gazed at them with interest as they explained the circumstances of their visit.

"So you see, Miss Brinkman," Witherspoon finished, "we'd be most grateful for any help you could give us."

"That's quite a tale, Inspector," she replied. "But I don't know what I can tell you that you don't already know. From what you've told me, the purser has already given you the details of Miss Daws's voyage. I don't know that I have anything to add to that."

Witherspoon stifled a sigh and glanced at Constable Barnes. He was

desperately hoping that Barnes could think of something to ask that might
be useful. Something that would nudge the woman's memory in some sort
of fashion. They had learned a lot of information about this case, but so
far, he'd not a clue as to who the killer might be.

Barnes gave a barely perceptible nod of his head and said, "Can you
verify that she wore the opal and diamond necklace all the time?"

"Probaby even when she bathed," she replied bluntly. She smiled slightly,
and the inspector knew it was because he was probably blushing. "Mirabelle
wouldn't let the thing out of her sight. She wore it all the time. She was
terrified someone might steal it or that she would lose the wretched thing."

"That's not an unreasonable fear," Witherspoon said.

"True," she agreed, "but if she was that frightened of losing it, she
ought to have had it locked in the ship's safe. Most of the women on board
brought their jewels with them, but we weren't in the habit of wearing
them continuously." She shook her head. "Mirabelle Daws was a most
unusual woman. On the surface, it would appear she simply didn't care
what people thought of her. Yet the fact that she flaunted that necklace
constantly rather showed that she did care. That she wanted everyone on
board to know she had plenty of money."

"That probably didn't make her very popular," Barnes muttered.

Judith nodded in agreement. "She was quite sad, really. I rather felt
sorry for her. I tried to help her socially. But it was impossible, I'm afraid.
By the end of the voyage, all the decent people on board had completely
cut her."

"Was it just wearin' the necklace that put people off?" Barnes asked.

"No. Most people were rather amused by that particular foible. It
wasn't what she did. It was her manner of speaking."

Witherspoon was incredulous. He knew the English were a tad snobbish, but that sounded absurd. "You mean they didn't like her accent?"

"Oh, no, contrary to what everyone believes, we're not so horribly class
ridden that most of us would ignore someone because of their speech,"
Judith explained. "People cut her because of what she said. People were
dreadfully shocked."

The inspector and Barnes both leaned forward in their chairs. Rather like
two old women getting ready for a particularly good morsel of gossip.

"Oh, dear," Witherspoon said, "I do hope it won't upset you to repeat it?"

"Hardly, Inspector." Her hazel eyes sparkled with amusement. "I spent many years as a nursing sister. There isn't much that upsets me. And apparently there wasn't much that upset Mirabelle Daws either. She talked constantly, told everyone her business and then dared them to disagree with her."

"What precisely was her business?" Barnes asked. He sounded just a bit impatient. "We were under the impression she was just comin' to visit her sister."

"She was," Judith replied. "And she was bound and determined to make her sister come back to Australia with her. The fact that the woman was properly married didn't make any difference to Mirabelle. She told everyone that she wasn't going to rest until Annabelle was on board a ship and heading home. She used to twirl those opals while she was speaking. It would have been amusing except that she was deadly serious."

"If she was violently opposed to her sister's marriage," Witherspoon asked, "why didn't she object before the fact? Why wait until her sister comes all the way to England and then follow her months later to bring her home? It's most odd, don't you think?"

"Not really," Judith said, "not when one understands Mirabelle's reasoning. She wasn't opposed to the marriage when it happened. It was only later, after Annabelle had come to England, that Mirabelle decided there was something odd going on. She implied that Eldon Prosper was keeping his wife a virtual prisoner. When I tried to get her to explain what she meant, all she would say was that she suspected that he was keeping her letters from her sister and not letting Annabelle write home."

"She hadn't had a letter from her sister since she'd been married?" Barnes surmised.

"That's right." Judith nodded. "Mirabelle said she'd only received one letter from Annabelle since she'd come to England and that one had been mailed the day her ship docked in Southampton. She was convinced that Annabelle was in some sort of trouble or stuck with one of those monstrous men for a husband. Mind you, I was quite sympathetic to Mirabelle. I suspect if I were in her situation, I'd have done the same thing. Especially if I'd come into a great deal of money, as the Daws family apparently has. But one thing I wouldn't have done was to tell everyone on board the ship that a man as rich and influential as Eldon Prosper was some sort of animal and that I was going to get my sister away from him if it was the last thing I did!" She shook her head in disbelief. "For an intelligent woman, that was quite stupid on Mirabelle's part. You can imagine what most people thought. Mind you, it was mainly the men who didn't want their wives around her. I think a lot of the women felt as I did."

"Do you think it's possible that her attitude about er . . . a marriage and that sort of thing might have offended someone so much that they would want to harm her?" Witherspoon thought it a weak motive for murder, but then again, one never knew.

Judith pursed her lips in thought. "I don't think so," she finally said. "People cut her, but they didn't go out of their way to be cruel. I don't think that there was any one particular man that was overly offended by Mirabelle's attitudes. No, I'd say they just wanted to keep their wives away from her."

"Did you see Miss Daws leaving the vessel?" Barnes asked.

"As a matter of fact, I did," Judith said. "There was a real crush on the quay. Relatives and friends were turning up and meeting people, that sort of thing. But as I was getting into a hansom, I saw Mirabelle talking to a young boy, rather I should say a street arab."

"Do you know where her luggage was at that point?" Barnes persisted.

"I'm not absolutely certain," she said hesitantly, "but I think there was a porter right behind her. He may have been carrying her things. She didn't have much, just a large case and a carpet bag. She'd told us she planned to buy some things in London. She spoke to the boy for a moment; then I saw him give her something. Perhaps it was a letter or a message. A few moments later, I saw her moving through the crowd. That's the last I saw of her."

Witherspoon nodded gratefully. They'd never found Mirabelle's baggage. The shipping line claimed she took it with her when she left the vessel.

"Is there anything else you can tell us?" Witherspoon asked. "Anything at all?"

Again, Judith hesitated. "I don't know if this is helpful, but she did tell me she was going straight up to London. The ship docked quite late in the afternoon. By the time it tied up and we passed through the formalities of disembarkation, it was late. Most of the passengers had made plans to stay over in Southampton and continue on the next day. But not Mirabelle. She said she was going up to London straightaway to have it out with Eldon Prosper."

"I guess she didn't know that he was out of town," Barnes mused. "Too bad. If she'd known that, she'd have stayed in Southampton that night, and she'd still be alive."

"But Mr. Prosper was in London that night," Judith exclaimed. "I know because Mirabelle had sent him a telegram when the ship docked in Cherbourg. Right after we docked here, she received a reply from him saying he'd see her that very night."

Witherspoon looked at the constable. Barnes grimaced. They were thinking the same thing. They hadn't checked Eldon Prosper's alibi as thoroughly as they should. "Are you sure, ma'am?" the inspector pressed. "We have it on good authority that Mr. Prosper was in Edinburgh that evening."

She shrugged. "I didn't actually read the message, but I did see Mirabelle coming out of the purser's office waving the envelope about. She was quite pleased. She told me it was all arranged, that she was going to meet him in London. Then she said, and this is a direct quote, gentlemen, she was going to 'have it out once and for all with the old bastard.'"

"This was right before the *Island Star* docked?" Witherspoon hadn't any idea why this was important, but in the past he'd learnt it was useful to have a person's "timeline," as he called it, absolutely correct.

"No, it was right after the ship docked," Judith answered. "Mirabelle and I said our farewells, and she went back to her cabin, presumably to gather her things. The last I saw of her was on the dock an hour or so later. Pity, I rather liked her. She was blunt and rather foolishly honest. But she didn't deserve to die alone and in a strange land." She stared off at the far wall for a few moments and then gave herself a small shake. Turning to Witherspoon, she said, "I hope you catch whoever killed her. I hope you catch them, and I hope they hang."

As soon as the inspector and Barnes had gone, Judith Brinkman walked to a door just a few feet behind the area where she'd been sitting and yanked it open. "Are you all right?"

"I'm jus' fine," Luty Belle Crookshank scrambled up off the floor of the small storage closet and wiped the dust off her bright orange skirts. "Jus' fine. Boy, you gotta powerful lot of information outta that woman. I was listenin' so hard, I was fit to bust. Who'da thought Prosper was in town the night of the murder?"

"Would you care to come out and have cup of tea?" Judith invited. "I believe you must be rather thirsty. You've been in there a good while."

Luty hurried out. "I've spent time in worse places. But I am thirsty. Can I help myself?" she asked as she headed for the tea trolly.

"Of course." Judith chuckled.

Luty grabbed a clean cup from the second shelf of the trolly, filled it with tea and took a long, soothing sip. Then she flopped down on the settee. "I was parched. Thanks."

Judith sat down in the chair the inspector had just vacated and looked at the elderly American with wry amusement. The woman's expensive hat was askew, a long line of white dust had settled on the shoulders of her orange and black striped jacket, and there was a smudge of ink on her nose.

"You might want to freshen up before you leave," she told Luty. "I'm sorry you had to go into that closet. I'm sure it wasn't very pleasant. It's quite dusty and closed in, but it's only used for storing a few of my late father's things."

Luty waved her hand dismissively. She'd actually gotten quite short of breath while she was inside the place. She didn't like enclosed spaces. To be more accurate, she darned well hated them. But she'd been stuck. Just when she and Judith Brinkman were fixin' to have a right good chat, there'd been a knock on the front door, and a second later Inspector Witherspoon and Constable Barnes were stompin' down the hall. Thank goodness they'd made a racket loud enough to waken the dead, otherwise Luty wouldn't have had time to beg Judith Brinkman to keep quiet about her and leap into that danged closet. "Don't worry about it, I'd rather be sittin' on a closet floor gettin' an earful than standing behind a thick oak door and strainin' to hear what was bein' said. I'm real obliged about you lettin' me do it in the first place. Not everyone would be as understandin' as you."

"Your story was most unusual," Judith admitted. "I've never met anyone who helped the police out with their investigations without the police actually knowing anything about it. Most odd, I'd say. But jolly good fun nonetheless."

CHAPTER 7

———◦◦◦◦———

Smythe glanced down the staircase to make sure the coast was clear and then hurried across the landing to Betsy's door. He didn't have much time. In less than fifteen minutes the others would be here for their late afternoon meeting. He wanted to have a word or two with the lass before everything started.

"Betsy," he whispered, knocking softly. "Are you in there?"

There was no reply. Blast, he thought, frowning ferociously at the door. He was sure he'd heard her going up the stairs not just two minutes ago. Why wasn't she answering? Surely, her nose wasn't still out of joint over that silly misunderstanding they'd had?

"I know you're in there, Betsy," he said quietly. "Look, lass, I'm sorry I didn't tell you about all them trips to Australia. But you've got to admit, when I finally told ya about 'em, you weren't very nice. I didn't take kindly to ya laughing at me. Now, if you'll just open up, we can talk about this like civilized people."

The door flew open, and Wiggins stuck his head out. "What trips to Australia?" he asked cheerfully.

"What are you doin' in Betsy's room?" Smythe demanded. "And where in blazes is she?"

"She's downstairs 'elpin' Mrs. Goodge get the tea ready for us. It's almost time for our meetin', ya know," Wiggins replied. "I nipped up 'ere to 'ave a go at her window. She said it were stickin' somethin' awful, and with this 'eat, she wanted it fixed so she could 'ave a spot of fresh air at night."

Smythe was incensed. "She asked *you* to fix her bloomin' window? Why in thunder didn't she ask me?" But he knew the answer to that. She was still mad as spit at him, that's why. Turning on his heel, he stomped toward the back stairs. "Just like a woman. No matter what ya do, ya can't please 'em. Try tellin' 'em the truth and they laugh at ya. Try fibbin' a bit to keep the peace, and they act like you've cut 'em to the quick."

Wiggins, who was right on his heels, asked, "Are you angry about something, Smythe?"

"No." He started down the stairs, determined that when he saw Betsy, he blooming well wouldn't do anymore apologizing. "Come on, let's get to the meetin'. I've got a lot to tell and then I've got plenty of investigatin' to do."

"Me too," Wiggins echoed. "I learned ever so much this morning. Almost as much as we found out last night in the pub."

The others were sitting around the table when they came into the kitchen. Fred leapt to his feet and darted across the kitchen as soon as he spotted his beloved Wiggins. Smythe gave a general nod to everyone and deliberately avoided looking at Betsy as he took his usual seat at the table.

"Leave off playin' with that silly dog," Mrs. Goodge ordered the footman. "We've got a lot to do today. My report alone is goin' to take a good while, and I've got some sources droppin' by after supper."

"It sounds as if we've no time to spare," Mrs. Jeffries said. She paused as Wiggins pulled out his chair and plopped down. "Perhaps we ought to hurry along with our tea."

"The tea's already poured." Mrs. Goodge began handing around the steaming cups. "And if you'll give your plates here, I'll fill 'em up." She snatched Wiggins's plate and slapped two pieces of buttered brown bread, a scone and a slice of seed cake onto it. Then she shoved it back to him and made a grab for Smythe's plate.

"Ta, Mrs. Goodge," Wiggins said happily.

"Yes, I believe that's quite a good idea," Mrs. Jeffries said. "Who would like to go first?"

"I think Smythe and I ought to," Wiggins said from around a mouthful of food. "We found out ever so much last night." He swallowed. "Accordin' to what we 'eard, there wasn't any reason for anyone to be scratchin' their 'eads over them garden keys. Jon Siler, the gardener, claims the place is unlocked 'alf the time as it is."

Mrs. Goodge, who'd just shoved a heaped plate of food under Smythe's nose, nodded vigorously in agreement. "I found out the same thing. My sources seemed to think that a number of residents on the square used the garden late at night for . . . well, how shall I put it? Assignations of an illicit nature."

"Humph, that's just a fancy way of sayin' there's some that was sneakin' around and doin' what they oughtn't to be doin'," Luty concluded. "Course that's been goin' on since the beginin' of time, I reckon. Now what I want to know is which one was it?"

It was Smythe who answered. "We heard it was Mr. Heckston. He's been carryin' on with Mrs. Prosper. They used to meet in the garden after Mr. Tavistock had taken his bulldog for a walk. Seems to me, it was right dangerous. I mean they coulda been caught."

"They was caught," Mrs. Goodge announced. "By Mrs. Heckston. I got this straight from the butcher's boy whose cousin is sister to Mrs. Heckston's tweeny. But how I found out isn't important."

"What happened?" Luty asked eagerly. "Did she catch 'em in the act?"

"Madam, please," Hatchet squawked indignantly. "There are young people present." He looked pointedly at Wiggins and Betsy.

"Don't be such an old stick, Hatchet. They know what I'm talkin' about." She waved him off and turned her attention to the cook. "Well," she demanded. "How did Mrs. Heckston catch 'em?"

"Not, as you call it, 'in the act.'" Behind her spectacles, Mrs. Goodge's eyes sparkled with amusement. "She simply woke up and found him gone. The first time it happened, she accepted his story that he couldn't sleep and had gone for a walk. But when it continued to happen, she got suspicious and followed him. I expect that when she saw Mrs. Prosper going into the garden a few moments after her husband, she realized he was lyin' through his teeth about being an insomniac."

"Cor blimey, that was a stupid lie to tell." Smythe shook his head, disgusted that one of his own gender could be so dumb.

"Maybe Mr. Heckston thought his wife was stupid enough to believe anything he told her," Betsy suggested. "Some men are like that, you know. They think you'll believe any old tale they make up." She hadn't looked at the coachman when she was speaking, but nonetheless, the barb struck home.

Smythe's eyes narrowed angrily.

Mrs. Jeffries realized that once again these two were at odds. She didn't mind their little tiffs when there wasn't a murder to investigate, but this was getting very tiresome. She decided to intervene. "I do think we ought to be a bit more systematic in our reporting," she said firmly. "Doesn't everyone agree? Otherwise we're going to be here all evening."

"Exactly, Mrs. Jeffries," Hatchet said. "It does appear that several of us have learned the same information."

"I 'ate it when that 'appens," Wiggins complained.

Mrs. Jeffries didn't particularly like it either, but there was little anyone could do about it. "Mrs. Goodge, why don't you continue?" she suggested.

"Not much more to tell, really." The cook shrugged. "That's about all I've heard so far. Exceptin' that Mrs. Prosper playin' about is pretty common knowledge. There's even some gossip that claims that the two of them are still seeing each other. One of the maids thought she heard someone in that vacant house on the square. She was sure it was Mr. Heckston and Mrs. Prosper."

"When was this?" Mrs. Jeffries asked. "The morning of the murder?"

"It was before that," Mrs. Goodge replied. "But it was after Mrs. Heckston caught them."

"How does her husband keep from findin' out?" Luty asked, her expression curious. "It seems to me that there's always them that likes to run tellin' tales on someone. If everyone knows, how come no one's spilt the beans?"

"Someone 'as," Wiggins put in. "Oh, sorry Mrs. Jeffries, I know it's not my turn."

"It's all right," Mrs. Jeffries waved him on.

"Well, accordin' to one of the rumours that I 'eard this mornin', Mr. Prosper knows and doesn't care. 'E's that besotted with the woman, 'e is."

"I can verify that information," Mrs. Jeffries added. She told them about her visit to Isadora Lucas.

"Watches out the window, does she?" Luty asked when Mrs. Jeffries had finished her recitation.

"Yes, I think she's a very lonely person, but on the other hand, if it wasn't for people like her, our task would be incredibly difficult."

"Did you learn anything else that may be of use?" Hatchet asked her. "It appears as if this Mrs. Lucas keeps quite an eye on that square."

"She does." Mrs. Jeffries cast her mind back, trying to recall everything that had been said. Finally, she shook her head. "She did confirm what Wiggins and Mrs. Goodge have told us about Mr. Heckston and Mrs. Prosper."

Smythe leaned forward. "All right, so we know that the Prosper woman and her neighbor were meetin' secretly in that garden. That still doesn't give any reason why someone would want to kill Mirabelle Daws. From what's been said, everyone knew about the two of 'em, so Mirabelle findin' out wouldn't matter. And 'ow could she find out? She was killed right after she got 'ere."

Mrs. Jeffries was thinking the same thing. "I don't know. We'll just have to keep on digging. Who would like to go next? Smythe?"

"Wiggins has already told ya what we learned." He gave them a few more details about the meeting with Jonathan Siler and Bill Trent. "And that's about all I found out for now. I didn't have much luck this morning."

He neglected to mention he'd made one of his dreaded trips to the bank this morning. He'd almost escaped, but then Mr. Pike, the bank manager, had popped out from behind a pillar just when Smythe was almost at the door. The bloke had gotten clever. Mr. Pike insisted that Smythe make some decisions about his investments. Smythe glanced at Betsy and tried a tiny half-smile. She didn't smile back. Blast, he thought. This ruddy money was becoming a misery. First he'd lived a lie with the others because he was rich as Croesus and couldn't let them know it, and now, it was putting a wedge between him and Betsy.

"Wiggins, do you have anything to add?" Mrs. Jeffries asked.

"Nah, just what I've already told ya."

"I might as well go next," Betsy said. She told them about her conversation with Alice Sparkle. Of course, she didn't tell them where the conversation had taken place or under what circumstances she'd learned the information. Not only would Smythe have a fit at the thought of her going into a pub, but even Mrs. Jeffries, for all her liberal ways, wouldn't take kindly to the idea of Betsy drinking gin at eleven o'clock in the morning.

"So Mrs. Prosper did know her sister was coming," Mrs. Jeffries mused.

"And apparently so did everyone else," Hatchet added. Betsy nodded in agreement. She ought to be feeling better about having been the one who discovered such an important clue. But it was hard to take pleasure in much of anything when she and Smythe were at odds. Plus her conscience was still smarting over her having bought all that gin for Alice. "Accordin' to Alice, it wasn't just Mrs. Prosper who didn't want her sister to come. It was Mrs. McCabe as well."

"That means both of them had a good reason to murder her," Luty said.

"So it would appear," Mrs. Jeffries said. "Anything else?"

"That's it," Betsy said. She cast a quick glance at Smythe, but he was glaring at the tabletop like he was trying to memorize the grain of the oak.

"If no one objects," Hatchet said, "I think I'd like to make my contribution now." He drew a long envelope out of his coat pocket, opened it and pulled out several sheets of paper. Laying them on the table, he said, "This is the passenger manifest from the *Island Star*. It came over by messenger while madam was out this afternoon. I thought perhaps we ought to have a look at it."

"That ain't necessary," Luty cut in. "I already knows what we needed to know about Mirabelle Daws's trip here from Australia." She grinned triumphantly at her butler. "But thanks jus' the same fer bringin' the thing. I'd forgotten I even asked for it."

"You did a great deal more than simply ask for it," Hatchet said from between clenched teeth. "You barged in on Lord Dyston practically in the middle of the night and demanded he get you a copy. The very least you can do is have a look at it."

"Oh, all right." Luty snatched up the pages and gave them a cursory inspection. "There, you satisified? Besides, I already told you I've heard plenty about Mirabelle's trip here. I got it straight from the horse's mouth."

"You spoke with Miss Brinkman, I presume," Hatchet asked stiffly. He was most put out that his own investigative efforts had come to naught on this case. Most put out, indeed.

Luty grinned. "Yup. She likes old ladies. She talked a blue streak while I was there." She neglected to mention that Miss Brinkman had talked that blue streak to Inspector Witherspoon while Luty sat on the floor of a storage closet. Some things were just too undignified to admit. "She told me that Mirabelle Daws wore that opal and diamond necklace all the time, had the manners of a field hand and a tongue like a shrew." She proceeded to give them all the details she'd learned that day.

When she'd finished, Mrs. Jeffries shook her head in amazement. "So Eldon Prosper knew Mirabelle was coming as well."

"And had sent her a telegram sayin' he'd meet her," Luty said eagerly. "For all we know, that telegram coulda told Mirabelle he'd meet her in the garden. He sure had a reason for not wantin' her to come."

"Yes, it seems he did." Mrs. Jeffries rubbed her chin. "This is perhaps the oddest case we've ever encountered."

"You can say that again," Mrs. Goodge agreed. "I can't make heads nor tails of anything. First the garden's locked and no one can get in or out without a key, then we find that having a key doesn't matter because the ruddy place is open half the time so people can sneak about late at night. Then we find out that everyone knew the victim was comin', and no one wanted her here. And no one's seen hide nor hair of the poor woman's luggage." She sighed heavily. "I do hope you've got your thinking cap ready, Mrs. Jeffries. You'll have a hard time figuring this one out."

Mrs. Jeffries was thinking the same thing. In the space of less than twenty-four hours they'd gone from having no suspects to having several. "I'm sure we'll be quite able to determine who the murderer is," she replied, refusing to take the sole credit for their crime-solving activities. "It will all come right in the end. It always does."

The inspector had debated about leaving his second interview with Eldon Prosper until the following morning, but he'd decided against that course of action. He and Barnes waited in the drawing room while the housekeeper fetched the master.

"Inspector." Prosper strode into the room, pausing long enough to draw the double oak doors closed behind him. "I hadn't expected to see you again so soon. Have you found the murderer yet?"

"No, sir, I'm sorry to say we haven't," Witherspoon replied.

"Then what are you doing here?" He asked. "I mean, why have you come back?"

"I'm afraid we've a few more questions to ask you, sir," the inspector said. "May we please sit down?"

"Of course. Make yourselves comfortable." He took the chair opposite the two policemen and crossed his legs. "I can't see how I can be of any help in this matter. Unfortunately, I didn't even know my sister-in-law."

"We're aware of that, sir," Witherspoon said. "But we still need to ask our questions. Now, sir, can you tell me where you were on the night or should I say the morning of the murder?"

Prosper's mouth gaped open slightly. "I've already told you that. I was out of town on business. In Edinburgh."

"We know what you've told us, sir," Barnes said. "Are you sure you wouldn't like to amend the statement you gave us? It's not too late to tell the truth. We know that you'd reason to dislike your sister-in-law."

Eldon's eyes widened. "I don't know what you're talking about. I tell you, I never met that woman. I didn't even know her."

"You don't have to know someone to want them dead," Witherspoon said softly. "You're lying, Mr. Prosper. We've had it on good authority that you were going to be in London that very evening. You had an appointment to meet your sister-in-law. She'd received a telegram from you when the ship docked at Southampton."

"That's not true," he cried. He leapt to his feet. "I'll thank you to leave my house. This isn't a convenient time just now. We've got the funeral to plan, and my wife is most upset."

"Mr. Prosper." Barnes got to his feet as well. He'd been a street copper for years. He didn't like intimidating people, but he could if he had to. "We can either finish the questions here, or you can come down to the station and help us with our inquiries there. Which is it going to be?"

"We can get verification from the ship's purser and the telegraph operator that Miss Daws received the telegram," Witherspoon said gently. "And we can also find out from your hotel in Edinburgh when you actually left."

Prosper said nothing for a moment. Then he sighed and sat down. "Oh what's the use? I should have known you'd find out. I didn't tell you the truth because I was terrified you wouldn't believe me."

"Tell us now," the inspector urged. "Tell us the truth and nothing else and I assure you, sir, if you're innocent of this crime, we'll not lay it on your doorstep simply to have the case closed. Now, why don't you start from the beginning. How did you know your sister-in-law was coming for a visit?"

He closed his eyes briefly. "I got a telegram from her a few days ago. It came to my office. I was quite surprised, really."

"What did it say, sir?" Barnes asked.

"It was very strange," he continued. "I wasn't quite sure what to make of it. Mirabelle insisted we meet in London on the night her ship came into Southampton. I was due to go to Edinburgh for a business trip, but at the last minute, I decided to change my plans. The telegram disturbed me. There was some sort of implication that I was holding Annabelle prisoner here."

"So you agreed to meet Mirabelle?" Witherspoon pressed. He wanted to make sure he understood the sequence of events.

"Oh, yes, I sent her a telegram care of the steamship line with instructions that it was to be given to her as soon as the ship docked. We were to meet at the Grand Hotel at nine o'clock that evening. I was there, but Mirabelle never arrived."

"Did you wait in the lobby, sir?" Barnes asked.

"Yes, several people saw me," he replied. "The bellman, the concierge, the night porter. A number of people can verify that I was there."

Witherspoon nodded. "What time did you leave?"

Prosper swallowed nervously. "I'm not sure. But it was very late."

"Was it past midnight?"

"It could have been."

"Did anyone see you leave?" Barnes pressed.

"Not that I'm aware of," Prosper stammered.

"So you can only account for your time up to midnight?" Witherspoon said. He didn't like the sound of that. Didn't like it at all.

"I suppose that's correct." Prosper said hesitantly.

Barnes leaned forward and looked Prosper directly in the eyes. "Where did you go after you left the hotel, sir?"

Prosper said nothing for a moment. "I went for a walk, Constable. As I've told you, this whole business with getting a telegram from that woman upset me greatly. When she didn't arrive, I decided that perhaps her ship had been late or that she'd missed the train or that something had detained her. I'd no idea she'd come to London and gone to Sheridan Square to get herself murdered."

Mrs. Jeffries was in a quandry. They'd learned an enormous amount of information in a very short time. Now the question was how to communicate what they knew to the inspector.

An even bigger question was whether they ought to tell him anything at all. He seemed to be doing quite nicely on his own. She sighed heavily and stared out the window of the drawing room. No, it wouldn't be right to deliberately keep anything from him. But really, it was quite amazing how very different he was from the shy, rather reticient man she'd come to work for over five years ago. Why, she could remember how she'd had to poke and prod and do all manner of things to get him to stick his nose into those horrible Kensington High Street murders.

He'd only been a clerk in the records room back then. She smiled as she remembered how none of the household had known what she was doing when she'd sent them all out and practically forced them to start asking questions. They hadn't realized what she was up to until Inspector Witherspoon was assigned the Knightsbridge murder of that Dr. Slocum. Not that Inspector Witherspoon had been assigned the Kensington killings; he hadn't. Pride welled up from deep inside her, her employer hadn't been assigned that case, but she'd made sure he got the credit for catching the killer. Now it seemed as though he was getting quite good at catching killers on his own.

She sighed again and dropped the edge of the velvet curtain she'd been holding as she stared out onto the empty street. Perhaps it was a good thing he'd become so proficient at solving homicides. Mrs. Jeffries was beginning to lose confidence in her own abilities to think the solution through.

She wandered slowly over to the settee and sank down. Leaning back against the cushion, she stared at the far wall as she let her mind deliberately go blank. Sometimes not thinking about the case produced the best results.

The soft ticking of the mantle clock filled the quiet room. Mrs. Jeffries tried her best not to think, but it was impossible. She wasn't tired enough to relax properly. Additionally, one part of her was listening for the inspector's footsteps coming up the front steps. Why would someone want Mirabelle Daws dead? There were plenty of motives, she told herself. But were any of them strong enough to kill over? Apparently so.

The sister-in-law might not have wanted Annabelle Daws to go back to Australia, but would she want her freedom badly enough to kill? That was a fairly radical way of obtaining one's freedom. Especially as Marlena McCabe didn't know one way or the other that Annabelle would, in fact, go home with her sister. Furthermore, Mrs. Jeffries suspected that given Luty's description of Mirabelle's behaviour on the ship, one could make the argument that the last thing any sane woman would want, would be to go and live with a dominating sister who controlled the purse strings.

And what about Mr. Prosper? Would he have been that frightened that his wife would really leave? Even in the rough-and-tumble world of Australia, a woman who'd run off from her husband wasn't treated kindly by society.

Mrs. Jeffries cocked her head to one side as she heard the distinctive clippity-clop of a hansom pulling up outside. She got up and hurried to the window. Peeking out, she saw her employer paying off the driver. She started for the front door. She'd see what all he'd come up with today, and then she'd have a jolly good long think in her own rooms.

"It's been the most amazing day." Witherspoon shoved another mouthful of mashed potato into his mouth.

She smiled, waiting patiently for him to swallow. Really, though, he'd done nothing but pat himself on the back since he'd come home. Then she caught herself and realized she was being most unfair. It wasn't the inspector's fault that his investigation was going along quite well while she couldn't make head nor tails out of theirs.

The inspector neatly sliced off a bit of chop and transferred it to his fork. "Judith Brinkman was most helpful, most helpful, indeed."

"Yes, it appears that she knew quite a bit about Miss Daws." She reached for the glass of sherry she'd poured herself before sitting down. "Did she give you any indication that there were other people who might have known the victim as well as she did?"

"There was a Lady Henrietta Morland and her butler who were hanging about a bit." Witherspoon said, "but apparently, Miss Daws was quite rude to them. Miss Brinkman says they were barely speaking by the time the ship docked at Cherbourg."

Drat, thought Mrs. Jeffries, that was one of the clues that Hatchet said he was going to pursue. He'd planned on going to the Morland home tomorrow. Now it sounded as if it would be a waste of time.

She was convinced now that the killer wasn't someone from the ship. If someone on board the vessel had wanted Mirabelle dead, it would have been easiest to cosh her over the head and dump her into the ocean in the dark of night. Instead, she'd been murdered in Sheridan Square. No one from the ship had any connections to the square, at least not as far as she or the household had learned.

"And then, of course, imagine my surprise when he jolly well admits to staying in a hotel just around the corner from the Sheridan Square," Witherspoon continued eagerly.

"What? What did you say?" Mrs. Jeffries could have smacked herself for not paying attention. "I'm sorry, I was thinking about what you mentioned a few moments ago. I'm afraid I didn't catch what you just said. Mr. Prosper stayed at a hotel? What hotel?"

Witherspoon smiled kindly at his housekeeper. "That's quite all right, Mrs. Jeffries. Our minds do tend to wander as we age. But as I was saying, Eldon Prosper claims he checked into the Webster Hotel on Armond Road. That's less than half a mile from the square. Well, he couldn't go home, now, could he? Everyone, including his wife, thought he was in Scotland on business."

Mrs. Jeffries kept the benign smile on her face with difficulty. She didn't mind the fact that she was getting older, but she certainly didn't have a "wandering" mind. "Are you going to verify his statement?"

"Of course." He waved his fork for emphasis. "Mind you, I don't think he realizes how much of a suspect he's become. He did have a strong motive for murdering Miss Daws."

"But, sir," she protested, "from what you've said, he had no reason to think his wife was going to go back to Australia with her sister. All he knew was that he'd received a rather odd telegram from the woman. Why do you think that could possibly mean he had a strong motive for wanting Mirabelle Daws dead?"

She didn't really want the answer to her question. She merely voiced the thought to make him stop and think about the situation for a moment.

"Well, uh." The inspector frowned. "I suppose you're right. All we've really got is Judith Brinkman's evidence of what Mirabelle said to her. Drat, I do wish she'd taken a look at the telegram . . ."

The inspector broke off as there was a loud knocking on the front door. "I wonder who on earth that could be?" Mrs. Jeffries jumped to her feet and started for the front door.

"Now, Mrs. Jeffries, please wait." Witherspoon tossed his serviette onto the table and leapt up. "I don't like you answering the door this time of night."

"I don't like either of ya answerin' at night," Smythe called as he shot past the housekeeper. He made it to the door first and pulled it open. "Cor blimey," he said in surprise. "It's that Inspector Nivens."

By this time, Inspector Witherspoon and Mrs. Jeffries were both right behind the coachman.

"You expectin' him, sir?" Smythe asked. Like everyone else in the household, he disliked Nivens.

"Of course he isn't expecting me," Nivens snapped. "I don't make it a habit to come calling at half past nine in the evening. Now if you'll get out of my way, I'll state my business and go. I've had a long day and I'm tired."

"Do come in, Inspector Nivens," Witherspoon said quickly as they all stepped back far enough to let their visitor pass. "Would you care for a cup of tea? Or perhaps a sherry?"

"That won't be necessary. Please dispense with the pleasantries, Witherspoon. As I said, I'm tired and in a hurry. Let's go into the drawing room."

"Yes, that's a jolly good idea." Whirling on his heel, the inspector took off at a fast trot back the way he'd just come.

Mrs. Jeffries and Smythe stared at the two policemen for a moment, and then both of them turned and followed. Luckily the direction of the drawing room was also the same direction as the back stairs. Without so much as a glance into the room, the two of them continued past the open double doors.

Smythe paused at the top of the landing and turned to the housekeeper. He jerked his head toward the drawing room and raised his eyebrows. Understanding his silent question perfectly, she nodded once. He took off immediately, taking care to make a racket as he went so that it sounded as if two people, not just one were going to the kitchen. As soon as the coachman's feet hit the first stair, Mrs. Jeffries started tiptoeing back up the hall. By the time Smythe had reached the bottom landing, she was right where she wanted to be, standing to one side of the open door. She angled her head so she could hear every word the two policemen said.

"Chief Inspector Barrows insisted I come around tonight," she heard Nivens say. "Though in my opinion, it could easily have waited until tomorrow. I don't have all that much news. But then again, he always seems to think your cases are so ruddy important."

Mrs. Jeffries glared in Nivens's direction. His manners certainly hadn't improved any since the last time she'd seen the fellow. Despite her adherence to certain Christian principles, it was people like Nigel Nivens who made it difficult to love thy neighbor. He was rude, obnoxious and desperately jealous of Inspector Witherspoon. He'd made no secret of the fact that he simply didn't believe their inspector was clever enough to have solved so many murders. Well, she thought, let him think what he likes. He can't prove we've been helping all along. Though she rather suspected he'd tried several times in the past. He'd never succeeded in getting the chief inspector to take his accusations seriously.

"Er, well." Witherspoon's voice was apologetic. "I say, I am sorry if coming here has caused you any inconvenience."

"It's caused me a great deal," Nivens said nastily, "but I really had no choice in the matter. You wanted to know if any of my people had heard about that opal and diamond necklace, right?"

"That's correct."

"You're in luck, them," Niven's voice stretched, as though he were yawning. "One of them has. I heard about it right before I left the Yard this evening."

"Excellent, Inspector Nivens," Witherspoon enthused. "I certainly didn't expect such a quick response."

"Why not?" Nivens demanded. "Unlike some people on the force, I actually know what I'm doing."

Mrs. Jeffries had to restrain herself from rushing in and giving the odious little toad a good boxing on his ears. The nerve of the fellow, insulting Inspector Witherspoon in his own home. Lucky for Nivens, their inspector was far too much a gentleman to take offense.

"I didn't mean to imply you didn't" Witherspoon hastily apologized again. "But I must say, don't you think you're being a bit harsh? I think most of the force does a jolly good job. But on to your information. Do tell me the details, sir. Did your source actually see the necklace?"

There was a long pause. Mrs. Jeffries could imagine Nivens's expression. By this time he was no doubt gaping like a goldfish, shocked that his nasty sarcasm went right past Inspector Witherspoon. She stifled a giggle. Served him right, she thought.

"No, he didn't actually see it," Nivens replied.

Mrs. Jeffries was sure his teeth were clenched.

"But he did hear about it," he continued. "It seems some woman was going round the less-reputable jewelers and inquiring as to the value of the piece."

"What woman?" Witherspoon asked. "Did your source get a name?"

Again there was a rather lengthy pause. Then Nivens said, "Don't be absurd, Witherspoon. The kind of jewelers I'm talking about don't ask that sort of question. Only an imbecile would give their right name when they were trying to fence a piece of jewelry obtained off a murdered corpse."

Mrs. Jeffries winced. Much as she loathed admitting it, Nivens had a point.

"You're quite correct," Witherspoon replied. "I wasn't thinking. Did your source get a description of this woman? I mean we must know some details."

"All I know is what I've already told you. Some woman has been trying to sell a necklace like the one you described."

"Oh, dear," Witherspoon said. "That's a start I suppose, but it's not quite what we were hoping for."

"I wasn't finished," Nivens said irritably. "My source told me that the jeweler in question directed the woman to someone else. A fence named Jon McGee. McGee operates out of a pub off the Commercial Docks. He's usually there most evenings."

"Gracious," Witherspoon yelped. "I'd best get cracking then. It's getting quite late."

"Calm down," Nivens ordered. "McGee won't be there tonight. He's in Birmingham and not due back until tomorrow. So even if your lady goes there this evening, she'll not find him."

"What's the name of the pub?"

"The Sailor's Whistle," Nivens said. "That's all I know. It's up to you to put a watch on the place and nab the woman. You'll have your killer then."

"I'm not sure I would go quite that far," Witherspoon demurred. "We may have someone who has a necklace to sell. We don't know that it's the right necklace, and even if it is, we don't know that the person trying to sell it is the killer."

Bravo, Inspector, Mrs. Jeffries thought. You tell him how a real homicide policeman thinks. He never makes assumptions without thoroughly looking at the evidence.

Nivens snorted loudly. "Whatever you say, Witherspoon," his voice dripping with sarcasm. "After all, you're the great homicide detective."

CHAPTER 8

Despite Mrs. Jeffries's doubts as to the veracity of Inspector Niven's statements, Witherspoon was utterly deaf to her hints that he ought to send a lad down to watch the pub just in case someone trying to fence an opal and diamond necklace happened to show up. As she wasn't supposed to have even heard that conversation, she had to be very careful about how hard she pressed the matter. But it was no good at all. The inspector was such an innocent. He took Nivens completely at his word.

"I'm sure Inspector Nivens doesn't mean to be so grumpy," he explained as he reached for his coat and hat. "He's just had a very long day."

"But don't you think, perhaps, you ought to, well, verify whatever it was he told you," she'd suggested.

"That's not necessary," Witherspoon whistled for Fred, who came bounding down the stairs with his tongue hanging out and his tail wagging furiously. "I'm sure Nivens's information is absolutely on the mark. He isn't the most pleasant of fellows, but I've never know him to deliberately lie. Come along, boy." He started for the back door. "Let's go walkies."

"We'd better make this quick," Smythe muttered as they heard the back door close behind the inspector. He'd had the others at the ready since Nivens had shown up. It was late and they were all tired, but none of them were willing to wait until tomorrow to find out what had gone on.

"Why?" Mrs. Goodge asked. She set a jug of lemonade out on the table and motioned for Betsy to put the tray of glasses down next to it. "He'll be gone a good forty-five minutes. All he does is stroll across the garden to Lady Cannonberry's. Fred'll get a nice tidbit from the kitchen and our inspector'll drink a couple of glasses of Harvey's. He's certainly taking his own sweet time with that courtship. How long's it been now? Four, five years?"

The entire household had given up trying to rush that relationship. Even though the two involved were very much enamored of one another, neither seemed in any hurry to change the present situation. As far as Mrs. Jeffries was concerned, that was just fine. The inspector had a right to make his own choices in his private life. Though she did feel a tad guilty because they'd not included Ruth in this investigation. Their neighbor, despite her aristocratic title, was the daughter of a simple vicar. She'd married well and now that she was widowed and in control of her money and her household, was quite a political radical. But that didn't stop her from being a wonderful neighbor and a good friend to the entire household. She was a fairly good snoop as well, Mrs. Jeffries thought. Too bad they'd been so rushed on this case. But that was the way things had worked out.

"Are we ready, then?" Wiggins asked as he flopped down in the chair next to Betsy. He reached for his glass, took a sip of lemonade and then yawned.

"This'll not take long," the housekeeper assured him. She noticed that Mrs. Goodge had dark circles under her eyes as well. The cook needed her rest. Getting up at the crack of dawn to bake and cook so she'd have food to "feed her sources" was getting harder on the elderly woman than Mrs. Jeffries had realized. "As I'm sure Smythe told you, I eavesdropped on the inspector and Nigel Nivens. But before I tell you about that, I'll tell you the other things I learned during dinner."

Taking care not to leave out even the smallest of details, she told them everything she and the inspector had discussed while he was eating his meal. Then she told them what she'd overheard from Nivens.

When she finished, Smythe started to get up, but she waved him back to his seat. "I know what you want to do," she said, "but I don't think it's necessary."

"Nivens hates our inspector," Smythe argued. "I wouldn't put it past him to do a bit o'sabotagin'. That necklace might be bein' fenced tonight. Someone ought to get over there . . ."

"I was worried about the same thing," she interrupted, "but upon reflection, I don't think Nivens is stupid enough to do something that obvious. He knows the chief inspector doesn't like or trust him, and if it came down to it, Chief Inspector Barrows would take our inspector's word over Nivens's. I think we can safely assume that he was telling the truth tonight. Besides, if he'd been lying and deliberately giving our inspector false information, he'd have been far more pleasant about the whole thing."

Smythe thought about it for a moment and then sank back down to his chair. "That's true." He chuckled. "Cor blimey, he was in a sorry old state. He were so niggled at having to come round, you could practically see the steam pourin' out of 'is ears."

"So what do we do now?" Betsy asked. "Seems like the inspector's learning as much as we are and doin' it quickly as well. From what he said, there's no point in our trying to hunt down anyone else that was on the ship with Mirabelle Daws, not if no one was even talking to her."

"Sometimes things aren't always what they seem," Mrs. Jeffries replied. "As you all well know, we really can't take anything for granted. No one may have been speaking to Miss Daws by the time she left the ship, but that doesn't mean the people on board didn't see something that could turn out to be important." She'd learned the hard way not to leave any stone unturned. "I know that Hatchet was going to try and contact Lady Henrietta Morland tomorrow . . ."

"'E's goin' on the train," Wiggins put in, "and it's a long ways."

"Colchester isn't that far," Mrs. Goodge said.

"But if it's goin' to be a waste of time, maybe I ought to nip over there tonight and tell 'im not to bother."

"Mrs. Jeffries hesitated and then shook her head firmly. "No. Let him go. He might learn something important. From what we know of the victim, she didn't hide her light under a bushel. She may have given Lady Henrietta Morland an interesting earful before she offended her."

"But would it have anything to do with her murder?" Mrs. Goodge asked softly.

"We won't know unless we ask," Mrs. Jeffries said firmly. They talked about the case for another ten minutes, but it was soon apparent that none of them had anything new to add to the matter.

Mrs. Goodge broke rank first. Yawning, she got up and stretched. "I think I'll turn in. It's gettin' late and I've got to be up early to bake another seed cake. Betsy, could you do us a favor, dear, and tidy up?"

"Of course, Mrs. Goodge." The maid smiled, "You go get some rest now. You've been on your feet for hours."

"I can help you," Mrs. Jeffries told Betsy.

But the maid would have none of it. "You've been on your feet all day too. I can handle this on my own. There isn't much to do. Just a few glasses and a jug to wash and put away."

As the housekeeper wasn't so much tired as desperate to get to the quiet of her room so that she could have a good long think, she smiled gratefully. "Thank you, dear. Smythe, will you lock up?"

"Sure, but I'll wait till the inspector's home. I'm not sure 'e took the back door key with 'im."

"That'll be fine." She got up and went towards the back stairs.

"Wait fer me." Wiggins leapt up too. "I'm knackered. Night, everyone," he called as he followed the housekeeper.

Betsy picked up a tray from the sideboard and began loading the empty glasses on it. She lifted the jug and peered inside. "Do you want the rest of this?" she asked Smythe.

"No, thanks, I'm not all that thirsty," he said softly.

"All right." She put the jug on the tray and went to the sink. Mrs. Goodge had left a sinkful of soapy water ready for her. Betsy carefully popped everything in the steamy liquid. She pretended not to notice when she heard the faint scrape of a chair and a moment later, Smythe standing close behind her.

"I'd like to talk to ya," he said softly.

"I'm not going anywhere until these things are washed and dried," she replied.

He cleared his throat. "There's something I've got to tell ya."

"Like I said, I'm not going anywhere at the moment."

"There's nothin' wrong with me hearin'," he said irritably. "I know what you've said. It's just that I don't want to be interrupted by the inspector." He reached to one side and whipped a clean tea towel off the rack. Then he picked up one of the glasses Betsy had just washed and put on the wooden draining board and began to dry it.

"What are you doing?" she asked.

"I'm 'elpin' with the cleanup so you and I can go somewhere private-like and talk."

"And just where would that be?" She plopped two more glasses on the board. "I'm not goin' to your room."

"I'd not ask ya to," he snapped, incensed that she would even think such a thing. "But there's a whole bloomin' garden outside, and it's a nice warm evening."

She rinsed off the jug and placed it next to the glasses. "The inspector'll be home soon."

"So what?" he said. "I've got the back door key. He'll come inside and go straight up to bed. He always leaves it fer me to lock up. Now, are you willin' to come out and talk?"

She thought about it for all of two seconds, and then she nodded. "All right, but not for too long. I'm tired."

Just at that moment, they heard the back door open. Fred came flying into the room first. He ran over to Betsy and Smythe to get petted. The inspector came in a few seconds later.

"Gracious, are you two still up?"

"We're just finishin'," Smythe said.

"Don't be too late," Witherspoon said as he headed towards the stairs. "I'm sure you're as tired as I am. Good night, sleep well. Come on, Fred, let's go upstairs. We all need our sleep."

Fred, who was enjoying Betsy's petting, reluctantly followed his master out of the kitchen.

Smythe waited till he heard the inspector's footsteps fade away. "Come on, then, let's go." He held out his hand.

Betsy took off her apron, tossed it onto the table and joined her hand with his. "All right, I'm ready."

Mrs. Jeffries sighed gratefully as she sank into her favorite chair. She hadn't lighted the lamps, but she'd kept the curtains open. The faint, pale glow of the gas lamps on the street below cast enough light into the room to keep it from being pitch black. She liked the quiet and the dark. It helped her think.

She leaned her head back and began to mentally go over each and every fact they knew about this case. Just the facts, she told herself firmly. She'd pick the other bits apart later. Right now she simply wanted it clear in her own mind what was indisputable. She cringed slightly, aware that she was forcing herself through this exercise because she was concerned that perhaps she wasn't quite as confident in herself as she used to be. Perhaps that was a product of getting older, or perhaps it was simply that this case was so terribly baffling.

She shook herself, determined not to give in to these ridiculous notions . . . she'd go over the facts and then she'd examine the other information they'd gathered, the gossip, the implications, everything. She'd pick it apart piece by piece, and then she'd put all the pieces back together and somehow, someway, some kind of a pattern would emerge.

It always had before.

But first, the facts. She straightened her spine and took a deep breath. Fact, two nights ago an Australian woman who'd never been to England before in her life got murdered in a locked garden. Fact, it happened between four and six in the morning. Fact, the victim was stabbed. Fact, there were no identifying papers on the woman's body. Fact, the woman had just come here from a ship. Fact, an opal and diamond necklace had been taken off her body.

Fact, fact, fact. Mrs. Jeffries snorted in disgust. This was getting her nowhere. She could sit here all night and list facts until the cows came home, but it wouldn't bring her a step closer to finding the killer. Absurd, really. What was she thinking? There was nothing wrong with her mind, and there was nothing wrong with this investigation. They simply hadn't found the key yet. But she would, oh yes, she promised herself, she would.

She relaxed back in her chair and instead of keeping her attention focused on the facts of the case, she let her mind drift where it would. Bits and pieces swam in and out of her consciousness, and she didn't try to put them in any proper order; she simply let them come as they would.

Eldon Prosper hadn't been in Edinburgh on the night of the murder. He had a reason to want Mirabelle dead, too. He was scared that with her newfound wealth she'd convince Annabelle to go back to Australia. But was he really that frightened of such a thing? Frightened enough to kill? And why was Mirabelle so set on coming to "rescue" her sister in the first place? She had no real evidence that Annabelle was being treated cruelly. Had she? And what about Annabelle Prosper's affair with her neighbor, Heckston? Why hadn't Prosper put a stop to that if he was so frightened of losing his wife? Apparently it was finally Mrs. Heckston who'd put a stop to it.

Mrs. Jeffries sat straight up in her chair. Good gracious, why hadn't she thought of it before? It was as plain as the nose on your face. Without thinking—for if she thought about it, she might not do it—she got up from her chair and dashed out of the room.

Hurrying down a short flight of stairs, she came to a halt outside Inspector Witherspoon's door. She knocked. "Inspector, I'd like to have a quick word with you."

The door opened a crack and Witherspoon, minus his spectacles and with a nightcap on, stuck his head out. "Is something wrong, Mrs. Jeffries?"

"No, sir," she smiled reassuringly. "It was just something you said, sir. Goodness, you are a sly one, sir. I mean I'd no idea you were going to send the investigation in that direction. Well done, sir. Well done, indeed. I'd have never thought of doing something that clever."

"Er, uh, thank you, Mrs. Jeffries." He gave her a thin, worried smile. "But I'm not sure I know exactly what you're referring to. I can't think of anything I said tonight. . . ."

"It was what you didn't say, sir," she said, beaming proudly at him. "Come now, sir. Do confess, or I shall never get any sleep."

"Er, I'm still rather unsure of what you could possibly mean . . ."

"Now, now, sir. Don't be coy with me." She chuckled indulgently. "Surely you're thinking what I'm thinking. Annabelle Prosper and Mirabelle Daws were sisters. Like most sisters, I suspect they resembled each other somewhat."

Witherspoon thought for a moment. Except for the fact that Mirabelle had been a distinctly chalky-white color when he'd seen her, there was a resemblance between the two women. "Yes, they were the same height and build," he said. His mind was trying to catch on to what Mrs. Jeffries was saying. Drat, he hated it when he'd been brilliant and then forgotten about it.

"Then of course, sir, you're going to do the obvious, aren't you? You're going to find out if Mirabelle Daws was the real victim."

"The real victim?" he repeated.

She clasped her hands together excitedly. "I knew it. I knew I was right and that I'd guessed what you're going to do next. You're going to ask about and find out if anyone had a reason to want Annabelle Daws Prosper dead."

The inspector's jaw dropped, and then he quickly clamped his mouth shut. "Well, yes, you're right, Mrs. Jeffries. That's precisely what I'm going to do. I ought to have known you'd be onto my tricks."

"Excellent, sir." She smiled broadly. "Thank you so much for telling me. Now I can sleep well tonight," she waved good night and hurried back to her rooms.

At least now she'd have him asking the right questions of the servants and the local residents, she thought as she quietly opened her door and stepped inside. It shouldn't be too long before the inspector discovered, as they had, that Annabelle Daws used the garden quite frequently to meet her lover. She shook her head in disgust as she sank down in her chair again. She'd been so blind when the real answer might be right under her nose. Mirabelle Prosper, despite the unusual circumstances that brought her to Sheridan Square at that time of night, might not have been the real victim.

No one had a motive to murder her. Yet a good number of people might have wanted Annabelle dead; Mrs. Heckston, Mr. Heckston, or even the woman's own husband. Perhaps he was tired of being cuckolded. Killing the wrong woman would be an easy mistake to make. Mrs. Jeffries knew that for a fact. It had happened at least twice just on the cases they'd investigated.

Smythe and Betsy sat at the wooden bench under the oak tree in the middle of the garden. It was a quiet, secluded place, perfect for sweethearts. A luminous moon peeked out from behind the branches of the tree, the scent of lavender and summer roses filled the air and in the distance, a night bird sang. But neither Betsy nor Smythe noticed the beauty of the summer night.

They were both too scared.

She was afraid Smythe was going to tell her he wasn't sweet on her anymore, and Smythe was terrified that once she knew the truth about his past, she'd feel differently about him.

"Go on, then," she said. She smoothed her skirt over her lap and then twined her hands together to keep them from shaking. "You said you wanted to talk."

"I'm not sure where to begin," he said softly.

"Start at the beginnin'," she advised. "That's what Mrs. Jeffries always tells us."

"Yeah, I reckon that's as good a place as any." He cleared his throat. "All right, then. Do you remember when you first came to the inspector's house?"

"I didn't exactly come there," she reminded him. "It was more like I collapsed on his doorstep." The memory was a hard and painful one, but she didn't shrink from it. Her sense of self, of pride, had grown greatly in the past few years. Perhaps it was because for the first time in her life, people she admired seemed to think she was worth something. She'd finally decided that having been born and raised in the poorest part of London wasn't anything to be ashamed of. She hadn't asked to go hungry or watch her younger sister die from starvation. That's what people didn't understand about being poor. It's not a condition that you decide upon. It's something that's thrust upon you, like the color of your hair or eyes. Her people had been decent and hardworking. Both her parents had labored long and hard to take care of their family. But they'd died, and she'd been faced with some ugly choices. Just when life had seemed the worst for her, just when it seemed there was no hope or mercy or compassion for people like her, she'd stumbled onto Inspector Witherspoon's door stoop.

"Sometimes I wonder how my life would have turned out if I'd sat down on Mrs. Collier's doorstep," Betsy mused. She was referring to one of the inspector's neighbors. "She's not a bad woman, but she'd have shooed me away, not taken me in like Inspector Witherspoon did. I was lucky."

"We were lucky, Betsy," he told her softly. "You were sick and half starved, but so stubborn about earnin' your keep that you tried to get up off your sickbed and help Mrs. Jeffries scrub floors. I remember how she had to give ya a right good tongue-lashin' to get ya back to bed."

"She was wonderful to me," Betsy said. "She talked the inspector into giving me a position, helped me learn how to speak properly and most importantly made me think I was worth something." She stopped and gave herself a small shake. This wasn't about her. "Of course I remember coming here. What of it?"

"Mrs. Jeffries hadn't been here long, as the inspector 'ad inherited the place from his Auntie Euphemia." Smythe said.

"I know that," she said. "You and Wiggins both worked for her, didn't you? Come on now, Smythe, what's this all about? Are you still annoyed with me because I didn't believe that silly story you was tryin' to tell me the other day?"

"It weren't a silly story, lass," he said calmly. "It were the truth. I wished you'da listened then. If you 'ad, this wouldn't be so hard."

Betsy said nothing. She simply stared out into the the night. In her heart of hearts she'd known he was telling the truth. He wasn't a liar. And in one part of her mind, she'd suspected there was more to him than he'd let on. To begin with, there were all those gifts everyone in the household received. Like when she lost her best pair of gloves this winter and then she'd found an even better pair lying out on her bed. And Mrs. Goodge's expensive medicine for her rheumatism. New bottles were always popping up in her room. No matter how many silly poems he wrote, Wiggins always had a fresh supply of nice notepaper. Even Mrs. Jeffries wasn't left out. The gift giver always made sure that she had the latest volume of Mr. Walt Whitman's poems.

She bit her lip. The clues had been right under her nose. She just hadn't wanted to see them. Everyone in the household received these gifts, except Smythe. And there were other things as well, like the times she'd seen him going through the post when he thought no one was looking. There'd always be a big white envelope for him. An envelope he'd hide in his pocket when he heard her coming. There had been so many things she could have asked him about. So many times when she could have confronted him about all the little mysteries surrounding him, but she hadn't. She hadn't wanted to admit it because admitting it would change things. She didn't want things to change.

"I've got lots of money, Betsy," he continued, when she didn't speak. "More than enough to take care of both of us for the rest of our lives."

"Are you rich?" she asked.

"Yeah." He licked his suddenly dry lips. She didn't look pleased. "I can give you anything you want, buy you a big house, we can travel, we can do whatever we want."

"I see." She knew that she ought to be happy. The man she cared about was telling her she'd never have to worry about being poor again. But somehow, all she felt was a sharp, searing pain in her heart. She swallowed the sudden lump in her throat. "I want things to be the way they were. You've lied to me all these years. You've lied to all of us. Why? Was it to make us look like fools?"

His heart broke as he heard the ragged misery in her voice. "Never, lass. It was never that. I never meant fer it to 'appen this way. You've got to believe me."

"How can I believe someone who's just admitted he's lied to me since the day we met?"

"I never meant fer it to happen," he continued doggedly. "I wasn't goin' to stay. I only stayed because I promised Euphemia I'd hang about a bit and make sure the inspector got settled in all right. He'd never had a big house or any money. So I stayed until after Mrs. Jeffries come and then you came and then before I knew it, we was out investigatin' murders and actin' like a family."

"But you still could have told us," Betsy insisted doggedly.

"You'd have treated me differently if I'd said anything," he insisted.

"We wouldn't. Luty Belle's got money, and we don't treat her any differently."

"Only because you've always known she had money," he argued. "If I'd come out and told everyone, you'd 'ave all acted like I didn't have a right to be here. Like I was takin' a good job away from some poor bloke that really needed it. I've 'eard the way you and Wiggins go on about that sort of thing, about people takin' jobs when they don't have to have one. I didn't want you turnin' on me. Not after I'd come to care for ya."

She said nothing. In the pale light, Smythe could see her expression. Her face seemed carved of stone. He wished she'd scream or cry or call him names. Temper or tears, he could handle that. Anything but this awful silence. "Say something," he begged.

With a barely perceptible nod, she shook her head as though she were shaking herself out of a dream. "What is there to say? You're rich. I'm poor. You've stayed on at the house because it was comfortable for you, I suppose. I don't know. I don't think I know anything anymore."

It was the God's truth. Betsy's world had suddenly started to collapse upon her. "If I can't trust you," she mused, "who on earth can I trust?" There was one part of her that wondered if he'd not told her the truth as a kind of test. To make sure she really cared about him and not his money. Maybe when she could feel something again, she'd get angry over that. She'd not made him jump through any hoops to win her affections. She couldn't understand why she was so hurt. Most women would be dancing for joy to find out that a man who was sweet on them was rich as sin, but she wasn't. Perhaps it was because in a life of hard times, she'd learned to hold herself back, to keep her feelings to herself. That was how she'd survived the awful streets of the East End.

But she'd opened herself to Smythe, shared things with him she'd never told another living soul, and now he was telling her he'd been lying to her for almost five years. It hurt. It hurt so much that it was almost hard to breathe. "I've got to go in now." She started to get up, but he placed his big hand on her arm and pulled her back down beside him.

"Don't hate me, lass," he whispered. "For all my money, it'd be worth nothin' if I lost you."

She looked down at his hand. "I don't think I hate you," she mumbled.

"But what I've told ya has changed yer feelings for me, hasn't it?" he asked. He prayed it wasn't true. But he was enough of a realist to know that this particular prayer didn't have a hope in Hades of being answered.

"I don't know how I feel," she admitted truthfully. She pulled away from him and stood up. She wasn't a fool, and she wasn't stupid enough to let hurt feelings and injured pride stand between her and a man she'd come to care deeply about. "I just don't know."

He threw caution to the winds. He loved her. Loved her more than he'd ever loved anything. "Will you marry me?" he asked. "You know how I feel about ya."

"Oh, Smythe," she sighed. "How can you ask me that now? I don't know what I feel anymore. I'm so confused I don't know if I'm comin' or goin'."

"Just think about it. That's all I'm asking." He stood up quickly and raised his hands in a supplicating gesture. "Don't answer right away. I know you've had a bit of a shock."

"A bit of a shock?" she echoed. "Is that what you call it? Let me ask you this. What if the tables were turned? What if I'd brought you out here tonight and told you something like this about me?"

"I'd try to be forgivin' and understandin'," he said quickly. He couldn't imagine Betsy telling him anything that would make him not love her.

"What if I told you I was married?" she asked. She knew exactly how to get to him.

"All right," he said, "I'd probably not be *that* understanding. But even if it was somethin' like that, I'd not just shut you out of my life, Betsy. I'd find a way for us to be together. Please, lass. What we've got is worth something."

Betsy knew that was true. But her sense of anger and betrayal went deep. Deeper, perhaps, than she could make him understand. "I need some time."

"How much time?"

"I don't know," she replied impatiently. "Enough to get over the shock and try and think clearly."

"I guess I can understand that."

She turned and started back toward the house. Her back was poker straight, and she held her head high, refusing to give in to the awful despair that threatened to overwhelm her. She was determined to get back to the safety of her room before she broke down and started crying.

"Betsy," he called softly. "Are you going to tell the others?"

She stopped but didn't turn to look at him. "That's for you to do."

"It's a bit of a mess," he said.

"But it's your mess, Smythe. You made it; now you clean it up."

CHAPTER 9

Hatchet knew he ought to be ashamed of himself, but he wasn't. Paying for information was a bit of a blow to his pride, but at his age, he'd decided his pride could stand it. In any case, one had to do what one had to do if one wanted results. Besides, he told himself, it wasn't as if madam hadn't crossed a palm with silver a time or two in the past.

He twisted slightly in his chair, vainly trying to find a more comfortable postion while he waited for his hostess to return. But the chair, like everything else in the drawing room, appeared to be on its last legs. The stuffing beneath the worn blue silk was knotted in some spots and nonexistent in others. No matter how one shifted or turned, it was dreadfully uncomfortable. The whole place was dreadfully uncomfortable, he decided.

And it smelled as well. The windows were caked with dirt and closed shut. The air was stale, with faint overtones of sour milk and mildewed cloth. Hatchet tried breathing through his mouth as he gazed curiously around the room.

The once-elegant home of the aristocratic Morlands had fallen on hard times. The delicate moldings on the high ceiling were cracked and broken in places, the gold and white striped wallpaper was faded, the chandelier was covered in cobwebs, and the thin velvet curtains were so stained with soot and grime that you had to squint to tell that they'd once been a lovely pale gold. But Hatchet wasn't one to look a gift horse in the mouth. The reason he was even sitting here at all was because he'd taken one look at the outside of the huge house and realized that the only things Lady Henrietta Morland had left were a worthless title and this mouldering pile of bricks.

If there was one thing he knew about aristocrats, it was that despite their disdain for money, when they didn't have it, they'd do anything to get it.

So he'd taken a gamble, and it appeared to have paid off.

The door creaked open and Lady Henrietta appeared. She was a tall, sparse woman with a hawk nose, deep-set watery hazel eyes and iron-gray hair pulled severely back in a top-knot. She was dressed in a long-sleeved, black bombazine dress. "Sorry to keep you waiting," she said brusquely. "But I had to take my medicine. Now, how much did you say your paper was willing to pay for my story?"

"Fifteen pounds, ma'am," he replied. Silently, he prayed to whatever deity might be listening that this woman actually knew something useful. This was an exorbitant amount of cash he was going to part with, and he wanted his money's worth. "Provided, of course, that you can verify you actually knew the victim, Miss Mirabelle Daws."

"Don't be absurd, man," she said curtly. "Of course I knew her. I knew her sister as well. Met each of them the same way, coming over from Australia on the *Island Star.*"

"I wasn't impuning your honesty, ma'am," Hatchet said quickly. "A lady of your class and background is obviously above reproach on matters of character. But it's my editor that needs convincing," he said conspiratorially. "Proof, as it were. He's an American."

"I can give you all the proof you need." She stared at him out of hard, shrewd eyes. "But I still don't understand why an American newspaper is interested in this murder. Don't they have enough of their own over there?"

"They do indeed, ma'am," he agreed. "But there is an enormous amount of interest in this particular one. It has what my editor calls 'human interest.'"

"Why?" Lady Henrietta walked towards a table next to the door. "Mirabelle Daws was a nobody. Why should anyone care how she got killed?" She opened the drawer in the table and pulled out a flat, white packet. Opening the packet, she slipped out a photograph, stared at it and nodded in satisfaction.

Hatchet watched her curiously. "I understand she was quite wealthy," he said.

Lady Henrietta snorted and tucked the photograph into the pocket of her skirt. "She had money, but she had no breeding. She kept house for her brother somewhere out in the outback. I believe she actually took in boarders while her brother was away working his mine." She advanced towards him, a malicious smile on her face. "The family were peasants, you know. Despite their mine and the property in the outback. Her sister was a lady's maid."

"I know." Hatchet smiled thinly. He was glad now that he'd only offered her fifteen pounds and not twenty-five. Hidebound old snob. It no longer bothered him that he'd obtained entry into this house under false pretenses. Since he'd gotten involved with the household at Upper Edmonton Gardens, his own ideas about the class system and right and wrong had completely changed. "That's one of the reasons my newspaper is so interested in the murder. Americans like what we call rags-to-riches stories," he explained eagerly. "They'll be fascinated with the story of the Daws women. One of them was essentially a mail-order bride, and the other was a murder victim."

"Mail-order bride? Humph, yes, I imagine that's what you'd call it. I call it disgusting. Annabelle Daws writes a few letters to a stupid rich Englishman and then ends up his wife. While her employer, that poor Mrs. Moulton, ended up so humiliated she couldn't even face coming back to England. It's not right, I tell you."

"What's not right?" he pressed.

"That people like that should have money," she cried. "Can you imagine it? Mrs. Moulton, a widow from one of the finest families in the realm, had to come home to England in a tiny closet of a cabin while her maid came back in a suite. It was utterly disgusting. A lady's maid, eating at the captain's table. Both of them did, you know. These days, all it takes is money. Breeding and lineage count for nothing. But at least Annabelle Daws had the good grace to know she was among her betters and kept her mouth shut."

"I take it Mirabelle didn't?" he asked. Hatchet had no idea if he was getting value for money, but he was certainly getting an earful and quite enjoying himself. Apparently, even thinking about the uppity Daws women was enough to make Lady Henrietta have a fit.

"She thought she was as good as the queen," Lady Henrietta snapped. "Had the nerve to lecture me on the value of hard work and how the decadent aristocrats had ruined the country. Can you believe it? Flounced about all over the ship, twirling those ridiculous opals and telling anyone who'd listen how she was going to England to straighten things out. Some of us tried to tell her that under English law you couldn't just waltz in and snatch an Englishman's wife, but she'd have none of it. Said English law was for fools and idiots, and she'd do whatever she had to to make sure her sister got away from that monster. It was shocking. Utterly shocking."

"But, ma'am, even English law doesn't compel a woman to live with a husband who treats her badly," Hatchet charged.

"She'd not get a penny of her husband's money if she left," Lady Henrietta cried wildly. She began pacing back and forth in front of the table. "Not one penny, and she'd not deserve it either."

Hatchet wasn't surprised by the woman's agitated behaviour. Strange as it was, it was quite in keeping with what he was sure was her character. She was the type who felt terribly upset by anyone even daring to suggest, through word or deed, the British class system wasn't perfect. Mirabelle Daws not only questioned it; she made it abundantly clear she'd no respect for it or aristocratic leeches like the Morland woman.

"I'm surprised the captain didn't have Miss Daws moved to another table," Hatchet said. His tone was only slightly sarcastic, but it went right past Lady Henrietta. "It appears her presence upset you greatly."

"Humph, I'd have thought so as well," she replied haughtily. "But the captain did nothing. He actually seemed to find the woman amusing. Well, he's going to regret that, I assure you. As soon as I returned, I wrote a letter to Hamilton-Dyston. They pay attention to my letters. My late husband was a shareholder in the company."

"That must bring you in a handsome dividend," Hatchet said. "They do quite well in the Australian trade." He was probing to see how a woman of her obviously limited means managed two expensive trips to Australia in the last year.

She had the good grace to look embarrassed. "Actually, we sold the shares before my dear husband passed away. But I do get to travel on their vessels whenever I want."

"I expect that's quite convenient for you, ma'am," he enthused. "Especially if you have business interests there."

"I have family that I go to visit," she replied. "My cousin has a very large holding outside of Sydney."

And Hatchet would bet his last penny that said cousin cringed every time Lady Henrietta showed up on the doorstep. "Is there anything else you can tell me about Mirabelle Daws?" He'd not really learned anything he didn't already know.

"Only that she was an ill-bred woman who shouldn't have ever left the outback."

"Like her sister?"

Lady Henrietta shrugged. "Annabelle was a bit better. But then she'd learned her manners from working for the Moultons."

"I take it you and Miss Daws were well acquainted by the time the vessel reached London. You certainly seem to know an awful lot about her."

"I don't become 'well acquainted' with persons of her sort."

Hatchet tried to ignore the sinking feeling in the pit of his stomach. He'd learned nothing. And he was out fifteen pounds. "I see." He rose to his feet.

Lady Henrietta's eyes widened in alarm as she watched him get up. "Where's my money?"

He started to reach his coat and the hesitated. "Uh, I say, this is awkward, but I do need some proof that you did actually know the victim." He fully intended to fulfil his end of the bargain, but he might as well get something tangible for his fifteen quid.

She reached into her pocket and took out the photograph. "This was taken on board the *Island Star*," she handed it to him. "The woman standing next to me was Mrs. Moulton. The person just to her right is Annabelle Daws. Is that proof enough for you?"

"I'd rather have a photograph of Mirabelle Daws."

"I don't have one of her. But you said you wanted proof I knew the Daws women. Well, this is a picture of Annabelle Daws."

"I suppose it'll do," he said. "Though a photograph of the murder victim would have been better." He pulled out several bills.

She stepped back. "Put them on the tray by the door," she instructed.

"As you wish, ma'am." He tucked the photograph in his pocket. "Thank you for seeing me. I'll be on my way now." He gave her a quick, barely perceptible head bob. Not because he had any genuine respect for her, but because it would be suspicious if he stopped playing his part now. That of an English gentleman forced to do something distasteful to make a living.

"I'll ring for Collins to see you out," she said, yanking on the frayed bellpull that dangled forlornly next to the door.

"There's no need," he protested. He rather suspected she'd only done it to make sure he didn't scarper without putting down the cash. "I can see myself out. Please don't trouble your staff."

"That's what he's here for," she replied arrogantly. "What did you say your name was again?"

Hatchet was ready for that question. "It was Puffy, ma'am. Rollo Puffy."

Wiggins thought his day couldn't get any worse. First, Smythe was as grouchy as a dog with a sore paw, Betsy was barely speakin' to anyone, Mrs. Goodge had caught him snatchin' one of her special sticky buns, and even Mrs. Jeffries was so preoccupied that she'd probably not heard a word he'd said when he'd left this morning.

And now this. He stared miserably at the young girl hurrying toward Charing Cross. He didn't know what to do. She was the tweeny he'd met that first day, the one he was sure knew more than she was telling. He'd popped along to Sheridan Square right early today and hit a spot of luck. He'd seen her sweepin' the front door stoop. Mind you, when he'd tried to talk to her, she'd not been real friendly. But he had learned that the funeral for that poor Miss Daws was tomorrow morning and that no one excepting the family was invited. Then she'd dropped the real news. She was leavin' that day. Taking the midday train home to her people and never setting foot in London again.

He'd tried to keep her talking, but he'd failed. Then Mrs. Prosper had come out and spoken to the girl. Wiggins couldn't hear much of what was said, just saw Fiona nod her head up and down a few times and then she'd said, 'Yes, Mrs. Prosper,' curtsied and hurried back inside.

Wiggins refused to give up. He knew this girl knew something. He'd hovered for hours waiting for her to come out. And it hadn't been easy either. The murder had made the residents of Sheridan Square nervous. Several people had come out and asked him his business. Luckily, the use of Inspector Witherspoon's name had worked like magic. Now he hoped that he wouldn't be in even more hot water when he got home. What if someone complained to the inspector?

The girl darted into the station. Considering that she was carrying a large carpetbag, she moved fairly quickly. Wiggins rushed after her. Just inside the huge door, he skidded to a halt. She was at the ticket counter. Directly above where she stood, there was a large clack board showing departure and arrival times. Wiggins smiled. There wasn't a train leaving for at least twenty minutes. Sighing in relief, he relaxed. At least she wasn't rushing off right this minute. Maybe now that she was away from the Prosper house, she'd not be so unfriendly.

He leaned against the wall and watched her. In a few moments, she had her ticket. Then she picked up the carpetbag and started for the platform.

Wiggins was relieved about that as well. He'd been worried she might head for the ladies' waiting room. He kept a close eye on her as she moved out into the cavernous station, and when he was sure he could follow her safely, he went after her.

"Are you sure we can't be seen from here?" the inspector asked for the third time. He and Barnes were standing behind a covered doorway in a warehouse across the street from the Sailor's Whistle. The pub was small and had a tiny window on each side of the door. It was crammed in between a derelict office building on one side and a cluttered wharf on the other.

"Absolutely, sir." He patted the wood that covered half of the recessed doorway. "We've had a bit of luck. They're goin' to be tearin' this place down in a couple of months. That's why they started boarding things up, sir. Wanted to make sure no one got in and took root."

"Yes," Witherspoon mused. "I suppose we have had our share of good fortune. You're absolutely certain there isn't any other way in or out of the pub?"

"Absolutely, sir," Barnes said patiently. "They used to have a bit of a wharf so that boats could pull up and let people in and out. But it rotted years ago, and they boarded over the back door. Take my word for it, sir. Whoever is fencing that necklace has to come in through the front door. Right under our noses as it were."

"Good." Witherspoon walked back out into the street. Barnes was right on his heels. "Then we'll be back this evening. If we hurry, we ought to have enough time to get a bite to eat. It might be quite a long night. We've no idea what time the woman might be showing up. How many lads are we leaving to watch the place?"

"Three, sir," Barnes replied. "None of them in uniform either. They're good coppers, sir. They'll not be spotted. Two of them are from around

this area. They're the ones I'm puttin' on the inside tonight. Tonight, of
course, we'll have several more on hand in case we have to make an arrest."

Mrs. Jeffries wasn't in a particularly good mood herself, so when she saw
Betsy's long face and Smythe's tight-lipped expression, she knew this meeting might not run smoothly.

"Let's get this done, then," Mrs. Goodge ordered as she placed the tea
tray on the table "I've got more people coming through here in an hour
or two, and I'll need this kitchen clear if I'm to get information out of
anyone."

Her tone was a tad testy, a sure sign that she'd not learned anything
useful either.

"I agree," Mrs. Jeffries said. "Quickly, everyone, take your seats." For
a few moments the only sounds were the scraping of chairs and the swish
of material as people took their places around the table. "Now, if no one
has anything to report . . ."

"I've got something to report," Hatchet said eagerly. It wasn't much,
but at least he'd come back with something. "I tracked down Lady Henrietta Morland," he continued. "She was on the same ship as Mirabelle
Daws. She was also on the same vessel as Annabelle Daws Prosper. She
knew both women."

"How very interesting," Mrs. Jeffries said. She forced herself to be
patient. Though what she was most interested in doing at this meeting was
making their plans for this evening's hunt at the Sailor's Whistle pub. She
fully intended that someone from this household would witness everything
that went on. "Did you learn anything new?"

Hatchet opened his mouth to reply and then clamped it shut again and
slumped in his chair. "Not really. I simply got confirmation of what Judith
Brinkman reported. Mirabelle Daws wasn't shy with expressing her opinion to all and sundry. But I did get a photograph," he reached in his pocket,
pulled it out and tossed it onto the tabletop. "Unfortunately, it's not one
of Mirabelle Daws."

"Who is it, then?" Betsy asked as she picked it up.

"Lady Henrietta and Annabelle Prosper," he replied. "Lady Henrietta's
on the right, the woman next to her is that Mrs. Moulton. Annabelle Daws
is standing a few feet back. She's the one in the dark shawl."

"How'd you get in to see this woman?" Luty demanded.

Hatchet smiled broadly. "That was easy. I pretended to be an American newspaper reporter doing a story on Mirabelle Daws. I used the name Rollo Puffy. That way, if Lady Henrietta said anything to Inspector Witherspoon, it would be the same name as madam so cleverly used when she sent the telegram."

"Touché, Hatchet." Luty laughed.

"Who's Rollo Puffy?" Betsy asked. She put the photograph down next to her teacup.

"I'll tell you later," Luty promised, "after the men leave for the pub tonight."

"Is that it, Hatchet?" Mrs. Jeffries asked quickly.

"I'm afraid so, ma'am," he admitted. He noticed that his photograph wasn't eliciting much interest. No one else even bothered to pick it up. He started to reach for it, fully intending to stuff it back in his coat pocket, when he was distracted by Wiggins.

"I've got something to say," the footman said eagerly. "I finally had a word with Fiona today. Caught her at the train station as she was fixin' to leave town."

"Who's Fiona?" Smythe asked.

"You remember, she were that tweeny I told ya about that first day," Wiggins said. "The one who I thought was hidin' something. I were right, she was hidin' somethin'. That's one of the reasons she's leavin' town. Scared, she is. Right scared that's she's goin' to be next."

Everyone leaned forward eagerly.

Wiggins, seeing that he now had their full attention, paused and reached for his tea.

"Get on with it, Wiggins," Mrs. Goodge ordered. "We've not got all night. Not only do I have my sources comin' in, but we've got to make some plans for this evening."

"I'm gettin' to it," he complained. Why was he always the one that got rushed? "Anyways, I saw Fiona outside the Prosper 'ouse, but I didn't get a chance to speak to 'er. Finally caught up with her at the railway station. At first, she weren't too friendly." He didn't tell them about her threatenin' to call the police on him when he'd first showed up. "But after we'd talked for a few minutes, she were willin' to tell me a few things." Again, he'd used the inspector's name. That and a cup of tea had calmed the girl considerably. "She was right nervous. Claimed that Mrs. Prosper were pretendin' she didn't want the girl to go because of the funeral bein' tomorrow."

"That's understandable," Mrs. Goodge put in. "A funeral reception takes a lot of work. They'll have a lot of people to cater for."

"But they'll not," Wiggins argued. "That's one of the reasons Fiona left. She thinks the whole bunch of 'em is actin' right strange. No one's goin' to the funeral but the immediate family. There's to be no reception at all. They're not even letting some of the people from the ship come. The purser sent his condolences and asked when the service would be, and Mrs. Prosper sent him a nasty note sayin' he shouldn't come, that it was to be family only. That Judith Brinkman wanted to come as well, and the Prospers did the same thing to her. Fiona says the whole thing gives her a funny feelin'."

"Why would the Prospers' lack of a funeral reception make the tweeny leave?" Betsy asked. "A private funeral isn't that unusual, especially as Mirabelle Daws didn't really know anyone here."

"It weren't just that," Wiggins continued. "It were a lot of things that scared Fiona. It seems that on the night of the murder, Fiona heard half the household up and down and out and about. Her room is just over the second floor, right over the family bedrooms. Well, Fiona couldn't sleep that night 'cause Sally, that's the girl she shares with, was snorin' somethin' awful. About half past four, she was wide awake and worryin' that she'd be dead tired the next day. All of a sudden, she hears the bedroom door below her creakin' open. Then she heard footsteps crossing the landing and going down the front stairs."

"Did she get up and see who it was?"

He shook his head. "No, she thought at the time that she knew who it was. She thought it was Mrs. Prosper sneakin' out to the garden to meet Mr. Heckston."

"Blimey, I guess everyone did know about those two," Smythe muttered softly.

"But it weren't Mrs. Prosper," Wiggins explained, "because fifteen or so minutes later, she heard another door open. This time, she did stick her head out to see what was goin' on. Well, blow me for a game of tin soldiers if she didn't get the surprise of her life."

"Who was it?" Betsy demanded.

"Eldon Prosper. That's who it was. Standing in the hallway big as life." Wiggins beamed proudly. "That's why she left town. She got up the next morning and mentioned Mr. Prosper's name to the housekeeper only to be told that he'd not come back from Edinburg. Then she found out about the murder. She claimed she tried to talk to Mrs. Prosper's maid about everything, about how she didn't like what was goin' on, but the maid refused to listen. But then Fiona says the woman drinks."

"She does," Betsy agreed.

"How'd you know?" Smythe asked sharply.

"I smelled it on her breath when we talked," Betsy said.

"Can I finish?" Wiggins asked. "Poor Fiona is in a right old state. Something funny were goin' on, and she'd no idea what."

"Who does she think did it?" Mrs. Goodge asked.

"She's no idea." Wiggins shrugged. "But considerin' how much comin' and goin' there was from that house that night, she thought it best to leave."

No one said anything for a moment. Finally, Mrs. Jeffries said, "That's very interesting, Wiggins. You've done very well. I'm just wondering if we ought to find a way to get this information to the inspector."

"Why don't we hold off on that, Mrs. J?" Smythe suggested. "Let's see what 'appens at the Sailor's Whistle tonight."

"That's probably a good idea," she replied. "If needed, we can always make sure the inspector knows the girl left the household suddenly. That alone would be cause enough for him to question her." She looked at Wiggins. "Why didn't she tell the police any of this when she was questioned before? Inspector Witherspoon always makes sure he talks to everyone."

Wiggins had asked the girl the same question. "She weren't questioned by our inspector. One of the uniformed lads did it. She said that she was afraid to say too much because both Mrs. Prosper and Mrs. McCabe kept hanging about the kitchen when the policeman was talking to 'er."

Mrs. Jeffries frowned in disapproval but said nothing. She'd thought the inspector went to great lengths to insure that everyone was questioned privately. Apparently, his standards were slipping a bit.

"But what does it mean?" Luty asked. "Like the boy says, there was so much comin' and goin' that night it's nigh on impossible to tell who mighta done the killin'."

"Who had the motive?" Mrs. Goodge added. "Seems to me that's where we ought to really start."

"Eldon Prosper, for one," Smythe said softly. "He was afraid Mirabelle would talk his wife into going back to Australia. That's a powerful motive for some men, the idea of losin' someone they love." He glanced at Betsy as he spoke. And this time she didn't look away.

"That Mrs. McCabe had a motive as well," Mrs. Goodge argued. "I think hers is even stronger. If Mrs. Prosper left, she'd be stuck home with her brother for the rest of her life, and we know she wanted to go off traveling with her friend."

"It seems to me that the only person who didn't have a motive is Mrs. Prosper," Hatchet commented.

"Perhaps she did," Mrs. Jeffries said. "Perhaps she didn't want her wanton behaviour with her neighbor, Mr. Heckston, getting back to her brother in Australia. After all, we know nothing of the brother. Perhaps if he knew Mrs. Prosper had been unfaithful to her marriage vows, he'd cut her off completely."

"But why should she care?" Betsy pointed out. "She knows her husband is so besotted with her that he'll not turn her out into the streets. He's rich as well. I don't think she'd murder her own sister on the off chance that the sister might spill the beans to a brother that's halfway 'round the world. Besides, from what we know of Mirabelle, I think there's a good chance her brother is much the same. He probably wouldn't care what Annabelle Prosper had been up to with her neighbor."

"You've got a point." Mrs. Jeffries nodded slowly. There were so many unexplained questions. So much that she didn't understand. But right now, there wasn't time to think about them. They had to decide how they were going to keep watch on the pub. Inspector Witherspoon might be doing quite well on this case, but she and the others weren't quite ready to give up. "If no one else has anything to add, perhaps we'd better discuss how we're going to deal with tonight's problem."

"I think Hatchet, Wiggins and I ought to nip out and keep an eye on the Sailor's Whistle. We can see who shows up to sell that necklace."

"Don't you mean you can see who the killer is?" Mrs. Goodge groused. She was annoyed that so far, she'd not added one useful clue to this investigation.

"We don't know that the person with the necklace is the murderer," Mrs. Jeffries insisted as she remembered the inspector's comment to Nivens. But even as the words left her lips, they had a hollow ring. The truth was, whoever showed up with the jewels probably had killed Mirabelle Daws. And the inspector had essentially come to that point without much help from any of them. It was depressing, but she refused to give in to it.

She glanced at Smythe and Betsy. She could tell by the way they occasionally smiled at each other that the ice between them was melting. She was fairly certain that there would be a big change coming from that direction. The idea didn't really displease her. It might make life a bit more interesting if those two came to their senses and realized they cared deeply for one another. Besides, she thought, even if they did get engaged or even married, that didn't mean their investigations would end. Betsy and Smythe loved snooping too much.

"We don't know that the person fencing the jewels ain't the killer either," Smythe pointed out. He got up. "There's a warehouse right across the street from the pub where we can see everything."

"Won't the police be using it?" Mrs. Jeffries asked.

"Probably." Smythe shrugged. "But they'll be on the ground floor. I've got us a way into the second floor. There's a right nice view from the window up there."

CHAPTER 10

"The inspector is doin' quite well on his own this time, isn't he?" Mrs. Goodge commented as soon as the men had left.

"Indeed he is," Mrs. Jeffries agreed. "But that's no reason for us not to do our best."

The cook didn't look convinced. "I suppose you're right," she replied slowly. "But I can't help thinkin' that I've wasted an awful lot of food in the past couple of days. I've not found out anything useful."

"Now don't be so down in the mouth," Luty chided. "We won't know what's useful and what's not until after we catch the killer. Besides, just because we ain't had much luck gettin' the jump on the inspector so far don't mean we ain't contributin'. Think of poor Hatchet. Drags his old bones all the way out to Colchester to see that Lady Henrietta, and he don't find out anything more than what we already know. But he didn't let that get him down none. He went ahead and went out tonight with the others. It's just like Hepzibah says; we don't know that the case is over just because the inspector is fixin' to grab some woman tryin' to sell a necklace. Besides, maybe no one will show at all tonight."

"Well said, Luty," the housekeeper commented. "By the way, now that Hatchet is gone, will you please tell us something? Who is Rollo Puffy?"

Luty laughed. "He was, or for all I know, still is, one of the best con men operating in the United States. He took Hatchet and a few others real good."

"What do you mean?" Betsy asked curiously. "Took him how?"

"For money," Luty replied. "Rollo Puffy cost poor old Hatchet three thousand dollars. Mind you, it was a number of years back, before we came to London. Hatchet had just come to work for me. My husband was still alive back in those days, and we had us a big house up on Nob Hill. Well, Hatchet had somehow met up with this real nice old feller named Rollo Puffy. Puffy claimed that he'd made a fortune in the lumber business up in the northwest and had come to San Francisco to sell this big, fancy yacht." She reached for the pot and poured herself more tea. "Anyway, Hatchet come in one evening sayin' that Puffy wanted to get shut of this yacht so danged bad, he was goin' to sell it real cheap. Puffy said he was goin' to buy an even bigger one and sail it back to Seattle. He didn't need two boats. Now the reason Hatchet told me and my husband about it was because we'd invested some of his money for him. We both thought it sounded fishy, but we didn't like to say nothin'. So we all got in the carriage and went down to the dock to have a look at the yacht." She smiled and shook her head at the memory. "It was a beauty. Over forty foot long and with the prettiest white and gold trim you ever saw. To make a long story short, Hatchet gave Puffy the money that night. Even though we thought the boat were pretty, we were against him doin' it. Just didn't stand to reason that even a rich man would sell something that valuable for three thousand dollars. But it was Hatchet's money, and he did as he wanted. He told us he was goin' to set sail for the Pacific islands. Give up butlerin' and see something of the world. But things didn't work out like that."

"What happened?" Mrs. Goodge asked eagerly.

"When he went back to the dock the next morning, the yacht was nowhere to be seen. But there were three other people there, and they was all madder than spit."

"I take it the man had sold the yacht to these three as well," Mrs. Jeffries said.

"Absolutely. And the reason the feller worked the scam so easy was that there really was a Rollo Puffy, and he really was an eccentric millionaire. He kept a huge suite at one of the fanciest hotels in town and had a letter of credit deposited at the Bank of California. This feller claimin' to be Puffy had moved into his suite at the Fremont Hotel and from the gossip I got later, even though the bank did try to hush it up, he'd used the line of credit too."

"But how did this man get away with pretending to be someone he wasn't?" Betsy asked.

"Easy." Luty grinned and put down her cup. "No one had ever seen Puffy. He was rich as sin, but he never came to town. Lots of fellows like him back in those days. Fellows that struck it rich back in the 1840s and 50s and didn't know what to do with all that money. Puffy had deposited the letter of credit and rented the rooms at the Fremont through an agent. But the agent was long gone by the time the sharpster come around pretendin' to be Puffy."

"Poor Hatchet," Mrs. Jeffries said sympathetically. "That must have been quite a blow to him. Losing all that money."

"It hurt his pride worse than his pocketbook," Luty replied. "But I didn't use Puffy's name on that telegram just to niggle at Hatchet. I used it because it's probably the last name on earth that'll ever be heard tell here in England. The last thing I'd ever want to do is make up a name and have some poor soul have to suffer for what we done."

"Did you hear something, sir?" Barnes asked Witherspoon. He stuck his head around the wooden partition and stared hard up and down the street. "I thought I heard a thumping noise."

"I expect it's just the sound of the bumpers hitting against the wharf," Witherspoon replied. He'd not heard anything.

"It sounded closer than that, sir. Almost like it was right over our heads."

"There's nothing over our heads, Constable. No one's been in this building for ages," Witherspoon said. "I expect there's so much rot upstairs that it wouldn't be safe to walk across the floor. Do you see anything yet?"

"Not yet, sir." Barnes stuck his head back in. He wasn't concerned that they would be spotted. To begin with, there wasn't anyone about, and secondly they were well hidden. "But he ought to be here soon. Accordin' to what Nivens's people told us, Jon McGee is back in town. He holds court here every night from eight o'clock on."

"Hmmm . . . yes. But it's almost eight, and we've not seen anyone go in except a few locals and our own lads. I don't think this McGee fellow could have slipped past us either, not from the description we got from the lads in K division."

"He'll be along soon, sir. And the minute he shows, we'll spot him. There's not too many peg-legged crooks working this part of London." Suddenly, Barnes cocked his ear toward the road and then stuck his ear toward the road and then stuck his head back out.

"Someone's comin' now, sir." He paused for a brief second. "It's him, sir. It's McGee. He and one of his mates are just coming past the wharf."

Witherspoon stuck his head out as well. Holding his breath, he watched the two men, one with a wooden peg leg, make their way toward the door of the Sailor's Whistle. "Excellent. Now all we have to do is wait for the lady to arrive, and we'll be right as rain."

"You're convinced that whoever shows up with the necklace is our killer, sir?" Barnes asked.

"Probably," the inspector replied. "But we'll have to see what happens, won't we? I don't want to make too many assumptions about tonight. I shouldn't like to arrest the wrong person." The inspector had a horror about that. He had a great deal of faith in the British justice system. But in a murder case where the penalty was probably going to be death, he wanted to make absolutely sure that for his part, he arrested the guilty party.

Witherspoon would rather see the guilty go free than an innocent person hang.

"Be quiet," Smythe hissed at Wiggins. "You keep thumping about like that, the inspector or one of his lads will be up here to see what's goin' on."

"I'm not movin' on purpose," Wiggins gave himself another hard shake and smacked at the air in front of him. "There's a spider on me somewhere."

"There's nothing on you," Hatchet soothed.

"Yes, there is." Wiggins jiggled up and down on the balls of his feet. "I walked through its ruddy web."

"Stop that or I'll box yer ears," Smythe whispered. "These floorboards are old as sin and creakin' like an old woman's bones."

"But the inspector and Constable Barnes is outside the building," Wiggins protested. "They can't 'ear nuthin'." But he did force himself to stand still. He slapped his hand to his neck, thinking he felt a tickle on his skin.

"Can you see, Smythe?" Hatchet asked. They'd wiped a fairly large amount of grime off the window. But the night was dark, and his eyes weren't as sharp as they used to be.

"The view's just fine. I think that's Jon McGee and one of his thugs goin' in now." He raised his hand and wiped at his cheek. This place was so filthy that even standing in it made you feel dirty. The very air itself reeked of grime and grit. It also reeked of lots of other things, most of them nasty. The river being so close didn't help much. In this part of town the water mainly smelled of rancid vegetation and rotting fish. "Stinks, doesn't it?" he commented idly.

"It shouldn't be for much longer," Hatchet replied. "Not if our lady wants to be home at a reasonable hour."

"Ouch." Wiggins slapped himself on the cheek, again thinking he'd felt something scuttling across his face.

"Let's just 'ope she doesn't change her mind on us," the coachman muttered.

From a distance, they heard the sound of a carriage turning into the street.

"That sounds like a cab," Smythe said, "and if it is, it's proably her. In this neighborhood, there ain't much carriage trade after dark."

Witherspoon's whole body stiffened as he watched the cab pull up on the narrow street in front of the pub. A heavily veiled woman stepped out. Despite the warmth of the summer evening, she carried a large fur muff. She handed the driver some coins, and they heard her murmur something to him. But her tone was too low for them to understand what she said.

"Right, ma'am," the driver replied. "I'll be back for you in fifteen minutes and not a moment later." He cracked the whip in the air and moved off.

The woman stood in front of the door and paused, probably to gather her courage, and went inside.

Witherspoon and Barnes didn't take their eyes off the door. "I think it's her, sir," the constable muttered.

"We'll know in a moment." Just as the words left Witherspoon's mouth, the door opened and a young man dressed in workingman's clothes stepped out. He looked straight at the two policemen and shook his head. Then he went back inside.

"It's her," Witherspoon said in relief. He really wanted this case finished. Even if this person wasn't the killer, at least apprehending her would bring them one step closer to solving the murder. He hoped.

The minutes ticked by. It got so quiet that they could hear the sound of the water lapping against the dilapidated wharf. Finally, after what seemed hours but was really only ten minutes or so, the door opened. Jon McGee and the veiled woman both stepped outside.

McGee took the woman's elbow, and they walked away from the pub, towards the wharf. Towards the darkness.

"Drat," Witherspoon murmured. "Now he's moved out of the light."

"I think that was the idea," Barnes said softly. He didn't like this. Didn't like it one bit. The constable held his breath as he watched the fence edging the woman farther and farther away from them.

McGee finally stopped. The two of them were now a good fifty feet off and standing in an area that was considerably darker than the spot outside the pub.

But there was still enough light to make out what few details Barnes discovered, as he watched McGee reach into his coat pocket and pull out a small packet. He extended it towards the woman. She reached for it, but he jerked back, keeping the packet just out of reach. "I'll have the other first," he told her.

Witherspoon nodded in satisfaction, glad that they could hear what was being said. McGee apparently felt so safe here that he didn't bother to lower his voice.

The woman said nothing; she merely reached into her muff and drew out a cloth bag. They made the exchange.

McGee started to open the bag. Barnes and Witherspoon stepped out into the street, and the constable blew long and hard on the whistle he'd had at the ready.

Policemen poured out into the street. The three in plain clothes rushed out of the pub, two more that had been hiding behind a pile of rubbish on the wharf leapt out, and three others came flying from around the corner.

McGee realized what was happening first. He spotted Barnes and Witherspoon closing in quickly. Grabbing the woman, he hurled her towards the two policemen and made a mad dash in the other direction, his wooden leg thumping wildly as he ran.

The woman gave an inelegant squawk as she flew through the air and slapped into Witherspoon. He managed to catch her around the waist and by throwing all his body weight forward, he kept them from hitting the pavement.

Barnes and three other policemen went flying after McGee. The fence bolted towards the intersection, watching over his shoulder as he ran. The constable saw what was happening first and shouted a warning at McGee, but to no avail. The fence went hurtling straight into the hansom cab that had just pulled around the corner.

The cabbie pulled hard on the reins, but there simply wasn't time to stop. McGee was lucky, though. Instead of actually being trampled, he was butted in the stomach by the panicked horse and sent flying. He landed a couple of feet away from two police constables. Moaning, he tried to get up, couldn't, and collapsed back onto the pavement.

"See about him, Barnes," Witherspoon yelled as he struggled to hold onto the woman. By now, she was pulling, pushing, shoving and doing all manner of unladylike things to get free of the inspector's grasp. But he held firm.

Two police constables leapt into the fray. Within a few moments, they had their quarry firmly, each one grasping one of the woman's arms. Witherspoon, adjusting his glasses, stepped back and surveyed the scene.

Barnes knelt down next to McGee, reached into the groaning man's coat pocket and took out the soft cloth bag. He opened the bag, reached in, and pulled out a long necklace. "I think this is it, sir," he called.

"I don't know how that got in my pocket," McGee argued. "That tart must have planted it on me."

"Is he going to be all right?" Witherspoon asked.

"He'll be fine, sir. I don't think he's even got any broken bones."

"Fat lot you know," McGee snapped. He rubbed his head. "This is a setup, this is. I'm an innocent businessman doing a bit o' legitimate business, and all of a sudden I'm set upon by coppers. It's your fault I run into that bleedin' hansom," he accused Barnes. "You'll be hearin' from my solicitor, you will."

"I didn't see him coming," cried the hansom driver. He'd stopped a few feet away and was staring openmouthed at the scene. "Oh my God, I've run over a cripple."

McGee's head shot up off the pavement. "Bugger off," he yelled at the hapless hansom driver. "I ain't no cripple, and if I wasn't layin' here surrounded by coppers, I'd get up and kick yer bloomin' arse all the way to Brighton."

The cab driver ignored him. "It wasn't my fault," he repeated as he looked at Barnes. "I couldn't stop. He come out of nowhere, he did. Ran smack into me."

"You'll be hearin' from my solicitor too," McGee screamed, incensed that the driver ignored his threats.

"Of course you couldn't stop," Barnes assured the driver. Then he looked down at McGee. "Save it for the judge," he said to him. He rose to his feet and signaled for two uniformed men to take over. Then he hurried back to the inspector.

He handed Witherspoon the necklace. "Looks like opals and diamonds to me, sir."

The inspector held them up. Even with just the faint light from the small pub windows, the stones separating the opals glittered in the night. "Indeed they do." He dropped the necklace back into the bag. Then he handed it back to Barnes. "We'll need this signed in as evidence. Now, let's see who we have here."

The woman, still standing between the two constables, said nothing. The inspector reached over and lifted her veil. He sighed as he stared into the frightened eyes of Marlena McCabe. "Mrs. McCabe," he said firmly. "You're under arrest for the murder of Mirabelle Daws."

Marlena McCabe didn't seem to grasp that she was under arrest for murder. "I tell you, I want to go home. My brother will be very worried about me."

Witherspoon sighed inwardly. His suspect was sitting quite calmly in the straight-backed chair on the other side of his desk. Constable Barnes was sitting to one side as was the young police constable who was taking down the woman's statement. Not that she'd said anything particularly useful yet.

He tried again. "Mrs. McCabe, you don't seem to understand how serious your predicament is. I must advise you that you're under arrest for murder. Do you understand?"

She continued to stare at him blankly, then all of a sudden, she seemed to realize that she was at a police station and that she was in serious straits. She shuddered, and her eyes filled with tears. "Dear God, this can't be happening."

Finally, he thought. "But I assure you, ma'am, it is happening. Now, we have some questions for you. How did you come to be in possession of Mirabelle Daws's necklace?" They'd not established that the necklace actually belonged to the victim as yet, but they weren't in court at the moment and consequently, he wasn't bound by the judge's rules. It was perfectly reasonable to make the assumption that the necklace did belong to the victim.

"I don't have to talk to you," she insisted. "I don't have to say anything."

"That's true," Witherspoon replied. "You're well within your rights to call for your solicitor. However," he leaned forward, his expression deadly serious, "if you are innocent, you're playing right into the real murderer's hands by not telling us everything you know."

The inspector had no idea what prompted him to say such a thing. He'd opened his mouth, and it had just popped out. Gracious, he didn't want Mrs. McCabe to think she wasn't under arrest. But before he could tell her that, she started to speak.

"She was already dead when I got there," she blurted. "I'll admit that I took the necklace, but I didn't kill her."

"What time did you arrive?" Barnes asked quickly.

She bit her lip. "It was about five, I think. I'm not absolutely sure."

"How did you know that Mirabelle Daws was in the garden?" Witherspoon asked.

"I didn't," she replied. She looked down at the floor. "It was only an accident that I happened to come upon her body. I'd gone out to the garden because I couldn't sleep."

Witherspoon knew she was lying.

"That's quite a coincidence, isn't it ma'am?" Barnes said softly.

"Coincidences happen," she said. She didn't look up from the floor. "Can I go home now? I really would like to have few hours to rest. Tomorrow is the funeral, you know. Even though it's just going to be family, I do want to look my best."

"No, ma'am," the inspector said, "I'm afraid you can't. Why didn't you call for help when you found the woman dead?"

"I don't know. I expect I ought to have called for the police. But I wasn't thinking properly." She looked up; her face wore a dazed, panicked expression. "I didn't wish to be involved. It is rather a shock, you know. Finding a body."

"If you were in such a state, ma'am," Witherspoon pressed, "then how was it that you had the presence of mind to take the necklace?"

She said nothing for a moment. "I know what you're trying to do. You're trying to make it look like I killed her. But I didn't. I didn't, I tell you."

Wearily Witherspoon shook his head. He glanced over at Barnes, who nodded. They had no other course of action. "Mrs. McCabe. We're going to send a message to your brother . . ."

"No, don't," she cried. "There's no need to drag Eldon into this. Please, can't you just let me go home?"

"You don't understand, ma'am," Barnes said gently. "You're not going home. You're under arrest. We thought you'd want your family to know where you were so they could get you some legal help."

She cocked her head to one side and stared at him. She looked utterly stunned, as though she couldn't believe what was happening. "Does that mean you're going to put me in prison?"

Witherspoon hated this part. "Yes, ma'am, I'm rather afraid it does."

"Marlena McCabe!" Mrs. Goodge snorted in disgust. "I'd have never thought it was her."

"Why not?" Betsy demanded. "She had a motive. She didn't want her sister-in-law going home to Australia."

"That's a pretty pathetic motive if ya ask me," Luty put in. "Killin' someone just so's ya don't get stuck takin' care of your kinfolk. If she'da had any gumption, she'da told her brother she was leavin' with or without his stupid allowance."

"I must admit, I'm rather surprised," Mrs. Jeffries mused.

"Ya coulda knocked us over with a feather, too," Wiggins said.

"I've no idea why we were all so surprised," Hatchet added, "it's not as though there are a huge number of female suspects in this case. But when the inspector lifted that veil, we were all very taken aback."

No one said anything for a moment. Everyone was too busy thinking about this evening's events. Mrs. Goodge finally broke the silence. "I suppose that's it then, it's over. The inspector did it without much help from us, and that's a fact." She looked at the housekeeper. "You've not passed on much of what we learned, have you?"

"Not really," Mrs. Jeffries admitted. "This time it didn't appear as if the inspector needed our assistance. He was almost always a step or two ahead of us."

Hatchet yawned. "Oh, I do beg your pardon." He apologized as he realized everyone was looking at him. "If there's nothing else, I suppose the madam and I ought to be getting home. It is very late."

Mrs. Jeffries smiled wearily. It was late. They were all tired and the case, for all intents and purposes, was probably solved. Then why did it feel so wrong? Why wasn't she secure in her own mind that justice would be done? "We're all very tired."

Wiggins suddenly stood up. "You're all goin' to think I'm addled, but there's something I've got to say. I don't think it's 'er. I don't think she killed that woman. There's somethin' 'ere that's not right."

"You only think that 'cause you don't want to admit we've not been much help on this one," Mrs. Goodge said briskly. She got up. "I'm going to bed. I suggest the rest of you do the same."

"We'd best be off too," Luty said.

Smythe and Betsy said their good-nights as well and within just a few moments, it was only Wiggins and Mrs. Jeffries left in the kitchen.

Mrs. Jeffries noticed the forgotten photograph. "Oh dear, Hatchet has forgotten this," she said, picking it up.

"I take it round to 'im tomorrow," Wiggins said glumly. "'Ere, give it to me."

She smiled at the footman and handed him the photograph. She knew just how he felt. "Wiggins, we can't always be right."

"I know, Mrs. Jeffries," he replied. "But there's somethin' funny 'ere. You feel it too. I could see it in yer face when we was all talkin'." He glanced at the picture in his hand. "But maybe I'm only seein' what I want to see."

"Perhaps so," she agreed. But that wasn't true. She did think there was something wrong. But before she gave Wiggins any false hope about the matter, she wanted to think about the case in the privacy of her room.

"Oh, well, best move on to other things." He lifted the picture up and looked at it. "Ever since Smythe and Betsy took me to that photography exhibition at the Crystal Palace, I've been right interested."

"I agree. It is best to move on to other things." She was delighted he was so easily diverted. She didn't want him brooding over the case all night.

Wiggins had a nice, long look. "Who did Hatchet say this was?"

Mrs. Jeffries leaned over and pointed to the two women in the foreground. "The older one is Lady Henrietta Morland, the woman next to her is Mrs. Moulton, and the one in the dark shawl in the background is Annabelle Prosper. Strange, isn't it, how life works out. I'll bet that Mrs. Moulton never thought her maid would end up paying for her passage back to England."

Wiggins continued to stare at the photograph, his expression puzzled. "Hatchet must have got it wrong," he finally said.

"Got what wrong?"

"Who the women are."

"What do you mean?" Mrs. Jeffries asked. But her heart had begun to beat faster, and her spirits were picking up by the seconds.

Wiggins pointed to the figure in the black shawl. "That's not Annabelle Prosper," he declared. "I saw Mrs. Prosper just today. When she come out of the house to give poor Fiona a talkin' to. That's not her." Then he pointed to the woman standing next to Lady Henrietta Morland. "This one is."

CHAPTER 11

"Are you sure?" Mrs. Jeffries wanted to be absolutely certain the lad wasn't making a mistake. "Both the women in the photograph are of the same height and build."

"I'm sure as I'm standin' 'ere talkin' to you. I got a good look at Mrs. Prosper when she come out of the 'ouse to have a natter at poor Fiona. That's 'er, all right," he insisted, pointing to the likeness of Abigail Moulton. "So Hatchet musta got it wrong. I tell ya, Mrs. J, I knew there were something right funny about this whole case. I knew it. I could feel it in my bones, so to speak."

But Mrs. Jeffries wasn't listening. She was thinking furiously. Was it possible? Could it be that once again, they'd made a grave error in their whole approach to this case? If what she suspected was true, then it explained so very much. They'd been concentrating on the wrong question all along. They should have been asking "why" Mirabelle Daws, a woman who'd never set foot in England before, had been murdered. Instead, they'd been concentrating on "who" had a reason to kill her. It was a reasonable mistake to make, but a mistake nonetheless. Mrs. Jeffries's only consolation was that they weren't the only ones concentrating on the wrong question. Inspector Witherspoon had made the same error.

Wiggins wasn't sure Mrs. Jeffries was listening anymore. So he raised his voice and poked her lightly in the arm. "And of course, I knew in me own mind that there was somethin' odd about the way it were all workin' out."

Startled out of her thoughts, she flinched. "Oh dear, I am sorry, Wiggins. I wasn't listening properly. I was thinking." She stared at the lad and hoped she wasn't wrong. If she was, then what she was going to do might be utterly, utterly stupid. But her instincts were screaming that she was right, and as she was always admonishing the inspector to trust his instincts, she was going to do the same with hers.

"That's all right, Mrs. Jeffries," he replied affably. "Sometimes my mind wanders too. Especially when Mrs. Goodge or Betsy is lecturin' me about washing under me fingernails . . . uh, what are you doin'?"

Mrs. Jeffries grabbed his hand and jerked him towards the door. "Hurry, Wiggins. We've not much time." She pulled him towards the back stairs.

"Time for what?" he asked as he stumbled after her. "Where are we goin'?"

"Upstairs," she replied. "We've got to get Smythe. You two have to get moving. The two of you need to get out of here right away."

"You mean before the inspector comes home?" Wiggins asked eagerly. He loved going out on adventures. "But shouldn't we wait so I can take Fred with me?" He especially loved adventures when he had his dog.

"Fred'll have to stay here," she replied. "We don't want the inspector to know you've gone out. I've got to talk to him before he goes to bed. I've got to tell him about Rollo Puffy. That's the only way this will work."

"The only way what will work?" Wiggins asked breathlessly.

"My plan. We've got to plant the idea, Wiggins. Otherwise, a guilty woman will get away with murder. Twice."

They'd reached the top landing. She dropped Wiggins's hand and dashed over to the door. She knocked. "Smythe, do hurry. We need your help."

Smythe was there in an instant. "What's wrong? What's goin' on?"

She took a minute to catch her breath. Then she reached for the photograph that dangled from Wiggins's fingers. Holding it up, she said, "The inspector is wrong. It wasn't Marlena McCabe that murdered Mirabelle Daws. It was this woman. Abigail Moulton. But we'll have to act quickly. I suspect she's not going to hang about much longer. You and Wiggins will have to move fast tonight."

Smythe was rebuttoning the shirt he'd just unbuttoned as he listened. "What do ya want us to do?"

"'Tis a perfect day for a funeral," Barnes said quietly. "Gray, bleak and overcast. I don't think we'll be seein' the sun today, sir."

Witherspoon nodded in agreement. He and the constable were standing in Manor Park Cemetery. It was a good ways out of town, and both Barnes and the inspector had been rather surprised that the Prospers had chosen to bury a family member so far away from their home. It had taken the funeral party a good two hours to get here.

"I don't think they'll care." He nodded towards the mourners who were standing around an open grave, less than a hundred feet away from them.

The hearse had pulled up a few feet from the grave, and the undertakers had taken out the plain, oak casket. A single wreath of daisies had been placed at the foot of the grave as the workmen solemnly lowered the coffin to its final resting place. A vicar stood at the head of the grave holding an open prayer book.

On the far side, Annabelle Daws Prosper, properly attired in black but wearing a chic hat without a veil, stood next to her husband. Mr. Prosper held his wife's arm. His sister clung to his other arm. Her eyes were red rimmed, her hair untidy, but she was properly dressed in mourning black even though she'd never known the dead woman. Behind them, the servants stood solemnly, their expressions grim. Though whether it was sorrow for the victim they felt or pity for themselves for being dragged all the way out here was impossible to tell.

The vicar began the short graveside service.

Barnes glanced nervously about. He was reassured to see two constables staying discreetly back next to a large crypt.

"Not to worry, Constable," Witherspoon reassured him. "I don't think she'll make a run for it."

"I'd not be too sure about that, sir," Barnes replied. "But if she does, we're ready. We've four constables stationed about the cemetery. That ought to be enough for one woman."

"Excuse me, Inspector Witherspoon." A familiar voice said from behind them.

Witherspoon and Barnes both whirled about and found themselves facing the purser from the *Island Star.* "Good day, sirs." The purser smiled broadly. He was a portly man with iron-gray hair and a cheerful countenance.

"Gracious," the inspector said. "It's Mr. Faversham, isn't it? What are you doing here, sir?"

Tom Faversham's bright smile was replaced with a puzzled expression.

"What am I doing here? But you sent me a telegram. You said it was urgent that I come. I've come all the way up from Southampton on the morning train and then taken another train out here. This isn't an easy place to find, you know."

"You received a telegram from me?" Witherspoon's brows drew together. "I'm afraid there's been a mistake, sir. I did no such thing."

"But the telegram said that if I didn't come, there would be a grave miscarriage of justice." Tom Faversham pursed his lips. "Do you think someone is having a joke at my expense, sir?"

"I expect so," Barnes put in quickly. He didn't want to be distracted by a ship's purser if the McCabe woman tried to make a run for it. "Too bad you've wasted your day, but as we've said, we didn't send a telegram. We are sorry you went to all the trouble of comin'."

"A miscarriage of justice," Witherspoon muttered. He didn't like the sound of that. For some odd reason, the story that his housekeeper had told him this morning popped into his head. Perhaps because she'd used the same words. He made a mental note to share the story with Constable Barnes. He'd find it quite amusing.

"It's all right, I suppose." Faversham shrugged philosophically, his irritation vanishing as quickly as it had come. "I wanted to come up to London anyway."

"You're taking this quite well, sir," Witherspoon said.

"Not really. I'd wanted to come to begin with, but Miss Annabelle, correction, Mrs. Prosper, sent me that note saying the funeral was for family only. But seein' as how I'm here, I might as well go over and pay my respects to Miss Annabelle."

Witherspoon looked over at the funeral party. The vicar had finished. He noticed that Annabelle Prosper had dropped her husband's arm.

"It looks like the service is finished," Witherspoon said. "You should have time to nip over before the family leaves. I'm sure Mrs. Prosper, or as you knew her, Miss Annabelle, will appreciate your condolences." From the corner of his eyes, he saw that the woman in question was staring at them, her attention focused on the purser.

Faversham started across the damp grass and then stopped suddenly. "I'm too late. She must have already gotten into the carriage."

Witherspoon pointed at Annabelle Prosper, who was now backing away from the funeral party as fast as she could. "She's right there."

Bewildered, the purser shook his head. "There's some mistake, Inspector. That woman isn't Annabelle Daws Prosper. It's Abigail Moulton."

The woman gave up any pretense of subtley. She turned and bolted in the opposite direction.

Barnes looked frantically at his superior. He hadn't a clue what was going on, but something strange was happening. "What should we do, sir?"

The funeral party gaped at the running woman. The two constables, who'd only been told to watch for a woman making a break for it, came bounding out from behind the crypt. They began the chase—she wouldn't get far. Their lives were filled with chasing fleeter-footed villains.

"After her," the inspector called. He and Barnes took off at a run. Eldon Prosper, shouting his wife's name, bounded behind them. Marlena McCabe, who'd finally come out of her stupor to realize something rather peculiar was going on, went running after her brother. The Prosper servants, not knowing what else to do, took off after the rest of them.

The only people left standing at the grave site were the vicar, who was staring openmouthed at the spectacle, and the undertaker's assistants, who weren't in the least surprised by the outburst. They'd seen plenty of strange goings-on at funerals.

Witherspoon and Barnes got there first. The woman was struggling hard, and the police constable, who was quite young and inexperienced, was turning a bright red as he tried to hang on to her without either hurting her or touching body parts that were considered sacrosanct.

"Let me go, you great oaf," she snapped.

"Let her go," Witherspoon instructed. It was a safe instruction as they were now surrounded by police constables.

She yanked her arm out of the constable's grip and turned to glare at Inspector Witherspoon. "I don't know what you think you're doing, but I'll have your job for this."

"Are you Abigail Moulton?" he asked. But he knew in his heart that she was.

"Don't be absurd. I'm Annabelle Prosper."

"You are not," Tom Faversham interrupted. "You're Abigail Moulton, and I can bring ten people here tomorrow to prove it. What have you done with Miss Annabelle? She got off the ship with you."

"I don't know what you're talking about."

"You know perfectly well what I'm on about," Faversham cried. "Where is she? Why isn't she here properly married to that Prosper fellow?"

The woman said nothing.

"Leave my wife alone," Eldon Prosper ordered. He tried to break through the small circle of constables but couldn't. "You've no right to handle her in such a fashion. No right at all. I'll have my solicitors on you, you can be sure of that."

"I'm afraid your wife is under arrest," Witherspoon replied.

"That's ridiculous," Prosper charged. "First you arrest my sister, and now you're trying to malign my wife. I'll not have it, I tell you. Annabelle, don't say a word to them. I'll bring Jackson to the station. We'll get this sorted out. You're not to worry about a thing, love. Not a thing."

Witherspoon ignored him. "Mrs. Abigail Moulton, you're under the arrest for the murder of Mirabelle Daws and Annabelle Daws. Constable, please caution her and take her down to the station."

Prosper protested the whole time they were leading her away. But in the end, he finally gave up and hurried off to get his solicitor.

"How did you know it was her?" Barnes asked as they walked back towards the grave site. "I mean, how did you know what was going to happen?" He was rather awed by the quick turn of events. He knew his inspector was brilliant, but this was above and beyond anything he'd ever seen. "I mean, uh, what did happen? Who's Abigail Moulton, and why would she want to murder Mirabelle Daws?"

Witherspoon sighed. "It's rather a long story, Constable. Luckily, I had a little chat with my housekeeper last night. She filled me in on some gossip she'd heard about the Daws women."

"I don't understand, sir," Barnes said. "How did you know something was goin' to happen today?"

"I didn't. But I think someone else did. Someone who badly wanted to see justice done in this case. I'll tell you all about it on the way back to the station." He closed his eyes and briefly thanked heaven for housekeepers who couldn't sleep. "I wouldn't have figured it out except that Mrs. Jeffries told me the most amusing story. Remember that telegram I received giving us the identity of the dead woman?"

"Yes, sir, if we'd not got that telegram, that Mrs. Moulton would have gotten away with murder. If we'd not found out the victim's identity, we'd never have solved this case."

"Right," Witherspoon agreed. "Well, the telegram was signed by a fellow named Rollo Puffy. My housekeeper told me she'd remembered where she'd heard that name before. You recall that Mrs. Jeffries used to be married to a police officer up in Yorkshire. He was always telling her tales he'd collected from all over the world. It seems that Rollo Puffy was once a rather rich eccentric in San Francisco. Then the name was used by quite a successful con artist. His specialty was pretending to be someone he wasn't."

"That's remarkable, sir," Barnes mumbled. He still didn't know what was going on or how the inspector had solved the case. Perhaps by the time they got back to the station, everything would begin to make sense.

They arrived back at the open grave. Witherspoon nodded politely to the vicar, knelt down and closed his eyes. Silently and earnestly he prayed for the soul of Mirabelle Daws.

"It was her, all right," Wiggins said excitedly. "You should 'ave seen it when she saw the purser comin' at 'er. She took off like a cat runnin' from the 'ounds."

"It was a right strange sight," Smythe agreed.

They were all gathered around the table at Upper Edmonton Gardens. Wiggins and Smythe, after a long and arduous night of rousting out witnesses, had hidden in the cemetery to watch the proceedings. They'd then nipped back to give their report.

"Seems to me you were lucky," Luty snipped. She was out of sorts because it was Hatchet's photograph that had saved the day. "What if that woman hadn't been Abigail Moulton? You'd have made a right fool of the inspector."

"But we knew it were 'er," Wiggins said eagerly. "That's why we were up all night. We 'ad to nip down to Southampton lickety split, roust Mr. Faversham and get 'im back up 'ere. But before he did his part at the cemetery, we stopped at Sheridan Square." He stuffed a piece of ginger cake in his mouth.

"Can't you wait to feed your face until you finish telling us what happened?" Betsy cried.

"The lad's starved," Smythe said. "It was a long night. But like he said, we stopped at Sheridan Square and waited for the funeral party to leave the Prosper 'ouse. That's when Tom Faversham confirmed the woman were Abigail Moulton and not Annabelle Prosper."

"Then you had him go on to the cemetery and pretend to get that telegram from the inspector?" Mrs. Goodge was still a bit puzzled over the sequence of events. "Is that right?"

"Right." Smythe nodded. "He was right 'appy to do it. Seems he liked the real Annabelle Prosper. When we explained what we thought might 'ave happened, he was keen to 'elp us." The coachman didn't bother to tell them he'd paid the man fifty quid for his trouble.

Hatchet raised his teacup to Mrs. Jeffries. "Madam, I salute you for a brilliant piece of detective work."

"I'll not take the credit for this one," she said stoutly. "All of you helped solve this puzzle."

"I still don't know that I understand what happened," the cook cried. "Why did Abigail Moulton kill Mirabelle Daws, and how come everyone thought she was Annabelle Daws?"

Mrs. Jeffries smiled sympathetically. "It is a complicated case because it really began when Annabelle came to England to marry Eldon Prosper. As you told us, Mrs. Goodge, Annabelle's former employer came on the ship with her. Abigail Moulton apparently realized that no one in England had ever seen Annabelle Daws. I think that she decided when they arrived here, rather than live as a disgraced widow and a poor relation, she'd take Annabelle's place. After all, she knew that Annabelle was coming here to marry a rich man and be the mistress of a fine house. Whereas she, disgraced by her husband's embezzlement and suicide, was going to have to go to the north of England and live with relatives who would probably make her life miserable. I suspect she decided to murder Annabelle before the ship even reached Southampton. She wanted to take her place."

"But how could she?" Betsy asked. "Surely Eldon Prosper would have realized the woman he'd married wasn't the woman he'd been corresponding with?"

"I imagine she had Annabelle's letters," Mrs. Jeffries replied.

"That stands to reason," Luty said thoughtfully. "Most women would hang on to the letters they got from the man they was fixin' to marry."

"Remember, Annabelle had been her maid. She'd probably confided all manner of things to Abigail," Hatchet added.

"Where would she get rid of the body?" Betsy asked.

"Oh, I imagine Annabelle Daws ended up in the Thames." Mrs. Jeffries shook her head sadly. "Poor woman never had a chance. Then, of course, when Abigail got the letter from Mirabelle saying she was coming for a

visit, she knew her masquerade would be exposed. She had to kill Mirabelle. So she sent her a message to meet her in the garden early in the
morning. I'm sure she knew about Mirabelle's concern for her. Mirabelle
made no secret of the fact that she thought something was wrong at the
Prosper household."

"So she sends her a mysterious note." Luty picked up the thought. "And
then lies in wait for her out in the garden. But how on earth did she think
she'd not get caught? A dead woman in a posh place like Sheridan Square
is goin' to raise a fuss."

"That's true," Mrs. Jeffries agreed. "But the fuss would die down when
the dead woman wasn't identified. That's what she was counting on. That
no one would know that it was Mirabelle Daws who was the victim. She'd
not realized that both her husband and her sister-in-law knew about Mirabelle's visit and had reasons of their own to fear it."

"What did she do with Mirabelle's things?" Wiggins asked.

"I'm not sure," the housekeeper said, "but I've a feeling that if the
police search that empty house on Sheridan Square they'll not only find
Mirabelle's things, but perhaps Annabelle's as well. We had a report that
noises had been heard in that place."

"I still think it's remarkable that you put it all together. madam,"
Hatchet said.

"Not really," Mrs. Jeffries said. "Actually, once Luty told us the story
of Rollo Puffy and then Wiggins identifed the woman in the photograph,
it was simple. After that, everything made sense. The fact that Mrs. Prosper
wouldn't respond to her sister's letters, those sudden hysterics at the
mortuary . . ."

"What about 'em?" Luty asked.

"Remember, the inspector said she was quite calm until they started
into the viewing room. Then she suddenly threw herself in her husband's
arms and got hysterical. But she did it just as the purser, who knew her as
Abigail Moulton, was coming out of that very room. She didn't want him
to see her, and she had to act fast. I think what really set it in my own
mind was when Wiggins said she'd sent the purser a note telling him not
to attend the funeral service. That was simply out of character for someone
of Annabelle's background."

"What about Mrs. McCabe and the necklace?" Hatchet asked.

"I think she's telling the truth, or at least a part of it."

"I think she spotted Mirabelle arrivin'," Mrs. Goodge put in.

"Remember, she was the one that heard the hansom cab arrive that morning and saw Mirabelle get out. I think she waited a bit to go out to the garden, not knowing exactly why Mirabelle was there, and then when she did go out, she saw the woman had been stabbed. So she took the necklace and ran."

"But why didn't she tell the police?" Betsy asked.

"Because she thought her brother 'ad done the killin'," Smythe said softly. "Remember, Fiona told Wiggins she'd seen Prosper that night. Probably Mrs. McCabe 'ad seen 'im too, and she didn't know that her sister-in-law wasn't Annabelle, so she didn't think she'd have a reason to murder the woman. Stands to reason she'd think it was her brother."

Mrs. Jeffries nodded in agreement. "You're right, Smythe. I do believe that's how it must have happened."

"How did you convince the inspector to go along?" Luty asked.

"I didn't." Mrs. Jeffries laughed. "I merely planted a few seeds last night when the inspector got home." She nodded appreciatively at the cook. "It's amazing how useful a bit of gossip turns out to be."

The inspector arrived home quite late that evening. He insisted on eating in the kitchen, rather than have the staff go to the trouble of bringing his dinner to the dining room.

"I say, this soup is excellent." He smiled appreciatively at the cook.

"Thank you, sir," Mrs. Goodge replied. "I thought you might be hungry, sir. Mrs. Jeffries told us you'd had quite an eventful day."

He'd given the housekeeper a brief synopsis when he was hanging up his coat and hat.

"Indeed it has been eventful," he replied. "And it looks as if it's going to be a long and arduous trial. Mrs. Prosper is being represented by one of the best legal firms in England."

"How can she afford that?" Wiggins asked. He was helping Mrs. Jeffries put the copper pot on the top shelf of the pine bureau.

"She can't, but her husband can," he said. "Eldon Prosper has plenty of money. Our task is not going to be an easy one. Not only must we prove that she murdered Mirabelle Daws, but that she murdered Annabelle as well."

"You mean that Mr. Prosper is still goin' to help the woman, knowin' that she killed 'is real fiancée?" Wiggins was shocked.

"I'm afraid so," Witherspoon sighed. "He told me he didn't care who the woman was; she was his wife, and he loved her. He's going to do whatever he can to save her. Well, he might be able to save her from hanging, but I don't think he'll save her from prison. Even without Annabelle's body, we've a strong case against her." He suddenly looked around the kitchen. "I say, where are Smythe and Betsy?"

"They're out in the garden, sir," Mrs. Jeffries replied. She brushed the dust off her hands and came towards the table. "As a matter of fact, I believe I hear them coming now." She had a strong feeling that an announcement of some kind might be in the offing.

A moment later, the two of them came into the kitchen. They were holding hands.

Mrs. Goodge looked knowingly at Mrs. Jeffries.

"Good evening, Smythe, Betsy." Witherspoon beamed at the two of them. Then he noticed their entwined fingers. "Oh dear, dear me. Smythe, do you really think you ought to be doing that?"

"I do, sir." Smythe grinned wickedly. "I'm glad everyone's 'ere. Betsy and I 'ave something to tell ya all." He looked at the maid. "Do ya want me to say it?"

Suddenly, shy, she nodded. "Go on, then."

He took a deep breath. "Betsy has done me the great honor of agreein' . . ."

"To get engaged," Betsy interrupted. "That's what we've agreed. We're going to be engaged."

"Gracious, how very wonderful," the inspector enthused. "I'm so pleased for the both of you."

"Congratulations," Mrs. Jeffries said. She smiled broadly, delighted her intuition had been on the mark. "I know the two of you will be happy. I think you're perfect for one another."

"Cor blimey," Wiggins cried. "It's about time."

"All the best to both of you," Mrs. Goodge added. "But you should have said something. I'd have made a special dinner for you. So when's the wedding to be?"

"Thank you, everyone," Betsy said. She gave her intended a fast, quick smile. "We haven't set a date yet."

Smythe, who seemed to be in a state of shock, simply stared at her.

It took a moment or two before Mrs. Jeffries realized that it wasn't simply a matter of the man being lovestruck. He really had been surprised.

"As a matter of fact." Betsy grabbed Smythe's hand. "We'd best go back outside and talk a bit more." She began tugging him toward the back hall. "We'll be right back."

As soon as they'd disappeared, Inspector Witherspoon looked at Mrs. Jeffries. "I say, did you notice that Smythe seemed to be a bit stunned?"

"Oh, that's normal, sir," Mrs. Jeffries replied. "All men act stunned when they realize they've actually gotten engaged."

"What are you playin' at?" Smythe hissed at Betsy as soon as they were out of earshot. "If ya don't want to marry me, all ya had to do was say so."

"Don't be daft," she whispered. She reached for the back door, yanked it open and jerked him outside. "Of course I want to marry you. But I suddenly realized what we were about to do."

Smythe glared at her. "What are you goin' on about? We were about to tell the others we wanted to be married."

"Right," she agreed, "and then you were goin' to tell them you were rich."

"So? Why shouldn't I tell 'em the truth? I'm right tired of livin' a lie, Betsy."

"I don't doubt it," she replied. "But think a minute. Where would that leave us? I'll tell you where we'd be. Living all on our own in some big fancy house without any murders to investigate, that's where. Are you ready to give it up?"

He frowned thoughtfully. "Why would we have to give up our investigatin'?"

"We wouldn't have to," Betsy said, "but you know as well as I do that it would be different. Oh, maybe not at first, but eventually things would start to change and before you knew it, we'd be too busy with out own lives to want to do any snooping about. Look, Smythe, you know I love you more than anything. But our investigations has made me feel right important. Like I'm contributing something to this world that only I can give . . . oh, I don't think I know how to explain it, but I know I'm not ready to give it up. Not yet. I don't want things to change. I'm not ready for it."

"I think I know what you're sayin'," he agreed slowly. "But how long exactly are ya thinkin' we ought to be engaged?"

"Not too long," Betsy said, delighted that he wasn't going to give her too much trouble. "Maybe a year or two. Just long enough for us to get some idea about how we'd be a part of things once we was married and livin' on our own."

Smythe was silent for a moment. "I guess you're right," he finally said. "I'm not ready to give up our investigatin' either, and once we was married, we would want our own place. All right, then, we'll be engaged for a bit. But just long enough to suss out how we're goin' to do things once we're married."

Betsy decided that was probably about as good a compromise as she was likely to get. She slipped her arms around his neck. "I'm so glad you understand, Smythe."

He pulled her close. At least, he thought, now that they were officially engaged, she'd be much easier to handle.

She smiled up at him. Now that they were engaged, she thought, he'd be so much easier to handle.

MRS. JEFFRIES
WEEDS THE PLOT

To Ann Ruggles,
with my heartfelt thanks and gratitude
for answering all my questions about dogs.

And to Oreo, Abby, and Clancy,
with thanks for the great stories
and the good laughs.

CHAPTER 1

"Really, I honestly don't know why Louisa won't believe me. I'm not making it up," Annabeth Gentry said to her maid. She was an attractive, blond woman in her late thirties. Her eyes were bright blue and she possessed a cheerful disposition and, usually, a ready smile. She wasn't smiling now.

"Of course you're not making it up, ma'am," her maid, Martha Dowling, replied. She put the tray she'd been carrying down on a table by the window and poured her mistress a cup of tea.

"I'm not usually in the habit of telling tales, am I?" Annabeth got up and began to pace the small sitting room.

"No, ma'am. Did Mrs. Cooksey actually say she thought you was lyin'?" Martha asked.

Annabeth stopped in front of the fireplace. "She didn't come right out and accuse me of making it up, but I could tell by the expression on her face that she didn't take my concerns seriously." Her shoulders slumped. "She thinks I'm getting fanciful. She said that unmarried women get funny ideas in their heads when they get to be my age."

"That's the silliest bit of nonsense I've ever heard," Martha snorted, handing the tea to her mistress. "You're one of the most sensible people I've ever met." She wasn't at all afraid of being reprimanded for her bluntness. Unlike most women of her class, Miss Gentry wasn't one to get annoyed over an honest answer.

"But it wasn't just Louisa," Annabeth wailed. She put the tea down on the mantel and began pacing again. "It was Reverend Cooksey, too. Now that the fuss about Miranda finding that body has died down, he thinks I miss being the center of attention."

"That's even sillier than Mrs. Cooksey's notion that you're getting strange fancies. It weren't your fault Miranda dug up that corpse. You didn't ask all them newspapers to interview you and put your name in the papers." Martha shook her head in disgust. She thought both the Cookseys fools. "I don't mean to be steppin' out of my place, ma'am, but you need help. You've almost been run down by a carriage, clouted on the head with a load of flyin' bricks, and someone's even tried to poison you. And that's just been in the last two weeks. You can't go on like this, ma'am. Whoever's doin' all this is goin' to get lucky soon and you're goin' to end up pushing up daisies."

"You believe me, then?" Annabeth asked quietly. "You don't think I'm making things up to get attention or that it's all my imagination?"

"Of course I believe you, ma'am," Martha replied. "I was there when them bricks come topplin' off the top of the garden wall and I was there when poor Miranda keeled over after she ate part of your scone. Good thing she didn't take more than a bite or she'd be a goner."

Annabeth shuddered. "That was a dreadful day." She glanced at the bloodhound. Miranda was lying in a shaft of sunlight streaming in through the lace curtains, enjoying the warm September sunshine.

"You'll not get any argument from me, ma'am. Pardon the expression, but poor Miranda was as sick as a dog. Of course, she *is* a dog, but she did look pitiful."

Hearing her name bandied about, Miranda raised her head and looked at the two women.

"We've got to do something, ma'am," Martha continued earnestly, "and we must do it quickly."

"You think I ought to go to the police?" Annabeth picked up her teacup and took a quick sip.

"That'll not do any good without proof, ma'am. If your own family won't believe you, you don't have much chance of convincin' the coppers."

"Then I don't see what I can do." Annabeth sighed heavily. "It's hopeless. I was so looking forward to moving into my new home, too. Now it appears as if I ought to move away, far away. Then maybe whoever is trying to kill me will give up."

Martha, being from a far less protected class than Miss Gentry, knew better than that. "'Course they won't, they'll just follow you. Mark my words, ma'am, if someone's wantin' to do you in, they'll only stop if you're six feet under or if you catch 'em first."

Annabeth's eyes widened. "Oh dear, I don't want to die. There are so many places I want to go. I've always wanted to travel, you know—"

"You're not goin' to die," Martha interrupted. When she was excited, her accent tended to revert to the one she'd been born to, not the one she'd acquired working as a ladies' maid. "We're goin' to catch the villain, that's what we're goin' to do. I think I know someone who could help."

"Help how?"

"Help by finding out who's trying to do you in, ma'am." Martha grinned. "Her name is Betsy. She's very good at detecting stuff, and even better, she works for Inspector Gerald Witherspoon of Scotland Yard. I know Betsy'll believe us, and what's more, she'll be able to do something about it."

Annabeth frowned in confusion. "She works for a police inspector?"

"She's his maid, ma'am, but don't let that fool you. She's also a right good snoop. Now, you just leave everything to me. We'll have you safe and sound in no time."

Mrs. Goodge, the cook, put the big brown teapot on the table next to a plate of buttered bread. She was a portly, gray-haired woman who'd cooked for some of the finest families in all of England. She now cooked for Inspector Gerald Witherspoon of Scotland Yard and she wouldn't have given up working for him to be the head cook at Buckingham Palace. Indeed she wouldn't.

"Are the others coming?" Betsy, the blond-haired maid, asked as she stepped into the kitchen. She smiled at the housekeeper and the cook.

Mrs. Jeffries, the housekeeper, smiled back. "Wiggins went to wash his hands. I haven't seen Smythe since breakfast, but I'm assuming he'll be here at the usual time. Do you have any idea where he's got to this morning?"

Betsy knew good and well where Smythe had gone, but she didn't really want to mention it to the others. Drat, this was awkward. The cook and the housekeeper were watching her inquiringly. "I think he went to the stables," she mumbled as she sat down. She hated telling lies. But she could hardly admit that her fiancé had gone to see his banker to check about his investments. Not when the rest of the household thought he was just a simple coachman. Drat, Smythe *was* a coachman, of course. He just happened to be a very rich one.

"I expect he'll be back shortly," Mrs. Jeffries said briskly. She was a motherly, plump woman dressed in a brown bombazine dress. She had dark brown eyes and auburn hair lightly streaked with gray. She smiled easily and often.

"Cor blimey, I'm starvin'." Wiggins, the apple-cheeked footman, rushed into the room and plopped down next to the cook. "Do we have to wait for Smythe? I've got ever so much to do this mornin'. I know it's warm outside, but it's already September and I want to get another coat of paint on the back windowsills before the cold sets in."

"Help yourself to something to eat," the housekeeper said as she began pouring the tea. "I'm sure Smythe won't mind if we start without him."

"What else do you have to do today?" the cook asked the footman. She eyed him suspiciously. She had a few chores in mind for the lad. The wet larder could use a good scrubbing, for example.

"After I finish the paintin'"—Wiggins stuffed a bite of bread into his mouth—"I was goin' to pop 'round and show Horace, Lady Cannonberry's footman, how to mix that new polish for the door brasses."

"That sounds like a very good idea," Mrs. Jeffries said. "Is Lady Cannonberry still gone?" Their neighbor, Ruth Cannonberry, was a good friend and she was also very special to Inspector Witherspoon.

"She's coming back on the fifteenth," Wiggins replied. He turned his head and glanced toward the hall as the back door opened. The soft murmur of voices and the sound of footsteps echoed clearly in the quiet kitchen.

"That's Smythe," Betsy said. She easily recognized his voice.

"He's got someone with him," Mrs. Goodge added.

"It's a woman," Betsy mumbled.

A moment later, the coachman, accompanied by a stranger, stepped into the kitchen. Smythe was a tall, muscular fellow with dark brown hair and heavy, rather brutal features. He smiled broadly as he spotted Betsy sitting at the kitchen table. "This young lady wants to 'ave a word with you," he said to her.

Betsy studied his companion. She was a tall, big-boned woman in her early twenties with dark hair and hazel eyes. She wore a pale lavender broadcloth dress and a short, thin brown jacket. The slender face under the serviceable broad-brimmed hat seemed vaguely familiar. Betsy didn't know who she was, yet the girl was smiling at her like they were old friends. "I'm sorry," Betsy said, "have we met before?"

"It's been a few years," the girl replied, "and I've filled out a bit. My name is Martha Dowling and we met when you come around to Mayfair when I worked for Mr. Vincent. Remember, you pretended to run into me accidentally like so you could ask me all them questions."

"Oh yes." Betsy grinned as she remembered. "Of course. You worked for Justin Vincent. Sad how that turned out."

Martha shrugged philosophically. "It couldn't be helped."

"How nice to see you again," Betsy said quickly. "Won't you sit down?" She gestured toward an empty chair.

"Thanks all the same," Martha replied. "But if it's all right with your housekeeper"—she nodded respectfully at Mrs. Jeffries—"I'd like to have word with you in private. It's a rather delicate matter, you see." She smiled nervously.

Betsy had an idea of why the woman had come. Apparently, she hadn't been as discreet with her investigating back in those days as she'd hoped. "A delicate matter? Does that mean you need my help?" she asked bluntly. "The kind of help you're not wanting to go to the police about, I suppose." She was relieved to think that was the reason Smythe had brought the woman inside. She trusted him, of course. But she was glad to know that Martha had come here to see her and wasn't someone from her fiancé's past.

The girl cast a quick, wary look at the others sitting around the table. "Uh . . . well . . ."

"Don't worry. You can speak in front of them." Betsy gestured at the others. "They know all about the circumstances of our last meeting. We have no secrets here." Except about money, she thought, glancing at Smythe, who looked away.

"It's all right, my dear," Mrs. Jeffries said kindly. She deliberately kept her tone informal. "If you're in some sort of trouble—"

"It's not me," Martha exclaimed quickly. "It's me mistress."

Mrs. Jeffries knew the others sensed an adventure in the making. Mrs. Goodge leaned forward with her head slightly cocked to the left so she could hear every word (Mrs. Jeffries suspected she'd gone a tad deaf in her right ear). Smythe, who'd been in the midst of taking his seat, went stock-still, and Wiggins had actually pulled his hand back from reaching for a slice of bread. Oh yes, Mrs. Jeffries thought, they'd caught the scent all right.

"What's wrong with yer mistress?" Wiggins asked. "'As she gone missin' or is someone tryin' to 'urt 'er?"

Martha gasped. "How'd you know?"

"We knows lots of things," Wiggins told her confidently. He patted the empty chair on his other side. "You come and 'ave a sit-down next to me. We'll get everything sorted out as right as rain."

Martha smiled in relief and sat down next to the lad.

Mrs. Jeffries quickly poured the girl a cup of tea. "Here, my dear. Have some refreshment. Then tell us what this is all about. Take your time."

"Ta." Martha's gaze darted quickly around the table over the top of the cup as she took a sip. "I'm not sure where to begin."

"Why don't you begin at the beginning?" Mrs. Goodge suggested. "That's always best."

"That's right," Wiggins added. "That's where I always like to start." He was eager to know everything about Martha. She was a bit taller than he and a bit older, but she was pretty.

"Right, then." Martha took a long, deep breath and sat her cup down. "I work for a lady named Annabeth Gentry. We live at number seventeen Orley Road in Hammersmith. It's a quiet life—well, usually it's quiet. Mind you, people did make a bit of fuss when Miranda and Miss Gentry got in the newspapers for finding that body. But that's passed and we're back to doin' what we always did. At least we were until bricks come flyin' off the wall and poison ended up in the scones—"

"Body?" Wiggins interrupted. "What body? And who's Miranda?"

The others were all staring intently at the girl.

"Oh, Miranda is Miss Gentry's dog," Martha said proudly. "She's a bloodhound. She's got the best nose in all of England. Miss Gentry has taught her to do all kinds of interestin' things. I don't think she quite had diggin' up dead bodies in mind when she was teachin' the pup all those tricks, but there you have it. Life's like that, innit? You never know what's going to happen. Here she and Miranda was just out doin' a bit of trainin' and all of a sudden the pup starts diggin' like a mad thing, and before you know it, Miranda had dug up that corpse."

"Miss Dowling, I'm sorry, please slow down. I'm afraid I'm getting confused," Mrs. Jeffries said softly. "You're going too quickly for me to take this all in. Are you saying someone is trying to kill Miss Gentry because her dog dug up a body?"

"Oh, no." Martha waved her hand in dismissal. "I'm sorry, I didn't mean to ramble on and on. I tend to do that when I'm nervous." She paused and took a deep breath. "Let me start again. Someone's trying to kill my mistress, but I don't think it has anything to do with Miranda finding that poor man's body. The police think whoever killed him and planted him on the side of the path is long gone."

"Do they know who he was?" Smythe asked.

Martha nodded. "Feller named Tim Porter. He were well known to the police. Been in and out of knick all the time for pickin' pockets and petty stuff like that."

The coachman made a mental note to have a good look into the circumstances of Porter's death. Despite what the girl said, he thought the attempts on this Miss Gentry's life might have a lot to do with finding a body.

"How was the man killed?" Mrs. Goodge pushed the plate of bread and butter toward the girl. "Help yourself."

"Ta," Martha said as she grabbed a slice. "The police said his throat had been slit." She took a bite of the bread. "But like I said, I don't think that could have anything to do with Miss Gentry's troubles. It weren't like Miranda was sniffin' about for the one that did the killin'. She just found the corpse."

"How long after discovering the body did the attempts on Miss Gentry's life begin?" Mrs. Jeffries asked.

Martha thought for a moment. "Let me see now. It would have been a week or so later. Yes, yes." She nodded eagerly, "That's right. Miranda found the body on August tenth and the attempts started about the seventeenth. I remember because the first one was the same day that Miss Gentry went to afternoon tea at her sister's house in Kensington. When she was on her way home, someone tried to run her down in a carriage. Right on the corner of the Brompton Road it was, and no one saw a bloomin' thing neither. Everyone said it happened too fast."

Wiggins's eyes were big as saucers. "What saved her?"

"She's a strong woman, is Miss Gentry. When she saw that coach-and-four bearin' down on her, she gave one almighty leap onto the pavement. Landed on her knees and scraped 'em real bad she did, but she was safe. The carriage kept on goin' down the Brompton Road."

"Could it have been an accident?" Mrs. Jeffries inquired. Before they got their hopes up, she wanted to be absolutely sure there really was something to investigate.

"At first we thought that's exactly what it was," Martha said earnestly. "You don't expect to get knocked about when you're walkin' in Kensington in broad daylight, do you? But when the other things started happening, that's when Miss Gentry got to thinking that the coach accident was no accident, if you get my meaning."

"Tell us about the other things." Betsy picked up her own cup and took a quick sip.

"A day or so after she was almost run down, a bunch of bricks come tumbling off the top of the garden wall right onto the spot where Miss Gentry was sittin'. Her head would've been crushed exceptin' for the fact that not two seconds before it happened, she dropped her spoon under the table and bent down to pick it up. It was the table that kept her from bein' coshed. As it was, she got her arm bruised pretty badly."

"Did anyone see who did it?" Smythe asked.

"No, more's the pity," Martha said. "It's a ten-foot wall, and by the time we'd rounded up the lad from next door to skivvy over and see what was what, there was no one there. But there was a ladder lying on the ground close by."

"That's a rather peculiar way to try and kill someone," Mrs. Jeffries mused. "How could the assailant know that Miss Gentry would be sitting in the, well . . . right spot?"

"It's where she always sat for tea," Martha exclaimed. "If the sun was shinin', she had tea there every day. Besides, it weren't one brick that come tumbling down, it were a whole lot of 'em. That's how come Miss Gentry got her arm bruised. When she realized what was happening she squeezed under the table, but she weren't quick enough to get her whole body under it."

"Maybe the mortar just come loose," Wiggins suggested.

"Them bricks had been pried loose," Martha insisted. "We went 'round to the school and had a look ourselves later that day."

"So it's a school yard on the other side," the cook said brightly. "That explains it, then; it was probably some silly schoolboy prank that went wrong."

"The school closed down right after Easter. There was no one there but the caretaker and he'd been taking a nap. Looked like someone had spent the better part of that Sunday afternoon chiseling the mortar out of them bricks and then waitin' till Miss Gentry was sittin' down in her spot before they pushed 'em over. You can take a look, the tea table is right beside that wall. If Miss Gentry hadn't reached for that spoon, she'd have been a goner."

Mrs. Jeffries leaned forward. "I'm sure you're right, my dear. Now, what about the scones being poisoned?"

"Not the scones, the cream." Martha sighed. "Mind you, Miranda'd be dead, too, if that fat old cat from down the street hadn't come into the garden and caught her attention before she ate the rest of Miss Gentry's scone."

"So it was the cream that was poisoned?" Mrs. Jeffries clarified. This was a most bizarre tale, but she'd learned in her life that merely because circumstances sounded odd didn't make them any less true.

"Right. There were just a thin layer spread on Miss Gentry's scone, she's not all that fond of it. But we'd run out of butter, so she used the cream . . . we were havin' guests that day and it were a good thing Miranda snatched that bite first and got sick, otherwise we'd have had a houseful of dead guests . . ." Her voice trailed off as she took in their expressions. Everyone looked thoroughly confused. "Look, I'm not explainin' things very well . . ."

"That's not true," Wiggins protested. "You're doin' a right good job if you ask me."

She flashed the footman a grateful smile. "That's kind of you to say, but the truth is, Miss Gentry could tell it all much better than me. I was wonderin' if I could bring her 'round this afternoon."

"I think that's a splendid idea," Mrs. Jeffries said quickly. She darted a fast look around the table; the others were nodding their agreement and she suspected they were thinking the same thing she was. By the time Martha and her mistress came back today, they could verify a number of things. "We'd be pleased to meet Miss Gentry and hear her story."

Martha smiled gratefully. "That's ever so wonderful. This is such a load off of my mind, it is."

"Why didn't you go to the police after the dog was poisoned?" Mrs. Goodge asked curiously.

"The mistress and I thought about it," Martha answered. "But we had no proof."

"You had the poisoned cream," Smythe pointed out softly.

"No, we didn't," Martha said. "When Miss Gentry and I went back out to the terrace after taking care of Miranda and getting rid of everyone, the cream pot was gone. That's how we knew it was poison! As I've said, my mistress can explain everything much better than I can."

"Actually," Mrs. Jeffries said quickly, "I do believe it would be best if one of us came to see you. Would Miss Gentry be available tomorrow morning?"

Martha's brow furrowed in confusion. Then she shrugged. "To get some help, she'll be available anytime you want. Tomorrow will be fine. What time?"

"Ten o'clock."

Martha stood up. She still looked a bit puzzled by the sudden change of plans, but apparently had decided to leave well enough alone.

"Before you go," Mrs. Jeffries said, "there's just one or two more questions we'd like to ask. It'll only take a moment."

"All right." Martha sat down and the housekeeper finished her questions. A few minutes later, Betsy escorted the girl to the back door.

As soon as the two women were out of sight, Smythe was on his feet and looking inquiringly at the housekeeper. She nodded and he disappeared in the opposite direction, up the stairs leading to the front door.

"You havin' Smythe follow her?" Wiggins asked in a loud whisper. He looked very disappointed. He'd have liked that job himself.

"I think that's best, don't you?" the housekeeper said quietly. "It'll give him the opportunity to see the layout of Miss Gentry's home firsthand."

"Why didn't he just offer to take her back himself?" Wiggins asked curiously. He wasn't quite as cynical as the others; he actually believed what people told him.

"Because we want to see for ourselves what's what," the cook said impatiently. "Following her will give Smythe a good chance to take the lay of the land, have a nice look around, and see just how far that wall actually is from the tea table."

"And sendin' her off like that'll give us a chance to find out if that dog really did find a dead body," Wiggins finished. He leapt to his feet, scooting the chair back loudly against the floor as he did so. "I can nip down to the station and have a word with Constable Griffiths. He'll know if some dog dug up a body."

"Mind how you talk to him," Betsy warned as she came back to the kitchen. Constable Griffiths had worked on a number of the inspector's cases. This wouldn't be the first time they'd used him for information. "He's no fool."

"Should we send someone to fetch Luty and Hatchet?" Mrs. Goodge asked.

Mrs. Jeffries considered the question. Luty Belle Crookshank and her butler, Hatchet, would be very annoyed to be kept out of an investigation. They were good friends of the household of Upper Edmonton Gardens and always helped with the inspector's cases. "I'm not sure we ought to involve them until we know for certain we've got something to investigate."

"Are you sure, Mrs. Jeffries?" Betsy pressed. "They'll both get their noses out of joint if they find out we've started snooping without them."

Mrs. Jeffries considered the maid's warning. "You're right, of course." She sighed. "They will be annoyed. But what if this is only a tempest in a teapot? What if this Miss Gentry is one of those very unfortunate and rather pathetic people who make up stories to get a little attention?"

"If that were true, would her maid have come all this way to ask for our help?" Betsy asked. "She seems to like her mistress, but I don't think she'd go to all this trouble unless she was certain Miss Gentry was really in danger."

"Don't be too sure of that," Mrs. Goodge put in. "I've known some really silly women who had equally silly maids."

Betsy shook her head. "Martha figured out what I was up to when she worked for Vincent, so she can't be too silly." The moment the words were out, she clamped her lips shut, wishing she'd kept her comment to herself or just agreed with the cook. She didn't like reminding the others that she was the one who'd questioned Martha on that case. She was the one who'd been a lot less clever than she'd thought. They weren't supposed to let anyone know they helped Inspector Witherspoon. No one. But this girl had sussed it out and it had been all Betsy's fault.

"Don't worry about it, Betsy," Mrs. Jeffries said softly. "Sometimes it's impossible to get information out of people without giving the game away, so to speak."

Betsy's shoulders sagged in relief. "You're not annoyed about it?"

"Don't be daft, girl," the cook interjected. "Of course we're not. We've all had to tell more than we wanted every once in a while."

"Martha Dowling isn't the first person to catch us out." Mrs. Jeffries smiled kindly. "And I doubt she'll be the last. Now stop fretting and let's have a good think about whether or not there's something else we can do before Wiggins and Smythe return."

But there wasn't anything to do except go about their normal routine. Betsy went upstairs to finish polishing the furniture, Mrs. Goodge mixed up her suet, and Mrs. Jeffries went upstairs to check the linen cupboard.

But all of them worked just a bit faster than usual and with their ears cocked toward the door. They wanted to be at the ready, as it were, when the males of the household returned.

The rest of the morning seemed to crawl by at a snail's pace. Mrs. Jeffries replenished the supply of dewberry-wood chips and counted out the week's linen supply. She laid the sheets, towels, and cleaning rags on the table outside the cupboard, then withdrew to her quarters to finish the household accounts.

She entered her rooms and kept the door open so that she could hear when someone arrived back with news. Sitting down at her desk, she drew the account book out of the top drawer, opened it, and diligently picked up the stack of receipts sitting underneath the brass angel paperweight. The greengrocer's bill was on the top. She picked it up, studied the items on the list, and then dropped it onto the ledge. This was utterly pointless. She simply couldn't concentrate. Her mind was already too occupied with that strange tale the girl had told them. She knew it was because investigating murder—or in this case, attempted murder—had become virtually second nature to all of them. The housekeeper smiled to herself. Even Smythe and Betsy, who'd just recently become engaged, had postponed getting married because they were afraid they'd have to give up their snooping. They hadn't come right out and admitted that this was behind their reluctance to set a wedding date, but Mrs. Jeffries was fairly certain. Once Smythe and Betsy were married, they'd no doubt want their own house and their own life. A life certainly far grander than the one they lived now. Smythe, despite his efforts to keep his circumstances a secret, was a wealthy man. None of the others in the household, save for herself and Betsy, knew about the coachman's fortune.

She picked up the greengrocer's bill and put it back under the paperweight. She reflected for a moment on the strange circumstances that had led them all to the household of Gerald Witherspoon. She'd been a policeman's widow from York who'd decided to come to London because she was bored. She'd quite deliberately found a position as housekeeper to a policeman. The inspector had been happily working in the records room, but once she'd gotten him investigating and then solving those horrible Kensington High Street killings, well, everything had fallen into place rather neatly.

Smythe and Wiggins were already here when the inspector and she had arrived. They'd worked for Witherspoon's late aunt Euphemia. The inspector, though he had very little use for either a footman or a coachman, kept them both on. He'd not only inherited this house from his aunt, he'd also inherited a substantial fortune. Mrs. Goodge had come along a few weeks later, and then one night, Betsy, half-starved and looking like death was dogging her very footsteps, ended up on the inspector's door stoop. Gerald Witherspoon, being the man he was, insisted on taking the girl in, feeding her, and then giving her a position as maid.

That was the beginning. Now they were family. And they loved to snoop. Not that their dear inspector ever realized he was getting help from his own household on his cases. He didn't. Occasionally, though, others did.

She was shaken from her reverie by the sound of the front door shutting downstairs. Someone was back. She leapt up and fairly flew down the front stairs.

"Oh, Inspector—" She caught herself and slowed down when she reached the landing on the first floor. Recovering her poise, she continued down the stairs at her normal pace. "I didn't think you'd be home so early. Is everything all right?"

"Quite all right, Mrs. Jeffries." Witherspoon took off his hat and moved toward the new brass coatrack he'd recently bought. "Chief Inspector Barrows is having a dinner party tonight."

"A dinner party, sir?" Mrs. Jeffries beat him to the coatrack by a couple of seconds. She extended her arm, took the inspector's bowler, and placed it on the top.

Gerald Witherspoon was a middle-aged man with a mustache and thinning dark hair. His complexion was light and his features sharp and rather fine-boned. Behind a pair of wire-rim spectacles, he had kindly hazel eyes. He frowned in confusion at his housekeeper. "Apparently I'm invited to this dinner party. But I don't recall receiving an invitation. Do you remember our receiving one?"

"No, sir, I don't. Was the chief inspector absolutely certain he'd sent the invitation?"

"That was the awful part, Mrs. Jeffries, I couldn't ask." He started toward the back stairs. "You see, I wasn't really paying attention to the conversation, when all of a sudden Inspector Nivens poked me in the ribs and asked what I was going to bring Mrs. Barrows for her birthday. It was most awkward. At that very moment the chief inspector turned and looked in our direction. He told me not to be late tonight, otherwise he'd be stuck talking to his wife's brother. It was obvious that a celebration was planned and that I'd been invited."

"Oh dear, that *is* awkward. Excuse me, sir." She was practically running to keep up with him. "But if you'd like a cup of tea, I'll be happy to bring it to the drawing room." Drat, she didn't want the inspector hanging about the kitchen when they were beginning an investigation. It would be just their bad luck to have Wiggins come flying through the back door talking up a blue streak about the case.

Witherspoon reached the top of the back stairs and started down. "I shall require far more than a cup of tea," he called over his shoulder. "I shall require the good graces of you dear ladies."

"Good graces?" she repeated. She charged down the back stairs behind him. "Whatever does that mean, sir?"

"It means I shall need your help." He reached the bottom step. "We've not much time."

Mrs. Goodge and Betsy glanced up from the table as the inspector and Mrs. Jeffries entered. Both of them, to their credit, managed to quickly mask their surprise. "This is a nice treat, sir," the cook said heartily. "Have you come home to have tea with us?" He sometimes did have tea with them, though usually that was on Sundays.

"I've come home to throw myself on your mercy," he said, pulling out the chair at the head of the table. "I'm in a bit of a muddle. I've been invited to Chief Inspector Barrows's dinner party tonight. It's his wife's birthday, so I must take a present, you see."

The women all stared at him blankly. It was so quiet they could hear the clip-clop of horses' hooves on the street outside.

"You've plenty of time to buy a present, sir," Betsy finally said. "It's not even three o'clock yet. The shops are open for another three hours."

"Yes, yes, I'm aware of that. But I've no idea what on earth to buy the woman. That's why I nipped home, you see. I was hoping one of you might suggest the proper sort of present one should buy for a superior's spouse."

The women cast quick, covert glances at one another. They understood their inspector's dilemma; this was, indeed, a very delicate matter. But they had a dilemma of their own they considered equally important—namely, to get Inspector Witherspoon out of their kitchen before Smythe or Wiggins came barging in.

Mrs. Goodge took the initiative. "It's quite simple, sir. You must buy her something nice, but not too personal."

Witherspoon shook his head eagerly. "That's what I thought, too. I was thinking perhaps I ought to get her a nice carpetbag."

"Oh, that's too expensive, sir," Mrs. Jeffries said quickly. Witherspoon's face fell. "You don't want to get her a gift that will be nicer than the one her husband gives her."

"How about a box of lace runners?" the cook suggested. "They've got some lovely ones at Hunts on the Kensington High Street."

"That's a wonderful idea," Mrs. Jeffries agreed. She didn't really care what the inspector bought Chief Inspector Barrows's wife; she simply wanted him out of the kitchen. "It's a perfect gift for Mrs. Barrows. One can never have enough lace runners."

The inspector brightened. "Good, then I'll get them. I'm so glad I came home; I'd have never thought of something like that. I was thinking I ought to buy her some gloves."

"You've got be careful buying things to wear, sir," Betsy said quickly. "Some women are real particular about what they like and what they don't like."

Witherspoon looked at the carriage clock on the pine sideboard. He got to his feet. "I ought to have plenty of time to nip out and get the present. Uh, what color do you think I ought to get?"

"They only come in white or cream," Mrs. Goodge replied. "Either will do."

"Excellent, excellent. Well, thank you, ladies, you've been enormously helpful." He turned toward the back door as it banged open and the sound of running footsteps could be heard. A moment later, Wiggins, closely followed by a panting Fred, the household dog, came bounding into the kitchen.

Upon seeing the inspector, Fred charged across the floor and began bouncing up and down enthusiastically.

"Hello, old boy." Witherspoon was devoted to the bundle of brown-and-black fur. If the truth were known, he was just a tad jealous of the relationship that Wiggins and the dog shared.

"Cor blimey, sir, we didn't expect to see you," Wiggins looked curiously at the others as the inspector and Fred indulged in their mutual admiration.

Mrs. Jeffries smiled briefly and then explained why the inspector had come home.

"The ladies have been most helpful," Witherspoon exclaimed as he gave the dog one last pat. "Most helpful indeed. I shall be home as soon as I've made my purchase. The chief inspector lives in St. John's Wood, so

I shall be needing the carriage tonight. Do be so kind as to let Smythe know." He was unable to resist giving the dog another stroke.

"We'll do that, sir." Mrs. Jeffries edged toward the hall, she wanted to get the man out of the house. Smythe wouldn't have much time to give his report if he had to go to the livery stable and get the carriage ready.

The inspector finally said his good-byes and, accompanied by Mrs. Jeffries, was soon heading toward the front door.

"What'll we do now?" Wiggins asked. He plopped down at the table and scratched the dog behind the ears. "Smythe's not gonna be pleased with 'avin' to cart the inspector around all evenin' on the first day of an investigation."

"It doesn't matter," Mrs. Goodge said. "We'll not be doing much tonight."

"We could 'ave a meeting with Luty and Hatchet," Wiggins suggested. "I think we'll want them to know what's goin' on."

Betsy shrugged. "It won't hurt Smythe to wait until tomorrow." She was secretly rather pleased that her beloved would spend the first night of the investigation driving the coach and not snooping about or shadowing that maid Martha. On several of their other murders, he'd been able to go out in the night and begin investigating while she and the other women had had to wait until the following day. For once, she might actually get the jump on him.

"Smythe's not goin' to like that." Wiggins grinned. "Especially after you 'ear what I found out down at the station. Constable Griffiths knew ever so much."

Just then Smythe came into the kitchen. "What am I not goin' to like?" he asked.

CHAPTER 2

Smythe wasn't pleased when he heard about the inspector's plans for the evening. "Bloomin' Ada," he muttered. "Why tonight? I wanted to talk to a few of my sources." Frowning, he plunked himself down at the table.

Mrs. Jeffries came back to the kitchen and took the chair the inspector had vacated only moments earlier. She turned to Wiggins. "I take it you believe Martha is telling the truth?"

"I 'ad a nice natter with Constable Griffiths," Wiggins replied. "That bloodhound did dig up a corpse. It was in the newspapers. But I guess none of us seen it."

"That's odd," Mrs. Jeffries murmured. "I generally make a note of things like bodies being found."

"He'd been murdered?" Mrs. Goodge prodded. Simply finding a body didn't guarantee one also found a murder.

"Throat was sliced like a butchered pig," the footman said cheerfully. "They don't 'ave a clue who done it, either. Like Martha said, he was a pickpocket. But Tim Porter wasn't much of anythin' else, if you know what I mean."

"Even petty thieves 'ave enemies," Smythe said.

"Yeah, but accordin' to Constable Griffiths, this bloke were known to avoid anythin' that was violent. Bit of a coward, so to speak."

The housekeeper nodded approvingly at the footman. "You've done very well. Did the constable share anything else with you?"

"You're not goin' to like this part." Wiggins's grin faded. "The case was given to Inspector Nivens on account of the victim bein' a known thief. No one expects he'll ever catch the killer. I'd bet against it myself."

"Indeed, that murderer has little to worry about, then," Mrs. Goodge snorted in derision. "Not if Nivens is on the hunt."

"Nivens couldn't find the back end of horse, not even if he was ridin' on it," Smythe muttered. "Let alone a murderer."

"They must not want to catch the killer." Betsy shook her head in disgust.

Mrs. Jeffries didn't try to stem the tide of anger directed at Inspector Nigel Nivens. He was an ambitious, self-serving little toad who was always trying to prove that Witherspoon had help in solving his cases. He went tattling to the chief inspector at the slightest pretext and used a system of informants to solve what few burglary cases he had each year. He was the sort of fellow you didn't want to sit next to on a long train trip. Nigel Nivens's favorite topic was Nigel Nivens. Mrs. Jeffries loathed him. And she suspected that the feeling was mutual. On more than one occasion, she'd had to dodge both him and his questions. "Well, let's hope that this case doesn't involve Nivens more than necessary. We don't want him interfering with our investigation. Anything else, Wiggins?"

The footman frowned thoughtfully. He didn't want to leave something out. "Not that I can remember. I 'ad to be right careful when I was askin' questions." He grinned at Betsy. "Wouldn't want the constable to get suspicious."

"Can I tell my bit now?" Smythe asked. There was only the barest hint of impatience in his tone.

"By all means," the housekeeper replied.

"I followed Martha to Orley Road. As she got to the front door, it opened and this tall woman poked her head out and started natterin' at the girl."

"The maid used the front door?" Mrs. Goodge's voice was only the smallest bit disapproving. Which actually showed how far she'd come since she'd begun investigating with the others. When they'd first come together, the cook would have been of the opinion that there were no circumstances which would justify a servant using the front door. Under the influence of Mrs. Jeffries and the rest of them, however, she'd lost much of her snobbish attitude. Indeed, there were moments when she was almost radical in her views.

Smythe nodded.

"Could you hear what she said?" Betsy asked.

"I was too far away. But I'll tell ya one thing, that woman looked mighty worried."

"Then what happened?" Mrs. Jeffries asked. She wanted to hurry him along. There might be things that needed doing before the inspector returned.

"I waited a few minutes and then I nipped around the corner so that I could see the back of the house. The school's deserted, all right. Place looks like it's falling down."

"Did you go inside?" Mrs. Jeffries was fairly certain she knew the answer already.

"Popped over the fence in two shakes of a lamb's tail. The caretaker weren't in sight, so I snooped about and had a good look at the wall dividing the school from the houses along Orley Road. There was two big indentions right there in the mud where a ladder'd been propped. You could still see 'em, and most importantly, there were a bunch of bricks missing from the top of the wall."

"What about the table?" Betsy asked. "If the wall is as high as Martha said it was, were you able to see where the table was?"

"I managed." He grinned at the maid. "I'm not a young'un, but no ten-foot wall will stop me from 'avin' a look. The table was pushed back away from the wall, but you could see by the scratch marks on the paving where it'd been. Any bricks dropping from the top could have clomped someone sitting there. Probably killed 'em, too."

"It still seems a very unreliable way to try and murder someone," Mrs. Jeffries mused.

"Maybe the killer's a stupid git," Wiggins suggested. "Not all murderers are smart—"

"We don't know that we have a murderer," the housekeeper interrupted. "All we know for certain is that Miss Gentry appears to be having some very unfortunate accidents." But she did know that they had a case; she could feel it in her bones.

"Three accidents in two weeks," the cook said. "That's an awful lot of bad luck if you ask me."

"What do we do now?" Betsy asked.

Everyone stared at Mrs. Jeffries. She thought about it for a moment and then said, "If all of you agree, I think we ought to proceed as we usually do."

There was a collective rumble of agreement.

"Should I go get Luty and Hatchet?" Wiggins asked. He started to get up but Mrs. Jeffries waved him back to his seat.

"That's a good idea," she said, "but do wait until after the inspector comes home. He may want to take Fred for a walk or something before he goes out. Besides, you've got to shine his good shoes and brush his dinner jacket."

Wiggins slumped back into his chair. "Can't someone else do that? I hate brushin' that jacket; all them little dusty bits go up my nose."

"There wouldn't be any dusty bits if you kept the inspector's closet aired properly," Mrs. Goodge retorted.

As the household really didn't need a footman, Mrs. Jeffries had assigned Wiggins some light valet duties. Not that their employer expected such service, but only to keep the lad busy.

"What are you complainin' about?" Smythe said. "I'm stuck drivin' him to a dinner party this evening instead of feelin' out my sources. Someone might have known something about our Miss Gentry's troubles. Count yourself lucky, lad."

Smythe glanced mournfully at Betsy. She smiled back at him. They both knew that when he came home with the inspector tonight, Betsy would have a cup of hot tea waiting for him. If the housekeeper and the cook were safely asleep, she'd have a kiss waiting for him as well.

"I think you could put that time to good use," Wiggins said.

Smythe cocked an eyebrow at the youth. "Do ya now?"

"If it's a party, they'll be lots of people comin' in hansoms and private carriages. Seems to me you could ask about and talk to some of the cabbies, see if anyone knows anything about that carriage accident."

"Fat chance, lad." Smythe laughed. "That 'appened over two weeks ago. The trail's gone cold, unless it were a paid job, and if that's the case, whoever did it ain't goin' to be talkin' about it in front of a bunch of cabbies."

"Besides, of all the things that have happened to Miss Gentry," Mrs. Jeffries added, "the incident with the carriage really could have been an accident. There are an awful lot of careless drivers about. But it was a rather good suggestion, Wiggins." She smiled kindly at the boy.

"Will you be going on your own to see Miss Gentry tomorrow?" the cook asked the housekeeper.

"No. If the rest of you are agreeable," Mrs. Jeffries replied, "I thought Betsy and I both should go. Two heads are better than one, you know.

And while one of us is asking questions, the other can be keeping a sharp eye out. One never knows what one can learn by being observant."

Orley Road was a short row of two-story redbrick houses with small, enclosed front gardens. The entire street was sandwiched between open fields on one side and the deserted school on the other.

Betsy and Mrs. Jeffries were at number 17 Orley Road at exactly ten o'clock the next morning. The small brass knocker had just banged against the wood when Martha threw open the door. "I'm ever so glad to see you," she said brightly. "I was afraid you might change your mind about comin'."

"We wouldn't have done that," Betsy assured her.

"Of course not," Mrs. Jeffries confirmed.

"Come in, then. Miss Gentry is all ready for you. She's in the drawing room."

Mrs. Jeffries and Betsy stepped inside. From the small entryway, a flight of stairs curved up sharply to the second floor. Martha led them down a short, carpeted hallway and into a bright, airy sitting room. Sunlight streamed in through the lace curtains, the walls were a pale yellow, and there was a green-and-gold carpet on the floor.

A tall woman with a nice smile and lovely blue eyes got up from a cream-and-rose chintz settee as the women entered. "Mrs. Jeffries? I'm Annabeth Gentry. Thank you so much for coming."

"We hope we'll be able to help you," the housekeeper replied. She judged the woman to be about thirty-five or forty. She introduced Betsy and the two of them sat down. Betsy had a quick look around. The room was nicely furnished but not cluttered. Two potted plants, a couple of nice pictures, an ottoman in the same shade of rose as the chair she was sitting on, and a matching set of bookcases on either side of the small fireplace.

"Martha told me all about you," Annabeth Gentry said as she resumed her seat, then turned her head toward the door. "Come in, Miranda; as you can see, we have visitors."

Betsy and Mrs. Jeffries both turned to look. A huge russet-colored bloodhound with a mournful face and enormously long ears loped into the room.

"What a lovely dog," Betsy exclaimed in delight. "So you're Miranda?"

The dog's tail wagged as she trotted over to give Betsy's outstretched hand a sniff. Betsy giggled and started petting the animal's shiny coat. "Oh, you're lovely, aren't you."

"She loves the attention." Annabeth laughed. The dog trotted over to her mistress and rubbed her big head against her knees. "That's right, she's my Miranda girl. She's just a bit spoiled, but she's so good-natured, I don't see any harm in it."

"She's the one that found the body?" Mrs. Jeffries asked gently, trying to get the investigation started.

"That's right. We were out taking a walk on those open fields off Loftus Road. I don't know if you know the area, but it's quite lovely. As there wasn't anyone about, I'd taken Miranda off the lead so she could have a bit of a run. All of a sudden she started sniffing the ground in that concentrated way she has and following it along the edge of the footpath for a good fifty feet. Then, just as suddenly, she turned sharply and stopped just inside a wooded area. She started digging frantically. When I saw the man's hand, I almost fainted. I called her away and went and got a policeman."

"Very wise of you, I'm sure." Mrs. Jeffries nodded. "And it was just after you and Miranda found that body that the attempts on your life began?"

"I really don't see how that poor man could be connected to what's happening to me." Annabeth sighed. "After the police arrived, I wasn't involved at all. They hustled me away very quickly. But I'm so confused now, I don't really know what to think. At first I thought I was just having a run of bad luck; it's not unheard of for horses to bolt. Then I was even willing to think that perhaps I was becoming accident-prone when those bricks started flying off the top of the wall; after all, it's an old wall. But when Miranda almost died from eating that poisoned cream, I knew for certain someone was really trying to kill me. You see, I was the one that should have eaten the cream. Not my poor hound."

"Tell us how this poisoning attempt took place," Betsy urged.

"I'm not sure I understand what you mean." Annabeth cocked her head to one side.

"We do need a few more details, Miss Gentry," Mrs. Jeffries explained. "Exactly when did it happen? Who was in the house? Where did the cream come from and how much of it had you consumed before Miranda helped herself?"

"Oh dear." She smiled apologetically. "I must sound as if I'm a dolt. Of course you need details. Let me see . . . well, it was the day before yesterday. My sister and her husband were visiting, so we were going to have tea outside. None of us particularly care for cream, but as we were having scones, Martha put it out along with the strawberry jam."

"Where did the cream come from?" Mrs. Jeffries asked. "I mean, why did you have it in the house if none of you care for it?"

"That's the strangest thing," Annabeth answered. "We don't know where it came from. But we didn't know we didn't know until after poor Miranda almost died from eating the wretched stuff, if you see what I mean. You see, when Martha went into the kitchen after searching for the curd, she saw a pot of cream on the table. Things have been a bit chaotic recently, what with getting ready for the move and all, so she naturally assumed I'd remembered we needed something for tea and purchased the cream. So she put it on the serving tray and brought it outside. When I saw the cream on the tray, I simply assumed that she'd nipped out and bought it herself. You see? Neither of us had actually bought the stuff, it was just here. But the circumstances were such that we didn't ask one another anything until after Miranda got ill."

Betsy thought she understood what the woman was saying. She glanced at Mrs. Jeffries. The housekeeper's expression revealed nothing. "Are you saying this pot of clotted cream just suddenly appeared on your kitchen table? Someone must have put it there."

"It makes no sense at all," Annabeth said eagerly. "That's what's so baffling to us, too."

Mrs. Jeffries looked at the huge hound, who was now lying at her mistress's feet. "Miranda doesn't seem to have been harmed by the experience."

"Only because she'd just eaten a mouthful of the stuff," Annabeth said. "I'd put a very small amount on my scone and then I'd cut it up into pieces. Just at that time, my sister and her husband arrived and I got up to go greet them. Miranda, naughty girl that she is, stretched up and grabbed one of the pieces of scone. Then Bruce, that's Mrs. Aylesworthy's cat, bounded into the yard and Miranda took off after him. A few minutes later, just as we were sitting down for tea, Miranda came slinking back. The poor darling was retching terribly. I didn't know what was the matter. I asked Martha if Miranda had eaten anything—"

"And I said all she'd had since her breakfast was that bit of scone," Martha added.

"How did you know for certain it was the cream?" Betsy asked. "Couldn't it have been the scones?"

"No, my brother-in-law and my sister both ate the scones and they didn't have cream, so I realized that whatever had made Miranda ill had been in the cream. By then I realized Miranda had been poisoned," Annabeth said. "I'm rather an expert on dogs, you see. I don't have any formal medical training, but I know enough to spot the symptoms of poisoning. As soon as I got rid of my relatives, I gave Miranda a thorough examination and then I sent Martha into the larder for the cream. We were going to take it to the police. But it had vanished."

"Who was in the house that day?" Betsy asked. She thought that was a reasonable place to start.

Annabeth's expression grew thoughtful. Absently, she reached down and petted the huge dog. "Well, let's see, there was Martha and myself, of course. My sister and her husband were here for tea . . . well, they were here for part of the tea; after Miranda retched all over the terrace, they took themselves off fairly quickly."

"What are their names?" Mrs. Jeffries asked.

"Reverend and Mrs. Cooksey." Annabeth grinned. "That's how they insist on introducing themselves. I always think of them as Harold and Louisa, but that tends to annoy them. Then my other sister and her husband popped in later that day. They're Elliot and Ethel Caraway. They'd stopped by to see how the renovations on the new house were going."

"Anyone else?"

"My new neighbor, Mr. Eddington; he came around to bring me the name of his painters. Oh, there were ever so many people here that day. I expect that's one of the reasons we didn't pay much attention to that wretched cream."

Betsy's head was spinning. She had dozens of questions to ask. From the expression on Mrs. Jeffries's face, she was certain the housekeeper had quite a few as well. "I know what you mean; some days there's so much coming and going you don't know what's what."

"Miss Gentry." Mrs. Jeffries smiled. "Let's put the issue of how the cream got into the house to one side. I've a few more things to ask, if you don't mind."

"But of course you do." Annabeth nodded vigorously. "That's why you've come. To help me. I must say, I'm ever so grateful. I don't think anyone else would take me seriously. Why, even my own sister didn't believe me."

"We believe you," Betsy said. "But like Mrs. Jeffries said, before we can do you any good at all, we'll have to ask you a lot of questions."

Martha started for the kitchen. "I'll get the kettle on. We'll all think better over a cup of tea."

Wiggins hoped that Mrs. Jeffries wouldn't get angry when she found out what he'd done, but he didn't fancy sitting around the kitchen with Mrs. Goodge, waiting for the others to get back. He stopped in front of the gate of what had been Helmsley's Grammar School for Boys and peeked through the rusted iron railings into the yard. The building was three stories tall and made of brick. Several of the top windows were broken and the eaves over the attic were missing bits of masonry. The aged gray-red cobblestones in the wide courtyard were split in spots and patches of grass pushed up between the cracks.

Wiggins sighed in disappointment. He wasn't sure what he expected to find here. Smythe had already had a good look about the place. "We might as well see what's what, Fred." He glanced at the animal standing patiently at his heels. Fred pricked his ears and woofed gently in agreement. "It looks deserted. But you never know, we might stumble onto something important."

He put his foot on the bottom rail of the gate and started to hoist himself up. The latch popped and the gate squeaked open. Fred trotted through, turned, and woofed at Wiggins, who was having a difficult time getting his foot out from between the railings. "'Ang on a minute," he told the dog. Not one to waste a lot of energy, Fred promptly sat down. Wiggins extricated his foot and squeezed through the opening.

To his left, the courtyard narrowed and wound to the back of the school. Two small, dilapidated sheds were on the far side and behind them was the wall which separated the school grounds from the neighboring houses. Wiggins glanced to his right; there was a high wall on the far side of the school building, and over it, he could see the spires of a church.

"Come on, Fred, let's have a look-see down by them buildings." He and Fred headed across the cobblestones. In the quiet morning, the heels of his heavy work shoes seemed horribly loud. He could even hear the click of Fred's nails against the stones. He stopped in front of the first building but it didn't look very interesting, so he continued on to the next. "This seems as good a place as any," he said to the dog. "Let's go 'round the back and see if we can spot them ladder marks in the dirt."

But Fred wasn't listening to Wiggins, he was staring at the shed they'd just passed. The hair on his back stood up and his ears had gone back. He was rooted to the spot.

A shiver of fear snaked up Wiggins's spine. They were now out of sight of the street and he suddenly felt very alone. He knelt down close to the dog's ear. "What is it, boy? What's wrong?" he whispered.

Not taking his gaze off the shed, Fred began to growl.

"Maybe we'd best get out of here," Wiggins said. He began rising to his feet and backing away. "Come on, boy, let's go."

But the dog didn't budge. His growl turned into a snarl.

From the inside of the shed, there was a loud, metallic thump.

Wiggins was no coward, but he knew in his bones that he and Fred had to get out of there. He didn't know how he knew it; he simply knew that if they didn't go now, something horrible would happen. He turned and started for the gate. "Come on, Fred," he hissed, "let's go."

Fred began to bark.

There was another frightening thump from the shed and then a loud whack as something banged against the door.

Wiggins reached down, picked up the dog, tucked him under his arm, and ran for the gate. Surprised, Fred stopped barking. He started up again a moment later, but by then, Wiggins had pushed the dog through the opening and was shimmying through himself. Wiggins heard the shed door opening. He knew he ought to look around, to get a look at whoever was behind him, but for the life of him, he was too scared.

Still barking, Fred tried to run back through the gate. Wiggins grabbed his collar and dragged him back. "Come on, boy," he called, frantically trying to keep the animal under control, "let's run. Come on, let's 'ave us a good run." Praying his tactic would work, he let go the collar and ran across the empty road. For a fraction of a second, Fred hesitated, then he took off after his beloved friend.

They ran down around the corner and onto Frithville Gardens and then onto the Uxbridge Road. Wiggins didn't stop till he and Fred were in sight of the railway lines and surrounded by people. He skidded to a halt when he reached the Albion Brewery and slumped against the side of the building. Sweat poured down his face as he took in huge gulps of air. He could feel the rough brick through his thin shirt. "Good dog." He reached down and petted the panting Fred. "You followed my lead. It's not that I'm a coward, Fred, but there was somethin' evil back there. I could feel it in me bones."

Fred woofed softly and wagged his tail.

"Now we've got to suss out what to do next," Wiggins said. He often talked to Fred. The fact that he was on a busy London street and that several passerbys were staring at him oddly didn't bother him in the least. "Someone's got to go back to that place." He started toward Shepherd's Bush Green. "I know there's somethin' wrong. But I'll have a devil of a time convincin' anyone to 'ave a look-see in that shed. What can I tell 'em? That I 'eard some funny noises? They'll wonder why I didn't 'ave a look myself." He stopped by a street lamp to let a handsome brougham pulled by two elegant gray horses go past. Wiggins knew that no one at Upper Edmonton Gardens would make fun of him for running away, nor would anyone consider him a coward. In truth, they'd probably tell him he'd acted wisely. But now that he was safely away from that place, he felt silly.

But he didn't feel silly enough to go back to that shed alone. Not by himself.

A costermonger pushing a creaky cart trundled past, leaving the pungent scent of mussels and jellied eels in its wake. Wiggins sighed and started across the road. "There's nothing for it, Fred," he said to the dog. "There's only one thing to do now. We've got to find Smythe."

"What do you think, Mrs. Jeffries?" Betsy asked as soon as they were out of earshot of the Gentry house.

"I think we'd best get everyone together and try to make some sense of all this," the housekeeper replied. They walked toward the omnibus stop at the top of the road. "But I've no doubt now that someone is trying to kill the woman."

"Should we involve the inspector?" Betsy stared up the road, her head bobbing from side to side as she tried to see if the omnibus was coming. But there was too much traffic to see much of anything.

"Not at this time," Mrs. Jeffries replied.

"Why?" Betsy looked at her curiously. "Don't you believe Miss Gentry?"

"Absolutely. But we've no proof. The poison cream disappeared and the other two incidents could both have been accidents. At least that's what the police will say. We need a bit more evidence before we involve the inspector. But I've no doubt we shall find it. Miss Gentry gave us plenty of information to begin our inquiry. Oh look, here comes the omnibus.

When we get on, why don't you continue on to the Kensington High Street and Knightsbridge."

Betsy laughed. "So that's why you wanted us to take the omnibus instead of walking. You want me to get Luty and Hatchet."

"Of course, have them back at Upper Edmonton Gardens by teatime. We've much to discuss."

Betsy frowned. "Will Smythe be back by then? For that matter, did he say where he was going today?" He'd been very closemouthed this morning and she, of course, had too much pride to pry. She wasn't going to become a nosy nellie simply because they'd got engaged. But she was just a tad hurt that he'd gone off without saying anything to her.

Mrs. Jeffries opened her coin purse and took out two ha'pennies and a sixpence. The omnibus pulled to a stop and the two women, holding tightly on to the wooden handrail, climbed aboard. There were two seats just inside. Mrs. Jeffries slid in by the window, leaving Betsy the one on the aisle. She handed the coins to the conductor and said, "One for Holland Park Road and one for the Kensington High Street."

Smythe wasn't in a good mood. He hung the harness on to the wall of the tack room and stepped into the stable proper. Howards, the livery where the inspector stabled his horses and carriage, was a large commercial concern, but at this time of day, it was relatively quiet.

He pulled the door shut behind him, locked it, and walked across the aisle to the stall where Bow and Arrow munched happily on their fresh oats. "Bloomin' Ada," he muttered to himself, "it's been a waste of a day. That's what I get for tryin' to be clever. A bleedin' wild goose chase."

"What kind of wild goose chase?" Wiggins asked as he and Fred popped around the corner and into view.

Surprised, Smythe started and then quickly caught himself. "What the blazes are you doin' 'ere?"

"I come to find you." Wiggins grinned. "I didn't know ya talked to yourself."

"I don't."

"Then who was ya talkin' to? The horses?"

"All right, every once in a while I talk to myself. What of it? Why was ya lookin' for me? Did Mrs. Jeffries send ya?"

Wiggins's smile faded. He looked down at the dog, who'd plopped down by his feet. "Uh, I need some 'elp with something."

"What are you on about, lad?" Smythe asked. He looked carefully at the boy; a line of sweat clung to his hairline and his face was flushed. Fred was panting like he'd run with the hounds of hell on his heels. "And let's get that dog some water. Fred's tongue's hangin' out."

They made their way to the pump in the front of the stable. The scent of horse and manure wasn't as strong out in the open air. Wiggins worked the handle and water gushed into the trough. Fred helped himself.

"Now, what's all this about, then?" Smythe asked softly. He could tell by the boy's expression that something serious was clouding his mind.

"You've got to promise not to laugh at me," Wiggins muttered. He kept his gaze on Fred.

"'Ave I ever laughed at you?"

Wiggins shook his head. "It's just that this sounds so silly, but it's not. It were real. I felt it. Something 'appened there. Somethin' awful. Fred felt it, too."

Smythe was genuinely alarmed now. Wiggins could go a bit foolish over a pretty lass, but he had good instincts. Alarmed, his voice was harsher than he intended. "What are you talkin' about? What's wrong?"

"I went over to that school you was at yesterday," Wiggins began. "The one next to that Miss Gentry's house."

"Why? I'd already had a good gander about the place, already said them bricks 'ad been pried off the top and pushed over the wall. What was you hopin' to find?"

Wiggins shrugged. "I'm not sure. But it wasn't like I 'ad anythin' else to do, so I went along and 'ad a look myself. Fred and I squeezed through the gate and we was just startin' down that bend toward the back when Fred stopped dead in his tracks and we 'eard somethin' comin' from the second shed."

"What do you mean, you 'eard somethin'? What'd ya 'ear?"

"I don't know what it was," Wiggins admitted. "But it scared me. Scared Fred, too. His hackles come up and his ears went back and then 'e started barkin'—"

"Well, what was it?"

"I don't know." Wiggins slumped his shoulders. "I got so scared I ran. I picked Fred up and ran like the devil. That's why I come 'ere to get you. I know somethin' bad was in that shed and I want you to come back with me."

Betsy arrived back at Upper Edmonton Gardens a few minutes before tea. Luty Belle Crookshank and her butler, Hatchet, accompanied her.

"We got here as quick as we could," Luty exclaimed. She was a small, thin elderly American woman with white hair, brown eyes so dark they looked almost black, and a razor-sharp mind. She loved bright clothes almost as much as she loved investigating crime. This afternoon she wore a huge hat decorated with yellow flowers and two bright purple plumes, a lavender dress with lace on the collars and cuffs, and a pair of outrageously huge amethyst earrings.

"Good day, everyone," Hatchet said politely as he followed Luty into the kitchen. "I hope all is well with the household." He was a tall man in his late fifties, with a full head of snow-white hair, a dignified demeanor, and a love of detective work that surpassed even his employer's.

"We are all well," Mrs. Jeffries replied. She nodded toward the others. "Do sit down and have some tea. We're just waiting for Wiggins and Smythe to come before we begin. They ought to be here any moment now." She looked at the maid. "What have you told them?"

"Just that Miss Gentry wants us to find out who is trying to kill her. That's all."

"Girl's lips were sealed tighter than a bank vault," Luty said. She took the empty seat next to the cook.

"To be fair, madam," Hatchet said as he slipped into the seat next to Mrs. Jeffries, "Miss Betsy explained that she wanted to wait until the others could be here to share what she and Mrs. Jeffries learned today."

"I wasn't trying to be mysterious," Betsy said earnestly. "I just didn't think Mrs. Jeffries would want us having to explain everything twice. Besides, Wiggins and Smythe'll be here soon. I'm sure of it. They know we were going to be having one of our meetings."

"Maybe we'd better leave Fred out 'ere," Wiggins suggested. "We could tie 'im to the inside of the gate."

"Why do that?" Smythe asked curiously. "Seems to me if you're right and there's somethin' amiss back at that shed, we'd do best to 'ave Fred with us."

Fred wagged his tail and woofed softly, as though he agreed with the coachman.

"Well, if ya think so, but he barked 'is 'ead off before." Wiggins started up the short drive to the gate.

"Wait a minute," Smythe ordered. "I thought you told me you run off like the 'ounds of 'ell was on yer 'eels?"

"I did."

"Then who closed the ruddy thing behind you?" Smythe asked.

Wiggins stared at the now-closed gate and shook his head. "I swear, it were open when I left. I was carryin' Fred and I didn't stop to pull it closed."

Smythe frowned at the latch. "It's not locked, just pulled up close together. This is gettin' interestin'." He edged the gate open and squeezed his big frame through.

Fred jumped through and Wiggins followed. Once they were all inside, Smythe stood for a moment. Cautiously, he looked to his left and then his right. Then he turned his attention to the derelict school building. His gaze started at the top and scanned the windows, assuring himself that none of the curtains moved or twitched. After he'd satisfied himself that they weren't being watched, he said, "Show me where you 'eard these noises at, then."

Wiggins started across the cobblestones. "It's just 'round there." Now that the moment was at hand, he hoped he wouldn't disgrace himself in front of the person he most admired. But as they headed for the shed, he found his steps slowing. Even Fred's frisky trot suddenly slowed to a much more sedate pace. He didn't like where this walk was heading.

From the corner of his eyes, Smythe saw Wiggins dropping behind. He knew then that the lad had really been frightened. But he didn't let that rattle him. Wiggins was a bit on the imaginative side. What did set the hair on the back of Smythe's neck prickling was when he noticed the dog's reaction. Cor blimey, he thought, what's going on here?

They reached the shed. Wiggins took a deep breath. Fred sniffed the crack under the door and whined softly. Smythe gave the door a gentle nudge. Slowly, it creaked open and a shaft of sunlight illuminated the dark space.

The inside of the place was covered with cobwebs and dust. A wooden bench with missing slats ran the length of the small room. In the dim light, it was hard to make out much detail, but Smythe could see where the dust on the stone floor had been disturbed.

"Do you see anything?" Wiggins asked.

"Just a lot of dirt and mess . . ." Smythe paused as he spotted a large mound on the far side of the room. He pushed the door open wide to get more light into the room. "Damn." He charged inside and flew over to the mound.

"What is it?" Wiggins cried as he followed quickly on Smythe's heels. Fred whined softly, hesitated, and then charged inside.

"It's a man." Smythe knelt down beside the bench, pulled the body onto its back, and began feeling for a pulse. He yanked open the man's shirt collar and skimmed his fingers across the flesh, hoping to feel the spark of life.

"Is he dead?" Wiggins's heart sank to his toes. He knew the answer already. And it was probably his fault.

Smythe said nothing for a moment; then he sighed and sat back on his heels. "'E's a goner, lad."

"Is there any blood?" Wiggins asked softly. He silently prayed that the man had died of natural causes. But deep in his bones, he knew that probably wasn't the case.

"No." Smythe straightened the collar back into place and tried vainly to smooth out the fabric. "But then there wouldn't be. There's bruises all over 'is throat. I'm no expert, but unlessin' 'e strangled 'imself, someone's murdered the poor bloke."

CHAPTER 3

"What's keeping them?" Mrs. Goodge asked irritably. "They knew we were going to be having a meeting this afternoon."

"I'm sure they'll be here any moment," Mrs. Jeffries said soothingly. "Smythe was going to take the horses for a run; you know how busy the roads get in the afternoons. There's always delays of one sort or another."

"What about Wiggins?" Luty asked. "Where in the dickens is he?"

The housekeeper took a sip of tea. "No one seems to know where Wiggins has gone. Apparently, Fred's with him."

"You ought to speak to him about that," Mrs. Goodge said. "He oughtn't to go off on his own without telling one of us where he's going and when he'll be back. What if the inspector needed him?"

"I'm sure the lad has a good reason for being tardy," Hatchet interjected.

"He'd better," the cook murmured. She hated it when Wiggins disappeared like this. She wouldn't for the world let anyone know, but she did worry so about the boy. He did have his head in the clouds so much of the time and anything could happen if you weren't careful. "Left here this morning without so much as a by-your-leave."

They all turned as they heard the back door opening and the sound of rushing footsteps in the hall.

Smythe flew into the kitchen, followed closely by Wiggins and Fred. "We've got trouble," the coachman said without preamble.

"What kind of trouble?" Mrs. Jeffries asked.

"There's a dead man in the school behind Miss Gentry's 'ouse. Looks to me like 'e's been strangled."

"I take it you haven't sent for the police," she stated calmly.

Smythe shook his head. "Not yet. We wanted to 'ave a word with you lot first."

"You're quite sure the victim was murdered?" she asked.

"There's a ring around the feller's throat," Smythe reported grimly. "Looks like a garrote of some kind was used."

"Any idea who the man is?" Mrs. Goodge asked.

"We think it's the caretaker," Wiggins added.

"How do you know?" Hatchet asked.

"When we rolled 'im over, these come tumblin' out of 'is pocket." Wiggins pulled a brass ring with several keys hanging from it out of his trouser pocket. "The back door of the school was open, too. Stands to reason, doesn't it; the caretaker would be the one with keys."

"Strange that an abandoned building would have a caretaker," Luty muttered. "Are you sure he ain't just some tramp that wandered in off the street?"

"We're not sure of anythin' yet," Smythe said. "We're only guessin'. But right now who the feller was isn't our problem; figuring out what we're going to tell the police is. We'd no business bein' there and now we've got to think of a way to get the police to that body without lettin' 'em know it were Wiggins and I that found it."

"You must go right to the inspector," Mrs. Goodge insisted.

"And what would we say when 'e asks what we was doin' there in the first place?" Smythe returned archly.

"What *were* you doing there?" Mrs. Jeffries asked curiously.

Smythe hesitated and then looked at the footman. Wiggins blushed a deep rosy color and looked at the dog sitting at his feet. "Smythe was there because I went and got 'im," he finally admitted. "I was there earlier, Mrs. Jeffries. I decided I'd nip along and 'ave a look while you was talkin' to Miss Gentry. I weren't followin' you or anythin' like that; I just thought I'd get a bit of jump on the case, so to speak."

"But Smythe had already been to the school and had a look around," Betsy pointed out.

"I know that," Wiggins explained. "But I didn't want to sit about 'ere waitin'. I was tryin' to 'elp."

"I'm sure you were, Wiggins," Mrs. Jeffries interjected. "Now, tell us how you came to find the body."

"'E didn't exactly find it," Smythe said. "'E 'eard some suspicious noises and, quite rightly, came along to 'Owards to get me."

"Suspicious noises?" Luty repeated. "What does that mean?"

"'E 'eard a few thumps comin' from the shed," Smythe explained, "and then Fred started barkin' his fool 'ead off. So the lad did the smart thing and took off before anyone got suspicious and came out to see what all the ruckus was about. It didn't take 'im long; 'Owards is only about twenty minutes away. We went back to the school and had a look in the shed; that's when we found the bloke."

It was quite obvious that Smythe and Wiggins were giving only a bare-bones version of the story. Consequently, no one said anything. Finally, after the silence stretched to an embarrassing length, Mrs. Jeffries said, "It's always best to avoid making a spectacle of oneself, especially if one suspects something untoward is afoot. It was clever of you to dash off and get Smythe. Two heads are always better than one in a precarious situation. Now, why don't the two of you sit down, have a cup of tea, and we'll come up with a way to get our inspector out to that corpse."

Inspector Gerald Witherspoon pushed the heavy iron gate open. "Do you think we ought to have brought some more men along, Constable Barnes?"

Barnes, a tall man with a craggy face and a headful of iron-gray hair under his policeman's helmet, glanced over his shoulder at the two constables trailing them. "If there really is a body, sir, we've enough men to secure the area and send off for the police surgeon."

"Oh, I'm sure there's a body," Witherspoon said. "That's not the sort of thing that Wiggins would make a mistake about."

"What was the lad doing in this neighborhood?" Barnes asked curiously.

"He said he was looking for a haberdashery." The inspector stopped abruptly and stared at the forlorn brick building which had once been a school. Following his footman's instructions, he turned his gaze to where the cobblestones wound around the corner and spotted the two sheds. "My housekeeper thinks I need a new bowler. She sent Wiggins off to check the prices. I suppose it's in there." He pointed to the farther shed.

"I'll just have a quick look, sir." Knowing his superior was quite squeamish when it came to death, Barnes hurried on ahead. He opened the door and stuck his head inside. "It's here, sir. Just where young Wiggins said it would be."

Witherspoon took a long, deep breath. He knew his duty. He had to examine the body. "All right, Constable, let's have at it." Together, he and Barnes stepped inside.

"Your dog must have a good nose," Barnes commented as he stepped around the bench. "It's a good seventy yards from the road to this shed."

"Fred didn't actually smell anything from the road." He laughed nervously. "Wiggins said he was feeling quite frisky, and as there weren't many people about, he'd let him off the lead. Well, you know how dogs are, he started dashing about and slipped through the fence. The lad went after him, but by this time Fred must have had some sort of scent because he ran up to the shed, began howling his head off, and started scratching at the door. It swung open and Fred ran inside. Well, of course, Wiggins had no choice but to go after him." Witherspoon sighed. "Poor lad, it was quite dreadful for him. He seemed very upset when he came to the station to tell me what happened. That's one of the reasons I didn't want him to accompany us back here. He's not one of us, you know. He's not used to some of the awful things we must deal with."

"Yes, sir," Barnes agreed dryly. But he didn't share his superior's opinion of Wiggins. It seemed to him the lad was quite capable of dealing with a wide variety of police like activity. The boy had been in at the arrest often enough. For that matter, half the inspector's household sometimes seemed to show up at the very moment when a bit of assistance was most needed. But Barnes was careful not to share his suspicions about the activities of the inspector's servants. Especially not around the station. There were some that were jealous of Witherspoon's success in solving murders.

"We'd better get on with it." The inspector stifled a shudder as he looked at the dead man's face. "Poor fellow. What an ugly place to die." At least this one wasn't oozing blood everywhere.

Constable Barnes knelt down on the other side and examined the body. He saw the ligature mark around the throat right away. "It's a murder, sir. You'll have to have a gander. The man's been strangled."

Somehow, the inspector wasn't surprised. Every corpse he came in contact with turned out to be a murder victim. "I was rather hoping the fellow had died of heart failure or some other natural cause." He sighed. "Send one of the constables back to the station for the surgeon and an ambulance. We'll need more lads as well. We'd best search the school and the grounds. We'll need to do a house-to-house in the neighborhood as well." He knelt beside the body and took a quick peek at the marks on the fellow's throat. "Let's go through his clothes."

"Right, sir." Barnes opened the man's jacket and stuck his fingers in the inside pocket. "Nothing here, sir."

Witherspoon held his breath and stuck his hand into the man's trouser pocket. He pulled out two ha'pennies and a shilling.

"What about your lad, sir?" Barnes asked. He was rifling through the other pocket, looking for anything which would identify the fellow. "You'll have to speak to him again."

Witherspoon frowned. "Wiggins? Why?"

"He's a witness, sir," Barnes said calmly.

"But he's told us everything he knows." The inspector stood up. He decided they could finish examining the victim's clothing after the police surgeon arrived.

"He thinks he has, sir." Barnes rose to his feet as well. "But as you always say, sir, 'People know more than they think they do.' That's one of the reasons you're so clever at catching killers. You're always digging for that extra bit of information."

"Ah yes." The inspector nodded vaguely. He wasn't sure he liked being reminded of all the things he'd said in the past. His housekeeper had a habit of doing the same thing. But then again, it was flattering to know that his constable listened when he spoke. But really, did he have to remember every single word? "Quite right. Much as I dislike upsetting the poor lad, I suppose we've no choice."

"What the dickens do we do now?" Luty demanded. "I don't want to waste any more time sittin' around this table. There's investigatin' to be done!"

"Patience, madam, patience," Hatchet said. "We can't investigate anything until we've decided what, precisely, it is we're to investigate."

"If you ask me, it's got to be the dead man," Mrs. Goodge said stoutly.

"But what about Miss Gentry, then?" Betsy asked. "Just because someone's been strangled, we can't ignore her problem. Someone is still trying to do her in."

"I think Miss Gentry's troubles must be related to the dead man," Hatchet interjected. "It would be a very big coincidence to have a murder and an attempted murder within a hundred yards of one another."

"I agree," Mrs. Jeffries said quickly. She was in a real quandary. On the one hand, it might be prudent to wait until after the inspector returned home this evening before they began their investigation, while on the other, she felt one should strike while the iron was hot. "And as at least one of the attempts on Miss Gentry appears to come from the school property, I think we can safely assume the incidents are related."

"Right, then." Smythe grinned widely. "Let's get crackin'."

"Before we do anything," Mrs. Jeffries said, "we need to discuss what we know. In the interests of logic, my suggestion is that we discuss the details that Miss Gentry gave us earlier today. Perhaps by then, Wiggins will have returned." She took a quick sip from her teacup.

"Do you think Miss Gentry might have killed this fellow?" Mrs. Goodge asked. "I mean, perhaps she found out he was the one trying to do her in and took matters into her own hands, so to say."

"That's possible, of course," the housekeeper said thoughtfully. "But I'm not sure it's likely. From what Wiggins told us, he heard noises in the shed at about the same time we were speaking with Miss Gentry."

"Now, just a fast minute here," Luty said. "You're forgettin' something. You haven't told Hatchet and me much of anything yet. Come on, tell us everything that's happened so far and don't be leavin' out any details."

"Oh dear, I *am* sorry. You're quite right. We have let things get out of hand a bit since you arrived." Mrs. Jeffries gave Luty and Hatchet a complete report. "So you see," she concluded, "we've got ourselves a very complicated case here."

"What did you find out from Miss Gentry this morning?" the cook asked. She needed names. Her methods of investigating depended on cajoling gossip out of visiting tradespeople and working a network of informants from one end of London to the other.

"We found out who benefits if Miss Gentry suddenly meets her Maker," Betsy announced. "And quite a few other things as well."

"What about the body her dog discovered?" Mrs. Goodge frowned. She already had that name, but one never knew what other name might pop up in connection with the pickpocket. "We mustn't forget him. He might have something to do with this mess."

"Miss Gentry had no dealings with Tim Porter before Miranda dug him up." Mrs. Jeffries said. "She claims she knows nothing about him. But we won't forget him. You're quite right, Porter may have more to do with this than meets the eye. Now, as Betsy was saying, the first thing we did was to find out who gains in the event of Miss Gentry's death." Of the murders they'd investigated, money was by far the most common motive for killing.

"What does she have to leave? I thought you said she was a spinster lady who lived in a little house over on Orley Road," the cook said.

"Is she rich?" Luty asked bluntly. She was always one to get to the heart of the matter.

"She is now," Betsy replied. "Miss Gentry just inherited a huge house and a large fortune."

"And her relatives aren't precisely pleased by her new circumstances," Mrs. Jeffries added. "She's got two married sisters, both of whom have already let it be known that they feel a single lady shouldn't be in charge of such wealth. They're putting pressure on her to let one of their husbands oversee Miss Gentry's money. But she's not having it. She wants to do it herself."

"Who left her the goods?" Smythe asked.

Betsy laughed. "Her almost mother-in-law. A woman named Clara Dempsey. A few years back, Miss Gentry was engaged to Cecil Dempsey, Clara's son. He died, so they never married. Miss Gentry kept on seeing Mrs. Dempsey. The women were very close. Miss Gentry helped take care of Mrs. Dempsey in the last years of her life, when the poor old thing was ill. No one knew it, but Mrs. Dempsey was rich. When she died, she left her big house and a huge number of stocks and bonds to Miss Gentry."

"She had a big house but no one knew she was rich?" Luty looked skeptical.

"The house is very run-down. Miss Gentry's having a lot of work done to fix it up."

"I take it that Miss Gentry has been pressured to make a will?" Hatchet said.

"Oh yes." Mrs. Jeffries smiled cynically. "As soon as her sisters heard about her inheritance, they hustled her to a solicitor and got a will drawn up. One of the sisters is married to a barrister."

"I'll bet he was the one who recommended which solicitor Miss Gentry used," Smythe finished.

Mrs. Jeffries smiled knowingly. "I know, it's all so predictable. But that's one of the sad commentaries about life. People often *are* predictable, especially where money is concerned. Now, we've got to decide how we want to investigate this matter."

"If you'll give me the names of Miss Gentry's relatives," Mrs. Goodge said, "I'll get cracking and see what my sources can find out. If one of them is a barrister, someone will know something."

"You oughta get an earful about him. No one ever says anything good about lawyers," Luty said. "I've got a pack of 'em working for me and there ain't a one of 'em I'd trust further than I could throw him."

"Really, madam." Hatchet sniffed disapprovingly. "Sir Oswald would be most offended to hear you speaking like that."

"Why don't we split the investigation in two?" Smythe suggested quickly. He didn't want anyone side-tracked by one of Luty and Hatchet's arguments, not this early in the game. "Wiggins and I can concentrate on finding out about the bloke that was strangled and the rest of you can concentrate on Miss Gentry."

No one said anything as they thought about his suggestion.

"I'm not sure that's a good idea," Mrs. Goodge finally murmured. "Surely the cases are connected."

Betsy looked doubtful. "I don't know, maybe we ought to do both at the same time."

"You're just scared you'll miss something," Smythe teased.

"It hasn't escaped my notice you're the one taking the actual murder," she shot back, "and leaving the rest of us to work on what might turn out to be a silly woman's imagination."

"I don't think so, Betsy," Mrs. Jeffries interjected. "As we discussed earlier, the cases have to be connected, and Smythe is right, we must have some way of going about our investigation in a way that won't leave us all confused."

Betsy didn't look convinced. "Oh, all right. I suppose it's the best we can do for now. But I'm reserving the right to poke my nose into the actual murder if it turns out Miss Gentry's making up tales."

"Me, too," Mrs. Goodge said. "Now, what's the name of Miss Gentry's two sisters and their husbands? I might as well get my sources sussin' out what's what."

"Ethel is married to Elliot Caraway. He's the barrister. They live in Kensington," Mrs. Jeffries explained. "The other sister is married to a vicar." She frowned. "Oh dear, I seem to have forgotten her name . . ."

"It's Louisa," Betsy said, "Louisa Cooksey. She's married to the Reverend Harold Cooksey. They live in Hammersmith, quite close to Miss Gentry."

"Where's his parish?" Hatchet asked.

"He doesn't have one," the housekeeper said. "Miss Gentry was a bit reticent about discussing her relatives. One can't blame her for that; it wouldn't be pleasant to think one's sister wanted you dead because you'd inherited a bit of money."

"And a house," Betsy reminded her.

"Where's the house at?" Luty asked.

"On the far side of the school, just beyond the church." Mrs. Jeffries took a sip of tea. "From what I gather, Mrs. Dempsey had lived there for many years. It needs quite a bit of repair. As I said, Miss Gentry is having a lot of work done, and apparently there's been a number of problems and delays in the past two weeks."

Luty nodded. "Fixing up an old house is always aggravating."

"If Miss Gentry spent a lot of time with her late fiancé's mother," Hatchet suggested, "perhaps I can ask about the neighborhood over there and see if there's anyone from her past with Mrs. Dempsey that wishes her harm."

Mrs. Jeffries stared at him in surprise. "Do you think that's worth your time?"

Hatchet hesitated. "I've no idea, but in many of our earlier investigations, it's sometimes been the one place we didn't look that produced the murderer. Besides, with Mrs. Goodge working her sources for information on Miss Gentry's family, Miss Betsy asking around the current neighborhood, and Smythe and Wiggins finding out about our murder victim, there isn't much left for me to do at this point."

"What about me?" Luty demanded. "I need something."

"Of course you do, madam," Hatchet said smoothly. "But if I know you, you'll play the innocent while all along you've already decided to find out everything you can about everyone's bank balance." He only said this because he knew this was precisely what his employer had planned.

"Hmmph," Luty snorted. "You think you know me so well." In truth, she was planning on having a chat with her sources in the City early the following morning. She might as well get some use out of those old windbags who were watching her money. God knows they all liked to talk; they bent her ear often enough about what she should and shouldn't do with her own cash.

"Precisely, madam." Hatchet gave a satisfied smile.

"Are we going to wait for Wiggins?" Mrs. Goodge glanced at the clock on the pine dresser. "It's getting late."

"'E ought to be back 'ere anytime now," Smythe replied. "He's 'ad plenty of time to get down to the station, say 'is piece, and get back."

"What if he went with the inspector back to that shed?" Betsy said.

Smythe's smile disappeared. "Bloomin' Ada, I 'ope 'e's enough sense not to go back to that ruddy place. Poor lad felt bad enough—"

"I'm not surprised," Mrs. Goodge interrupted. "Finding a body isn't very pleasant, the lad'll be having nightmares if he's not careful."

"It wasn't just findin' the corpse that upset him—" Smythe broke off as they heard the back door open. Fred, who'd been having a nap at the coachman's feet, jumped up and raced down the hall.

"Hello, boy." Wiggins's muffled voice could be heard. A moment later, he popped into the room. "It's done. The inspector and Constable Barnes is on their way."

"I take it the inspector believed your story?" Mrs. Jeffries asked. To her way of thinking, that was the key.

"He believed me all right. But Inspector Nivens was givin' me some funny looks."

"Nivens was there?" Mrs. Jeffries didn't like the sound of that.

"It's a funny thing." Wiggins frowned. "'E spotted me comin' in the building as 'e was leavin', but instead of goin' on about 'is business, 'e turned heel and followed me right up to the inspector's desk. 'Ung about the whole time I was there."

"That's not good." Smythe shot the housekeeper a worried look.

"It most certainly isn't."

"You think he's onto us?" Luty asked.

"I don't know," Mrs. Jeffries admitted honestly. "But the fact that he followed Wiggins back inside is worrying."

"We'll 'ave to be doubly careful, won't we?" Smythe said. "Sounds to me like Nivens is going to be watchin' this investigation pretty sharp like."

"That's true," Betsy said brightly. "But he'll only be concerned about the murdered man. He doesn't know about Miss Gentry. So the only people who have to be careful are you and Wiggins."

Mrs. Jeffries had a cold supper laid in the dining room and was standing at the ready when Inspector Witherspoon came home. "Good evening, sir."

"Good evening, Mrs. Jeffries. I'm so sorry to be late."

"That's quite all right, sir." She reached for his bowler. "We expected you wouldn't be home on time for dinner. Wiggins told us what happened. I've a cold supper laid out, sir."

"Would it be too much trouble if we had a glass of sherry first?" Witherspoon asked hopefully.

"That would be splendid, sir," she replied. Her spirits soared. She couldn't believe her good luck. An invitation for a sherry together was a sure sign the inspector wanted to have one of his "chats" about the case.

They went into the drawing room and Witherspoon dropped into his favorite armchair. The lamps had already been lighted and the room was suffused with a pale, golden glow. Mrs. Jeffries went to the mahogany sideboard and got the elegant Waterford crystal sherry glasses off of the top shelf. She pulled open the bottom cabinet and removed a bottle of Harvey's. She filled both glasses to the brim. Putting her sherry on the table next to the settee, she handed the inspector his glass. "Here you are, sir. Just what the doctor ordered after a long, hard day at work." She wanted to get right onto the subject at hand. "It must have been a really dreadful day for you, sir."

"Perhaps, but it was a great deal worse for the poor fellow who got himself strangled." He took a quick gulp of his drink.

She pretended to be surprised. "Strangled? Oh dear, you mean he was murdered? All Wiggins said was he'd seen a dead body. He seemed so upset, we didn't press him for details; we just assumed that whoever it was had died of natural causes."

"I'm afraid not. There was quite a wide ligature mark about the fellow's throat." He shuddered.

"How very sad, sir." She clucked her tongue sympathetically. "I don't suppose you've been able to identify him?"

"Oh yes, that was quite easy. His name was Stanley McIntosh. He was a caretaker of a grammar school. Which, by the way, has been closed since Easter."

"So he was strangled, sir?"

"It certainly looked like it."

"Do you have any idea who might have murdered the poor man?" She asked this as a matter of course.

He sighed. "Not as yet. We sent police constables to do a house-to-house in the local area, but so far, we've not turned up much."

"Did this Mr. McIntosh live in the school itself?"

"He had a room off the kitchen. Actually, they'd converted the dry larder into a bedroom for the fellow. We searched the room but we came up with nothing."

"Could robbery have been the motive, sir?" she asked innocently.

"I doubt it, the school is virtually nothing more than an empty shell and the victim had nothing of value in his room. Quite sad, really, nothing but a few old rags for clothes and some postcards he'd kept under his bed in a cigar box." He closed his eyes and shook his head. "Not much to show for a man's life. But whatever modest means he had, however humble his position and circumstances, no one had the right to kill him. To take his life."

"I agree, sir," she said softly. From any other man, the sentiment expressed by him would have sounded false or silly, but Mrs. Jeffries knew he meant every single word. He would do everything in his power to bring the killer to justice. "I know you'll catch the murderer, sir. You always do."

"I certainly hope so, Mrs. Jeffries. But I must admit, I'm not overly optimistic about our chances. There seems no reason for this killing."

"But there never seems to be a reason for murder, sir," she protested. "Not in the beginning of a case. What's got you so pessimistic about this one?"

He smiled wanly. "I don't really know. There was just something so depressing about the whole situation. Here was this poor wretch of a man living in that awful little room. There weren't any curtains, or pictures or books or carpeting or anything to brighten his miserable existence, just this silly cigar box with a few postcards that he'd probably drug out of dustbins." He sighed and shook his head again. "Why would anyone want to kill someone who had so little? It seems so pointless and cruel, I simply don't understand, Mrs. Jeffries."

Mrs. Jeffries gazed at him sympathetically. He really was a sensitive person. She understood exactly what he meant. "Life is often cruel, Inspector," she said softly. "And it's because of this random misery that what you do is so important. You'll find the person who took this McIntosh's life and you'll put them in prison so they can't ever hurt anyone again."

"I'm flattered by your faith in me." He sighed again, but this time he didn't sound quite so depressed. "I only hope I can justify it."

"You've never failed in the past, sir," she reminded him, "and there's no reason to think you'll fail on this case. Now, sir, do tell me what you've learned so far. You know how I love hearing all the details." She held her breath, hoping she'd managed to shift his mood.

He hesitated for a moment and then he swallowed the bait. "Well, we did learn a few things today. There weren't any witnesses, of course, but one of the neighbors said they'd seen Mr. McIntosh crossing the school yard earlier today."

"Earlier today?" she repeated. She wanted something a bit more specific.

"Around a quarter to eleven." Witherspoon took another drink of sherry. "So far, that's the last time anyone saw him alive."

"Except for the killer," she said. "It would have been nice if your witness had seen someone going into the school yard."

"That would certainly make my task a great deal easier." He drained his glass and got to his feet. "Perhaps we'll come up with something soon. Not all of the lads doing the house-to-house had reported in by the time I left the station. So there's still hope. Someone may have seen something."

Mrs. Jeffries suddenly remembered that Smythe and Wiggins had been at the school. She hoped it wouldn't be their bad luck that someone had seen one of them. But she managed to give the inspector an encouraging smile. "Let's hope so, sir. Did you find any evidence of what actually, uh, strangled the victim?" She might as well get as many details as possible.

Witherspoon started toward the dining room. "We think the killer must have used rope. The marks on the throat certainly weren't caused by hands."

"Why do you think it was rope, sir?" she asked as she followed him into the dining room.

Witherspoon pulled out his chair and sat down. "There was a length of it tossed into the corner. Of course, we won't know the cause of death until the postmortem is completed. But Dr. Bosworth assured me that he'll have the results by tomorrow."

Mrs. Jeffries's spirits lifted. "Dr. Bosworth. He's doing the autopsy?"

"Oh yes; Dr. Potter's gout has flared up again and the district doctor's got a broken arm. I had Barnes send over to St. Thomas's for Dr. Bosworth. I'm sure the chief inspector won't object. It's not good to delay the postmortem, you know. I mean"—he yanked his serviette off the table and onto his lap—"we think the man was strangled, but we don't know for certain, if you get my meaning."

"Yes, sir, I believe I do," Mrs. Jeffries agreed. She deliberately kept her expression casual, but she was delighted that Dr. Bosworth would be doing the autopsy. He'd helped them on several of the inspector's cases.

"I'm not very hungry," the inspector said as he reached for his fork, "but I suppose I should eat something."

"Absolutely, sir," she assured him. "You must keep up your strength. You've much to do in the next few days."

Smythe had the uncomfortable feeling that someone was watching him as he slipped around the corner of Orley Road. Yet when he looked over his shoulder, he saw nothing. "I'm gettin' fanciful," he muttered to himself. Yet the feeling persisted as he continued up the road and around the bend to a pub he'd spotted. It was a plain, honest workingman's pub called the White Hare. He pushed into the public bar and took a good, long look around before moving up to the bar. "I'll have a pint of your best bitter," he told the publican.

The room was crowded with workers, shop assistants, day laborers, and even a few bank clerks in their suits and ties.

"Here you are." The barman slid his glass of beer across the counter.

"Ta." Smythe slapped down his money, picked up his beer, and headed toward an empty chair in the corner. "This spot taken?" he asked a ruddy-faced man sitting at the table.

"It's yours if you want it," the fellow replied.

Smythe sat down and sipped his beer. He didn't try to start a conversation, he simply sat there keeping his ears open.

"Blast and damn, that bitch's got a sharp tongue," the man at the table next to him said to his companion. "A bit late with the ready and she's wantin' to toss me out on me ear."

"You know how women are," his companion replied, "they want to know the rent's been paid. Can't blame her for that."

Thinking this conversation wasn't particularly interesting, Smythe turned his head slightly, the better to hear the conversation going on behind him.

"Ada told me she weren't in the least surprised old McIntosh got done in, what with him bein' such a secretive sort." The voice was female and sharp.

Smythe turned his head and looked behind him. Two women were sitting at the table in the corner. One had frizzy blond hair stuck up in a knot on the top of her head and the other had dark brown hair. It was the frizzy blonde that was doing the talking. "He might have looked as poor as a church mouse, but believe me, he could come up with the money when he—" She broke off as she saw Smythe staring at her.

He decided to plunge straight ahead. There was no point in being coy. "Sorry," he said quickly, "I couldn't 'elp overhearin'. Are you talkin' about that poor bloke that got 'imself murdered yesterday?"

Frizzy blonde cocked her head to one side and appraised him shrewdly. "What's it to you?"

Smythe suddenly realized the entire room had gone quiet. He wasn't sure what to do next. He looked around the room and noticed that people weren't just staring at him curiously, there was open hostility on most of their faces. "I was just wonderin'," he finally said. "Bein' curious, that's all."

"You'd do best to mind your own business," the man at his own table said. "Being too curious about Stan McIntosh can get a man killed."

Smythe wasn't going to let this lot intimidate him. He stared hard at the man who'd spoken until the fellow looked away. The others turned back to their own business.

Blast, he thought, there goes my chance to get anything out of this lot. Asking any more questions here would be a waste of his time. These people had closed ranks. Something was going on. Something the police wouldn't have a hope in Hades of getting out of any of them. If he wanted to find out what was happening here, there was only one thing left for him to do.

He'd have to make a trip to the East End docks.

He needed to see Blimpey Groggins.

CHAPTER 4

"They're the most awful gossips," Ida Leahcock said to Mrs. Goodge. "They'd talk the hind legs off a dog, they would. Those tea cakes are very nice, Mrs. Goodge, begging your pardon. I don't suppose you'd part with the recipe, would you?"

The cook hesitated, torn between hoarding her own precious recipes and wanting to keep Ida talking. "Of course you can have it," she said with a bright smile. "Please, do help yourself to another." She'd give Ida the recipe all right, minus an important ingredient or two. "Now, you were saying about the Adderly twins, the ones that was going on and on about that Reverend Cook."

"Reverend Cooksey," Ida corrected as she reached across the table and snatched up another tea cake. She was a thin, sparse woman with steel-gray hair done up in a skinny bun, a pointy nose, and a pair of sharp brown eyes that could spot a pickpocket or a petty thief at twenty paces. On the back of her right hand she had a birthmark in the shape of a hedgehog. "Eliza Adderly was the one that told me all about him. Mind you, she only found out because she works for the Cookseys and she happened to overhear Mrs. Cooksey giving the reverend a right earful." She paused long enough to stuff half the tea cake into her mouth.

Mrs. Goodge forced herself to keep smiling. She wasn't going to let the woman's piggish manners put her off. It wasn't often in an investigation that information as good as this dropped right into her lap, so to speak. Well, it hadn't exactly dropped into her lap; she'd sent a street Arab with a note over to invite Ida to tea after learning the Cookseys lived in Hammersmith.

Ida Leahcock owned Lanhams, a café just outside the Shepherd's Bush station. Every working person in the area stopped in for tea. Ida knew them all. Back more years than she liked to remember, Mrs. Goodge and Ida had once been kitchen maids together. Mrs. Goodge had minded her work, kept herself decent, and climbed the ranks to end up a highly respected cook. Ida had been caught kissing a stable boy in the back garden and tossed out without a reference. But that hadn't stopped her from being successful. She'd ended up owning half a dozen small, but lucrative cafés. Mrs. Goodge had run into the woman at the greengrocer's one morning. They'd both been reaching for the same apple. She recognized the hedgehog birthmark on Ida's hand right away. It hadn't taken more than five minutes of chat before Mrs. Goodge realized that Ida Leahcock, the kitchen maid dismissed in scandal all those years ago, was now a successful business-woman. More importantly, she was a walking gold mine of information. "An earful?" Mrs. Goodge prompted.

Ida snickered. "Apparently she doesn't have much respect for his being a man of the cloth. I heard the two of them had a right old slinging match, they did. Eliza told me she almost run out of the house in fright as they was screaming at each other so loud. Mind you, Eliza's a bit of twit. Scared of her own shadow, she is. You know what I mean. Remember that green girl that worked at Morgan's with us? The one with the buckteeth and the runny nose. Eliza reminds me of her."

Mrs. Goodge didn't have a clue whom Ida was referring to but she'd die a thousand deaths rather than admit her memory wasn't as keen as the other woman's. "Indeed I do," she said heartily. "Frightened of the wind, she was."

Ida nodded in agreement. "That's right. Well, Eliza didn't run outside, she just hid in the kitchen until the shouting died down. She may be a ninny, but she wanted her wages and this happened on the last day of the quarter."

"What were they arguing about, anyway?" Mrs. Goodge reached for the teapot and poured more tea for Ida.

"Ta. Seems that Mrs. Cooksey was giving the reverend what for about him being out of a position. Said she couldn't hold her head up no more and that he ought to be ashamed of himself for not being able to provide for his wife."

"I've never heard of such a thing!" Mrs. Goodge clucked her tongue in disapproval. "You don't say—a vicar out of work. Doesn't the church have to find them a parish?"

"That's what I always thought," Ida said. "But maybe it's not true."

Mrs. Goodge made a mental note to find out exactly how the Church of England's bishops appointed vicars. There was something amiss here, she could feel it. "Maybe there's just too many vicars and not enough parishes," she suggested.

"That's not it." Ida waved her hand dismissively. "He's probably had his hand in the till or been messing about with the choirboys. Mark my words, it'll be scandal that's got him out of a job."

Mrs. Goodge tried to look shocked, but the truth was, she really wasn't. She'd once believed that people in positions of authority were true and good and honorable. But since she'd gotten involved in investigating murders, she'd found it was often those people in authority who lied, cheated, and worst of all, killed.

"That's usually how these things turn out," Ida continued cheerfully. "Didn't Eliza have any idea why he'd not got a parish?"

"That silly goose," Ida snorted. "Even after hearing that screaming match, Eliza still thinks the good reverend is taking a long rest for his health."

Smythe scowled at the two pickpockets standing in front of the Admiral Nelson pub. Blast, he thought as the two scurried out of his way, trust Blimpey to pick a place not fit for man nor beast.

The pub was in the East End, on St. George Street. It was close enough to the Tobacco Dock to smell it. This was an area of London that reeked of poverty and was plagued with crime, misery, and pain. The only good thing that ever came out of here, he thought as he elbowed his way through the crowded public bar, was Betsy. He knew she'd been born not far from here. He thanked God every day that she'd gotten out and landed on the inspector's doorstep. He refused even to think of what her life would have been like if she'd stayed in the East End.

He heard a familiar laugh. Turning, he spotted a portly man with ginger-colored hair sitting at one of the few tables. Blimpey saw him and winked.

"Nice to see you my friend." Blimpey patted the chair next to him. The day was warm but he had a bright red scarf dangling around his neck over his dirty brown-and-white-checkered coat. A battered porkpie hat was sitting forlornly on the table. "It's been a while since you and I've crossed paths."

Smythe raised an eyebrow. "It's not been that long. What'll you have?" he asked, glancing at Blimpey's empty glass. He knew the rules. Blimpey expected to be well supplied while you conducted business.

"Gin." Blimpey nodded at the barman. "And bring us two pints of the best bitter as well. You still drink beer, don't you?"

"That'll be fine." Smythe yanked out the chair and sat down. "I've just not got a lot of time."

"You're always in a hurry," Blimpey chided him. "That's what's wrong with this world, people are always in a bloody rush. They ought to slow down a bit, take time to exchange a few kind words with their fellowman."

Smythe rolled his eyes. "The only thing you ever exchange with your fellowman is a bit of coin. Now let's get down to it. I've got someone I want you to find out about. Fellow is named Stan McIntosh—"

"The bloke that got killed?" Blimpey's cheerful grin vanished.

"How'd you hear about it? It's not been in the papers."

Blimpey gave him a pitying look and Smythe realized how stupid he sounded. Of course Blimpey had heard about the murder. Blimpey heard about everything criminal in this town. That's why Smythe had come to him. The man had been a petty thief, but he'd soon realized that his incredible memory could earn him a great deal more than simple thieving. Besides, thievery was a dangerous occupation. Blimpey had a natural distaste for violence and an ability to organize snippets of information that went far beyond his meager education. Before you could say "Bob's-your-uncle," he had a network of informants that stretched from Spitalfields to Putney. He collected information the way a dog collected fleas. Then he sold it to whoever would pay for it. Smythe was one of his best customers.

"Why are you so interested in this McIntosh?" Blimpey eyed him speculatively.

"Here ya are, fellers." A buxom barmaid put their drinks on the table. "A gin and two pints of the best."

"Thanks." Smythe reached into his shirt pocket, took out some coins, and handed them to the woman.

"Thanks," she replied when she saw what he'd given her. She rushed off before he could ask for change.

He stared steadily at Blimpey. He wasn't about to answer questions as to why he wanted information. That wasn't part of their arrangement. But despite his scowl, he didn't blame the fellow for trying it on. Gathering information was the man's stock-in-trade.

Blimpey gave in gracefully. "No harm in askin'. A healthy curiosity is what makes life worth livin'. That's what I always say. You need the goods on anyone else?"

Smythe hesitated. He knew he shouldn't be sticking his oar in the Gentry investigation. After all, it had been his suggestion that they separate the murder from the attempted murder. But as he was here anyway, why not get his money's worth. "Yeah, there is." He thought for a moment, trying to recall all the names that had been bandied about the kitchen during their meeting. "Find out what you can about some people who live over in Hammersmith and Kensington."

"What's the names?"

"Reverend Harold Cooksey and his wife, Louisa. They live in Hammersmith. The other one's a barrister and his wife by the name of Caraway—"

"Elliot Caraway?" Blimpey interrupted.

"You've heard of 'im?" Smythe was shocked.

Blimpey sneered. "He took the brief for a friend of mine in a stolen-goods case. Poor bloke was innocent but he ended up doing six years in the Scrubs."

"Bad luck," Smythe murmured.

"Luck had nothin' to do with it." Blimpey's eyes flashed angrily. "Caraway's an idiot and poor Rysington got six years for a crime he didn't commit. And it weren't the first time it had happened, either. Word I got is Caraway's so bad he can't get criminal briefs at all anymore. Stupid old git."

"Well, find out what you can about the bloke and about the other names I give you." He threw back the rest of his beer and started to get up, when he remembered there'd been another guest in Miss Gentry's house the day the dog had been poisoned. "And find out what you can about a fellow named Eddington, too. Phillip Eddington."

"Where does 'e live?" Blimpey asked.

"I'm not sure . . . wait a minute, it's on Forest Street. On the other side of St. Matthew's Church."

"Right." Blimpey finished off his gin and got to his feet. "Meet me back here tomorrow evening around eight, I ought to have something for ya by then."

"I knew that this case was going to be quite difficult, Constable," Witherspoon said to Barnes as they made their way down Forest Street. "I had a bad feeling about it."

"You always think that, sir," Barnes replied, "and we always end up solvin' the case. Besides, sir, we've done quite well. At least we found one person who had business dealings with the deceased. It's a start, isn't it?"

"Yes." Witherspoon sighed and started up the steps of a large, Georgian house. "We've got a place to begin. Let's see what this Mr. Eddington may know." He banged the heavy brass knocker against the polished white door.

The door opened a moment later. "Yes? Can I help you?" A gray-haired woman wearing a soiled white apron and holding a cleaning rag in her hand stared curiously at Barnes.

"We'd like to see Mr. Eddington," Witherspoon said. "We're—"

"Who is it, Jane?" a voice from inside the house interrupted.

"It's the coppers," Jane screeched. She threw the door open wide.

Witherspoon winced then quickly recovered as a middle-aged man with dark curly hair worn straight back from his broad face came down the wide hall. "Why, goodness, it *is* the police." He sounded very surprised.

"They want to see you, sir," Jane said, eager to learn more.

"Thank you, Jane, you may go now and finish cleaning the stove. I'll see the gentlemen into the drawing room."

Jane's round, eager face crumbled in disappointment. Then she nodded glumly and shuffled off toward the back of the house. Eddington turned back to the policemen. "Gentlemen, do come in."

"Thank you." Witherspoon and Barnes stepped inside the foyer. "I do hate to trouble you, sir, but we'd like to ask you a few questions regarding a Mr. Stanley McIntosh."

"Who?"

"I take it you are Phillip Eddington?" Witherspoon wanted to make sure he was talking to the right person.

"I am, indeed." He frowned slightly. "But I don't know what this is all about. Perhaps we ought to go into the drawing room." He turned and led the way.

They followed; their footsteps sounded loud on the polished wood floor. They went through a double oak door into a formal drawing room. It was large and pleasant but not opulently furnished. There was a plain brown settee with a matching set of chairs. Several tables, a bookcase full of books on the end wall, plain white muslin curtains at the windows, and framed hunting prints on the walls. "Do please sit down," Eddington instructed, gesturing at the settee.

As soon as they'd sat down, Constable Barnes whipped out his little brown notebook. He looked expectantly at his superior.

Witherspoon cleared his throat. "I'm Inspector Gerald Witherspoon and this is Constable Barnes. We've come to ask you a few questions regarding Mr. Stanley McIntosh. He was the caretaker at Helmsley's Grammar School. We've reason to believe that you knew Mr. McIntosh."

Clearly puzzled, Eddington stared at them for a few moments and then his expression brightened in understanding. "Oh, you're talking about old Stan. Of course, how silly of me. I'm sorry. I didn't quite realize who you meant. I did know him, actually. As a matter of fact, I saw him just yesterday. What's this all about, inspector? Is he in some sort of trouble?"

His voice had a slight inflection to it, one that the inspector couldn't quite place. Almost, but not quite, an accent. "What was your business with Mr. McIntosh, sir?"

"I would hardly call it business, Inspector. More like charity." Eddington shrugged. "I felt sorry for the poor chap. He'd mentioned the board of governors at Helmsley's had found a buyer for the property and his job might be coming to an end. I wanted to see if he wanted some work."

"He was going to lose his position?" Witherspoon wondered why the secretary of the board of governors hadn't mentioned that fact when they'd spoken earlier today.

"That's what he told me." Eddington smiled kindly. "I'm sorry, I didn't really know him very well. But, you know how it is, I'd seen him in passing and I'd spoken to him a time or two, exchanged pleasantries, that sort of thing. The last time we spoke, he mentioned that he was going to be out of work. I've got a bit of painting that needs to be done around here and I thought he might like a go at it. It's not exactly a position, but I thought it might help him make ends meet until he could find another job."

"So you went over to the school to see if he wanted to work for you?" the inspector clarified.

"That's right." Eddington relaxed back against the cushions.

"What time was this, sir?" Constable Barnes asked.

"Oh"—Eddington's face creased thoughtfully—"let me see, it must have been about eleven-thirty or so. Oh dear, I'm not exactly sure what time it was. But it was late in the morning. Before noon."

"You saw Mr. McIntosh?"

He shook his head. "Actually, no. I stuck my head in the back door and called out, but there was no answer. I tried several times but I never found the fellow. What's all this about, Inspector?"

"I'm afraid the reason Mr. McIntosh never answered you was because he was dead."

Eddington's mouth gaped open. "Dead? Gracious, that's terrible."

"Sorry to say, he was murdered, sir. That's why we're here making inquiries."

They met back at Upper Edmonton Gardens at four o'clock for their meeting. Betsy was the last to arrive. "I'm sorry to be so late," she said, tossing her beloved one of her warm smiles as she rushed across the kitchen to put away her things. "But I was doing ever so well."

"That's excellent, Betsy," Mrs. Jeffries said. She was sitting at the head of the table. "Hurry and sit down so we can get started. It looks as if we've all something to report."

"I don't," Smythe admitted easily. "So far I've not turned up a ruddy thing." He didn't mind letting the others have their moment of glory. His turn would be coming. Blimpey hadn't failed him yet and he had no doubt he'd give them an earful at tomorrow's meeting.

"Well, who's gonna go first?" Luty asked eagerly. Since she was bouncing up and down in her chair, it was obvious to everyone she was bursting to talk.

"Patience, madam," Hatchet said. "We'll all have our say in good time."

"I think we ought to let Luty talk," Wiggins said. "Looks to me like she's got somethin' real interestin' to tell us."

"That's right nice of you, boy." Luty patted his arm. "And I do have somethin' interestin' to say. But I expect the rest of you do, too."

Mrs. Jeffries poured Betsy's tea and handed it to her as the maid took her place next to Smythe. She'd seen the warm, intimate smile the girl had given the coachman and was delighted the two of them were getting along so well. Sometimes on their investigations, Betsy had a tendency to be too competitive with him and Smythe could be a tad overprotective of her. "If everyone else agrees, why don't you go first, Luty."

"Seein' as how no one is raisin' a fuss, I believe I will." She paused to take a deep breath. "As this case is gettin' complicated, I made me out a list." She pulled a rolled-up piece of paper out of the bright red sleeve of her dress. "I know we decided to keep things separate, but I had old Teddyworth's ear, so I decided to kill two birds with one stone and find out all I could about the people in both situations."

"Huh?" Wiggins said. "Who's Teddyworth?"

"One of Madam's bankers," Hatchet said smoothly. "He's well connected in the City."

"Thank you, Hatchet," Luty said tartly. Turning her head, she gave the butler a wide smile. "I did a little checking into our murder victim's finances."

Hatchet snorted. "He was a caretaker, madam. He could hardly have had 'finances' as far as the City was concerned."

"Fat lot you know," Luty shot back. "He had a deposit account at the West London Commercial Bank over on Sloane Square. Had a hundred and thirty-five pounds in it."

"I stand corrected, madam," Hatchet said loftily. "Now we know that the man had a veritable fortune, I'm sure we should conclude that's the reason he was murdered. Do tell us who his beneficiaries might be."

"Hatchet, you don't have to be so sarcastic," Luty said. "I know it ain't a fortune. But it's something. Now, if it's all the same to you, I'll get on with my report. This McIntosh fellow wasn't the only one I found out about." She squinted at the paper she'd just unrolled. "Our Miss Gentry has plenty, too. Her fortune's valued at a hundred thousand pounds."

"Gracious, that *is* an enormous amount." Mrs. Jeffries wasn't sure what this meant, but she knew it meant something. That much money often attracted trouble.

"Just so you'll know, I did a bit of snoopin' about Miss Gentry, wanted to make sure we could trust her, if you know what I mean," Luty continued. "She was livin' on the edge of poverty, gettin' by all these years on a tiny inheritance from her mother, when all of a sudden the woman who would have been her mother-in-law up and dies and leaves her sittin' pretty."

"Exactly how did Mrs. Dempsey die?" Mrs. Goodge asked.

It was Mrs. Jeffries who answered. "Pneumonia. I already checked. The death wasn't considered suspicious. She was over eighty and had been ill a long time."

"Annabeth Gentry took care of Mrs. Dempsey," Betsy protested. "She had no idea of what Mrs. Dempsey was worth; no one did."

"I ain't sayin' she killed the old woman," Luty said. "I'm just sayin' how she come to have all that cash. It's no wonder someone's tryin' to kill her."

"Money isn't the only motive for murder," Smythe put in. "Just because Miss Gentry inherited a bundle doesn't mean that's the reason someone's tryin' to do 'er in."

"It's a darned good motive, though," Luty argued.

"I still think it's got somethin' to do with her findin' that Tim Porter," Wiggins put in. "That's when it began."

"I agree," Mrs. Jeffries said.

"But yesterday you said we ought to keep things separate," Mrs. Goodge reminded her.

"I know. But after thinking about it all night, I changed my opinion. But let's let Luty finish and then we can discuss it."

"Thank you, Hepzibah," Luty said. "Now, as I was sayin', Annabeth Gentry inherited an estate big enough to choke a horse—"

"When, exactly, did she get this inheritance?" The housekeeper wanted to get the facts straight in her mind.

"About six months ago," Luty replied.

"Who stands to inherit from Miss Gentry?" Smythe asked softly.

"I don't know," Luty admitted. "But as she ain't married, it's probably her sisters."

"We need to find out for certain," Mrs. Jeffries said. "It could well be important."

"I've got my sources workin' on that very question," Mrs. Goodge said.

"Excellent," Mrs. Jeffries said. "Then we can continue. Luty, anything else?"

"Only that the Caraways are broke," Luty replied. "I've still got my sources"—she shot the cook a quick grin—"workin' on finding out if the good reverend's broke, too, but I haven't heard back from them yet."

"If you're finished, madam," Hatchet interjected, "I'd like to speak next."

"I'm done," she replied.

Hatchet smiled apologetically at the others. "Do forgive me for jumping in, but I believe my information might complement madam's quite nicely."

"Go on," Mrs. Jeffries said.

"As you'll recall, my task was to go to Miss Gentry's soon-to-be new abode on Forest Street and ask about. I must say, I wasn't overly enthusiastic about the assignment, but on the whole, I must admit it went rather well . . . it's quite amazing what the local people know."

"Local people? For goodness' sakes, it's only a quarter of a mile from where she lives now," Luty said impatiently.

"I know that, madam," he chided. "I'm simply trying to give everyone a bit of understanding about the circumstances. We've all admitted this is going to be a most complicated case."

"Yes, Hatchet, that's true," Mrs. Jeffries said. "It's very complex." But she rather agreed with Luty, Hatchet was being very long-winded.

"Thank you." He smiled at the housekeeper. Luty snorted softly. "As I was saying, it's quite amazing what the local people can tell you. I had a most enlightening conversation with one Mr. Jonathan Parradom, one of the local tradesmen."

"What did you find out?" Mrs. Jeffries's voice was just the slightest bit impatient.

"It seems that Miss Gentry's troubles didn't start with the attempts on her life; she's also had a terrible run of bad luck on getting her new home refurbished."

"What do you mean?" Mrs. Goodge asked. "Everyone has troubles with builders."

"Miss Gentry was due to move into the place at the beginning of this month. But in the past two weeks, she's been delayed. First by a flood in the kitchen and then by a fire on the upper floors."

"Both of these things have happened since her dog found Tim Porter's body?" Mrs. Jeffries mused.

Hatchet nodded slowly. "Once I heard that, I, too, began to think that it all must be connected somehow. No one has this much bad luck."

"We need to be careful here," Mrs. Jeffries warned. "Remember, we've made assumptions in other cases and the results weren't what we'd hoped." In one awful case, by acting on theories that appeared to be true but really weren't, they'd done very badly in their investigation. Why, they'd actually had the case solved by the inspector with virtually no help from them.

Mrs. Jeffries was determined that this wasn't going to happen again. "But, still, my instincts are telling me it's all connected somehow."

Betsy sighed. "We've got to keep our minds sharp."

"Agreed," Hatchet said somberly.

"Have you finished?" Mrs. Jeffries asked.

"Yes, I believe so." Hatchet sighed. He'd picked up another rumor or two, but after hearing Mrs. Jeffries's warning, he decided to determine if they were true before he confided in the others. They really must be on their guard.

"I've got some bits to tell," Mrs. Goodge said before anyone else could speak up. "I found out that it's true that Reverend Cooksey doesn't have a parish. Furthermore, it's not by choice." She gave them all the details she'd learned from Ida Leahcock. When she finished, she poured herself another cup of tea.

"So if 'e doesn't 'ave a church," Wiggins asked, "'ow's he makin' a livin'?"

"He could be independently wealthy," Hatchet suggested.

"If he was wealthy, why would his wife be shouting at him about being a bad provider," Betsy pointed out. "Besides, I found a few things about the Cookseys today, too, and about the Caraways. They've been trying to get Miss Gentry to turn control of her inheritance over to one of her brother-in-laws ever since Mrs. Dempsey died. But she's having none of it. She's handling it herself."

"Good for her. Did you find out anything else?" Mrs. Jeffries asked.

"A bit," Betsy replied. "Miss Gentry is well liked about the neighborhood. All the tradesmen and shopkeepers have nothing but good to say about her."

"Excellent, Betsy. Is that it?" The maid nodded her head, and Mrs. Jeffries turned her attention to Wiggins. "How about you? Did you find out any more about Stan McIntosh?"

"A little," Wiggins replied. "McIntosh pretty much kept to 'imself. The local people didn't know too much about 'im. 'E took care of the school grounds and tried to keep the place from fallin' apart until the board of governors can sell the property."

"Has he been there a long time?" Mrs. Goodge took another sip of tea.

"No one knew exactly 'ow long," Wiggins said. "But I know 'e was workin' there while it still 'ad pupils. The locals didn't know much about the feller. I think I ought to find out if any of the staff or students from the school is still about the area."

"What good would that do?" Mrs. Goodge asked.

Wiggins shrugged. "Maybe one of the students would know something about McIntosh. Children are right nosy, you know. They know all sorts of things."

"I think that's a splendid idea," Mrs. Jeffries said. "Until we learn something more about the victim, we'll never find out how these cases are connected."

"Can I go next?" Smythe asked.

"I thought you said you didn't have anything to report," Betsy said. She watched his face suspiciously. It would be just like the man to pretend like he'd not got a thing and then to drop a big surprise on them.

"I don't," he said earnestly. "I mean, I don't have any facts. But somethin' odd 'appened and I think you ought to know about it."

"What is it?"

Smythe told them about his visit to the local pub. About how the locals had not only closed ranks, but had been openly hostile. "I don't know what got their backs up," he finished. "I was bein' right careful in what I said. Do you think it's important?"

Mrs. Jeffries thought about it for a moment before she answered. "I'm not sure. It could just be the natural inclination of a group to close ranks against an outsider—"

"It's important," Hatchet said. "Oh, I'm sorry, Mrs. Jeffries, I didn't mean to interrupt you."

"That's quite all right." She waved his apology away. "But I am curious as to your reasons."

"Yeah, so am I," Luty added.

"Well," Hatchet began, "Smythe was in a pub. Now, it was probably the local, but pubs are used to having people come and go. And in a case like this, a case of murder, everyone in the place should have been talking about it. But they weren't. I find that very strange."

"So do I," Smythe said. "And I think I'll make it my business to find out why everyone got so niggled just by my mentionin' McIntosh's name."

"Be careful, Smythe," Betsy said. "I've got a bad feeling about it." The words slipped out before she could stop herself. She was always trying to stop him from being overprotective of her and here she was doing the same to him.

He gave her a knowing grin. She could feel a flush creeping up her cheeks.

"I'm sure Smythe will take great care," Mrs. Jeffries soothed.

"Now, does anyone else have anything to add?" She waited a moment but no one spoke. "As I said earlier, I think we now ought to proceed with our investigation based on the assumption that all these events are somehow connected."

"But you warned us not to jump to conclusions," Mrs. Goodge protested. "You pointed out that we'd been wrong in the past when we did that."

"I know." Mrs. Jeffries wasn't sure how to explain this part. "But I've given this a great deal of thought and it's the timing that makes me believe everything is connected. Nothing happened until Miranda found that body. Then, all of a sudden, Miss Gentry has three attempts made on her life, her new house has a fire and a flood, and there's another murder less than a hundred yards from where she lives. I don't think it's a coincidence. But I'm willing to change my opinion if the rest of you think I'm wrong."

"I think you're right," Luty said softly. "Like was said earlier, no one has as much bad luck as Miss Gentry unlessin' there's someone behind it."

"I agree," Betsy said. "There's someone behind all this."

"And it ain't goin' to be easy to find out who it is," Smythe added.

"We'll find 'em," Wiggins said cheerfully. "We always do."

"Right, then." Mrs. Jeffries smiled at the others. "We go forward on the assumption that the cases are connected. Does anyone else have anything they'd like to report?"

No one did. But they stayed on for another half hour going over the details of the cases and deciding on what they'd do next. By the time Luty and Hatchet left, it was getting dark. Mrs. Jeffries didn't expect the inspector home for dinner until quite late. She felt quite safe going upstairs to her rooms to have a think about everything they'd discussed.

But she was only halfway up the landing when she heard the front door open. "Hello, hello," Witherspoon called out cheerfully.

Mrs. Jeffries turned and hurried back down the stairs. "Hello, sir. I didn't expect you home till much later."

"I thought I'd pop in to have a bit of supper," he explained as he took off his bowler. "I've a brief meeting this evening with Chief Inspector Barrows. He wants a report on the case."

"Isn't that an odd time to be seeing your chief inspector?" she asked. She spotted Betsy coming up the stairs. As soon as the maid realized the inspector had come home early, she did an about-face and went back the way she'd just come. Mrs. Jeffries was confident that the girl would tell the cook to prepare a tray.

"Usually, yes, but he's going to Birmingham tomorrow and wanted to get a report before he left. Er, do you think Mrs. Goodge will be able to put something together for me? I'm quite hungry."

"I'm sure we can get you a decent meal, sir," she replied. "If you'd like to go into the drawing room, I'll bring some tea while you're waiting." She hurried down to the kitchen. Betsy and Mrs. Goodge were busy preparing a cold supper.

"I've some cold chicken and half a loaf of bread," the cook said. "It'll have to do."

"Don't you have any of those treacle tarts left?" Betsy asked. "I saw some in the larder earlier today."

Mrs. Goodge hesitated. "Well, all right, I'll give him a tart. But only one. I'm saving the rest for my sources."

Mrs. Jeffries gaped at the cook. For her to hoard her precious tarts for her investigative sources rather than the master of the house was truly a measure of how much she'd changed.

"I know, I know, I really oughtn't to do such a thing," Mrs. Goodge said. "But those treacle tarts get people talking."

"It's all right, Mrs. Goodge," the housekeeper said. "I'll take the tea up. Betsy, bring the tray up in ten minutes."

She took the inspector his tea. "Here you are, sir. Now, how was your day? Did you get any information from the uniformed lads?"

"They did their best, but they didn't learn all that much. But we did have a witness that had seen one of the neighbors in the school yard close to the time the poor fellow must have been killed."

"Really, sir," she said. She silently prayed that the witness hadn't seen Wiggins. Or if it they had, that they'd not given an account that differed too much from what the footman had told the inspector. That could get very awkward.

"Yes, fellow named Phillip Eddington. He lives just on the other side of the church." Witherspoon took a quick sip of his tea.

Mrs. Jeffries tried to remember exactly where she'd heard that name before.

"Nice man, very cooperative. He admitted to going along to see Stan McIntosh that very morning."

"What was his business with the victim?"

"He was trying to help the fellow out." Witherspoon sighed. "He said that McIntosh had told him that the school was being sold and that he was losing his position. Mr. Eddington had a bit of work for him. Nothing permanent, mind you. Just a bit of painting on the third floor of his home."

"Do you think Mr. Eddington is telling the truth?" Mrs. Jeffries still couldn't remember where she'd heard that name.

The inspector shrugged. "I've no idea. But he doesn't appear to have any reason to dislike McIntosh. I can't imagine why he'd want the fellow dead. Do you think supper will be much longer?"

"I believe I hear Betsy now, sir." She got up and started for the dining room. She was determined to get as much information as possible out of the inspector before he left for the station. "How unfortunate that Mr. Eddington wasn't really all that much help," she said.

"Oh, I wouldn't say that." Witherspoon smiled at Betsy as she put the loaded tray on the dining table. "He gave me the name of someone who'd had some nasty words with McIntosh."

Betsy and Mrs. Jeffries exchanged glances.

"If I didn't have to see the chief inspector this evening, I'd pop along and interview her this very evening," Witherspoon continued as he pulled out a chair and sat down.

"Her, sir? You mean it's a woman."

"That's right, according to Mr. Eddington, one of the neighbors on the other side of the school had some rather heated words with Stan McIntosh only a few days before he was killed. I believe she accused him of chucking bricks at her head. Her name is Gentry. Annabeth Gentry."

CHAPTER 5

"What'll we do?" Betsy whispered as she and Mrs. Jeffries went down to the kitchen.

"I don't see that we can do anything right at the moment. But I share your concern. We certainly don't want Miss Gentry saying anything to the inspector about us."

Mrs. Goodge looked up as they came into the kitchen. "I thought you were going to keep the inspector company while he ate," she said.

"We've got a bit of a problem," Mrs. Jeffries replied. "We may need Wiggins or Smythe."

"Smythe's gone to the stables," the cook said.

"But I'm 'ere, Mrs. Jeffries." Wiggins, with Fred in tow, walked in from the back hall. From the expressions on their faces, he could tell something was amiss. "What's wrong?"

"The inspector is going to be interviewing Miss Gentry tomorrow about Stan McIntosh," Betsy blurted, "and we don't want her saying anything about us."

"Why on earth would the inspector want to talk to her about him?" Wiggins asked. "We know she didn't 'ave nuthin' to do with him bein' killed. You two was with 'er when the murder took place."

"We can't tell the inspector that we know she didn't do it," Betsy said. "He'd want to know what we were doing there in the first place."

"But this may be just what we want to happen," Mrs. Jeffries exclaimed. "As a matter of fact, I'm sure it is."

"What?" Betsy frowned. "I don't understand. You want the inspector to speak to Miss Gentry?"

"Of course; that's the only way to get this investigation moving along properly. We can only ask questions in the most roundabout of ways. The inspector can actually interrogate people and come up with suspects. In case you've not noticed, we've plenty of murders and attempted murders but virtually no suspects."

"That's the bloomin' truth," the cook muttered. She snapped open a clean tea towel and laid it over the plate of treacle tarts she was hoarding for her sources. "At least if he talks to Miss Gentry, he can start interviewin' those relatives of hers."

"Good, I'm glad you agree. But right now our immediate concern is to make sure that Miss Gentry says nothing to the inspector about coming to us for help. That's why I'm glad you're here, Wiggins. I want you to nip over to her house and tell her the inspector will be interviewing her tomorrow. Make it clear that she should say nothing about us—" She broke off as she realized she couldn't leave this matter to Wiggins. She'd have to go herself and she'd have to do it tonight. "Never mind. On second thought, I'll have to go over there myself."

"Tonight?" Mrs. Goodge glanced toward the window at the far end of the kitchen. "But it's almost half past six. You haven't had supper yet."

"That's all right, I'll wait till the inspector's gone back to the station and then I'll take a hansom."

"I'll go with ya," Wiggins said. "You don't want to be out at night. They never did catch that Ripper fellow, you know."

"There's no need to do that," she protested. But she was touched nonetheless.

"It's not a good idea for you to be out alone at night," he insisted. "Fred and I'll ride along with ya. We can wait outside if ya like, but I don't think you should go on yer own. Like I said, they never caught that Ripper bloke. He could still be lurkin' about, and even if 'e's not, there's been two killings in that neighborhood."

"Wiggins is right," Betsy added. "You must take him and Fred."

Mrs. Jeffries gave in gracefully. "All right. Thank you, Wiggins, I'd be pleased to have you and Fred accompany me. I don't think it'll be necessary for you to wait outside, though."

Smythe sidled up to the pub bar and slapped a shilling onto the counter. "What'll you 'ave?" he asked his companion.

"Gin and water," Ned McCluskey replied. He was a young man with dark brown hair, haunted gray eyes, and the look of someone who didn't know where his next meal was coming from. It was a fair assessment of his life. As a simple laborer, he never knew from one day to the next if he'd find work and have money for food.

Smythe nodded at the barman and gave him their orders. When the drinks came, he picked them up and jerked his chin toward an empty table in the corner. "Let's sit down and have a chat."

"Thanks," Ned said as soon as they'd sat down on the rough wooden stools. He picked up his glass and drained it. "Ahh . . . that's good. It's been so long since I've 'ad a drink."

Smythe sipped his beer. "You can 'ave another, if ya want." He waited for the gray eyes to narrow in suspicion, but Ned was just happy to have a drink. He didn't much care why a complete stranger was buying it for him. "So 'ow long you been workin' at that 'ouse? If you don't mind me askin'?"

Ned shrugged. "Just for the past couple of days. There was a fire up on the third floor and it made an awful bleedin' mess. Boris 'ired me and my mate Jack to clean the rooms and get it ready to be redone and painted."

"A fire? What 'appened?" Smythe deliberately made his own accent more pronounced. He thought Ned would be more open to answering his questions if he thought he was talking to one of his own. He'd had a bit of luck running into the fellow. He'd been on his way back from Howards when he impulsively decided to take a quick look at Annabeth Gentry's new house on Forest Street. He'd spotted Ned and another man coming out the front door. Following them, he'd seen the other man board an omnibus. Ned had started walking. Smythe had caught up with him and struck up a casual conversation. He knew Betsy might worry about him being home so late, but blooming Ada, he couldn't let an opportunity like this pass him by.

"No one actually said what caused the fire." Ned wiped a lock of hair off his forehead. "But Boris seemed to think it were set deliberately."

"Cor blimey," Smythe exclaimed. "Want another gin?"

Ned nodded eagerly and Smythe waved the barmaid over. He was determined to keep the man talking. "Another round 'ere," he told the woman.

"That's right generous of you, mate," Ned said happily. He didn't much care why the big fellow wanted to buy him drinks, he'd keep pouring them down his throat as long as the bloke kept buying. "Now, like I was tellin' ya, Boris thinks the fire were set deliberately."

"Is Boris the boss, then?"

"Oh yeah. He's the guv." He smiled at the barmaid as she put their fresh drinks on the table. "Ta."

Smythe handed her a pound note. "Let me know when this runs out," he said.

"Just give me a nod when you're ready for another round." She grinned easily.

"Now"—Smythe turned his attention back to Ned—"why does your guv think the fire wasn't an accident?"

"Well, mainly, because of the flood in the kitchen." He grinned. "I know it don't make much sense. But just a week or so before the fire, there was a flood in the ruddy kitchen. The builder told the owner the flood was caused by a loose pipe in the water pump, but that weren't true. Someone had deliberately uncapped the main pipes leadin' from the sink to the wet larder. But the builder wasn't goin' to admit someone 'ad done somethin' daft like that, now, was 'e? For sure the owner woulda blamed it on one of the builder's men and none of 'em would admit to doin' it. So when there was a fire upstairs, Boris nipped up and had a right good look around before Mr. Shoals—that's the builder—could get there. Boris said he couldn't see anythin' up there that could have started a fire like that."

"How would Boris know?" Smythe finished off his beer.

"'E's got eyes, don't 'e?" Ned replied. "'E's not stupid. Fires don't just start themselves when there's no reason for that fire to start in the first place."

"What do ya mean?"

"The only people up there that day were the workmen. It was a warm day," he explained. "None of the fireplaces had been used, there weren't any candles or lime lamps or even gas lamps lit. So what could have started it? Boris was curious enough that 'e 'ad a nice long look about the place. 'E found an empty tin of coal oil in the garden, 'e did. He reckoned some-one had poured it on the curtains and lit a match."

"Maybe one of the workmen was usin' it for something," Smythe speculated.

"Boris would 'ave known if they'd been usin' coal oil on the job, he's the guv."

"Did Boris tell anyone what he'd found?"

"He told Mr. Shoals and 'e said 'e'd look into it, but I don't think 'e did. He was just happy that the owner didn't make a fuss. Mind you, Shoals isn't a complete fool. 'E's been lucky the owner ain't taken 'im to court over all the damage. 'E finally put a night watchman onto the place right after the fire. Fellow stays there from the time we leave until the morning."

"So there's always someone on the premises?"

"That's right." Ned grinned broadly. "Shoals wasn't worried about the owner so much as 'e was scared somethin' else strange would 'appen. Some barrister fellow did show up after the fire and raised a ruckus. But Miss Gentry, she's the owner, soon quieted the bloke down. Still, it shook Shoals up to 'ave a lawyer sniffin' about the place."

"You can bring your dog inside," Annabeth said cheerfully. "I'm sure Miranda won't hurt him. She's a very gentle animal."

Wiggins gaped at Miss Gentry. He didn't wish to be rude, but he certainly wasn't worried about that bloodhound hurting Fred. Fred could look after himself, thank you very much.

"That's very kind of you, Miss Gentry," Mrs. Jeffries said quickly. She could tell by the footman's expression that he was rather offended.

Upon hearing her name, Miranda trotted down the short hallway to the foyer. Fred's lip curled back, but he didn't growl. The bloodhound simply wagged her tail, looking for all the world like she wanted to be his friend. "Be nice, now, Fred," Wiggins chided the dog. Fred gave his tail one perfunctory wag and stared up at his master.

"Shall we move into the drawing room?" Annabeth said. "Martha's out visiting her young man's family, so I'm afraid it's just me and Miranda here."

"You're all alone?" Mrs. Jeffries didn't like the sound of that.

For a moment Annabeth was taken aback. "Oh dear, I see what you mean. That sounds rather foolish considering I came to you for help because someone was trying to kill me. But honestly, I'm not in the least nervous. Miranda's here with me. She can be quite ferocious if necessary." She patted her on the head and Miranda wagged her tail proudly.

"So can Fred," Wiggins put in. "'E can be right nasty if I don't hold 'im back when 'e smells trouble." Annabeth smiled at Wiggins as they moved down the short hall and entered the drawing room.

Mrs. Jeffries sat down on the settee while Wiggins took the chair next to the door. Fred flopped onto the floor and stared at the bloodhound, who was now studiously ignoring him. "I know you're probably wondering why we've come," the housekeeper said.

"I rather thought you might have some progress to report," Annabeth said eagerly. She'd sat down on the love seat. Miranda curled up on the rug beside her and closed her eyes.

"We've made some progress," Mrs. Jeffries replied. "But that's not why we're here. Actually, we have it on good authority that Inspector Witherspoon will be here tomorrow to interview you about Stan McIntosh's murder."

"He's going to interview me?" Annabeth's eyes widened in shock. "Good gracious, why? I barely knew the man."

Miranda's head came up. Fred, seeing the other dog move, rose up to a sitting position.

"According to what I've learned, I think it's because someone told the inspector you'd had words with Mr. McIntosh." Mrs. Jeffries watched her carefully, wanting to see how she'd react.

Annabeth's brows came together. "Words? Well, I did get a bit annoyed with the man, but I'd hardly say we had 'words.'"

"Why'd you get angry at 'im, miss?" Wiggins asked. He didn't think Mrs. Jeffries would mind him asking a question or two. "If you don't mind me askin'."

"Because he told me to get off the school's property," she replied. "I didn't mind that so much. After all, that's his job. What I got annoyed about was his refusal to even listen to me when I tried to explain why I was there."

"When was this?" Mrs. Jeffries asked.

Annabeth thought for a moment. "Oh dear, I suppose it was the day before he was killed."

Mrs. Jeffries carefully kept her expression blank. "Why, exactly, were you on the school grounds?"

"I wanted to have another look at the wall. I wanted to see the exact spot where those bricks had been loosened."

"Beggin' your pardon, miss," Wiggins said, "but didn't you tell us you'd been around and 'ad a look the day it 'appened?"

"Of course, but on the day it happened, I only had a rather cursory look at the wall. I wanted to have a good look this time."

"What were you hoping to see?" Mrs. Jeffries asked. Gracious, she had gotten off track, so to speak. But hearing Miss Gentry's account of what happened was quite interesting.

"I wanted to see if there were any marks along the top of the wall. So I took Miranda and we went around to the school. I slipped in through the gate and went around to the wall. We'd only been there a few moments when Stan McIntosh came charging out and ordered us off the property. I tried to explain, of course, but he was so rude." Her eyes flashed angrily as she recalled the incident. "He actually tried to grab my arm and drag me off the premises. Luckily, Miranda was having none of that. The moment he touched me she growled and bared her teeth. He let go quick enough then, I can tell you that. Of course, I didn't want Miranda to chew the man up, so I called her off and we left."

No one said anything when she'd finished. The only sound in the room was the click of nails against the wooden floor as Fred shifted positions. Finally, Mrs. Jeffries said, "I see."

Annabeth bit her lip. "Oh dear, do you think I ought to have mentioned this before. I didn't see that it was important. That's why I said nothing. I wasn't trying to hide anything. I was just so terribly worried about everything, you see. And no one, not even my own relatives, seemed to believe me."

"It's always best that we know everything," Mrs. Jeffries said softly. "Unfortunately, the incident was a bit more important than you think."

"Oh dear." Annabeth's brows drew together. "What should I tell him?"

"The truth," Mrs. Jeffries replied. "As a matter of fact, I think you ought to tell him everything."

"Everything? You mean about the attempts on my life and asking for your help—"

"Everything but that bit," Wiggins interjected. He glanced at Mrs. Jeffries. "I'm right, aren't I? She oughtn't to say anything about us being involved."

"That's right," the housekeeper replied. "Tell the inspector everything except the fact that we're involved. He doesn't know we . . . uh . . . well . . ."

"He doesn't know he has assistance on his cases from all of you." Annabeth laughed. "My lips are sealed, Mrs. Jeffries. I'll not say a word." Her smile faded abruptly. "That doesn't mean you'll stop trying to help me, does it? I'm sure your inspector is quite a nice man, but frankly, I've not much faith the police will be able to find the person who's doing this to me. They haven't found the person who killed that poor Mr. Porter."

"Don't worry. We'll still be on the case," Mrs. Jeffries assured her.

"Do you think my troubles are connected to McIntosh's murder?" Annabeth idly reached down and patted Miranda on the head. "I hope not. It's not quite fair, you know. I didn't really know him."

"Fair or not, Miss Gentry," Mrs. Jeffries replied, "there's a very good possibility your troubles and his murder are connected. In any case, it can't hurt to have the police asking a few questions." She almost mentioned that she thought the real connection was Tim Porter's murder, but she decided to keep that to herself for a bit longer. "By the way, what do you know about Phillip Eddington?"

"I don't know much about him at all," Annabeth said thoughtfully. "He seems a nice man. He's been a bit of an absent neighbor, I believe he travels a lot on business—" She was interrupted by knocking on the front door.

Miranda shot to her feet. So did Fred.

Annabeth got up, her expression puzzled. "Now, who can that be at this time of the evening?"

"Maybe it's Martha," Wiggins suggested. He reached down and took a firm grip on Fred's lead.

"Martha comes in the back door and she has her own key." She started for the hallway. Miranda trotted along at her heels.

"Do be careful, Miss Gentry. You don't know who is out there. Perhaps you ought to peek out the window before you open up," Mrs. Jeffries warned.

"Excellent idea." Annabeth stopped before she reached the door and hurried over to the front window, which looked out on the road. She pulled the curtains back. "It's the police."

"The police?" Alarmed, Mrs. Jeffries sprang to her feet. "Are you certain?"

"Oh yes; there's an older constable in uniform and another gentleman in plain clothes."

"Does he have a mustache and is he wearing a bowler hat?" She was already heading for the hall.

Annabeth dropped the curtain. "Yes. Is it your inspector?"

"Cor blimey." Wiggins jumped up and dashed after Mrs. Jeffries, who was now flying toward the back of the house.

"It's him all right," the housekeeper hissed over her shoulder. "If it's all the same to you, we'll go out the back door."

I won't mention a word to your inspector about knowing you," she whispered loudly. She gave them a final wave and turned toward the front door.

Mrs. Jeffries, Wiggins, and Fred dashed into the kitchen and hurried toward the back door. Grabbing the handle, she twisted and pulled the door open just as she heard a familiar voice coming from the front of the house.

By this time, Fred had gotten into the spirit of the game and fairly bounced along at Wiggin's heels. Until he heard that voice from the front. He skidded to a halt halfway through the back door. As Mrs. Jeffries was in the process of pulling it closed, she almost caught him dead center between the door and the frame. "Oh no, come along, Fred," she whispered urgently.

Fred, who was now very confused, tried backing up into the kitchen. "Come on, boy," Wiggins ordered. He reached down and grabbed the dog's collar.

But the house was small and the inspector's voice rang loud and clear in the quiet night.

"We're so sorry to disturb you, Miss Gentry," Witherspoon said. "But we'd like to ask you a few questions. Oh my, what a nice dog. Is it a bloodhound?"

Fred stiffened and tried to pull back into the house, toward the voice he knew and loved.

"Get him out, Wiggins," Mrs. Jeffries whispered. "We mustn't be found here."

"Come on, Fred," Wiggins hissed. He gave the collar another tug, but he didn't pull very hard. He didn't want to hurt the animal.

Confused, Fred looked back toward the sound of the inspector's voice then back at Wiggins. He barked softly. From down the hall, Miranda, hearing Fred, began to bark, too.

"Gracious," they heard the inspector say. "What's wrong with your dog? She seems most agitated."

Mrs. Jeffries leaned down, grabbed Fred's collar, and yanked him out the door.

From inside, Witherspoon looked curiously toward the kitchen. "I say, is everything all right? It sounds like there's something at the back of your house."

"It's cats, Inspector." Annabeth smiled up at him as she straightened up from petting her hound. "Miranda gets a bit agitated when she hears them."

"I could have sworn I heard a dog back there," Constable Barnes said.

"You probably did," Annabeth replied. "There's one or two strays in the neighborhood that like to chase the cats. Let's go into the drawing room, gentlemen. We might as well sit down."

Witherspoon and Barnes were soon seated in almost the exact same spots as Mrs. Jeffries and Wiggins had been a minute earlier. Barnes whipped open his little brown notebook and looked expectantly at the inspector.

"Do forgive us for coming so late, ma'am," Witherspoon said. "But we saw your lights on and thought that perhaps you wouldn't mind answering a few questions."

"About that poor man from next door?" She shook her head sympathetically. "He wasn't a very nice person, but he certainly didn't deserve to be murdered."

The inspector watched her carefully. "You knew Mr. McIntosh, then?"

"I didn't really know him, Inspector," she replied. "We'd met. But it wasn't a particularly pleasant meeting. As a matter of fact, I had words with him on the day before he died."

"Words, ma'am, you mean in the sense of an argument?" Barnes asked.

"Quite." She smiled at the constable and then patted Miranda on the head. "He chased me off the school's property and he wouldn't listen when I tried to tell him what I was doing there and why it was so important I have a look at the back wall."

Witherspoon sat up straighter. "Would you mind explaining yourself, ma'am?"

"Not at all, Inspector. There's a wall that separates my property from the school."

"Yes, ma'am, we know that. The uniformed officers did come around and ask you if you'd seen or heard anything unusual at the time of Mr. McIntosh's death."

Annabeth flushed in embarrassment. "I know. I ought to have told you about it then, but honestly, the police constable that came around asking questions was very rude."

"Rude, ma'am?" Witherspoon was genuinely surprised. The lads were trained to always be polite. Especially to women. "I'm sorry to hear that. I assure you, we'll look into it. Do please continue."

"As I said, there's a wall that separates my garden from the school. I'd gone over there to have a look at it and Mr. McIntosh caught me. He ordered me off the property. Apparently I didn't move as quickly as he wanted because he grabbed my arm and began physically shoving me toward the front gate. When he did that, Miranda raised a terrible fuss. She'd have gone for him if I hadn't called her off. McIntosh let me go and I left. That's all there was to it."

Witherspoon glanced at Barnes. Eddington hadn't mentioned the dog. "Why did you want to look at the wall? Is there some sort of property dispute?"

"Oh no, not at all. As a matter of fact, I rather liked having the school there. But I needed to look at the wall to see if there were any marks along the top where the bricks had come loose."

"I don't quite follow."

"Of course you don't." She smiled. "It doesn't make a lot of sense until you know the whole story. But you see, I wanted to see for myself if there was evidence that the bricks had been pried loose or if the assassin was clever enough to loosen them without leaving any marks."

Witherspoon gaped at her. "Assassin?"

"That's right. Someone is trying to kill me."

"Cor blimey, all of a sudden there 'e was, big as life at the front door. Mrs. Jeffries and I 'ad to scarper, that was for sure." Wiggins was once again telling the others about their close call. Now that they were safely back in the kitchen of Upper Edmonton Gardens, he thought the whole affair quite an adventure.

"Seems to me you two were lucky." Mrs. Goodge clucked her tongue.

"Indeed we were," Mrs. Jeffries said. She cocked her head to one side and looked at Fred, who'd curled up on the floor beside Wiggins's chair. "We almost got caught because of Fred."

As if to apologize, Fred thumped his tail.

"But all's well that ends well," Wiggins said happily.

"Are you goin' to wait up for the inspector?" Betsy asked.

"Absolutely. I want to know what he thinks about the attempts on Annabeth Gentry's life."

"You think he'll take 'em seriously?" Smythe asked.

"Yes, I do." Mrs. Jeffries drummed her fingers lightly against the table. "At least I hope he'll take her seriously. It will make our task so much easier if he sees that there must be some connection between Stan McIntosh's murder and the attempts on Annabeth's life."

"Let's not be forgettin' the murder of Tim Porter," Wiggins put in. "Seems to me that's what started the whole mess."

Mrs. Jeffries frowned. "Oh dear, I didn't tell Miss Gentry to mention that fact to the inspector."

"You can do that if she forgets to mention it," Mrs. Goodge said easily. "Remember, her dog finding Porter's body was in the newspapers. Once her name is mentioned, you can tell him you read about it."

"You're right, of course."

"Seein' as we're all 'ere, I might as well tell ya what I found out this evenin'." Smythe kept his tone casual, but he was watching Betsy out of the corner of his eye.

"What do you mean?" Betsy cuffed him lightly on the arm. "Is that why you were so late getting home? You were supposed to be at the stables, not snooping about." She considered it most unfair that just because he was male he could go out investigating in the evenings, while she was stuck in the house until morning.

"I did go to Howards, but the stable lad 'ad already taken the horses for their run, and as I knew you weren't expectin' me back anytime soon . . ." He let his voice trail off.

"Oh, just tell us what you found out," Betsy said irritably.

He grinned. "I 'ad a bit of luck tonight. I went over to Miss Gentry's house on Forest Street just as the workmen were comin' out. I managed to strike up a conversation with one of 'em and we went to a pub. Not the one I'd gone to before," he added hastily. "Anyway, like I said, I got this bloke to talkin' and he gave me an earful about what's been goin' on at Miss Gentry's new 'ouse." He told them everything that he'd learned from Ned.

"So the workmen don't think the fire or the flood was an accident," Mrs. Jeffries mused.

"Ned's guv was certain the fire was deliberately started."

"But why?" Wiggins asked. "It don't make sense . . . if someone was tryin' to kill Miss Gentry, why try and burn down 'er 'ouse when she's not even in it?"

"Nothing about these cases makes sense," Betsy agreed. "Not yet, anyway. But they will. There's something here that connects everything. Something that we'll find if we just keep looking."

Mrs. Goodge looked skeptical. "I hope you're right. But for the life of me, I can't see what it could be."

"Good evening, sir," Mrs. Jeffries said cheerfully.

"Gracious, Mrs. Jeffries, you certainly didn't have to wait up for me," he said, handing her his hat. "It's terribly late. It must be after ten. You really ought to have retired for the evening."

"I'm not in the least tired, sir," she replied. But he looked exhausted. "Would you care for a cup of tea?"

"Not tonight," he replied. He headed for the staircase. "I'm quite tired. I believe I'll go right up."

"Are you sure, sir?" she hurried after him. "Perhaps you'd like some warm milk to help you fall asleep."

"Oh, I shan't have any trouble falling asleep tonight," Witherspoon called over his shoulder. "I shall see you in the morning."

Mrs. Jeffries gave in gracefully. The poor man was tired, so she'd let him have his rest. She checked that all the doors were locked and then she went up to her rooms. As was her custom, she didn't light the lamps, but instead went over to the window. In the darkness, she stared at the gas lamp across the road. The light glowed softly, casting pale shadows into the night. This was the strangest case. She was sure the murder of Stan McIntosh was connected to the attempts on Annabeth Gentry's life and Porter's murder. But how? That was the critical question.

She made a mental note to drop a hint to the inspector pointing out that the events must be connected. She frowned. If the inspector started asking questions about the Porter case, he'd draw Inspector Nivens's wrath. That was simply something they'd have to deal with if it happened. And what about the accidents at Annabeth's new home? Wiggins had made a good point. Annabeth hadn't been there when the fire and the flood happened, so one could safely say that neither incident was part of the continued attempt on her life. But what was the point if they were not accidents—if, instead, they were deliberate attempts to destroy the house? But why do that? Surely there was nothing hidden in the house. It had been empty since Mrs. Dempsey's death, six months ago. If there was something incriminating to someone in the house, there'd been ample time to get it out. Mrs. Jeffries sighed. Nothing made sense as yet. But she wasn't giving up. They'd find the connection. She was sure of it.

"Kippers, how delightful." The inspector sat down at the dining table and fluffed his serviette onto his lap. He picked up his knife and spread butter on the steaming fish on his plate.

Mrs. Jeffries poured him a cup of tea. "Mrs. Goodge thought you'd need an especially good breakfast this morning. You had such a long day yesterday. Did you have a good meeting with the chief inspector?"

"I didn't meet with him at all." Witherspoon spiked a large piece of kipper with his fork. "He got called away at the last minute, so I went along and took a statement from Annabeth Gentry. She's the woman Mr. Eddington saw having words with Stan McIntosh shortly before McIntosh was murdered."

"Really, sir? How very interesting. Was she able to give you any useful information?"

Witherspoon swallowed his food and reached for his teacup. "Actually, it was quite extraordinary. She readily admitted to talking to McIntosh and, I might add, she claims she was handled most rudely by the fellow, then she told me she was a victim herself. She said someone's been trying to kill her for the past two weeks."

As Mrs. Jeffries wasn't supposed to know anything about Miss Gentry, she feigned surprise. "Goodness, sir, that is extraordinary. Did you believe her?"

"Well . . ." He looked doubtful. "I'm not sure what to believe. The way she described the attempts on her life could lead one to think she's simply imagining that a few accidents are really quite sinister attempts to kill her. Except for one thing. There have been some corresponding accidents at her new home, a home, by the way, that she's not even moved into as yet."

Mrs. Jeffries couldn't believe her ears. The inspector was willing to believe Annabeth Gentry because of the accidents at her house? "Goodness, sir, it sounds as if the poor woman has had a string of bad luck."

"Yes, extraordinary, isn't it. She had a flood and a fire in the new place." He waved a piece of toast for emphasis. "Mark my words, Mrs. Jeffries, something sinister is afoot. If it were simply those incidents which have happened to her, it would be one thing, but to also have the additional burden of having your home almost destroyed twice at the same time. Mark my words, something is terribly, terribly wrong. I'm determined to get to the bottom of it."

Mrs. Jeffries smiled politely. She'd have to bring another fact to his attention. She was sure Miss Gentry must have mentioned Miranda finding that corpse. It was a very pertinent fact. Surely the inspector would see the connection. Surely.

"And of course, the investigation on McIntosh isn't going all that well," he continued. "No one, not even the board of governors at the school, seems to know much about the fellow."

"Didn't the board get his references before they hired him?" Mrs. Jeffries pushed the extra serving of kippers closer to his plate. As long as she kept him eating, he'd talk.

"That's the odd thing, he wasn't hired by the board. He was hired by the headmaster. A Mr. Needs. We haven't been able to locate him."

"Do you know how long he worked for the school?"

He shrugged. "Two years. As to what he did before that, we've no idea. But we'll keep trying to find Mr. Needs and hope he can help with some answers."

"Absolutely, sir. It's just as you always say: when you're dealing with a murder, the first and best place to start is with the victim."

He blinked in surprise. "Er, yes, I suppose I did say that." Sometimes he couldn't remember all the things he'd said. Indeed, at times he was amazed by his own insight and intelligence. He certainly didn't feel very intelligent or perceptive. "But you know, Mrs. Jeffries, despite some of the things I say, when I'm working, I generally feel very muddled, as though I was trying to solve a murder using jumbled bits and pieces of information. It's most disconcerting."

Mrs. Jeffries suspected her employer was having grave doubts about his abilities. She was having none of that. "Nevertheless, sir. It doesn't matter how jumbled up the pieces are, you always end up putting them in order. It's simply what you do, sir. You catch killers."

CHAPTER 6

"This case is more twisted than a miner's whiskers. I can't make heads nor tails of it," Luty said. They were seated around the kitchen table at Upper Edmonton Gardens. Luty and Hatchet had been given a full report on everything that had transpired.

"This case might be complicated, but it's not impossible," Mrs. Goodge declared stoutly. "I think we're doing quite well. We've learned ever so much just in twenty-four hours and now we've got the inspector snooping about in Miss Gentry's troubles. Is he really going to interview her sisters and their husbands?"

"He has no choice," Mrs. Jeffries replied. "The inspector knows the motives behind most murders. Greed is number one, and now Miss Gentry has a fortune. She's no husband or children, so unless dictated otherwise by the terms of her will, her sisters get it all if she should die."

"And it looks like at least one of them could use the money." Mrs. Goodge sniffed disapprovingly. "According to the gossip I heard, the Cook-seys' creditors are starting to be a bit heavy-handed. He's behind in his mortgage payments, and reverend or not, the building society wants their money."

Smythe started to open his mouth and then thought the better of it. He'd wait until after he spoke to Blimpey Groggins before he said anything.

"What were you going to say, Smythe?" Betsy asked with a smile.

He thought quickly. "Oh, I was just wonderin' when the inspector was goin' to interview Miss Gentry's sisters and their 'usbands? I'll bet they'll be surprised."

"No doubt," Mrs. Jeffries said. "But it must be done. Even if there is a connection between the attempts on Miss Gentry's life and the murders of Porter and Stan McIntosh, her sisters are, essentially, the only suspects. So far, they're the only ones who stand to benefit. No one appears to have had any reason to murder either Porter or McIntosh. At least, as far as we know at this point. In answer to your question, Smythe, I believe he's going to be seeing both sisters today."

"I'll keep a sharp eye out," Betsy said. "I'm going over to the Caraways' and the Cookseys' neighborhoods today. I don't want to run into the inspector or Constable Barnes."

"I ought to have more information about their finances by our afternoon meetin'," Luty declared. "We know they're both pretty hard up, maybe by our meetin' we'll know if either of 'em are in hot enough financial water to commit murder."

"I thought I'd 'ave a snoop-about lookin' for information on McIntosh and Porter," Smythe said casually. He had only the barest twinge of conscience that he was going to be paying for the information. What was the point of having money if you couldn't do some good with it? "Maybe if I ask enough questions, we can suss out who wanted them two dead."

"I've got nuthin' to report," Wiggins said glumly.

"No luck finding any former pupils or staff from the school?" Mrs. Jeffries asked. She took a quick sip of tea.

"Not yet," Wiggins admitted. "But I'm not givin' up. I'll find someone who knows something."

"Of course you will," the cook assured him. She got up and began clearing the tea things. She didn't want to rush the others, but she did have people stopping by. The rag-and-bones man was going to be passing through about ten this morning and the boy from the greengrocer's up on the Shepherds Bush Road would be here with their order about ten-thirty.

"We'd best get started, then. We don't want to waste our day." Mrs. Jeffries rose to her feet. She could tell that Mrs. Goodge wanted her kitchen to herself.

"Will you be here today, Mrs. Jeffries?" Betsy asked.

"I'm be out for a while this morning," she replied. "But I ought to be back by early this afternoon. Why?"

"No reason." The maid shrugged. "I just wanted to be sure that someone would be here to help Mrs. Goodge with the tea. If it's all the same to you, I might be a bit late getting back today." She was determined to learn something useful. No matter how long she had to stay out.

"I ought to be home in plenty of time to help," the housekeeper assured her.

"You'll be 'ere for tea, won't you?" Smythe asked. He kept his tone casual, but they both knew he'd get worried if she was late.

"I'll be here," she promised him. "But you're not to get concerned if I'm a few minutes late."

"You do realize I don't have to speak to you at all." Elliot Caraway stared coldly at Witherspoon and Barnes. He was a short, pudgy man with wavy brown hair and a high forehead. He had a pencil-thin mustache, blue eyes, and looked to be in his mid-forties.

"That's not precisely true," the inspector replied. "Under the latest Judge's Rules, you do. However, you don't have to say anything that will incriminate yourself." Gracious, this man was a barrister. He really ought to be better versed in legal procedures.

They were in the drawing room of the Caraway home at number 11 Redden Hill Road. The house was a narrow two-story brick building with a tiny front garden. Though the place was in a decent neighborhood and certainly wasn't derelict, it had a faint air of benign neglect. The brown wool carpet was threadbare in spots, the rust-colored settee sagged ever so slightly, and the cream-and-brown flowered curtains were yellowed with age.

"You don't need to lecture me about the law, Inspector," Caraway snapped. He sat behind a desk at the far end of the room. He'd not asked the two policemen to sit down. "I know the Judge's Rules and I know precisely what my rights are. Please keep in mind that I'm speaking with you voluntarily and of my own free will. Now, please, get on with it. I've not got all day. I'm a busy man."

"Due in court today, sir?" Barnes asked politely. The constable had done some checking on Caraway. He knew the man hadn't seen the inside of a courtroom for three months.

Caraway sniffed disdainfully. "That's none of your concern, Constable! What is this all about?" He addressed his question to the inspector.

"It's about your sister-in-law, sir."

"My sister-in-law?"

"Your wife's sister, sir," Witherspoon said. "Miss Annabeth Gentry. Do you have any idea why someone would wish to do her harm?"

"Harm?" Caraway's brows drew together. "That's the most ridiculous thing I've ever heard. Why would anyone want to hurt her?"

"That's what we'd like to know." The inspector smiled slightly. "We have reason to believe there have been several attempts on her life."

"Attempts on her life," he scoffed. "Did she tell you that? Gentleman, you're wasting your time on a fool's errand. Annabeth is cursed with a vivid imagination. It comes from having too much time on her hands. She should marry. Taking care of a husband would give her something useful to do with life."

"The incidents she described to us don't appear to be something she imagined, sir," the inspector replied. He didn't particularly like this man. He was rude, arrogant, and far too quick to dismiss the problems of others. He should have at least listened to them before passing judgment.

"What incidents? That nonsense about almost being hit by a carriage?"

"That and others, sir." Barnes was careful not to give out any details.

"I can't believe you're taking this seriously." Caraway leaned forward on his elbows and steepled his fingers together. The pose was supposed to make him look thoughtful. "If you'll forgive my being so blunt, Annabeth is prone to . . . well . . . shall we say she's a bit overly dramatic. As a matter of fact, my wife and I are seriously worried about her. She's not as strong as she appears to be."

"She seemed quite a fit and sensible woman, sir," Witherspoon said. "But we're not here to discuss the particulars of Miss Gentry's health. I understand you were present a few days ago at a tea party at Miss Gentry's, is that correct?"

Caraway straightened up in his chair. "We had tea with her last week."

"Did you have reason to go into the kitchen, sir?" Barnes asked softly.

"The kitchen?" Caraway looked puzzled by the question. "Of course not; why on earth would I?"

"The maid says she saw you coming out of the kitchen just after you and your wife arrived at the house," Barnes said. He looked up from his notebook.

"That's absurd—oh wait, I did pop into the kitchen for a moment. I, uh, needed to wash my hands. The water closet in the hall was occupied, so I went and used the sink in the kitchen. I'd quite forgotten."

"As the constable had been bluffing about the maid seeing Caraway, he was quite pleased with himself. "When you were in the kitchen, did you happen to notice if there was a pot of cream on the table?"

"A pot of cream?" Caraway repeated. "I didn't notice, Constable. But I assume it's not unusual to find food in the kitchen. Look, this is a peculiar line of questioning. What's this all about?"

"Did you notice if the back door was open?" Witherspoon asked. Barnes's questions had gotten him into the spirit of the interview.

"Caraway hesitated. "I don't think I remember—wait, I do recall. It was open. I remember because I looked out and noticed the table on the terrace had been set for tea. I was annoyed about that, because if we were going to have tea outside, it meant that Annabeth was going to let that wretched dog join us."

"You don't like the dog, sir?" Witherspoon prodded. He wasn't sure he trusted people that didn't like dogs. But, of course, he wouldn't let his personal feelings interfere with his investigation.

"I like Miranda well enough," Caraway replied. "But Annabeth's got the animal dreadfully spoiled. She claims the animal is trained. To hear her tell it, the dog can practically do anything except cook a five-course meal, but it's a lot of silly nonsense if you ask me."

"Bloodhounds are quite easily trained, sir," Barnes said. "The police use them often to do tracking."

"Naturally, I know that, Constable," Caraway said. "But Miranda isn't a properly trained hound. Annabeth's got some absurd notions that she can train the dog on her own with hand gestures and bits of bacon. But it's all nonsense. Dogs are like women, sir, they need a firm hand and plenty of guidance."

"The dog did find a body," Witherspoon reminded him.

"Yes, well, even a broken clock is correct twice a day," Caraway sat back in his chair. "Inspector, are we almost finished?"

"Did you know a man named Stan McIntosh?" The inspector thought he'd toss that question in. One never knew what one would find out if one didn't ask.

"No. Is there any reason I should?"

"None at all, sir," Witherspoon said. "He worked at the school next door to Miss Gentry's."

Caraway stared at him blankly.

The inspector wondered if the chap ever read the newspapers. "Stan McIntosh was found murdered two days ago. I thought you might have read about it."

"I rarely read the gutter press, Inspector."

"It was in the *Times,*" Witherspoon said. He decided to try a different tactic. "When will your wife be home, sir? We'd like a word with her as well."

"My wife? What do you want with her? She knows nothing."

"She may know something. She does visit her sister, doesn't she?" Barnes said softly. "We'd be remiss in our duty if we didn't interview her."

"She'll be home this afternoon. But I shall insist on being present," Caraway warned.

"Why? Is there some reason you don't want your wife to speak with us alone?" The inspector surprised himself by the question. He'd no idea where it came from, it simply popped out. He generally wasn't quite this blunt with people. But the truth was, there was something about this fellow that put him off. The moment the thought entered his head, he was a little ashamed. An officer of the law oughtn't to let personal feelings dictate the way he asked questions. That was terribly prejudicial.

"Don't be absurd, man." A dull flush crept up Caraway's cheeks. "Of course there isn't any reason she oughtn't to speak with you. It's simply I don't want her upset, so I must insist on being present. You are suggesting, after all, that her sister's life is in danger." Glaring at them, he got to his feet. "Good day, gentlemen."

"It's all the same to me if you want to buy me a cup of tea." The older woman stared at Wiggins suspiciously. But she sat down in the chair the footman had pulled out for her. "I'm in no 'urry to get 'ome."

Wiggins took a deep breath. He'd spent most of the day trying to find someone connected to Helmsley's Grammar School. He'd almost given up when the lad working at the greengrocer's had remembered that Stella Avery had once been a chairwoman at the school. Luckily for Wiggins, Stella still cleaned at a theater in Notting Hill Gate. He'd managed to find her just as she was leaving work for the day. "I'll get us some tea," he told her.

"And a biscuit," she ordered. "I'm 'ungry."

He took his time getting their tea and biscuits from the serving lady behind the counter. He was desperately trying to think of the best way to ask his questions. Stella Avery seemed a tad cranky.

He made his way toward the back of the small café. It was late afternoon and too early for the supper trade, so the place was empty. Stella Avery watched him out of sunken, brown eyes. Stringy strands of iron-gray hair poked out of the sides of her tattered bonnet, her complexion was sallow, and she was wearing a dingy, gray day dress that was badly wrinkled and had a button missing from the sleeve. She'd put her rolled-up apron on the table.

Wiggins put the tray down, served her, and then took a seat across from her. "I appreciate your agreein' to talk to me," he began.

"You said you'd pay me fer my trouble," she reminded him. "A shillin' and a cup of tea, that's what you said. I'll take it now, please."

Wiggins fumbled in the pocket of his shirt and pulled out the coin. "'Ere ya are. Now, what can you tell me about Stan McIntosh?"

As he was paying for the information, he saw no reason to beat about the bush. He felt just a bit uncomfortable with the situation, he'd never paid someone to talk to him before, but it was the only way the woman had agreed to speak to him.

"What do ya want to know?" She picked up her tea and took a sip. "He was a pig of a man. I didn't like 'im much and neither did anyone else. What else ya want to know?"

He couldn't think of what to ask. So he asked the obvious. "Do you know of anyone who would want to kill 'im?"

She laughed, revealing a row of uneven, rotten teeth "Most of the pupils wouldna minded the old sod dyin' but I doubt they'd 'ave 'ad the nerve to kill the bastard.'

"It couldn't be any of them. Why would they wait till now?" he mused. "The school's been closed for almost a term."

"It closed down at the end of Easter. Place was losin' money. Couldn't keep any students." She chewed her biscuit slowly.

"Did the staff dislike 'im, too?" Wiggins asked.

"Everyone disliked 'im but the head. He was always runnin' to 'im with tales about what everyone was doin'. Couldn't mind 'is own business if you know what I mean. 'E was such a nosey parker that one of the neighbors even 'ired McIntosh to keep an eye on 'is 'ouse when he was gone."

"Cor blimey, why'd 'e do that?"

"'E didn't want to come back and find 'is furniture gone." She shrugged and took another gulp of tea. "What else ya want to know?"

Wiggins tried to think of more questions, but it was difficult. Generally, he had to be so careful when he was investigating that he didn't have time to actually think about what to ask; it was usually just keep them chatting and get what you could. "Did 'e ever 'ave any visitors or anythin' like that?

Or did you ever see or 'ear of 'im goin' off and meetin' someone. What'd 'e do on 'is day out?"

"'Ow should I know? I didn't live at the bleedin' place. I was just a cleaner."

Wiggins flushed. "Sorry. I guess I was just 'opin' you'd know a bit more. It's important, you see. This McIntosh fellow got 'imself murdered and the police ain't askin' the right questions. My guv wanted me to do some snoopin' about so's an innocent person don't get nicked for it." He crossed his fingers under the table as he told this lie and silently hoped the inspector would forgive him.

Stella's hard expression softened. "Who's yer guv?"

Wiggins was waiting for this one. "I'm not allowed to say, 'e don't want anyone knowin' 'e's lookin' into this murder." He glanced over his shoulder at the almost empty café and then leaned across the table. "I can tell ya this," he whispered. "'E's someone known for wantin' justice. Someone who's not afraid to do a bit of lookin' on 'is own to make sure the innocent don't suffer."

"Are ya 'aving me on?" she demanded. But despite her harsh tone, she wanted to believe him. He could see it in her sad, tired eyes. She wanted to believe that somewhere out in what was for her a hard, cruel world, there really was a champion of justice.

A feeling of elation he'd never experienced before swept through him. He'd played about with a few of the details, but basically, he'd told the truth. He and others at Upper Edmonton Gardens were champions of justice. Maybe they didn't get their names in the newspapers and maybe they'd started their snooping because they were bored or they wanted to help their inspector, but now that they'd done it for a while, they were doing it for the best of reasons.

Justice. A commodity generally in short supply for people like Stella Avery. "Would I pay you for what you know if I was 'avin' you on?" he asked. "Stan McIntosh might 'ave been a right miserable person, but no one 'ad the right to kill 'im."

She hesitated briefly. "Well, bein' as you put it like that, I do sort of remember seein' some funny things goin' on a time or two."

"What kind of things?"

She glanced down at her empty cup. "Get me some more tea and I'll give ya what I know about old Stan."

"I'll get us both another cup." He picked up their cups and went to the counter. "Can we 'ave two more, please?"

"And some more biscuits," Stella called. "I want one of them kinds that's got chocolate on it."

"She's a right old tartar, she is," declared Eliza Adderly, maid to the Reverend Cooksey and his wife. "It's not that I mind hard work, I don't, but working for that woman is awful."

"Is she mean to you, then? Is that why you're going home?" Betsy glanced around the ladies' waiting room at St. Pancras station. She'd followed Eliza Adderly here and then struck up a conversation.

Eliza pursed her lips and shook her head. She was a tall, red-haired girl with a pale complexion and bright blue eyes. "It's my day out. I'm going to Little Chalfont to see my gran." She snorted. "If she'd had her way, I'd have had to be back tonight, but the reverend said I could stay over until tomorrow as I didn't get a day out last week. I'm only staying long enough to get a reference. Then I'm off."

Betsy tried to see the departure board through the window of the waiting room, but she was sitting at the wrong angle. "When's your train, then? I'm stuck here for a bit." She smiled and shrugged. "It's nice having some company."

Eliza laughed. "Oh, my train's not for another hour. I came early just so that I could get out of the house. Those two were getting ready to have another quarrel."

Betsy pretended to be shocked. "How awful for you. What a strange way for a vicar to behave. I always thought they were nice men."

"Those two go at it like cats and dogs." Eliza leaned forward eagerly. "Used to be they just fussed about money. About how it was all his fault they were destitute and about how she was always spending. But now they've got something even better to fight about. Mrs. Cooksey's sister inherited a fortune a few months ago and now they're always fighting over how they can get it away from her."

Betsy's jaw dropped and this time she wasn't pretending surprise. While she wasn't shocked that the good vicar and his wife were after Annabeth Gentry's fortune, she was amazed to learn they were stupid enough to discuss the matter in front of witnesses. "Gracious, they talk of such things in front of you?"

"Oh, they start out talking all quiet like, but before five minutes is gone they're screaming at each other like a couple of fishwives."

"That's terrible. How do they think they're going to get this poor woman's money?"

Eliza shrugged her thin shoulders. "First they tried to talk her into letting Reverend Cooksey handle it for her, to take over the investments and the business part. But Miss Gentry is a spinster lady and she's lived on her own a good long while. She told them both she'd handle her own affairs." Eliza laughed again. "They were both madder than wet cats when she wouldn't give in on that one. Then they said they thought it would be a good idea if they all moved into Miss Gentry's big house together . . . but Miss Gentry wasn't havin' that either and told them so straight out. There was a right old dustup about that one, I can tell you that. Mrs. Cooksey just about screamed her head off at her husband—said he'd jumped the gun and if he'd left things to her, they'd be sitting pretty now."

"What'd she mean by that?" Betsy didn't try to be cautious in her questioning. Eliza Adderly was a talker; either that, or life at the Cookseys was unimaginably lonely.

"She didn't say; about that time, Reverend Cooksey must have remembered I was in the house, too, because he told her to lower her voice. For once, she actually listened and did what he asked."

"Why are they so badly off?" Betsy asked. "You said he's a vicar."

"Oh, he is," Eliza replied. "But he's not got a parish. That's another thing they fight about. Accordin' to Mrs. Cooksey, that's all his fault, too. He used to be the vicar of St. Andrew's over in Clapham. But something happened and he and Mrs. Cooksey had to leave."

Betsy made a mental note to find out what had happened in Clapham. Vicars didn't just lose parishs like they lost buttons. There had to be a reason. "You poor dear, it must be awful for you, living in a house like that."

Eliza shrugged. "It's not for much longer. Like I say, I'm just stayin' long enough for a reference."

"Will they give you one?" Betsy asked. "Some people get right nasty when you give notice."

"They'll give me one, all right," Eliza said flatly. "If they don't, I'll go right to that nice Miss Gentry and tell her what they're plannin' on doin' next."

"This is goin' to cost you a pretty penny," Blimpey Groggins said bluntly. "It weren't easy findin' out about either man."

"If it'd been easy, I wouldn't 'ave 'ired you." Smythe shrugged. He wasn't concerned about the cost. Blimpey wasn't cheating him; it probably had cost the man a pretty penny. "Why was it so 'ard findin' out the goods on Porter? He was known to the police, 'e was a thief."

"Actually, the fellow was a pickpocket." Blimpey picked up his drink and took a sip. They were in the public bar of the Admiral Nelson. "Quite a good one, by all accounts."

"Then 'ow come 'e's dead?" Smythe asked. "Sounds to me like 'e picked the wrong pocket and got 'is throat slit for his trouble."

Blimpey frowned and shook his head. "I don't think so. Porter was a pro."

"Any idea on who might 'ave killed 'im?" Smythe knew that Blimpey's sources were likely to have far more information than they shared with the police.

"That's the funny part: no one knows. Word is that Porter made it a point to get along well with his . . . uh . . . associates. Went out of his way to avoid makin' enemies."

"Maybe it was one of 'is marks that killed 'im," Smythe mused.

"It's possible, but not very likely." Blimpey took another sip. "Most marks don't even know they've been hit till they go to empty their pockets for bed. 'Course, there is one thing else—Porter had come into a bit of money. He was flashin' a wad of notes about two days before he died and he told one of his mates that there was more to come."

"Flashin' notes? From liftin' purses?" Smythe exclaimed. "Come on, pull the other one. No one's that bleedin' good." The good citizens of London had been contending with pickpockets since the Romans. Most of them never carried large amounts of cash on their person.

Blimpey hesitated.

"Go on, tell me. You must 'ave some idea what Porter was up to, and it weren't pickin' pockets."

"I don't want to set you on the wrong track," Blimpey said. "But it sounds to me like he was blackmailin' someone."

"You said Porter went out of his way to keep things nice and tranquil. Blackmail generally makes you a few enemies."

"That's one of the reasons I wasn't sure I ought to say anything. Blackmail would be out of character for Porter. But that doesn't mean he didn't do it."

"So what you're tellin' me is that it sounds like 'e was puttin' the screws to someone, but from what you've 'eard, Porter didn't generally have the guts to take on anyone who was likely to give 'im any grief."

"That's about the size of it." Blimpey waved at the barman. "You want another?"

Smythe shook his head. "I've 'ad enough, thanks. If Porter was blackmailin' someone, could you find out who?"

"My sources are workin' on that as we speak," Blimpey replied. "Mind you, that doesn't mean we'll find out anythin' worthwhile."

"Fair enough. Did you get anything on McIntosh?" Smythe took a quick sip from his beer.

Blimpey shrugged. "Not much. He worked as a caretaker at Helmsley's Grammar School for a couple of years. Before that, no one seems to have heard of him. But one rumor I got is that he was a seaman of some kind."

"Nobody 'as any idea why 'e was murdered?"

Perplexed, Blimpey shook his head. "Not yet. But I'm workin' on it."

"You don't 'ave much, do you?" Smythe muttered. He didn't really blame Blimpey. The man wasn't a miracle worker, but Smythe did hate having to go to this evening's meeting with so little information.

Blimpey's expression soured. "I ain't failed you yet, have I? Just give me a day or two and I'll know more about Stan McIntosh than his own mother."

"Don't be so bleedin' touchy," Smythe shot back. "You're the one that said this was goin' to cost me a pretty penny. You can't blame me for wantin' to get my money's worth."

"You'll get your money's worth," he promised. "Just give us a day or two."

"Fine, you've got it. Did you hear anything on that other matter?"

"Elliot Caraway?" Blimpey grinned. "Oh, I heard plenty about him. I was right, you know. He's about ready to be tossed out of his chambers. He's not had a brief in months and he's dead broke."

"What's he livin' on?"

"Credit, I expect." Blimpey shrugged. "Word I 'eard is that some relative of his wife's inherited a bundle and he's schemin' to get his hands on it."

"Could he do that?" Smythe asked curiously.

"When there's money involved, you can do all sorts of things. Mind you, with his skills in front of the bench, I don't think there's much chance he'd get a bloomin' cent out of her. It's been years since he won a case." He shrugged philosophically. "But that probably won't stop him from bringing the poor woman to court."

"On what grounds? You can't just go haulin' people into court willy-nilly. You've got to 'ave a reason."

"I don't know. You want me to find out?"

Smythe thought about it for a few seconds. He had no doubt it was Annabeth Gentry whom the barrister wanted to drag into court. He didn't think he needed Blimpey pursuing that line of inquiry. If a case was filed against Miss Gentry, they'd be the first to know. She'd tell them herself. "Nah, don't bother. What else 'ave you got for me?"

"Not much," Blimpey said. "I've still got my feelers out on that vicar and his wife. I'll let you know when I hear something, and as for that Phillip Eddington fellow, the only thing I could get on him was that he seems to travel out of the country a lot."

"Doing what?"

Blimpey grinned. "He goes off to Nova Scotia a time or two a year and does pretty much the same as you: he checks on his investments."

"You wanted to see me, sir?" Inspector Witherspoon stuck his head in Chief Inspector Barrows's office. "Oh sorry, sir. I didn't realize you had someone with you." He nodded politely to Nigel Nivens, who was sitting in a straight-backed chair opposite the chief's desk.

"Come in, Witherspoon." The chief waved him toward the empty chair next to Nivens. "Have a seat. This won't take a moment."

"Thank you, sir." He gave Nivens a friendly smile.

Stone-faced, Nivens stared back at him out of his cold, gray eyes. He was a portly, pale-skinned man with dirty blond hair worn straight back, a weak chin, and a large nose.

The inspector's smile faltered.

Chief Inspector Barrows cleared his throat. "Witherspoon, Inspector Nivens has brought it to my attention that you're asking questions about the Porter murder. Is that true?"

It took a moment before the inspector realized what the chief was talking about. "Oh yes, but I'm not really asking questions about that murder; it's more along the lines of trying to find out if it has anything to do with another case I'm working on—the McIntosh murder."

"That's ridiculous," Nivens snapped. "There's no evidence that Stan McIntosh had anything to do with Tim Porter. Porter was a thief. That one is mine, so I'll thank you to keep your paws off it."

"If you don't mind," Barrows said sarcastically, "I'll handle this matter." He directed his words at Nivens. He didn't like the man. But Nivens had made a career of being politically well connected and the chief couldn't completely ignore his complaints. But no matter how many friends in high places that Nivens had, Barrows wasn't going to pull his best homicide detective off a case just because he might have stepped on Nivens's patch. Chief Inspector Barrows had no idea how someone like Gerald Witherspoon actually solved murders; all he knew was the man got results. That was all that mattered. "You say you were only asking questions about Porter in connection with the McIntosh murder?"

"Yes, sir. Well, there was another matter that appeared to be connected. I was looking into that as well."

Barrows raised an eyebrow. "What other matter?"

"It was in my daily report, sir." Witherspoon pointed to a stack of papers on the side of the chief's desk. "I put it there this afternoon."

"Oh, uh, yes, well, I've not had time to read the dailies, so just tell me about it."

Nivens snorted faintly.

"It's one of our witnesses in the McIntosh case, sir. A neighbor to the victim. She was seen having words with the fellow on the day before he was killed. When I interviewed her, she claimed there'd been several attempts on her life."

"What's that got to do with Tim Porter?" Nivens asked harshly.

"The woman's name is Annabeth Gentry. Her bloodhound was the one that dug up Porter's body," Witherspoon explained. "So, of course, I began to suspect that it's all related somehow. Miss Gentry's dog finds a body; that's victim number one. Then there are attempts on her life, that's number two, and then, lo and behold, someone murders the caretaker next door. I mean, I don't think we're discussing a series of unrelated coincidences here. There must be some connection."

"Rubbish," Nivens snapped. "I remember Annabeth Gentry. I interviewed her. She's a silly spinster who fancies her dog is smarter than most people. If someone was trying to kill her, why didn't she contact me? I'm the officer in charge of the Porter case."

Witherspoon had asked her that very question. She'd been quite blunt in her reply. She'd thought Inspector Nivens rude, bombastic, and worst of all, he'd not liked her dog. "I don't think Miss Gentry quite realizes there might be a connection between finding that body and the attempts on her life," he hedged. "As I was there to interview her about the McIntosh murder, she told me about the attempts on her own life."

"How many attempts?" Barrows asked.

"Three."

"All since she found the body?"

"Right."

Barrows nodded. "There's a connection. There has to be."

Witherspoon hesitated. "Well, there is something else you ought to know. Miss Gentry inherited a substantial amount of money recently."

"What's that got to do with anything?" Nivens barked. "The attempts on her life are obviously tied to Tim Porter, so I should be taking over that investigation as well."

"Not so fast." Barrows lifted his hand. "Witherspoon is right. If the woman received a large inheritance, she may have a whole passel of relatives trying to murder her. God knows that's happened often enough in the past. There might not be a connection to the Porter case at all."

"But, sir," Nivens protested, "how likely is that?"

Barrows shrugged. Things were getting very complicated. He wasn't even sure whether Witherspoon was defending his poking his nose into Nivens's case because there was a connection between the cases or because there wasn't. He didn't care, either. But he did care about catching killers. "We don't know. But I'm not taking him off the case. As a matter of fact, I'm beginning to think that maybe he ought to be investigating the Porter murder as well."

Nivens shot to his feet. "That's my case. You can't do that."

"But I can," Barrows said calmly. "You've had it for two weeks and you're no closer to an arrest than the day that dog dug up the corpse."

CHAPTER 7

"Who would like to go first?" Mrs. Jeffries asked.

Mrs. Goodge waved her hand. "Let me. My report is short. Truth is, I didn't have much luck today at all. The only thing I heard was that there was some foreign man who went to the Helmsley's Grammar School looking for his cousin. He was surprised it was empty and a school. Fellow kept insisting to the woman down at the post office that that was the address where he'd sent his letters." She waved her hands dismissively. "It isn't very useful, I know."

"What kind of foreigner?" Wiggins asked.

"What difference does it make?" the cook retorted. "It doesn't have anything to do with our case. According to Mrs. Pavel at the post office, it wasn't the first time some foreigner come in with the wrong address for a relative. But if you must know, he was an American or maybe a Canadian. They sound so much alike it's hard to be sure." She sighed loudly. "I know it's not much."

"Nonsense," Mrs. Jeffries said stoutly. "As we've found out before, everything is useful. We never know what detail will be the one that provides the vital clue for solving the case. Perhaps one of us ought to have a word with Mrs. Pavel. Who knows what we'll learn. I'm not sure what this means, but it could be significant."

"Can I go next?" Wiggins waved his hand in the air. "I found out a lot today."

Mrs. Jeffries glanced around the table. "As no one appears to object, go ahead."

He grinned and took a deep breath. "All right, then. I found a woman who used to clean at the school. She knew McIntosh. 'E wasn't much liked. Seems 'e liked runnin' to the 'eadmaster and tellin' on people."

"I'll bet the students hated that." Betsy laughed.

"Not just the students," Wiggins said. "The staff did, too. From what Stella told me, just about everyone 'ated the fellow. But I don't think any of them killed 'im. The school's been closed since spring term."

"Maybe someone was biding his time," Luty suggested. "I knew a miner once who waited twenty years to shoot the man who jumped his claim. Waited till the fellow was walkin' up the aisle of the church for his weddin' and then he shot him right in the back."

"Why'd he wait so long?" Betsy asked

"He wanted to wait till the happiest day of the feller's life before he killed him, least that's what he said at his trial."

"I don't think McIntosh was killed on the happiest day of 'is life," Wiggins said with a frown. "From what Stella said, 'e was 'appiest when 'e was tellin' tales on someone."

"Did she know what McIntosh had done before he was the caretaker?" Hatchet asked.

"He worked at sea."

"Like a sailor?" Betsy asked.

"'E weren't really a sailor, 'e worked for passenger liners. More like a porter or a steward. You know, fetchin' and carryin' and doin' for the passengers. But he stopped doin' that and got a job as the caretaker at the school."

"I wonder why he gave up the sea," Luty murmured. "Can you find out what passenger line he worked for?"

Wiggins nodded eagerly. "I expect I can. Stella give me the address of one of the cooks from the school. I'm 'aving a word with 'er tomorrow."

"You've learned a great deal, Wiggins," Mrs. Jeffries said. "Who would like to go next?"

"I might as well," Betsy volunteered. "I found that maid that worked for the Cookseys." She glanced at the cook. "The one you heard about."

"The one that was scared of her own shadow." Mrs. Goodge nodded.

"She didn't act scared when I was with her," Betsy said. "What's more, she was a real talker, too. I didn't even have to come up with any reason for asking so many questions." She told the others everything she'd learned from Eliza Adderly. "And when I asked her if they'd give her a reference," she finished, "Eliza told me they had to, that if they didn't, she'd go right to Miss Gentry and tell her what the Cookseys planned to do next." She took a quick sip of her tea.

"Don't stop now," Luty demanded. "Go on."

"That's just it," Betsy admitted glumly. "That's the one thing she didn't tell. Another girl from Eliza's village happened to come into the waiting room just then and I couldn't get anything more out of her."

"Maybe you can manage to run into her again," Luty suggested.

"I thought about that, but I don't think I can manage it. She wasn't sure which train she was taking back and I can't spend my whole day hanging about the St. Pancras station." Betsy wanted to get over to Clapham and pay a visit to St. Andrew's. She wasn't going to waste her precious investigating hours waiting for Eliza Adderly to turn up. Especially since she thought the maid might have been exaggerating just a bit. But she didn't want to share this with the others. She might be wrong.

"But you've got to find out," Wiggins insisted. "It might be right important."

"Maybe you can manage to see her again after she's come back to the Cookseys'," Hatchet suggested. "From what we know of their financial circumstances, they don't have a large staff."

"They don't," Betsy agreed. "They used to have a cook but she quit last month. Now it's just Eliza."

"Then it would be my guess that this young lady does most of the errands for the household," Hatchet said.

"She does." Betsy brightened immediately. "I know because she was complaining about having to go to the fishmongers for Mrs. Cooksey before she left. She was afraid she'd get on the train smelling of fish. I'll wait until early tomorrow morning and then have another try at it. If there's shopping to be done, she'll be doing it then."

"Can I go now?" Smythe asked. He had a lot of information to share with the others.

"By all means," Mrs. Jeffries replied.

He told them what he'd learned from Blimpey Groggins without, of course, mentioning where he'd got the information. "So you see, not even the street toughs 'ave any idea who killed Porter."

"Is your . . . er . . . source a reliable one?" Mrs. Jeffries hated to ask such a question, but it was necessary. "Oh dear, that sounds awful."

"No offense taken." The coachman grinned broadly. "I know what you're askin'. Take my word, the source is a good one. If 'e says no one on the streets knows anythin' about this murder, it's the truth."

Luty frowned in confusion. "The one thing I don't understand is why your source thinks Porter was blackmailing someone. There's lots of other ways to get a wad of bills—"

"I know," Smythe interrupted. "My source weren't sure, 'e were only tossing the idea out because it seemed to be the only one that fit. But you're right, there's lots of ways to get money."

"But Porter is alleged to have said there was more coming," Hatchet reminded them, "and that implies that he had access to a steady source of cash. He wouldn't have made such a statement if he'd been referring to robbery or pickpocketing. The first is too risky and the second is too unreliable."

"So what we know is that no one knows why Tim Porter was murdered and there is some evidence he was also a blackmailer," Mrs. Jeffries said.

Smythe nodded. "That's about it. I've got my sources workin' on who Porter's victim might 'ave been."

"Maybe it was Stan McIntosh," Luty ventured.

"Now, madam, let's not jump to conclusions. We've no evidence the two men even knew one another," Hatchet warned.

"I know that," Luty replied. "But it would sure make this case easier if that was so."

"But even if it were McIntosh that murdered Porter, we'd still have the problem of who killed McIntosh," Mrs. Goodge said. "And so far, we've no idea."

"But we will," Mrs. Jeffries said firmly. "No matter how complicated this case gets, we'll keep digging until we find the truth."

Inspector Witherspoon smiled gratefully as he accepted the glass of sherry. "Thank you, Mrs. Jeffries."

"You look like you've had a very tiring day, sir," she said, taking her usual seat.

"Indeed it was, Mrs. Jeffries. I must say, it wasn't too awful until right at the very end. There was a bit of a scene in the chief inspector's office."

Alarmed, she stared at him. "A scene, sir?"

"I'm afraid so." He sighed and took a sip of his sherry. "Inspector

Nivens seemed to feel I was trespassing on his case. I don't know how he found out so quickly, but he'd heard I was asking questions about the Porter murder. He wasn't pleased."

"I'm sure he wasn't, sir," she replied. Nivens had probably had an apoplectic fit.

"Luckily, the chief understood my reasoning, you know, about the cases being related."

Mrs. Jeffries wondered precisely how the inspector had explained the connection. "You told him about Miss Gentry?"

"Of course. Well, I think Miss Gentry's case is connected—" He broke off and frowned. "I mean . . . oh drat. I'm not sure what I mean anymore. But somehow, I believe that Miss Gentry being threatened is connected to McIntosh's death. It seems to me those threats must be somehow connected to her dog finding that pickpocket's body. Oh dear, you see how confusing it's becoming. But luckily, the chief quite understood." He took another quick gulp of sherry. "Unfortunately, Inspector Nivens didn't quite see the situation in the same light. He was rather unhappy with me. I was going to offer to share any information I received with him, about the Porter matter, but for some odd reason, the chief decided it would be best if I took a hand in that investigation as well."

"I think that's a jolly good idea, sir." She fought hard to keep her expression neutral. It wouldn't do to let him see she was elated at the thought of Nivens being out in the cold.

"I'm flattered by your faith in me, Mrs. Jeffries." Witherspoon sighed again. "But I'm not sure it's justified. I've no idea what to do next. Even with the new information I received from Inspector Nivens, it's all still so muddled and confusing."

Mrs. Jeffries knew his confidence was slipping. She had no doubt that this was due to the confrontation with Inspector Nivens. Witherspoon was no coward, but he hated doing anything underhanded or unfair. She was quite certain that Nivens, knowing Inspector Witherspoon's good character as he did, had taken very unfair advantage of the situation and made all sorts of ridiculous allegations. "It might be muddled, sir, but you'll soon sort it out. You always do."

"In the past I have." He drained his glass. "But as Inspector Nivens pointed out, one can't be right all the time. I'm bound to fail eventually."

"Nonsense," Mrs. Jeffries said briskly. She was furious, but she didn't allow it show. "You have a gift, sir. An inner voice that guides you. Of course you won't fail. I think it's quite unfair of Inspector Nivens to make you doubt yourself like this."

"Oh, now, we mustn't blame Inspector Nivens, he had good reason to be upset. He'd made some progress on the Porter case, and of course, it is still his case, so to speak."

"But he's not made enough progress, sir," Mrs. Jeffries said. Drat, the fool was still on the case. "Otherwise the chief wouldn't have asked you to lend a hand."

"I'm sure Inspector Nivens is doing his best. Perhaps he simply needs more time," Witherspoon replied. "As I said, he's made some progress on the case. He'd found out that Tim Porter hadn't been working his usual pickpocket routes."

"Where had he been?" Mrs. Jeffries asked.

Witherspoon frowned. "Inspector Nivens hadn't found that out. But he'd not been picking pockets, that was for certain. No one had seen him on the streets for a good week prior to his death."

"Inspector Nivens actually managed to determine the right time of death?"

"The body hadn't been in the ground more than a day before it was found." The Inspector suppressed a shudder. "And taking that fact, along with witness statements of the last time Porter was seen, means it was easier to pinpoint the time of death."

"Pardon my saying so, sir. But if that's all Inspector Nivens found out in two weeks, it's not very good." She watched him closely as she spoke, hoping to tell by his expression if there was more to come.

"I know." He sighed again. "But perhaps it'll be the best anyone can do. There are some murders that can't be solved, Mrs. Jeffries."

"And there are plenty that can," she told him. "Anyway, sir, other than a rather dismal meeting with Inspector Nivens, how did your day go?"

He brightened a little. "Quite well, actually. I think we're making progress." He told her whom he'd interviewed, what they'd said, and more importantly, what was left unsaid. Mrs. Jeffries listened carefully. She took each and every fact and tucked it away in her mind. Despite her bravado with the inspector, she knew these murders were going to be difficult to solve.

But she refused to believe that it was going to be impossible.

"And, of course, when I went back to the Caraway house to interview Mrs. Caraway, she'd not come home yet. I'll have to try again tomorrow.

I tell you, Mrs. Jeffries, it's shocking how little respect some people have for the police."

"Dreadfully shocking, sir," she agreed. She clucked her tongue in reproof. "And didn't you say that Elliot Caraway was a barrister?"

"Which means he ought to know better," Witherspoon replied.

Mrs. Jeffries wanted him to know that Caraway was in dire financial straits. Of course, she couldn't come right out and tell him. "I'm sure he does, sir. But it *is* a puzzle, isn't it. You'd think that as he's a barrister, he'd be more sympathetic to any officer of the court. But then again, perhaps he's not had much luck in front of the bench and he blames the police for his failures. You know what I mean, sir. Perhaps he's lost a number of criminal cases. Goodness, sir, how very odd . . . Porter was a criminal and Caraway is a barrister. Do you think it's possible they knew one another?" She hadn't meant to plant that particular seed, but now that she had, she decided perhaps she'd see what grew. Maybe there had been a connection between Porter and Caraway.

Witherspoon stared at her for a moment. "Why, Mrs. Jeffries, that's a wonderful idea. I'll certainly look into it right away."

She didn't want him thinking she was giving him "wonderful" ideas. That could lead to all sorts of consequences. "It's very nice of you to say so, sir, but let's be honest here. We both know I was merely saying what you were already thinking—" She held up her hand as he opened his mouth to protest. "Now, now, sir, don't be so modest. Even if the thought wasn't precisely in your head the moment I spoke, you know good and well that by tomorrow morning you'd have been thinking along those lines. Just like you'll be thinking about how important it is to find out what you can about Miss Gentry's relations. After all, sir, as you always say, there are many motives for murder, but the usual ones generally turn out to be correct."

He now looked positively puzzled. "Er, uh . . . yes, I suppose I do say that. Uh, I didn't, perchance, happen to mention what I meant when I said it, did I?"

Knowing she'd succeeded in getting him so muddled he wouldn't remember where any ideas had come from, she laughed. "You're so amusing, sir. I must say I think it's remarkable that you've still got your sense of humor after a hard day's work. You meant that in each and every murder, if one kept the most basic motives in mind, one could generally find the killer."

He smiled weakly, but his eyes were still confused. "Oh yes. Well, yes, of course."

"So in the case of the attempted murder of Miss Gentry, the first thing one would do is find out who benefited from her death and, equally important, what their financial circumstances are now. Am I correct, sir?"

He nodded. But he still looked a bit confused. Mrs. Jeffries wasn't one to waste an opportunity. The timing was perfect. This was her chance to let him know what they'd learned about these strange cases. The inspector was tired, confused, and slightly tipsy, as he had returned home with a very empty stomach and it was quite a large sherry she'd given him. She reached for his empty glass. "Let me get you another drink, sir. I think after today's events you could use one."

"'Ere, let me 'elp with that," Smythe said from the open door of the inspector's bedroom early the next morning. The inspector had already left for the day.

Betsy looked up from the tangle of linens she'd just pulled off the double brass bed. "I'm just changing his sheets. It'll not take a minute."

He pushed into the room. "It'll go even faster with two of us doin' it. Don't look so surprised. I do know 'ow to make a bed." It bothered him that she worked so hard. He had enough money that she'd never have to turn her hand for the rest of her days if that's what she wanted. But they'd decided that neither of them was ready to give up their investigating and so they'd decided on a long engagement. He just hoped it wouldn't be too long. He loved the lass more than life itself.

Betsy laughed and slapped the neatly folded clean sheet onto the center of the mattress. "All right, then. Give us a hand." She unfolded the sheet, grabbed the edges, and gave it a good shake. She giggled at his efforts to grab the linen on his side.

He finally got his fingers on it. "Are you going to try making contact with Eliza Adderly this morning?"

She nodded. "Pull that end up tighter. I'll find Eliza. But now that I think about it, she might have just been talking. You know, trying to make herself sound important."

"Why do you say that?" He tucked his edge of the sheet under the mattress.

She finished her side and then turned and picked up the clean top sheet she'd left on the chair by the window. "I don't know. The thought just suddenly occurred to me last night before I fell asleep. Once I'd thought of it, the surer I was that it might be true." Sometimes she didn't know how to explain things properly. She was sure there must be words that described what she'd felt, but she didn't know what they were.

"I know what ya mean." He grabbed the edge of the top sheet she tossed in his direction. "Sometimes the oddest things pop into my 'ead just before I'm noddin' off and it generally turns out to be right. But I still think ya ought to 'ave another word with the girl."

"I'm going to," Betsy assured him. She finished tucking the top sheet in and reached for the blanket. "Then I thought I'd pop over to Miss Gentry's neighborhood and see if anyone knows any more about the Caraways or the Cookseys." She frowned. "Seems strange to me that the only suspects we've got in this case is people that didn't even know the murder victim."

"You talkin' about McIntosh or Porter?"

"Either of them," she replied. "That's not right. Someone's got to know something about McIntosh. Everyone's got friends or relations somewhere."

"Maybe Wiggins will 'ave a bit of luck with the cook. Maybe she knew a thing or two more about the fellow." Smythe carefully spread his half of the blanket onto his side of the bed. "Actually, I was thinkin' of 'avin' a go at findin' out a bit more about Porter."

"Good." Betsy gave him one of her beautiful smiles. "He's a bit of a dark horse."

He didn't return it. He stared at her for a long moment.

Her smile faded. "What's wrong?"

"I'm wonderin' how long we ought to be engaged. You know how I feel about you, Betsy." He took care to enunciate his words properly, especially as he was talking to her. She'd never mentioned his lack of formal education or the way he spoke, but he knew she respected bettering yourself and he was determined to be everything she wanted in a man.

She'd been dreading this discussion. "And you know how I feel about you. I love you with all my heart. But I don't want to give up our investigating. Not yet."

"Maybe we wouldn't 'ave to . . ." His voice trailed off as he saw her shake her head.

"We would," she said fiercely. "Once we were married, you'd not be content for me to keep on being a maid. You'd want us to have our own home. Once we did that, we'd be gone and that would be it. You're a rich man"—she glanced up to make sure none of the others were passing by the open door—"and you'd not want me fetching and carrying for someone else, even our inspector."

What she said was true. He was rich and he did want to give her a home of her own. He wanted to give her everything. But he didn't want to give up their investigations any more than she did. He sighed. "All right, we'll wait. But not forever, lass. I do want to marry you."

"And I want to marry you," she said softly. "But we've plenty of time, Smythe. There's no rush." She didn't tell him she'd been giving their future a lot of thought. She realized something he didn't, or perhaps something he did, but wouldn't face.

She knew that no matter how big a house he bought her and no matter how much money he had, if they stayed in England, he'd always be a coachman and she'd always be a maid. But that was something they could talk about at another time. Right now she was glad she'd gotten him off the subject of setting a date for their wedding. Their investigations were too precious to give up yet. Being a part of them made her feel like she was contributing to something important. Something noble. She wasn't willing to give it up. Not even for love. Not yet.

Mrs. Goodge balled her hand into a fist, drew her arm back, and let fly with a punch. The dough crumpled on its side. She let fly with another punch and it flattened completely. "I did hear something this morning, but I don't think it's got naught to do with our case," she said casually. She wasn't sure the tidbit she'd heard was worth sharing with the others. Truth was, she'd been sorely disappointed in the bits and pieces she'd picked up.

"What's that?" Mrs. Jeffries prodded. She could see that the cook was in one of her dark moods. She sometimes got that way when she'd not had much luck with her sources. The housekeeper always tried to jolly her out of them. "Come now, Mrs. Goodge, do tell. I'm the only one here, so no matter how trivial you think it is, I'd like to hear it."

"Well . . ." The cook picked up a clean tea towel and draped it over the bowl of bread dough. "Mrs. Macklingberg, she used to do a bit of cleaning for that Mrs. Dempsey—"

"The Mrs. Dempsey that left Annabeth Gentry her house?"

"That's right. Michael, the butcher's boy, told me that Mrs. Macklingberg had told him that Mrs. Dempsey had gone a bit childish in her dotage."

"Childish how?"

"She'd started seeing things. She used to point at the mirror in the parlor and ask Mrs. Macklingberg to invite someone who wasn't even there to tea."

"She saw people in the mirror that weren't there?" Mrs. Jeffries clarified. Unfortunately, Mrs. Goodge was right, this didn't have anything to do with their case. But she wasn't going to cut the cook short. She'd hear her out.

"Yes, poor old thing. It must have been awful for her. She saw men in the mirrors that weren't there and a few days before her death she'd started seeing monsters in the garden."

"How very sad." Mrs. Jeffries shook her head sympathetically. "I wonder what kind of creatures haunted the poor woman."

"Gargoyles." Mrs. Goodge shrugged. "Mrs. Macklingberg overheard her asking her neighbor if he'd seen the gargoyles digging out in the gardens. Eddington was quite polite about the whole thing; he very calmly replied that he'd only arrived home that very morning, so he couldn't have seen a thing."

"How awful to spend your last months on this earth with your mind going like that." She shuddered and sent up a silent prayer that God would take her fast, painlessly, and with all her faculties intact.

"It wasn't as bad as it could have been," the cook said. "She died very quickly after that."

"Old age does have some blessings." Mrs. Jeffries rose to her feet. She had a number of things to take care of this morning. "The body simply wears out."

"Let's hope our bodies go before our minds give out," the cook said. "I don't think I fancy people treating me as if I were a dim-witted child."

"Mr. Eddington, we came as soon as we got your message." Witherspoon smiled politely. He'd not planned on starting his day here, but when he'd got to the station, there'd been a message that Mr. Eddington might have more information for them. At this point in the investigation, Witherspoon would take any clues he could get.

Eddington gave a short, deprecating bark of a laugh. "Inspector, that's good of you, but it certainly isn't urgent. I don't even know if my information is useful in your investigation. Oh dear, where are my manners? You don't want to stand about out here on the doorstep. Do come in." He pulled the door wider and the inspector and Barnes stepped inside.

They followed him into the drawing room. He sat down on the settee and gestured for them to sit as well. As soon as they were settled, Barnes whipped out his notebook.

Witherspoon gave the man an encouraging smile. "Now, sir, what do you have for us?" He prayed it was something really useful. He didn't think he'd ever been this muddled on a case before.

Eddington looked embarrassed. "This is awkward, Inspector. Most awkward. But it's something I thought you ought to know. It's about Miss Gentry." He paused. "I don't think her dog really found that body."

Witherspoon blinked. "I assure you, sir, the dog did find a body. I checked."

He shook his head briskly. "Forgive me, Inspector. I'm not very good at explaining this. What I meant to say was that I think she may have known this Porter fellow before he died. Well, of course, if she did, then perhaps her dog finding the body wasn't as remarkable a feat as everyone thinks."

"Are you implying that Annabeth Gentry murdered Tim Porter?" Barnes asked. His expression was frankly skeptical.

Eddington looked pained. A slow, red flush crept up his cheeks. "I know it sounds awful and I've agonized over whether or not I ought to mention it. Miss Gentry seems a very nice woman. She took wonderful care of Mrs. Dempsey before she died. I honestly don't know what it means, sir. But I do know my duty and I finally realized I had to tell the truth."

"Exactly what is the truth?" Witherspoon asked.

Eddington took a deep breath. "I saw Annabeth Gentry giving a strange man money. They were standing in the churchyard. The next day, she and her dog found Porter's body. I think the man she was giving money to was Tim Porter."

Barnes looked up from his notebook. "Why do you think it was Porter?"

Eddington sighed. "I travel a lot, gentlemen. On business. Consequently, I tend to save my newspapers and read them when I get home. That's why I didn't come forward sooner." He reached for a newspaper on the top of the table next to the settee and waved it at the policemen. "I only read the newspaper account last night. It said Porter was wearing a gray workingman's shirt when he was dug up. The man Miss Gentry was giving money to in the churchyard had on that kind of shirt."

Witherspoon glanced at Barnes. The constable's expression gave nothing away. "I see."

"I'm not accusing her of murder, Inspector," Eddington said quickly. "I almost decided to say nothing. But as I said, I know my duty. My conscience demanded that I tell you what I'd seen. This Porter sounds a disagreeable fellow, but he didn't deserve to be murdered in cold blood."

"I agree," Witherspoon replied. He gave himself a shake. By rights, he'd investigated enough murders that nothing ought to have surprised him. But this did. He simply couldn't think of what this new information might mean. Annabeth Gentry didn't seem like a murderer. For goodness' sakes, she had a dog. But he'd learned in the past that appearances could be deceptive. And even killers could have a dog. "What time of day was it that you saw Miss Gentry?"

"I'm not sure I remember the precise time." Eddington frowned thoughtfully. "Let me see, it was when I was out taking some air after breakfast. Yes, it must have been about ten o'clock."

"Did anyone else see Miss Gentry? Any of your servants or the gardener perhaps?" Witherspoon wanted as many witnesses as possible before he trotted over to Miss Gentry's and began questioning her about Tim Porter.

"I do the gardening, Inspector," Eddington replied. "I enjoy it and it keeps one fit. As I said, I travel a great deal in my business. I only have an occasional cleaner come in, so there wasn't any staff to see Miss Gentry. Look, I've a great deal of admiration and respect for the woman. She spent an enormous amount of time with poor Mrs. Dempsey before she died. And I think it's tragic that now that she's inherited the house and Mrs. Dempsey's money, there's been so many awful things happening to prevent her from moving into her new home and enjoying it. I didn't tell you what I saw because I wished to slander the woman, but only because I thought it was my civic duty."

"We weren't doubting you, sir," Witherspoon said. "We merely wanted to get as much information as possible before we questioned Miss Gentry again. If someone else saw her with Porter, that would be most useful to know."

"You might ask the vicar," Eddington said. "When I turned around to go back inside a few moments later, I noticed he'd come into the church-yard."

"Was Miss Gentry still with Porter at that point?" Barnes asked.

"I don't remember," Eddington admitted. "At the time, I thought nothing of the incident."

Witherspoon thought that odd. "Why not, sir? Surely a respectable woman handing money to a disreputable man is something that one doesn't see every day."

"I thought she was paying someone to work on the house," Eddington explained. "She'd hired some of the workmen herself, you know."

"She didn't employ a builder?"

"She did. But she'd also hired some laborers to do some of the unskilled work. At the time, that's what I thought she'd done."

Barnes looked up from his scribbling. "What kind of business are you in, sir?"

Eddington looked surprised. "Investments, sir. I find opportunities for a group of Canadian and American businessmen to invest their capital in. Why? Is it relevant?"

Barnes smiled. "No, sir. I was merely curious. I've always thought it would be nice to have a position where one could travel."

Witherspoon stared at the constable in surprise. Barnes was a home-body. He didn't even like the short train ride to Essex to visit his own relatives.

"Travel does broaden the mind," Eddington said. "But it also has some disadvantages. I won't have a wife to comfort me in my old age. I'm never in one place long enough to court a lady. More's the pity."

"Who are you?" The woman stuck her head out and glared at Wiggins with small, piggy eyes. "What da you want?"

He tried not to stare. She had the fattest face he'd ever seen. "I'm just wantin' to talk to you," he said. He held up a brown paper parcel. "I've brought you some buns. If you'll let me in, I'll share 'em with you." He thanked his lucky stars that Stella had warned him to bring food.

"You ain't said who you are?" She licked her lips as she stared at the parcel.

Wiggins didn't want to stand on the doorstep of the derelict row house a moment longer than necessary. "My name's Wiggins. Stella Avery sent me. She said you could 'elp me."

"Stella sent you?" The woman stepped back and pulled the door open. "Why didn't you say so? Come on in."

Wiggins stepped inside. The hallway was dim and smelled of boiled cabbage and rotting carpet.

"Close the door," she ordered.

He did as she instructed and hurried after her. She was the fattest woman he'd ever seen. The sides of her body brushed the walls as she waddled down the short hall. They came into a small, dismal sitting room. White curtains hung limply at the narrow window and the rose-colored settee was faded with age. A paint-splattered table and a spindly chair were the only other furniture in the room. Through an open door he could see one bare table and chair in the tiny kitchen.

"My name's Cora Babbel." She waved him toward the only chair. "Have a seat. Then tell us why you've come."

Swallowing hard, he sat down. "My name's Wiggins and Stella Avery said you might be able to 'elp me."

Her attention was fixed on the parcel. "Let's have them buns you promised," she said, reaching across the small space that separated them.

Wiggins handed them over. "Please, 'elp yourself." This was the most depressing place he'd ever seen and he'd been in some pretty awful places. He wondered how this woman managed to live.

"I've got a small pension," she suddenly announced. She unwrapped the parcel, tossing the string that held it together onto the floor.

Wiggins started in surprise. "How'd you know what I was thinkin'?"

She stared at him as she stuffed a bite of bun in her mouth. "Your face does your talking for you. What you was thinkin' was written as clear as the day is bright. Now, why'd Stella send you to me?"

Wiggins was glad she hadn't offered him one of the buns. "She said you might be able to tell me about Stan McIntosh."

"You with the police?"

"No."

"Then why'd you want to know about Stan?" She picked up the second bun and stuffed it in her mouth.

"Because I'm workin' for someone who's trying to catch 'is killer," Wiggins explained. He didn't think giving this woman the speech about justice for the common person would do much good. "And I'm bein' paid to ask questions."

"You're a private inquiry agent?" Her expression was skeptical.

He shook his head. "I'm just bein' paid to ask a few questions, that's all. You know anything about Stan or not?"

She laughed and reached for another bun. "Oh, I know plenty about old Stan. Plenty."

CHAPTER 8

Inspector Witherspoon wasn't certain what the proper etiquette was when someone deliberately kept the police waiting. As it was a lady, he didn't wish to be rude, but he didn't want the police to be made fools of either. He sighed inwardly as he glanced at Constable Barnes. "Do you think she'll be much longer?"

They were sitting in the Caraway drawing room. They'd been there for over twenty minutes and Mrs. Caraway still hadn't put in an appearance.

Barnes shrugged. "If she's not here soon, sir, we'd best go. There's a number of other people we've got to see today. We've still got the Cookseys to interview and you wanted to see Miss Gentry. Plus there's the former school secretary. He's supposed to have Stan McIntosh's references. I'd like to get a look at them, sir. We need to talk to someone who knew McIntosh."

"He is a bit of a mystery, isn't he?" Witherspoon said. "And of course, you're right. We do need to get cracking." He rose to his feet and started toward the hall, intending to call the maid and instruct her to have Mrs. Caraway come to the station. But he stopped abruptly and leapt to his left. A plump, blond whirlwind of a woman almost toppled him over as she charged into the room.

"What are you doing?" she demanded as she dodged to one side of Witherspoon. "Haven't you any manners? You almost knocked me over."

"I'm most dreadfully sorry," the inspector apologized quickly "I didn't expect you to come through the door so fast."

"It's my house, I can come through the door as fast as I please. I'm Ethel Caraway. I take it you're the police." She glanced at Barnes as she spoke.

"Correct, madam." Witherspoon moved back to the settee. "If you don't mind, we'd like to ask you a few questions."

"Of course I mind, but Elliot insisted I answer your questions. It is, of course, an utter waste of time." She didn't sit down; she simply crossed her arms over her chest and stared at them coldly.

"I believe, madam," the inspector said softly, "that we're the best judges of whether or not we're wasting time." He sincerely hoped that Ethel Caraway was wrong.

She snorted indelicately and walked to a chair. "Get on with it then." She sat down.

He wondered why she was being so very disagreeable. After all, it was her sister they were trying to help. "Mrs. Caraway, do you know a man by the name of Stan McIntosh?"

"Certainly not. Why would I? What's he got to do with Annabeth's tale of someone trying to kill her?"

"What makes you think that's why we're here?" Barnes asked.

"My husband. That's what he said you wanted," she retorted promptly.

Witherspoon realized this interview wasn't going at all well. She'd been rude, but he wanted to get as much information out of her as possible. "Mrs. Caraway, we're not here to inconvenience you. We've several very difficult cases and they might be related to one another. Your cooperation would be very helpful."

"I *am* cooperating," she replied. "But I don't see how Annabeth's wild stories have anything to do with that caretaker being killed."

"We've reason to believe there might be a connection," the inspector insisted softly. He didn't know why he felt that way, but all of a sudden he was absolutely certain that all of it was connected. The words of his housekeeper flooded into his mind. *You have a gift, sir,* she'd said. *You've an instinct for catching killers* . . . Well, he thought, perhaps that wasn't exactly what she'd said, but it had been something like that.

Barnes watched Ethel Caraway as Witherspoon spoke. Something flickered in her eyes, something that looked very much like fear. She knew something. The constable was sure of it.

"I don't know anything about Stan McIntosh and I've certainly no idea why anyone would want to kill him," she stated firmly.

"Have you ever been to the school?" The inspector had no idea where that question had come from; he'd simply opened his mouth and it had popped out.

"Certainly not," Mrs. Caraway replied. "That's the most preposterous thing I've ever heard. Why would I go to that tumbledown wreck of a school to see that disreputable-looking man—"

"How do you know he's disreputable looking?" Witherspoon asked.

"He's the caretaker," she cried. "Of course he's disreputable looking. He wears those filthy old clothes and doesn't cut his hair properly . . ." Her voice trailed off as she realized what she'd revealed.

"The only way you could know how his hair was cut, ma'am, was if you'd seen him," Barnes pointed out.

She recovered quickly. "You didn't ask if I'd seen him, Constable. You asked if I knew him. Of course I've seen him."

Witherspoon asked, "Where were you on Thursday morning?"

She was surprised by the question. "This past Thursday? I was at home."

"Was there anyone here with you?"

"I was alone, Inspector."

"What about your maid?" Witherspoon pressed.

She hesitated for the briefest of moments. "It was her day out," she finally said. "I've no idea what you're leading up to, but I assure you, I had nothing to do with the man's murder. Why would I want to kill a perfect stranger?"

"We're merely exploring possibilities, madam," he said quickly. "Have you ever heard of a man named Tim Porter?"

She frowned. "You mean the person Miranda dug up?"

"Yes, had you ever heard of him before your sister's dog . . . uh, dug him up."

"No. Why would I? From what I understand, he was a pickpocket. I don't generally consort with such persons."

"Excuse me, madam." The maid poked her head in the drawing room. "Miss Gentry is here. Shall I show her in?"

"Oh, it's all right." Annabeth Gentry popped into the room. "I'm family. Of course I can come in . . ." Her face broadened into a smile when she saw the inspector and Constable Barnes. "Goodness, how nice to see you again, Inspector, Constable."

Ethel Caraway closed her eyes briefly and sighed. "Annabeth, you really ought to wait to be announced. Even with family."

"Nonsense," Annabeth said cheerfully. "Can I bring Miranda in? I promise she'll behave. She's sitting right outside and you know how lonely she gets."

"Dogs don't belong in drawing rooms," Ethel Caraway retorted. Annabeth's face fell. "Oh, all right," she said, relenting, "bring the creature in, but mind that she behaves herself."

"She'll be good as gold." Annabeth hurried toward the door. "She's ever so well trained."

Ethel Caraway sighed. "We spoil Annabeth dreadfully. But that dog means the world to her. You don't mind, do you, Inspector? Constable?"

Both men looked surprised to have been asked. Witherspoon spoke first. "Of course not, ma'am. We both like dogs. I've got one at home."

Annabeth swept back in with Miranda trotting by her side. The dog wasn't on a lead. But she stayed right next to her mistress. Annabeth took a chair to one side of her sister. "Sit," she instructed the dog.

Miranda sat.

"See, I told you she'd behave." Annabeth looked at the inspector as she spoke. "You'll appreciate this, as you've got an animal at home. But I've found the most wonderful way of training Miranda . . ."

Ethel Caraway sighed theatrically. "We know, dear. Come now, Annabeth, I'm sure the inspector and the constable aren't interested in your training methods."

"Actually," Barnes said, "I'd like to hear a bit more about them. The police use bloodhounds for tracking, sometimes—"

"Miranda would be a wonderful tracker," Annabeth exclaimed. She clasped her hands with excitement. "I've been working on teaching her to follow a trail. You know, laying down bits of food and then praising her when she—"

"Annabeth, please, the police are here to talk to me. We need to get on with it." Ethel Caraway glared at her sister. "Now do let us continue."

"I'm sorry." She smiled apologetically. "I do get carried away."

The inspector suddenly had an idea. It would let him kill two birds with one stone, he somehow felt. He smiled at Miss Gentry. "I say, would you show us exactly where Miranda dug up Porter's body?" he asked.

"Of course," she replied, but her expression was puzzled. "I don't mind taking you there. But I didn't think it was important. That other police inspector said not to bother when I offered to show him."

"Excuse me, miss." Barnes frowned. "Are you saying that Inspector Nivens didn't view the body where it was actually found?"

"No, by the time he was on the case, they'd already taken the body away. He said he'd seen it and that where it was found wasn't important."

Barnes gaped at her as though he couldn't believe his ears. Even the inspector was stunned.

"But the surrounding area was searched?" Witherspoon pressed.

"Oh, I think the constables had a look." Annabeth shrugged. "I don't really know. They bundled me off as soon as they got there. Why? Is it important?"

"Yes, Miss Gentry, it's very important." Witherspoon rose to his feet. He made a mental note to ask Miss Gentry about Eddington's report of seeing her in the churchyard, but for right now, getting to the scene where Porter's body was found was the most important order of the day.

"What's going on here?" Ethel Caraway demanded. "Are you finished with me?"

"For the moment, ma'am." Witherspoon turned his attention to Annabeth Gentry. "Are you free now? Can you show us where you found the body?"

Hatchet glanced over his shoulder and then climbed up on a carved gravestone next to the wall which separated the churchyard from the houses on Forest Street. He had a moment's guilt but he quickly squelched it. Since Mr. Edmund Pearsons had gone to meet his Maker over fifty years ago, Hatchet didn't see why the fellow should object to helping out a bit. After all, this was a murder investigation.

He stood on tiptoe and craned his neck to see over the top. He wasn't sure what he was looking for, but as his contribution to the case so far had been fairly limited, he was rather desperate to see something. All his other sources had dried up, and he couldn't get anyone new to talk to him, so he'd ended up here in the churchyard next to Annabeth Gentry's new home.

He could see the communal garden behind the two tall houses on Forest Street. The gardens had been terribly neglected. The grass was overgrown by a good three inches. The trees and hedges planted along the length of the back wall were wild and overgrown and didn't look like they'd been pruned since George III was on the throne.

From behind him, he heard the rustle of footsteps. "Excuse me, sir. May I be of some assistance?"

Hatchet whirled around. A short, rotund fellow dressed all in black smiled at him. It was the vicar. His bald head gleamed in the midday sun and his brown eyes twinkled merrily. "I'm Father Jerridan." The priest extended his hand.

"Good day, Father." Hatchet shook hands with him, realized he was still standing on the top of poor old Pearson's monument, and leapt off. "Do please excuse me, I meant no disrespect to the grave. I was . . . curious about the garden next door, that's all."

"That's quite all right," the priest replied. "No need to apologize. Is there something I can help you with?"

"Yes, Father, there is." Hatchet hesitated, not certain of what to say to the vicar. He didn't want to lie to a man of the cloth, but he did want information. "Do you happen to know a Miss Annabeth Gentry?"

"I've met Miss Gentry," he replied. "Fine woman. She was engaged at one time to the son of one of our flock. Poor fellow died. Miss Gentry was very good to his mother. Mrs. Dempsey's last years were made far happier by the companionship she received from the woman who would have been her daughter-in-law." The priest's eyes narrowed suspiciously. "Tell me, sir, what's your interest in Miss Gentry?"

Hatchet wanted to be as truthful as possible, yet he also wanted to protect Miss Gentry from wagging tongues. "Lately Miss Gentry has been frightened by some very unfortunate incidents."

"Unfortunate incidents? What kind of incidents?"

"It's rather delicate, Father," Hatchet hedged. "I'm sure you understand. It's quite confidential."

"I'm a man of the cloth, sir. I know how to hold my tongue."

"Let's just say she has reason to believe some individual may be trying to do her harm."

"You mean someone is threatening her?" The priest's bushy eyebrows rose. "Then you're a private inquiry agent? Oh dear, how very awful for Miss Gentry. As I said, she's a fine woman. Well, what can I tell you? Ask away. I'll do what I can to help."

"Thank you, sir." Hatchet gave him a grateful smile. "You'll be doing Miss Gentry a great service and I know I can trust your discretion in this matter." He had only the barest of qualms about questioning a priest under false pretenses. After all, catching a murderer was more important than correcting the erroneous impression that he was a private inquiry agent. Nevertheless, he resolved to put a couple of pounds in the church collection box. "Do you know of anyone who doesn't like Miss Gentry?"

"Oh, no, no, everyone around her quite admires and likes her. She's very kind. Well, perhaps I shouldn't say everyone, her brother-in-law is a bit of a bother, but I mustn't speak ill of a fellow priest."

"Her brother-in-law has been annoying her?" Hatchet pressed.

"No, no, He's only looking out for Miss Gentry's best interests. He'd never hurt her." The priest clamped his mouth and gave him a strained smile.

Hatchet knew he'd get nothing more from Father Jerridan about the Reverend Harold Cooksey. The priesthood didn't discuss one of their own to outsiders. But he wasn't going to let that stop him. "So there's no one who you know of that would wish Miss Gentry harm?"

"I don't wish to tell tales out of school, but I don't think her neighbor is all that fond of her." Father Jerridan jerked his ample chins in the direction of Forest Street. "She's not even moved in yet and they've had words."

"Words? You mean they've had an argument?"

"That's putting it a bit too strongly," he replied. "You know, I'm probably making a mountain out of a molehill. Perhaps I oughtn't to have said anything. It was such a minor incident."

Hatchet didn't want the good father to get tongue-tied at this point. "Please continue, it might be very important."

"Well . . ." He shrugged. "It's so silly I'm not sure I ought to repeat it. They've gotten along quite well since Mr. Eddington moved in two years ago. It isn't as if I really thought Mr. Eddington didn't like Miss Gentry. I just happened to overhear him asking her to please keep her dog on a lead when she came to inspect the work at the new house."

"Mr. Eddington doesn't like dogs?"

"That's what struck me as so odd about the request." He stroked his chin. "The only other time I saw the two of them together was right after Miss Gentry got the dog, about six months ago, just after Mrs. Dempsey had passed away. At that time, I rather got the impression Mr. Eddington was an animal lover. He seemed very fond of the dog then."

"Where were they when you saw them?" Hatchet asked.

"Right here." The father gestured at the churchyard. "Miss Gentry and Miranda were on their way over to Forest Street and Mr. Eddington was taking a shortcut through the churchyard to the road. They met right here in the middle."

"Shortcut?"

"Oh yes. There's a gate just over there that connects the two properties." Father Jerridan pointed farther down the wall. Sure enough, there was a slender, wrought-iron gate. "It's an ancient right-of-way between the properties. Very few people know about it. But some do. The residents of Forest Street have been trying to get the right-of-way revoked for the past couple of years. Well, Mr. Eddington has; he's not a member of our church. But Mrs. Dempsey refused. She used the gate every Sunday until her health gave out."

Hatchet silently apologized to Mr. Pearsons. If he'd been using his eyes properly, he needn't have trampled on the fellow's grave! "I take it Mr. Eddington didn't like people being able to cut across his property."

"But that's what's so silly about the fuss he's been making. The right-of-way doesn't go anywhere but to the communal garden on Forest Street. There's no right-of-way past the houses and onto Forest Street itself. It literally ends at the garden edge."

"In other words, the right-of-way only benefits the people who live on Forest Street," Hatchet clarified.

"That's right, and there's only three houses there."

"Then why was Mr. Eddington upset enough to try and get it revoked?"

"Oh, sometimes tramps use the side entryway to the church when the weather is bad. They sleep there because it's partly enclosed and it provides a bit of protection from the wet. They're not supposed to, of course. But frankly"—he flushed slightly—"I look the other way. Our Lord did tell us that what we did to the least of our brothers, we did to him."

"Why would Mr. Eddington object to anyone sleeping there? You said he wasn't a member of your church, so why would he care?"

"The side entry is just opposite the gate. You can see right through to the gardens if you've a mind to." Father Jerridan sighed. "I'd thought he'd let the issue go, but a few weeks back, Mr. Eddington spotted another fellow having a sleep there, so I expect he'll be worrying Miss Gentry to get the right-of-way revoked again. I don't know why it bothers the fellow so much; he's not even here most of the time. He travels quite a bit on business. But perhaps that's one of the reasons he values his privacy. He does seem to come and go at the oddest times."

Hatchet nodded. "Did Miss Gentry agree to his request?"

"She said her dog was very well trained and that Mr. Eddington needn't worry." Father Jerridan looked troubled. "But I don't think he believed her. Mr. Eddington's face had gone red and he looked angry enough to pop."

"You saw him?" Hatchet asked.

The priest blushed. "Oh dear, I'm afraid I've been caught haven't I? Inadvertent eavesdropping is bad enough, but spying is even worse, isn't it?"

"Don't be so hard on yourself, Father," Hatchet said.

Father Jerridan glanced at his watch. "Oh dear, I must be running along, I'm going to be dreadfully late to the Ladies' Missionary Society meeting." He tossed Hatchet an apologetic smile and started toward the front gate.

Hatchet wasn't about to let him escape. "Father, wait. Can I walk with you? I've a few more questions to ask, if you don't mind."

"You'll have to hurry," the priest called over his shoulder as he reached the front gate. "Mrs. Vohinkle gets awfully annoyed if I'm late."

"We're not more than a quarter mile from your new home, are we?" Inspector Witherspoon said to Annabeth Gentry.

"It's over a mile if you go by the roads," she replied. "But if you use the footpath through there"—she pointed to her left, toward an empty field that opened up off a row of small houses—"it's a ten-minute walk."

They stood on the footpath that wound through open fields on the edge of Hammersmith. They were separated from the grim walls of Wormwood Scrubs Prison by a good half mile. In the distance, the whistle of a train chugging down the Great Western Railway Line shattered the silence.

Witherspoon glanced at Barnes, trying to read his expression. They were going to be stepping on some toes here. Searching a crime site that should have already been searched by another officer wouldn't make either of them popular with Inspector Nivens. If they found nothing, well, then perhaps Witherspoon would leave it out of his daily report. But he had a feeling they would find something.

He could have kicked himself for being so precipitous. But gracious, when he heard the site hadn't been thoroughly searched, he hadn't thought about the ramifications of dashing over here and doing the job properly. If Nivens got wind of it he wouldn't like it at all. He'd think it made him look incompetent and he'd strike back any way he could.

Witherspoon wasn't concerned for himself. But the constable didn't have a fortune. He relied on his salary to support his wife. The inspector knew he was a bit slow when it came to the internal politics of Scotland Yard, but even he understood that Inspector Nivens had enough friends in high places to do a lot of damage to a policeman's career. He would make a nasty enemy. "Er, Constable, if you'd like, Miss Gentry can show me the site and I can search it on my own . . ."

"Four eyes are better than two, sir," Barnes said calmly. "And we may have to do some digging. But I appreciate the thought, sir, and if I may say, sir, I, too, have a few friends at Whitehall."

Clearly confused, Miss Gentry glanced from one of them to another. But she was too polite to ask any questions. "It's just over there." She pointed at a spot up the footpath.

They followed her to a copse of trees and shrubs bordering the footpath. She and the dog led the way in amongst the trees. Once inside, tall brush grew up against the trees, making the area hidden and private. A perfect place to bury a body.

"It's just here." Miss Gentry stopped at the edge of a circle of disturbed earth. There was still enough light to see the site clearly, and the actual spot where the body had been dug out was only partially filled in. They stared down at it.

Annabeth relaxed her hold on Miranda's lead and the dog edged closer and shoved her nose onto the ground. Keeping her head down, she sniffed her way around the circle.

"It's all right, girl." Miss Gentry called the dog back to her side. "She must still smell the corpse," she said.

Witherspoon was glad that his sense of smell wasn't as keen as the bloodhound's. He knelt down and studied the area. It looked like a hole filled with dirt.

Barnes walked to the other side and looked at Annabeth. "Exactly how was the body lying when you found him?"

She frowned slightly, as though she were trying to remember. "Well, let me see. I didn't get that good a look at it. Once Miranda started digging and I realized what it was, I dashed off to find a policeman. But I believe the head was at this end." She pointed to the closest edge of the hole. "Yes, that's right, because I remember seeing the man's hair. At first I thought it was some sort of animal, then I saw his hand."

"Right, then." Witherspoon took a deep breath and plunged his fingers into the damp soil. He began scooping earth out onto the perimeter.

"Exactly what is it you're looking for?" Miss Gentry asked.

"We're not sure," Barnes replied. He, too, was digging in the soil on his side of the makeshift grave. "Anything the victim may have had on him could have dropped under the body. When he was killed or when he was buried. We'll have to dig all this out."

"Can I help?" Annabeth asked.

"I don't think that would be a good idea," Witherspoon replied. "But thank you very much all the same."

Miranda watched them curiously. Suddenly she bounded over and began sniffing the dirt at the end of the grave where the feet would have been. She began pawing the spot.

"I think you ought to dig there," Annabeth said. "She's found something. Something that probably belonged to the dead man."

"How on earth could she do that?" Witherspoon asked curiously.

"She's a very smart dog," Annabeth replied. "She's still got the scent. There's something buried there, mark my words."

As the inspector's back was starting to hurt, he was willing to take the chance that the dog might actually be onto something. He shifted to the far end. "Can I have a look?" He gently shoved Miranda out of his way and began digging where the dog's nose had just been. For a few moments he found nothing, then his fingers brushed against metal. "I've got something." He got a grip on the object, brushed away more dirt, and yanked it out of the earth.

Barnes, Miss Gentry, and Miranda crowded around him to have a look, effectively blocking his light. "What is it, sir?" the constable asked.

Witherspoon held up a small, dirt-encrusted change purse. "It's a woman's purse," Miss Gentry exclaimed.

The inspector could see it was a purse, but that was all. "How can you tell it belongs to a woman?"

"Have a good look, sir." She bent closer and pointed to a spot right beneath the clasp. "It's made of blue velvet. I don't think there are many men who would carry a blue velvet coin purse."

"She's right, sir." Barnes squinted at the purse. "Why don't you open it."

"Good idea." He popped open the clasp and looked inside the small bag. "There's nothing here but some coins . . ." He pulled out the biggest coin and stared at it. "It's not English." He held it up to get a better look. "It's a Canadian nickel . . . gracious, how extraordinary."

"What's the other one, sir?" Barnes asked.

"A penny. Canadian as well. Now, how on earth did Porter end up with a woman's purse and Canadian coins?"

"Looks to me like he was just doing his job. He was a pickpocket, sir"—Barnes rose to his feet and dusted off his knees—"and it looks like he picked a Canadian pocket right before he was killed."

Smythe couldn't believe his luck. She was going into a pub. He'd spotted the frizzy blond-haired woman when he was on his way down the Uxbridge Road. He'd recognized her as the woman who'd been sitting behind him at the White Hare Pub. She'd been talking about Stan McIntosh to her friend. He dodged around a fruit vendor pushing a handcart and across the narrow walkway to the pub.

It wasn't the nicest pub he'd been in, but it wasn't the worst either. There was sawdust on the floor, a sagging bar, and an empty fireplace. Most of the plain wooden tables were taken. The blonde was sitting hunched over a glass of gin by the one nearest the fireplace.

Smythe went to the bar and ordered a beer and a glass of gin. "Ta," he said to the barmaid when she slid the glasses in front of him. Tossing her some coins, he picked up the gin and headed for the blonde. "Mind if I join ya?" he asked.

She stared at him for a second before her gaze shifted to the gin in his right hand. "Not unless that gin's for me," she replied.

"It's for you." He slid the drink in front of her and sat down on the hard wooden stool. "I'd like to ask you a couple of questions if you don't mind."

She tossed back the gin. "You're the bloke that was at the White Hare the other night. The one askin' all them questions about Stan."

"I didn't ask all that many questions," he countered. "You lot closed ranks on me before I got my curiosity satisfied."

She laughed, revealing a set of yellowed, chipped teeth. "We weren't closin' ranks, man. Everyone was just scared, that's all. Last time anyone was in the pub talkin' about Stan McIntosh, he ended up dead."

"And who would that be?" Smythe asked innocently.

Her eyes narrowed shrewdly. "Oh, I think you know who I'm talkin' about all right, don't you, big fellow? Otherwise, you'd not be botherin' to ask questions. You with the police or are you one of them private inquiry agents?"

"Neither," he replied. He was getting a little confused. She seemed more than willing to talk and that made him uneasy. "I'm just a curious sort." He reached in his shirt pocket and pulled out a five-pound note.

Her eyes widened. "If you answer my questions and tell me the truth, ya can 'ave this."

"Ask away, big fellow. My name's Emmy Flynt. What's yours?"

"Smythe," he replied. "Nice to meet ya, Emmy. Now, who was askin' questions about McIntosh that ended up dead?" He asked the question even though he knew the answer.

"Little sod named Tim Porter," she shot back, her gaze still on the note. "Pickpocket, he was. A little whiles back he come around askin' questions about Stan McIntosh; the next thing we 'eard was that some woman had found Porter's body over in them fields beyond Ellerelie Road. Scared us it did. No one liked McIntosh. He was always a bit of a bad one."

Smythe nodded. He could understand why they'd kept quiet. They might have heard McIntosh was dead, but that didn't mean all his friends were, and to these people, crooks tended to run in packs "So you knew 'im, did ya?"

"I worked in the laundry over at the grammar school before it closed. I met him there. Didn't like him much, no one did."

"What did you mean about McIntosh having money?"

"Huh?" She stared at him in confusion. "Whaddaya mean?"

"You said that old Stan could come up with a bit of the ready when he wanted to," he reminded her. "You said it to your friend that night at the White Hart. I 'eard ya."

She shrugged. "I didn't mean nuthin', I was just talkin'." She reached for the note.

Smythe snatched it out of reach. He knew she was lying. "Come on, now, what d'ya take me for? Tell me the truth and ya can 'ave the money."

Emmy worried her lower lip with her teeth, as though she were waging some awful internal battle with herself. "Oh, all right, then. But you're to keep what I tell ya to yourself. I've got a reputation in these parts and I aim to keep my name decent. Stan liked me. But I didn't like him all that much, if you get my meaning. He weren't overly fond of soap and water, you know. Puts a girl right off, that does. Anyway, the, uh . . . only way I'd have anything to do with him was if he paid me, you understand?" she finished belligerently. Then she looked away, unable to hold his gaze.

Smythe understood all right. She supplemented her income with a bit of prostitution. He didn't look down on her for it. He felt sorry for Emmy. You did what you had to do to survive. "I understand," he said softly, "and I'll keep my mouth shut. What else can you tell me about Stan McIntosh?"

"What do you want to know? I wasn't with him that often. But I know he's got plenty of money . . ."

"How do you know that?" Smythe asked. McIntosh flashing a bit of cash to pay for a woman was one thing, having a lot of money was a very different matter.

"Because he told me he did," she retorted. "He liked to talk a bit, did Stan. Especially afterward. He told me once the school closed and the place were sold, he'd be off to a life of luxury. Said he'd never have to fetch or carry for anyone again."

Smythe shook his head. "Was he just talkin', do ya think?" He didn't see how a few pounds in the bank made a fortune, and to anyone's knowledge, that was all McIntosh had.

"Nah, he was tellin' the truth. Stan was a talker but he wasn't a liar."

"Did 'e ever say where this money was?"

She shrugged. "Didn't ask, did I. Frankly, I didn't want to know too much about Stan McIntosh. Seemed healthier that way."

CHAPTER 9

It was quite late in the afternoon before everyone arrived back at Upper Edmonton Gardens for their daily meeting. Luty was fairly bursting with excitement, Wiggins's cheeks were pink, Hatchet's eyes sparkled, and Smythe looked like the cat that had just got the cream.

Mrs. Goodge and Betsy wore almost identical glum expressions. Apparently, it hadn't been a very good day for either of them.

"I don't think we've much time this evening," Mrs. Jeffries said without preamble. "So let's get right to it. I'd like to go first if no one objects." She paused for a brief moment and then continued. She held up a set of keys. The keys that Wiggins and Smythe had found on McIntosh's body. "I've been trying to think what we ought to do with these. I don't think they're particularly important evidence, but I do think the police ought to know about them."

"Cor blimey." Smythe made a face. "I can't believe we forgot about 'em. Maybe I ought to nip over and plant 'em somewhere in the school."

"That's a good idea," she replied. "The inspector said the school was thoroughly searched, so I think our best course of action is to plant them on the grounds. Then we must make sure our inspector finds them. But for the life of me, I can't think of how we're going to do that without being too obvious."

"We'll find a way," Wiggins put in confidently. "We always do. Is that all you've got, Mrs. Jeffries?"

She had a great deal more, but she wasn't quite ready to share her ideas with the others yet. It was a bit too premature. "I'm finished. Would you care to go next?"

"I'd be right pleased." Wiggins told them about his visit with Cora Babbel. He was a true gentleman and he didn't mention her size. "She was the cook at Helmsley's Grammar until it closed. She had rooms on the far side of the kitchen. She said that Stan McIntosh was a right odd one and that no one at the school liked 'im."

"We know that already," Mrs. Goodge said irritably. She could tell the others all had plenty to report, while she had practically nothing.

"But what you don't know is that 'e used to sneak out at night," Wiggins said. "Cora told me McIntosh would wait until the place were locked up tighter than a drum and then slip out the back door."

"Was he meeting a woman?" Smythe asked.

Wiggins shook his head. "No, that's what Cora thought at first. But one night she followed him. She was angry at him because he'd run to the headmaster with some tale about her stealing food from the school kitchen and sellin' it on the side."

"So she was trying to get the goods on him, was she?" Luty chuckled. "Good for her."

Wiggins grinned. "She didn't come out and admit it, but I think that's what she was doin'. Anyway, when she got outside, she saw it were a man McIntosh was meeting. The fellow was carrying something; Cora couldn't make out what it was, but it was something with a long handle, like a broom. They headed off toward the gate leading to the churchyard. Cora was goin' to follow 'em but she must've made some noise, because all of a sudden they stopped and turned in her direction. She had time to duck behind a bush, but it scared her, so when they went on, she went back inside."

"I wonder who it was he was meeting," Mrs. Jeffries murmured.

"I wonder what it was he was carrying," Hatchet added. "Somehow, I don't think it was a broom."

"What else has a long handle?" Betsy asked. She wanted to contribute something useful, even if it was just questions.

"Maybe he was meeting Tim Porter," Mrs. Goodge suggested. "Maybe that's the connection between Porter and McIntosh. They were up to something together."

"That's possible," Mrs. Jeffries murmured. "But if they were up to something together, what was it?"

"More importantly, who killed 'em?" Smythe said. He glanced at Betsy. Her brow was furrowed in concentration and he could almost see her mind working. He hoped she wasn't up to anything. There'd been a time or two in the past when she'd done things that put her in danger.

"Go on, Wiggins," Mrs. Jeffries ordered. "We're short on time here. The inspector might be home any minute."

"That's really about it," Wiggins said. "Cora didn't 'ave much else to say about Stan." He rather thought that McIntosh's night activities was an important clue. "The only other thing she mentioned was that he wouldn't let anyone else get the mail."

"What do you mean?" Hatchet asked. "How could he stop anyone from picking it up once it was shoved in the slot through the door."

"School had one of them locked baskets over their door slot," he explained. He referred to a square, woven metal device placed over the slot. It was hinged on one side and could be locked. "McIntosh kept the keys and he wouldn't let anyone, not even the 'ead, 'ave 'em. Said unlockin' the basket and getting the mail was 'is job and 'is job alone."

"Hmmph," Mrs. Goodge snorted faintly. "Sounds like he put on airs."

"Is that it?" Mrs. Jeffries inquired. Wiggins nodded and she looked around the table. "Who'd like to be next?"

"I'll have a go," Luty said. "Stan McIntosh worked for Gibbens Steamship Lines. They go between here and Canada. Before that, he worked for the White Star Line on the North America run. He was a passenger steward up until two years ago. Then he suddenly up and quits."

"That must have been when he got the job at Helmsley's," Betsy said.

"It would 'ave been," Wiggins interjected. "Cora said McIntosh come to the place about then."

"Why would you give up a job traveling to go and be a caretaker at a school that was going broke?" Smythe asked. "I know stewards don't make a fortune, but that's got to be a better job than caretakin' at that ruddy school."

"Maybe he got tired of travelin' and wanted to settle down," Luty suggested. "Whatever it was, he quit and come to London. I also found out that no one knows anything about that Mr. Eddington. I asked my bankers and all my other sources in the City and no one's ever heard of Eddington or his investment group. I think that's mighty suspicious."

"Madam, many investors prefer to remain anonymous," Hatchet told her. "Besides, Mr. Eddington says his investors are Canadian and American. It's no wonder your sources haven't heard of them. They're foreigners.'

"Seems like this case is filled with people no one's ever heard of," Betsy muttered. "Almost like they just popped up out of the earth."

"Is that it, Luty?" Mrs. Jeffries asked in an effort to hurry things along.

"That's all I have." She gave her butler a disgusted look. "Why don't we let Hatchet go next, looks to me like he's gonna pop a collar button if he don't get it out."

"Thank you, madam." Hatchet beamed at his employer. "If no one objects, I do have some interesting tidbits to share." He told them about his visit to St. Matthew's and his lucky meeting with Father Jerridan. He left out the part about masquerading as a private inquiry agent.

No one spoke when he'd finished. Finally, Mrs. Jeffries broke the silence. "I don't know what it means," she said, "but I'm sure it means something. But I don't think a minor dispute about Miss Gentry's dog being on a lead is really a good motive for attempted murder." But the moment the words were out of her mouth, something niggled at the back of her mind.

"Neither do I," Hatchet replied. "But so far, he's the only person we've found that has any reason to dislike Miss Gentry."

"But he doesn't have any connection with Porter or McIntosh," Mrs. Goodge put in, "so if he's the one trying to kill Miss Gentry, then her case doesn't have a thing to do with the other murders."

"I can't believe that's true," Mrs. Jeffries replied. The idea she'd just glimpsed had disappeared as quickly as it had come. She frowned slightly and resolved to try to get it back when she was alone in her rooms.

Smythe noticed the housekeeper's expression. "Are you all right, Mrs. Jeffries?"

She gave him an quick smile. "I'm fine; I was just thinking of something. But it wasn't important. Would you like to go next?"

Smythe nodded. He told them about his meeting with Emmy Flynt. He didn't mention her being a prostitute. "So it clears up why they all closed ranks on me at the White Hart that night. The last person who'd been in there askin' questions about McIntosh was Tim Porter and he ended up dead. They weren't coverin' somethin' up, they was scared."

"But by then they knew that McIntosh was dead," Luty pointed out. "So why was they scared?"

"They knew McIntosh was dead but they'd no idea who killed 'im; no one does. They'd assumed McIntosh might 'ave killed Porter because of 'is askin' all them questions about McIntosh. Then McIntosh 'imself was killed and none of 'em knew what to think except that there was someone out there killin' people left and right. Believe it or not, they was warnin' me, tryin' to do me a good turn."

"Did Emmy know how much money McIntosh had?" Betsy asked.

"No, but she was fairly sure 'e weren't lyin' to 'er about goin' off and livin' in luxury."

From upstairs, they heard the front door open. Mrs. Jeffries leapt to her feet. "Oh drat, that's probably the inspector. I hadn't expected him home so early."

"I'll get his tray ready." Mrs. Goodge dashed toward the wet larder. "Come on, Betsy, give me a hand."

"We'll meet back here tomorrow morning," Mrs. Jeffries called over her shoulder as she dashed for the stairs. "I have a feeling we'll have more information to share by then."

The inspector was in the drawing room by the time she arrived upstairs. "Good evening, sir. This is nice, you're home early."

"I'm going back out again," he replied. "Constable Barnes and I want to have a word with Reverend Cooksey and his wife. They don't live far from here."

"That's too bad, sir. You look as if you're tired. But Mrs. Goodge will have a tray ready in a few moments, sir. Would you like tea or sherry?"

"I'd love a sherry . . ." He hesitated. "But as I'm still on duty, as it were, I don't suppose I ought to. I've had the most bizarre day, Mrs. Jeffries." He told her about his rather unsatisfactory interview with Ethel Caraway and about going to search the spot where Tim Porter's body had been found.

"What did you do with the coin purse, sir?" Mrs. Jeffries asked curiously.

"Constable Barnes nipped down to the station and logged it in as evidence. I expect there will be some trouble about that. Inspector Nivens won't be pleased about our search."

"Then he should have searched it properly himself, sir," she retorted. She didn't think her inspector would hear one word from Nivens. Even he wasn't stupid enough to raise a fuss over evidence he'd have found if he'd been doing his duty. "So, sir, any ideas?"

"If you mean do I have any ideas about who the killer is or even whether or not the cases are connected, well, the answer has got to be no. I've not a clue." He sighed. "But I refuse to give up."

"That's the spirit, sir. Why, your tenacity has already paid off. You found that purse."

"Yes, but the purse may not have anything to do with Porter's murder. As Constable Barnes pointed out, Tim Porter was a pickpocket. He'd probably pinched the purse before he was killed."

"Excuse me, sir. If I remember correctly, don't pickpockets get rid of the purse as soon as they take the money out? Aren't they afraid of getting caught with an item that's so easy to identify?" She could hardly mention that her sources had made it clear that Porter hadn't been picking pockets on the day he'd been killed.

Witherspoon's brows drew together. "Why, you're right. That means that unless the murder took place within minutes of his picking some Canadian woman's pocket, that purse is some sort of clue."

"Now you just have to figure out what kind of clue it is," she said cheerfully. "By the way, have you found out any more about Stan McIntosh's background? You didn't say if you'd met with the secretary of the board and got his references."

"Oh, drat. I do hope the secretary will forgive me; in the excitement of the search, I completely forgot I was supposed to meet with the man. I'll have to do it first thing tomorrow morning. Ah . . ." He cocked his ear toward the hall. "Is that my dinner coming up the stairs?"

Betsy popped her head into the drawing room. "I've got your tray, sir."

"Excellent." He got up and followed the maid to the dining room. Mrs. Jeffries followed a bit more slowly. She had much to think about.

The Reverend Harold Cooksey didn't look pleased to be disturbed. He was a tall, thin man with a ruddy complexion and wisps of gray hair circling his bald head. His thin lips pursed disapprovingly as he looked down his nose at the two policemen in his small drawing room. "I was just about to do evening prayers, sir," he said to Witherspoon. "This isn't at all convenient."

"We're sorry to interrupt your devotions, sir," the inspector replied, "but we've come around twice in the past two days and neither you nor your wife were at home. We have some questions we'd like you to answer."

"Oh, let's get it over with, Harold." Louisa Cooksey, an older, fatter, and rather meaner-looking version of Miss Gentry, glared at the two policemen. "It's only Annabeth's silly nonsense they want to talk about."

"We take Miss Gentry's problems quite seriously, I assure you," Witherspoon replied. He was amazed that the same family could produce three such different women. "Do either of you know of anyone who would wish to harm Miss Gentry?"

"Absolutely not," Louisa Cooksey replied. "Why would anyone wish to hurt her?"

"She imagines things," the reverend added. "We worry about her health, don't we, my dear?" He addressed the last part to his wife.

"Indeed we do," Mrs. Cooksey affirmed. "She's quite delicate, you know. She oughtn't to be living on her own."

"Do either of you know a man named Stan McIntosh?" Barnes asked. He didn't like these two.

"No," the reverend replied. "Is there any reason why we should?"

Barnes didn't answer; he looked at Mrs. Cooksey. "Ma'am?"

"I saw him a time or two," she admitted. "You are talking about the caretaker of that school, correct?"

"Yes, ma'am. You saw him? When?"

"Well, I guess it was the day that poor Miranda got so ill. I saw him going into the school just as we were passing by in a hansom. But that hardly counts, does it?"

"Was he carrying anything, ma'am?" Barnes persisted.

"Not that I remember," she said.

The inspector looked at Reverend Cooksey. "Have you ever met a man named Tim Porter?"

"Isn't that the fellow Miranda dug up?"

"Yes, did either you or your wife know him?" The inspector was fairly certain he knew how they'd answer, but one could never be sure until one asked.

Louisa Cooksey's eyes narrowed angrily. "He was a pickpocket, Inspector, hardly the sort of person we'd be acquainted with."

"We don't know the man," the reverend stated. "We never heard of him until all this fuss started. Look, Inspector, how much longer is this likely to take? I've an appointment this evening and I don't wish to be late."

Witherspoon glanced at Barnes. He snapped his notebook closed, a sure indication that he had no more questions to ask. The inspector couldn't think of anything else to ask them. Once again, it was a bit of a dead end. "I believe we're finished, sir. Oh, just one more thing. On the day you stopped by Miss Gentry's to have tea, the day Miranda took ill, did you happen to notice if the back door was open?"

Both the reverend and his wife answered at the same time.

"It was open," she said.

"Closed," he stated firmly.

Mrs. Jeffries waited up for the inspector, but it was so late by the time he returned home that she got only the barest details out of him about his visit with the Cookseys. She wished him a good night at the top of the staircase and went to her rooms.

She didn't bother to light the lamps. She wanted the darkness. She wanted to put her mind at ease and let the information they had gathered about his case flow about in her head until it made sense.

She sat down in her chair and closed her eyes. Then she forced her body to relax. Little by little, the bits and pieces began to coalesce and form themselves into the beginnings of a pattern. Porter was murdered first and then McIntosh. So she decided that she could safely assume that the same person killed them both. It was finding Porter's body that had involved Annabeth Gentry, so now the killer or killers were trying to murder her, but they wanted her murder to look like an accident. Why?

She sighed and opened her eyes. The pattern she'd thought was forming shifted suddenly in her head and now nothing made sense. Annabeth Gentry's death was supposed to look like an accident. That could only mean that whoever it was who was trying to kill her didn't want the police to investigate her death. And they wouldn't if the coroner ruled it was an accident.

Then why, she asked herself, hadn't the killer cared about the police investigating Porter's and McIntosh's deaths? They might have been poor and had no family to raise a fuss— She stopped as the idea that had come to her earlier took root in her mind. The answer, she realized, was simple. The killer hadn't cared because there was nothing that could connect him or her with Porter and McIntosh. Those poor wretches had lived solitary lives, with virtually no connection to anyone or anything. How had Betsy put it? *As if they'd popped up on the face of the earth.* The police would do their best, but after a few weeks, other cases would demand their attention and they'd certainly put these murders on the back burner. Neither man had anyone to look after his interests. No one really cared that they'd been killed.

But Annabeth Gentry was different. She had friends and relatives to demand that the police keep looking no matter how long it took. And the killer didn't want the police looking too closely into her death, because there was something in her life that connected her directly to the murderer. But what?

Mrs. Jeffries sighed and got up. She'd best get ready for bed. Maybe she'd think of something before she fell asleep.

Holding her shoes in one hand, Betsy tiptoed down the back stairs. If she was quick about this, she could get over to the school, have a look 'round, and be back in time for breakfast.

The floorboard on the bottom stepped creaked loudly. She stopped, cocked her head up the stairs, and listened for a moment. But she heard nothing. She continued on into the kitchen, put her shoes down on the chair, and then crept over to the pine sideboard. She'd seen Mrs. Jeffries put McIntosh's keys in the top drawer. She pulled it open and frowned. No keys. She pushed aside a ball of twine, a tin of sealing wax, and two rusted door hinges.

"Looking for these?" Smythe asked softly.

Betsy jumped and whirled around. Her beloved stood there, holding up McIntosh's key ring.

"What are you doing down here?" she snapped. "You scared me to death. Don't go sneaking up on a body like that, it's not healthy."

"More's the point, what are you doin' down 'ere at this 'our of the mornin'? And don't try tellin' me any tales, lass, you're fully dressed and wearin' your cloak, so I know you've taken it into yer 'ead to go out and 'ave a snoop on your own."

She debated arguing with him, but she didn't want to waste the time. "All right, what if I *was* going out? So what? It's morning. I can go out and do a bit of snooping on my own, I don't need your permission."

He glared at her. She raised her chin a notch and glared right back. Defeated because she wasn't in the least intimidated, he sighed. "I knew you were up to somethin'."

Betsy wasn't sure she liked that. "How?"

"Your face, lass. You were thinkin' about what you was goin' to do when we were 'avin' our meetin' yesterday. I could tell you were plottin' and schemin' about somethin'."

"I wasn't plotting anything," she retorted. "I was thinking we oughtn't to lose a perfectly good opportunity."

"To search the school ourselves," he said. "Yeah, the same thing crossed my mind."

She brightened immediately, delighted at the way their minds had come to the same conclusion. "Well, let's get moving, then. We've only got a couple of hours before the others get up."

He wanted to stay angry at her, wanted to give her a good talking-to about worrying him and trying to go off on her own. But the truth was, she looked so sweet and eager standing there with that shiny expression on her pretty face that he didn't have the heart to keep chewing on her. "All right, we'll go. But I want you to promise me you'll not do something this daft again."

Betsy was already grabbing her hat off the hat stand and heading for the back door. "It wasn't daft. You said so yourself."

"I said I 'ad the same idea to search the place, I didn't say it weren't daft to try and sneak off on your own." He was practically running to catch up with her. "And I want your promise, Betsy."

She gave in because she didn't want him nattering at her all the way to the school. "Oh, all right, I promise the next time I have an idea to go off, I'll tell you first." She threw the latch on the back door and stepped outside.

Smythe pulled the door shut behind him as he followed. He wasn't sure, but he had the distinct impression he'd won that round far too easily.

Though it was early morning, the sun hadn't risen yet. They made their way to Holland Park Road and Smythe waved a hansom cab. He had the cab stop one street short of the grammar school. He'd learned to be cautious and there was no point in leaving a trail.

"We'll walk from 'ere," he told Betsy as he helped her down.

"Good idea," she agreed. Five minutes later, they were slipping through the heavy gates of the school.

"Let's go around to the back door," he whispered. Betsy nodded and they slipped around the side of the building. Smythe noticed that Betsy deliberately kept her gaze off the sheds. She'd not admit it in a million years, but he knew she was glad he'd come. In the dim light, this place was right scary.

Stan McIntosh's keys got them into the kitchen. The sun was just cresting the horizon, so there was enough light to get around without hurting themselves. The kitchen was huge. The floors were a gray slat, scratched and worn by years of shuffling feet. On the far wall were the sinks, greened with age and smelling of rotten vegetables. Above them, the wooden slats of the drying racks were broken and bent. Cobwebs hung from the ceiling, cupboards with doors askew lined the other wall, and a huge cooker, blackened with grim and soot, stood just the other side of the back door.

"McIntosh's rooms were supposedly off the kitchen," Smythe murmured. He noticed that Betsy hadn't left his side. As a matter of fact, if the lass got any closer, they'd be joined at the hip. "Come on, let's have a gander over 'ere." He started for the hallway opposite the cooker.

"But the police already searched his room," Betsy insisted. "I think we ought to have a good hunt around the school."

"All right, where would you hide something?" He swept his hands out in an arcing motion. "This place isn't exactly small."

"Well, we don't know that he had anything to hide," she replied. Drat, she hated it when he was right. The building was huge. It would take them hours to do a proper search.

"Then why the dickens are we 'ere?" He put his hands on his hips.

"Because he might have something here that'll give us a clue to this case," she shot back. "Oh, come on, you're right, let's start with his room. From what little we know of McIntosh, if he did have something to hide, he'd probably want to put it where he could keep an eye on it. His room's in the dry larder. That's what the inspector told Mrs. Jeffries."

They went down the short hall past the wet larder. Betsy wrinkled her nose. The wet larder smelled of rotten meat and boiled cabbage. She wondered how anyone could have stood living here. But sure enough, Stan McIntosh had turned the dry larder into his room.

"It's not much in the way of comfort," Smythe murmured. A simple iron bedstead covered with an ugly, green wool blanket and a pathetically small pillow was shoved up against one wall. A huge steamer trunk was at the foot of the bed and there was a small table and a chair in the far corner. There were no windows in the room.

"How'd he stand it?" Betsy asked. "The smell from the larder is enough to choke a horse. Why'd he stay down here? There must be dozens of bedrooms upstairs; why would he take this one?"

"Who knows? Maybe he didn't 'ave any choice."

"I don't believe that." Betsy stepped farther into the room. "He was here all alone, how would anyone know where he slept or what room he took for his own?"

"Come on, let's have a hunt." Smythe moved over to the bed, picked up the mattress, and peeked underneath.

Betsy did nothing; she simply stood where she was, shaking her head in consternation. "Look at this place. It's got dust everywhere—" She broke off as she realized the dust around the base of the trunk hadn't been disturbed. But the dust everywhere else in the room had. "Smythe," she said softly. "Let's have a go at the trunk."

Smythe cocked an eyebrow at her. "The police aren't stupid, lass. They'll have looked in there."

"I don't mean *in* the trunk, I mean under it." She rushed over and began pushing at the heavy thing.

"'Ere, you'll 'urt yourself; let me." Smythe got on the other side and shoved it out of the way. He didn't know what his beloved expected to find. But he'd humor her. "See, there's nothing here. Just an empty floor."

But Betsy had dropped to her knees and practically had her nose to the floorboards. She pressed on one, then another and another. As she put pressure on one side of one of the boards, the back of it lifted. "See, the nails have been taken out of these." She gestured at the floor. "He's got something hidden here."

Smythe dropped down beside her. With his big hands and quick fingers, it took less than two minutes to pry half a dozen floorboards out of their way. They looked inside, but it was still far too dark to see anything. "Here goes." He plunged his hand down into the hole. "There's something 'ere." He grabbed what felt like a piece of carpet and pulled hard. But it was too big to come through. "Pull out some more boards," he ordered. But Betsy was already doing that.

"There, try it again," she said as she pried two more out.

This time it came up in a cloud of dust and dirt. Smythe sneezed and plopped it down on the floor by the truck. He brushed the dirt off the side. "It's a woman's carpetbag."

"An expensive one, too," Betsy said. "Come on, let's open it."

He brushed more dust off the thing and popped the brass clasp at the top. The bag wasn't locked. It sprang open and they peeked inside. On the top was a flat leather case. "Let's have a look." Smythe took it out and flipped it open. A small, flat object that looked like a notebook fell out. He picked it up and studied it for a moment.

"Well, what is it?"

"It's a diary." He cocked his head and squinted at the fine print on the inside of the first page. "It belongs to a Miss Deborah Baker of Halifax, Nova Scotia."

CHAPTER 10

"I do wish you'd let me know what you were planning," Mrs. Jeffries said. There was just a hint of irritation in her tone. "If you had, we might have worked out some sort of plan. As it is now, we'll have to come up with a way to get this evidence to the inspector."

"I'm sorry, Mrs. Jeffries," Smythe said. "We shouldn't 'ave gone off like that—"

"It was my fault," Betsy interrupted. "All my fault. Smythe caught me trying to slip out early this morning and insisted on coming with me."

"It's no one's fault." The housekeeper laughed. Gracious, these two were adults. She had no right to berate them for taking a bit of initiative. "Forgive me, I have no right to chastise either of you for plunging ahead with the investigation. As a matter of fact, I should have thought to suggest we search the school well before this. However, we do need to come up with some way to get Inspector Witherspoon back to that room. Are you sure you put everything back in the hiding place?"

"We did," Smythe assured her. "We were right careful, too. After we'd had a good hunt through this woman's bag, I realized the best thing to do would be to let our inspector find it."

Mrs. Goodge put a fresh pot of tea on the table. "I still don't see what all the fuss is about. Who is this Deborah Baker anyway? How does she fit in with the whole mess, that's what I want to know."

"We don't know who she is," Mrs. Jeffries replied. "But I think it's important evidence. Betsy and Smythe also found a ticket stub from the passenger liner the *Laura Gibbens*. She's one of the Gibbens Steamship Line fleet and that's where McIntosh worked."

"All that proves is that McIntosh is a thief and that he stole some woman's carpetbag," the cook retorted. "I don't see how it has any bearing on our case." She gasped as Fred, his muzzle and paws covered with dirt, came trotting into the kitchen. "You wretched dog," she shrieked, "have you been out digging up my daffodil bulbs?"

Fred started guiltily and tried to slink under the table.

Wiggins leapt to his feet. "I'm sure 'e weren't botherin' your bulbs, Mrs. Goodge. 'E's a good dog, 'e is. But I'll just run 'ave a quick look." He took off down the hall toward the garden. Fred, his ears pinned back, took off like a shot behind him.

"He better not have dug them up again," Mrs. Goodge muttered darkly. "That's twice I've planted them and I'm not goin' to do it a third time. I'll have his head."

"It's a dog's nature to dig, Mrs. Goodge," Smythe said helpfully.

The back door opened and then they heard, "You're a bad boy, Fred," Wiggins was scolding, "and you'd best go and apologize to Mrs. Goodge."

"Oh dear," Mrs. Jeffries said to the cook. "I do believe that Fred's in a bit of trouble. Why don't you plant the next batch in pots and put them up on the garden wall where Fred can't reach them."

Trying to control her temper, Mrs. Goodge took a long, deep breath. "I tell you, if he wasn't so handy in our investigations, I'd have that dog's hide." She was bluffing, of course. They all knew she was fond of Fred. He was getting a bit plump from all the treats she slipped him.

"Sorry, Mrs. Goodge," Wiggins said morosely as he and the dog returned. "It looks like he's done it again." This time, Fred did slink under the table.

"Oh bother, shouting at the stupid beast doesn't do any good." She gave a quick glare under the table. "Let's get on with our meeting. As I was saying, all finding that ticket stub proves is that McIntosh is a thief."

"That can't be it," Betsy said. "The sailing date on the ticket is from last year, and McIntosh wasn't working as a steward then. He'd been at Helmsley's for two years. So where did it come from?"

"And more importantly, where is Miss Baker?" Mrs. Jeffries muttered. She was staring at Fred's dusty paw prints on the kitchen floor. An idea was taking root in her mind, an idea that was so farfetched that it might possibly be true. But she needed a few more facts before she said anything. "For the time being, let's put the problem of the carpetbag to one side. There are one or two other matters we need to know before we can move ahead."

Smythe regarded her levelly. "You know who the killer is, don't you?"

"I have a theory," she admitted, "but I won't discuss it until I'm a bit more sure."

"Oh, come on, Mrs. Jeffries, give us a clue," Wiggins pleaded.

"I can't. Not until I know more. I could so easily be wrong. I don't want to ruin our whole investigation at this point. If I am mistaken, it might completely fuzzy up our thinking and we'll never get this case solved." She got to her feet. "Luty and Hatchet will be here right after breakfast. I need to plant an idea or two in the inspector's mind before he goes out this morning. Then we'll get cracking. If I'm right, we've much to do and very little time to do it in."

She wasn't deliberately keeping them in suspense, but she was serious about not wanting to prejudice their thinking if she was wrong. She'd learned in the past that once a theory was advanced and acted on, it was difficult to let it go, even if it turned out to be wrong.

She left the others in the kitchen and took the inspector's breakfast tray up to the dining room. He was sitting down as she entered the room. "Good morning, sir. How are you?"

"Fine, thank you. Gracious, that smells delicious." He smiled approvingly as Mrs. Jeffries took the plate of fried eggs and bacon off the tray and placed it in front of him. She put his toast rack down next to his bread plate and then filled his cup with tea. "What's on your agenda today, sir?"

He sighed around a mouthful of egg. "I'm going to have another go at Miss Gentry. I completely forgot to ask her something rather important yesterday."

"And what was that, sir?" She poured herself a cup of tea and sat down next to the inspector. He hated eating alone.

"Just what I mentioned yesterday—that Mr. Eddington claimed he'd seen her giving money to some man in the churchyard. He thinks the man was probably Tim Porter."

"Yes, sir, you did mention that. Mr. Eddington seemed under the impression that the dog finding Porter's body wasn't accidental, right?"

Witherspoon nodded. "Honestly, I don't see how Miss Gentry could have murdered the fellow and carried him all that way up that footpath. I mean, can you see her humping along like some crippled monster, dragging a corpse and a shovel with her."

"Crippled monster?"

He laughed. "I'm sorry, I suddenly had this image of Miss Gentry with

Porter's corpse thrown over one shoulder and a long-handled shovel over the other. Ridiculous, I know. Oh dear, you must think me monstrous myself that I can laugh at such a thing. Of course murder isn't funny."

"You're not at all monstrous. Sometimes the only way to keep the horror of something at bay is to laugh at it. I was wondering, sir, exactly what do you know about Mr. Eddington?"

Witherspoon took a sip of tea. "He travels a lot on business."

"Hmm, you mentioned that he doesn't have much staff in his home? That's odd, isn't it?"

"As I said, he's gone a great deal of the time."

"That's what I mean. From what you said about the homes on Forest Street, they're quite large. I should think he'd have someone looking in on his place from time to time. The way you described him, it's almost as if the man doesn't want anyone about the place."

"Perhaps he likes his privacy," Witherspoon murmured. But she could tell the idea of looking further into the background of Phillip Eddington was taking root.

"Oh, I'm sure he does, sir. I was just curious, that's all. As you always say, there's generally more to someone than meets the eyes. As a matter of fact, I happened to overhear some gossip about him the other day." She told him about Eddington's attempts to have the right-of-way revoked. "That is so strange, sir. Why should he care about some ancient right-of-way if he's gone so often?"

"Why indeed?" Witherspoon muttered.

"Does he have offices in the City?"

"No, uh, he doesn't," the inspector replied. "I do believe I ought to have another word with the fellow. Clear up a few bits and pieces. Perhaps I'll call round and see him after I've seen McIntosh's references and had word with Miss Gentry."

"That's probably quite a good idea, sir," she replied.

Mr. Malcolm Beadle stared at Witherspoon over the top of his spectacles. "I believe we had an appointment for four o'clock yesterday afternoon, sir." The secretary of the board of governors of Helmsley's Grammar School was not happy. His hazel eyes were cold and his thin lips pursed in disapproval. "I'm a busy man, sir. I do not appreciate having my time wasted."

They were in Beadle's book-lined study in St. John's Wood. Malcolm Beadle was sitting behind a huge, mahogany desk. Barnes and Witherspoon were standing in front of him like recalcitrant schoolboys.

Constable Barnes was getting annoyed. It was disgraceful how some people had such a lack of respect for the police. "We were called away on a matter of some urgency, sir," he replied before his superior could utter another apology. "The fact of the matter is, sir, police emergencies take precedence over appointments."

"But we are most dreadfully sorry," Witherspoon said for the third time. "We'll not take up much more of your morning. There's just one or two things we need." He frowned thoughtfully as the question he was going to ask flew right out of his head.

"May we sit down, sir?" Barnes asked.

"Hmmph," Beadle snorted, and jerked his head toward two chairs. "Sit down."

"Thank you." Barnes smiled slightly. "You said you'd provide us with a copy of Stan McIntosh's references. Do you have it?"

Beadle picked up a piece of paper from off the desk and handed it toward the now sitting policemen. Barnes had to get up to reach it. "Thank you."

Witherspoon finally remembered what it was he was going to ask. "Is the school going to be sold soon?"

Beadle frowned, an act that brought his bushy brown eyesbrows almost together over his nose. "Sold? We've no intention of selling it, Inspector. Whatever gave you that idea?"

"Uh, one of the neighbors mentioned that Mr. McIntosh had said the school was to be sold. Perhaps he was mistaken."

"The property isn't being sold; it's being let and turned into a girls' school come the first of the year. McIntosh knew that. The new tenants had agreed to keep him on if he wanted to stay. He worked cheap and kept the windows from being broken by hooligans."

"Thank you, Mr. Beadle. You've been most helpful." Witherspoon rose to his feet. Constable Barnes stayed seated, his gaze on the paper in his hand. "Uh, Constable, perhaps we'd better go. We don't want to take up any more of Mr. Beadle's time."

Barnes handed the references to Witherspoon. "You'd better have a look at this before we go, sir. You may have a few more questions for Mr. Beadle."

Witherspoon scanned the sheet quickly. There were only four names on it. The last name was Phillip Eddington of number 1 Forest Street. "Good gracious. He never mentioned this."

"What is it?" Beadle asked.

"These names, sir, did you actually contact them before you hired McIntosh?"

"Of course; I wrote all of them personally. We wouldn't hire someone without checking references."

"Did Mr. Eddington reply to your inquiry?" Barnes asked.

"All of them replied. Otherwise we'd have not given McIntosh the position. Do you want to see the letters?"

"Indeed we do, sir," Witherspoon replied. "It's very important."

Luty shook her head in disbelief. "We should've searched that place way before this." She grinned at Betsy. "Smart girl. I wish I'da thought of it."

Betsy giggled. "Thanks, but it was really frightening. I'd have lost my nerve if Smythe hadn't been with me." She could admit it as he wasn't here at the moment. Mrs. Jeffries had sent him out on some mysterious errand.

"What should we do next?" Hatchet addressed the question to Mrs. Jeffries. But she didn't seem to hear him. She was staring at the wall with great concentration.

In truth, she wasn't listening. The idea that had come to her earlier simply wouldn't go away. But it was so bizarre. She was in a real quandary. She was sure she was right, but what if she was mistaken? Still, there couldn't be any other answer. Everything pointed in that one single direction.

Everything. The fire and flood at Miss Gentry's house on Forest Street, poor old Mrs. Dempsey seeing gargoyles in the garden, McIntosh sneaking out at night for secret meetings, the tramp sleeping in the church entryway, the entryway with a view of the communal gardens at Forest Street. No, she shook her head. It could only mean one thing. But how to prove it? That was the question. There was really only one way.

"Mrs. Jeffries," Hatchet said softly.

"Oh dear, I *am* sorry. What did you say?"

"I said, what do we do now?" He smiled at her. "You seem very lost in your thoughts. Is there something you'd like to share with us?"

"Mrs. Jeffries knows who the killer is," Betsy stated. "But she won't say yet."

"Only because I'm not completely certain. I do wish Smythe would come back. If what I think is true, then I'm fairly certain the information Smythe may come back with will prove it."

"We can be patient, Mrs. Jeffries," Hatchet said. "I say, Mrs. Goodge, may I have another one of your delicious buns?"

The cook shoved the plate toward him. "Help yourself." She was dying of curiosity.

"'Ow long do we 'ave to wait?" Wiggins asked plaintively. He and Fred had kept a very low profile; they were both still in the doghouse over the daffodils.

"Not much longer, I hope."

From the street, they heard the distinct sounds of a carriage stopping in front of the house. "That sounds like Smythe now," Mrs. Jeffries said. Her spirits lifted enormously. "I told him to bring the carriage back with him. I expect we'll need it." She knew they would. She'd instructed him to bring the vehicle only if he was able to confirm what she suspected.

A few moments later, Smythe bounded into the kitchen. "You were right, Mrs. Jeffries, he's goin' to run. I followed him to Cook's. I overheard him buyin' tickets on the *Sarah Maine;* she sails at first tide tomorrow morning from Southampton." He flashed Betsy a quick smile and dropped into the chair next to her. "The 'ouse is up for sale as well, I spotted the sign in the front garden when I followed 'im home."

"Who we talkin' about here?" Luty demanded.

"I do believe it's time you shared your ideas with us, Mrs. Jeffries," Hatchet interjected. "Things appear to be getting very interesting."

"What's goin' on?" Mrs. Goodge asked. "Who's he been following all morning?"

"Cor blimey, Mrs. Jeffries, don't keep us in the dark," Wiggins complained. "We wants to 'elp."

Mrs. Jeffries held up her hand. "I'm sorry, I wasn't being deliberately mysterious. I asked Smythe to follow Phillip Eddington. I'm fairly certain he's our killer, but proving it is going to take a great deal of cleverness and luck. Now, we must act fast if we're going to keep him from leaving the country."

"Tell us what we need to do," Hatchet said.

"First of all," Mrs. Jeffries replied, "Smythe, you and Wiggins need to go get Miss Gentry. Tell her she must write the inspector a note that he is to meet her at Forest Street right away. She must tell him it's urgent. But you're not to bring the note here. Smythe, you take the note and find the inspector. Tell the inspector that Miss Gentry brought the note here to the house and that she begged you to take it to him. Then be sure you tell him that as Luty and Hatchet were here, Hatchet and Wiggins insisted on accompanying Miss Gentry back to Forest Street. We can always claim she was nervous and upset and didn't want to go there on her own."

"I get it." Smythe rose to his feet. "That way, we can 'ave Wiggins and Hatchet at the ready if the inspector is delayed."

"Correct. If I'm right, Phillip Eddington is a killer. I don't want Miss Gentry at that house alone with him next door. This way, we'll have a good excuse for them being there with her when the inspector arrives."

Wiggins and Hatchet got up and the three of then turned to go. "Take Fred with you," Mrs. Jeffries insisted. "For what I've got in mind, he'll come in handy.'

Fred, who'd been curled up in disgrace under Wiggins's chair, came wiggling out as he heard his name. His tail thumped against the kitchen floor.

"Come on, boy." Wiggins called the dog.

"And be sure and have Miss Gentry bring Miranda as well. If her nose is as good as I think it is, she's going to catch our killer for us." If Mrs. Jeffries was wrong, they might all end up disgraced. But that was a risk she was willing to take to stop a murderer from leaving the country.

"Anything else?" Smythe asked.

Mrs. Jeffries thought for a moment. She wanted to make sure she hadn't forgotten anything important. "Yes, when Miss Gentry gets to Forest Street, have her and the dog go directly to the garden. That's very important. Miranda and Fred both need to be out there when the inspector arrives. That may be the only way this situation is going to work."

"What about Eddington?" Smythe asked. "Should we keep an eye on him?" He didn't see how they could, but if it was necessary, he'd think of something.

"No, don't worry. Even if he leaves the premises when he sees the inspector, he won't get far. Not once the police have the evidence I pray is there."

"Uh, Mrs. Jeffries, what's Miss Gentry to say when the inspector asks why it was so urgent she meet him?" Wiggins asked.

Mrs. Jeffries smiled. "She's to tell him she's fairly sure she knows why someone was trying to kill her."

"And why's that?" Hatchet prompted. Like the rest of them, he was curious.

"Because someone didn't want Miranda in the communal garden. That's where the bodies are buried, you see. Miranda is actually quite good at digging up corpses. She's got the best nose in London."

"Miss Gentry's not home," Martha explained. "She's taken Miranda out for a walk."

"Cor blimey," Wiggins muttered. "That's all we need. Our plan'll be ruined."

"What's this about, then?" Martha asked suspiciously. "Why do you need Miss Gentry? You're not goin' to arrest her, are you?"

"We're not the police, Martha," Smythe retorted. "We're tryin' to 'elp 'er. Besides, why would the police be wantin' to arrest 'er anyway?"

"Don't pay me any mind, I'm acting like a goose. I expect I'm rattled over what happened." Martha made a disgusted face. "Them two sisters of hers was by early this morning. They was saying all sorts of nasty things. They said Miss Gentry's goin' to get in trouble for making false claims to the police about someone wanting to kill her. They caused quite a ruckus, they did. They was shouting and carrying on so loudly that Miranda started barking. Mind you, I think the dog knew them hags was tormenting Miss Gentry and that was her way of gettin' shut of them. Mind you, I—"

"Do you know when Miss Gentry is due back?" Hatchet interrupted. Annabeth Gentry's domestic troubles were not of paramount importance at this moment. Finding her was.

Martha scowled. She didn't like being interrupted. "She didn't say when she'd be back," she snapped.

"Do you know where she went, then?" Smythe pressed. "It's urgent that we find her. We think we've found out who's been trying to kill her."

Martha gaped at him. "Why didn't you say that in the first place? I don't know exactly where she's gone, but I do know her usual walking spots. She's either gone to the footpath this side of the scrubs—"

"Why would she go there? Isn't that where Miranda found Porter's corpse?" Wiggins asked incredulously. "Seems to me if someone is tryin' to kill you, you don't go walking all on your own in lonely places."

"I said she *might* have gone there," Martha replied tartly. "But she's probably over at the commons." She waved her hand in the general direction of Shepherd's Bush Green. "If she's not there, try the footpath. If she's not at either of them places, then I don't know where she is."

"Thanks, Martha," Smythe said. "If she comes home, tell her to stay right here. It's urgent we find her."

They dashed back to the carriage. "What'll we do if we can't find her?" Wiggins asked.

"We'll find her," Smythe promised. "Mark my words, we'll find her."

"I hope she's all right," Hatchet said. He looked a bit worried. "You don't think she could have possibly come to some harm, do you?" He didn't need to remind the others that their involvement in this case had started because someone was trying to kill Miss Gentry.

"Of course not," Smythe said, but the thought had crossed his mind.

But their fears turned out to be for naught, as they found her less than five minutes later walking up the Uxbridge Road toward home.

Within twenty minutes, they'd explained what had to be done, and Smythe, after dropping them off, was on his way to find the inspector.

"I say, Smythe," Witherspoon began as he and Barnes climbed out of the carriage, "Miss Gentry didn't happen to explain why it was so urgent I meet her here, did she?"

Smythe shook his head. "No sir, she only said it were right important. Said it were a matter of life and death and that you'd know what she meant."

As instructed, he'd brought the inspector and Barnes to Miss Gentry's house on Forest Street. He only hoped the housekeeper was right about everything and they wouldn't end up looking incredibly foolish.

"Well, I can't say that I do," Witherspoon murmured. "But as I was coming over here anyway, it doesn't matter."

"You were comin' 'ere, sir?" Smythe deliberately kept the question casual. "That's a bit of a coincidence, isn't it?"

"Not really. You see we found out this morning that Mr. Eddington was one of the names Stan McIntosh gave as a reference to get his job at the school. I'm a bit curious as to why Mr. Eddington never mentioned that to us and as to why he lied."

"We don't know that he did lie, sir," Barnes pointed out. "Maybe McIntosh was the one lying about the school being sold. Take a look at that, sir." He pointed toward the front garden of number one, Eddington's house.

"Gracious, it's a 'For Sale' sign. Mr. Eddington never mentioned he was selling his house." Witherspoon didn't like this. He didn't like it one bit. First the lie and now this. He was beginning to think that perhaps Mr. Eddington wasn't what he appeared to be. "I do believe we ought to have a word with him right now." He started toward the walkway to number one.

"But, sir," Smythe yelled, "don't you think we ought to see if Miss Gentry's all right first? She was in a bit of state when she came to the 'ouse, sir. That's why Mrs. Jeffries insisted that Wiggins and Hatchet come back here with 'er. They didn't think she ought to be alone."

Witherspoon hesitated. "Yes, yes, of course you're right. We must see to the lady." He started toward the open front door of number two.

"It was right convenient that Wiggins and Mr. Hatchet were there when Miss Gentry showed up, wasn't it?" Barnes said as they fell in step behind the inspector.

Smythe swallowed. The constable was no fool. "Luty and Hatchet had dropped by to 'ave tea," he said. "They come to visit quite often."

"So I've noticed," Barnes replied. They walked up the steps and into the foyer. The place was obviously still being redone. Paint buckets and ladders cluttered the long hallway leading to the back of the house. Drop cloths were scattered about the floors and the scent of fire hung heavily in the air. "They always seem to be around when the inspector's about to solve a case."

They crossed the huge, empty kitchen and reached the back door. "Uh, yeah," Smythe said. He didn't know what to say next. "It's right fortunate, innit?"

Barnes laughed softly. "Don't look so worried, man. I think the inspector's a very lucky man to have such a devoted staff."

Smythe breathed a sigh of relief as they came out into the garden. There was a small, paved terrace outside the kitchen that ran for ten feet on either side of the door. Beyond that was the garden proper. Annabeth Gentry, Hatchet, and Wiggins were standing in the middle of the grass.

Miranda, nose to the ground, was following some sort of trail. Fred was sniffing the ground behind her.

"Hello, Inspector," Annabeth called, waving to him. "Thank you so much for coming."

From the corner of his eye, Smythe saw Miranda circling a patch of dirt at the far edge of the grass. The spot was just under a tree, near the back wall.

He glanced at Miss Gentry and the others. If they'd done as they were instructed, they'd probably arrived here only a few minutes ahead of them. He'd dropped them off at Orley Road and told them to wait an hour before going into the garden. He'd needed the time to find the inspector and get him over here.

"Good day, Miss Gentry, I understand you wanted to see me," Witherspoon said. "The constable and I came as soon as we got your message." For the life of him, he couldn't see anything that looked the least dangerous.

"Thank you, Inspector." Annabeth's smile faltered a bit. She looked at Wiggins. "It was good of you to come so quickly. I'm very grateful."

It was at that moment that Miranda started to dig.

CHAPTER 11

The inspector waited politely for Miss Gentry to continue speaking. She merely smiled at him.

"Hello, sir," Wiggins called.

"Inspector." Hatchet smiled and nodded. "Nice to see you, sir."

Bewildered, Witherspoon glanced around the garden. What on earth was this about? There certainly didn't seem to be anything going on here that could be construed as a matter of life and death. Except for the fact that Miranda appeared to be digging quite a large hole, the day was extraordinarily quiet. "Uh, Miss Gentry, from what I understand, you seemed to feel something was very much amiss this morning."

"That's quite right, Inspector, I did." She smiled and danced toward the two dogs. Her snout deep in the hole, Miranda was digging furiously. Fred, his nose less than an inch from the ground, was circling the area in a rapid figure-eight sort of motion. "You see, I suddenly had an idea."

"An idea," the inspector prompted. "What kind of idea?"

Barnes was now watching the dogs.

"Well, uh, about why someone might be trying to kill me. You see, it all started with me finding that fellow's body."

The dirt stopped flying out of the hole and Miranda buried her snout in the ground. She grabbed something between her teeth.

Fred began circling and crept up close to the other dog. His whole body went rigid.

Witherspoon, not noticing the dogs, kept his attention on Miss Gentry. "Yes, I know that. We're quite certain the threats on your life are connected to Tim Porter."

"But that's just it, sir," she began slowly. She was trying to say it just right. Mrs. Jeffries's instructions had been very explicit. "I don't think they're connected to this Porter business at all." She broke off and pointed behind the inspector. "Look, there's my neighbor Mr. Eddington."

Eddington had stepped out onto his terrace. His gaze raked the garden, taking in the two policemen, Miss Gentry, and the others, and then he spotted the dogs. A look of horror spread across his face.

"I say, Mr. Eddington," Witherspoon called to him. "I'd like a word with you, sir. I'll pop over in a few minutes, if that's all right."

But Eddington didn't answer. He turned on his heel and bolted back to the house. Smythe started as though he meant to go after him, but Barnes held up his hand and whispered, "Wait. Do nothing yet."

"How rude," Witherspoon muttered, and turned his attention back to Miss Gentry. "I'm sorry. Uh, what were you saying? Something about digging up Porter's body . . ."

But Annabeth Gentry wasn't paying any attention to the inspector. She was gaping at Miranda. The dog had wrestled something out of the ground and was gripping it between her teeth. But the object was buried deep, and despite the dog's efforts, it wouldn't come all the way out.

Fred, seeing the brown, dirt-covered thing in Miranda's mouth, barked jealously and charged the bloodhound in an effort to get her to share. Miranda dropped it and growled at Fred.

"Oh dear," Witherspoon exclaimed. "We can't have this. Whatever's the matter? What's wrong with those two? It's not like Fred to be so aggressive." Afraid that his beloved dog would get bitten, the inspector charged across the grass. "Come on now, Fred, back off. Whatever it is Miranda's found, it's hers." He got close to the animals and stopped dead. "Oh, my good gracious!" he cried. "Constable, you'd best come help. Wiggins, call Fred back. Miss Gentry, call Miranda. Get them away from that thing immediately!"

"What is it, sir?" Barnes had already started across the scruffy grass.

"It's a human arm, Constable, and from what I can see here, it appears to be attached to a body."

It was well past dinnertime by the time Smythe, Wiggins, and Hatchet returned to Upper Edmonton Gardens. They told the women what had happened.

"It were ever so exciting," Wiggins said. "By the time they finished this evening, that dog 'ad found three bodies. Fred 'elped, a bit. Well, 'e tried to. But the inspector kept 'olding him back."

"Only three?" Mrs. Jeffries asked. "Thank goodness. I was afraid there would be far more."

Smythe looked at the women suspiciously. "You're all mighty calm about this. What's goin' on? 'Ave you been up to somethin'?"

"We didn't sit here twiddlin' our thumbs while you all was gone, that's for sure," Luty said. "After Hepzibah told us who she thought the killer was, we finished puttin' the rest of the puzzle together. Betsy and I went over to Hampton House, to see my friend Skidmore—"

"You mean Lord Skidmore," Hatchet interrupted. He looked at the men. "He owns majority shares in a number of steamship lines. For some odd reason, he finds Madam quite amusing."

"He likes me." Luty grinned. "What's more, he's fast, discreet, and he knows how to do a body a favor."

Betsy giggled. "He got us the information we needed right away and he gave us tea."

Smythe's eyes narrowed. "What kind of information could 'e give ya? Oh, I git it, did 'e know anything about that ticket we found in Deborah Baker's things?"

"That and more," Luty replied. "It's amazin' what you can learn by lookin' at a manifest. There's no record of a Deborah Baker on that voyage of the *Laura Gibbens* last year."

"Does that mean she wasn't on the ship?"

"We think she traveled under another name," Mrs. Jeffries said. "A married name. You see, there wasn't a Deborah Baker on that vessel, but there was a Mr. and Mrs. Phillip Essex on board. I'm willing to bet Phillip Essex is really Phillip Eddington."

"Cor blimey," Wiggins muttered. "I'll bet she's one of them women buried in his back garden."

"Probably," Luty said. "But that ain't all we learned. We also found out that Eddington and McIntosh go way back. They'd known each other since McIntosh was a steward. Eddington was a passenger on at least three of McIntosh's voyages. Now you fellas finish your story. We're not tryin' to steal your thunder."

"Hmm, madam, I suspect that's precisely what you're trying to do," Hatchet replied. He looked at Mrs. Jeffries. "Perhaps you'd be so kind as to tell us how you figured it out. I'm afraid that even with the discovery of the bodies, I still don't see how it's all connected."

"Neither did I until Fred dug up Mrs. Goodge's daffodil bulbs," Mrs. Jeffries replied. "That's when it all fell into place."

"What's them bulbs got to do with it?" Wiggins asked.

Mrs. Jeffries laughed and poured herself another cup of tea. "It wasn't the bulbs that were important, it was the digging. That's what I finally realized this morning. You see, it wasn't Porter's murder that precipitated the attempts on Miss Gentry's life, it was her dog digging up his body. Once I started from that point, from the fact that it was the dog that was a threat to someone, and not Miss Gentry, then it all made sense."

"Tell them how you figured out it was Eddington," Mrs. Goodge prompted.

"He was the only person it could be," Mrs. Jeffries said. "If he'd just been content with trying to kill Miss Gentry, we'd never have figured it out. But it was the sabotage to her new home that pointed the finger directly at him."

"I don't understand," Smythe said.

"I asked myself why would anyone sabotage a house, and there was only one reason. To keep someone from moving into it? But someone already lived on Forest Street and nothing was happening to him—"

"I get it," Wiggins interrupted. "That means he must be the one doin' the sabotagin'."

"Right. He is the only person who lives on Forest Street and he wants to keep it that way. Once Porter's body was found, Eddington realized that he was in grave danger if Miss Gentry and her bloodhound moved into their new home. He did everything in his power to keep Miranda out of that garden. He even had a confrontation with Miss Gentry to try and get her to agree to keep the dog on a lead."

"Now we know why," Betsy said. "He didn't want her digging up what he'd buried there."

Mrs. Jeffries took a quick sip of tea. "I was sure that Eddington was the killer, but I didn't know why until today. After Luty and Betsy told me about seeing that name on the manifest, I had an idea it must have something to do with killing for profit. But I'm still not sure how he managed it."

"Well, he killed at least three women," Hatchet said slowly. "At least that was the body count before we left this afternoon."

"Where was Eddington?" Mrs. Jeffries asked.

"He scarpered," Smythe answered. "Good thing 'e did, too. It were 'im takin' off like that that convinced the inspector 'e's the killer."

"That and the fact that Miss Gentry insisted he's the one that's been trying to keep her out of the house on Forest Street," Hatchet added.

"Do they have any idea where he's gone?"

"Probably to the train station," Smythe said. "I managed to whisper to Miss Gentry to tell the inspector she'd gotten suspicious of Eddington and followed him to Cook's. She told the inspector she'd watched him buy that steamship ticket." He didn't add that he was sure Constable Barnes had overheard him. He'd share that little nugget with the others later.

"I only hope the inspector manages to catch the fellow before he gets out of the country," Mrs. Jeffries said. "We can't let him get away. He's evil. Absolutely evil."

"The inspector will get 'im, Mrs. Jeffries," Smythe assured her. "Now, you still 'aven't told us everything. 'Ow you knew it were him behind everything. Did 'e kill Porter and McIntosh?"

"He probably killed McIntosh," she said. "But I'm fairly certain McIntosh killed Porter. Your source was right, Smythe, Porter probably was blackmailing McIntosh. Do you recall Father Jerridan telling Hatchet about tramps sleeping in the entryway of St. Matthew's Church? We think it must have been Porter and that he witnessed McIntosh and Eddington burying one of the bodies in the garden. We'll never know for certain, of course, but it does make sense. It would explain Porter's bragging that there was more money coming his way."

"Especially if McIntosh paid him off a time or two so he'd let his guard down," Betsy put in. "It'd be easier to lure him up that footpath if he wasn't suspicious of you."

"Why did he have that purse on him?" Smythe wondered.

"We think he must've slipped into the garden after they'd buried the body and dug it up," Mrs. Goodge said. She didn't want to be left out just because she'd not gone with Luty and Betsy. "You know, so he'd have something real to wave under McIntosh's nose."

"Why do you think he approached McIntosh?" Hatchet asked. "Why not Eddington?" He still wasn't clear on a number of things, but he was patient.

"He probably thought McIntosh would be easier. He probably didn't have the nerve to go knocking on Eddington's front door. He'd be much more comfortable going after someone of his own class. Besides, remember what happened to Smythe at the White Hare pub," Betsy explained. "Porter went there asking questions about McIntosh. Maybe we'll never know for sure, but he went to McIntosh instead of Eddington."

Smythe smiled at Betsy and then turned to Mrs. Jeffries. "All right, if McIntosh killed Porter to keep his mouth shut, why would Eddington kill McIntosh? If your theory is right and they'd known each other for years, why would Eddington want to kill 'im now?"

"We're not certain," Mrs. Jeffries replied. "But I suspect it's because Eddington decided to move on."

"He didn't just put his house on the market today," Mrs. Goodge interjected. "One of my sources told me he'd been to see the estate agent toward the middle of August, just a few days after Porter's body was found."

"So he killed McIntosh so there wouldn't be any loose ends about?" Wiggins frowned in confusion. "But why was Eddington killing women in the first place? That's what I want to know."

"I have an idea," Mrs. Jeffries said, "but we won't know for sure about his motives until we hear what the inspector has to say." She glanced anxiously at the clock. "I do hope that Eddington didn't catch a train to the coast. They'll have a devil of a time catching the fellow if he gets out of the country."

They caught Eddington as he tried to board a train for Southampton. He saw them coming, and for a moment Witherspoon thought he might make a run for it.

But he didn't. Perhaps it was the dozen men converging on the platform that convinced him he hadn't a hope of escape.

Eddington smiled slightly but said nothing as Witherspoon and Barnes approached. A porter, halfway down the train steps to the platform, saw the police and quickly disappeared inside. Gentlemen in top hats grabbed their ladies and stepped out of the way as the police constables made a wide circle around their quarry.

The train whistle shrilled just as they reached him. The inspector waited for quiet. "Phillip Eddington, you're under arrest for murder," Witherspoon said somberly. "Constable, take him into custody."

Barnes pulled out his handcuffs. Eddington sighed, dropped his bag, and held out his wrists. "I'm surprised you caught me," he said conversationally, still smiling at Witherspoon. "You struck me as being a bit dim."

"You were wrong," Barnes said. He finished cuffing Eddington and then knelt down next to the bag the criminal had been carrying. It was a large black leather traveling case with a wide silver clasp. "What's this, then? Shall I open it, Inspector?"

"Yes," Witherspoon replied. He wondered why people always underestimated him. But then again, perhaps it wasn't a bad thing. After all, Eddington had been caught. But being thought a dim sort of fellow wasn't very pleasant. The inspector pushed that silly notion out of his mind. He'd concentrate on the task at hand.

Barnes pushed the clasp. "It's locked." Eddington still continued to smile. The constable reached up and stuck his hand into the man's coat pocket. He pulled out a handful of bills, some coins, and a small silver key. He handed the bills and coins to another police constable. "Make sure this is logged in properly." Then he knelt down, unlocked the case, and gave a long, low whistle. "It looks like Mr. Eddington was preparing for a long trip. The case is full of money, sir. Five-and ten-pound notes."

"Let's get him down to the station," Witherspoon said, "and see what he has to say for himself."

"I've nothing to say, Inspector," Eddington told him calmly. "Absolutely nothing."

It was well past eleven that night before the inspector arrived home. As he'd seen the kitchen lamps from the street, he went to that room first. "Gracious"—he stopped just inside the door and stared at the crowd around his table—"you're all here."

"'Course we are," Luty said firmly. "We want to know what happened. You can't have something exciting like diggin' up bodies happen and then expect us to go home without findin' out if you caught that Eddington feller."

They all watched him carefully. He looked dreadfully tired, but he didn't appear to be annoyed. As a matter of fact, he looked almost pleased. "That sounds reasonable. I expect I'd be dying of curiosity myself. I say, is there anything to eat? I'm famished."

Mrs. Goodge, who'd been almost asleep before the inspector arrived, got to her feet. "I've got some nice buns right here, sir." She pulled a covered plate off the counter and slid it onto the table. Mrs. Jeffries, who'd slipped out of her chair when she heard him coming, said, "Do sit down and have some tea, sir. Let me pour you a cup."

"That would be lovely." He sat down and waited for them to finish preparing his snack. He picked up a bun and took a huge bite. "That's wonderful," he said as soon as he'd swallowed. "I expect you're wondering what happened."

"That's why we waited here half the night," Luty replied. She didn't want to rush him, but she did wish he'd get on with it.

"We arrested Phillip Eddington at the train station," Witherspoon said. "At first he refused to tell us anything at all. But when we confronted him with all the evidence we had against him, he confessed."

"Three bodies is a lot of evidence," Hatchet said grimly. He closed his eyes and shuddered. Watching them being dug out of the ground this afternoon had been quite gruesome.

"Oh, it wasn't the bodies," Witherspoon said. "It was the marriage licenses. The fellow had quite a collection of them at the bottom of his bag. In the past fifteen years, he's married and murdered seven different women." He shook his head in disbelief.

"Good gracious, sir. I thought there was only three bodies," Mrs. Goodge exclaimed.

"Three bodies at the house in Forest Street," the inspector replied. "But there's four more buried at his home in Halifax. We've wired the Canadian authorities. We're waiting to hear back from them about what they find."

"Cor blimey, 'ow'd 'e get away with that?"

"To hear him tell it"—Witherspoon sighed—"it was very easy. Eddington was careful when he picked his victims. He'd find a woman who had money and no relatives. After a short courtship, he'd propose marriage and the lady would agree. But as part of his proposal, he'd tell his victim that he had to go back to England to manage his estate, or, if the victim was English, that he had to return to Canada to manage the family business. The unlucky woman would generally give him her money to take to his bankers because, after all, she wasn't going to be coming back. Once he had their cash, they'd sail off for either England or Canada. He always made sure he arrived in London in the dead of night. He wanted to be certain no one saw him. Before the poor woman realized what was happening, he'd cosh her over the head and then strangle her to finish the job." He broke off and shook his head sadly. "Poor ladies. They never stood a chance. Then, with the help of Stan McIntosh, he'd bury them in the garden. His plan worked perfectly."

"But that's monstrous!" Hatchet cried. "Surely someone must have suspected he was up to something?"

"Who was there to suspect?" the inspector asked. "He made sure his victims were somewhat alone in the world and he always made sure he arrived in either Halifax or London late at night so that no one ever spotted him with his wife."

"But what about the ship? Surely people on the ship noticed him and his wife."

"He used an assumed name. But that wasn't quite as foolproof as he hoped. He admitted that's how he and McIntosh started working together. Eddington always traveled on different steamship lines, but he didn't realize that the staff frequently moved from one line to another. He had to cut McIntosh in on the scheme when McIntosh recognized him from an earlier trip on another vessel."

"I'm amazed he's gotten away with it for so long." Mrs. Goodge clucked her tongue. "Fifteen years. Seven women. That's awful. Didn't any of them have friends or relatives that inquired about them?"

"He took care of that," Witherspoon said. "As I said, Stan McIntosh was his accomplice. We found a box of postcards under McIntosh's bed. We're fairly certain that McIntosh used those cards to send off to the victims' friends. Pretending to be the victim, he'd write those cards and send them off. Her friends would receive cards saying married life was wonderful and she couldn't be happier."

"But how could McIntosh do that? People know each other's handwriting," Betsy said.

Witherspoon smiled sadly. "We've done some checking. McIntosh served three years in jail in New York for forgery."

"But didn't these people ever write back?"

"Of course. Eddington gave the women he duped the wrong address. He used the Helmsley Grammar School address as his own. They, in turn, gave that address to their friends before they left. McIntosh intercepted the letters."

Mrs. Jeffries nodded. That explained why McIntosh wouldn't let anyone else get the mail. "Didn't people get suspicious when the cards stopped coming?"

"Possibly. But not enough to do anything about it. He was counting on the fact that we live in a busy, impersonal world. People come and go so much more than they used to. They drift apart. Remember, he picked women who hadn't any close relatives. He was bragging about that, about how clever he was to pick people that no one really cared about." Witherspoon closed his eyes briefly. "He used the newspapers to refine his search. He'd read the obituaries and probate news to see who'd died and left an estate. He hunted his victims on both sides of the Atlantic with the cunning and malice of the devil himself. He took ruthless advantage of women who were alone in the world and without anyone to see to their safety. But he wasn't quite as clever as he thought; several people had started making inquiries."

"Poor Miss Gentry. Lucky she didn't become one of his victims," Mrs. Goodge said.

"She was lucky, indeed," Witherspoon agreed. "He admitted trying to kill her. He stole a coach and tried to run her down. When that didn't work, he had McIntosh chuck those bricks off the wall at her head. He couldn't afford for Miranda to start nosing around in his garden. Not with all those bodies."

"Why not just kill the dog?" Hatchet asked.

"Constable Barnes asked him that," the inspector replied. "He said he'd tried. But that he couldn't get close enough to the animal to do it any harm."

"Why didn't he move the bodies?" Luty asked.

"He couldn't. Not with the workmen coming and going at Miss Gentry's place. Especially after the vandalism. The builder had someone staying there some nights. Eddington couldn't be sure he wouldn't be seen." He sighed deeply. "The man is a monster, and God forgive me for saying it, but I'm glad he's going to hang. I thank the Lord we caught him before he could hurt anyone else."

"*You* caught him, sir," Mrs. Jeffries said gently. She could see he was very affected by the horror of this case. For that matter, now that they'd heard the gruesome details, they were all horrified as well. "Why don't you go up to bed, sir. You look exhausted."

"I *am* tired." He got up and gave them a tired smile. "I want to thank all of you for your help. You did right in taking care of Miss Gentry today. I shudder to think what would have happened if she'd gone to that garden alone."

A bit guilty, they all glanced at one another, but the inspector didn't appear to notice. "I believe we should all have a bit of a holiday when this is over," he continued. "Perhaps we'll go to the country."

"That would be lovely, sir," Mrs. Jeffries replied.

He started for the back stairs. Fred left Wiggins and trotted after the inspector. Perhaps he sensed the man needed a bit of comfort.

"Excuse me, sir," Mrs. Jeffries said. "Was Eddington responsible for the poisoned cream that Miranda ate?"

"He says he wasn't and he's no reason to lie. He's going to hang anyway. Admitting one more attempt on Miss Gentry's life won't make any difference in his sentence." He smiled sadly and continued toward the stairs.

"Thank you, sir. Good night." Mrs. Jeffries turned to the others. "Well, what a horrifying story this has turned out to be."

"No, it woulda only been really awful if that varmint had got away with it and went on to kill a bunch more women." Luty got up. "Let's get goin', Hatchet. You're fallin' asleep in your chair."

"I most certainly am not." He tossed Luty a quick frown and then looked at Mrs. Jeffries. "What about that poisoned cream? If Eddington didn't do it, who did?"

"One of her relatives, I expect," Mrs. Jeffries mused.

"What are we going to do, then?" Betsy asked. "They might try again."

"Not if we tell her," the housekeeper replied. "She can make it very clear to her family that in the event of her death, there's to be a full police investigation. I don't think they'll have another go at her. Not now. They've had the police around once. They'll probably be too frightened to try it again. But just to be on the safe side, I believe we'll have her mention that she's a number of friends who will raise quite a fuss if she disappears or comes to harm."

"Good," Mrs. Goodge said stoutly. "That's what we've all got to do. Especially us women who are alone in the world. We've got to keep an eye out for one another. That's the only way any of us will be safe."

"Amen to that, Mrs. Goodge," Mrs. Jeffries agreed. "Amen to that."

Printed in the United States
by Baker & Taylor Publisher Services